BEAUTY

AND THE

BEAST

AND OTHER
CLASSIC
FAIRY TALES

BEAUTY

AND THE

BEAST

AND OTHER
CLASSIC
FAIRY TALES

BARNES & NOBLE

NEW YORK

Compilation © 2016 by Sterling Publishing Co., Inc.

Cover illustration © 2016 by Sterling Publishing Co., Inc.

This 2016 edition printed for Barnes & Noble
by Sterling Publishing Co., Inc.

ISBN 978-1-4351-6127-6

Barnes & Noble, Inc.
122 Fifth Avenue
New York, NY 10011

Manufactured in China

8 10 9 7

www.sterlingpublishing.com

Cover illustration by Laurel Long
Cover design by Patrice Kaplan
Endpapers: *A Garden with a Rose Arch* by Edith Helena Adie/
Private Collection/© Mallett Gallery, London, UK/
Bridgeman Images

Contents

BEAUTIES CONTINUED

BEASTS

BEASTS CONTINUED

Introduction

The first known published text of the classic fairy tale "Beauty and the Beast" was written by Gabrielle-Suzanne Barbot de Villeneuve in 1740 and collected in her compilation *La Jeune Américaine et les contes marins*. To say that the story met with favor is an understatement. By 1756, "Beauty and the Beast" was so well known that Jeanne-Marie Leprince de Beaumont wrote an abridged edition of it that would become the popular version included in collections of fairy tales throughout the nineteenth century (although Andrew Lang went back to de Villeneuve's original for his groundbreaking anthology *The Blue Fairy Book*, first published in 1891 as the beginning of a twelve-book series that would revolutionize the anthologizing of fairy tales for young readers). Fifteen years later, Jean-François Marmontel and André Ernest Modeste Grétry adapted de Villeneuve's story as the book for the opera *Zémire et Azor*, the start of more than two centuries of extraliterary treatments that now include Jean Cocteau's famous 1946 film *La Belle et la Bête*, Walt Disney's 1991 animated feature *Beauty and the Beast*, and countless other cinematic, television, stage, and musical variations on the story's theme.

More than 4,000 years after it became part of the oral storytelling tradition, it is easy to understand why "Beauty and the Beast" continues to be one of the most popular fairy tales of all time, and a seemingly inexhaustible source of inspiration for artists working in all mediums. Its theme of the power of unconditional love is one that never grows old. And one can see in its narrative the components of so many similar fairy tales: the gratification of a simple request that proves to have a terrible price; the young heroine who pines to be delivered from the miserable circumstances of her life; the hero afflicted by a terrible curse to be reviled and misunderstood by all who encounter him; the transformative power of a beauty that is more than skin deep; and the love that conquers all and ensures that everyone will live happily ever after.

Beauty and the Beast and Other Classic Fairy Tales is a celebration of de Villeneuve's classic story and the impact that it has had on fairy tales told across cultures and over the centuries. Its contents are evenly—though far from rigidly—divided into the two character types juxtaposed in the story's title. The book leads with "Beauties" because fairy tales positively teem with them. Beauties frequently play the heroines in traditional romantic tales who need to be rescued from fates worse than death, occasionally at the hands (or other appendages) of beasts. In some stories they are spoils won by men whose own plain looks are less than beautiful, but who win them by outwitting rivals for their hand, or by expressing their affection in ways more genuine and heartfelt than do more comely suitors. Although in most stories beauty of face is an index to beauty of soul, this is not always the case. The beautiful princess in "The Frog King," who thinks herself a victim of an unfair bargain, shows a cruel and spiteful side that her king-in-frog's-clothing patiently helps her to tame. In a small number of these stories outward physical beauty seems a compensation for an ugly disposition and unappealing attitude that no amount of kindliness or instruction can alter.

The "Beasts" section of this book is a veritable bestiary of the many animal types to be found in the fairy and folktale tradition. Some of these stories are struck from the mold of the classic animal fables of Aesop in which animals are endowed with the personality quirks that humans project upon them: i.e., cunning foxes, clever cats, courageous lions, mischievous monkeys, and so forth. Often these creatures are the heroes and villains of their own stories, with nary a human in sight. Other stories feature humans contending with monsters of myth and legend: dragons, giant serpents, drakens, people-eating nundas, and evil tanukis. The beasts in these tales invariably bring out the best and worst in human behavior from their opponents.

Some of the stories collected in this volume will be very well known even to readers who are not well acquainted with fairy tales. Are there any readers so unfamiliar with fairy tale classics such as "Cinderella," "Snow-White and the Seven Dwarfs," and the title tale that they would not immediately know the reason for their inclusion? But many of the selections will offer the same pleasures experienced when reading those classics for the first time. The beauties and the beasts on display in these tales represent the polar extremes of the character types in which fairy tales commonly traffic. And it is between those extremes that all manner of the magical and the marvelous occur.

Beauty and the Beast

(From *The Blue Fairy Book*)

Once upon a time, in a very far-off country, there lived a merchant who had been so fortunate in all his undertakings that he was enormously rich. As he had, however, six sons and six daughters, he found that his money was not too much to let them all have everything they fancied, as they were accustomed to do.

But one day a most unexpected misfortune befell them. Their house caught fire and was speedily burnt to the ground, with all the splendid furniture, the books, pictures, gold, silver, and precious goods it contained; and this was only the beginning of their troubles. Their father, who had until this moment prospered in all ways, suddenly lost every ship he had upon the sea, either by dint of pirates, shipwreck, or fire. Then he heard that his clerks in distant countries, whom he trusted entirely, had proved unfaithful; and at last from great wealth he fell into the direst poverty.

All that he had left was a little house in a desolate place at least a hundred leagues from the town in which he had lived, and to this he was forced to retreat with his children, who were in despair at the idea of leading such a different life. Indeed, the daughters at first hoped that their friends, who had been so numerous while they were rich, would insist on their staying in their houses now they no longer possessed one. But they soon found that they were left alone, and that their former friends even attributed their misfortunes to their own extravagance, and showed no intention of offering them any help. So nothing was left for them but to take their departure to the cottage, which stood in the midst of a dark forest, and seemed to be the most dismal place upon the face of the earth. As they were too poor to have any servants, the girls had to work hard, like peasants, and the sons, for their part, cultivated the fields to earn their living. Roughly clothed, and living in the simplest way, the girls regretted unceasingly the luxuries and amusements of their former life; only the youngest tried to be brave and cheerful. She had been as sad as anyone when misfortune overtook her father, but, soon recovering her natural gaiety, she set to work to make the best of things, to amuse her father and brothers as well as she could, and to try to persuade her sisters to join her in dancing and singing. But they would do nothing of the sort, and, because she was not as doleful as themselves, they declared that this miserable life was all she was fit for. But she was really far prettier and cleverer than they were; indeed, she was so lovely that she was always called Beauty. After two years, when they were all beginning to get used to their new life, something happened to disturb their tranquility. Their father received the news that one of his ships, which he had believed to be lost, had come safely into port with a rich cargo. All the sons and daughters at once thought that their poverty was at an end, and wanted to set out directly for the town; but their father, who was more prudent, begged them to wait a little, and, though it was harvest time, and he could ill be spared, determined to go himself first, to make inquiries. Only the youngest daughter had any doubt but that they would soon again be as rich as they were before, or at least rich enough to live comfortably in some town where they would find amusement and gay companions once more. So they all loaded their father with commissions for jewels and dresses which it would have taken a fortune to buy; only Beauty, feeling sure that it was of no use, did not ask for anything. Her father, noticing her silence, said: "And what shall I bring for you, Beauty?"

"The only thing I wish for is to see you come home safely," she answered.

But this only vexed her sisters, who fancied she was blaming them for having asked for such costly things. Her father, however, was pleased, but as he thought that at her age she certainly ought to like pretty presents, he told her to choose something.

"Well, dear father," she said, "as you insist upon it, I beg that you will bring me a rose. I have not seen one since we came here, and I love them so much."

So the merchant set out and reached the town as quickly as possible, but only to find that his former companions, believing him to be dead, had divided between them the goods which the ship had brought; and after six months of trouble and expense he found himself as poor as when he started, having been able to recover only just enough to pay the cost of his journey. To make matters worse, he was obliged to leave the town in the most terrible weather, so that by the time he was within a few leagues of his home he was almost exhausted with cold and fatigue. Though he knew it would take some hours to get through the forest, he was so anxious to be at his journey's end that he resolved to go on; but night overtook him, and the deep snow and bitter frost made it impossible for his horse to carry him any further. Not a house was to be seen; the only shelter he could get was the hollow trunk of a great tree, and there he crouched all the night which seemed to him the longest he had ever known. In spite of his weariness the howling of the wolves kept him awake, and even when at last the day broke he was not much better off, for the falling snow had covered up every path, and he did not know which way to turn.

At length he made out some sort of track, and though at the beginning it was so rough and slippery that he fell down more than once, it presently became easier, and led him into an avenue of trees which ended in a splendid castle. It seemed to the merchant very strange that no snow had fallen in the avenue, which was entirely composed of orange trees, covered with flowers and fruit. When he reached the first court of the castle he saw before him a flight of agate steps, and went up them, and passed through several splendidly furnished rooms. The pleasant warmth of the air revived him, and he felt very hungry; but there seemed to be nobody in all this vast and splendid palace whom he could ask to give him something to eat. Deep silence reigned everywhere, and at last, tired of roaming through empty rooms and galleries, he stopped in a room smaller than the rest, where a clear fire was burning and a couch was drawn up close to it. Thinking that this must be prepared for someone who was expected, he sat down to wait till he should come, and very soon fell into a sweet sleep.

When his extreme hunger wakened him after several hours, he was still alone; but a little table, upon which was a good dinner, had been drawn up close to him, and, as he had eaten nothing for twenty-four hours, he lost no time in beginning his meal, hoping that he might soon have an opportunity of thanking his considerate entertainer, whoever it might be. But no one appeared, and even after another long sleep, from which he awoke completely refreshed, there was no sign of anybody, though a fresh meal of dainty cakes and fruit was prepared upon the little table at his elbow. Being naturally timid, the silence began to terrify him, and he resolved to search once more through all the rooms; but it was of no use. Not even a servant was to be seen; there was no sign of life in the palace! He began to wonder what he should do, and to amuse himself by pretending that all the treasures he saw were his own, and considering how he would divide them among his children. Then he went down into the garden, and though it was winter everywhere else, here the sun shone, and the birds sang, and the flowers bloomed, and the air was soft and sweet. The merchant, in ecstasies with all he saw and heard, said to himself:

"All this must be meant for me. I will go this minute and bring my children to share all these delights."

In spite of being so cold and weary when he reached the castle, he had taken his horse to the stable and fed it. Now he thought he would saddle it for his homeward journey, and he turned down the path which led to the stable. This path had a hedge of roses on each side of it, and the merchant thought he had never seen or smelt such exquisite flowers. They reminded him of his promise to Beauty, and he stopped and had just gathered one to take to her when he was startled by a strange noise behind him. Turning round, he saw a frightful Beast, which seemed to be very angry and said, in a terrible voice:

"Who told you that you might gather my roses? Was it not enough that I allowed you to be in my palace and was kind to you? This is the way you show your gratitude, by stealing my flowers! But your insolence shall not go unpunished." The merchant, terrified by these furious words, dropped the fatal rose, and, throwing himself on his knees, cried: "Pardon me, noble sir. I am truly grateful to you for your hospitality, which was so magnificent that I could not imagine that you would be offended by my taking such a little thing as a rose." But the Beast's anger was not lessened by this speech.

"You are very ready with excuses and flattery," he cried; "but that will not save you from the death you deserve."

"Alas!" thought the merchant, "if my daughter could only know what danger her rose has brought me into!"

And in despair he began to tell the Beast all his misfortunes, and the reason of his journey, not forgetting to mention Beauty's request.

"A king's ransom would hardly have procured all that my other daughters asked," he said; "but I thought that I might at least take Beauty her rose. I beg you to forgive me, for you see I meant no harm."

The Beast considered for a moment, and then he said, in a less furious tone:

"I will forgive you on one condition—that is, that you will give me one of your daughters."

"Ah!" cried the merchant, "if I were cruel enough to buy my own life at the expense of one of my children's, what excuse could I invent to bring her here?"

"No excuse would be necessary," answered the Beast. "If she comes at all she must come willingly. On no other condition will I have her. See if any one of them is courageous enough, and loves you well enough to come and save your life. You seem to be an honest man, so I will trust you to go home. I give you a month to see if either of your daughters will come back with you and stay here, to let you go free. If neither of them is willing, you must come alone, after bidding them good-bye for ever, for then you will belong to me. And do not imagine that you can hide from me, for if you fail to keep your word I will come and fetch you!" added the Beast grimly.

The merchant accepted this proposal, though he did not really think any of his daughters could be persuaded to come. He promised to return at the time appointed, and then, anxious to escape from the presence of the Beast, he asked permission to set off at once. But the Beast answered that he could not go until next day.

"Then you will find a horse ready for you," he said. "Now go and eat your supper, and await my orders."

The poor merchant, more dead than alive, went back to his room, where the most delicious supper was already served on the little table which was drawn up before a blazing fire. But he was too terrified to eat, and only tasted a few of the dishes, for fear the Beast should be angry if he did not obey his orders. When he had finished he heard a great noise in the next room, which he knew meant that the Beast was coming. As he could do nothing to escape his visit, the only thing that remained was to seem as little afraid as possible; so when the Beast appeared and asked roughly if he had supped well, the merchant answered humbly that he had, thanks to his host's kindness. Then the Beast warned him to remember their agreement, and to prepare his daughter exactly for what she had to expect.

"Do not get up to-morrow," he added, "until you see the sun and hear a golden bell ring. Then you will find your breakfast waiting for you here, and the horse you are to ride will be ready in the courtyard. He will also bring

5

you back again when you come with your daughter a month hence. Farewell. Take a rose to Beauty, and remember your promise!"

The merchant was only too glad when the Beast went away, and though he could not sleep for sadness, he lay down until the sun rose. Then, after a hasty breakfast, he went to gather Beauty's rose, and mounted his horse, which carried him off so swiftly that in an instant he had lost sight of the palace, and he was still wrapped in gloomy thoughts when it stopped before the door of the cottage.

His sons and daughters, who had been very uneasy at his long absence, rushed to meet him, eager to know the result of his journey, which, seeing him mounted upon a splendid horse and wrapped in a rich mantle, they supposed to be favourable. He hid the truth from them at first, only saying sadly to Beauty as he gave her the rose:

"Here is what you asked me to bring you; you little know what it has cost."

But this excited their curiosity so greatly that presently he told them his adventures from beginning to end, and then they were all very unhappy. The girls lamented loudly over their lost hopes, and the sons declared that their father should not return to this terrible castle, and began to make plans for killing the Beast if it should come to fetch him. But he reminded them that he had promised to go back. Then the girls were very angry with Beauty, and said it was all her fault, and that if she had asked for something sensible this would never have happened, and complained bitterly that they should have to suffer for her folly.

Poor Beauty, much distressed, said to them:

"I have, indeed, caused this misfortune, but I assure you I did it innocently. Who could have guessed that to ask for a rose in the middle of summer would cause so much misery? But as I did the mischief it is only just that I should suffer for it. I will therefore go back with my father to keep his promise."

At first nobody would hear of this arrangement, and her father and brothers, who loved her dearly, declared that nothing should make them let her go; but Beauty was firm. As the time drew near she divided all her little possessions between her sisters, and said good-bye to everything she loved, and when the fatal day came she encouraged and cheered her father as they mounted together the horse which had brought him back. It seemed to fly rather than gallop, but so smoothly that Beauty was not frightened; indeed, she would have enjoyed the journey if she had not feared what might happen to her at the end of it. Her father still tried to persuade her to go back, but in vain. While they were talking the night fell, and then, to their great surprise, wonderful colored lights began to shine in all directions, and splendid fireworks blazed out before them; all the forest was illuminated by them, and even felt pleasantly warm, though it had been bitterly cold before. This lasted until they reached the avenue of orange trees, where were statues holding flaming torches, and when they got nearer to the palace they saw that it was illuminated from the roof to the ground, and music sounded softly from the courtyard. "The Beast must be very hungry," said Beauty, trying to laugh, "if he makes all this rejoicing over the arrival of his prey."

But, in spite of her anxiety, she could not help admiring all the wonderful things she saw.

The horse stopped at the foot of the flight of steps leading to the terrace, and when they had dismounted her father led her to the little room he had been in before, where they found a splendid fire burning, and the table daintily spread with a delicious supper.

The merchant knew that this was meant for them, and Beauty, who was rather less frightened now that she had passed through so many rooms and seen nothing of the Beast, was quite willing to begin, for her long ride had made her very hungry. But they had hardly finished their meal when the noise of the Beast's footsteps was heard approaching, and Beauty clung to her father in terror, which became all the greater when she saw how frightened he was. But when the Beast really appeared, though she trembled at the sight of him, she made a great effort to hide her terror, and saluted him respectfully.

This evidently pleased the Beast. After looking at her he said, in a tone that might have struck terror into the boldest heart, though he did not seem to be angry:

"Good-evening, old man. Good-evening, Beauty."

The merchant was too terrified to reply, but Beauty answered sweetly:

"Good-evening, Beast."

"Have you come willingly?" asked the Beast. "Will you be content to stay here when your father goes away?"

Beauty answered bravely that she was quite prepared to stay.

"I am pleased with you," said the Beast. "As you have come of your own accord, you may stay. As for you, old man," he added, turning to the merchant, "at sunrise to-morrow you will take your departure. When the bell rings get up quickly and eat your breakfast, and you will find the same horse waiting to take you home; but remember that you must never expect to see my palace again."

Then turning to Beauty, he said:

"Take your father into the next room, and help him to choose everything you think your brothers and sisters would like to have. You will find two traveling-trunks there; fill them as full as you can. It is only just that you should send them something very precious as a remembrance of yourself."

Then he went away, after saying, "Good-bye, Beauty; good-bye, old man"; and though Beauty was beginning to think with great dismay of her father's departure, she was afraid to disobey the Beast's orders; and they went into the next room, which had shelves and cupboards all round it. They were greatly surprised at the riches it contained. There were splendid dresses fit for a queen, with all the ornaments that were to be worn with them; and when Beauty opened the cupboards she was quite dazzled by the gorgeous jewels that lay in heaps upon every shelf. After choosing a vast quantity, which she divided between her sisters—for she had made a heap of the wonderful dresses for each of them—she opened the last chest, which was full of gold.

"I think, father," she said, "that, as the gold will be more useful to you, we had better take out the other things again, and fill the trunks with it." So they did this; but the more they put in the more room there seemed to be, and at last they put back all the jewels and dresses they had taken out, and Beauty even added as many more of the jewels as she could carry at once; and then the trunks were not too full, but they were so heavy that an elephant could not have carried them!

"The Beast was mocking us," cried the merchant; "he must have pretended to give us all these things, knowing that I could not carry them away."

"Let us wait and see," answered Beauty. "I cannot believe that he meant to deceive us. All we can do is to fasten them up and leave them ready."

So they did this and returned to the little room, where, to their astonishment, they found breakfast ready. The merchant ate his with a good appetite, as the Beast's generosity made him believe that he might perhaps venture to come back soon and see Beauty. But she felt sure that her father was leaving her for ever, so she was very sad when the bell rang sharply for the second time, and warned them that the time had come for them to part. They went down into the courtyard, where two horses were waiting, one loaded with the two trunks, the other for him to ride. They were pawing the ground in their impatience to start, and the merchant was forced to bid Beauty a hasty farewell; and as soon as he was mounted he went off at such a pace that she lost sight of him in an instant. Then Beauty began to cry, and wandered sadly back to her own room. But she soon found that she was very sleepy, and as she had nothing better to do she lay down and instantly fell asleep. And then she dreamed that she was walking by a brook bordered with trees, and lamenting her sad fate, when a young prince, handsomer than anyone she had ever seen, and with a voice that went straight to her heart, came and said to her, "Ah, Beauty! you are not so unfortunate as you suppose. Here you will be rewarded for all you have suffered elsewhere. Your every wish shall be gratified. Only try to find me out, no matter how I may be disguised, as I love you dearly, and in making me happy you will find your own happiness. Be as true-hearted as you are beautiful, and we shall have nothing left to wish for."

"What can I do, Prince, to make you happy?" said Beauty.

"Only be grateful," he answered, "and do not trust too much to your eyes. And, above all, do not desert me until you have saved me from my cruel misery."

After this she thought she found herself in a room with a stately and beautiful lady, who said to her:

"Dear Beauty, try not to regret all you have left behind you, for you are destined to a better fate. Only do not let yourself be deceived by appearances."

Beauty found her dreams so interesting that she was in no hurry to awake, but presently the clock roused her by calling her name softly twelve times, and then she got up and found her dressing-table set out with everything she could possibly want; and when her toilet was finished she found dinner was waiting in the room next to hers. But dinner does not take very long when you are all by yourself, and very soon she sat down cozily in the corner of a sofa, and began to think about the charming Prince she had seen in her dream.

"He said I could make him happy," said Beauty to herself.

"It seems, then, that this horrible Beast keeps him a prisoner. How can I set him free? I wonder why they both told me not to trust to appearances? I don't understand it. But, after all, it was only a dream, so why should I trouble myself about it? I had better go and find something to do to amuse myself."

So she got up and began to explore some of the many rooms of the palace.

The first she entered was lined with mirrors, and Beauty saw herself reflected on every side, and thought she had never seen such a charming room. Then a bracelet which was hanging from a chandelier caught her eye, and on taking it down she was greatly surprised to find that it held a portrait of her unknown admirer, just as she had seen him in her dream. With great delight she slipped the bracelet on her arm, and went on into a gallery of pictures, where she soon found a portrait of the same handsome Prince, as large as life, and so well painted that as she studied it he seemed to smile kindly at her. Tearing herself away from the portrait at last, she passed through into a room which contained every musical instrument under the sun, and here she amused herself for a long while in trying some of them, and singing until she was tired. The next room was a library, and she saw everything she had ever wanted to read, as well as everything she had read, and it seemed to her that a whole lifetime would not be enough to even read the names of the books, there were so many. By this time it was growing dusk, and wax candles in diamond and ruby candlesticks were beginning to light themselves in every room.

Beauty found her supper served just at the time she preferred to have it, but she did not see anyone or hear a sound, and, though her father had warned her that she would be alone, she began to find it rather dull.

But presently she heard the Beast coming, and wondered tremblingly if he meant to eat her up now.

However, as he did not seem at all ferocious, and only said gruffly:

"Good-evening, Beauty," she answered cheerfully and managed to conceal her terror. Then the Beast asked her how she had been amusing herself, and she told him all the rooms she had seen.

Then he asked if she thought she could be happy in his palace; and Beauty answered that everything was so beautiful that she would be very hard to please if she could not be happy. And after about an hour's talk Beauty began to think that the Beast was not nearly so terrible as she had supposed at first. Then he got up to leave her, and said in his gruff voice:

"Do you love me, Beauty? Will you marry me?"

"Oh! what shall I say?" cried Beauty, for she was afraid to make the Beast angry by refusing.

"Say 'yes' or 'no' without fear," he replied.

"Oh! no, Beast," said Beauty hastily.

"Since you will not, good-night, Beauty," he said. And she answered, "Good-night, Beast," very glad to find that her refusal had not provoked him. And after he was gone she was very soon in bed and asleep, and dreaming of her unknown Prince. She thought he came and said to her:

"Ah, Beauty! why are you so unkind to me? I fear I am fated to be unhappy for many a long day still."

And then her dreams changed, but the charming Prince figured in them all; and when morning came her first thought was to look at the portrait, and see if it was really like him, and she found that it certainly was.

This morning she decided to amuse herself in the garden, for the sun shone, and all the fountains were playing; but she was astonished to find that every place was familiar to her, and presently she came to the brook where the myrtle trees were growing where she had first met the Prince in her dream, and that made her think more than ever that he must be kept a prisoner by the Beast. When she was tired she went back to the palace, and found a new room full of materials for every kind of work—ribbons to make into bows, and silks to work into flowers. Then there was an aviary full of rare birds, which were so tame that they flew to Beauty as soon as they saw her, and perched upon her shoulders and her head.

"Pretty little creatures," she said, "how I wish that your cage was nearer to my room, that I might often hear you sing!"

So saying she opened a door, and found, to her delight, that it led into her own room, though she had thought it was quite the other side of the palace.

There were more birds in a room farther on, parrots and cockatoos that could talk, and they greeted Beauty by name; indeed, she found them so entertaining that she took one or two back to her room, and they talked to her while she was at supper; after which the Beast paid her his usual visit, and asked her the same questions as before, and then with a gruff "good-night" he took his departure, and Beauty went to bed to dream of her mysterious Prince. The days passed swiftly in different amusements, and after a while Beauty found out another strange thing in the palace, which often pleased her when she was tired of being alone. There was one room which she had not noticed particularly; it was empty, except that under each of the windows stood a very comfortable chair; and the first time she had looked out of the window it had seemed to her that a black curtain prevented her from seeing anything outside. But the second time she went into the room, happening to be tired, she sat down in one of the chairs, when instantly the curtain was rolled aside, and a most amusing pantomime was acted before her; there were dances, and colored lights, and music, and pretty dresses, and it was all so gay that Beauty was in ecstasies. After that she tried the other seven windows in turn, and there was some new and surprising entertainment to be seen from each of them, so that Beauty never could feel lonely any more. Every evening after supper the Beast came to see her, and always before saying good-night asked her in his terrible voice:

"Beauty, will you marry me?"

And it seemed to Beauty, now she understood him better, that when she said, "No, Beast," he went away quite sad. But her happy dreams of the handsome young Prince soon made her forget the poor Beast, and the only thing that at all disturbed her was to be constantly told to distrust appearances, to let her heart guide her, and not her eyes, and many other equally perplexing things, which, consider as she would, she could not understand.

So everything went on for a long time, until at last, happy as she was, Beauty began to long for the sight of her father and her brothers and sisters; and one night, seeing her look very sad, the Beast asked her what was the matter. Beauty had quite ceased to be afraid of him. Now she knew that he was really gentle in spite of his ferocious looks and his dreadful voice. So she answered that she was longing to see her home once more. Upon hearing this the Beast seemed sadly distressed, and cried miserably.

"Ah! Beauty, have you the heart to desert an unhappy Beast like this? What more do you want to make you happy? Is it because you hate me that you want to escape?"

"No, dear Beast," answered Beauty softly, "I do not hate you, and I should be very sorry never to see you any more, but I long to see my father again. Only let me go for two months, and I promise to come back to you and stay for the rest of my life."

The Beast, who had been sighing dolefully while she spoke, now replied:

"I cannot refuse you anything you ask, even though it should cost me my life. Take the four boxes you will find in the room next to your own, and fill them with everything you wish to take with you. But remember your promise and come back when the two months are over, or you may have cause to repent it, for if you do not come in good time you will find your faithful Beast dead.

The Frog-King

(FROM *GRIMM'S COMPLETE FAIRY TALES*)

In old times when wishing still helped one, there lived a king whose daughters were all beautiful, but the youngest was so beautiful that the sun itself, which has seen so much, was astonished whenever it shone in her face. Close by the King's castle lay a great dark forest, and under an old lime-tree in the forest was a well; and when the day was very warm, the King's child went out into the forest and sat down by the side of the cool fountain, and when she was dull she took a golden ball, and threw it up on high and caught it, and this ball was her favorite plaything.

Now it so happened that on one occasion the princess's golden ball did not fall into the little hand which she was holding up for it, but on to the ground beyond, and rolled straight into the water. The King's daughter followed it with her eyes, but it vanished; and the well was deep—so deep that the bottom could not be seen. On this she began to cry, and cried louder and louder, and could not be comforted.

And as she thus lamented some one said to her, "What ails thee, King's daughter? Thou weepest so that even a stone would show pity."

She looked round to the side from whence the voice came, and saw a frog stretching forth its thick, ugly head from the water. "Ah! old water-splasher, is it thou?" said she; "I am weeping for my golden ball, which has fallen into the well."

"Be quiet, and do not weep," answered the frog, "I can help thee, but what wilt thou give me if I bring thy plaything up again?"

"Whatever thou wilt have, dear frog," said she—"My clothes, my pearls and jewels, and even the golden crown which I am wearing."

The frog answered, "I do not care for thy clothes, thy pearls and jewels, or thy golden crown, but if thou wilt love me and let me be thy companion and play-fellow, and sit by thee at thy little table, and eat off thy little golden plate, and drink out of thy little cup, and sleep in thy little bed—if thou wilt promise me this I will go down below, and bring thee thy golden ball up again."

"Oh yes," said she, "I promise thee all thou wishest, if thou wilt but bring me my ball back again." She, however, thought, "How the silly frog does talk! He lives in the water with the other frogs, and croaks, and can be no companion to any human being!"

But the frog when he had received this promise, put his head into the water and sank down, and in a short while came swimming up again with the ball in his mouth, and threw it on the grass. The King's daughter was delighted to see her pretty plaything once more, and picked it up, and ran away with it. "Wait, wait," said the frog. "Take me with thee. I can't run as thou canst." But what did it avail him to scream his croak, croak, after her, as loudly as he could? She did not listen to it, but ran home and soon forgot the poor frog, who was forced to go back into his well again.

The next day when she had seated herself at table with the King and all the courtiers, and was eating from her little golden plate, something came creeping splish splash, splish splash, up the marble staircase, and when it had got to the top, it knocked at the door and cried, "Princess, youngest princess, open the door for me."

She ran to see who was outside, but when she opened the door, there sat the frog in front of it. Then she slammed the door to, in great haste, sat down to dinner again, and was quite frightened. The King saw plainly that her heart was beating violently, and said, "My child, what art thou so afraid of? Is there perchance a giant outside who wants to carry thee away?"

"Ah, no," replied she. "It is no giant but a disgusting frog."

"What does a frog want with thee?"

"Ah, dear father, yesterday as I was in the forest sitting by the well, playing, my golden ball fell into the water. And because I cried so, the frog brought it out again for me, and because he so insisted, I promised him he should be my companion, but I never thought he would be able to come out of his water! And now he is outside there, and wants to come in to me."

In the meantime it knocked a second time, and cried,

> "Princess! youngest princess!
> Open the door for me!
> Dost thou not know what thou saidst to me
> Yesterday by the cool waters of the fountain?

Princess, youngest princess!
Open the door for me!"

Then said the King, "That which thou hast promised must thou perform. Go and let him in."

She went and opened the door, and the frog hopped in and followed her, step by step, to her chair. There he sat and cried, "Lift me up beside thee."

She delayed, until at last the King commanded her to do it. When the frog was once on the chair he wanted to be on the table, and when he was on the table he said, "Now, push thy little golden plate nearer to me that we may eat together."

She did this, but it was easy to see that she did not do it willingly. The frog enjoyed what he ate, but almost every mouthful she took choked her.

At length he said, "I have eaten and am satisfied; now I am tired, carry me into thy little room and make thy little silken bed ready, and we will both lie down and go to sleep."

The King's daughter began to cry, for she was afraid of the cold frog which she did not like to touch, and which was now to sleep in her pretty, clean little bed. But the King grew angry and said, "He who helped thee when thou wert in trouble ought not afterwards to be despised by thee."

So she took hold of the frog with two fingers, carried him upstairs, and put him in a corner. But when she was in bed he crept to her and said, "I am tired, I want to sleep as well as thou, lift me up or I will tell thy father."

Then she was terribly angry, and took him up and threw him with all her might against the wall. "Now, thou wilt be quiet, odious frog," said she.

But when he fell down he was no frog but a King's son with beautiful kind eyes. He by her father's will was now her dear companion and husband. Then he told her how he had been bewitched by a wicked witch, and how no one could have delivered him from the well but herself, and that to-morrow they would go together into his kingdom. Then they went to sleep, and next morning when the sun awoke them, a carriage came driving up with eight white horses, which had white ostrich feathers on their heads, and were harnessed with golden chains, and behind stood the young King's servant Faithful Henry.

Faithful Henry had been so unhappy when his master was changed into a frog that he had caused three iron bands to be laid round his heart, lest it should burst with grief and sadness. The carriage was to conduct the young King into his Kingdom. Faithful Henry helped them both in, and placed himself behind again, and was full of joy because of this deliverance. And when they had driven a part of the way the King's son heard a cracking behind him as if something had broken. So he turned round and cried, "Henry, the carriage is breaking."

"No, master, it is not the carriage. It is a band from my heart, which was put there in my great pain when you were a frog and imprisoned in the well."

Again and once again while they were on their way something cracked, and each time the King's son thought the carriage was breaking; but it was only the bands which were springing from the heart of faithful Henry because his master was set free and was happy.

The Wonderful Sheep

(From *The Blue Fairy Book*)

Once upon a time—in the days when the fairies lived—there was a king who had three daughters, who were all young, and clever, and beautiful; but the youngest of the three, who was called Miranda, was the prettiest and the most beloved.

The King, her father, gave her more dresses and jewels in a month than he gave the others in a year; but she was so generous that she shared everything with her sisters, and they were all as happy and as fond of one another as they could be.

Now, the King had some quarrelsome neighbors, who, tired of leaving him in peace, began to make war upon him so fiercely that he feared he would be altogether beaten if he did not make an effort to defend himself. So he collected a great army and set off to fight them, leaving the Princesses with their governess in a castle where news of the war was brought every day—sometimes that the King had taken a town, or won a battle, and, at last, that he had altogether overcome his enemies and chased them out of his kingdom, and was coming back to the castle as quickly as possible, to see his dear little Miranda whom he loved so much.

The three Princesses put on dresses of satin, which they had had made on purpose for this great occasion, one green, one blue, and the third white; their jewels were the same colors. The eldest wore emeralds, the second turquoises, and the youngest diamonds, and thus adorned they went to meet the King, singing verses which they had composed about his victories.

When he saw them all so beautiful and so gay he embraced them tenderly, but gave Miranda more kisses than either of the others.

Presently a splendid banquet was served, and the King and his daughters sat down to it, and as he always thought that there was some special meaning in everything, he said to the eldest:

"Tell me why you have chosen a green dress."

"Sire," she answered, "having heard of your victories I thought that green would signify my joy and the hope of your speedy return."

"That is a very good answer," said the King; "and you, my daughter," he continued, "why did you take a blue dress?"

"Sire," said the Princess, "to show that we constantly hoped for your success, and that the sight of you is as welcome to me as the sky with its most beautiful stars."

"Why," said the King, "your wise answers astonish me; and you, Miranda. What made you dress yourself all in white?"

"Because, sire," she answered, "white suits me better than anything else."

"What!" said the King angrily, "was that all you thought of, vain child?"

"I thought you would be pleased with me," said the Princess; "that was all."

The King, who loved her, was satisfied with this, and even pretended to be pleased that she had not told him all her reasons at first.

"And now," said he, "as I have supped well, and it is not time yet to go to bed, tell me what you dreamed last night."

The eldest said she had dreamed that he brought her a dress, and the precious stones and gold embroidery on it were brighter than the sun.

The dream of the second was that the King had brought her a spinning wheel and a distaff, that she might spin him some shirts.

But the youngest said: "I dreamed that my second sister was to be married, and on her wedding-day, you, father, held a golden ewer and said: 'Come, Miranda, and I will hold the water that you may dip your hands in it.'"

The King was very angry indeed when he heard this dream, and frowned horribly; indeed, he made such an ugly face that everyone knew how angry he was, and he got up and went off to bed in a great hurry; but he could not forget his daughter's dream. "Does the proud girl wish to make me her slave?" he said to himself. "I am not surprised at her choosing to dress herself in white satin without a thought of me. She does not think me worthy of her consideration! But I will soon put an end to her pretensions!"

He rose in a fury, and although it was not yet daylight, he sent for the Captain of his Bodyguard, and said to him:

"You have heard the Princess Miranda's dream? I consider that it means strange things against me, therefore I order you to take her away into the forest and kill her, and, that I may be sure it is done, you must bring me her heart and her tongue. If you attempt to deceive me you shall be put to death!"

The Captain of the Guard was very much astonished when he heard this barbarous order, but he did not dare to contradict the King for fear of making him still more angry, or causing him to send someone else, so he answered that he would fetch the Princess and do as the King had said. When he went to her room they would hardly let him in, it was so early, but he said that the King had sent for Miranda, and she got up quickly and came out; a little black girl called Patypata held up her train, and her pet monkey and her little dog ran after her. The monkey was called Grabugeon, and the little dog Tintin.

The Captain of the Guard begged Miranda to come down into the garden where the King was enjoying the fresh air, and when they got there, he pretended to search for him, but as he was not to be found, he said:

"No doubt his Majesty has strolled into the forest," and he opened the little door that led to it and they went through.

By this time the daylight had begun to appear, and the Princess, looking at her conductor, saw that he had tears in his eyes and seemed too sad to speak.

"What is the matter?" she said in the kindest way. "You seem very sorrowful."

"Alas! Princess," he answered, "who would not be sorrowful who was ordered to do such a terrible thing as I am? The King has commanded me to kill you here, and carry your heart and your tongue to him, and if I disobey I shall lose my life."

The poor Princess was terrified, she grew very pale and began to cry softly.

Looking up at the Captain of the Guard with her beautiful eyes, she said gently:

"Will you really have the heart to kill me? I have never done you any harm, and have always spoken well of you to the King. If I had deserved my father's anger I would suffer without a murmur, but, alas! he is unjust to complain of me, when I have always treated him with love and respect."

"Fear nothing, Princess," said the Captain of the Guard. "I would far rather die myself than hurt you; but even if I am killed you will not be safe: we must find some way of making the King believe that you are dead."

"What can we do?" said Miranda; "unless you take him my heart and my tongue he will never believe you."

The Princess and the Captain of the Guard were talking so earnestly that they did not think of Patypata, but she had overheard all they said, and now came and threw herself at Miranda's feet.

"Madam," she said, "I offer you my life; let me be killed, I shall be only too happy to die for such a kind mistress."

"Why, Patypata," cried the Princess, kissing her, "that would never do; your life is as precious to me as my own, especially after such a proof of your affection as you have just given me."

"You are right, Princess," said Grabugeon, coming forward, "to love such a faithful slave as Patypata; she is of more use to you than I am, I offer you my tongue and my heart most willingly, especially as I wish to make a great name for myself in Goblin Land."

"No, no, my little Grabugeon," replied Miranda, "I cannot bear the thought of taking your life."

"Such a good little dog as I am," cried Tintin, "could not think of letting either of you die for his mistress. If anyone is to die for her it must be me."

And then began a great dispute between Patypata, Grabugeon, and Tintin, and they came to high words, until at last Grabugeon, who was quicker than the others, ran up to the very top of the nearest tree, and let herself fall, head first, to the ground, and there she lay—quite dead!

The Princess was very sorry, but as Grabugeon was really dead, she allowed the Captain of the Guard to take her tongue; but, alas! it was such a little one—not bigger than the Princess's thumb—that they decided sorrowfully that it was of no use at all: the King would not have been taken in by it for a moment!

"Alas! my little monkey," cried the Princess, "I have lost you, and yet I am no better off than I was before."

"The honor of saving your life is to be mine," interrupted Patypata, and, before they could prevent her, she had picked up a knife and cut her head off in an instant.

But when the Captain of the Guard would have taken her tongue it turned out to be quite black, so that would not have deceived the King either.

"Am I not unlucky?" cried the poor Princess; "I lose everything I love, and am none the better for it."

"If you had accepted my offer," said Tintin, "you would only have had me to regret, and I should have had all your gratitude."

Miranda kissed her little dog, crying so bitterly, that at last she could bear it no longer, and turned away into the forest. When she looked back the Captain of the Guard was gone, and she was alone, except for Patypata, Grabugeon, and Tintin, who lay upon the ground. She could not leave the place until she had buried them in a pretty little mossy grave at the foot of a tree, and she wrote their names upon the bark of the tree, and how they had all died to save her life. And then she began to think where she could go for safety—for this forest was so close to her father's castle that she might be seen and recognized by the first passer-by, and, besides that, it was full of lions and wolves, who would have snapped up a princess just as soon as a stray chicken. So she began to walk as fast as she could, but the forest was so large and the sun was so hot that she nearly died of heat and terror and fatigue; look which way she would there seemed to be no end to the forest, and she was so frightened that she fancied every minute that she heard the King running after her to kill her. You may imagine how miserable she was, and how she cried as she went on, not knowing which path to follow, and with the thorny bushes scratching her dreadfully and tearing her pretty frock to pieces.

At last she heard the bleating of a sheep, and said to herself:

"No doubt there are shepherds here with their flocks; they will show me the way to some village where I can live disguised as a peasant girl. Alas! it is not always kings and princes who are the happiest people in the world. Who could have believed that I should ever be obliged to run away and hide because the King, for no reason at all, wishes to kill me?"

So saying she advanced toward the place where she heard the bleating, but what was her surprise when, in a lovely little glade quite surrounded by trees, she saw a large sheep; its wool was as white as snow, and its horns shone like gold; it had a garland of flowers round its neck, and strings of great pearls about its legs, and a collar of diamonds; it lay upon a bank of orange-flowers, under a canopy of cloth of gold which protected it from the heat of the sun. Nearly a hundred other sheep were scattered about, not eating the grass, but some drinking coffee, lemonade, or sherbet, others eating ices, strawberries and cream, or sweetmeats, while others, again, were playing games. Many of them wore golden collars with jewels, flowers, and ribbons.

Miranda stopped short in amazement at this unexpected sight, and was looking in all directions for the shepherd of this surprising flock, when the beautiful sheep came bounding toward her.

"Approach, lovely Princess," he cried; "have no fear of such gentle and peaceable animals as we are."

"What a marvel!" cried the Princess, starting back a little. "Here is a sheep that can talk."

"Your monkey and your dog could talk, madam," said he; "are you more astonished at us than at them?"

"A fairy gave them the power to speak," replied Miranda. "So I was used to them."

"Perhaps the same thing has happened to us," he said, smiling sheepishly. "But, Princess, what can have led you here?"

"A thousand misfortunes, Sir Sheep," she answered. "I am the unhappiest princess in the world, and I am seeking a shelter against my father's anger."

"Come with me, madam," said the Sheep; "I offer you a hiding-place which you only will know of, and where you will be mistress of everything you see."

"I really cannot follow you," said Miranda, "for I am too tired to walk another step."

The Sheep with the golden horns ordered that his chariot should be fetched, and a moment after appeared six goats, harnessed to a pumpkin, which was so big that two people could quite well sit in it, and was all lined with cushions of velvet and down. The Princess stepped into it, much amused at such a new kind of carriage, the King of the Sheep took his place beside her, and the goats ran away with them at full speed, and only stopped when they reached a cavern, the entrance to which was blocked by a great stone. This the King touched with his foot, and immediately it fell down, and he invited the Princess to enter without fear. Now, if she had not been so alarmed by everything that had happened, nothing could have induced her to go into this frightful cave, but she was so afraid of what might be behind her that she would have thrown herself even down a well at this moment. So, without hesitation, she followed the Sheep, who went before her, down, down, down, until she thought they must come out at the other side of the world—indeed, she was not sure that he wasn't leading her into Fairyland. At last she saw before her a great plain, quite covered with all sorts of flowers, the scent of which seemed to her nicer than anything she had ever smelled before; a broad river of orange-flower water flowed round it and fountains of wine of every kind ran in all directions and made the prettiest little cascades and brooks. The plain was covered with the strangest trees, there were whole avenues where partridges, ready roasted, hung from every branch, or, if you preferred pheasants, quails, turkeys, or rabbits, you had only to turn to the right hand or to the left and you were sure to find them. In places the air was darkened by showers of lobster-patties, white puddings, sausages, tarts, and all sorts of sweetmeats, or with pieces of gold and silver, diamonds and pearls. This unusual kind of rain, and the pleasantness of the whole place, would, no doubt, have attracted numbers of people to it, if the King of the Sheep had been of a more sociable disposition, but from all accounts it is evident that he was as grave as a judge.

As it was quite the nicest time of the year when Miranda arrived in this delightful land the only palace she saw was a long row of orange trees, jasmines, honeysuckles, and musk-roses, and their interlacing branches made the prettiest rooms possible, which were hung with gold and silver gauze, and had great mirrors and candlesticks, and most beautiful pictures. The Wonderful Sheep begged that the Princess would consider herself queen over all that she saw, and assured her that, though for some years he had been very sad and in great trouble, she had it in her power to make him forget all his grief.

"You are so kind and generous, noble Sheep," said the Princess, "that I cannot thank you enough, but I must confess that all I see here seems to me so extraordinary that I don't know what to think of it."

As she spoke a band of lovely fairies came up and offered her amber baskets full of fruit, but when she held out her hands to them they glided away, and she could feel nothing when she tried to touch them.

"Oh!" she cried, "what can they be? Whom am I with?" and she began to cry.

At this instant the King of the Sheep came back to her, and was so distracted to find her in tears that he could have torn his wool.

"What is the matter, lovely Princess?" he cried. "Has anyone failed to treat you with due respect?"

"Oh! no," said Miranda; "only I am not used to living with sprites and with sheep that talk, and everything here frightens me. It was very kind of you to bring me to this place, but I shall be even more grateful to you if you will take me up into the world again."

"Do not be afraid," said the Wonderful Sheep; "I entreat you to have patience, and listen to the story of my misfortunes. I was once a king, and my kingdom was the most splendid in the world. My subjects loved me, my neighbors envied and feared me. I was respected by everyone, and it was said that no king ever deserved it more.

"I was very fond of hunting, and one day, while chasing a stag, I left my attendants far behind; suddenly I saw the animal leap into a pool of water, and I rashly urged my horse to follow it, but before we had gone many steps I felt an extraordinary heat, instead of the coolness of the water; the pond dried up, a great gulf opened before me, out of which flames of fire shot up, and I fell helplessly to the bottom of a precipice.

"I gave myself up for lost, but presently a voice said: 'Ungrateful Prince, even this fire is hardly enough to warm your cold heart!'

"'Who complains of my coldness in this dismal place?' I cried.

"'An unhappy being who loves you hopelessly,' replied the voice, and at the same moment the flames began to flicker and cease to burn, and I saw a fairy, whom I had known as long as I could remember, and whose ugliness had always horrified me. She was leaning upon the arm of a most beautiful young girl, who wore chains of gold on her wrists and was evidently her slave.

"'Why, Ragotte,' I said, for that was the fairy's name, 'what is the meaning of all this? Is it by your orders that I am here?'

"'And whose fault is it,' she answered, 'that you have never understood me until now? Must a powerful fairy like myself condescend to explain her doings to you who are no better than an ant by comparison, though you think yourself a great king?'

"'Call me what you like,' I said impatiently; 'but what is it that you want—my crown, or my cities, or my treasures?'

"'Treasures!' said the fairy, disdainfully. 'If I chose I could make any one of my scullions richer and more powerful than you. I do not want your treasures, but,' she added softly, 'if you will give me your heart—if you will marry me—

I will add twenty kingdoms to the one you have already; you shall have a hundred castles full of gold and five hundred full of silver, and, in short, anything you like to ask me for.'

" 'Madam Ragotte,' said I, 'when one is at the bottom of a pit where one has fully expected to be roasted alive, it is impossible to think of asking such a charming person as you are to marry one! I beg that you will set me at liberty, and then I shall hope to answer you fittingly.'

" 'Ah!' said she, 'if you really loved me you would not care where you were—a cave, a wood, a fox-hole, a desert, would please you equally well. Do not think that you can deceive me; you fancy you are going to escape, but I assure you that you are going to stay here and the first thing I shall give you to do will be to keep my sheep—they are very good company and speak quite as well as you do.

"As she spoke she advanced, and led me to this plain where we now stand, and showed me her flock, but I paid little attention to it or to her; to tell the truth, I was so lost in admiration of her beautiful slave that I forgot every-thing else, and the cruel Ragotte, perceiving this, turned upon her so furious and terrible a look that she fell lifeless to the ground.

"At this dreadful sight I drew my sword and rushed at Ragotte, and should certainly have cut off her head had she not by her magic arts chained me to the spot on which I stood; all my efforts to move were useless, and at last, when I threw myself down on the ground in despair, she said to me, with a scornful smile:

" 'I intend to make you feel my power. It seems that you are a lion at present, I mean you to be a sheep.'

"So saying, she touched me with her wand, and I became what you see. I did not lose the power of speech, or of feeling the misery of my present state.

" 'For five years,' she said, 'you shall be a sheep, and lord of this pleasant land, while I, no longer able to see your face, which I loved so much, shall be better able to hate you as you deserve to be hated.'

"She disappeared as she finished speaking, and if I had not been too unhappy to care about anything I should have been glad that she was gone.

"The talking sheep received me as their king, and told me that they, too, were unfortunate princes who had, in different ways, offended the revenge-ful fairy, and had been added to her flock for a certain number of years; some more, some less. From time to time, indeed, one regains his own proper form and goes back again to his place in the upper world; but the other beings whom you saw are the rivals or the enemies of Ragotte, whom she has imprisoned for a hundred years or so; though even they will go back at last. The young slave of whom I told you about is one of these; I have seen her often, and it has been a great pleasure to me. She never speaks to me, and if I were nearer to her I know I should find her only a shadow, which would be very annoying. However, I noticed that one of my companions in misfortune was also very attentive to this little sprite, and I found out that he had been her lover, whom the cruel Ragotte had taken away from her long before; since then I have cared for, and thought of, nothing but how I might regain my freedom. I have often been in the forest; that is where I have seen you, lovely Princess, sometimes driving your chariot, which you did with all the grace and skill in the world; sometimes riding to the chase on so spirited a horse that it seemed as if no one but yourself could have managed it, and sometimes running races on the plain with the Princesses of your Court—running so lightly that it was you always who won the prize. Oh! Princess, I have loved you so long, and yet how dare I tell you of my love! what hope can there be for an unhappy sheep like myself?"

Miranda was so surprised and confused by all that she had heard that she hardly knew what answer to give to the King of the Sheep, but she managed to make some kind of little speech, which certainly did not forbid him to hope, and said that she should not be afraid of the shadows now she knew that they would some day come to life again. "Alas!" she continued, "if my poor Patypata, my dear Grabugeon, and pretty little Tintin, who all died for my sake, were equally well off, I should have nothing left to wish for here!"

Prisoner though he was, the King of the Sheep had still some powers and privileges.

"Go," said he to his Master of the Horse, "go and seek the shadows of the little black girl, the monkey, and the dog: they will amuse our Princess."

And an instant afterward Miranda saw them coming towards her, and their presence gave her the greatest pleasure, though they did not come near enough for her to touch them.

The King of the Sheep was so kind and amusing, and loved Miranda so dearly, that at last she began to love him too. Such a handsome sheep, who was so polite and considerate, could hardly fail to please, especially if one knew that he was really a king, and that his strange imprisonment would soon come to an end. So the Princess's days passed very gaily while she waited for the happy time to come. The King of the Sheep, with the help of all the flock, got up balls, concerts, and hunting parties, and even the shadows joined in all the fun, and came, making believe to be their own real selves.

One evening, when the couriers arrived (for the King sent most carefully for news—and they always brought the very best kinds), it was announced that the sister of the Princess Miranda was going to be married to a great Prince, and that nothing could be more splendid than all the preparations for the wedding.

"Ah!" cried the young Princess, "how unlucky I am to miss the sight of so many pretty things! Here am I imprisoned under the earth, with no company but sheep and shadows, while my sister is to be adorned like a queen and surrounded by all who love and admire her, and everyone but myself can go to wish her joy!"

"Why do you complain, Princess?" said the King of the Sheep. "Did I say that you were not to go to the wedding? Set out as soon as you please; only promise me that you will come back, for I love you too much to be able to live without you."

Miranda was very grateful to him, and promised faithfully that nothing in the world should keep her from coming back. The King caused an escort suitable to her rank to be got ready for her, and she dressed herself splendidly, not forgetting anything that could make her more beautiful. Her chariot was of mother-of-pearl, drawn by six dun-colored griffins just brought from the other side of the world, and she was attended by a number of guards in splendid uniforms, who were all at least eight feet high and had come from far and near to ride in the Princess's train.

Miranda reached her father's palace just as the wedding ceremony began, and everyone, as soon as she came in, was struck with surprise at her beauty and the splendor of her jewels. She heard exclamations of admiration on all sides; and the King her father looked at her so attentively that she was afraid he must recognize her; but he was so sure that she was dead that the idea never occurred to him.

However, the fear of not getting away made her leave before the marriage was over. She went out hastily, leaving behind her a little coral casket set with emeralds. On it was written in diamond letters: "Jewels for the Bride," and when they opened it, which they did as soon as it was found, there seemed to be no end to the pretty things it contained. The King, who had hoped to join the unknown Princess and find out who she was, was dreadfully disappointed when she disappeared so suddenly, and gave orders that if she ever came again the doors were to be shut that she might not get away so easily. Short as Miranda's absence had been, it had seemed like a hundred years to the King of the Sheep. He was waiting for her by a fountain in the thickest part of the forest, and the ground was strewn with splendid presents which he had prepared for her to show his joy and gratitude at her coming back.

As soon as she was in sight he rushed to meet her, leaping and bounding like a real sheep. He caressed her tenderly, throwing himself at her feet and kissing her hands, and told her how uneasy he had been in her absence, and how impatient for her return, with an eloquence which charmed her.

After some time came the news that the King's second daughter was going to be married. When Miranda heard it she begged the King of the Sheep to allow her to go and see the wedding as before. This request made him feel very sad, as if some misfortune must surely come of it, but his love for the Princess being stronger than anything else he did not like to refuse her.

"You wish to leave me, Princess," said he; "it is my unhappy fate—you are not to blame. I consent to your going, but, believe me, I can give you no stronger proof of my love than by so doing."

The Princess assured him that she would only stay a very short time, as she had done before, and begged him not to be uneasy, as she would be quite as much grieved if anything detained her as he could possibly be.

So, with the same escort, she set out, and reached the palace as the marriage ceremony began. Everybody was delighted to see her; she was so pretty that they thought she must be some fairy princess, and the Princes who were there could not take their eyes off her.

The King was more glad than anyone else that she had come again, and gave orders that the doors should all be shut and bolted that very minute. When the wedding was all but over the Princess got up quickly, hoping to slip away unnoticed among the crowd, but, to her great dismay, she found every door fastened.

She felt more at ease when the King came up to her, and with the greatest respect begged her not to run away so soon, but at least to honor him by staying for the splendid feast which was prepared for the Princes and Princesses. He led her into a magnificent hall, where all the Court was assembled, and himself taking up the golden bowl full of water, he offered it to her that she might dip her pretty fingers into it.

At this the Princess could no longer contain herself; throwing herself at the King's feet, she cried out:

"My dream has come true after all—you have offered me water to wash my hands on my sister's wedding day, and it has not vexed you to do it."

The King recognized her at once—indeed, he had already thought several times how much like his poor little Miranda she was.

"Oh! my dear daughter," he cried, kissing her, "can you ever forget my cruelty? I ordered you to be put to death because I thought your dream portended the loss of my crown. And so it did," he added, "for now your sisters are both married and have kingdoms of their own—and mine shall be for you." So saying he put his crown on the Princess's head and cried:

"Long live Queen Miranda!"

All the Court cried: "Long live Queen Miranda!" after him, and the young Queen's two sisters came running up, and threw their arms round her neck, and kissed her a thousand times, and then there was such a laughing and crying, talking and kissing, all at once, and Miranda thanked her father, and began to ask after everyone—particularly the Captain of the Guard, to whom she owed so much; but, to her great sorrow, she heard that he was dead. Presently they sat down to the banquet, and the King asked Miranda to tell them all that had happened to her since the terrible morning when he had sent the Captain of the Guard to fetch her. This she did with so much spirit that all the guests listened with breathless interest. But while she was thus enjoying herself with the King and her sisters, the King of the Sheep was waiting impatiently for the time of her return, and when it came and went, and no Princess appeared, his anxiety became so great that he could bear it no longer.

"She is not coming back any more," he cried. "My miserable sheep's face displeases her, and without Miranda what is left to me, wretched creature that I am! Oh! cruel Ragotte; my punishment is complete."

For a long time he bewailed his sad fate like this, and then, seeing that it was growing dark, and that still there was no sign of the Princess, he set out as fast as he could in the direction of the town. When he reached the palace he asked for Miranda, but by this time everyone had heard the story of her adventures, and did not want her to go back again to the King of the Sheep, so they refused sternly to let him see her. In vain he begged and prayed them to let him in; though his entreaties might have melted hearts of stone they did not move the guards of the palace, and at last, quite broken-hearted, he fell dead at their feet.

In the meantime the King, who had not the least idea of the sad thing that was happening outside the gate of his palace, proposed to Miranda that she should be driven in her chariot all round the town, which was to be illuminated with thousands and thousands of torches, placed in windows and balconies, and in all the grand squares. But what a sight met her eyes at the very entrance of the palace! There lay her dear, kind sheep, silent and motionless, upon the pavement!

She threw herself out of the chariot and ran to him, crying bitterly, for she realized that her broken promise had cost him his life, and for a long, long time she was so unhappy that they thought she would have died too.

So you see that even a princess is not always happy—especially if she forgets to keep her word; and the greatest misfortunes often happen to people just as they think they have obtained their heart's desires!

The Story of Ciccu

(FROM *THE PINK FAIRY BOOK*)

Once upon a time there lived a man who had three sons. The eldest was called Peppe, the second Alfin, and the youngest Ciccu. They were all very poor, and at last things got so bad that they really had not enough to eat. So the father called his sons, and said to them, "My dear boys, I am too old to work any more, and there is nothing left for me but to beg in the streets."

"No, no!" exclaimed his sons; "that you shall never do. Rather, if it must be, would we do it ourselves. But we have thought of a better plan than that."

"What is it?" asked the father.

"Well, we will take you in the forest, where you shall cut wood, and then we will bind it up in bundles and sell it in the town." So their father let them do as they said, and they all made their way into the forest; and as the old man was weak from lack of food his sons took it in turns to carry him on their backs. Then they built a little hut where they might take shelter, and set to work. Every morning early the father cut his sticks, and the sons bound them in bundles, and carried them to the town, bringing back the food the old man so much needed.

Some months passed in this way, and then the father suddenly fell ill, and knew that the time had come when he must die. He bade his sons fetch a lawyer, so that he might make his will, and when the man arrived he explained his wishes.

"I have," said he, "a little house in the village, and over it grows a fig-tree. The house I leave to my sons, who are to live in it together; the fig-tree I divide as follows. To my son Peppe I leave the branches. To my son Alfin I leave the trunk. To my son Ciccu I leave the fruit. Besides the house and tree, I have an old coverlet, which I leave to my eldest son. And an old purse, which I leave to my second son. And a horn, which I leave to my youngest son. And now farewell."

Thus speaking, he laid himself down, and died quietly. The brothers wept bitterly for their father, whom they loved, and when they had buried him they began to talk over their future lives. "What shall we do now?" said they. "Shall we live in the wood, or go back to the village?" And they made up their minds to stay where they were and continue to earn their living by selling firewood.

One very hot evening, after they had been working hard all day, they fell asleep under a tree in front of the hut. And as they slept there came by three fairies, who stopped to look at them.

"What fine fellows!" said one. "Let us give them a present."

"Yes, what shall it be?" asked another.

"This youth has a coverlet over him," said the first fairy. "When he wraps it round him, and wishes himself in any place, he will find himself there in an instant."

Then said the second fairy: "This youth has a purse in his hand. I will promise that it shall always give him as much gold as he asks for."

Last came the turn of the third fairy. "This one has a horn slung round him. When he blows at the small end the seas shall be covered with ships. And if he blows at the wide end they shall all be sunk in the waves." So they vanished, without knowing that Ciccu had been awake and heard all they said.

The next day, when they were all cutting wood, he said to his brothers, "That old coverlet and the purse are no use to you; I wish you would give them to me. I have a fancy for them, for the sake of old times." Now Peppe and Alfin were very fond of Ciccu, and never refused him anything, so they let him have the coverlet and the purse without a word. When he had got them safely Ciccu went on, "Dear brothers, I am tired of the forest. I want to live in the town, and work at some trade."

"O Ciccu! stay with us," they cried. "We are very happy here; and who knows how we shall get on elsewhere?"

"We can always try," answered Ciccu; "and if times are bad we can come back here and take up wood-cutting." So saying he picked up his bundle of sticks, and his brothers did the same.

But when they reached the town they found that the market was over-stocked with firewood, and they did not sell enough to buy themselves a dinner, far less to get any food to carry home. They were wondering sadly what they should do when Ciccu said, "Come with me to the inn and let us have something to eat." They were so hungry by this time that they did not care much whether they paid for it or not, so they followed Ciccu, who gave his orders to the host. "Bring us three dishes, the nicest that you have, and a good bottle of wine."

"Ciccu! Ciccu!" whispered his brothers, horrified at this extravagance, "are you mad? How do you ever mean to pay for it?"

"Let me alone," replied Ciccu; "I know what I am about." And when they had finished their dinner Ciccu told the others to go on, and he would wait to pay the bill.

The brothers hurried on, without needing to be told twice, "for," thought they, "he has no money, and of course there will be a row."

When they were out of sight Ciccu asked the landlord how much he owed, and then said to his purse, "Dear purse, give me, I pray you, six florins," and instantly six florins were in the purse. Then he paid the bill and joined his brothers.

"How did you manage?" they asked.

"Never you mind," answered he. "I have paid every penny," and no more would he say. But the other two were very uneasy, for they felt sure something must be wrong, and the sooner they parted company with Ciccu the better. Ciccu understood what they were thinking, and, drawing forty gold pieces from his pocket, he held out twenty to each, saying, "Take these and turn them to good account. I am going away to seek my own fortune." Then he embraced them, and struck down another road.

He wandered on for many days, till at length he came to the town where the king had his court. The first thing Ciccu did was to order himself some fine clothes, and then buy a grand house, just opposite the palace.

Next he locked his door, and ordered a shower of gold to cover the staircase, and when this was done, the door was flung wide open, and everyone came and peeped at the shining golden stairs. Lastly the rumor of these wonders reached the ears of the king, who left his palace to behold these splendors with his own eyes. And Ciccu received him with all respect, and showed him over the house.

When the king went home he told such stories of what he had seen that his wife and daughter declared that they must go and see them too. So the king sent to ask Ciccu's leave, and Ciccu answered that if the queen and the princess would be pleased to do him such great honor he would show them anything they wished. Now the princess was as beautiful as the sun, and when Ciccu looked upon her his heart went out to her, and he longed to have her to wife. The princess saw what was passing in his mind, and how she could make use of it to satisfy her curiosity as to the golden stairs; so she praised him and flattered him, and put cunning questions, till at length Ciccu's head was quite turned, and he told her the whole story of the fairies and their gifts. Then she begged him to lend her the purse for a few days, so that she could have one made like it, and so great was the love he had for her that he gave it to her at once.

The princess returned to the palace, taking with her the purse, which she had not the smallest intention of ever restoring to Ciccu. Very soon Ciccu had spent all the money he had by him, and could get no more without the help of his purse. Of course, he went at once to the king's daughter, and asked her if she had done with it, but she put him off with some excuse, and told him to come back next day. The next day it was the same thing, and the next, till a great rage filled Ciccu's heart instead of the love that had been there. And when night came he took in his hand a thick stick, wrapped himself in the coverlet, and wished himself in the chamber of the princess. The princess was asleep, but Ciccu seized her arm and pulled her out of bed, and beat her till she gave back the purse. Then he took up the coverlet, and wished he was safe in his own house.

No sooner had he gone than the princess hastened to her father and complained of her sufferings. Then the king rose up in a fury, and commanded Ciccu to be brought before him. "You richly deserve death," said he, "but I will allow you to live if you will instantly hand over to me the coverlet, the purse, and the horn."

What could Ciccu do? Life was sweet, and he was in the power of the king; so he gave up silently his ill-gotten goods, and was as poor as when he was a boy.

While he was wondering how he was to live it suddenly came into his mind that this was the season for the figs to ripen, and he said to himself, "I will go and see if the tree has borne well." So he set off home, where his brothers still lived, and found them living very uncomfortably, for they had spent all their money, and did not know how to make any more. However, he was pleased to see that the fig-tree looked in splendid condition, and was full of fruit. He ran and fetched a basket, and was just feeling the figs, to make sure which of them were ripe, when his brother Peppe called to him, "Stop! The figs of course are yours, but the branches they grow on are mine, and I forbid you to touch them."

Ciccu did not answer, but set a ladder against the tree, so that he could reach the topmost branches, and had his foot already on the first rung when he heard the voice of his brother Alfin: "Stop! the trunk belongs to me, and I forbid you to touch it!"

Then they began to quarrel violently, and there seemed no chance that they would ever cease, till one of them said, "Let us go before a judge." The others agreed, and when they had found a man whom they could trust Ciccu told him the whole story.

"This is my verdict," said the judge. "The figs in truth belong to you, but you cannot pluck them without touching both the trunk and the branches. Therefore you must give your first basketful to your brother Peppe, as the price of his leave to put your ladder against the tree; and the second basketful to your brother Alfin, for leave to shake his boughs. The rest you can keep for yourself."

And the brothers were contented, and returned home, saying one to the other, "We will each of us send a basket of figs to the king. Perhaps he will give us something in return, and if he does we will divide it faithfully between us." So the best figs were carefully packed in a basket, and Peppe set out with it to the castle.

On the road he met a little old man who stopped and said to him, "What have you got there, my fine fellow?"

"What is that to you?" was the answer; "mind your own business." But the old man only repeated his question, and Peppe, to get rid of him, exclaimed in anger, "Dirt."

"Good," replied the old man; "dirt you have said, and dirt let it be."

Peppe only tossed his head and went on his way till he got to the castle, where he knocked at the door. "I have a basket of lovely figs for the king," he said to the servant who opened it, "if his majesty will be graciously pleased to accept them with my humble duty."

The king loved figs, and ordered Peppe to be admitted to his presence, and a silver dish to be brought on which to put the figs. When Peppe uncovered his basket sure enough a layer of beautiful purple figs met the king's eyes, but underneath there was nothing but dirt. "How dare you play me such a trick?" shrieked the king in a rage. "Take him away, and give him fifty lashes." This was done, and Peppe returned home, sore and angry, but determined to say nothing about his adventure. And when his brothers asked him what had happened he only answered, "When we have all three been I will tell you."

A few days after this more figs were ready for plucking, and Alfin in his turn set out for the palace. He had not gone far down the road before he met the old man, who asked him what he had in his basket.

"Horns," answered Alfin, shortly.

"Good," replied the old man; "horns you have said, and horns let it be."

When Alfin reached the castle he knocked at the door and said to the servant: "Here is a basket of lovely figs, if his majesty will be good enough to accept them with my humble duty."

The king commanded that Alfin should be admitted to his presence, and a silver dish to be brought on which to lay the figs. When the basket was uncovered some beautiful purple figs lay on the top, but underneath there was nothing but horns. Then the king was beside himself with passion, and screamed out, "Is this a plot to mock me? Take him away, and give him a hundred and fifty lashes!" So Alfin went sadly home, but would not tell anything about his adventures, only saying grimly, "Now it is Ciccu's turn."

Ciccu had to wait a little before he gathered the last figs on the tree, and these were not nearly so good as the first set. However, he plucked them, as they had agreed, and set out for the king's palace. The old man was still on the road, and he came up and said to Ciccu, "What have you got in that basket?"

"Figs for the king," answered he.

"Let me have a peep," and Ciccu lifted the lid. "Oh, do give me one, I am so fond of figs," begged the little man.

"I am afraid if I do that the hole will show," replied Ciccu, but as he was very good-natured he gave him one. The old man ate it greedily and kept the stalk in his hand, and then asked for another and another and another till he had eaten half the basketful. "But there are not enough left to take to the king," murmured Ciccu.

"Don't be anxious," said the old man, throwing the stalks back into the basket; "just go on and carry the basket to the castle, and it will bring you luck."

Ciccu did not much like it; however he went on his way, and with a trembling heart rang the castle bell. "Here are some lovely figs for the king," said he, "if his majesty will graciously accept them with my humble duty."

When the king was told that there was another man with a basket of figs he cried out, "Oh, have him in, have him in! I suppose it is a wager!" But Ciccu uncovered the basket, and there lay a pile of beautiful ripe figs. And the king was delighted, and emptied them himself on the silver dish, and gave five florins to Ciccu, and offered besides to take him into his service. Ciccu accepted gratefully, but said he must first return home and give the five florins to his brothers.

When he got home Peppe spoke: "Now we will see what we each have got from the king. I myself received from him fifty lashes."

"And I a hundred and fifty," added Alfin.

"And I five florins and some sweets, which you can divide between you, for the king has taken me into his service." Then Ciccu went back to the Court and served the king, and the king loved him.

The other two brothers heard that Ciccu had become quite an important person, and they grew envious, and thought how they could put him to shame. At last they came to the king and said to him, "O king! your palace is beautiful indeed, but to be worthy of you it lacks one thing—the sword of the Man-eater."

"How can I get it?" asked the king.

"Oh, Ciccu can get it for you; ask him."

So the king sent for Ciccu and said to him, "Ciccu, you must at any price manage to get the sword of the Man-eater."

Ciccu was very much surprised at this sudden command, and he walked thoughtfully away to the stables and began to stroke his favorite horse, saying to himself, "Ah, my pet, we must bid each other good-bye, for the king has sent me away to get the sword of the Man-eater." Now this horse was not like other horses, for it was a talking horse, and knew a great deal about many things, so it answered, "Fear nothing, and do as I tell you. Beg the king to give you fifty gold pieces and leave to ride me, and the rest will be easy." Ciccu believed what the horse said, and prayed the king to grant him what he asked. Then the two friends set out, but the horse chose what roads he pleased, and directed Ciccu in everything.

It took them many days' hard riding before they reached the country where the Man-eater lived, and then the horse told Ciccu to stop a group of old women who were coming chattering through the wood, and offer them each a shilling if they would collect a number of mosquitos and tie them up in a bag. When the bag was full Ciccu put it on his shoulder and stole into the house of the Man-eater (who had gone to look for his dinner) and let them all out in his bedroom. He himself hid carefully under the bed and waited. The Man-eater came in late, very tired with his long walk, and flung himself on the bed, placing his sword with its shining blade by his side. Scarcely had he lain down than the mosquitos began to buzz about and bite him, and he rolled from side to side trying to catch them, which he never could do, though they always seemed to be close to his nose. He was so busy over the mosquitos that he did not hear Ciccu steal softly out, or see him catch up the sword. But the horse heard and stood ready at the door, and as Ciccu came flying down the stairs and jumped on his back he sped away like the wind, and never stopped till they arrived at the king's palace.

The king had suffered much pain in his absence, thinking that if the Man-eater ate Ciccu, it would be all his fault. And he was so overjoyed to have him safe that he almost forgot the sword which he had sent him to bring. But the two brothers did not love Ciccu any better because he had succeeded when they hoped he would have failed, and one day they spoke to the king. "It is all very well for Ciccu to have got possession of the sword, but it would have been far more to your majesty's honor if he had captured the Man-eater himself." The king thought upon these words, and at last he said to Ciccu,

"Ciccu, I shall never rest until you bring me back the Man-eater himself. You may have any help you like, but somehow or other you must manage to do it." Ciccu felt very much cast, down at these words, and went to the stable to ask advice of his friend the horse. "Fear nothing," said the horse; "just say you want me and fifty pieces of gold." Ciccu did as he was bid, and the two set out together.

When they reached the country of the Man-eater, Ciccu made all the church bells toll and a proclamation to be made. "Ciccu, the servant of the king, is dead." The Man-eater soon heard what everyone was saying, and was glad in his heart, for he thought, "Well, it is good news that the thief who stole my sword is dead." But Ciccu bought an axe and a saw, and cut down a pine tree in the nearest wood, and began to hew it into planks.

"What are you doing in my wood?" asked the Man-eater, coming up.

"Noble lord," answered Ciccu, "I am making a coffin for the body of Ciccu, who is dead."

"Don't be in a hurry," answered the Man-eater, who of course did not know whom he was talking to, "and perhaps I can help you"; and they set to work sawing and fitting, and very soon the coffin was finished.

Then Ciccu scratched his ear thoughtfully, and cried, "Idiot that I am! I never took any measures. How am I to know if it is big enough? But now I come to think of it, Ciccu was about your size. I wonder if you would be so good as just to put yourself in the coffin, and see if there is enough room."

"Oh, delighted!" said the Man-eater, and laid himself at full length in the coffin. Ciccu clapped on the lid, put a strong cord round it, tied it fast on his horse, and rode back to the king. And when the king saw that he really had brought back the Man-eater, he commanded a huge iron chest to be brought, and locked the coffin up inside.

Just about this time the queen died, and soon after the king thought he should like to marry again. He sought everywhere, but he could not hear of any princess that took his fancy. Then the two envious brothers came to him and said, "O king! there is but one woman that is worthy of being your wife, and that is she who is the fairest in the whole world."

"But where can I find her?" asked the king

"Oh, Ciccu will know, and he will bring her to you."

Now the king had got so used to depending on Ciccu, that he really believed he could do everything. So he sent for him and said, "Ciccu, unless within eight days you bring me the fairest in the whole world, I will have you hewn into a thousand pieces." This mission seemed to Ciccu a hundred times worse than either of the others, and with tears in his eyes he took his way to the stables.

"Cheer up," laughed the horse; "tell the king you must have some bread and honey, and a purse of gold, and leave the rest to me."

Ciccu did as he was bid, and they started at a gallop.

After they had ridden some way, they saw a swarm of bees lying on the ground, so hungry and weak that they were unable to fly. "Get down, and give the poor things some honey," said the horse, and Ciccu dismounted. By-and-bye they came to a stream, on the bank of which was a fish, flapping feebly about in its efforts to reach the water. "Jump down, and throw the fish into the water; he will be useful to us," and Ciccu did so. Farther along the hillside they saw an eagle whose leg was caught in a snare. "Go and free that eagle from the snare; he will be useful to us"; and in a moment the eagle was soaring up into the sky.

At length they came to the castle where the fairest in the world lived with her parents. Then said the horse, "You must get down and sit upon that stone, for I must enter the castle alone. Directly you see me come tearing by with the princess on my back, jump up behind, and hold her tight, so that she does not escape you. If you fail to do this, we are both lost." Ciccu seated himself on the stone, and the horse went on to the courtyard of the castle, where he began to trot round in a graceful and elegant manner. Soon a crowd collected first to watch him and then to pat him, and the king and queen and princess came with the rest. The eyes of the fairest in the world brightened as she looked, and she sprang on the horse's saddle, crying, "Oh, I really must ride him a little!" But the horse made one bound forward, and the princess was forced to hold tight by his mane, lest she should fall off. And as they dashed past the stone where Ciccu was waiting for them, he swung himself up and held her round the waist. As he put his arms round her waist, the fairest in the world unwound the veil from her head and cast it to the ground, and then she drew a ring from her finger and flung it into the stream. But she said nothing, and they rode on fast, fast.

The king of Ciccu's country was watching for them from the top of a tower, and when he saw in the distance a cloud of dust, he ran down to the steps so as to be ready to receive them. Bowing low before the fairest in the world, he spoke: "Noble lady, will you do me the honor to become my wife?"

But she answered, "That can only be when Ciccu brings me the veil that I let fall on my way here."

And the king turned to Ciccu and said, "Ciccu, if you do not find the veil at once, you shall lose your head."

Ciccu, who by this time had hoped for a little peace, felt his heart sink at this fresh errand, and he went into the stable to complain to the faithful horse.

"It will be all right," answered the horse when he had heard his tale; "just take enough food for the day for both of us, and then get on my back."

They rode back all the way they had come till they reached the place where they had found the eagle caught in the snare; then the horse bade Ciccu to call three times on the king of the birds, and when he replied, to beg him to fetch the veil which the fairest in the world had let fall.

"Wait a moment," answered a voice that seemed to come from somewhere very high up indeed. "An eagle is playing with it just now, but he will be here with it in an instant"; and a few minutes after there was a sound of wings, and an eagle came fluttering towards them with the veil in his beak. And Ciccu saw it was the very same eagle that he had freed from the snare. So he took the veil and rode back to the king.

Now the king was enchanted to see him so soon, and took the veil from Ciccu and flung it over the princess, crying, "Here is the veil you asked for, so I claim you for my wife."

"Not so fast," answered she. "I can never be your wife till Ciccu puts on my finger the ring I threw into the stream." Ciccu, who was standing by expecting something of the sort, bowed his head when he heard her words, and went straight to the horse.

"Mount at once," said the horse; "this time it is very simple," and he carried Ciccu to the banks of the little stream. "Now, call three times on the emperor of the fishes, and beg him to restore you the ring that the princess dropped."

Ciccu did as the horse told him, and a voice was heard in answer that seemed to come from a very long way off.

"What is your will?" it asked; and Ciccu replied that he had been commanded to bring back the ring that the princess had flung away, as she rode past.

"A fish is playing with it just now," replied the voice; "however, you shall have it without delay."

And sure enough, very soon a little fish was seen rising to the surface with the lost ring in his mouth. And Ciccu knew him to be the fish that he had saved from death, and he took the ring and rode back with it to the king.

"That is not enough," exclaimed the princess when she saw the ring; "before we can be man and wife, the oven must be heated for three days and three nights, and Ciccu must jump in." And the king forgot how Ciccu had served him, and desired him to do as the princess had said.

This time Ciccu felt that no escape was possible, and he went to the horse and laid his hand on his neck. "Now it is indeed good-bye, and there is no help to be got even from you," and he told him what fate awaited him.

But the horse said, "Oh, never lose heart, but jump on my back, and make me go till the foam flies in flecks all about me. Then get down, and scrape off the foam with a knife. This you must rub all over you, and when you are quite covered, you may suffer yourself to be cast into the oven, for the fire will not hurt you, nor anything else." And Ciccu did exactly as the horse bade him, and went back to the king, and before the eyes of the fairest in the world he sprang into the oven.

And when the fairest in the world saw what he had done, love entered into her heart, and she said to the king, "One thing more: before I can be your wife, you must jump into the oven as Ciccu has done."

"Willingly," replied the king, stooping over the oven. But on the brink he paused a moment and called to Ciccu, "Tell me, Ciccu, how did you manage to prevent the fire burning you?"

Now Ciccu could not forgive his master, whom he had served so faithfully, for sending him to his death without a thought, so he answered, "I rubbed myself over with fat, and I am not even singed."

When he heard these words, the king, whose head was full of the princess, never stopped to inquire if they could be true, and smeared himself over with fat, and sprang into the oven. And in a moment the fire caught him, and he was burned up.

Then the fairest in the world held out her hand to Ciccu and smiled, saying, "Now we will be man and wife." So Ciccu married the fairest in the world, and became king of the country.

The Story of the Queen of the Flowery Isles

(FROM *THE GRAY FAIRY BOOK*)

There once lived a queen who ruled over the Flowery Isles, whose husband, to her extreme grief, died a few years after their marriage. On being left a widow she devoted herself almost entirely to the education of the two charming princesses, her only children. The elder of them was so lovely that as she grew up her mother greatly feared she would excite the jealousy of the Queen of all the Isles, who prided herself on being the most beautiful woman in the world, and insisted on all rivals bowing before her charms.

In order the better to gratify her vanity she had urged the king, her husband, to make war on all the surrounding islands, and as his greatest wish was to please her, the only conditions he imposed on any newly-conquered country was that each princess of every royal house should attend his court as soon as she was fifteen years old, and do homage to the transcendent beauty of his queen.

The Queen of the Flowery Isles, well aware of this law, was fully determined to present her daughter to the proud queen as soon as her fifteenth birthday was past.

The queen herself had heard a rumor of the young princess's great beauty, and awaited her visit with some anxiety, which soon developed into jealousy, for when the interview took place it was impossible not to be dazzled by such radiant charms, and she was obliged to admit that she had never beheld anyone so exquisitely lovely.

Of course she thought in her own mind "excepting myself!" for nothing could have made her believe it possible that anyone could eclipse her.

But the outspoken admiration of the entire court soon undeceived her, and made her so angry that she pretended illness and retired to her own rooms, so as to avoid witnessing the princess's triumph. She also sent word to the Queen of the Flowery Isles that she was sorry not to be well enough to see her again, and advised her to return to her own states with the princess, her daughter.

This message was entrusted to one of the great ladies of the court, who was an old friend of the Queen of the Flowery Isles, and who advised her not to wait to take a formal leave but to go home as fast as she could.

The Queen was not slow to take the hint, and lost no time in obeying it. Being well aware of the magic powers of the incensed queen, she warned her daughter that she was threatened by some great danger if she left the palace for any reason whatever during the next six months.

The princess promised obedience, and no pains were spared to make the time pass pleasantly for her.

The six months were nearly at an end, and on the very last day a splendid fête was to take place in a lovely meadow quite near the palace. The princess, who had been able to watch all the preparations from her window, implored her mother to let her go as far as the meadow; and the queen, thinking all risks must be over, consented, and promised to take her there herself.

The whole court was delighted to see their much-loved princess at liberty, and everyone set off in high glee to join in the fête.

The princess, overjoyed at being once more in the open air, was walking a little in advance of her party when suddenly the earth opened under her feet and closed again after swallowing her up!

The queen fainted away with terror, and the younger princess burst into floods of tears and could hardly be dragged away from the fatal spot, whilst the court was overwhelmed with horror at so great a calamity.

Orders were given to bore the earth to a great depth, but in vain; not a trace of the vanished princess was to be found.

She sank right through the earth and found herself in a desert place with nothing but rocks and trees and no sign of any human being. The only living creature she saw was a very pretty little dog, who ran up to her and at once began to caress her. She took him in her arms, and after playing with him for a little put him down again, when he started off in front of her, looking round from time to time as though begging her to follow.

She let him lead her on, and presently reached a little hill, from which she saw a valley full of lovely fruit trees, bearing flowers and fruit together.

The ground was also covered with fruit and flowers, and in the middle of the valley rose a fountain surrounded by a velvety lawn.

The princess hastened to this charming spot, and sitting down on the grass began to think over the misfortune which had befallen her, and burst into tears as she reflected on her sad condition.

The fruit and clear fresh water would, she knew, prevent her from dying of hunger or thirst, but how could she escape if any wild beast appeared and tried to devour her?

At length, having thought over every possible evil which could happen, the princess tried to distract her mind by playing with the little dog. She spent the whole day near the fountain, but as night drew on she wondered what she should do, when she noticed that the little dog was pulling at her dress.

She paid no heed to him at first, but as he continued to pull her dress and then run a few steps in one particular direction, she at last decided to follow him; he stopped before a rock with a large opening in the center, which he evidently wished her to enter.

The princess did so and discovered a large and beautiful cave lit up by the brilliancy of the stones with which it was lined, with a little couch covered with soft moss in one corner. She lay down on it and the dog at once nestled at her feet. Tired out with all she had gone through she soon fell asleep.

Next morning she was awakened very early by the songs of many birds. The little dog woke up too, and sprang round her in his most caressing manner. She got up and went outside, the dog as before running on in front and turning back constantly to take her dress and draw her on.

She let him have his way and he soon led her back to the beautiful garden where she had spent part of the day before. Here she ate some fruit, drank some water of the fountain, and felt as if she had made an excellent meal. She walked about among the flowers, played with her little dog, and at night returned to sleep in the cave.

In this way the princess passed several months, and as her first terrors died away she gradually became more resigned to her fate. The little dog, too, was a great comfort, and her constant companion.

One day she noticed that he seemed very sad and did not even caress her as usual. Fearing he might be ill she carried him to a spot where she had seen him eat some particular herbs, hoping they might do him good, but he would not touch them. He spent all the night, too, sighing and groaning as if in great pain.

At last the princess fell asleep, and when she awoke her first thought was for her little pet, but not finding him at her feet as usual, she ran out of the cave to look for him. As she stepped out of the cave she caught sight of an old man, who hurried away so fast that she had barely time to see him before he disappeared.

This was a fresh surprise and almost as great a shock as the loss of her little dog, who had been so faithful to her ever since the first day she had seen him. She wondered if he had strayed away or if the old man had stolen him.

Tormented by all kinds of thoughts and fears she wandered on, when suddenly she felt herself wrapped in a thick cloud and carried through the air. She made no resistance and before very long found herself, to her great surprise, in an avenue leading to the palace in which she had been born. No sign of the cloud anywhere.

As the princess approached the palace she perceived that everyone was dressed in black, and she was filled with fear as to the cause of this mourning. She hastened on and was soon recognized and welcomed with shouts of joy. Her sister hearing the cheers ran out and embraced the wanderer, with tears of happiness, telling her that the shock of her disappearance had been so terrible that their mother had only survived it a few days. Since then the younger princess had worn the crown, which she now resigned to her sister to whom it by right belonged.

But the elder wished to refuse it, and would only accept the crown on condition that her sister should share in all the power.

The first acts of the new queen were to do honor to the memory of her dear mother and to shower every mark of generous affection on her sister. Then, being still very grieved at the loss of her little dog, she had a careful search made for him in every country, and when nothing could be heard of him she was so grieved that she offered half her kingdom to whoever should restore him to her.

Many gentlemen of the court, tempted by the thought of such a reward, set off in all directions in search of the dog; but all returned empty-handed to the queen, who, in despair, announced that since life was unbearable without her little dog, she would give her hand in marriage to the man who brought him back.

The prospect of such a prize quickly turned the court into a desert, nearly every courtier starting on the quest. Whilst they were away the queen was informed one day that a very ill-looking man wished to speak with her. She desired him to be shown into a room where she was sitting with her sister.

On entering her presence he said that he was prepared to give the queen her little dog if she on her side was ready to keep her word.

The princess was the first to speak. She said that the queen had no right to marry without the consent of the nation, and that on so important an occasion the general council must be summoned. The queen could not say anything against this statement; but she ordered an apartment in the palace to be given to the man, and desired the council to meet on the following day.

Next day, accordingly, the council assembled in great state, and by the princess's advice it was decided to offer the man a large sum of money for the dog, and should he refuse it, to banish him from the kingdom without seeing the queen again. The man refused the price offered and left the hall.

The princess informed the queen of what had passed, and the queen approved of all, but added that as she was her own mistress she had made up her mind to abdicate her throne, and to wander through the world till she had found her little dog.

The princess was much alarmed by such a resolution, and implored the queen to change her mind. Whilst they were discussing the subject, one of the chamberlains appeared to inform the queen that the bay was covered with ships. The two sisters ran to the balcony, and saw a large fleet in full sail for the port.

In a little time they came to the conclusion that the ships must come from a friendly nation, as every vessel was decked with gay flags, streamers, and pennons, and the way was led by a small ship flying a great white flag of peace.

The queen sent a special messenger to the harbor, and was soon informed that the fleet belonged to the Prince of the Emerald Isles, who begged leave to land in her kingdom, and to present his humble respects to her. The queen at once sent some of the court dignitaries to receive the prince and bid him welcome.

She awaited him seated on her throne, but rose on his appearance, and went a few steps to meet him; then begged him to be seated, and for about an hour kept him in close conversation.

The prince was then conducted to a splendid suite of apartments, and the next day he asked for a private audience. He was admitted to the queen's own sitting-room, where she was sitting alone with her sister.

After the first greetings the prince informed the queen that he had some very strange things to tell her, which she only would know to be true.

"Madam," said he, "I am a neighbor of the Queen of all the Isles; and a small isthmus connects part of my states with hers. One day, when hunting a stag, I had the misfortune to meet her, and not recognizing her, I did not stop to salute her with all proper ceremony. You, Madam, know better than anyone how revengeful she is, and that she is also a mistress of magic. I learnt both facts to my cost. The ground opened under my feet, and I soon found myself in a far distant region transformed into a little dog, under which shape I had the honor to meet your Majesty. After six months, the queen's vengeance not being yet satisfied, she further changed me into a hideous old man, and in this form I was so afraid of being unpleasant in your eyes, Madam, that I hid myself in the depths of the woods, where I spent three months more. At the end of that time I was so fortunate as to meet a benevolent fairy who delivered me from the proud queen's power, and told me all your adventures and where to find you. I now come to offer you a heart which has been entirely yours, Madam, since first we met in the desert."

A few days later a herald was sent through the kingdom to proclaim the joyful news of the marriage of the Queen of the Flowery Isles with the young prince. They lived happily for many years, and ruled their people well.

As for the bad queen, whose vanity and jealousy had caused so much mischief, the Fairies took all her power away for a punishment.

How to Tell a True Princess

(FROM *THE YELLOW FAIRY BOOK*)

There was once upon a time a Prince who wanted to marry a Princess, but she must be a true Princess. So he traveled through the whole world to find one, but there was always something against each. There were plenty of Princesses, but he could not find out if they were true Princesses. In every case there was some little defect, which showed the genuine article was not yet found. So he came home again in very low spirits, for he had wanted very much to have a true Princess. One night there was a dreadful storm; it thundered and lightened and the rain streamed down in torrents. It was fearful! There was a knocking heard at the Palace gate, and the old King went to open it.

There stood a Princess outside the gate; but oh, in what a sad plight she was from the rain and the storm! The water was running down from her hair and her dress into the points of her shoes and out at the heels again. And yet she said she was a true Princess!

"Well, we shall soon find that!" thought the old Queen. But she said nothing, and went into the sleeping-room, took off all the bed-clothes, and laid a pea on the bottom of the bed. Then she put twenty mattresses on top of the pea, and twenty eider-down quilts on the top of the mattresses. And this was the bed in which the Princess was to sleep.

The next morning she was asked how she had slept.

"Oh, very badly!" said the Princess. "I scarcely closed my eyes all night! I am sure I don't know what was in the bed. I laid on something so hard that my whole body is black and blue. It is dreadful!"

Now they perceived that she was a true Princess, because she had felt the pea through the twenty mattresses and the twenty eider-down quilts.

No one but a true Princess could be so sensitive.

So the Prince married her, for now he knew that at last he had got hold of a true Princess. And the pea was put into the Royal Museum, where it is still to be seen if no one has stolen it. Now this is a true story.

The Princess Who Was Hidden Underground

(FROM *THE VIOLET FAIRY BOOK*)

Once there was a king who had great riches, which, when he died, he divided among his three sons. The two eldest of these lived in rioting and feasting, and thus wasted and squandered their father's wealth till nothing remained, and they found themselves in want and misery. The youngest of the three sons, on the contrary, made good use of his portion. He married a wife and soon they had a most beautiful daughter, for whom, when she was grown up, he caused a great palace to be built underground, and then killed the architect who had built it. Next he shut up his daughter inside, and then sent heralds all over the world to make known that he who should find the king's daughter should have her to wife. If he were not capable of finding her then he must die. Many young men sought to discover her, but all perished in the attempt.

After many had met their death thus, there came a young man, beautiful to behold, and as clever as he was beautiful, who had a great desire to attempt the enterprise. First he went to a herdsman, and begged him to hide him in a sheepskin, which had a golden fleece, and in this disguise to take him to the king. The shepherd let himself be persuaded so to do, took a skin having a golden fleece, sewed the young man in it, putting in also food and drink, and so brought him before the king.

When the latter saw the golden lamb, he asked the herd: "Will you sell me this lamb?"

But the herd answered: "No, oh king; I will not sell it; but if you find pleasure therein, I will be willing to oblige you, and I will lend it to you, free of charge, for three days, after that you must give it back to me."

This the king agreed to do, and he arose and took the lamb to his daughter. When he had led it into her palace, and through many rooms, he came to a shut door. Then he called "Open, Sartara Martara of the earth!"

and the door opened of itself. After that they went through many more rooms, and came to another closed door. Again the king called out: "Open, Sartara Martara of the earth!" and this door opened like the other, and they came into the apartment where the princess dwelt, the floor, walls, and roof of which were all of silver.

When the king had embraced the princess, he gave her the lamb, to her great joy. She stroked it, caressed it, and played with it.

After a while the lamb got loose, which, when the princess saw, she said: "See, father, the lamb is free."

But the king answered: "It is only a lamb, why should it not be free?"

Then he left the lamb with the princess, and went his way.

In the night, however, the young man threw off the skin. When the princess saw how beautiful he was, she fell in love with him, and asked him: "Why did you come here disguised in a sheepskin like that?"

Then he answered: "When I saw how many people sought you, and could not find you, and lost their lives in so doing, I invented this trick, and so I am come safely to you."

The princess exclaimed: "You have done well so to do; but you must know that your wager is not yet won, for my father will change me and my maidens into ducks, and will ask you, 'Which of these ducks is the princess?' Then I will turn my head back, and with my bill will clean my wings, so that you may know me."

When they had spent three days together, chatting and caressing one another, the herd came back to the king, and demanded his lamb. Then the king went to his daughter to bring it away, which troubled the princess very much, for she said they had played so nicely together.

But the king said: "I cannot leave it with you, my daughter, for it is only lent to me." So he took it away with him, and gave it back to the shepherd.

Then the young man threw the skin from off him, and went to the king, saying: "Sire, I am persuaded I can find your daughter."

When the king saw how handsome he was, he said: "My lad, I have pity on your youth. This enterprise has already cost the lives of many, and will certainly be your death as well."

But the young man answered, "I accept your conditions, oh king; I will either find her or lose my head."

Thereupon he went before the king, who followed after him, till they came to the great door. Then the young man said to the king: "Speak the words that it may open."

And the king answered: "What are the words? Shall I say something like this: 'Shut; shut; shut'?"

"No," said he; "say 'Open, Sartara Martara of the earth.'"

When the king had so said, the door opened of itself, and they went in, while the king gnawed his moustache in anger. Then they came to the second door, where the same thing happened as at the first, and they went in and found the princess.

Then spoke the king and said: "Yes, truly, you have found the princess. Now I will turn her as well as all her maidens into ducks, and if you can guess which of these ducks is my daughter, then you shall have her to wife."

And immediately the king changed all the maidens into ducks, and he drove them before the young man, and said: "Now show me which is my daughter."

Then the princess, according to their understanding, began to clean her wings with her bill, and the lad said: "She who cleans her wings is the princess."

Now the king could do nothing more but give her to the young man to wife, and they lived together in great joy and happiness.

Graciosa and Percinet

(FROM *THE RED FAIRY BOOK*)

Once upon a time there lived a King and Queen who had one charming daughter. She was so graceful and pretty and clever that she was called Graciosa, and the Queen was so fond of her that she could think of nothing else.

Everyday she gave the Princess a lovely new frock of gold brocade, or satin, or velvet, and when she was hungry she had bowls full of sugar-plums, and at least twenty pots of jam. Everybody said she was the happiest Princess in the world. Now there lived at this same court a very rich old duchess whose name was Grumbly. She was more frightful than tongue can tell;

her hair was red as fire, and she had but one eye, and that not a pretty one! Her face was as broad as a full moon, and her mouth was so large that everybody who met her would have been afraid they were going to be eaten up, only she had no teeth. As she was as cross as she was ugly, she could not bear to hear everyone saying how pretty and how charming Graciosa was; so she presently went away from the court to her own castle, which was not far off. But if anybody who went to see her happened to mention the charming Princess, she would cry angrily:

"It's not true that she is lovely. I have more beauty in my little finger than she has in her whole body."

Soon after this, to the great grief of the Princess, the Queen was taken ill and died, and the King became so melancholy that for a whole year he shut himself up in his palace. At last his physicians, fearing that he would fall ill, ordered that he should go out and amuse himself; so a hunting party was arranged, but as it was very hot weather the King soon got tired, and said he would dismount and rest at a castle which they were passing.

This happened to be the Duchess Grumbly's castle, and when she heard that the King was coming she went out to meet him, and said that the cellar was the coolest place in the whole castle if he would condescend to come down into it. So down they went together, and the King seeing about two hundred great casks ranged side by side, asked if it was only for herself that she had this immense store of wine.

"Yes, sire," answered she, "it is for myself alone, but I shall be most happy to let you taste some of it. Which do you like, canary, St. Julien, champagne, hermitage sack, raisin, or cider?"

"Well," said the King, "since you are so kind as to ask me, I prefer champagne to anything else."

Then Duchess Grumbly took up a little hammer and tapped upon the cask twice, and out came at least a thousand crowns.

"What's the meaning of this?" said she smiling.

Then she tapped the next cask, and out came a bushel of gold pieces.

"I don't understand this at all," said the Duchess, smiling more than before.

Then she went on to the third cask, tap, tap, and out came such a stream of diamonds and pearls that the ground was covered with them.

"Ah!" she cried, "this is altogether beyond my comprehension, sire. Someone must have stolen my good wine and put all this rubbish in its place."

"Rubbish, do you call it, Madam Grumbly?" cried the King. "Rubbish! why there is enough there to buy ten kingdoms."

"Well," said she, "you must know that all those casks are full of gold and jewels, and if you like to marry me it shall all be yours."

Now the King loved money more than anything else in the world, so he cried joyfully:

"Marry you? why with all my heart! to-morrow if you like."

"But I make one condition," said the Duchess; "I must have entire control of your daughter to do as I please with her."

"Oh certainly, you shall have your own way; let us shake hands upon the bargain," said the King.

So they shook hands and went up out of the cellar of treasure together, and the Duchess locked the door and gave the key to the King.

When he got back to his own palace Graciosa ran out to meet him, and asked if he had had good sport.

"I have caught a dove," answered he.

"Oh! do give it to me," said the Princess, "and I will keep it and take care of it."

"I can hardly do that," said he, "for, to speak more plainly, I mean that I met the Duchess Grumbly, and have promised to marry her."

"And you call her a dove?" cried the Princess. "*I* should have called her a screech owl."

"Hold your tongue," said the King, very crossly. "I intend you to behave prettily to her. So now go and make yourself fit to be seen, as I am going to take you to visit her."

So the Princess went very sorrowfully to her own room, and her nurse, seeing her tears, asked what was vexing her.

"Alas! who would not be vexed?" answered she, "for the King intends to marry again, and has chosen for his new bride my enemy, the hideous Duchess Grumbly."

"Oh, well!" answered the nurse, "you must remember that you are a Princess, and are expected to set a good example in making the best of whatever happens. You must promise me not to let the Duchess see how much you dislike her."

At first the Princess would not promise, but the nurse showed her so many good reasons for it that in the end she agreed to be amiable to her step-mother.

Then the nurse dressed her in a robe of pale green and gold brocade, and combed out her long fair hair till it floated round her like a golden mantle, and put on her head a crown of roses and jasmine with emerald leaves.

When she was ready nobody could have been prettier, but she still could not help looking sad.

Meanwhile the Duchess Grumbly was also occupied in attiring herself. She had one of her shoe heels made an inch or so higher than the other, that she might not limp so much, and put in a cunningly made glass eye in the place of the one she had lost. She dyed her red hair black, and painted her face. Then she put on a gorgeous robe of lilac satin lined with blue, and a yellow petticoat trimmed with violet ribbons, and because she had heard that queens always rode into their new dominions, she ordered a horse to be made ready for her to ride.

While Graciosa was waiting until the King should be ready to set out, she went down all alone through the garden into a little wood, where she sat down upon a mossy bank and began to think. And her thoughts were so doleful that very soon she began to cry, and she cried, and cried, and forgot all about going back to the palace, until she suddenly saw a handsome page standing before her. He was dressed in green, and the cap which he held in his hand was adorned with white plumes. When Graciosa looked at him he went down on one knee, and said to her:

"Princess, the King awaits you."

The Princess was surprised, and, if the truth must be told, very much delighted at the appearance of this charming page, whom she could not remember to have seen before. Thinking he might belong to the household of the Duchess, she said:

"How long have you been one of the King's pages?"

"I am not in the service of the King, madam," answered he, "but in yours."

"In mine?" said the Princess with great surprise. "Then how is it that I have never seen you before?"

"Ah, Princess!" said he, "I have never before dared to present myself to you, but now the King's marriage threatens you with so many dangers that I have resolved to tell you at once how much I love you already, and I trust that in time I may win your regard. I am Prince Percinet, of whose riches you may have heard, and whose fairy gift will, I hope, be of use to you in all your difficulties, if you will permit me to accompany you under this disguise."

"Ah, Percinet!" cried the Princess, "is it really you? I have so often heard of you and wished to see you. If you will indeed be my friend, I shall not be afraid of that wicked old Duchess any more."

So they went back to the palace together, and there Graciosa found a beautiful horse which Percinet had brought for her to ride. As it was very spirited he led it by the bridle, and this arrangement enabled him to turn and look at the Princess often, which he did not fail to do. Indeed, she was so pretty that it was a real pleasure to look at her. When the horse which the Duchess was to ride appeared beside Graciosa's, it looked no better than an old cart horse, and as to their trappings, there was simply no comparison between them, as the Princess's saddle and bridle were one glittering mass of diamonds. The King had so many other things to think of that he did not notice this, but all his courtiers were entirely taken up with admiring the Princess and her charming Page in green, who was more handsome and distinguished-looking than all the rest of the court put together.

When they met the Duchess Grumbly she was seated in an open carriage trying in vain to look dignified. The King and the Princess saluted her, and her horse was brought forward for her to mount. But when she saw Graciosa's she cried angrily:

"If that child is to have a better horse than mine, I will go back to my own castle this very minute. What is the good of being a Queen if one is to be slighted like this?"

Upon this the King commanded Graciosa to dismount and to beg the Duchess to honor her by mounting her horse. The Princess obeyed in silence, and the Duchess, without looking at her or thanking her, scrambled up upon the beautiful horse, where she sat looking like a bundle of clothes, and eight officers had to hold her up for fear she should fall off.

Even then she was not satisfied, and was still grumbling and muttering, so they asked her what was the matter.

"I wish that Page in green to come and lead the horse, as he did when Graciosa rode it," said she very sharply.

And the King ordered the Page to come and lead the Queen's horse. Percinet and the Princess looked at one another, but said never a word, and then he did as the King commanded, and the procession started in great pomp. The Duchess was greatly elated, and as she sat there in state would not have wished to change places even with Graciosa. But at the moment when it was least expected the beautiful horse began to plunge and rear and kick, and finally to run away at such a pace that it was impossible to stop him.

At first the Duchess clung to the saddle, but she was very soon thrown off and fell in a heap among the stones and thorns, and there they found her, shaken to a jelly, and collected what was left of her as if she had been a broken glass. Her bonnet was here and her shoes there, her face was scratched, and her fine clothes were covered with mud. Never was a bride seen in such a dismal plight. They carried her back to the palace and put her to bed, but as soon as she recovered enough to be able to speak, she began to scold and rage, and declared that the whole affair was Graciosa's fault, that she had contrived it on purpose to try and get rid of her, and that if the King would not have her punished, she would go back to her castle and enjoy her riches by herself.

At this the King was terribly frightened, for he did not at all want to lose all those barrels of gold and jewels. So he hastened to appease the Duchess, and told her she might punish Graciosa in any way she pleased.

Thereupon she sent for Graciosa, who turned pale and trembled at the summons, for she guessed that it promised nothing agreeable for her. She looked all about for Percinet, but he was nowhere to be seen; so she had no choice but to go to the Duchess Grumbly's room. She had hardly got inside the door when she was seized by four waiting women, who looked so tall and strong and cruel that the Princess shuddered at the sight of them, and still more when she saw them arming themselves with great bundles of rods, and heard the Duchess call out to them from her bed to beat the Princess without mercy. Poor Graciosa wished miserably that Percinet could only know what was happening and come to rescue her. But no sooner did they begin to beat her than she found, to her great relief, that the rods had changed to bundles of peacock's feathers, and though the Duchess's women went on till they were so tired that they could no longer raise their arms from their sides, yet she was not hurt in the least. However, the Duchess thought she must be black and blue after such a beating; so Graciosa, when she was released, pretended to feel very bad, and went away into her own room, where she told her nurse all that had happened, and then the nurse left her, and when the Princess turned round there stood Percinet beside her. She thanked him gratefully for helping her so cleverly, and they laughed and were very merry over the way they had taken in the Duchess and her waiting-maids; but Percinet advised her still to pretend to be ill for a few days, and after promising to come to her aid whenever she needed him, he disappeared as suddenly as he had come.

The Duchess was so delighted at the idea that Graciosa was really ill, that she herself recovered twice as fast as she would have done otherwise, and the wedding was held with great magnificence. Now as the King knew that, above all other things, the Queen loved to be told that she was beautiful, he ordered that her portrait should be painted, and that a tournament should be held, at which all the bravest knights of his court should maintain against all comers that Grumbly was the most beautiful princess in the world.

Numbers of knights came from far and wide to accept the challenge, and the hideous Queen sat in great state in a balcony hung with cloth of gold to watch the contests, and Graciosa had to stand up behind her, where her loveliness was so conspicuous that the combatants could not keep their eyes off her. But the Queen was so vain that she thought all their admiring glances were for herself, especially as, in spite of the badness of their cause, the King's knights were so brave that they were the victors in every combat.

However, when nearly all the strangers had been defeated, a young unknown knight presented himself. He carried a portrait, enclosed in a bow encrusted with diamonds, and he declared himself willing to maintain against them all that the Queen was the ugliest creature in the world, and that the Princess whose portrait he carried was the most beautiful.

So one by one the knights came out against him, and one by one he vanquished them all, and then he opened the box, and said that, to console them, he would show them the portrait of his Queen of Beauty, and when he did so everyone recognized the Princess Graciosa. The unknown knight then saluted her gracefully and retired, without telling his name to anybody. But Graciosa had no difficulty in guessing that it was Percinet.

As to the Queen, she was so furiously angry that she could hardly speak; but she soon recovered her voice, and overwhelmed Graciosa with a torrent of reproaches.

"What!" she said, "do you dare to dispute with me for the prize of beauty, and expect me to endure this insult to my knights? But I will not bear it, proud Princess. I will have my revenge."

"I assure you, Madam," said the Princess, "that I had nothing to do with it and am quite willing that you shall be declared Queen of Beauty."

"Ah! you are pleased to jest, popinjay!" said the Queen, "but it will be my turn soon!"

The King was speedily told what had happened, and how the Princess was in terror of the angry Queen, but he only said: "The Queen must do as she pleases. Graciosa belongs to her!"

The wicked Queen waited impatiently until night fell, and then she ordered her carriage to be brought. Graciosa, much against her will, was forced into it, and away they drove, and never stopped until they reached a great forest, a hundred leagues from the palace. This forest was so gloomy, and so full of lions, tigers, bears, and wolves, that nobody dared pass through it even by daylight, and here they set down the unhappy Princess in the middle of the black night, and left her in spite of all her tears and entreaties. The Princess stood quite still at first from sheer bewilderment, but when the last sound of the retreating carriages died away in the distance she began to run aimlessly hither and thither, sometimes knocking herself against a tree, sometimes tripping over a stone, fearing every minute that she would be eaten up by the lions. Presently she was too tired to advance another step, so she threw herself down upon the ground and cried miserably:

"Oh, Percinet! where are you? Have you forgotten me altogether?"

She had hardly spoken when all the forest was lighted up with a sudden glow. Every tree seemed to be sending out a soft radiance, which was clearer than moonlight and softer than daylight, and at the end of a long avenue of trees opposite to her the Princess saw a palace of clear crystal which blazed like the sun. At that moment a slight sound behind her made her start round, and there stood Percinet himself.

"Did I frighten you, my Princess?" said he. "I come to bid you welcome to our fairy palace, in the name of the Queen, my mother, who is prepared to love you as much as I do." The Princess joyfully mounted with him into a little sledge, drawn by two stags, which bounded off and drew them swiftly to the wonderful palace, where the Queen received her with the greatest kindness, and a splendid banquet was served at once. Graciosa was so happy to have found Percinet, and to have escaped from the gloomy forest and all its terrors, that she was very hungry and very merry, and they were a gay party. After supper they went into another lovely room, where the crystal walls were covered with pictures, and the Princess saw with great surprise that her own history was represented, even down to the moment when Percinet found her in the forest.

"Your painters must indeed be diligent," she said, pointing out the last picture to the Prince.

"They are obliged to be, for I will not have anything forgotten that happens to you," he answered.

When the Princess grew sleepy, twenty-four charming maidens put her to bed in the prettiest room she had ever seen, and then sang to her so sweetly that Graciosa's dreams were all of mermaids, and cool sea waves, and caverns, in which she wandered with Percinet; but when she woke up again her first thought was that, delightful as this fairy palace seemed to her, yet she could not stay in it, but must go back to her father. When she had been dressed by the four-and-twenty maidens in a charming robe which the Queen had sent for her, and in which she looked prettier than ever, Prince Percinet came to see her, and was bitterly disappointed when she told him what she had been thinking. He begged her to consider again how unhappy the wicked Queen would make her, and how, if she would but marry him, all the fairy palace would be hers, and his one thought would be to please her. But, in spite of everything he could say, the Princess was quite determined to go back, though he at last persuaded her to stay eight days, which were so full of pleasure and amusement that they passed like a few hours. On the last day, Graciosa, who had often felt anxious to know what was going on in her father's palace, said to Percinet that she was sure that he could find out for her, if he would, what reason the Queen had given her father for her sudden disappearance. Percinet at first offered to send his courier to find out, but the Princess said:

"Oh! Isn't there a quicker way of knowing than that?"

"Very well," said Percinet, "you shall see for yourself."

So up they went together to the top of a very high tower, which, like the rest of the castle, was built entirely of rock-crystal.

There the Prince held Graciosa's hand in his, and made her put the tip of her little finger into her mouth, and look towards the town, and immediately she saw the wicked Queen go to the King, and heard her say to him, "That miserable Princess is dead, and no great loss either. I have ordered that she shall be buried at once."

And then the Princess saw how she dressed up a log of wood and had it buried, and how the old King cried, and all the people murmured that the

Queen had killed Graciosa with her cruelties, and that she ought to have her head cut off. When the Princess saw that the King was so sorry for her pretended death that he could neither eat nor drink, she cried:

"Ah, Percinet! take me back quickly if you love me."

And so, though he did not want to at all, he was obliged to promise that he would let her go.

"You may not regret me, Princess," he said sadly, "for I fear that you do not love me well enough; but I foresee that you will more than once regret that you left this fairy palace where we have been so happy."

But, in spite of all he could say, she bade farewell to the Queen, his mother, and prepared to set out; so Percinet, very unwillingly, brought the little sledge with the stags and she mounted beside him. But they had hardly gone twenty yards when a tremendous noise behind her made Graciosa look back, and she saw the palace of crystal fly into a million splinters, like the spray of a fountain, and vanish.

"Oh, Percinet!" she cried, "what has happened? The palace is gone."

"Yes," he answered, "my palace is a thing of the past; you will see it again, but not until after you have been buried."

"Now you are angry with me," said Graciosa in her most coaxing voice, "though after all I am more to be pitied than you are."

When they got near the palace the Prince made the sledge and themselves invisible, so the Princess got in unobserved, and ran up to the great hall where the King was sitting all by himself. At first he was very much startled by Graciosa's sudden appearance, but she told him how the Queen had left her out in the forest, and how she had caused a log of wood to be buried. The King, who did not know what to think, sent quickly and had it dug up, and sure enough it was as the Princess had said. Then he caressed Graciosa, and made her sit down to supper with him, and they were as happy as possible. But someone had by this time told the wicked Queen that Graciosa had come back, and was at supper with the King, and in she flew in a terrible fury. The poor old King quite trembled before her, and when she declared that Graciosa was not the Princess at all, but a wicked impostor, and that if the King did not give her up at once she would go back to her own castle and never see him again, he had not a word to say, and really seemed to believe that it was not Graciosa after all. So the Queen in great triumph sent for her waiting women, who dragged the unhappy Princess away and shut her up in a garret; they took away all her jewels and her pretty dress, and gave her a rough cotton frock, wooden shoes, and a little cloth cap. There was some straw in a corner, which was all she had for a bed, and they gave her a very little bit of black bread to eat. In this miserable plight Graciosa did indeed regret the fairy palace, and she would have called Percinet to her aid, only she felt sure he was still vexed with her for leaving him, and thought that she could not expect him to come.

Meanwhile the Queen had sent for an old Fairy, as malicious as herself, and said to her:

"You must find me some task for this fine Princess which she cannot possibly do, for I mean to punish her, and if she does not do what I order, she will not be able to say that I am unjust." So the old Fairy said she would think it over, and come again the next day. When she returned she brought with her a skein of thread, three times as big as herself; it was so fine that a breath of air would break it, and so tangled that it was impossible to see the beginning or the end of it.

The Queen sent for Graciosa, and said to her:

"Do you see this skein? Set your clumsy fingers to work upon it, for I must have it disentangled by sunset, and if you break a single thread it will be the worse for you." So saying she left her, locking the door behind her with three keys.

The Princess stood dismayed at the sight of the terrible skein. If she did but turn it over to see where to begin, she broke a thousand threads, and not one could she disentangle. At last she threw it into the middle of the floor, crying:

"Oh, Percinet! this fatal skein will be the death of me if you will not forgive me and help me once more."

And immediately in came Percinet as easily as if he had all the keys in his own possession.

"Here I am, Princess, as much as ever at your service," said he, "though really you are not very kind to me."

Then he just stroked the skein with his wand, and all the broken threads joined themselves together, and the whole skein wound itself smoothly off in the most surprising manner, and the Prince, turning to Graciosa, asked if there was nothing else that she wished him to do for her, and if the time would never come when she would wish for him for his own sake.

"Don't be vexed with me, Percinet," she said. "I am unhappy enough without that."

"But why should you be unhappy, my Princess?" cried he. "Only come with me and we shall be as happy as the day is long together."

"But suppose you get tired of me?" said Graciosa.

The Prince was so grieved at this want of confidence that he left her without another word.

The wicked Queen was in such a hurry to punish Graciosa that she thought the sun would never set; and indeed it was before the appointed time that she came with her four Fairies, and as she fitted the three keys into the locks she said:

"I'll venture to say that the idle minx has not done anything at all—she prefers to sit with her hands before her to keep them white."

But, as soon as she entered, Graciosa presented her with the ball of thread in perfect order, so that she had no fault to find, and could only pretend to discover that it was soiled, for which imaginary fault she gave Graciosa a blow on each cheek, that made her white and pink skin turn green and yellow. And then she sent her back to be locked into the garret once more.

Then the Queen sent for the Fairy again and scolded her furiously. "Don't make such a mistake again; find me something that it will be quite impossible for her to do," she said.

So the next day the Fairy appeared with a huge barrel full of the feathers of all sorts of birds. There were nightingales, canaries, goldfinches, linnets, tomtits, parrots, owls, sparrows, doves, ostriches, bustards, peacocks, larks, partridges, and everything else that you can think of. These feathers were all mixed up in such confusion that the birds themselves could not have chosen out their own. "Here," said the Fairy, "is a little task which it will take all your prisoner's skill and patience to accomplish. Tell her to pick out and lay in a separate heap the feathers of each bird. She would need to be a fairy to do it."

The Queen was more than delighted at the thought of the despair this task would cause the Princess. She sent for her, and with the same threats as before locked her up with the three keys, ordering that all the feathers should be sorted by sunset. Graciosa set to work at once, but before she had taken out a dozen feathers she found that it was perfectly impossible to know one from another.

"Ah! well," she sighed, "the Queen wishes to kill me, and if I must die I must. I cannot ask Percinet to help me again, for if he really loved me he would not wait till I called him, he would come without that."

"I am here, my Graciosa," cried Percinet, springing out of the barrel where he had been hiding. "How can you still doubt that I love you with all my heart?"

Then he gave three strokes of his wand upon the barrel, and all the feathers flew out in a cloud and settled down in neat little separate heaps all round the room.

"What should I do without you, Percinet?" said Graciosa gratefully. But still she could not quite make up her mind to go with him and leave her father's kingdom for ever; so she begged him to give her more time to think of it, and he had to go away disappointed once more.

When the wicked Queen came at sunset she was amazed and infuriated to find the task done. However, she complained that the heaps of feathers were badly arranged, and for that the Princess was beaten and sent back to her garret. Then the Queen sent for the Fairy once more, and scolded her until she was fairly terrified, and promised to go home and think of another task for Graciosa, worse than either of the others.

At the end of three days she came again, bringing with her a box.

"Tell your slave," said he, "to carry this wherever you please, but on no account to open it. She will not be able to help doing so, and then you will be quite satisfied with the result." So the Queen came to Graciosa, and said:

"Carry this box to my castle, and place it upon the table in my own room. But I forbid you on pain of death to look at what it contains."

Graciosa set out, wearing her little cap and wooden shoes and the old cotton frock, but even in this disguise she was so beautiful that all the passers-by wondered who she could be. She had not gone far before the heat of the sun and the weight of the box tired her so much that she sat down to rest in the shade of a little wood which lay on one side of a green meadow. She was carefully holding the box upon her lap when she suddenly felt the greatest desire to open it.

"What could possibly happen if I did?" she said to herself. "I should not take anything out. I should only just see what was there."

And without farther hesitation she lifted the cover.

Instantly out came swarms of little men and women, no taller than her finger, and scattered themselves all over the meadow, singing and dancing, and playing the merriest games, so that at first Graciosa was delighted and watched them with much amusement. But presently, when she was rested and wished to go on her way, she found that, do what she would, she could not get them back into their box. If she chased them in the meadow they fled into the wood, and if she pursued them into the wood they dodged round trees and behind sprigs of moss, and with peals of elfin laughter scampered back again into the meadow.

At last, weary and terrified, she sat down and cried.

"It is my own fault," she said sadly. "Percinet, if you can still care for such an imprudent Princess, do come and help me once more."

Immediately Percinet stood before her.

"Ah, Princess!" he said, "but for the wicked Queen I fear you would never think of me at all."

"Indeed I should," said Graciosa; "I am not so ungrateful as you think. Only wait a little and I believe I shall love you quite dearly."

Percinet was pleased at this, and with one stroke of his wand compelled all the willful little people to come back to their places in the box, and then rendering the Princess invisible he took her with him in his chariot to the castle.

When the Princess presented herself at the door, and said that the Queen had ordered her to place the box in her own room, the governor laughed heartily at the idea.

"No, no, my little shepherdess," said he, "that is not the place for you. No wooden shoes have ever been over that floor yet."

Then Graciosa begged him to give her a written message telling the Queen that he had refused to admit her. This he did, and she went back to Percinet, who was waiting for her, and they set out together for the palace. You may imagine that they did not go the shortest way, but the Princess did not find it too long, and before they parted she had promised that if the Queen was still cruel to her, and tried again to play her any spiteful trick, she would leave her and come to Percinet for ever.

When the Queen saw her returning she fell upon the Fairy, whom she had kept with her, and pulled her hair, and scratched her face, and would really have killed her if a Fairy could be killed. And when the Princess presented the letter and the box she threw them both upon the fire without opening them, and looked very much as if she would like to throw the Princess after them. However, what she really did do was to have a great hole as deep as a well dug in her garden, and the top of it covered with a flat stone. Then she went and walked near it, and said to Graciosa and all her ladies who were with her:

"I am told that a great treasure lies under that stone; let us see if we can lift it."

So they all began to push and pull at it, and Graciosa among the others, which was just what the Queen wanted; for as soon as the stone was lifted high enough, she gave the Princess a push which sent her down to the bottom of the well, and then the stone was let fall again, and there she was a prisoner. Graciosa felt that now indeed she was hopelessly lost, surely not even Percinet could find her in the heart of the earth.

"This is like being buried alive," she said with a shudder. "Oh, Percinet! if you only knew how I am suffering for my want of trust in you! But how could I be sure that you would not be like other men and tire of me from the moment you were sure I loved you?"

As she spoke she suddenly saw a little door open, and the sunshine blazed into the dismal well. Graciosa did not hesitate an instant, but passed through into a charming garden. Flowers and fruit grew on every side, fountains plashed, and birds sang in the branches overhead, and when she reached a great avenue of trees and looked up to see where it would lead her, she found herself close to the palace of crystal. Yes! there was no mistaking it, and the Queen and Percinet were coming to meet her.

"Ah, Princess!" said the Queen, "don't keep this poor Percinet in suspense any longer. You little guess the anxiety he has suffered while you were in the power of that miserable Queen."

The Princess kissed her gratefully, and promised to do as she wished in everything, and holding out her hand to Percinet, with a smile, she said:

"Do you remember telling me that I should not see your palace again until I had been buried? I wonder if you guessed then that, when that happened, I should tell you that I love you with all my heart, and will marry you whenever you like?"

Prince Percinet joyfully took the hand that was given him, and, for fear the Princess should change her mind, the wedding was held at once with the greatest splendor, and Graciosa and Percinet lived happily ever after.

The White Slipper

(FROM *THE ORANGE FAIRY BOOK*)

Once upon a time there lived a king who had a daughter just fifteen years old. And *what* a daughter!

Even the mothers who had daughters of their own could not help allowing that the princess was much more beautiful and graceful than any of them; and, as for the fathers, if one of them ever beheld her by accident he could talk of nothing else for a whole day afterwards.

Of course the king, whose name was Balancin, was the complete slave of his little girl from the moment he lifted her from the arms of her dead mother; indeed, he did not seem to know that there was anyone else in the world to love.

Now Diamantina, for that was her name, did not reach her fifteenth birthday without proposals for marriage from every country under heaven; but be the suitor who he might, the king always said him nay.

Behind the palace a large garden stretched away to the foot of some hills, and more than one river flowed through. Hither the princess would come each evening towards sunset, attended by her ladies, and gather herself the flowers that were to adorn her rooms. She also brought with her a pair of scissors to cut off the dead blooms, and a basket to put them in, so that when the sun rose next morning he might see nothing unsightly. When she had finished this task she would take a walk through the town, so that the poor people might have a chance of speaking with her, and telling her of their troubles; and then she would seek out her father, and together they would consult over the best means of giving help to those who needed it.

But what has all this to do with the White Slipper? my readers will ask.

Have patience, and you will see.

Next to his daughter, Balancin loved hunting, and it was his custom to spend several mornings every week chasing the boars which abounded in the mountains a few miles from the city. One day, rushing downhill as fast

71

as he could go, he put his foot into a hole and fell, rolling into a rocky pit of brambles. The king's wounds were not very severe, but his face and hands were cut and torn, while his feet were in a worse plight still, for, instead of proper hunting boots, he only wore sandals, to enable him to run more swiftly.

In a few days the king was as well as ever, and the signs of the scratches were almost gone; but one foot still remained very sore, where a thorn had pierced deeply and had festered. The best doctors in the kingdom treated it with all their skill; they bathed, and poulticed, and bandaged, but it was in vain. The foot only grew worse and worse, and became daily more swollen and painful.

After everyone had tried his own particular cure, and found it fail, there came news of a wonderful doctor in some distant land who had healed the most astonishing diseases. On inquiring, it was found that he never left the walls of his own city, and expected his patients to come to see him; but, by dint of offering a large sum of money, the king persuaded the famous physician to undertake the journey to his own court.

On his arrival the doctor was led at once into the king's presence, and made a careful examination of his foot.

"Alas! your majesty," he said, when he had finished, "the wound is beyond the power of man to heal; but though I cannot cure it, I can at least deaden the pain, and enable you to walk without so much suffering."

"Oh, if you can only do that," cried the king, "I shall be grateful to you for life! Give your own orders; they shall be obeyed."

"Then let your majesty bid the royal shoemaker make you a shoe of goat-skin very loose and comfortable, while I prepare a varnish to paint over it of which I alone have the secret!" So saying, the doctor bowed himself out, leaving the king more cheerful and hopeful than he had been for long.

The days passed very slowly with him during the making of the shoe and the preparation of the varnish, but on the eighth morning the physician appeared, bringing with him the shoe in a case. He drew it out to slip on the king's foot, and over the goat-skin he had rubbed a polish so white that the snow itself was not more dazzling.

"While you wear this shoe you will not feel the slightest pain," said the doctor. "For the balsam with which I have rubbed it inside and out has, besides its healing balm, the quality of strengthening the material it touches, so that, even were your majesty to live a thousand years, you would find the slipper just as fresh at the end of that time as it is now."

The king was so eager to put it on that he hardly gave the physician time to finish. He snatched it from the case and thrust his foot into it, nearly weeping for joy when he found he could walk and run as easily as any beggar boy.

"What can I give you?" he cried, holding out both hands to the man who had worked this wonder. "Stay with me, and I will heap on you riches greater than ever you dreamed of." But the doctor said he would accept nothing more than had been agreed on, and must return at once to his own country, where many sick people were awaiting him. So king Balancin had to content himself with ordering the physician to be treated with royal honors, and desiring that an escort should attend him on his journey home.

For two years everything went smoothly at court, and to king Balancin and his daughter the sun no sooner rose than it seemed time for it to set. Now, the king's birthday fell in the month of June, and as the weather happened to be unusually fine, he told the princess to celebrate it in any way that pleased her. Diamantina was very fond of being on the river, and she was delighted at this chance of delighting her tastes. She would have a merry-making such as never had been seen before, and in the evening, when they were tired of sailing and rowing, there should be music and dancing, plays and fireworks. At the very end, before the people went home, every poor person should be given a loaf of bread and every girl who was to be married within the year a new dress.

The great day appeared to Diamantina to be long in coming, but, like other days, it came at last. Before the sun was fairly up in the heavens the princess, too full of excitement to stay in the palace, was walking about the streets so covered with precious stones that you had to shade your eyes before you could look at her. By-and-by a trumpet sounded, and she hurried home, only to appear again in a few moments walking by the side of her father down to the river. Here a splendid barge was waiting for them, and from it they watched all sorts of races and feats of swimming and diving. When these were over the barge proceeded up the river to the field where the dancing and concerts were to take place, and after the prizes had been given away to the winners, and the loaves and the dresses had been distributed by the princess, they bade farewell to their guests, and turned to step into the barge which was to carry them back to the palace.

Then a dreadful thing happened. As the king stepped on board the boat one of the sandals of the white slipper, which had got loose, caught in a nail that was sticking out, and caused the king to stumble. The pain was great, and unconsciously he turned and shook his foot, so that the sandals gave way, and in a moment the precious shoe was in the river.

It had all occurred so quickly that nobody had noticed the loss of the slipper, not even the princess, whom the king's cries speedily brought to his side.

"What is the matter, dear father?" asked she. But the king could not tell her; and only managed to gasp out: "My shoe! my shoe!" While the sailors stood round staring, thinking that his majesty had suddenly gone mad.

Seeing her father's eyes fixed on the stream, Diamantina looked hastily in that direction. There, dancing on the current, was the point of something white, which became more and more distant the longer they watched it. The king could bear the sight no more, and, besides, now that the healing ointment in the shoe had been removed the pain in his foot was as bad as ever; he gave a sudden cry, staggered, and fell over the bulwarks into the water.

In an instant the river was covered with bobbing heads all swimming their fastest towards the king, who had been carried far down by the swift current. At length one swimmer, stronger than the rest, seized hold of his tunic, and drew him to the bank, where a thousand eager hands were ready to haul him out. He was carried, unconscious, to the side of his daughter, who had fainted with terror on seeing her father disappear below the surface, and together they were placed in a coach and driven to the palace, where the best doctors in the city were awaiting their arrival.

In a few hours the princess was as well as ever; but the pain, the wetting, and the shock of the accident, all told severely on the king, and for three days he lay in a high fever. Meanwhile, his daughter, herself nearly mad with grief, gave orders that the white slipper should be sought for far and wide; and so it was, but even the cleverest divers could find no trace of it at the bottom of the river.

When it became clear that the slipper must have been carried out to sea by the current, Diamantina turned her thoughts elsewhere, and sent messengers in search of the doctor who had brought relief to her father, begging him to make another slipper as fast as possible, to supply the place of the one which was lost. But the messengers returned with the sad news that the doctor had died some weeks before, and, what was worse, his secret had died with him.

In his weakness this intelligence had such an effect on the king that the physicians feared he would become as ill as before. He could hardly be persuaded to touch food, and all night long he lay moaning, partly with pain, and partly over his own folly in not having begged the doctor to make him several dozens of white slippers, so that in case of accidents he might always have one to put on. However, by-and-by he saw that it was no use weeping and wailing, and commanded that they should search for his lost treasure more diligently than ever.

What a sight the river banks presented in those days! It seemed as if all the people in the country were gathered on them. But this second search was no more fortunate than the first, and at last the king issued a proclamation that whoever found the missing slipper should be made heir to the crown, and should marry the princess.

Now many daughters would have rebelled at being disposed of in the manner; and it must be admitted that Diamantina's heart sank when she heard what the king had done. Still, she loved her father so much that she desired his comfort more than anything else in the world, so she said nothing, and only bowed her head.

Of course the result of the proclamation was that the river banks became more crowded than before; for all the princess's suitors from distant lands flocked to the spot, each hoping that he might be the lucky finder. Many times a shining stone at the bottom of the stream was taken for the slipper itself, and every evening saw a band of dripping downcast men returning homewards. But one youth always lingered longer than the rest, and night would still see him engaged in the search, though his clothes stuck to his skin and his teeth chattered.

One day, when the king was lying on his bed racked with pain, he heard the noise of a scuffle going on in his antechamber, and rang a golden bell that stood by his side to summon one of his servants.

"Sire," answered the attendant, when the king inquired what was the matter, "the noise you heard was caused by a young man from the town, who has had the impudence to come here to ask if he may measure your majesty's foot, so as to make you another slipper in place of the lost one."

"And what have you done to the youth?" said the king.

"The servants pushed him out of the palace, and, added a few blows to teach him not to be insolent," replied the man.

"Then they did very ill," answered the king, with a frown. "He came here from kindness, and there was no reason to maltreat him."

"Oh, my lord, he had the audacity to wish to touch your majesty's sacred person—he, a good-for-nothing boy, a mere shoemaker's apprentice, perhaps! And even if he could make shoes to perfection they would be no use without the soothing balsam."

The king remained silent for a few moments, then he said:

"Never mind. Go and fetch the youth and bring him to me. I would gladly try any remedy that may relieve my pain."

So, soon afterwards, the youth, who had not gone far from the palace, was caught and ushered into the king's presence.

He was tall and handsome and, though he professed to make shoes, his manners were good and modest, and he bowed low as he begged the king not only to allow him to take the measure of his foot, but also to suffer him to place a healing plaster over the wound.

Balancin was pleased with the young man's voice and appearance, and thought that he looked as if he knew what he was doing. So he stretched out his bad foot which the youth examined with great attention, and then gently laid on the plaster.

Very shortly the ointment began to soothe the sharp pain, and the king, whose confidence increased every moment, begged the young man to tell him his name.

"I have no parents; they died when I was six, sire," replied the youth, modestly. "Everyone in the town calls me Gilguerillo, because, when I was little, I went singing through the world in spite of my misfortunes. Luckily for me I was born to be happy."

"And you really think you can cure me?" asked the king.

"Completely, my lord," answered Gilguerillo.

"And how long do you think it will take?"

"It is not an easy task; but I will try to finish it in a fortnight," replied the youth.

A fortnight seemed to the king a long time to make one slipper. But he only said:

"Do you need anything to help you?"

"Only a good horse, if your majesty will be kind enough to give me one," answered Gilguerillo. And the reply was so unexpected that the courtiers could hardly restrain their smiles, while the king stared silently.

"You shall have the horse," he said at last, "and I shall expect you back in a fortnight. If you fulfill your promise you know your reward; if not, I will have you flogged for your impudence."

Gilguerillo bowed, and turned to leave the palace, followed by the jeers and scoffs of everyone he met. But he paid no heed, for he had got what he wanted.

He waited in front of the gates till a magnificent horse was led up to him, and vaulting into the saddle with an ease which rather surprised the attendant, rode quickly out of the town amidst the jests of the assembled crowd, who had heard of his audacious proposal. And while he is on his way let us pause for a moment and tell who he is.

Both father and mother had died before the boy was six years old; and he had lived for many years with his uncle, whose life had been passed in the study of chemistry. He could leave no money to his nephew, as he had a son of his own; but he taught him all he knew, and at his death Gilguerillo entered an office, where he worked for many hours daily. In his spare time, instead of playing with the other boys, he passed hours poring over books, and because he was timid and liked to be alone he was held by everyone to be a little mad. Therefore, when it became known that he had promised to cure the king's foot, and had ridden away—no one knew where—a roar of laughter and mockery rang through the town, and jeers and scoffing words were sent after him.

But if they had only known what were Gilguerillo's thoughts they would have thought him madder than ever.

The real truth was that, on the morning when the princess had walked through the streets before making holiday on the river Gilguerillo had seen her from his window, and had straightway fallen in love with her. Of course he felt quite hopeless. It was absurd to imagine that the apothecary's nephew could ever marry the king's daughter; so he did his best to forget her, and study harder than before, till the royal proclamation suddenly filled him with hope. When he was free he no longer spent the precious moments poring over books, but, like the rest, he might have been seen wandering along the banks of the river, or diving into the stream after something that lay glistening in the clear water, but which turned out to be a white pebble or a bit of glass.

And at the end he understood that it was not by the river that he would win the princess; and, turning to his books for comfort, he studied harder than ever.

There is an old proverb which says: "Everything comes to him who knows how to wait." It is not all men who know how to wait, any more than it is all men who can learn by experience; but Gilguerillo was one of the few and instead of thinking his life wasted because he could not have the thing he wanted most, he tried to busy himself in other directions. So, one day, when he expected it least, his reward came to him.

He happened to be reading a book many hundreds of years old, which told of remedies for all kinds of diseases. Most of them, he knew, were merely invented by old women, who sought to prove themselves wiser than other people; but at length he came to something which caused him to sit up straight in his chair, and made his eyes brighten. This was the description of a balsam—which would cure every kind of sore or wound—distilled from a plant only to be found in a country so distant that it would take a man on foot two months to go and come back again.

When I say that the book declared that the balsam could heal every sort of sore or wound, there were a few against which it was powerless, and it gave certain signs by which these might be known. This was the reason why Gilguerillo demanded to see the king's foot before he would undertake to cure it; and to obtain admittance he gave out that he was a shoemaker. However, the dreaded signs were absent, and his heart bounded at the thought that the princess was within his reach.

Perhaps she was; but a great deal had to be accomplished yet, and he had allowed himself a very short time in which to do it.

He spared his horse only so much as was needful, yet it took him six days to reach the spot where the plant grew. A thick wood lay in front of him, and, fastening the bridle tightly to a tree, he flung himself on his hands and knees and began to hunt for the treasure. Many time he fancied it was close to him, and many times it turned out to be something else; but, at last, when light was fading, and he had almost given up hope, he came upon a large bed of the plant, right under his feet! Trembling with joy, he picked every scrap he could see, and placed it in his wallet. Then, mounting his horse, he galloped quickly back towards the city.

It was night when he entered the gates, and the fifteen days allotted were not up till the next day. His eyes were heavy with sleep, and his body ached with the long strain, but, without pausing to rest, he kindled a fire on his hearth, and quickly filling a pot with water, threw in the herbs and left them to boil. After that he lay down and slept soundly.

The sun was shining when he awoke, and he jumped up and ran to the pot. The plant had disappeared and in its stead was a thick syrup, just as the book had said there would be. He lifted the syrup out with a spoon, and after spreading it in the sun till it was partly dry, poured it into a small flask of crystal. He next washed himself thoroughly, and dressed himself, in his best clothes, and putting the flask in his pocket, set out for the palace, and begged to see the king without delay.

Now Balancin, whose foot had been much less painful since Gilguerillo had wrapped it in the plaster, was counting the days to the young man's return; and when he was told Gilguerillo was there, ordered him to be admitted at once. As he entered, the king raised himself eagerly on his pillows, but his face fell when he saw no signs of a slipper.

"You have failed, then?" he said, throwing up his hands in despair.

"I hope not, your majesty; I think not," answered the youth. And drawing the flask from his pocket, he poured two or three drops on the wound.

"Repeat this for three nights, and you will find yourself cured," said he. And before the king had time to thank him he had bowed himself out.

Of course the news soon spread through the city, and men and women never tired of calling Gilguerillo an impostor, and prophesying that the end of the three days would see him in prison, if not on the scaffold. But Gilguerillo paid no heed to their hard words, and no more did the king, who took care that no hand but his own should put on the healing balsam.

On the fourth morning the king awoke and instantly stretched out his wounded foot that he might prove the truth or falsehood of Gilguerillo's remedy. The wound was certainly cured on that side, but how about the other? Yes, that was cured also; and not even a scar was left to show where it had been!

Was ever any king so happy as Balancin when he satisfied himself of this?

Lightly as a deer he jumped from his bed, and began to turn head over heels and to perform all sorts of antics, so as to make sure that his foot was in truth as well as it looked. And when he was quite tired he sent for his daughter, and bade the courtiers bring the lucky young man to his room.

"He is really young and handsome," said the princess to herself, heaving a sigh of relief that it was not some dreadful old man who had healed her father; and while the king was announcing to his courtiers the wonderful cure that had been made, Diamantina was thinking that if Gilguerillo looked so well in his common dress, how much improved by the splendid garments of a king's son. However, she held her peace, and only watched with amusement when the courtiers, knowing there was no help for it, did homage and obeisance to the chemist's boy.

Then they brought to Gilguerillo a magnificent tunic of green velvet bordered with gold, and a cap with three white plumes stuck in it; and at the sight of him so arrayed, the princess fell in love with him in a moment. The wedding was fixed to take place in eight days, and at the ball afterwards nobody danced so long or so lightly as king Balancin.

He Wins Who Waits

(FROM *THE OLIVE FAIRY BOOK*)

Once upon a time there reigned a king who had an only daughter. The girl had been spoiled by everybody from her birth, and, besides being beautiful, was clever and willful, and when she grew old enough to be married she refused to have anything to say to the prince whom her father favored, but declared she would choose a husband for herself. By long experience the king knew that when once she had made up her mind, there was no use expecting her to change it, so he inquired meekly what she wished him to do.

"Summon all the young men in the kingdom to appear before me a month from to-day," answered the princess; "and the one to whom I shall give this golden apple shall be my husband."

"But, my dear—" began the king, in tones of dismay.

"The one to whom I shall give this golden apple shall be my husband," repeated the princess, in a louder voice than before. And the king understood the signal, and with a sigh proceeded to do her bidding.

The young men arrived—tall and short, dark and fair, rich and poor. They stood in rows in the great courtyard in front of the palace, and the princess, clad in robes of green, with a golden veil flowing behind her, passed before them all, holding the apple. Once or twice she stopped and hesitated, but in the end she always passed on, till she came to a youth near the end of the last row. There was nothing specially remarkable about him, the bystanders thought; nothing that was likely to take a girl's fancy. A hundred others were handsomer, and all wore finer clothes; but he met the princess's eyes frankly and with a smile, and she smiled too, and held out the apple.

"There is some mistake," cried the king, who had anxiously watched her progress, and hoped that none of the candidates would please her. "It is impossible that she can wish to marry the son of a poor widow, who has not a farthing in the world! Tell her that I will not hear of it, and that she must go through the rows again and fix upon someone else"; and the princess went through the rows a second and a third time, and on each occasion she gave the apple to the widow's son. "Well, marry him if you will," exclaimed the angry king; "but at least you shall not stay here." And the princess answered nothing, but threw up her head, and taking the widow's son by the hand, they left the castle.

That evening they were married, and after the ceremony went back to the house of the bridegroom's mother, which, in the eyes of the princess, did not look much bigger than a hen-coop.

The old woman was not at all pleased when her son entered bringing his bride with him.

"As if we were not poor enough before," grumbled she. "I dare say this is some fine lady who can do nothing to earn her living." But the princess stroked her arm, and said softly:

"Do not be vexed, dear mother; I am a famous spinner, and can sit at my wheel all day without breaking a thread."

And she kept her word; but in spite of the efforts of all three, they became poorer and poorer; and at the end of six months it was agreed that the husband should go to the neighboring town to get work. Here he met a merchant who was about to start on a long journey with a train of camels laden with goods of all sorts, and needed a man to help him. The widow's son begged that he would take him as a servant, and to this the merchant assented, giving him his whole year's salary beforehand. The young man returned home with the news, and next day bade farewell to his mother and his wife, who were very sad at parting from him.

"Do not forget me while you are absent," whispered the princess as she flung her arms round his neck; "and as you pass by the well which lies near the city gate, stop and greet the old man you will find sitting there. Kiss his hand, and then ask him what counsel he can give you for your journey."

Then the youth set out, and when he reached the well where the old man was sitting he asked the questions as his wife had bidden him.

"My son," replied the old man, "you have done well to come to me, and in return remember three things: 'She whom the heart loves, is ever the most beautiful.' 'Patience is the first step on the road to happiness.' 'He wins who waits.'"

The young man thanked him and went on his way. Next morning early the caravan set out, and before sunset it had arrived at the first halting place, round some wells, where another company of merchants had already encamped. But no rain had fallen for a long while in that rocky country, and both men and beasts were parched with thirst. To be sure, there *was* another well about half a mile away, where there was always water; but to get it you had to be lowered deep down, and, besides, no one who had ever descended that well had been known to come back.

However, till they could store some water in their bags of goat-skin, the caravans dared not go further into the desert, and on the night of the arrival of the widow's son and his master, the merchants had decided to offer a large reward to anyone who was brave enough to go down into the enchanted well and bring some up. Thus it happened that at sunrise the young man was aroused from his sleep by a herald making his round of the camp, proclaiming that every merchant present would give a thousand piastres to the man who would risk his life to bring water for themselves and their camels.

The youth hesitated for a little while when he heard the proclamation. The story of the well had spread far and wide, and long ago had reached his ears. The danger was great, he knew; but then, if he came back alive, he would be the possessor of eighty thousand piastres. He turned to the herald who was passing the tent:

"*I* will go," said he.

"What madness!" cried his master, who happened to be standing near. "You are too young to throw away your life like that. Run after the herald and tell him you take back your offer." But the young man shook his head, and the merchant saw that it was useless to try and persuade him.

"Well, it is your own affair," he observed at last. "If you must go, you must. Only, if you ever return, I will give you a camel's load of goods and my best mule besides." And touching his turban in token of farewell, he entered the tent.

Hardly had he done so than a crowd of men were seen pouring out of the camp.

"How can we thank you!" they exclaimed, pressing round the youth. "Our camels as well as ourselves are almost dead of thirst. See! here is the rope we have brought to let you down."

"Come, then," answered the youth. And they all set out.

On reaching the well, the rope was knotted securely under his arms, a big goat-skin bottle was given him, and he was gently lowered to the bottom of the pit. Here a clear stream was bubbling over the rocks, and, stooping down, he was about to drink, when a huge Arab appeared before him, saying in a loud voice:

"Come with me!"

The young man rose, never doubting that his last hour had come; but as he could do nothing, he followed the Arab into a brilliantly lighted hall, on the further side of the little river. There his guide sat down, and drawing towards him two boys, he said to the stranger:

"I have a question to ask you. If you answer it right, your life shall be spared. If not, your head will be forfeit, as the head of many another has been before you. Tell me: which of my two children do I think the handsomer."

The question did not seem hard, for while the one boy was as beautiful a child as ever was seen, his brother was ugly. But, just as the youth was going to speak, the old man's counsel flashed into the youth's mind, and he replied hastily: "The one whom we love best is always the handsomest."

"You have saved me!" cried the Arab, rising quickly from his seat, and pressing the young man in his arms. "Ah! if you could only guess what I have suffered from the stupidity of all the people to whom I have put that question, and I was condemned by a wicked genius to remain here until it was answered! But what brought you to this place, and how can I reward you for what you have done for me?"

"By helping me to draw enough water for my caravan of eighty merchants and their camels, who are dying for want of it," replied the youth.

"That is easily done," said the Arab. "Take these three apples, and when you have filled your skin, and are ready to be drawn up, lay one of them on the ground. Half-way to the earth, let fall another, and at the top, drop the third. If you follow my directions no harm will happen to you. And take, besides, these three pomegranates, green, red and white. One day you will find a use for them!"

The young man did as he was told, and stepped out on the rocky waste, where the merchants were anxiously awaiting him. Oh, how thirsty they all were! But even after the camels had drunk, the skin seemed as full as ever.

Full of gratitude for their deliverance, the merchants pressed the money into his hands, while his own master bade him choose what goods he liked, and a mule to carry them.

So the widow's son was rich at last, and when the merchant had sold his merchandise, and returned home to his native city, his servant hired a man by whom he sent the money and the mule back to his wife.

"I will send the pomegranates also," thought he, "for if I leave them in my turban they may some day fall out," and he drew them out of his turban. But the fruit had vanished, and in their places were three precious stones, green, white, and red.

For a long time he remained with the merchant, who gradually trusted him with all his business, and gave him a large share of the money he made. When his master died, the young man wished to return home, but the widow begged him to stay and help her; and one day he awoke with a start, to remember that twenty years had passed since he had gone away.

"I want to see my wife," he said next morning to his mistress. "If at any time I can be of use to you, send a messenger to me; meanwhile, I have told Hassan what to do." And mounting a camel he set out.

Now, soon after he had taken service with the merchant a little boy had been born to him, and both the princess and the old woman toiled hard all day to get the baby food and clothing. When the money and the pomegranates arrived there was no need for them to work any more, and the princess saw at once that they were not fruit at all, but precious stones of great value. The old woman, however, not being accustomed, like her daughter-in-law, to the sight of jewels, took them only for common fruit, and wished to give them to the child to eat. She was very angry when the princess hastily took them from her and hid them in her dress, while she went to the market and bought the three finest pomegranates she could find, which she handed the old woman for the little boy.

Then she bought beautiful new clothes for all of them, and when they were dressed they looked as fine as could be. Next, she took out one of the precious stones which her husband had sent her, and placed it in a small silver box. This she wrapped up in a handkerchief embroidered in gold, and filled the old woman's pockets with gold and silver pieces.

"Go, dear mother," she said, "to the palace, and present the jewel to the king, and if he asks you what he can give you in return, tell him that you want a paper, with his seal attached, proclaiming that no one is to meddle with anything you may choose to do. Before you leave the palace distribute the money among the servants."

The old woman took the box and started for the palace. No one there had ever seen a ruby of such beauty, and the most famous jeweler in the town was summoned to declare its value. But all he could say was:

"If a boy threw a stone into the air with all his might, and you could pile up gold as high as the flight of the stone, it would not be sufficient to pay for this ruby."

At these words the king's face fell. Having once seen the ruby he could not bear to part with it, yet all the money in his treasury would not be enough to buy it. So for a little while he remained silent, wondering what offer he could make the old woman, and at last he said:

"If I cannot give you its worth in money, is there anything you will take in exchange?"

"A paper signed by your hand, and sealed with your seal, proclaiming that I may do what I will, without let or hindrance," answered she promptly. And the king, delighted to have obtained what he coveted at so small a cost, gave her the paper without delay. Then the old woman took her leave and returned home.

The fame of this wonderful ruby soon spread far and wide, and envoys arrived at the little house to know if there were more stones to sell. Each king was so anxious to gain possession of the treasure that he bade his messenger outbid all the rest, and so the princess sold the two remaining stones for a sum of money so large that if the gold pieces had been spread out they would have reached from here to the moon. The first thing she did was to build a palace by the side of the cottage, and it was raised on pillars of gold, in which were set great diamonds, which blazed night and day. Of course the news of this palace was the first thing that reached the king her father, on his return from the wars, and he hurried to see it. In the doorway stood a young man of twenty, who was his grandson, though neither of them knew it, and so pleased was the king with the appearance of the youth, that he carried him back to his own palace, and made him commander of the whole army.

Not long after this, the widow's son returned to his native land. There, sure enough, was the tiny cottage where he had lived with his mother, but the gorgeous building beside it was quite new to him. What had become of his wife and his mother, and who could be dwelling in that other wonderful place. These were the first thoughts that flashed through his mind; but not wishing to betray himself by asking questions of passing strangers, he climbed up into a tree that stood opposite the palace and watched.

By-and-by a lady came out, and began to gather some of the roses and jessamine that hung about the porch. The twenty years that had passed since he had last beheld her vanished in an instant, and he knew her to be his own wife, looking almost as young and beautiful as on the day of their parting. He was about to jump down from the tree and hasten to her side, when she was joined by a young man who placed his arm affectionately round her neck. At this sight the angry husband drew his bow, but before he could let fly the arrow, the counsel of the wise man came back to him: "Patience is the first step on the road to happiness." And he laid it down again.

At this moment the princess turned, and drawing her companion's head down to hers, kissed him on each cheek. A second time blind rage filled the heart of the watcher, and he snatched up his bow from the branch where it hung, when words, heard long since, seemed to sound in his ears:

"He wins who waits." And the bow dropped to his side. Then, through the silent air came the sound of the youth's voice:

"Mother, can you tell me nothing about my father? Does he still live, and will he never return to us?"

"Alas! my son, how can I answer you?" replied the lady. "Twenty years have passed since he left us to make his fortune, and, in that time, only once have I heard aught of him. But what has brought him to your mind just now?"

"Because last night I dreamed that he was here," said the youth, "and then I remembered what I have so long forgotten, that I *had* a father, though even his very history was strange to me. And now, tell me, I pray you, all you can concerning him."

And standing under the jessamine, the son learnt his father's history, and the man in the tree listened also.

"Oh," exclaimed the youth, when it was ended, while he twisted his hands in pain, "I am general-in-chief, you are the king's daughter, and we have the most splendid palace in the whole world, yet my father lives we know not where, and for all we can guess, may be poor and miserable. To-morrow I will ask the king to give me soldiers, and I will seek him over the whole earth till I find him."

Then the man came down from the tree, and clasped his wife and son in his arms. All that night they talked, and when the sun rose it still found them talking. But as soon as it was proper, he went up to the palace to pay his homage to the king, and to inform him of all that had happened and who they all really were. The king was overjoyed to think that his daughter, whom he had long since forgiven and sorely missed, was living at his gates, and was, besides, the mother of the youth who was so dear to him. "It was written beforehand," cried the monarch. "You are my son-in-law before the world, and shall be king after me."

And the man bowed his head.

He had waited; and he had won.

The Three Snake-Leaves

(FROM *THE GREEN FAIRY BOOK*)

There was once a poor man who could no longer afford to keep his only son at home. So the son said to him, "Dear father, you are so poor that I am only a burden to you; I would rather go out into the world and see if I can earn my own living." The father gave him his blessing and took leave of him with much sorrow. About this time the King of a very powerful kingdom was carrying on a war; the youth therefore took service under him and went on the campaign. When they came before the enemy, a battle took place, there was some hot fighting, and it rained bullets so thickly that his comrades fell around him on all sides. And when their leader fell too the rest wished to take to flight; but the youth stepped forward and encouraged them and called out, "We must not let our country be ruined!" Then others followed him, and he pressed on and defeated the enemy. When the King heard that he had to thank him alone for the victory, he raised him higher than anyone else in rank, gave him great treasures and made him the first in the kingdom.

The King had a daughter who was very beautiful, but she was also very capricious. She had made a vow to marry no one who would not promise her that if she died first, he would allow himself to be buried alive with her. "If he loves me truly," she used to say, "what use would life be to him then?" At the same time she was willing to do the same, and if he died first to be buried with him. This curious vow had up to this time frightened away all suitors, but the young man was so captivated by her beauty, that he hesitated at nothing and asked her hand of her father. "Do you know," asked the King, "what you have to promise?" "I shall have to go into her grave with her," he answered, "if I outlive her, but my love is so great that I do not think of the risk." So the King consented, and the wedding was celebrated with great splendor.

Now, they lived for a long time very happily with one another, but then it came to pass that the young Queen fell seriously ill, and no doctor could save her. And when she lay dead, the young King remembered what he had promised, and it made him shudder to think of lying in her grave alive, but there was no escape. The King had set guards before all the gates, and it was not possible to avoid his fate.

When the day arrived on which the corpse was to be laid in the royal vault, he was led thither, then the entrance was bolted and closed up.

Near the coffin stood a table on which were placed four candles, four loaves of bread, and four bottles of wine. As soon as this provision came to an end he would have to die. So he sat there full of grief and misery, eating every day only a tiny bit of bread, and drinking only a mouthful of wine, and he watched death creeping nearer and nearer to him. One day as he was sitting staring moodily in front of him, he saw a snake creep out of the corner towards the corpse. Thinking it was going to touch it, he drew his sword and saying, "As long as I am alive you shall not harm her," he cut it in three pieces. After a little time a second snake crept out of the corner, but when it saw the first one lying dead and in pieces it went back and came again soon, holding three green leaves in its mouth. Then it took the three bits of the snake and laid them in order, and put one of the leaves on each wound. Immediately the pieces joined together, the snake moved itself and became alive and then both hurried away. The leaves remained lying on the ground, and it suddenly occurred to the unfortunate man who had seen everything, that the wonderful power of the leaves might also be exercised upon a human being.

So he picked up the leaves and laid one of them on the mouth and the other two on the eyes of the dead woman. And scarcely had he done this, before the blood began to circulate in her veins, then it mounted and brought color back to her white face. Then she drew her breath, opened her eyes, and said, "Ah! where am I?" "You are with me, dear lady," he answered, and told her all that had happened, and how he had brought her to life again. He then gave her some wine and bread, and when all her strength had returned she got up, and they went to the door and knocked and called so loudly that the guards heard them, and told the King. The King came himself to open the door, and there he found both happy and well, and he rejoiced with them that now all trouble was over. But the young King gave the three snake-leaves to a servant, saying to him, "Keep them carefully for me, and always carry them with you; who knows but that they may help us in a time of need!"

It seemed, however, as if a change had come over the young Queen after she had been restored to life, and as if all her love for her husband had faded from her heart. Some time afterwards, when he wanted to take a journey over the sea to his old father, and they were on board the ship, she forgot the great love and faithfulness he had shown her and how he had saved her from death, and fell in love with the captain. And one day when the young King was lying asleep, she called the captain to her, and seized the head of the sleeping King and made him take his feet, and together they threw him into the sea. When they had done this wicked deed, she said to him, "Now let us go home and say that he died on the journey. I will praise you so much to my father that he will marry me to you and make you the heir to the throne." But the faithful servant, who had seen everything, let down a little boat into the sea, unobserved by them, and rowed after his master while the traitors sailed on. He took the drowned man out of the water, and with the help of the three snake-leaves which he carried with him, placing them on his mouth and eyes, he brought him to life again.

They both rowed as hard as they could night and day, and their little boat went so quickly that they reached the old King before the other two did.

He was much astonished to see them come back alone, and asked what had happened to them. When he heard the wickedness of his daughter, he said, "I cannot believe that she has acted so wrongly, but the truth will soon come to light." He made them both go into a secret chamber, and let no one see them.

Soon after this the large ship came in, and the wicked lady appeared before her father with a very sad face. He said to her, "Why have you come back alone? Where is your husband?"

"Ah, dear father," she replied, "I have come home in great grief; my husband fell ill on the voyage quite suddenly, and died, and if the good captain had not given me help, I should have died too. He was at his death-bed and can tell you everything."

The King said, "I will bring the dead to life again," and he opened the door of the room and called them both out. The lady was as if thunderstruck when she caught sight of her husband; she fell on her knees and begged for mercy. But the King said, "You shall have no mercy. He was ready to die with you, and restored you to life again; but you killed him when he was sleeping, and shall receive your deserts."

So she and her accomplice were put in a ship which was bored through with holes, and were drawn out into the sea, where they soon perished in the waves.

The Story of the Seven Simons

(FROM *THE CRIMSON FAIRY BOOK*)

Far, far away, beyond all sorts of countries, seas and rivers, there stood a splendid city where lived King Archidej, who was as good as he was rich and handsome. His great army was made up of men ready to obey his slightest wish; he owned forty times forty cities, and in each city he had ten palaces with silver doors, golden roofs, and crystal windows. His council consisted of the twelve wisest men in the country, whose long beards flowed down over their breasts, each of whom was as learned as a whole college. This council always told the king the exact truth.

Now the king had everything to make him happy, but he did not enjoy anything because he could not find a bride to his mind.

One day, as he sat in his palace looking out to sea, a great ship sailed into the harbor and several merchants came on shore. Said the king to himself: "These people have traveled far and beheld many lands. I will ask them if they have seen any princess who is as clever and as handsome as I am."

So he ordered the merchants to be brought before him, and when they came he said: "You have traveled much and visited many wonders. I wish to ask you a question, and I beg you to answer truthfully.

"Have you anywhere seen or heard of the daughter of an emperor, king, or a prince, who is as clever and as handsome as I am, and who would be worthy to be my wife and the queen of my country?"

The merchants considered for some time. At last the eldest of them said: "I have heard that across many seas, in the Island of Busan, there is a mighty king, whose daughter, the Princess Helena, is so lovely that she can certainly not be plainer than your Majesty, and so clever that the wisest greybeard cannot guess her riddles."

"Is the island far off, and which is the way to it?"

"It is not near," was the answer. "The journey would take ten years, and we do not know the way. And even if we did, what use would that be? The princess is no bride for you."

"How dare you say so?" cried the king angrily.

"Your Majesty must pardon us; but just think for a moment. Should you send an envoy to the island he will take ten years to get there and ten more to return—twenty years in all. Will not the princess have grown old in that time and have lost all her beauty?"

The king reflected gravely. Then he thanked the merchants, gave them leave to trade in his country without paying any duties, and dismissed them.

After they were gone the king remained deep in thought. He felt puzzled and anxious; so he decided to ride into the country to distract his mind, and sent for his huntsmen and falconers. The huntsmen blew their horns, the falconers took their hawks on their wrists, and off they all set out across country till they came to a green hedge. On the other side of the hedge stretched a great field of maize as far as the eye could reach, and the yellow ears swayed to and fro in the gentle breeze like a rippling sea of gold.

The king drew rein and admired the field. "Upon my word," said he, "whoever dug and planted it must be good workmen. If all the fields in my kingdom were as well cared for as this, there would be more bread than my people could eat." And he wished to know to whom the field belonged.

Off rushed all his followers at once to do his bidding, and found a nice, tidy farmhouse, in front of which sat seven peasants, lunching on rye bread and drinking water. They wore red shirts bound with gold braid, and were so much alike that one could hardly tell one from another.

The messengers asked: "Who owns this field of golden maize?" And the seven brothers answered: "The field is ours."

"And who are you?"

"We are King Archidej's laborers."

These answers were repeated to the king, who ordered the brothers to be brought before him at once. On being asked who they were, the eldest said, bowing low:

"We, King Archidej, are your laborers, children of one father and mother, and we all have the same name, for each of us is called Simon. Our father taught us to be true to our king, and to till the ground, and to be kind to our neighbors. He also taught each of us a different trade which he thought might be useful to us, and he bade us not neglect our mother earth, which would be sure amply to repay our labor."

The king was pleased with the honest peasant, and said: "You have done well, good people, in planting your field, and now you have a golden harvest. But I should like each of you to tell me what special trades your father taught you."

"My trade, O king!" said the first Simon, "is not an easy one. If you will give me some workmen and materials I will build you a great white pillar that shall reach far above the clouds."

"Very good," replied the king. "And you, Simon the second, what is your trade?"

"Mine, your Majesty, needs no great cleverness. When my brother has built the pillar I can mount it, and from the top, far above the clouds, I can see what is happening: in every country under the sun."

"Good," said the king; "and Simon the third?"

"My work is very simple, sire. You have many ships built by learned men, with all sorts of new and clever improvements. If you wish it I will build you quite a simple boat—one, two, three, and it's done! But my plain little home-made ship is not grand enough for a king. Where other ships take a year, mine makes the voyage in a day, and where they would require ten years mine will do the distance in a week."

"Good," said the king again; "and what has Simon the fourth learnt?"

"My trade, O king, is really of no importance. Should my brother build you a ship, then let me embark in it. If we should be pursued by an enemy I can seize our boat by the prow and sink it to the bottom of the sea. When the enemy has sailed off, I can draw it up to the top again."

"That is very clever of you," answered the king; "and what does Simon the fifth do?"

"My work, your Majesty, is mere smith's work. Order me to build a smithy and I will make you a cross-bow, but from which neither the eagle in the sky nor the wild beast in the forest is safe. The bolt hits whatever the eye sees."

"That sounds very useful," said the king. "And now, Simon the sixth, tell me your trade."

"Sire, it is so simple I am almost ashamed to mention it. If my brother hits any creature I catch it quicker than any dog can. If it falls into the water I pick it up out of the greatest depths, and if it is in a dark forest I can find it even at midnight."

The king was much pleased with the trades and talk of the six brothers, and said: "Thank you, good people; your father did well to teach you all these things. Now follow me to the town, as I want to see what you can do. I need such people as you about me; but when harvest time comes I will send you home with royal presents."

The brothers bowed and said: "As the king wills." Suddenly the king remembered that he had not questioned the seventh Simon, so he turned to him and said: "Why are you silent? What is your handicraft?"

And the seventh Simon answered: "I have no handicraft, O king; I have learnt nothing. I could not manage it. And if I do know how to do anything it is not what might properly be called a real trade—it is rather a sort of performance; but it is one which no one—not the king himself—must watch me doing, and I doubt whether this performance of mine would please your Majesty."

"Come, come," cried the king; "I will have no excuses, what is this trade?"

"First, sire, give me your royal word that you will not kill me when I have told you. Then you shall hear."

"So be it, then; I give you my royal word."

Then the seventh Simon stepped back a little, cleared his throat, and said: "My trade, King Archidej, is of such a kind that the man who follows it in your kingdom generally loses his life and has no hopes of pardon. There is only one thing I can do really well, and that is—to steal, and to hide the smallest scrap of anything I have stolen. Not the deepest vault, even if its lock were enchanted, could prevent my stealing anything out of it that I wished to have."

When the king heard this he fell into a passion. "I will *not* pardon you, you rascal," he cried; "I will shut you up in my deepest dungeon on bread and water till you have forgotten such a trade. Indeed, it would be better to put you to death at once, and I've a good mind to do so."

"Don't kill me, O king! I am really not as bad as you think. Why, had I chosen, I could have robbed the royal treasury, have bribed your judges to let me off, and built a white marble palace with what was left. But though I know how to steal I don't do it. You yourself asked me my trade. If you kill me you will break your royal word."

"Very well," said the king, "I will not kill you. I pardon you. But from this hour you shall be shut up in a dark dungeon. Here, guards! away with him to the prison. But you six Simons follow me and be assured of my royal favor."

So the six Simons followed the king. The seventh Simon was seized by the guards, who put him in chains and threw him in prison with only bread and water for food. Next day the king gave the first Simon carpenters, masons, smiths and laborers, with great stores of iron, mortar, and the like, and Simon began to build. And he built his great white pillar far, far up into the clouds, as high as the nearest stars; but the other stars were higher still.

Then the second Simon climbed up the pillar and saw and heard all that was going on through the whole world. When he came down he had all sorts of wonderful things to tell. How one king was marching in battle against another, and which was likely to be the victor. How, in another place, great rejoicings were going on, while in a third people were dying of famine. In fact there was not the smallest event going on over the earth that was hidden from him.

Next the third Simon began. He stretched out his arms, once, twice, thrice, and the wonder-ship was ready. At a sign from the king it was launched, and floated proudly and safely like a bird on the waves. Instead of ropes it had wires for rigging, and musicians played on them with fiddle bows and made lovely music. As the ship swam about, the fourth Simon seized the prow with his strong hand, and in a moment it was gone—sunk to the bottom of the sea. An hour passed, and then the ship floated again, drawn up by Simon's left hand, while in his right he brought a gigantic fish from the depth of the ocean for the royal table.

Whilst this was going on the fifth Simon had built his forge and hammered out his iron, and when the king returned from the harbor the magic cross-bow was made.

His Majesty went out into an open field at once, looked up into the sky and saw, far, far away, an eagle flying up towards the sun and looking like a little speck.

"Now," said the king, "if you can shoot that bird I will reward you."

Simon only smiled; he lifted his cross-bow, took aim, fired, and the eagle fell. As it was falling the sixth Simon ran with a dish, caught the bird before it fell to earth and brought it to the king.

"Many thanks, my brave lads," said the king; "I see that each of you is indeed a master of his trade. You shall be richly rewarded. But now rest and have your dinner."

The six Simons bowed and went to dinner. But they had hardly begun before a messenger came to say that the king wanted to see them. They obeyed at once and found him surrounded by all his court and men of state.

"Listen, my good fellows," cried the king, as soon as he saw them. "Hear what my wise counselors have thought of. As you, Simon the second, can see the whole world from the top of the great pillar, I want you to climb up and to see and hear. For I am told that, far away, across many seas, is the great kingdom of the Island of Busan, and that the daughter of the king is the beautiful Princess Helena."

Off ran the second Simon and clambered quickly up the pillar. He gazed around, listened on all sides, and then slid down to report to the king.

"Sire, I have obeyed your orders. Far away I saw the Island of Busan. The king is a mighty monarch, but full of pride, harsh and cruel. He sits on his throne and declares that no prince or king on earth is good enough for his lovely daughter, that he will give her to none, and that if any king asks for her hand he will declare war against him and destroy his kingdom."

"Has the king of Busan a great army?" asked King Archidej; "is his country far off?"

"As far as I could judge," replied Simon, "it would take you nearly ten years in fair weather to sail there. But if the weather were stormy we might say twelve. I saw the army being reviewed. It is not so *very* large—a hundred thousand men at arms and a hundred thousand knights. Besides these, he has a strong bodyguard and a good many cross-bowmen. Altogether you may say another hundred thousand, and there is a picked body of heroes who reserve themselves for great occasions requiring particular courage."

The king sat for some time lost in thought. At last he said to the nobles and courtiers standing round: "I am determined to marry the Princess Helena, but how shall I do it?"

The nobles, courtiers and counselors said nothing, but tried to hide behind each other. Then the third Simon said:

"Pardon me, your Majesty, if I offer my advice. You wish to go to the Island of Busan? What can be easier? In my ship you will get there in a week instead of in ten years. But ask your council to advise you what to do when you arrive—in one word, whether you will win the princess peacefully or by war?"

But the wise men were as silent as ever.

The king frowned, and was about to say something sharp, when the Court Fool pushed his way to the front and said: "Dear me, what are all you clever people so puzzled about? The matter is quite clear. As it seems it will not take long to reach the island why not send the seventh Simon? He will steal the fair maiden fast enough, and then the king, her father, may consider how he is going to bring his army over here—it will take him ten years to do it!— no less! What do you think of my plan?"

"What do I think? Why, that your idea is capital, and you shall be rewarded for it. Come, guards, hurry as fast as you can and bring the seventh Simon before me."

Not many minutes later, Simon the seventh stood before the king, who explained to him what he wished done, and also that to steal for the benefit of his king and country was by no means a wrong thing, though it was very wrong to steal for his own advantage.

The youngest Simon, who looked very pale and hungry, only nodded his head.

"Come," said the king, "tell me truly. Do you think you could steal the Princess Helena?"

"Why should I not steal her, sire? The thing is easy enough. Let my brother's ship be laden with rich stuffs, brocades, Persian carpets, pearls and jewels. Send me in the ship. Give me my four middle brothers as companions, and keep the two others as hostages."

When the king heard these words his heart became filled with longing, and he ordered all to be done as Simon wished. Every one ran about to do his bidding; and in next to no time the wonder-ship was laden and ready to start.

The five Simons took leave of the king, went on board, and had no sooner set sail than they were almost out of sight. The ship cut through the waters like a falcon through the air, and just a week after starting sighted the Island of Busan. The coast appeared to be strongly guarded, and from afar the watchman on a high tower called out: "Halt and anchor! Who are you? Where do you come from, and what do you want?"

The seventh Simon answered from the ship: "We are peaceful people. We come from the country of the great and good King Archidej, and we bring foreign wares—rich brocades, carpets, and costly jewels, which we wish to show to your king and the princess. We desire to trade—to sell, to buy, and to exchange."

The brothers launched a small boat, took some of their valuable goods with them, rowed to shore and went up to the palace. The princess sat in a rose-red room, and when she saw the brothers coming near she called her nurse and other women, and told them to inquire who and what these people were, and what they wanted.

The seventh Simon answered the nurse: "We come from the country of the wise and good King Archidej," said he, "and we have brought all sorts of goods for sale. We trust the king of this country may condescend to welcome us, and to let his servants take charge of our wares. If he considers them worthy to adorn his followers we shall be content."

This speech was repeated to the princess, who ordered the brothers to be brought to the red-room at once. They bowed respectfully to her and displayed some splendid velvets and brocades, and opened cases of pearls and precious stones. Such beautiful things had never been seen in the island,

and the nurse and waiting women stood bewildered by all the magnificence. They whispered together that they had never beheld anything like it. The princess too saw and wondered, and her eyes could not weary of looking at the lovely things, or her fingers of stroking the rich soft stuffs, and of holding up the sparkling jewels to the light.

"Fairest of princesses," said Simon. "Be pleased to order your waiting-maids to accept the silks and velvets, and let your women trim their head-dresses with the jewels; these are no special treasures. But permit me to say that they are as nothing to the many colored tapestries, the gorgeous stones and ropes of pearls in our ship. We did not like to bring more with us, not knowing what your royal taste might be; but if it seems good to you to honor our ship with a visit, you might condescend to choose such things as were pleasing in your eyes."

This polite speech pleased the princess very much. She went to the king and said: "Dear father, some merchants have arrived with the most splendid wares. Pray allow me to go to their ship and choose out what I like."

The king thought and thought, frowned hard and rubbed his ear. At last he gave consent, and ordered out his royal yacht, with 100 cross-bows, 100 knights, and 1,000 soldiers, to escort the Princess Helena.

Off sailed the yacht with the princess and her escort. The brothers Simon came on board to conduct the princess to their ship, and, led by the brothers and followed by her nurse and other women, she crossed the crystal plank from one vessel to another.

The seventh Simon spread out his goods, and had so many curious and interesting tales to tell about them, that the princess forgot everything else in looking and listening, so that she did not know that the fourth Simon had seized the prow of the ship, and that all of a sudden it had vanished from sight, and was racing along in the depths of the sea.

The crew of the royal yacht shouted aloud, the knights stood still with terror, the soldiers were struck dumb and hung their heads. There was nothing to be done but to sail back and tell the king of his loss.

How he wept and stormed! "Oh, light of my eyes," he sobbed; "I am indeed punished for my pride. I thought no one good enough to be your husband, and now you are lost in the depths of the sea, and have left me alone! As for all of you who saw this thing—away with you! Let them be put in irons and lock them up in prison, whilst I think how I can best put them to death!"

Whilst the King of Busan was raging and lamenting in this fashion, Simon's ship was swimming like any fish under the sea, and when the island was well out of sight he brought it up to the surface again. At that moment the princess recollected herself. "Nurse," said she, "we have been gazing at these wonders only too long. I hope my father won't be vexed at our delay."

She tore herself away and stepped on deck. Neither the yacht nor the island was in sight! Helena wrung her hands and beat her breast. Then she changed herself into a white swan and flew off. But the fifth Simon seized his bow and shot the swan, and the sixth Simon did not let it fall into the water but caught it in the ship, and the swan turned into a silver fish, but Simon lost no time and caught the fish, when, quick as thought, the fish turned into a black mouse and ran about the ship. It darted towards a hole, but before it could reach it Simon sprang upon it more swiftly than any cat, and then the little mouse turned once more into the beautiful Princess Helena.

Early one morning King Archidej sat thoughtfully at his window gazing out to sea. His heart was sad and he would neither eat nor drink. His thoughts were full of the Princess Helena, who was as lovely as a dream. Is that a white gull he sees flying towards the shore, or is it a sail? No, it is no gull, it is the wonder-ship flying along with billowing sails. Its flags wave, the fiddlers play on the wire rigging, the anchor is thrown out and the crystal plank laid from the ship to the pier. The lovely Helena steps across the plank. She shines like the sun, and the stars of heaven seem to sparkle in her eyes.

Up sprang King Archidej in haste: "Hurry, hurry," he cried. "Let us hasten to meet her! Let the bugles sound and the joy bells be rung!"

And the whole Court swarmed with courtiers and servants. Golden carpets were laid down and the great gates thrown open to welcome the princess.

King Archidej went out himself, took her by the hand and led her into the royal apartments.

"Madam," said he, "the fame of your beauty had reached me, but I had not dared to expect such loveliness. Still I will not keep you here against your will. If you wish it, the wonder-ship shall take you back to your father and your own country; but if you will consent to stay here, then reign over me and my country as our queen."

What more is there to tell? It is not hard to guess that the princess listened to the king's wooing, and their betrothal took place with great pomp and rejoicings.

The brothers Simon were sent again to the Island of Busan with a letter to the king from his daughter to invite him to their wedding. And the wonder-ship arrived at the Island of Busan just as all the knights and soldiers who had escorted the princess were being led out to execution.

Then the seventh Simon cried out from the ship: "Stop! stop! I bring a letter from the Princess Helena!"

The King of Busan read the letter over and over again, and ordered the knights and soldiers to be set free. He entertained King Archidej's ambassadors hospitably, and sent his blessing to his daughter, but he could not be brought to attend the wedding.

When the wonder-ship got home King Archidej and Princess Helena were enchanted with the news it brought.

The king sent for the seven Simons. "A thousand thanks to you, my brave fellows," he cried. "Take what gold, silver, and precious stones you will out of my treasury. Tell me if there is anything else you wish for and I will give it you, my good friends. Do you wish to be made nobles, or to govern towns? Only speak."

Then the eldest Simon bowed and said: "We are plain folk, your Majesty, and understand simple things best. What figures should we cut as nobles or governors? Nor do we desire gold. We have our fields which give us food, and as much money as we need. If you wish to reward us then grant that our land may be free of taxes, and of your goodness pardon the seventh Simon. He is not the first who has been a thief by trade and he will certainly not be the last."

"So be it," said the king; "your land shall be free of all taxes, and Simon the seventh is pardoned."

Then the king gave each brother a goblet of wine and invited them to the wedding feast. And *what* a feast that was!

What the Rose Did to the Cypress

(FROM *THE BROWN FAIRY BOOK*)

Once upon a time a great king of the East, named Saman-lālpōsh, had three brave and clever sons—Tahmāsp, Qamās, and Almās-ruh-baksh. One day, when the king was sitting in his hall of audience, his eldest son, Prince Tahmāsp, came before him, and after greeting his father with due respect, said: "O my royal father! I am tired of the town; if you will give me leave, I will take my servants to-morrow and will go into the country and hunt on the hill-skirts; and when I have taken some game I will come back, at evening-prayer time." His father consented, and sent with him some of his own trusted servants, and also hawks, and falcons, hunting dogs, cheetahs and leopards.

At the place where the prince intended to hunt he saw a most beautiful deer. He ordered that it should not be killed, but trapped or captured with a noose. The deer looked about for a place where he might escape from the ring of the beaters, and spied one unwatched close to the prince himself. It bounded high and leaped right over his head, got out of the ring, and tore like the eastern wind into the waste. The prince put spurs to his horse and pursued it; and was soon lost to the sight of his followers. Until the world-lighting sun stood above his head in the zenith he did not take his eyes off the deer; suddenly it disappeared behind some rising ground, and with all his search he could not find any further trace of it. He was now drenched in sweat, and he breathed with pain; and his horse's tongue hung from its mouth with thirst. He dismounted and toiled on, with bridle on arm, praying and casting himself on the mercy of heaven. Then his horse fell and surrendered its life to God. On and on he went across the sandy waste, weeping and with burning breast, till at length a hill rose into sight. He mustered his strength and climbed to the top, and there he found a giant tree whose foot kept firm the wrinkled earth, and whose crest touched the very heaven. Its branches had put forth a glory of leaves, and there were grass and a spring underneath it, and flowers of many colors.

Gladdened by this sight, he dragged himself to the water's edge, drank his fill, and returned thanks for his deliverance from thirst.

He looked about him and, to his amazement, saw close by a royal seat. While he was pondering what could have brought this into the merciless desert, a man drew near who was dressed like a faqīr, and had bare head and feet, but walked with the free carriage of a person of rank. His face was kind, and wise and thoughtful, and he came on and spoke to the prince.

"O good youth! how did you come here? Who are you? Where do you come from?"

The prince told everything just as it had happened to him, and then respectfully added: "I have made known my own circumstances to you, and now I venture to beg you to tell me your own. Who are you? How did you come to make your dwelling in this wilderness?"

To this the faqīr replied: "O youth! it would be best for you to have nothing to do with me and to know nothing of my fortunes, for my story is fit neither for telling nor for hearing." The prince, however, pleaded so hard to be told, that at last there was nothing to be done but to let him hear.

"Learn and know, O young man! that I am King Janāngīr of Babylon, and that once I had army and servants, family and treasure; untold wealth and belongings. The Most High God gave me seven sons who grew up well versed in all princely arts. My eldest son heard from travelers that in Turkistān, on the Chinese frontier, there is a king named Quimūs, the son of Tīmūs, and that he has an only child, a daughter named Mihr-afrūz, who, under all the azure heaven, is unrivaled for beauty. Princes come from all quarters to ask her hand, and on one and all she imposes a condition. She says to them: 'I know a riddle; and I will marry anyone who answers it, and will bestow on him all my possessions. But if a suitor cannot answer my question I cut off his head and hang it on the battlements of the citadel.' The riddle she asks is, 'What did the rose do to the cypress?'

"Now, when my son heard this tale, he fell in love with that unseen girl, and he came to me lamenting and bewailing himself. Nothing that I could say had the slightest effect on him. I said: 'Oh my son! if there must be fruit of this fancy of yours, I will lead forth a great army against King Quimūs.

If he will give you his daughter freely, well and good; and if not, I will ravage his kingdom and bring her away by force.' This plan did not please him; he said: 'It is not right to lay a kingdom waste and to destroy a palace so that I may attain my desire. I will go alone; I will answer the riddle, and win her in this way.' At last, out of pity for him, I let him go. He reached the city of King Quimūs. He was asked the riddle and could not give the true answer; and his head was cut off and hung upon the battlements. Then I mourned him in black raiment for forty days.

"After this another and another of my sons were seized by the same desire, and in the end all my seven sons went, and all were killed. In grief for their death I have abandoned my throne, and I abide here in this desert, withholding my hand from all State business and wearing myself away in sorrow."

Prince Tahmāsp listened to this tale, and then the arrow of love for that unseen girl struck his heart also. Just at this moment of his ill-fate his people came up, and gathered round him like moths round a light. They brought him a horse, fleet as the breeze of the dawn; he set his willing foot in the stirrup of safety and rode off. As the days went by the thorn of love rankled in his heart, and he became the very example of lovers, and grew faint and feeble. At last his confidants searched his heart and lifted the veil from the face of his love, and then set the matter before his father, King Saman-lāl-pōsh. "Your son, Prince Tahmāsp, loves distractedly the Princess Mihr-afrūz, daughter of King Quimūs, son of Tīmūs." Then they told the king all about her and her doings. A mist of sadness clouded the king's mind, and he said to his son: "If this thing is so, I will in the first place send a courier with friendly letters to King Quimūs, and will ask the hand of his daughter for you. I will send an abundance of gifts, and a string of camels laden with flashing stones and rubies of Badakhsham. In this way I will bring her and her suite, and I will give her to you to be your solace. But if King Quimūs is unwilling to give her to you, I will pour a whirlwind of soldiers upon him, and I will bring to you, in this way, that most consequential of girls." But the prince said that this plan would not be right, and that he would go himself, and would answer the riddle. Then the king's wise men said: "This is a very weighty matter; it would be best to allow the prince to set out accompanied by some persons in whom you have confidence. Maybe he will repent and come back." So King Saman ordered all preparations for the journey to be made, and then Prince Tahmāsp took his leave and set out, accompanied by some of the courtiers, and taking with him a string of two-humped and raven-eyed camels laden with jewels, and gold, and costly stuffs.

By stage after stage, and after many days' journeying, he arrived at the city of King Quimūs. What did he see? A towering citadel whose foot kept firm the wrinkled earth, and whose battlements touched the blue heaven. He saw hanging from its battlements many heads, but it had not the least effect upon him that these were heads of men of rank; he listened to no advice about laying aside his fancy, but rode up to the gate and on into the heart of the city. The place was so splendid that the eyes of the ages have never seen its like, and there, in an open square, he found a tent of crimson satin set up, and beneath it two jeweled drums with jeweled sticks. These drums were put there so that the suitors of the princess might announce their arrival by beating on them, after which some one would come and take them to the king's presence. The sight of the drums stirred the fire of Prince Tahmāsp's love. He dismounted, and moved towards them; but his companions hurried after and begged him first to let them go and announce him to the king, and said that then, when they had put their possessions in a place of security, they would enter into the all important matter of the princess. The prince, however, replied that he was there for one thing only; that his first duty was to beat the drums and announce himself as a suitor, when he would be taken, as such, to the king, who would then give him proper lodgment. So he struck upon the drums, and at once summoned an officer who took him to King Quimūs.

When the king saw how very young the prince looked, and that he was still drinking of the fountain of wonder, he said: "O youth! leave aside this fancy which my daughter has conceived in the pride of her beauty. No one can answer her riddle, and she has done to death many men who had had no pleasure in life nor tasted its charms. God forbid that your spring also should be ravaged by the autumn winds of martyrdom." All his urgency, however, had no effect in making the prince withdraw. At length it was settled between them that three days should be given to pleasant hospitality and that then should follow what had to be said and done. Then the prince went to his own quarters and was treated as became his station.

King Quimūs now sent for his daughter and for her mother, Gulrukh, and talked to them. He said to Mihrafrūz: "Listen to me, you cruel flirt! Why do you persist in this folly? Now there has come to ask your hand a prince of the east, so handsome that the very sun grows modest before the splendor of his face; he is rich, and he has brought gold and jewels, all for you, if you will marry him. A better husband you will not find."

But all the arguments of father and mother were wasted, for her only answer was: "O my father! I have sworn to myself that I will not marry, even if a thousand years go by, unless someone answers my riddle, and that I will give myself to that man only who does answer it."

The three days passed; then the riddle was asked: "What did the rose do to the cypress?" The prince had an eloquent tongue, which could split a hair, and without hesitation he replied to her with a verse: "Only the Omnipotent has knowledge of secrets; if any man says, 'I know' do not believe him."

Then a servant fetched in the polluted, blue-eyed headsman, who asked: "Whose sun of life has come near its setting?" took the prince by the arm, placed him upon the cloth of execution, and then, all merciless and stony-hearted, cut his head from his body and hung it on the battlements.

The news of the death of Prince Tahmāsp plunged his father into despair and stupefaction. He mourned for him in black raiment for forty days; and then, a few days later, his second son, Prince Qamās, extracted from him leave to go too; and he, also, was put to death. One son only now remained, the brave, eloquent, happy-natured Prince Almās-ruh-bakhsh. One day, when his father sat brooding over his lost children, Almās came before him and said: "O father mine! the daughter of King Quimūs has done my two brothers to death; I wish to avenge them upon her." These words brought his father to tears. "O light of your father!" he cried, "I have no one left but you, and now you ask me to let you go to your death."

"Dear father!" pleaded the prince, "until I have lowered the pride of that beauty, and have set her here before you, I cannot settle down or indeed sit down off my feet."

In the end he, too, got leave to go; but he went a without a following and alone. Like his brothers, he made the long journey to the city of Quimūs the son of Tīmūs; like them he saw the citadel, but he saw there the heads of Tahmāsp and Qamās. He went about in the city, saw the tent and the drums, and then went out again to a village not far off. Here he found out a very old man who had a wife 120 years old, or rather more. Their lives were coming to their end, but they had never beheld the face of child of their own. They were glad when the prince came to their house, and they dealt with him as with a son. He put all his belongings into their charge, and fastened his horse in their out-house. Then he asked them not to speak of him to anyone, and to keep his affairs secret. He exchanged his royal dress for another, and next morning, just as the sun looked forth from its eastern oratory, he went again into the city. He turned over in his mind without ceasing how he was to find out the meaning of the riddle, and to give them a right answer, and who could help him, and how to avenge his brothers. He wandered about the city, but heard nothing of service, for there was no one in all that land who understood the riddle of Princess Mihr-afrūz.

One day he thought he would go to her own palace and see if he could learn anything there, so he went out to her garden-house. It was a very splendid place, with a wonderful gateway, and walls like Alexander's ramparts. Many gate-keepers were on guard, and there was no chance of passing them. His heart was full of bitterness, but he said to himself: "All will be well! it is here I shall get what I want." He went round outside the garden wall hoping to find a gap, and he made supplication in the Court of Supplications and prayed, "O Holder of the hand of the helpless! show me my way."

While he prayed he bethought himself that he could get into the garden with a stream of inflowing water. He looked carefully round, fearing to be seen, stripped, slid into the stream and was carried within the great walls. There he hid himself till his loin cloth was dry. The garden was a very Eden, with running water among its lawns, with flowers and the lament of doves and the jug-jug of nightingales. It was a place to steal the senses from the brain, and he wandered about and saw the house, but there seemed to be no one there. In the forecourt was a royal seat of polished jasper, and in the middle of the platform was a basin of purest water that flashed like a mirror. He pleased himself with these sights for a while, and then went back to the garden and hid himself from the gardeners and passed the night. Next morning he put on the appearance of a madman and wandered about till he came to a lawn where several pert-faced girls were amusing themselves. On a throne, jeweled and overspread with silken stuffs, sat a girl the splendor of whose beauty lighted up the place, and whose ambergris and attar perfumed the whole air. "That must be Mihr-afrūz," he thought, "she is indeed lovely." Just then one of the attendants came to the water's edge to fill a cup, and though the prince was in hiding, his face was reflected in the water. When she saw this image she was frightened, and let her cup fall into the stream, and thought, "Is it an angel, or a peri, or a man?" Fear and trembling took hold of her, and she screamed as women scream. Then some of the other girls came and took her to the princess who asked: "What is the matter, pretty one?"

"O princess! I went for water, and I saw an image, and I was afraid." So another girl went to the water and saw the same thing, and came back with the same story. The princess wished to see for herself; she rose and paced to the spot with the march of a prancing peacock. When she saw the image she said to her nurse: "Find out who is reflected in the water, and where he lives." Her words reached the prince's ear, he lifted up his head; she saw him and beheld beauty such as she had never seen before. She lost a hundred hearts to him, and signed to her nurse to bring him to her presence. The prince let himself be persuaded to go with the nurse, but when the princess questioned him as to who he was and how he had got into her garden, he behaved like a man out of his mind—sometimes smiling, sometimes crying, and saying: "I am hungry," or words misplaced and random, civil mixed with the rude.

"What a pity!" said the princess, "he is mad!" As she liked him she said: "He is my madman; let no one hurt him." She took him to her house and told him not to go away, for that she would provide for all his wants. The prince thought, "It would be excellent if here, in her very house, I could get the answer to her riddle; but I must be silent, on pain of death."

Now in the princess's household there was a girl called Dil-arām; she it was who had first seen the image of the prince. She came to love him very much, and she spent day and night thinking how she could make her affection known to him. One day she escaped from the princess's notice and went to the prince, and laid her head on his feet and said: "Heaven has bestowed on you beauty and charm. Tell me your secret; who are you, and how did you come here? I love you very much, and if you would like to leave this place I will go with you. I have wealth equal to the treasure of the miserly Qarūn." But the prince only made answer like a man distraught, and told her nothing. He said to himself, "God forbid that the veil should be taken in vain from my secret; that would indeed disgrace me." So, with streaming eyes and burning breast, Dil-arām arose and went to her house and lamented and fretted.

Now whenever the princess commanded the prince's attendance, Dil-arām, of all the girls, paid him attention and waited on him best. The princess noticed this, and said: "O Dil-arām! you must take my madman into your charge and give him whatever he wants." This was the very thing Dilarām had prayed for. A little later she took the prince into a private place and she made him take an oath of secrecy, and she herself took one and swore, "By Heaven! I will not tell your secret. Tell me all about yourself so that I may help you to get what you want." The prince now recognized in her words the perfume of true love, and he made compact with her. "O lovely girl! I want to know what the rose did to the cypress. Your mistress cuts off men's heads because of this riddle; what is at the bottom of it, and why does she do it?" Then Dil-arām answered: "If you will promise to marry me and to keep me always among those you favor, I will tell you all I know, and I will keep watch about the riddle."

"O lovely girl," rejoined he, "if I accomplish my purpose, so that I need no longer strive for it, I will keep my compact with you. When I have this woman in my power and have avenged my brothers, I will make you my solace."

"O wealth of my life and source of my joy!" responded Dil-arām, "I do not know what the rose did to the cypress; but so much I know that the person who told Mihr-afrūz about it is a negro whom she hides under her throne. He fled here from Wāq of the Caucasus—it is there you must make inquiry; there is no other way of getting at the truth." On hearing these words, the prince said to his heart, "O my heart! your task will yet wear away much of your life."

He fell into long and far thought, and Dil-arām looked at him and said: "O my life and my soul! do not be sad. If you would like this woman killed, I will put poison into her cup so that she will never lift her head from her drugged sleep again."

"O Dil-arām! such a vengeance is not manly. I shall not rest till I have gone to Wāq of the Caucasus and have cleared up the matter." Then they repeated the agreement about their marriage, and bade one another good-bye.

The prince now went back to the village, and told the old man that he was setting out on a long journey, and begged him not to be anxious, and to keep safe the goods which had been entrusted to him.

The prince had not the least knowledge of the way to Wāq of the Caucasus, and was cast down by the sense of his helplessness. He was walking along by his horse's side when there appeared before him an old man of serene countenance, dressed in green and carrying a staff, who resembled Khizr. The prince thanked heaven, laid the hands of reverence on his breast and salaamed. The old man returned the greeting graciously, and asked: "How fare you? Whither are you bound? You look like a traveler."

"O revered saint! I am in this difficulty: I do not know the way to Wāq of the Caucasus." The old man of good counsel looked at the young prince and said: "Turn back from this dangerous undertaking. Do not go; choose some other task! If you had a hundred lives you would not bring one out safe from this journey." But his words had no effect on the prince's resolve. "What object have you," the old man asked, "in thus consuming your life?"

"I have an important piece of business to do, and only this journey makes it possible. I must go; I pray you, ill God's name, tell me the way."

When the saint saw that the prince was not to be moved, he said: "Learn and know, O youth! that Wāq of Qāf is in the Caucasus and is a dependency of it. In it there are jins, demons, and peris. You must go on along this road till it forks into three; take neither the right hand nor the left, but the middle path. Follow this for a day and a night. Then you will come to a column on which is a marble slab inscribed with Cufic characters. Do what is written there; beware of disobedience." Then he gave his good wishes for the journey and his blessing, and the prince kissed his feet, said good-bye, and, with thanks to the Causer of Causes, took the road.

After a day and a night he saw the column rise in silent beauty to the heavens. Everything was as the wise old man had said it would be, and the prince, who was skilled in all tongues, read the following Cufic inscription: "O travelers! be it known to you that this column has been set up with its tablet to give true directions about these roads. If a man would pass his life in ease and pleasantness, let him take the right-hand path. If he take the left, he will have some trouble, but he will reach his goal without much delay. Woe to him who chooses the middle path! if he had a thousand lives he would not save one; it is very hazardous; it leads to the Caucasus, and is an endless road. Beware of it!"

The prince read and bared his head and lifted his hands in supplication to Him who has no needs, and prayed, "O Friend of the traveler! I, Thy servant, come to Thee for succor. My purpose lies in the land of Qāf and my road is full of peril. Lead me by it." Then he took a handful of earth and cast it on his collar, and said: "O earth! be thou my grave; and O vest! be thou my winding-sheet!" Then he took the middle road and went along it, day after day, with many a silent prayer, till he saw trees rise from the weary waste of sand. They grew in a garden, and he went up to the gate and found it a slab of beautifully worked marble, and that near it there lay sleeping, with his head on a stone, a negro whose face was so black that it made darkness round him. His upper lip, arched like an eyebrow, curved upwards to his nostrils and his lower hung down like a camel's. Four millstones formed his shield, and on a box-tree close by hung his giant sword. His loin-cloth was fashioned of twelve skins of beasts, and was bound round his waist by a chain of which each link was as big as an elephant's thigh.

The prince approached and tied up his horse near the negro's head. Then he let fall the Bismillah from his lips, entered the garden and walked through it till he came to the private part, delighting in the great trees, the lovely verdure, and the flowery borders. In the inner garden there were very many deer. These signed to him with eye and foot to go back, for that this was enchanted ground; but he did not understand them, and thought their pretty gestures were a welcome. After a while he reached a palace which had a porch more splendid than Caesar's, and was built of gold and silver bricks. In its midst was a high seat, overlaid with fine carpets, and into it opened eight doors, each having opposite to it a marble basin.

Banishing care, Prince Almās walked on through the garden, when suddenly a window opened and a girl, who was lovely enough to make the moon writhe with jealousy, put out her head. She lost her heart to the good looks of the prince, and sent her nurse to fetch him so that she might learn where he came from and how he had got into her private garden where even lions and wolves did not venture. The nurse went, and was struck with amazement at the sun-like radiance of his face; she salaamed and said: "O youth! welcome! the lady of the garden calls you; come!" He went with her and into a palace which was like a house in Paradise, and saw seated on the royal carpets of the throne a girl whose brilliance shamed the shining sun. He salaamed; she rose, took him by the hand and placed him near her. "O young man! who are you? Where do you come from? How did you get into this garden?" He told her his story from beginning to end, and Lady Latīfa replied: "This is folly! It will make you a vagabond of the earth, and lead you to destruction. Come, cease such talk! No one can go to the Caucasus. Stay with me and be thankful, for here is a throne which you can share with me, and in my society you can enjoy my wealth. I will do whatever you wish; I will bring here King Qulmūs and his daughter, and you can deal with them as you will."

110

"O Lady Latīfa," he said, "I have made a compact with heaven not to sit down off my feet till I have been to Wāq of Qāf and have cleared up this matter, and have taken Mihr-afrūz from her father, as brave men take, and have put her in prison. When I have done all this I will come back to you in state and with a great following, and I will marry you according to the law." Lady Latīfa argued and urged her wishes, but in vain; the prince was not to be moved. Then she called to the cupbearers for new wine, for she thought that when his head was hot with it he might consent to stay. The pure, clear wine was brought; she filled a cup and gave to him. He said: "O most enchanting sweetheart! it is the rule for the host to drink first and then the guest." So to make him lose his head, she drained the cup; then filled it again and gave him. He drank it off, and she took a lute from one of the singers and played upon it with skill which witched away the sense of all who heard. But it was all in vain; three days passed in such festivities, and on the fourth the prince said: "O joy of my eyes! I beg now that you will bid me farewell, for my way is long and the fire of your love darts flame into the harvest of my heart. By heaven's grace I may accomplish my purpose, and, if so, I will come back to you."

Now she saw that she could not in any way change his resolve, she told her nurse to bring a certain casket which contained, she said, something exhilarating which would help the prince on his journey. The box was brought, and she divided off a portion of what was within and gave it to the prince to eat. Then, and while he was all unaware, she put forth her hand to a stick fashioned like a snake; she said some words over it and struck him so sharply on the shoulder that he cried out; then he made a pirouette and found that he was a deer.

When he knew what had been done to him he thought, "All the threads of affliction are gathered together; I have lost my last chance!" He tried to escape, but the magician sent for her goldsmith, who, coming, overlaid the deer-horns with gold and jewels. The kerchief which that day she had had in her hand was then tied round its neck, and this freed it from her attentions.

The prince-deer now bounded into the garden and at once sought some way of escape. It found none, and it joined the other deer, which soon made it their leader. Now, although the prince had been transformed into the form of a deer, he kept his man's heart and mind. He said to himself, "Thank heaven that the Lady Latīfa has changed me into this shape, for at least deer are beautiful." He remained for some time living as a deer among the rest, but at length resolved that an end to such a life must be put ill some way. He looked again for some place by which he could get out of the magic garden. Following round the wall he reached a lower part; he remembered the Divine Names and flung himself over, saying, "Whatever happens is by the will of God." When he looked about he found that he was in the very same place he had jumped from; there was the palace, there the garden and the deer! Eight times he leaped over the wall and eight times found himself where he had started from; but after the ninth leap there was a change, there was a palace and there was a garden, but the deer were gone.

Presently a girl of such moon-like beauty opened a window that the prince lost to her a hundred hearts. She was delighted with the beautiful deer, and cried to her nurse: "Catch it! if you will I will give you this necklace, every pearl of which is worth a kingdom." The nurse coveted the pearls, but as she was three hundred years old she did not know how she could catch a deer. However, she went down into the garden and held out some grass, but when she went near the creature ran away. The girl watched with great excitement from the palace window, and called: "O nurse, if you don't catch it, I will kill you!" "I am killing myself," shouted back the old woman. The girl saw that nurse tottering along and went down to help, marching with the gait of a prancing peacock. When she saw the gilded horns and the kerchief she said: "It must be accustomed to the hand, and be some royal pet!" The prince had it in mind that this might be another magician who could give him some other shape, but still it seemed best to allow himself to be caught. So he played about the girl and let her catch him by the neck. A leash was brought, fruits were given, and it was caressed with delight. It was taken to the palace and tied at the foot of the Lady Jamīla's raised seat, but she ordered a longer cord to be brought so that it might be able to jump up beside her.

When the nurse went to fix the cord she saw tears falling from its eyes, and that it was dejected and sorrowful. "O Lady Jamīla! this is a wonderful deer, it is crying; I never saw a deer cry before." Jamīla darted down like a flash of lightning, and saw that it was so. It rubbed its head on her feet and then shook it so sadly that the girl cried for sympathy. She patted it and said: "Why are you sad, my heart? Why do you cry, my soul? Is it because I have caught you? I love you better than my own life." But, spite of her comforting, it cried the more. Then Jamīla said: "Unless I am mistaken, this is the work of my wicked sister Latīfa, who by magic art turns servants of God into beasts of the field." At these words the deer uttered sounds, and laid its head on her feet. Then Jamīla was sure it was a man, and said: "Be comforted, I will restore you to your own shape." She bathed herself and ordered the deer to be bathed, put on clean raiment, called for a box which stood in an alcove, opened it and gave a portion of what was in it to the deer to eat. Then she slipped her hand under her carpet and produced a stick to which she said something. She struck the deer hard, it pirouetted and became Prince Almās.

The broidered kerchief and the jewels lay upon the ground. The prince prostrated himself in thanks to heaven and Jamīla, and said: "O delicious person! O Chinese Venus! how shall I excuse myself for giving you so much trouble? With what words can I thank you?" Then she called for a clothes-wallet and chose out a royal dress of honor. Her attendants dressed him in it, and brought him again before the tender-hearted lady. She turned to him a hundred hearts, took his hand and seated him beside her, and said: "O youth! tell me truly who you are and where you come from, and how you fell into the power of my sister."

Even when he was a deer the prince had much admired Jamīla now he thought her a thousand times more lovely than before. He judged that in truth alone was safety, and so told her his whole story. Then she asked: "O Prince Almās-ruh-bakhsh, do you still wish so much to make this journey to Wāq of Qāf? What hope is there in it? The road is dangerous even near here, and this is not yet the borderland of the Caucasus. Come, give it up! It is a great risk, and to go is not wise. It would be a pity for a man like you to fall into the hands of jins and demons. Stay with me, and I will do whatever you wish."

"O most delicious person!" he answered, "you are very generous, and the choice of my life lies in truth in your hands; but I beg one favor of you. If you love me, so do I too love you. If you really love me, do not forbid me to make this journey, but help me as far as you can. Then it may be that I shall succeed, and if I return with my purpose fulfilled I will marry you according to the law, and take you to my own country, and we will spend the rest of our lives together in pleasure and good companionship. Help me, if you can, and give me your counsel."

"O very stuff of my life," replied Jamīla, "I will give you things that are not in kings' treasuries, and which will be of the greatest use to you. First, there are the bow and arrows of his Reverence the Prophet Salih. Secondly, there is the Scorpion of Solomon (on whom be peace), which is a sword such as no king has; steel and stone are one to it; if you bring it down on a rock it will not be injured, and it will cleave whatever you strike. Thirdly, there is the dagger which the sage Tīmūs himself made; this is most useful, and the man who wears it would not bend under seven camels' loads. What you have to do first is to get to the home of the Simurgh, and to make friends with him. If he favors you, he will take you to Wāq of Qāf; if not, you will never get there, for seven seas are on the way, and they are such seas that if all the kings of the earth, and all their vazīrs, and all their wise men considered for a thousand years, they would not be able to cross them."

"O most delicious person! where is the Simurgh's home? How shall I get there?"

"O new fruit of life! you must just do what I tell you, and you must use your eyes and your brains, for if you don't you will find yourself at the place of the negroes, who are a bloodthirsty set; and God forbid they should lay hands on your precious person."

Then she took the bow and quiver of arrows, the sword, and the dagger out of a box, and the prince let fall a *Bismillāh*, and girt them all on. Then Jamīla of the houri-face, produced two saddle-bags of ruby-red silk, one filled with roasted fowl and little cakes, and the other with stones of price. Next she gave him a horse as swift as the breeze of the morning, and she said: "Accept all these things from me; ride till you come to a rising ground, at no great distance from here, where there is a spring. It is called the Place of Gifts, and you must stay there one night. There you will see many wild beasts—lions, tigers, leopards, apes, and so on. Before you get there you must capture some game. On the long road beyond there dwells a lion-king, and if other beasts did not fear him they would ravage the whole country and let no one pass. The lion is a red transgressor, so when he comes rise and do him reverence; take a cloth and rub the dust and earth from his face, then set the game you have taken before him, well cleansed, and lay the hands of respect on your breast. When he wishes to eat, take your knife and cut pieces of the meat and set them before him with a bow. In this way you will enfold that lion-king in perfect friendship, and he will be most useful to you, and you will be safe from molestation by the negroes. When you go on from the Place of Gifts, be sure you do not take the right-hand road; take the left, for the other leads by the negro castle, which is known as the Place of Clashing

Swords, and where there are forty negro captains each over three thousand or four thousand more. Their chief is Taramtāq. Further on than this is the home of the Simurgh."

Having stored these things in the prince's memory, she said: "You will see everything happen just as I have said." Then she escorted him a little way; they parted, and she went home to mourn his absence.

Prince Almās, relying on the Causer of Causes, rode on to the Place of Gifts and dismounted at the platform. Everything happened just as Jamīla had foretold; when one or two watches of the night had passed, he saw that the open ground around him was full of such stately and splendid animals as he had never seen before. By-and-by, they made way for a wonderfully big lion, which was eighty yards from nose to tail-tip, and was a magnificent creature. The prince advanced and saluted it; it proudly drooped its head and forelocks and paced to the platform. Seventy or eighty others were with it, and now encircled it at a little distance. It laid its right paw over its left, and the prince took the kerchief Jamīla had given him for the purpose, and rubbed the dust and earth from its face; then brought forward the game he had prepared, and crossing his hands respectfully on his breast stood waiting before it. When it wished for food he cut off pieces of the meat and put them in its mouth. The serving lions also came near and the prince would have stayed his hand, but the king-lion signed to him to feed them too. This he did, laying the meat on the platform. Then the king-lion beckoned the prince to come near and said: "Sleep at ease; my guards will watch." So, surrounded by the lion-guard, he slept till dawn, when the king lion said good-bye, and gave him a few of his own hairs and said: "When you are in any difficulty, burn one of these and I will be there." Then it went off into the jungle.

Prince Almās immediately started; he rode till he came to the parting of the ways. He remembered quite well that the right-hand way was short and dangerous, but he bethought himself too that whatever was written on his forehead would happen, and took the forbidden road. By-and-by he saw a castle, and knew from what Jamīla had told him that it was the Place of Clashing Swords. He would have liked to go back by the way he had come, but courage forbade, and he said, "What has been preordained from eternity will happen to me," and went on towards the castle. He was thinking of tying his horse to a tree which grew near the gate when a negro came out and spied him. "Ha!" said the wretch to himself, "this is good; Taram-taq has not eaten man-meat for a long time, and is craving for some. I will take this creature to him." He took hold of the prince's reins, and said: "Dismount, man-child! Come to my master. He has wanted to eat man-meat this long time back." "What nonsense are you saying?" said the prince, and other such words. When the negro understood that he was being abused, he cried: "Come along! I will put you into such a state that the birds of the air will weep for you." Then the prince drew the Scorpion of Solomon and struck him—struck him on the leathern belt and shore him through so that the sword came out on the other side. He stood upright for a little while, muttered some words, put out his hand to seize the prince, then fell in two and surrendered his life.

There was water close at hand, and the prince made his ablution, and then said: "O my heart! a wonderful task lies upon you." A second negro came out of the fort, and seeing what had been done, went back and told his chief. Others wished to be doubled, and went out, and of every one the Scorpion of Solomon made two. Then Taram-tāq sent for a giant negro named Chil-māq, who in the day of battle was worth three hundred, and said to him: "I shall thank you to fetch me that man."

Chil-māq went out, tall as a tower, and bearing a shield of eight mill-stones, and as he walked he shouted: "Ho! blunder-head! by what right do you come to our country and kill our people? Come! make two of me." As the prince was despicable in his eyes, he tossed aside his club and rushed to grip him with his hands. He caught him by the collar, tucked him under his arm and set off with him to Taram-tāq. But the prince drew the dagger of Tīmūs and thrust it upwards through the giant's armpit, for its full length. This made Chil-māq drop him and try to pick up his club; but when he stooped the mighty sword shore him through at the waist.

When news of his champion's death reached Taram-tāq he put himself at the head of an army of his negroes and led them forth. Many fell before the magic sword, and the prince labored on in spite of weakness and fatigue till he was almost worn out. In a moment of respite from attack he struck his fire-steel and burned a hair of the king-lion; and he had just succeeded in this when the negroes charged again and all but took him prisoner. Suddenly from behind the distant veil of the desert appeared an army of lions led by their king. "What brings these scourges of heaven here?" cried the negroes. They came roaring up, and put fresh life into the prince. He fought on, and when he struck on a belt the wearer fell in two, and when on a head he cleft to the waist. Then the ten thousand mighty lions joined the fray and tore in pieces man and horse.

Taram-tāq was left alone; he would have retired into his fort, but the prince shouted: "Whither away, accursed one? Are you fleeing before me?" At these defiant words the chief shouted back, "Welcome, man! Come here and I will soften you to wax beneath my club." Then he hurled his club at the prince's head, but it fell harmless because the prince had quickly spurred his horse forward. The chief, believing he had hit him, was looking down for him, when all at once he came up behind and cleft him to the waist and sent him straight to hell.

The king-lion greatly praised the dashing courage of Prince Almās. They went together into the Castle of Clashing Swords and found it adorned and fitted in princely fashion. In it was a daughter of Taram-tāq, still a child. She sent a message to Prince Almās saying, "O king of the world! choose this slave to be your handmaid. Keep her with you; where you go, there she will go!" He sent for her and she kissed his feet and received the Mussulman faith at his hands. He told her he was going on a long journey on important business, and that when he came back he would take her and her possessions to his own country, but that for the present she must stay in the castle. Then he made over the fort and all that was in it to the care of the lion, saying: "Guard them, brother! let no one lay a hand on them." He said good-bye, chose a fresh horse from the chief's stable and once again took the road.

After traveling many stages and for many days, he reached a plain of marvelous beauty and refreshment. It was carpeted with flowers—roses, tulips, and clover; it had lovely lawns, and among them running water. This choicest place of earth filled him with wonder. There was a tree such as he had never seen before; its branches were alike, but it bore flowers and fruit of a thousand kinds. Near it a reservoir had been fashioned of four sorts of stone—touchstone, pure stone, marble, and loadstone. In and out of it flowed water like attar. The prince felt sure this must be the place of the Simurgh; he dismounted, turned his horse loose to graze, ate some of the food Jamīla had given him, drank of the stream and lay down to sleep.

He was still dozing when he was aroused by the neighing and pawing of his horse. When he could see clearly he made out a mountain-like dragon whose heavy breast crushed the stones beneath it into putty. He remembered the Thousand Names of God and took the bow of Salih from its case and three arrows from their quiver. He bound the dagger of Tīmūs firmly to his waist and hung the scorpion of Solomon round his neck. Then he set an arrow on the string and released it with such force that it went in at the monster's eye right up to the notch. The dragon writhed on itself, and belched forth an evil vapor, and beat the ground with its head till the earth quaked. Then the prince took a second arrow and shot into its throat. It drew in its breath and would have sucked the prince into its maw, but when he was within striking distance he drew his sword and, having committed himself to God, struck a mighty blow which cut the creature's neck down to the gullet. The foul vapor of the beast and horror at its strangeness now overcame the prince, and he fainted. When he came to himself he found that he was drenched in the gore of the dead monster. He rose and thanked God for his deliverance.

The nest of the Simurgh was in the wonderful tree above him, and in it were young birds; the parents were away searching for food. They always told the children, before they left them, not to put their heads out of the nest; but, to-day, at the noise of the fight below, they looked down and so saw the whole affair. By the time the dragon had been killed they were very hungry and set up a clamor for food. The prince therefore cut up the dragon and fed them with it, bit by bit, till they had eaten the whole. He then washed himself and lay down to rest, and he was still asleep when the Simurgh came home. As a rule, the young birds raised a clamor of welcome when their parents came near, but on this day they were so full of dragon-meat that they had no choice, they had to go to sleep.

As they flew nearer, the old birds saw the prince lying under the tree and no sign of life in the nest. They thought that the misfortune which for so many earlier years had befallen them had again happened and that their nestlings had disappeared. They had never been able to find out the murderer, and now suspected the prince. "He has eaten our children and sleeps after it; he must die," said the father-bird, and flew back to the hills and clawed up a huge stone which he meant to let fall on the prince's head. But his mate said, "Let us look into the nest first for to kill an innocent person would condemn us at the Day of Resurrection." They flew nearer, and presently the young birds woke and cried, "Mother, what have you brought for us?" and they told the whole story of the fight, and of how they were alive only by the favor of the young man under the tree, and of his cutting up the dragon and of their eating it. The mother-bird then remarked, "Truly, father! you were about to do a strange thing, and a terrible sin has been averted from you." Then the Simurgh flew off to a distance with the great stone and dropped it. It sank down to the very middle of the earth.

Coming back, the Simurgh saw that a little sunshine fell upon the prince through the leaves, and it spread its wings and shaded him till he woke. When he got up he salaamed to it, who returned his greeting with joy and gratitude, and caressed him and said: "O youth, tell me true! who are you, and where are you going? And how did you cross that pitiless desert where never yet foot of man had trod?" The prince told his story from beginning to end, and finished by saying: "Now it is my heart's wish that you should help me to get to Wāq of the Caucasus. Perhaps, by your favor, I shall accomplish my task and avenge my brothers." In reply the Simurgh first blessed the deliverer of his children, and then went on: "What you have done no child of man has ever done before; you assuredly have a claim on all my help, for every year up till now that dragon has come here and has destroyed my nestlings, and I have never been able to find who was the murderer and to avenge myself. By God's grace you have removed my children's powerful foe. I regard you as a child of my own. Stay with me; I will give you everything you desire, and I will establish a city here for you, and will furnish it with every requisite; I will give you the land of the Caucasus, and will make its princes subject to you. Give up the journey to Wāq, it is full of risk, and the jins there will certainly kill you." But nothing could move the prince, and seeing this the bird went on: "Well, so be it! When you wish to set forth you must go into the plain and take seven head of deer, and must make water-tight bags of their hides and keep their flesh in seven portions. Seven seas lie on our way—I will carry you over them; but if I have not food and drink we shall fall into the sea and be drowned. When I ask for it you must put food and water into my mouth. So we shall make the journey safely."

The prince did all as he was told, then they took flight; they crossed the seven seas, and at each one the prince fed the Simurgh. When they alighted on the shore of the last sea, it said: "O my son! there lies your road; follow it to the city. Take thee three feathers of mine, and, if you are in a difficulty, burn one and I will be with you in the twinkling of an eye."

The prince walked on in solitude till he reached the city. He went in and wandered about through all quarters, and through bazaars and lanes and squares, in the least knowing from whom he could ask information about the riddle of Mihr-afrūz. He spent seven days thinking it over in silence. From the first day of his coming he had made friends with a young cloth-merchant, and a great liking had sprung up between them. One day he said abruptly to his companion: "O dear friend! I wish you would tell me what the rose did to the cypress, and what the sense of the riddle is." The merchant started, and exclaimed: "If there were not brotherly affection between us, I would cut off your head for asking me this!" "If you meant to kill me," retorted the prince, "you would still have first to tell me what I want to know." When the merchant saw that the prince was in deadly earnest, he said: "If you wish to hear the truth of the matter you must wait upon our king. There is no other way; no one else will tell you. I have a well-wisher at the Court, named Farrūkh-fāl, and will introduce you to him." "That would be excellent," cried the prince. A meeting was arranged between Farrūkhfāl and Almās, and then the amir took him to the king's presence and introduced him as a stranger and traveler who had come from afar to sit in the shadow of King Sinaubar.

Now the Simurgh had given the prince a diamond weighing thirty misqāls, and he offered this to the king, who at once recognized its value, and asked where it had been obtained. "I, your slave, once had riches and state and power; there are many such stones in my country. On my way here I was plundered at the Castle of Clashing Swords, and I saved this one thing only, hidden in my bathing-cloth." In return for the diamond, King Sinaubar showered gifts of much greater value, for he remembered that it was the last possession of the prince. He showed the utmost kindness and hospitality, and gave his vazīr orders to install the prince in the royal guest-house. He took much pleasure in his visitor's society; they were together every day and spent the time most pleasantly. Several times the king said: "Ask me for something, that I may give it you." One day he so pressed to know what would pleasure the prince, that the latter said: "I have only one wish, and that I will name to you in private." The king at once commanded every one to withdraw, and then Prince Almās said: "The desire of my life is to know what the rose did to the cypress, and what meaning there is in the words." The king was astounded. "In God's name! if anyone else had said that to me I should have cut off his head instantly." The prince heard this in silence, and presently so beguiled the king with pleasant talk that to kill him was impossible.

Time flew by, the king again and again begged the prince to ask some gift of him, and always received this same reply: "I wish for your Majesty's welfare, what more can I desire?" One night there was a banquet, and cupbearers carried round gold and silver cups of sparkling wine, and singers with sweetest voices contended for the prize. The prince drank from the king's own cup, and when his head was hot with wine he took a lute from one of the musicians and placed himself on the carpet border and sang and sang till he witched away the sense of all who listened. Applause and compliments rang from every side. The king filled his cup and called the prince and gave it him and said: "Name your wish! it is yours." The prince drained off the wine and answered: "O king of the world! learn and know that I have only one aim in life, and this is to know what the rose did to the cypress."

"Never yet," replied the king, "has any man come out from that question alive. If this is your only wish, so be it; I will tell you. But I will do this on one condition only, namely, that when you have heard you will submit yourself to death." To this the prince agreed, and said: "I set my foot firmly on this compact."

The king then gave an order to an attendant; a costly carpet overlaid with European velvet was placed near him, and a dog was led in by a golden and jeweled chain and set upon the splendid stuffs. A band of fair girls came in and stood round it in waiting.

Then, with ill words, twelve negroes dragged in a lovely woman, fettered on hands and feet and meanly dressed, and they set her down on the bare floor. She was extraordinarily beautiful, and shamed the glorious sun. The king ordered a hundred stripes to be laid on her tender body; she sighed a long sigh. Food was called for and table-cloths were spread. Delicate meats were set before the dog, and water given it in a royal cup of Chinese crystal. When it had eaten its fill, its leavings were placed before the lovely woman and she was made to eat of them. She wept and her tears were pearls; she smiled and her lips shed roses. Pearls and flowers were gathered up and taken to the treasury.

"Now," said the king, "you have seen these things and your purpose is fulfilled." "Truly," said the prince, "I have seen things which I have not understood; what do they mean, and what is the story of them? Tell me and kill me."

Then said the king: "The woman you see there in chains is my wife; she is called Gul, the Rose, and I am Sinaubar, the Cypress. One day I was hunting and became very thirsty. After great search I discovered a well in a place so secret that neither bird nor beast nor man could find it without labor. I was alone, I took my turban for a rope and my cap for a bucket. There was a good deal of water, but when I let down my rope, something caught it, and I could not in any way draw it back. I shouted down into the well: 'O! servant of God! whoever you are, why do you deal unfairly with me? I am dying of thirst, let go! in God's name.' A cry came up in answer, 'O servant of God! we have been in the well a long time; in God's name get us out!' After trying a thousand schemes, I drew up two blind women. They said they were peris, and that their king had blinded them in his anger and had left them in the well alone.

" 'Now,' they said, 'if you will get us the cure for our blindness we will devote ourselves to your service, and will do whatever you wish.'

" 'What is the cure for your blindness?'

" 'Not far from this place,' they said, 'a cow comes up from the great sea to graze; a little of her dung would cure us. We should be eternally your debtors. Do not let the cow see you, or she will assuredly kill you.'

"With renewed strength and spirit I went to the shore. There I watched the cow come up from the sea, graze, and go back. Then I came out of my hiding, took a little of her dung and conveyed it to the peris. They rubbed it on their eyes, and by the Divine might saw again.

"They thanked heaven and me, and then considered what they could do to show their gratitude to me. 'Our perī-king,' they said, 'has a daughter whom he keeps under his own eye and thinks the most lovely girl on earth. In good sooth, she has not her equal! Now we will get you into her house and you must win her heart, and if she has an inclination for another, you must drive it out and win her for yourself. Her mother loves her so dearly that she has no ease but in her presence, and she will give her to no one in marriage. Teach her to love you so that she cannot exist without you. But if the matter becomes known to her mother she will have you burned in the fire. Then you must beg, as a last favor, that your body may be anointed with oil so that you may burn the more quickly and be spared torture. If the perī-king allows this favor, we two will manage to be your anointers, and we will put an oil on you such that if you were a thousand years in the fire not a trace of burning would remain.'

"In the end the two perīs took me to the girl's house. I saw her sleeping daintily. She was most lovely, and I was so amazed at the perfection of her beauty that I stood with senses lost, and did not know if she were real or a dream. When at last I saw that she was a real girl, I returned thanks that I, the runner, had come to my goal, and that I, the seeker, had found my treasure.

"When the perī opened her eyes she asked in affright: 'Who are you? Have you come to steal? How did you get here? Be quick! save yourself from this whirlpool of destruction, for the demons and perīs who guard me will wake and seize you.'

"But love's arrow had struck me deep, and the girl, too, looked kindly on me. I could not go away. For some months I remained hidden in her house. We did not dare to let her mother know of our love. Sometimes the girl was very sad and fearful lest her mother should come to know. One day her father said to her: 'Sweetheart, for some time I have noticed that your beauty is not what it was. How is this? Has sickness touched you? Tell me that I may seek a cure.' Alas! there was now no way of concealing the mingled delight and anguish of our love; from secret it became known. I was put in prison and the world grew dark to my rose, bereft of her lover.

"The perī-king ordered me to be burnt, and said: 'Why have you, a man, done this perfidious thing in my house?' His demons and perīs collected amber-wood and made a pile, and would have set me on it, when I remembered the word of life which the two perīs I had rescued had breathed into my ear, and I asked that my body might be rubbed with oil to release me the sooner from torture. This was allowed, and those two contrived to be the anointers. I was put into the fire and it was kept up for seven days and nights. By the will of the Great King it left no trace upon me. At the end of a week the perī-king ordered the ashes to be cast upon the dust-heap, and I was found alive and unharmed.

"Perīs who had seen Gul consumed by her love for me now interceded with the king, and said: 'It is clear that your daughter's fortunes are bound up with his, for the fire has not hurt him. It is best to give him the girl, for they love one another. He is King of Wāq of Qāf, and you will find none better.'

"To this the king agreed, and made formal marriage between Gul and me. You now know the price I paid for this faithless creature. O prince! remember our compact."

"I remember," said the prince; "but tell me what brought Queen Gul to her present pass?"

"One night," continued King Sinaubar, "I was aroused by feeling Gul's hands and feet, deadly cold, against my body. I asked her where she had been to get so cold, and she said she had had to go out. Next morning, when I went to my stable I saw that two of my horses, Windfoot and Tiger, were thin and worn out. I reprimanded the groom and beat him. He asked where his fault lay, and said that every night my wife took one or other of these horses and rode away, and came back only just before dawn. A flame kindled in my heart, and I asked myself where she could go and what she could do. I told the groom to be silent, and when next Gul took a horse from the stable to saddle another quickly and bring it to me. That day I did not hunt, but stayed at home to follow the matter up. I lay down as usual at night and pretended to fall asleep. When I seemed safely off Gul got up and went to the stable as her custom was. That night it was Tiger's turn. She rode off on him, and I took Windfoot and followed. With me went that dog you see, a faithful friend who never left me.

"When I came to the foot of those hills which lie outside the city I saw Gul dismount and go towards a house which some negroes have built there. Over against the door was a high seat, and on it lay a giant negro, before whom she salaamed. He got up and beat her till she was marked with weals, but she uttered no complaint. I was dumfounded, for once when I had struck her with a rose stalk she had complained and fretted for three days! Then the negro said to her: 'How now, ugly one and shaven head! Why are you so late, and why are you not wearing wedding garments?' She answered him: 'That person did not go to sleep quickly, and he stayed at home all day, so that I was not able to adorn myself. I came as soon as I could.' In a little while he called her to sit beside him; but this was more than I could bear. I lost control of myself and rushed upon him. He clutched my collar and we grappled in a death struggle. Suddenly she came behind me, caught my feet and threw me. While he held me on the ground, she drew out my own knife and gave it to him. I should have been killed but for that faithful dog which seized his throat and pulled him down and pinned him to the ground. Then I got up and despatched the wretch. There were four other negroes at the place; three I killed and the fourth got away, and has taken refuge beneath the throne of Mihr-afrūz, daughter of King Quimūs. I took Gul back to my palace, and from that time till now I have treated her as a dog is treated, and I have cared for my dog as though it were my wife. Now you know what the rose did to the cypress; and now you must keep compact with me."

"I shall keep my word," said the prince; "but may a little water be taken to the roof so that I may make my last ablution?"

To this request the king consented. The prince mounted to the roof, and, getting into a corner, struck his fire-steel and burned one of the Sirurgh's feathers in the flame. Straightway it appeared, and by the majesty of its presence made the city quake. It took the prince on its back and soared away to the zenith.

After a time King Sinaubar said: "That young man is a long time on the roof; go and bring him here." But there was no sign of the prince upon the roof; only, far away in the sky, the Simurgh was seen carrying him off. When the king heard of his escape he thanked heaven that his hands were clean of this blood.

Up and up flew the Simurgh, till earth looked like an egg resting on an ocean. At length it dropped straight down to its own place, where the kind prince was welcomed by the young birds and most hospitably entertained. He told the whole story of the rose and the cypress, and then, laden with gifts which the Simurgh had gathered from cities far and near, he set his face for the Castle of Clashing Swords. The king-lion came out to meet him; he took the negro chief's daughter—whose name was also Gul—in lawful marriage, and then marched with her and her possessions and her attendants to the Place of Gifts. Here they halted for a night, and at dawn said good-bye to the king-lion and set out for Jamīla's country.

When the Lady Jamīla heard that Prince Almās was near, she went out, with many a fair handmaid, to give him loving reception. Their meeting was joyful, and they went together to the garden-palace. Jamīla summoned all her notables, and in their presence her marriage with the prince was solemnized. A few days later she entrusted her affairs to her vazīr, and made preparation to go with the prince to his own country. Before she started she restored all the men whom her sister, Latīfa, had bewitched, to their own forms, and received their blessings, and set them forward to their homes. The wicked Latīfa herself she left quite alone in her garden-house. When all was ready they set out with all her servants and slaves, all her treasure and goods, and journeyed at ease to the city of King Quimūs.

When King Quimūs heard of the approach of such a great company, he sent out his vazīr to give the prince honorable meeting, and to ask what had procured him the favor of the visit. The prince sent back word that he had no thought of war, but he wrote: "Learn and know, King Quimūs, that I am here to end the crimes of your insolent daughter who has tyrannously done to death many kings and kings' sons, and has hung their heads on your citadel. I am here to give her the answer to her riddle." Later on he entered the city, beat boldly on the drums, and was conducted to the presence.

The king entreated him to have nothing to do with the riddle, for that no man had come out of it alive. "O king!" replied the prince, "it is to answer it that I am here; I will not withdraw."

Mihr-afrūz was told that one man more had staked his head on her question, and that this was one who said he knew the answer. At the request of the prince, all the officers and notables of the land were summoned to hear his reply to the princess. All assembled, and the king and his queen Gul-rukh, and the girl and the prince were there.

The prince addressed Mihr-afrūz: "What is the question you ask?"

"What did the rose do to the cypress?" she rejoined.

The prince smiled, and turned and addressed the assembly.

"You who are experienced men and versed in affairs, did you ever know or hear and see anything of this matter?"

"No!" they answered, "no one has ever known or heard or seen aught about it; it is an empty fancy."

"From whom, then, did the princess hear of it? This empty fancy it is that has done many a servant of God to death!"

All saw the good sense of his words and showed their approval. Then he turned to the princess: "Tell us the truth, princess; who told you of this thing? I know it hair by hair, and in and out; but if I tell you what I know, who is there that can say I speak the truth? You must produce the person who can confirm my words."

Her heart sank, for she feared that her long-kept secret was now to be noised abroad. But she said merely: "Explain yourself."

"I shall explain myself fully when you bring here the negro whom you hide beneath your throne."

Here the king shouted in wonderment: "Explain yourself, young man! What negro does my daughter hide beneath her throne?"

"That," said the prince, "you will see if you order to be brought here the negro who will be found beneath the throne of the princess."

Messengers were forthwith dispatched to the garden house, and after awhile they returned bringing a negro whom they had discovered in a secret chamber underneath the throne of Mihr-afrūz, dressed in a dress of honor, and surrounded with luxury. The king was overwhelmed with astonishment, but the girl had taken heart again. She had had time to think that perhaps the prince had heard of the presence of the negro, and knew no more. So she said haughtily: "Prince! you have not answered my riddle."

"O most amazingly impudent person," cried he, "do you not yet repent?"

Then he turned to the people, and told them the whole story of the rose and the cypress, of King Sinaubar and Queen Gul. When he came to the killing of the negroes, he said to the one who stood before them: "You, too, were present."

"That is so; all happened as you have told it!"

There was great rejoicing in the court and all through the country over the solving of the riddle, and because now no more kings and princes would be killed. King Quimūs made over his daughter to Prince Almās, but the latter refused to marry her, and took her as his captive. He then asked that the heads should be removed from the battlements and given decent burial. This was done. He received from the king everything that belonged to Mihr-afrūz; her treasure of gold and silver; her costly stuffs and carpets; her household plenishing; her horses and camels; her servants and slaves.

Then he returned to his camp and sent for Dil-arām, who came bringing her goods and chattels, her gold and her jewels. When all was ready, Prince Almās set out for home, taking with him Jamīla, and Dil-arām and Gul, daughter of Tarām-taq, and the wicked Mihr-afrūz, and all the belongings of the four, packed on horses and camels, and in carts without number.

As he approached the borders of his father's country word of his coming went before him, and all the city came forth to give him welcome. King Saman-lāl-pōsh—Jessamine, wearer of rubies—had so bewept the loss of his sons that he was now blind. When the prince had kissed his feet and received his blessing, he took from a casket a little collyrium of Solomon, which the Simurgh had given him, and which reveals the hidden things of earth, and rubbed it on his father's eyes. Light came, and the king saw his son.

Mihr-afrūz was brought before the king, and the prince said: "This is the murderer of your sons; do with her as you will." The king fancied that the prince might care for the girl's beauty, and replied: "You have humbled her; do with her as you will."

Upon this the prince sent for four swift and strong horses, and had the negro bound to each one of them; then each was driven to one of the four quarters, and he tore in pieces like muslin.

This frightened Mihr-afrūz horribly, for she thought the same thing might be done to herself. She cried out to the prince: "O Prince Almās! what is hardest to get is most valued. Up till now I have been subject to no man, and no man had had my love. The many kings and kings' sons who have died at my hands have died because it was their fate to die like this. In this matter I have not sinned. That was their fate from eternity; and from the beginning it was predestined that my fate should be bound up with yours."

The prince gave ear to the argument from pre-ordainment, and as she was a very lovely maiden he took her too in lawful marriage. She and Jamīla, set up house together, and Dil-arām and Gul set up theirs; and the prince passed the rest of his life with the four in perfect happiness, and in pleasant and sociable entertainment.

Now has been told what the rose did to the cypress.

Finished, finished, finished!

The Robber Bridegroom

(FROM *GRIMM'S COMPLETE FAIRY TALES*)

There was once on a time a miller, who had a beautiful daughter, and as she was grown up, he wished that she was provided for, and well married. He thought, "If any good suitor comes and asks for her, I will give her to him."

Not long afterwards, a suitor came, who appeared to be very rich, and as the miller had no fault to find with him, he promised his daughter to him. The maiden, however, did not like him quite so much as a girl should like the man to whom she is engaged, and had no confidence in him. Whenever she saw, or thought of him, she felt a secret horror.

Once he said to her, "Thou art my betrothed, and yet thou hast never once paid me a visit." The maiden replied, "I know not where thy house is." Then said the bridegroom, "My house is out there in the dark forest."

She tried to excuse herself and said she could not find the way there. The bridegroom said, "Next Sunday thou must come out there to me; I have already invited the guests, and I will strew ashes in order that thou mayst find thy way through the forest."

When Sunday came, and the maiden had to set out on her way, she became very uneasy, she herself knew not exactly why, and to mark her way she filled both her pockets full of peas and lentils. Ashes were strewn at the entrance of the forest, and these she followed, but at every step she threw a couple of peas on the ground. She walked almost the whole day until she reached the middle of the forest, where it was the darkest, and there stood a solitary house, which she did not like, for it looked so dark and dismal. She went inside it, but no one was within, and the most absolute stillness reigned. Suddenly a voice cried,

> "Turn back, turn back, young maiden dear,
> 'Tis a murderer's house you enter here."

The maiden looked up, and saw that the voice came from a bird, which was hanging in a cage on the wall. Again it cried,

> "Turn back, turn back, young maiden dear,
> 'Tis a murderer's house you enter here."

Then the young maiden went on farther from one room to another, and walked through the whole house, but it was entirely empty and not one human being was to be found. At last she came to the cellar, and there sat an extremely aged woman, whose head shook constantly.

"Can you not tell me," said the maiden, "if my betrothed lives here?"

"Alas, poor child," replied the old woman, "whither hast thou come? Thou art in a murderer's den. Thou thinkest thou art a bride soon to be married, but thou wilt keep thy wedding with death. Look, I have been forced to put a great kettle on there, with water in it, and when they have thee in their power, they will cut thee to pieces without mercy, will cook thee, and eat thee, for they are eaters of human flesh. If I do not have compassion on thee, and save thee, thou art lost."

Thereupon the old woman led her behind a great hogshead where she could not be seen. "Be as still as a mouse," said she, "do not make a sound, or move, or all will be over with thee. At night, when the robbers are asleep, we will escape; I have long waited for an opportunity."

Hardly was this done, than the godless crew came home. They dragged with them another young girl. They were drunk, and paid no heed to her screams and lamentations. They gave her wine to drink, three glasses full, one glass of white wine, one glass of red, and a glass of yellow, and with this her heart burst in twain. Thereupon they tore off her delicate raiment, laid her on a table, cut her beautiful body in pieces and strewed salt thereon. The poor bride behind the cask trembled and shook, for she saw right well what fate the robbers had destined for her.

One of them noticed a gold ring on the little finger of the murdered girl, and as it would not come off at once, he took an axe and cut the finger off, but it sprang up in the air, away over the cask and fell straight into the bride's bosom. The robber took a candle and wanted to look for it, but could not find it. Then another of them said, "Hast thou looked behind the great hogshead?" But the old woman cried, "Come and get something to eat, and leave off looking till the morning, the finger won't run away from you."

Then the robbers said, "The old woman is right," and gave up their search, and sat down to eat, and the old woman poured a sleeping-draught in their wine, so that they soon lay down in the cellar, and slept and snored.

When the bride heard that, she came out from behind the hogshead, and had to step over the sleepers, for they lay in rows on the ground, and great was her terror lest she should waken one of them. But God helped her, and she got safely over. The old woman went up with her, opened the doors, and they hurried out of the murderers' den with all the speed in their power. The wind had blown away the strewn ashes, but the peas and lentils had sprouted and grown up, and showed them the way in the moonlight. They walked the whole night, until in the morning they arrived at the mill, and then the maiden told her father everything exactly as it had happened.

When the day came when the wedding was to be celebrated, the bridegroom appeared, and the Miller had invited all his relations and friends. As they sat at table, each was bidden to relate something. The bride sat still, and said nothing. Then said the bridegroom to the bride, "Come, my darling, dost thou know nothing? Relate something to us like the rest."

She replied, "Then I will relate a dream. I was walking alone through a wood, and at last I came to a house, in which no living soul was, but on the wall there was a bird in a cage which cried,

"Turn back, turn back, young maiden dear,
 'Tis a murderer's house you enter here."

"And this it cried once more. My darling, I only dreamt this. Then I went through all the rooms, and they were all empty, and there was something so horrible about them! At last I went down into the cellar, and there sat a very very old woman, whose head shook; I asked her, 'Does my bridegroom live in this house?' She answered, 'Alas poor child, thou hast got into a murderer's den, thy bridegroom does live here, but he will hew thee in pieces, and kill thee, and then he will cook thee, and eat thee.' My darling, I only dreamt this. But the old woman hid me behind a great hogshead, and, scarcely was I hidden, when the robbers came home, dragging a maiden with them, to whom they gave three kinds of wine to drink, white, red, and yellow, with which her heart broke in twain. My darling, I only dreamt this. Thereupon they pulled off her pretty clothes, and hewed her fair body in pieces on a table, and sprinkled them with salt. My darling, I only dreamt this. And one of the robbers saw that there was still a ring on her little finger, and as it was hard to draw off, he took an axe and cut it off, but the finger sprang up in the air, and sprang behind the great hogshead, and fell in my bosom. And there is the finger with the ring!" And with these words she drew it forth, and showed it to those present.

The robber, who had during this story become as pale as ashes, leapt up and wanted to escape, but the guests held him fast, and delivered him over to justice. Then he and his whole troop were executed for their infamous deeds.

Lovely Ilonka

(FROM *THE CRIMSON FAIRY BOOK*)

There was once a king's son who told his father that he wished to marry.
 "No, no!" said the king; "you must not be in such a hurry. Wait till you have done some great deed. My father did not let me marry till I had won the golden sword you see me wear."

The prince was much disappointed, but he never dreamed of disobeying his father, and he began to think with all his might what he could do. It was no use staying at home, so one day he wandered out into the world to try his luck, and as he walked along he came to a little hut in which he found an old woman crouching over the fire.

"Good evening, mother. I see you have lived long in this world; do you know anything about the three bulrushes?"

"Yes, indeed, I've lived long and been much about in the world, but I have never seen or heard anything of what you ask. Still, if you will wait till to-morrow I may be able to tell you something."

Well, he waited till the morning, and quite early the old woman appeared and took out a little pipe and blew in it, and in a moment all the crows in the world were flying about her. Not one was missing. Then she asked if they knew anything about the three bulrushes, but not one of them did.

The prince went on his way, and a little further on he found another hut in which lived an old man. On being questioned the old man said he knew nothing, but begged the prince to stay overnight, and the next morning the old man called all the ravens together, but they too had nothing to tell.

The prince bade him farewell and set out. He wandered so far that he crossed seven kingdoms, and at last, one evening, he came to a little house in which was an old woman.

"Good evening, dear mother," said he politely.

"Good evening to you, my dear son," answered the old woman. "It is lucky for you that you spoke to me or you would have met with a horrible death. But may I ask where are you going?"

"I am seeking the three bulrushes. Do you know anything about them?"

"I don't know anything myself, but wait till to-morrow. Perhaps I can tell you then." So the next morning she blew on her pipe, and lo! and behold every magpie in the world flew up. That is to say, all the magpies except one who had broken a leg and a wing. The old woman sent after it at once, and when she questioned the magpies the crippled one was the only one who knew where the three bulrushes were.

Then the prince started off with the lame magpie. They went on and on till they reached a great stone wall, many, many feet high.

"Now, prince," said the magpie, "the three bulrushes are behind that wall."

The prince wasted no time. He set his horse at the wall and leaped over it. Then he looked about for the three bulrushes, pulled them up and set off with them on his way home. As he rode along one of the bulrushes happened to knock against something. It split open and, only think! out sprang a lovely girl, who said: "My heart's love, you are mine and I am yours; do give me a glass of water."

But how could the prince give it her when there was no water at hand? So the lovely maiden flew away. He split the second bulrush as an experiment and just the same thing happened.

How careful he was of the third bulrush! He waited till he came to a well, and there he split it open, and out sprang a maiden seven times lovelier than either of the others, and she too said: "My heart's love, I am yours and you are mine; do give me a glass of water."

This time the water was ready and the girl did not fly away, but she and the prince promised to love each other always. Then they set out for home.

They soon reached the prince's country, and as he wished to bring his promised bride back in a fine coach he went on to the town to fetch one. In the field where the well was, the king's swineherds and cowherds were feeding their droves, and the prince left Ilonka (for that was her name) in their care.

Unluckily the chief swineherd had an ugly old daughter, and whilst the prince was away he dressed her up in fine clothes, and threw Ilonka into the well.

The prince returned before long, bringing with him his father and mother and a great train of courtiers to escort Ilonka home. But how they all stared when they saw the swineherd's ugly daughter! However, there was nothing for it but to take her home; and, two days later, the prince married her, and his father gave up the crown to him.

But he had no peace! He knew very well he had been cheated, though he could not think how. Once he desired to have some water brought him from the well into which Ilonka had been thrown. The coachman went for it and, in the bucket he pulled up, a pretty little duck was swimming. He looked wonderingly at it, and all of a sudden it disappeared and he found a dirty looking girl standing near him. The girl returned with him and managed to get a place as housemaid in the palace.

Of course she was very busy all day long, but whenever she had a little spare time she sat down to spin. Her distaff turned of itself and her spindle span by itself and the flax wound itself off; and however much she might use there was always plenty left.

When the queen—or, rather, the swineherd's daughter—heard of this, she very much wished to have the distaff, but the girl flatly refused to give it to her. However, at last she consented on condition that she might sleep one night in the king's room. The queen was very angry, and scolded her well; but as she longed to have the distaff she consented, though she gave the king a sleeping draught at supper.

Then the girl went to the king's room looking seven times lovelier than ever. She bent over the sleeper and said: "My heart's love, I am yours and you are mine. Speak to me but once; I am your Ilonka." But the king was so sound asleep he neither heard nor spoke, and Ilonka left the room, sadly thinking he was ashamed to own her.

Soon after the queen again sent to say that she wanted to buy the spindle. The girl agreed to let her have it on the same conditions as before; but this time, also, the queen took care to give the king a sleeping draught. And once more Ilonka went to the king's room and spoke to him; whisper as sweetly as she might she could get no answer.

Now some of the king's servants had taken note of the matter, and warned their master not to eat and drink anything that the queen offered him, as for two nights running she had given him a sleeping draught. The queen had no idea that her doings had been discovered; and when, a few days later, she wanted the flax, and had to pay the same price for it, she felt no fears at all.

At supper that night the queen offered the king all sorts of nice things to eat and drink, but he declared he was not hungry, and went early to bed.

The queen repented bitterly her promise to the girl, but it was too late to recall it; for Ilonka had already entered the king's room, where he lay anxiously waiting for something, he knew not what. All of a sudden he saw a lovely maiden who bent over him and said: "My dearest love, I am yours and you are mine. Speak to me, for I am your Ilonka."

At these words the king's heart bounded within him. He sprang up and embraced and kissed her, and she told him all her adventures since the moment he had left her. And when he heard all that Ilonka had suffered, and how he had been deceived, he vowed he would be revenged; so he gave orders that the swineherd, his wife and daughter should all be hanged; and so they were.

The next day the king was married, with great rejoicings, to the fair Ilonka; and if they are not yet dead—why, they are still living.

The Swineherd

(FROM *THE YELLOW FAIRY BOOK*)

There was once a poor Prince. He possessed a kingdom which, though small, was yet large enough for him to marry on, and married he wished to be.

Now it was certainly a little audacious of him to venture to say to the Emperor's daughter, "Will you marry me?" But he did venture to say so, for his name was known far and wide. There were hundreds of princesses who would gladly have said "Yes," but would she say the same?

Well, we shall see.

On the grave of the Prince's father grew a rose-tree, a very beautiful rose-tree. It only bloomed every five years, and then bore but a single rose, but oh, such a rose! Its scent was so sweet that when you smelt it you forgot all your cares and troubles. And he had also a nightingale which could sing as if all the beautiful melodies in the world were shut up in its little throat. This rose and this nightingale the Princess was to have, and so they were both put into silver caskets and sent to her.

The Emperor had them brought to him in the great hall, where the Princess was playing "Here comes a duke a-riding" with her ladies-in-waiting. And when she caught sight of the big caskets which contained the presents, she clapped her hands for joy.

"If only it were a little pussy cat!" she said. But the rose-tree with the beautiful rose came out.

"But how prettily it is made!" said all the ladies-in-waiting.

"It is more than pretty," said the Emperor, "it is charming!"

But the Princess felt it, and then she almost began to cry.

"Ugh! Papa," she said, "it is not artificial, it is *real*!"

"Ugh!" said all the ladies-in-waiting, "it is real!"

135

"Let us see first what is in the other casket before we begin to be angry," thought the Emperor, and there came out the nightingale. It sang so beautifully that one could scarcely utter a cross word against it.

"*Superbe! charmant!*" said the ladies-in-waiting, for they all chattered French, each one worse than the other.

"How much the bird reminds me of the musical snuff-box of the late Empress!" said an old courtier. "Ah, yes, it is the same tone, the same execution!"

"Yes," said the Emperor; and then he wept like a little child.

"I hope that this, at least, is not real?" asked the Princess.

"Yes, it is a real bird," said those who had brought it.

"Then let the bird fly away," said the Princess; and she would not on any account allow the Prince to come.

"But he was nothing daunted. He painted his face brown and black, drew his cap well over his face, and knocked at the door. "Good-day, Emperor," he said. "Can I get a place here as servant in the castle?"

"Yes," said the Emperor, "but there are so many who ask for a place that I don't know whether there will be one for you; but, still, I will think of you. Stay, it has just occurred to me that I want someone to look after the swine, for I have so very many of them."

And the Prince got the situation of Imperial Swineherd. He had a wretched little room close to the pigsties; here he had to stay, but the whole day he sat working, and when evening was come he had made a pretty little pot. All round it were little bells, and when the pot boiled they jingled most beautifully and played the old tune—

> "Where is Augustus dear?
> Alas! he's not here, here, here!"

But the most wonderful thing was, that when one held one's finger in the steam of the pot, then at once one could smell what dinner was ready in any fire-place in the town. That was indeed something quite different from the rose.

Now the Princess came walking past with all her ladies-in-waiting, and when she heard the tune she stood still and her face beamed with joy, for she also could play "Where is Augustus dear?"

It was the only tune she knew, but that she could play with one finger.

"Why, that is what I play!" she said. "He must be a most accomplished Swineherd! Listen! Go down and ask him what the instrument costs."

And one of the ladies-in-waiting had to go down; but she put on wooden clogs. "What will you take for the pot?" asked the lady-in-waiting.

"I will have ten kisses from the Princess," answered the Swineherd.

"Heaven forbid!" said the lady-in-waiting.

"Yes, I will sell it for nothing less," replied the Swineherd.

"Well, what does he say?" asked the Princess.

"I really hardly like to tell you," answered the lady-in-waiting.

"Oh, then you can whisper it to me."

"He is disobliging!" said the Princess, and went away. But she had only gone a few steps when the bells rang out so prettily—

"Where is Augustus dear?
Alas! he's not here, here, here."

"Listen!" said the Princess. "Ask him whether he will take ten kisses from my ladies-in-waiting."

"No, thank you," said the Swineherd. "Ten kisses from the Princess, or else I keep my pot."

"That is very tiresome!" said the Princess. "But you must put yourselves in front of me, so that no one can see."

And the ladies-in-waiting placed themselves in front and then spread out their dresses; so the Swineherd got his ten kisses, and she got the pot.

What happiness that was! The whole night and the whole day the pot was made to boil; there was not a fire-place in the whole town where they did not know what was being cooked, whether it was at the chancellor's or at the shoemaker's.

The ladies-in-waiting danced and clapped their hands.

"We know who is going to have soup and pancakes; we know who is going to have porridge and sausages—isn't it interesting?"

"Yes, very interesting!" said the first lady-in-waiting.

"But don't say anything about it, for I am the Emperor's daughter."

"Oh, no, of course we won't!" said everyone.

The Swineherd—that is to say, the Prince (though they did not know he was anything but a true Swineherd)—let no day pass without making something, and one day he made a rattle which, when it was turned round, played all the waltzes, gallops, and polkas which had ever been known since the world began.

"But that is *superbe*!" said the Princess as she passed by. "I have never heard a more beautiful composition. Listen! Go down and ask him what this instrument costs; but I won't kiss him again."

"He wants a hundred kisses from the Princess," said the lady-in-waiting who had gone down to ask him.

"I believe he is mad!" said the Princess, and then she went on; but she had only gone a few steps when she stopped.

"One ought to encourage art," she said. "I am the Emperor's daughter! Tell him he shall have, as before, ten kisses; the rest he can take from my ladies-in-waiting."

"But we don't at all like being kissed by him," said the ladies-in-waiting.

"That's nonsense," said the Princess; "and if I can kiss him, you can too. Besides, remember that I give you board and lodging."

So the ladies-in-waiting had to go down to him again.

"A hundred kisses from the Princess," said he, "or each keeps his own."

"Put yourselves in front of us," she said then; and so all the ladies-in-waiting put themselves in front, and he began to kiss the Princess.

"What can that commotion be by the pigsties?" asked the Emperor, who was standing on the balcony. He rubbed his eyes and put on his spectacles. "Why those are the ladies-in-waiting playing their games; I must go down to them."

So he took off his shoes, which were shoes though he had trodden them down into slippers. What a hurry he was in, to be sure!

As soon as he came into the yard he walked very softly, and the ladies-in-waiting were so busy counting the kisses and seeing fair play that they never noticed the Emperor. He stood on tiptoe.

"What is that?" he said, when he saw the kissing; and then he threw one of his slippers at their heads just as the Swineherd was taking his eighty-sixth kiss.

"Be off with you!" said the Emperor, for he was very angry. And the Princess and the Swineherd were driven out of the empire.

Then she stood still and wept; the Swineherd was scolding, and the rain was streaming down.

"Alas, what an unhappy creature I am!" sobbed the Princess.

"If only I had taken the beautiful Prince! Alas, how unfortunate I am!"

And the Swineherd went behind a tree, washed the black and brown off his face, threw away his old clothes, and then stepped forward in his splendid dress, looking so beautiful that the Princess was obliged to courtesy.

"I now come to this. I despise you!" he said. "You would have nothing to do with a noble Prince; you did not understand the rose or the nightingale, but you could kiss the Swineherd for the sake of a toy. This is what you get for it!" And he went into his kingdom and shut the door in her face, and she had to stay outside singing—

> "Where's my Augustus dear?
> Alas! he's not here, here, here!"

The Satin Surgeon

(FROM *THE OLIVE FAIRY BOOK*)

Once upon a time there was a very rich and powerful king who, in spite of having been married several times, had only two daughters.

The elder was extremely plain—she squinted and was hunchbacked; but at the same time she was very clever and amusing, so, though at heart both spiteful and untruthful, she was her father's favorite.

The younger princess, on the other hand, was both lovely and sweet-tempered, and those who knew her well could hardly say whether her charming face or pleasant manners was the more attractive.

The neighboring country was governed by a young emperor, who, though not much over twenty years of age, had shown great courage in battle, and, had he wished it, might very likely have conquered the whole world. Luckily he preferred peace to war, and occupied his time with trying to rule his own kingdom well and wisely. His people were very anxious that he should marry, and as the two princesses were the only ladies to be heard of suitable age and rank, the emperor sent envoys to their father's court to ask for the hand of one of them in marriage. But, as he was resolved only to marry a woman whom he could love and be happy with, he determined to see the lady himself before making up his mind. For this purpose he set out in disguise not long after the departure of his ambassadors, and arrived at the palace very soon after they did; but as he had foolishly kept his plan secret, he found, when he reached the court, that they had already made proposals for the elder princess.

Now the emperor might just as well have gone openly, for his presence soon became known; and when the king heard of it he prepared to receive him royally, though of course he had to pretend that he had no idea who he was. So it was settled that the ambassadors should present their master under the name of one of the princes, and in this manner he was received by the king.

At night there was a grand ball at which the young emperor was able to see the two princesses and to make their acquaintance. The ugly face and figure and spiteful remarks of the elder displeased him so greatly that he felt he could not marry her even if she owned ten kingdoms, whilst the sweet face and gentle manners of the younger sister charmed him so much that he would gladly have shared his throne with her had she been only a simple shepherdess.

He found it very difficult to conceal his thoughts and to pay the elder princess the amount of attention due to her, though he did his best to be polite; while all he saw or heard during the next few days only increased his love for her younger sister, and at last he confessed that his dearest wish was to make her his wife, if she and her father would grant his desire.

He had commanded his ambassadors to put off their farewell audience for a little time, hoping that the king might perceive the state of his feelings; but when it could be deferred no longer, he bade them propose in his name for the younger princess.

On hearing this news, so different from what he had been led to expect, the king who—as we have said before—was devoted to his elder daughter and entirely under her influence, could hardly contain his displeasure. Directly the audience was over he sent for the princess and told her of the insolent proposal the emperor had made for her sister. The princess was even more furious than her father, and after consulting together they decided to send the younger daughter to some distant place out of reach of the young emperor; but *where* this should be they did not quite know. However, at length, after they had both racked their brains to find a suitable prison, they fixed on a lonely castle called the Desert Tower, where they thought she would be quite safe.

Meantime, it was thought best to let the court gaieties go on as usual, and orders were given for all sorts of splendid entertainments; and on the day that was fixed for carrying off the princess, the whole court was invited to a great hunt in the forest.

The emperor and the young princess were counting the hours till this morning, which promised to be so delightful, should dawn. The king and his guest arrived together at the meeting-place, but what was the surprise and distress of the young man at not seeing the object of his love among the ladies present. He waited anxiously, looking up and down, not hearing anything that the king said to him; and when the hunt began and she still was absent, he declined to follow, and spent the whole day seeking her, but in vain.

On his return, one of his attendants told him that some hours before he had met the princess's carriage, escorted by a troop of soldiers who were riding on each side, so that no one could get speech of her. He had followed them at a distance, and saw them stop at the Desert Tower, and on its return he noticed that the carriage was empty. The emperor was deeply grieved by this news. He left the court at once, and ordered his ambassadors to declare war the very next day, unless the king promised to set free the princess. And more than this, no sooner had he reached his own country than he raised a large army, with which he seized the frontier towns, before his enemy had had time to collect any troops. But, ere he quitted the court, he took care to write a letter to his beloved princess, imploring her to have patience and trust to him; and this he gave into the hands of his favorite equerry, who would he knew lay down his life in his service.

With many precautions the equerry managed to examine the surroundings of the tower, and at last discovered, not only where the princess lodged, but that a little window in her room looked out on a desolate plot full of brambles.

Now the unhappy princess was much annoyed that she was not even allowed to take the air at this little window, which was the only one in her room. Her keeper was her elder sister's former nurse, a woman whose eyes never slept. Not for an instant could she be induced to stir from the side of the princess, and she watched her slightest movement.

One day, however, the spy was for once busy in her room writing an account of the princess to her elder sister, and the poor prisoner seized the opportunity to lean out of the window. As she looked about her she noticed a man hidden among the bushes, who stepped forward as soon as he caught sight of her, and showed her a letter, which he took from his jerkin. She at once recognized him as one of the emperor's attendants, and let down a long string, to which he tied the letter. You can fancy how quickly she drew it up again, and luckily she had just time to read it before her jailer had finished her report and entered the room.

The princess's delight was great, and next day she managed to write an answer on a sheet of her note book, and to throw it down to the equerry, who hastened to carry it back to his master. The emperor was so happy at having news of his dear princess, that he resolved, at all risks, to visit the Desert Tower himself, if only to see her for a moment. He ordered his equerry to ask leave to visit her, and the princess replied that she should indeed rejoice to see him, but that she feared that her jailer's watchfulness would make his journey useless, unless he came during the short time when the old woman was writing alone in her own room.

Naturally, the bare idea of difficulties only made the emperor more eager than ever. He was ready to run any risks, but, by the advice of the equerry, he decided to try cunning rather than force. In his next letter he enclosed a sleeping powder, which the princess managed to mix with her jailer's supper, so that when the emperor reached the tower in the evening the princess appeared fearlessly at her window on hearing his signal. They had a long and delightful conversation, and parted in the fond hope that their meeting had not been observed. But in this they were sadly mistaken. The watchful eyes of the old nurse were proof against any sleeping draught—she had seen and heard all; and lost no time in writing to report everything to her mistress.

The news made the spiteful little hunchback furious, and she resolved to be cruelly revenged for the contempt with which the emperor had treated her. She ordered her nurse to pretend not to notice what might be passing, and meantime she had a trap made so that if the emperor pushed his way through the brambles at the foot of the tower, it would not only catch him, as if he were a mouse, but would let loose a number of poisoned arrows, which would pierce him all over. When it was ready, the trap was hidden among the brambles without being observed by the princess.

That same evening the emperor hurried to the tower with all the impatience of love. As he came near he heard the princess break into a long, joyous peal of laughter. He advanced quickly to give the usual signal, when suddenly his foot trod on something, he knew not what. A sharp, stinging pain ran through him, and he turned white and faint, but, luckily, the trap had only opened a little way, and only a few of the arrows flew out. For a moment he staggered, and then fell to the ground covered with blood.

Had he been alone he would have died very shortly, but his faithful squire was close at hand, and carried his master off to the wood where the rest of his escort were waiting for him. His wounds were bound up, and some poles were cut to make a rough litter, and, almost unconscious, the emperor was borne away out of his enemy's country to his own palace.

All this time the princess was feeling very anxious. She had been whiling away the hours before this meeting by playing with a little pet monkey, which had been making such funny faces that, in spite of her troubles, she had burst into the hearty laugh overheard by the emperor. But by-and-by she grew restless, waiting for the signal which never came, and, had she dared, would certainly have rebelled when her jailer, whom she believed to be fast asleep, ordered her to go to bed at once.

A fortnight passed, which was spent in great anxiety by the poor girl, who grew thin and weak with the uncertainty. At the end of this period, when the nurse went to her room one morning as usual in order to write her daily report, she carelessly left the key in the door. This was perceived by the princess, who turned it upon her so quickly and quietly that she never found out she was locked in till she had finished writing, and got up to seek her charge.

Finding herself free, the princess flew to the window, and to her horror saw the arrows lying about among the bloodstained brambles. Distracted with terror she slipped down the stairs and out of the tower, and ran for some time along a path, when with great good luck she met the husband of her own nurse, who had only just learned of her imprisonment, and was on his way to try and find out whether he could serve her. The princess begged him to get her some men's clothes while she awaited him in a little wood close by. The good man was overjoyed to be of use, and started at once for the nearest town, where he soon discovered a shop where the court lackeys were accustomed to sell their masters' cast-off clothes. The princess dressed herself at once in the disguise he had brought, which was of rich material and covered with precious stones; and, putting her own garments into a bag, which her servant hung over his shoulders, they both set out on their journey.

This lasted longer than either of them expected. They walked by day as far as the princess could manage, and by night they slept in the open air. One evening they camped in a lovely valley watered by a rippling stream, and towards morning the princess was awakened by a charming voice singing one of the songs of her own childhood. Anxious to find out where the sound came from, she walked to a thicket of myrtles, where she saw a little boy with a quiver at his back and an ivory bow in his hand, singing softly to himself as he smoothed the feathers of his shafts.

"Are you surprised at seeing my eyes open?" he asked, with a smile. "Ah! I am not always blind. And sometimes it is well to know what sort of a heart needs piercing. It was I who sent out my darts the day that you and the emperor met, so, as I have caused the wound, I am in duty bound to find the cure!"

Then he gave her a little bottle full of a wonderful salve with which to dress the emperor's wounds when she found him.

"In two days you can reach his palace," he said. "Do not waste time, for sometimes time is life."

The princess thanked the boy with tears in her eyes, and hastened to awake her guide so that they might start, and set off at once on their way.

As the boy had foretold, in two days the tower and walls of the city came in sight, and her heart beat wildly at the thought that she would soon be face to face with the emperor, but on inquiring after his health she learned, to her horror, that he was sinking fast. For a moment her grief was so great that she nearly betrayed herself. Then, calling all her courage to her aid, she announced that she was a doctor, and that if they would leave him in her charge for a few days she would promise to cure him.

Now, in order to make a good appearance at court the new doctor resolved to have an entire suit made of pale blue satin. She bought the richest, most splendid stuff to be had in the shops, and summoned a tailor to make it for her, engaging to pay him double if he would finish the work in two hours. Next she went to the market, where she bought a fine mule, bidding her servant see that its harness was adorned with trappings of blue satin also.

Whilst all was being made ready the princess asked the woman in whose house she lived whether she knew any of the emperor's attendants, and found to her satisfaction that her cousin was his majesty's chief valet. The doctor then bade the woman inform everyone she met that on hearing of the emperor's illness a celebrated surgeon had hastened to attend him, and had undertaken to cure him entirely; declaring himself prepared to be burnt alive in case of failure.

The good woman, who loved nothing better than a bit of gossip, hurried to the palace with her news. Her story did not lose in telling. The court physicians were very scornful about the new-comer, but the emperor's attendants remarked that as, in spite of their remedies, his majesty was dying before their eyes, there could be no harm in consulting this stranger.

So the lord chamberlain begged the young doctor to come and prescribe for the royal patient without delay; and the doctor sent a message at once, that he would do himself the honor to present himself at the palace, and he lost no time in mounting his mule and setting out. As the people and soldiers saw him ride past they cried out:

"Here comes the Satin Surgeon! Look at the Satin Surgeon! Long live the Satin Surgeon!" And, on arriving, he was announced by this name, and at once taken to the sick room of the dying man.

The emperor was lying with his eyes closed, and his face as white as the pillow itself; but directly he heard the new-comer's voice, he looked up and smiled, and signed that he wished the new doctor to remain near him. Making a low bow, the Satin Surgeon assured the emperor that he felt certain of curing his malady, but insisted that everyone should leave the room except the emperor's favorite equerry. He then dressed the wounds with the magic salve which the boy had given him, and it so relieved the emperor's pain that he slept soundly all that night.

When morning broke, the courtiers and doctors hurried to the emperor's chamber, and were much surprised to find him free of pain. But they were promptly ordered out of the room by the Satin Surgeon, who renewed the dressings with such good results that next morning the emperor was nearly well, and able to leave his bed. As he grew stronger, his thoughts dwelt more and more on the cause of all his sufferings, and his spirits grew worse as his health grew better. The face and voice of his new doctor reminded him of the princess who had, he imagined, betrayed him, and caused him such dreadful torture; and, unable to bear the thought, his eyes filled with tears.

The doctor noticed his sad countenance and did all he could to enliven his patient with cheerful talk and amusing stories, till at last he won the emperor's confidence and heard all the story of his love for a lady who had treated him cruelly, but whom, in spite of everything, he could not help loving.

The Satin Surgeon listened with sympathy, and tried to persuade the emperor that possibly the princess was not so much to blame as might appear; but, eager though the sick man was to believe this, it took a long while to persuade him of it. At length a day came when the emperor was nearly well, and for the last time the doctor dressed the wounds with the precious salve. Then, both patient and surgeon, being wearied out with something they could not explain, fell asleep and slept for hours.

Early next morning, the princess, having decided to resume her own clothes which she had brought with her in a bag, dressed herself with great care and put on all her jewels so as to make herself look as lovely as possible. She had just finished when the emperor awoke, feeling so strong and well that he thought he must be dreaming, nor could he believe himself to be awake when he saw the princess draw aside his curtains.

For some minutes they gazed at each other, unable to speak, and then they only uttered little gasps of joy and thankfulness. By-and-by the princess told him the whole story of her adventures since their last interview at the Desert Tower; and the emperor, weak as he was, threw himself at her feet with vows of love and gratitude, without ever giving a thought to the fact that the household and court physicians were awaiting their summons in the ante-room.

The emperor, anxious to prove how much he owed to the Satin Surgeon, opened his door himself, and great was everyone's surprise and joy at seeing him in such perfect health. Like good courtiers, they hastened in to praise and compliment the Satin Surgeon, but what was their astonishment on finding that he had disappeared, leaving in his place the loveliest princess in the whole world.

"Whilst thanking the surgeon for his miraculous cure, you might at the same time do homage to your empress," observed the emperor. He wished to have the marriage celebrated the same day, but the princess declared that she must wait to get her father's permission first.

Messengers were therefore instantly dispatched to the neighboring capital, and soon returned with the king's consent, for he had lately discovered all the mischief caused by his elder daughter.

The spiteful princess was so furious at the failure of her plans that she took to her bed, and died in a fit of rage and jealousy. No one grieved for her, and the king, being tired of the fatigues of Government, gave up his crown to his younger daughter; so the two kingdoms henceforth became one.

The Enchanted Wreath

(From *The Orange Fairy Book*)

Once upon a time there lived near a forest a man and his wife and two girls; one girl was the daughter of the man, and the other the daughter of his wife; and the man's daughter was good and beautiful, but the woman's daughter was cross and ugly. However, her mother did not know that, but thought her the most bewitching maiden that ever was seen.

One day the man called to his daughter and bade her come with him into the forest to cut wood. They worked hard all day, but in spite of the chopping they were very cold, for it rained heavily, and when they returned home, they were wet through. Then, to his vexation, the man found that he had left his axe behind him, and he knew that if it lay all night in the mud it would become rusty and useless. So he said to his wife:

"I have dropped my axe in the forest, bid your daughter go and fetch it, for mine has worked hard all day and is both wet and weary."

But the wife answered:

"If your daughter is wet already, it is all the more reason that *she* should go and get the axe. Besides, she is a great strong girl, and a little rain will not hurt her, while *my* daughter would be sure to catch a bad cold."

By long experience the man knew there was no good saying any more, and with a sigh he told the poor girl she must return to the forest for the axe.

The walk took some time, for it was very dark, and her shoes often stuck in the mud, but she was brave as well as beautiful and never thought of turning back merely because the path was both difficult and unpleasant. At last, with her dress torn by brambles that she could not see, and her face scratched by the twigs on the trees, she reached the spot where she and her father had been cutting in the morning, and found the axe in the place he had left it. To her surprise, three little doves were sitting on the handle, all of them looking very sad.

"You poor little things," said the girl, stroking them. "Why do you sit there and get wet? Go and fly home to your nest, it will be much warmer

147

than this; but first eat this bread, which I saved from my dinner, and perhaps you will feel happier. It is my father's axe you are sitting on, and I must take it back as fast as I can, or I shall get a terrible scolding from my stepmother." She then crumbled the bread on the ground, and was pleased to see the doves flutter quite cheerfully towards it.

"Good-bye," she said, picking up the axe, and went her way homewards.

By the time they had finished all the crumbs the doves felt much better, and were able to fly back to their nest in the top of a tree.

"That is a good girl," said one; "I really was too weak to stretch out a wing before she came. I should like to do something to show how grateful I am."

"Well, let us give her a wreath of flowers that will never fade as long as she wears it," cried another.

"And let the tiniest singing birds in the world sit among the flowers," rejoined the third.

"Yes, that will do beautifully," said the first. And when the girl stepped into her cottage a wreath of rosebuds was on her head, and a crowd of little birds were singing unseen.

The father, who was sitting by the fire, thought that, in spite of her muddy clothes, he had never seen his daughter looking so lovely; but the stepmother and the other girl grew wild with envy.

"How absurd to walk about on such a pouring night, dressed up like that," she remarked crossly, and roughly pulled off the wreath as she spoke, to place it on her own daughter. As she did so the roses became withered and brown, and the birds flew out of the window.

"See what a trumpery thing it is!" cried the stepmother; "and now take your supper and go to bed, for it is near upon midnight."

But though she pretended to despise the wreath, she longed none the less for her daughter to have one like it.

Now it happened that the next evening the father, who had been alone in the forest, came back a second time without his axe. The stepmother's heart was glad when she saw this, and she said quite mildly:

"Why, you have forgotten your axe again, you careless man! But now *your* daughter shall stay at home, and *mine* shall go and bring it back"; and throwing a cloak over the girl's shoulders, she bade her hasten to the forest.

With a very ill grace the damsel set forth, grumbling to herself as she went; for though she wished for the wreath, she did not at all want the trouble of getting it.

By the time she reached the spot where her stepfather had been cutting the wood the girl was in a very bad temper indeed, and when she caught sight of the axe, there were the three little doves, with drooping heads and soiled, bedraggled feathers, sitting on the handle.

"You dirty creatures," cried she, "get away at once, or I will throw stones at you!" And the doves spread their wings in a fright and flew up to the very top of a tree, their bodies shaking with anger.

"What shall we do to revenge ourselves on her?" asked the smallest of the doves, "we were never treated like that before."

"Never," said the biggest dove. "We must find some way of paying her back in her own coin!"

"I know," answered the middle dove; "she shall never be able to say anything but 'dirty creatures' to the end of her life."

"Oh, how clever of you! That will do beautifully," exclaimed the other two. And they flapped their wings and clucked so loud with delight, and made such a noise, that they woke up all the birds in the trees close by.

"What in the world is the matter?" asked the birds sleepily.

"That is *our* secret," said the doves.

Meanwhile the girl had reached home crosser than ever; but as soon as her mother heard her lift the latch of the door she ran out to hear her adventures. "Well, did you get the wreath?" cried she.

"Dirty creatures!" answered her daughter.

"Don't speak to me like that! What do you mean?" asked the mother again.

"Dirty creatures!" repeated the daughter, and nothing else could she say.

Then the woman saw that something evil had befallen her, and turned in her rage to her stepdaughter.

"*You* are at the bottom of this, I know," she cried; and as the father was out of the way she took a stick and beat the girl till she screamed with pain and went to bed sobbing.

If the poor girl's life had been miserable before, it was ten times worse now, for the moment her father's back was turned the others teased and tormented her from morning till night; and their fury was increased by the sight of her wreath, which the doves had placed again on her head.

Things went on like this for some weeks, when, one day, as the king's son was riding through the forest, he heard some strange birds singing more sweetly than birds had ever sung before. He tied his horse to a tree, and followed where the sound led him, and, to his surprise, he saw before him a beautiful girl chopping wood, with a wreath of pink rose-buds, out of which the singing came. Standing in the shelter of a tree, he watched her a long while, and then, hat in hand, he went up and spoke to her.

"Fair maiden, who are you, and who gave you that wreath of singing roses?" asked he, for the birds were so tiny that till you looked closely you never saw them.

"I live in a hut on the edge of the forest," she answered, blushing, for she had never spoken to a prince before. "As to the wreath, I know not how it came there, unless it may be the gift of some doves whom I fed when they were starving!" The prince was delighted with this answer, which showed the goodness of the girl's heart, and besides he had fallen in love with her beauty, and would not be content till she promised to return with him to the palace, and become his bride. The old king was naturally disappointed at his son's choice of a wife, as he wished him to marry a neighboring princess; but as from his birth the prince had always done exactly as he liked, nothing was said and a splendid wedding feast was got ready.

The day after her marriage the bride sent a messenger, bearing handsome presents to her father, and telling him of the good fortune which had befallen her. As may be imagined, the stepmother and her daughter were so filled with envy that they grew quite ill, and had to take to their beds, and nobody would have been sorry if they had never got up again; but that did not happen. At length, however, they began to feel better, for the mother invented a plan by which she could be revenged on the girl who had never done her any harm.

Her plan was this. In the town where she had lived before she was married there was an old witch, who had more skill in magic than any other witch she knew. To this witch she would go and beg her to make her a mask with the face of her stepdaughter, and when she had the mask the rest would be easy. She told her daughter what she meant to do, and although the daughter could only say "dirty creatures," in answer, she nodded and smiled and looked well pleased.

Everything fell out exactly as the woman had hoped. By the aid of her magic mirror the witch beheld the new princess walking in her gardens in a dress of green silk, and in a few minutes had produced a mask so like her, that very few people could have told the difference. However, she counseled the woman that when her daughter first wore it—for that, of course, was what she intended her to do—she had better pretend that she had a toothache, and cover her head with a lace veil. The woman thanked her and paid her well, and returned to her hut, carrying the mask under her cloak.

In a few days she heard that a great hunt was planned, and the prince would leave the palace very early in the morning, so that his wife would be alone all day. This was a chance not to be missed, and taking her daughter with her she went up to the palace, where she had never been before. The princess was too happy in her new home to remember all that she had suffered in the old one, and she welcomed them both gladly, and gave them quantities of beautiful things to take back with them. At last she took them down to the shore to see a pleasure boat which her husband had had made for her; and here, the woman seizing her opportunity, stole softly behind the girl and pushed her off the rock on which she was standing, into the deep water, where she instantly sank to the bottom. Then she fastened the mask on her daughter, flung over her shoulders a velvet cloak, which the princess had let fall, and finally arranged a lace veil over her head.

"Rest your cheek on your hand, as if you were in pain, when the prince returns," said the mother; "and be careful not to speak, whatever you do. I will go back to the witch and see if she cannot take off the spell laid on you by those horrible birds. Ah! why did I not think of it before!"

No sooner had the prince entered the palace than he hastened to the princess's apartments, where he found her lying on the sofa apparently in great pain.

"My dearest wife, what is the matter with you?" he cried, kneeling down beside her, and trying to take her hand; but she snatched it away, and pointing to her cheek murmured something he could not catch.

"What is it? tell me! Is the pain bad? When did it begin? Shall I send for your ladies to bath the place?" asked the prince, pouring out these and a dozen other questions, to which the girl only shook her head.

"But I can't leave you like this," he continued, starting up, "I must summon all the court physicians to apply soothing balsams to the sore place!" And as he spoke he sprang to his feet to go in search of them. This so frightened the pretended wife, who knew that if the physicians once came near her the trick would at once be discovered, that she forgot her mother's counsel not to speak, and forgot even the spell that had been laid upon her, and catching hold of the prince's tunic, she cried in tones of entreaty: "Dirty creatures!"

The young man stopped, not able to believe his ears, but supposed that pain had made the princess cross, as it sometimes does. However, he guessed somehow that she wished to be left alone, so he only said:

"Well, I dare say a little sleep will do you good, if you can manage to get it, and that you will wake up better to-morrow."

Now, that night happened to be very hot and airless, and the prince, after vainly trying to rest, at length got up and went to the window. Suddenly he beheld in the moonlight a form with a wreath of roses on her head rise out of the sea below him and step on to the sands, holding out her arms as she did so towards the palace.

"That maiden is strangely like my wife," thought he; "I must see her closer!" And he hastened down to the water. But when he got there, the princess, for she indeed it was, had disappeared completely, and he began to wonder if his eyes had deceived him.

The next morning he went to the false bride's room, but her ladies told him she would neither speak nor get up, though she ate everything they set before her. The prince was sorely perplexed as to what could be the matter with her, for naturally he could not guess that she was expecting her mother to return every moment, and to remove the spell the doves had laid upon her, and meanwhile was afraid to speak lest she should betray herself. At length he made up his mind to summon all the court physicians; he did not tell her what he was going to do, lest it should make her worse, but he went himself and begged the four learned leeches attached to the king's person to follow him to the princess's apartments. Unfortunately, as they entered, the princess was so enraged at the sight of them that she forgot all about the doves, and shrieked out: "Dirty creatures! dirty creatures!" which so offended the physicians that they left the room at once, and nothing that the prince could say would prevail on them to remain. He then tried to persuade his wife to send them a message that she was sorry for her rudeness, but not a word would she say.

Late that evening, when he had performed all the tiresome duties which fall to the lot of every prince, the young man was leaning out of his window, refreshing himself with the cool breezes that blew off the sea. His thoughts went back to the scene of the morning, and he wondered if, after all, he had not made a great mistake in marrying a low-born wife, however beautiful she might be. How could he have imagined that the quiet, gentle girl who had been so charming a companion to him during the first days of their marriage, could have become in a day the rude, sulky woman, who could not control her temper even to benefit herself. One thing was clear, if she did not change her conduct very shortly he would have to send her away from court.

He was thinking these thoughts, when his eyes fell on the sea beneath him, and there, as before, was the figure that so closely resembled his wife, standing with her feet in the water, holding out her arms to him.

"Wait for me! Wait for me! Wait for me!" he cried; not even knowing he was speaking. But when he reached the shore there was nothing to be seen but the shadows cast by the moonlight.

A state ceremonial in a city some distance off caused the prince to ride away at daybreak, and he left without seeing his wife again.

"Perhaps she may have come to her senses by to-morrow," said he to himself; "and, anyhow, if I am going to send her back to her father, it might be better if we did not meet in the meantime!" Then he put the matter from his mind, and kept his thoughts on the duty that lay before him.

It was nearly midnight before he returned to the palace, but, instead of entering, he went down to the shore and hid behind a rock. He had scarcely done so when the girl came out of the sea, and stretched out her arms towards his window. In an instant the prince had seized her hand, and though she made a frightened struggle to reach the water—for she in her turn had had a spell laid upon her—he held her fast.

"You are my own wife, and I shall never let you go," he said. But the words were hardly out of his mouth when he found that it was a hare that he was holding by the paw. Then the hare changed into a fish, and the fish into a bird, and the bird into a slimy wriggling snake. This time the prince's hand nearly opened of itself, but with a strong effort he kept his fingers shut, and drawing his sword cut off its head, when the spell was broken, and the girl stood before him as he had seen her first, the wreath upon her head and the birds singing for joy.

The very next morning the stepmother arrived at the palace with an ointment that the old witch had given her to place upon her daughter's tongue, which would break the dove's spell, if the rightful bride had really been drowned in the sea; if not, then it would be useless. The mother assured her that she had seen her stepdaughter sink, and that there was no fear that she would ever come up again; but, to make all quite safe, the old woman might bewitch the girl; and so she did. After that the wicked stepmother traveled all through the night to get to the palace as soon as possible, and made her way straight into her daughter's room.

"I have got it! I have got it!" she cried triumphantly, and laid the ointment on her daughter's tongue.

"Now what do you say?" she asked proudly.

"Dirty creatures! dirty creatures!" answered the daughter; and the mother wrung her hands and wept, as she knew that all her plans had failed.

At this moment the prince entered with his real wife. "You both deserved death," he said, "and if it were left to me, you should have it. But the princess has begged me to spare your lives, so you will be put into a ship and carried off to a desert island, where you will stay till you die."

Then the ship was made ready and the wicked woman and her daughter were placed in it, and it sailed away, and no more was heard of them. But the prince and his wife lived together long and happily, and ruled their people well.

Princess Rosette

(FROM *THE RED FAIRY BOOK*)

Once upon a time there lived a King and Queen who had two beautiful sons and one little daughter, who was so pretty that no one who saw her could help loving her. When it was time for the christening of the Princess, the Queen—as she always did—sent for all the fairies to be present at the ceremony, and afterwards invited them to a splendid banquet.

When it was over, and they were preparing to go away, the Queen said to them:

"Do not forget your usual good custom. Tell me what is going to happen to Rosette."

For that was the name they had given the Princess.

But the fairies said they had left their book of magic at home, and they would come another day and tell her.

"Ah!" said the Queen, "I know very well what that means—you have nothing good to say; but at least I beg that you will not hide anything from me."

So, after a great deal of persuasion, they said:

"Madam, we fear that Rosette may be the cause of great misfortunes to her brothers; they may even meet with their death through her; that is all we have been able to foresee about your dear little daughter. We are very sorry to have nothing better to tell you."

Then they went away, leaving the Queen very sad, so sad that the King noticed it, and asked her what was the matter.

The Queen said that she had been sitting too near the fire, and had burnt all the flax that was upon her distaff.

"Oh! is that all?" said the King, and he went up into the garret and brought her down more flax than she could spin in a hundred years. But the Queen still looked sad, and the King asked her again what was the matter. She answered that she had been walking by the river and had dropped one of her green satin slippers into the water.

"Oh! if that's all," said the King, and he sent to all the shoe-makers in his kingdom, and they very soon made the Queen ten thousand green satin slippers, but still she looked sad. So the King asked her again what was the matter, and this time she answered that in eating her porridge too hastily she had swallowed her wedding-ring. But it so happened that the King knew better, for he had the ring himself, and he said:

"Oh I you are not telling me the truth, for I have your ring here in my purse."

Then the Queen was very much ashamed, and she saw that the King was vexed with her; so she told him all that the fairies had predicted about Rosette, and begged him to think how the misfortunes might be prevented.

Then it was the King's turn to look sad, and at last he said:

"I see no way of saving our sons except by having Rosette's head cut off while she is still little."

But the Queen cried that she would far rather have her own head cut off, and that he had better think of something else, for she would never consent to such a thing. So they thought and thought, but they could not tell what to do, until at last the Queen heard that in a great forest near the castle there was an old hermit, who lived in a hollow tree, and that people came from far and near to consult him; so she said:

"I had better go and ask his advice; perhaps he will know what to do to prevent the misfortunes which the fairies foretold."

She set out very early the next morning, mounted upon a pretty little white mule, which was shod with solid gold, and two of her ladies rode behind her on beautiful horses. When they reached the forest they dismounted, for the trees grew so thickly that the horses could not pass, and made their way on foot to the hollow tree where the hermit lived. At first when he saw them coming he was vexed, for he was not fond of ladies; but when he recognized the Queen, he said:

"You are welcome, Queen. What do you come to ask of me?"

Then the Queen told him all the fairies had foreseen for Rosette, and asked what she should do, and the hermit answered that she must shut the Princess up in a tower and never let her come out of it again. The Queen thanked and rewarded him, and hastened back to the castle to tell the King. When he heard the news he had a great tower built as quickly as possible, and there the Princess was shut up, and the King and Queen and her two brothers went to see her every day that she might not be dull. The eldest brother was called "the Great Prince," and the second "the Little Prince." They loved their sister dearly, for she was the sweetest, prettiest princess who was ever seen, and the least little smile from her was worth more than a hundred pieces of gold. When Rosette was fifteen years old the Great Prince went to the King and asked if it would not soon be time for her to be married, and the Little Prince put the same question to the Queen.

Their majesties were amused at them for thinking of it, but did not make any reply, and soon after both the King and the Queen were taken ill, and died on the same day. Everybody was sorry, Rosette especially, and all the bells in the kingdom were tolled.

Then all the dukes and counselors put the Great Prince upon a golden throne, and crowned him with a diamond crown, and they all cried, "Long live the King!" And after that there was nothing but feasting and rejoicing.

The new King and his brother said to one another:

"Now that we are the masters, let us take our sister out of that dull tower which she is so tired of."

They had only to go across the garden to reach the tower, which was very high, and stood up in a corner. Rosette was busy at her embroidery, but when she saw her brothers she got up, and taking the King's hand cried:

"Good morning, dear brother. Now that you are King, please take me out of this dull tower, for I am so tired of it."

Then she began to cry, but the King kissed her and told her to dry her tears, as that was just what they had come for, to take her out of the tower and bring her to their beautiful castle, and the Prince showed her the pocketful of sugar plums he had brought for her, and said:

"Make haste, and let us get away from this ugly tower, and very soon the King will arrange a grand marriage for you."

When Rosette saw the beautiful garden, full of fruit and flowers, with green grass and sparkling fountains, she was so astonished that not a word could she say, for she had never in her life seen anything like it before. She looked about her, and ran hither and thither gathering fruit and flowers, and her little dog Frisk, who was bright green all over, and had but one ear, danced before her, crying "Bow-wow-wow," and turning head over heels in the most enchanting way.

Everybody was amused at Frisk's antics, but all of a sudden he ran away into a little wood, and the Princess was following him, when, to her great delight, she saw a peacock, who was spreading his tail in the sunshine. Rosette thought she had never seen anything so pretty. She could not take her eyes off him, and there she stood entranced until the King and the Prince came up and asked what was amusing her so much. She showed them the peacock, and asked what it was, and they answered that it was a bird which people sometimes ate.

"What!" said the Princess, "do they dare to kill that beautiful creature and eat it? I declare that I will never marry any one but the King of the Peacocks, and when I am Queen I will take very good care that nobody eats any of my subjects."

At this the King was very much astonished.

"But, little sister," said he, "where shall we find the King of the Peacocks?"

"Oh! wherever you like, sire," she answered, "but I will never marry any one else."

After this they took Rosette to the beautiful castle, and the peacock was brought with her, and told to walk about on the terrace outside her windows, so that she might always see him, and then the ladies of the court came to see the Princess, and they brought her beautiful presents—dresses and ribbons and sweetmeats, diamonds and pearls and dolls and embroidered slippers, and she was so well brought up, and said, "Thank you!" so prettily, and was so gracious, that everyone went away delighted with her.

Meanwhile the King and the Prince were considering how they should find the King of the Peacocks, if there was such a person in the world. And first of all they had a portrait made of the Princess, which was so like her that you really would not have been surprised if it had spoken to you. Then they said to her:

"Since you will not marry anyone but the King of the Peacocks, we are going out together into the wide world to search for him. If we find him for you we shall be very glad. In the meantime, mind you take good care of our kingdom."

Rosette thanked them for all the trouble they were taking on her account, and promised to take great care of the kingdom, and only to amuse herself by looking at the peacock, and making Frisk dance while they were away.

So they set out, and asked everyone they met—

"Do you know the King of the Peacocks?"

But the answer was always, "No, no."

Then they went on and on, so far that no one has ever been farther, and at last they came to the Kingdom of the Cockchafers.

They had never before seen such a number of cockchafers, and the buzzing was so loud that the King was afraid he should be deafened by it. He asked the most distinguished-looking cockchafer they met if he knew where they could find the King of the Peacocks.

"Sire," replied the cockchafer, "his kingdom is thirty thousand leagues from this; you have come the longest way."

"And how do you know that?" said the King.

"Oh!" said the cockchafer, "we all know you very well, since we spend two or three months in your garden every year."

Thereupon the King and the Prince made great friends with him, and they all walked arm-in-arm and dined together, and afterwards the cockchafer showed them all the curiosities of his strange country, where the tiniest green leaf costs a gold piece and more. Then they set out again to finish their journey, and this time, as they knew the way, they were not long upon the road. It was easy to guess that they had come to the right place, for they saw peacocks in every tree, and their cries could be heard a long way off:

When they reached the city they found it full of men and women who were dressed entirely in peacocks' feathers, which were evidently thought prettier than anything else.

They soon met the King, who was driving about in a beautiful little golden carriage which glittered with diamonds, and was drawn at full speed by twelve peacocks. The King and the Prince were delighted to see that the King of the Peacocks was as handsome as possible. He had curly golden hair and was very pale, and he wore a crown of peacocks' feathers.

When he saw Rosette's brothers he knew at once that they were strangers, and stopping his carriage he sent for them to speak to him. When they had greeted him they said:

"Sire, we have come from very far away to show you a beautiful portrait."

So saying they drew from their traveling bag the picture of Rosette.

The King looked at it in silence a long time, but at last he said:

"I could not have believed that there was such a beautiful Princess in the world!"

"Indeed, she is really a hundred times as pretty as that," said her brothers.

"I think you must be making fun of me," replied the King of the Peacocks.

"Sire," said the Prince, "my brother is a King, like yourself. He is called 'the King,' I am called 'the Prince,' and that is the portrait of our sister, the Princess Rosette. We have come to ask if you would like to marry her. She is as good as she is beautiful, and we will give her a bushel of gold pieces for her dowry."

"Oh! with all my heart," replied the King, "and I will make her very happy. She shall have whatever she likes, and I shall love her dearly; only I warn you that if she is not as pretty as you have told me, I will have your heads cut off."

"Oh! certainly, we quite agree to that," said the brothers in one breath.

"Very well. Off with you into prison, and stay there until the Princess arrives," said the King of the Peacocks.

And the Princes were so sure that Rosette was far prettier than her portrait that they went without a murmur. They were very kindly treated, and that they might not feel dull the King came often to see them. As for Rosette's portrait that was taken up to the palace, and the King did nothing but gaze at it all day and all night.

As the King and the Prince had to stay in prison, they sent a letter to the Princess telling her to pack up all her treasures as quickly as possible, and come to them, as the King of the Peacocks was waiting to marry her; but they did not say that they were in prison, for fear of making her uneasy.

When Rosette received the letter she was so delighted that she ran about telling everyone that the King of the Peacocks was found, and she was going to marry him.

Guns were fired, and fireworks let off. Everyone had as many cakes and sweetmeats as he wanted. And for three days everybody who came to see the Princess was presented with a slice of bread-and-jam, a nightingale's egg, and some hippocras. After having thus entertained her friends, she distributed her dolls among them, and left her brother's kingdom to the care of the wisest old men of the city, telling them to take charge of everything, not to spend any money, but save it all up until the King should return, and above all, not to forget to feed her peacock. Then she set out, only taking with her nurse, and the nurse's daughter, and the little green dog Frisk.

They took a boat and put out to sea, carrying with them the bushel of gold pieces, and enough dresses to last the Princess ten years if she wore two every day, and they did nothing but laugh and sing. The nurse asked the boatman:

"Can you take us, can you take us to the Kingdom of the Peacocks?"

But he answered:

"Oh no! oh no!"

Then she said:

"You must take us, you must take us."

And he answered:

"Very soon, very soon."

Then the nurse said:

"Will you take us? will you take us?"

And the boatman answered:

"Yes, yes."

Then she whispered in his ear:

"Do you want to make your fortune?"

And he said:

"Certainly I do."

"I can tell you how to get a bag of gold," said she.

"I ask nothing better," said the boatman.

"Well," said the nurse, "to-night, when the Princess is asleep, you must help me to throw her into the sea, and when she is drowned I will put her beautiful clothes upon my daughter, and we will take her to the King of the Peacocks, who will be only too glad to marry her, and as your reward you shall have your boat full of diamonds."

The boatman was very much surprised at this proposal, and said:

"But what a pity to drown such a pretty Princess!"

However, at last the nurse persuaded him to help her, and when the night came and the Princess was fast asleep as usual, with Frisk curled up on his own cushion at the foot of her bed, the wicked nurse fetched the boatman and her daughter, and between them they picked up the Princess, feather bed, mattress, pillows, blankets and all, and threw her into the sea, without even waking her. Now, luckily, the Princess's bed was entirely stuffed with phoenix feathers, which are very rare, and have the property of always floating upon water, so Rosette went on swimming about as if she had been in a boat. After a little while she began to feel very cold, and turned round so often that she woke Frisk, who started up, and, having a very good nose, smelt the soles and herrings so close to him that he began to bark. He barked so long and so loud that he woke all the other fish, who came swimming up round the Princess's bed, and poking at it with their great heads. As for her, she said to herself:

"How our boat does rock upon the water! I am really glad that I am not often as uncomfortable as I have been to-night."

The wicked nurse and the boatman, who were by this time quite a long way off, heard Frisk barking, and said to each other:

"That horrid little animal and his mistress are drinking our health in sea-water now. Let us make haste to land, for we must be quite near the city of the King of the Peacocks."

The King had sent a hundred carriages to meet them, drawn by every kind of strange animal. There were lions, bears, wolves, stags, horses, buffaloes, eagles, and peacocks. The carriage intended for the Princess Rosette had six blue monkeys, which could turn summersaults, and dance on a tight-rope, and do many other charming tricks. Their harness was all of crimson velvet with gold buckles, and behind the carriage walked sixty beautiful ladies chosen by the King to wait upon Rosette and amuse her.

The nurse had taken all the pains imaginable to deck out her daughter. She put on her Rosette's prettiest frock, and covered her with diamonds from head to foot. But she was so ugly that nothing could make her look nice, and what was worse, she was sulky and ill-tempered, and did nothing but grumble all the time.

When she stepped from the boat and the escort sent by the King of the Peacocks caught sight of her, they were so surprised that they could not say a single word.

"Now then, look alive," cried the false Princess. "If you don't bring me something to eat I will have all your heads cut off!"

Then they whispered one to another:

"Here's a pretty state of things! she is as wicked as she is ugly. What a bride for our poor King! She certainly was not worth bringing from the other end of the world!"

But she went on ordering them all about, and for no fault at all would give slaps and pinches to everyone she could reach.

As the procession was so long it advanced but slowly, and the nurse's daughter sat up in her carriage trying to look like a Queen. But the peacocks, who were sitting upon every tree waiting to salute her, and who had made up their minds to cry, "Long live our beautiful Queen!" when they caught sight of the false bride could not help crying instead:

"Oh! how ugly she is!"

Which offended her so much that she said to the guards:

"Make haste and kill all these insolent peacocks who have dared to insult me."

But the peacocks only flew away, laughing at her.

The rogue of a boatman, who noticed all this, said softly to the nurse:

"This is a bad business for us, gossip; your daughter ought to have been prettier."

But she answered:

"Be quiet, stupid, or you will spoil everything."

Now they told the King that the Princess was approaching.

"Well," said he, "did her brothers tell me truly? Is she prettier than her portrait?"

"Sire," they answered, "if she were as pretty that would do very well."

"That's true," said the King; "I for one shall be quite satisfied if she is. Let us go and meet her." For they knew by the uproar that she had arrived, but they could not tell what all the shouting was about. The King thought he could hear the words:

"How ugly she is! How ugly she is!" and he fancied they must refer to some dwarf the Princess was bringing with her. It never occurred to him that they could apply to the bride herself.

The Princess Rosette's portrait was carried at the head of the procession, and after it walked the King surrounded by his courtiers. He was all impatience to see the lovely Princess, but when he caught sight of the nurse's daughter he was furiously angry, and would not advance another step. For she was really ugly enough to have frightened anybody.

"What!" he cried, "have the two rascals who are my prisoners dared to play me such a trick as this? Do they propose that I shall marry this hideous creature? Let her be shut up in my great tower, with her nurse and those who brought her here; and as for them, I will have their heads cut off."

Meanwhile the King and the Prince, who knew that their sister must have arrived, had made themselves smart, and sat expecting every minute to be summoned to greet her. So when the jailer came with soldiers, and carried them down into a black dungeon which swarmed with toads and bats, and where they were up to their necks in water, nobody could have been more surprised and dismayed than they were.

"This is a dismal kind of wedding," they said; "what can have happened that we should be treated like this? They must mean to kill us."

And this idea annoyed them very much. Three days passed before they heard any news, and then the King of the Peacocks came and berated them through a hole in the wall.

"You have called yourselves King and Prince," he cried, "to try and make me marry your sister, but you are nothing but beggars, not worth the water you drink. I mean to make short work with you, and the sword is being sharpened that will cut off your heads!"

"King of the Peacocks," answered the King angrily, "you had better take care what you are about. I am as good a King as yourself, and have a splendid kingdom and robes and crowns, and plenty of good red gold to do what I like with. You are pleased to jest about having our heads cut off; perhaps you think we have stolen something from you?"

At first the King of the Peacocks was taken aback by this bold speech, and had half a mind to send them all away together; but his Prime Minister declared that it would never do to let such a trick as that pass unpunished, everybody would laugh at him; so the accusation was drawn up against them, that they were impostors, and that they had promised the King a beautiful Princess in marriage who, when she arrived, proved to be an ugly peasant girl.

This accusation was read to the prisoners, who cried out that they had spoken the truth, that their sister was indeed a Princess more beautiful than the day, and that there was some mystery about all this which they could not fathom. Therefore they demanded seven days in which to prove their innocence, The King of the Peacocks was so angry that he would hardly even grant them this favor, but at last he was persuaded to do so.

While all this was going on at court, let us see what had been happening to the real Princess. When the day broke she and Frisk were equally astonished at finding themselves alone upon the sea, with no boat and no one to help them. The Princess cried and cried, until even the fishes were sorry for her.

"Alas!" she said, "the King of the Peacocks must have ordered me to be thrown into the sea because he had changed his mind and did not want to marry me. But how strange of him, when I should have loved him so much, and we should have been so happy together!"

And then she cried harder than ever, for she could not help still loving him. So for two days they floated up and down the sea, wet and shivering with the cold, and so hungry that when the Princess saw some oysters she caught them, and she and Frisk both ate some, though they didn't like them at all. When night came the Princess was so frightened that she said to Frisk:

"Oh! Do please keep on barking for fear the soles should come and eat us up!"

Now it happened that they had floated close in to the shore, where a poor old man lived all alone in a little cottage. When he heard Frisk's barking he thought to himself:

"There must have been a shipwreck!" (for no dogs ever passed that way by any chance), and he went out to see if he could be of any use. He soon saw the Princess and Frisk floating up and down, and Rosette, stretching out her hands to him, cried:

"Oh! Good old man, do save me, or I shall die of cold and hunger!"

When he heard her cry out so piteously he was very sorry for her, and ran back into his house to fetch a long boat-hook. Then he waded into the water up to his chin, and after being nearly drowned once or twice he at last succeeded in getting hold of the Princess's bed and dragging it on shore.

Rosette and Frisk were joyful enough to find themselves once more on dry land, and the Princess thanked the old man heartily; then, wrapping herself up in her blankets, she daintily picked her way up to the cottage on her little bare feet. There the old man lighted a fire of straw, and then drew from an old box his wife's dress and shoes, which the Princess put on, and thus roughly clad looked as charming as possible, and Frisk danced his very best to amuse her.

The old man saw that Rosette must be some great lady, for her bed coverings were all of satin and gold. He begged that she would tell him all her history, as she might safely trust him. The Princess told him everything, weeping bitterly again at the thought that it was by the King's orders that she had been thrown overboard.

"And now, my daughter, what is to be done?" said the old man. "You are a great Princess, accustomed to fare daintily, and I have nothing to offer you but black bread and radishes, which will not suit you at all. Shall I go and tell the King of the Peacocks that you are here? If he sees you he will certainly wish to marry you."

"Oh no!" cried Rosette, "he must be wicked, since he tried to drown me. Don't let us tell him, but if you have a little basket give it to me."

The old man gave her a basket, and tying it round Frisk's neck she said to him: "Go and find out the best cooking-pot in the town and bring the contents to me."

Away went Frisk, and as there was no better dinner cooking in all the town than the King's, he adroitly took the cover off the pot and brought all it contained to the Princess, who said:

"Now go back to the pantry, and bring the best of everything you find there."

So Frisk went back and filled his basket with white bread, and red wine, and every kind of sweetmeat, until it was almost too heavy for him to carry.

When the King of the Peacocks wanted his dinner there was nothing in the pot and nothing in the pantry. All the courtiers looked at one another in dismay, and the King was terribly cross.

"Oh well!" he said, "if there is no dinner I cannot dine, but take care that plenty of things are roasted for supper."

When evening came the Princess said to Frisk:

"Go into the town and find out the best kitchen, and bring me all the nicest morsels that are being roasted upon the spit."

Frisk did as he was told, and as he knew of no better kitchen than the King's, he went in softly, and when the cook's back was turned took everything that was upon the spit, As it happened it was all done to a turn, and looked so good that it made him hungry only to see it. He carried his basket to the Princess, who at once sent him back to the pantry to bring all the tarts and sugar plums that had been prepared for the King's supper.

The King, as he had had no dinner, was very hungry and wanted his supper early, but when he asked for it, lo and behold it was all gone, and he had to go to bed half-starved and in a terrible temper. The next day the same thing happened, and the next, so that for three days the King got nothing at all to eat, because just when the dinner or the supper was ready to be served it mysteriously disappeared. At last the Prime Minister began to be afraid that the King would be starved to death, so he resolved to hide himself in some dark corner of the kitchen, and never take his eyes off the cooking-pot. His surprise was great when he presently saw a little green dog with one ear slip softly into the kitchen, uncover the pot, transfer all its contents to his basket, and run off. The Prime Minister followed hastily, and tracked him all through the town to the cottage of the good old man; then he ran back to the King and told him that he had found out where all his dinners and suppers went. The King, who was very much astonished, said he should like to go and see for himself. So he set out, accompanied by the Prime Minister and a guard of archers, and arrived just in time to find the old man and the Princess finishing his dinner.

The King ordered that they should be seized and bound with ropes, and Frisk also.

When they were brought back to the palace some one told the King, who said:

"To-day is the last day of the respite granted to those impostors; they shall have their heads cut off at the same time as these stealers of my dinner." Then the old man went down on his knees before the King and begged for time to tell him everything. While he spoke the King for the first time looked attentively at the Princess, because he was sorry to see how she cried, and when he heard the old man saying that her name was Rosette, and that she had been treacherously thrown into the sea, he turned head over heels three times without stopping, in spite of being quite weak from hunger, and ran to embrace her, and untied the ropes which bound her with his own hands, declaring that he loved her with all his heart.

Messengers were sent to bring the Princes out of prison, and they came very sadly, believing that they were to be executed at once: the nurse and her daughter and the boatman were brought also. As soon as they came in Rosette ran to embrace her brothers, while the traitors threw themselves down before her and begged for mercy. The King and the Princess were so happy that they freely forgave them, and as for the good old man he was splendidly rewarded, and spent the rest of his days in the palace. The King of the Peacocks made ample amends to the King and Prince for the way in which they had been treated, and did everything in his power to show how sorry he was.

The nurse restored to Rosette all her dresses and jewels, and the bushel of gold pieces; the wedding was held at once, and they all lived happily ever after—even to Frisk, who enjoyed the greatest luxury, and never had anything worse than the wing of a partridge for dinner all the rest of his life.

The Boys with the Golden Stars

(FROM *THE VIOLET FAIRY BOOK*)

Once upon a time what happened did happen: and if it had not happened, you would never have heard this story.

Well, once upon a time there lived an emperor who had half a world all to himself to rule over, and in this world dwelt an old herd and his wife and their three daughters, Anna, Stana, and Laptitza.

Anna, the eldest, was so beautiful that when she took the sheep to pasture they forgot to eat as long as she was walking with them. Stana, the second, was so beautiful that when she was driving the flock the wolves protected the sheep. But Laptitza, the youngest, with a skin as white as the foam on the milk, and with hair as soft as the finest lamb's wool, was as beautiful as both her sisters put together—as beautiful as she alone could be.

One summer day, when the rays of the sun were pouring down on the earth, the three sisters went to the wood on the outskirts of the mountain to pick strawberries. As they were looking about to find where the largest berries grew they heard the tramp of horses approaching, so loud that you would have thought a whole army was riding by. But it was only the emperor going to hunt with his friends and attendants.

They were all fine handsome young men, who sat their horses as if they were part of them, but the finest and handsomest of all was the young emperor himself.

As they drew near the three sisters, and marked their beauty, they checked their horses and rode slowly by.

"Listen, sisters!" said Anna, as they passed on. "If one of those young men should make me his wife, I would bake him a loaf of bread which should keep him young and brave for ever."

"And if I," said Stana, "should be the one chosen, I would weave my husband a shirt which will keep him unscathed when he fights with dragons; when he goes through water he will never even be wet; or if through fire, it will not scorch him."

"And I," said Laptitza, "will give the man who chooses me two boys, twins, each with a golden star on his forehead, as bright as those in the sky."

And though they spoke low the young men heard, and turned their horses' heads.

"I take you at your word, and mine shall you be, most lovely of empresses!" cried the emperor, and swung Laptitza and her strawberries on the horse before him.

"And I will have you," "And I you," exclaimed two of his friends, and they all rode back to the palace together.

The following morning the marriage ceremony took place, and for three days and three nights there was nothing but feasting over the whole kingdom. And when the rejoicings were over the news was in everybody's mouth that Anna had sent for corn, and had made the loaf of which she had spoken at the strawberry beds. And then more days and nights passed, and this rumor was succeeded by another one—that Stana had procured some flax, and had dried it, and combed it, and spun it into linen, and sewed it herself into the shirt of which she had spoken over the strawberry beds.

Now the emperor had a stepmother, and she had a daughter by her first husband, who lived with her in the palace. The girl's mother had always believed that her daughter would be empress, and not the "Milkwhite Maiden," the child of a mere shepherd. So she hated the girl with all her heart, and only bided her time to do her ill.

But she could do nothing as long as the emperor remained with his wife night and day, and she began to wonder what she could do to get him away from her.

At last, when everything else had failed, she managed to make her brother, who was king of the neighboring country, declare war against the emperor, and besiege some of the frontier towns with a large army. This time her scheme was successful. The young emperor sprang up in wrath the moment he heard the news, and vowed that nothing, not even his wife, should hinder his giving them battle. And hastily assembling whatever soldiers happened to be at hand he set off at once to meet the enemy. The other king had not reckoned on the swiftness of his movements, and was not ready to receive him. The emperor fell on him when he was off his guard, and routed his army completely. Then when victory was won, and the terms of peace hastily drawn up, he rode home as fast as his horse would carry him, and reached the palace on the third day.

But early that morning, when the stars were growing pale in the sky, two little boys with golden hair and stars on their foreheads were born to Laptitza. And the stepmother, who was watching, took them away, and dug a hole in the corner of the palace, under the windows of the emperor, and put them in it, while in their stead she placed two little puppies.

The emperor came into the palace, and when they told him the news he went straight to Laptitza's room. No words were needed; he saw with his own eyes that Laptitza had not kept the promise she had made at the strawberry beds, and, though it nearly broke his heart, he must give orders for her punishment.

So he went out sadly and told his guards that the empress was to be buried in the earth up to her neck, so that everyone might know what would happen to those who dared to deceive the emperor.

Not many days after, the stepmother's wish was fulfilled. The emperor took her daughter to wife, and again the rejoicings lasted for three days and three nights.

Let us now see what happened to the two little boys.

The poor little babies had found no rest even in their graves. In the place where they had been buried there sprang up two beautiful young aspens, and the stepmother, who hated the sight of the trees, which reminded her of her crime, gave orders that they should be uprooted. But the emperor heard of it, and forbade the trees to be touched, saying, "Let them alone; I like to see them there! They are the finest aspens I have ever beheld!"

And the aspens grew as no aspens had grown before. In each day they added a year's growth, and each night they added a year's growth, and at dawn, when the stars faded out of the sky, they grew three years' growth in the twinkling of an eye, and their boughs swept across the palace windows. And when the wind moved them softly, the emperor would sit and listen to them all the day long.

The stepmother knew what it all meant, and her mind never ceased from trying to invent some way of destroying the trees. It was not an easy thing, but a woman's will can press milk out of a stone, and her cunning will overcome heroes. What craft will not do soft words may attain, and if these do not succeed there still remains the resource of tears.

One morning the empress sat on the edge of her husband's bed, and began to coax him with all sorts of pretty ways.

It was some time before the bait took, but at length—even emperors are only men!

"Well, well," he said at last, "have your way and cut down the trees; but out of one they shall make a bed for me, and out of the other, one for you!"

And with this the empress was forced to be content. The aspens were cut down next morning, and before night the new bed had been placed in the emperor's room.

Now when the emperor lay down in it he seemed as if he had grown a hundred times heavier than usual, yet he felt a kind of calm that was quite new to him. But the empress felt as if she was lying on thorns and nettles, and could not close her eyes.

When the emperor was fast asleep, the bed began to crack loudly, and to the empress each crack had a meaning. She felt as if she were listening to a language which no one but herself could understand.

"Is it too heavy for you, little brother?" asked one of the beds.

"Oh, no, it is not heavy at all," answered the bed in which the emperor was sleeping. "I feel nothing but joy now that my beloved father rests over me."

"It is very heavy for me!" said the other bed, "for on me lies an evil soul."

And so they talked on till the morning, the empress listening all the while.

By daybreak the empress had determined how to get rid of the beds. She would have two others made exactly like them, and when the emperor had gone hunting they should be placed in his room. This was done and the aspen beds were burnt in a large fire, till only a little heap of ashes was left.

Yet while they were burning the empress seemed to hear the same words, which she alone could understand.

Then she stooped and gathered up the ashes, and scattered them to the four winds, so that they might blow over fresh lands and fresh seas, and nothing remain of them.

But she had not seen that where the fire burnt brightest two sparks flew up, and, after floating in the air for a few moments, fell down into the great river that flows through the heart of the country. Here the sparks had turned into two little fishes with golden scales, and one was so exactly like the other that everyone could tell at the first glance that they must be twins. Early one morning the emperor's fishermen went down to the river to get some fish for their master's breakfast, and cast their nets into the stream. As the last star twinkled out of the sky they drew them in, and among the multitude of fishes lay two with scales of gold, such as no man had ever looked on.

They all gathered round and wondered, and after some talk they decided that they would take the little fishes alive as they were, and give them as a present to the emperor.

"Do not take us there, for that is whence we came, and yonder lies our destruction," said one of the fishes.

"But what are we to do with you?" asked the fisherman.

"Go and collect all the dew that lies on the leaves, and let us swim in it. Then lay us in the sun, and do not come near us till the sun's rays shall have dried off the dew," answered the other fish.

The fisherman did as they told him—gathered the dew from the leaves and let them swim in it, then put them to lie in the sun till the dew should be all dried up.

And when he came back, what do you think he saw? Why, two boys, two beautiful young princes, with hair as golden as the stars on their foreheads, and each so like the other, that at the first glance every one would have known them for twins.

The boys grew fast. In every day they grew a year's growth, and in every night another year's growth, but at dawn, when the stars were fading, they grew three years' growth in the twinkling of an eye. And they grew in other things besides height, too. Thrice in age, and thrice in wisdom, and thrice in knowledge. And when three days and three nights had passed they were twelve years in age, twenty-four in strength, and thirty-six in wisdom.

"Now take us to our father," said they. So the fisherman gave them each a lambskin cap which half covered their faces, and completely hid their golden hair and the stars on their foreheads, and led them to the court.

By the time they arrived there it was midday, and the fisherman and his charges went up to an official who was standing about. "We wish to speak with the emperor," said one of the boys.

"You must wait until he has finished his dinner," replied the porter.

"No, while he is eating it," said the second boy, stepping across the threshold.

The attendants all ran forward to thrust such impudent youngsters outside the palace, but the boys slipped through their fingers like quicksilver, and entered a large hall, where the emperor was dining, surrounded by his whole court.

"We desire to enter," said one of the princes sharply to a servant who stood near the door.

"That is quite impossible," replied the servant.

"Is it? let us see!" said the second prince, pushing the servants to right and left.

But the servants were many, and the princes only two. There was the noise of a struggle, which reached the emperor's ears.

"What is the matter?" asked he angrily.

The princes stopped at the sound of their father's voice.

"Two boys who want to force their way in," replied one of the servants, approaching the emperor.

"To *force* their way in? Who dares to use force in my palace? What boys are they?" said the emperor all in one breath.

"We know not, O mighty emperor," answered the servant, "but they must surely be akin to you, for they have the strength of lions, and have scattered the guards at the gate. And they are as proud as they are strong, for they will not take their caps from their heads."

The emperor, as he listened, grew red with anger.

"Thrust them out," cried he. "Set the dogs after them."

"Leave us alone, and we will go quietly," said the princes, and stepped backwards, weeping silently at the harsh words. They had almost reached the gates when a servant ran up to them.

"The emperor commands you to return," panted he: "the empress wishes to see you."

The princes thought a moment: then they went back the way they had come, and walked straight up to the emperor, their caps still on their heads.

He sat at the top of a long table covered with flowers and filled with guests. And beside him sat the empress, supported by twelve cushions. When the princes entered one of the cushions fell down, and there remained only eleven.

"Take off your caps," said one of the courtiers.

"A covered head is among men a sign of honor. We wish to seem what we are."

"Never mind," said the emperor, whose anger had dropped before the silvery tones of the boy's voice. "Stay as you are, but tell me *who* you are! Where do you come from, and what do you want?"

"We are twins, two shoots from one stem, which has been broken, and half lies in the ground and half sits at the head of this table. We have traveled a long way, we have spoken in the rustle of the wind, have whispered in the wood, we have sung in the waters, but now we wish to tell you a story which you know without knowing it, in the speech of men."

And a second cushion fell down.

"Let them take their silliness home," said the empress.

"Oh, no, let them go on," said the emperor. "You wished to see them, but I wish to hear them. Go on, boys, sing me the story."

The empress was silent, but the princes began to sing the story of their lives.

"There was once an emperor," began they, and the third cushion fell down.

When they reached the warlike expedition of the emperor three of the cushions fell down at once.

And when the tale was finished there were no more cushions under the empress, but the moment that they lifted their caps, and showed their golden hair and the golden stars, the eyes of the emperor and of all his guests were bent on them, and they could hardly bear the power of so many glances.

And there happened in the end what should have happened in the beginning. Laptitza sat next her husband at the top of the table. The stepmother's daughter became the meanest sewing maid in the palace, the stepmother was tied to a wild horse, and every one knew and has never forgotten that whoever has a mind turned to wickedness is sure to end badly.

Fairer-than-a-Fairy

(FROM *THE YELLOW FAIRY BOOK*)

Once there lived a King who had no children for many years after his marriage. At length heaven granted him a daughter of such remarkable beauty that he could think of no name so appropriate for her as "Fairer-than-a-Fairy."

It never occurred to the good-natured monarch that such a name was certain to call down the hatred and jealousy of the fairies in a body on the child, but this was what happened. No sooner had they heard of this presumptuous name than they resolved to gain possession of her who bore it, and either to torment her cruelly, or at least to conceal her from the eyes of all men.

The eldest of their tribe was entrusted to carry out their revenge. This Fairy was named Lagree; she was so old that she only had one eye and one tooth left, and even these poor remains she had to keep all night in a strengthening liquid. She was also so spiteful that she gladly devoted all her time to carrying out all the mean or ill-natured tricks of the whole body of fairies.

With her large experience, added to her native spite, she found but little difficulty in carrying off Fairer-than-a-Fairy. The poor child, who was only seven years old, nearly died of fear on finding herself in the power of this hideous creature. However, when after an hour's journey underground she found herself in a splendid palace with lovely gardens, she felt a little reassured, and was further cheered when she discovered that her pet cat and dog had followed her.

The old Fairy led her to a pretty room which she said should be hers, at the same time giving her the strictest orders never to let out the fire which was burning brightly in the grate. She then gave two glass bottles into the Princess's charge, desiring her to take the greatest care of them, and having enforced her orders with the most awful threats in case of disobedience, she vanished, leaving the little girl at liberty to explore the palace and grounds and a good deal relieved at having only two apparently easy tasks set her.

Several years passed, during which time the Princess grew accustomed to her lonely life, obeyed the Fairy's orders, and by degrees forgot all about the court of the King her father.

One day, whilst passing near a fountain in the garden, she noticed that the sun's rays fell on the water in such a manner as to produce a brilliant rainbow. She stood still to admire it, when, to her great surprise, she heard a voice addressing her which seemed to come from the center of its rays. The voice was that of a young man, and its sweetness of tone and the agreeable things it uttered, led one to infer that its owner must be equally charming; but this had to be a mere matter of fancy, for no one was visible.

The beautiful Rainbow informed Fairer-than-a-Fairy that he was young, the son of a powerful king, and that the Fairy, Lagree, who owed his parents a grudge, had revenged herself by depriving him of his natural shape for some years; that she had imprisoned him in the palace, where he had found his confinement hard to bear for some time, but now, he owned, he no longer sighed for freedom since he had seen and learned to love Fairer-than-a-Fairy.

He added many other tender speeches to this declaration, and the Princess, to whom such remarks were a new experience, could not help feeling pleased and touched by his attentions.

The Prince could only appear or speak under the form of a Rainbow, and it was therefore necessary that the sun should shine on water so as to enable the rays to form themselves.

Fairer-than-a-Fairy lost no moment in which she could meet her lover, and they enjoyed many long and interesting interviews. One day, however, their conversation became so absorbing and time passed so quickly that the Princess forgot to attend to the fire, and it went out. Lagree, on her return, soon found out the neglect, and seemed only too pleased to have the opportunity of showing her spite to her lovely prisoner. She ordered Fairer-than-a-Fairy to start next day at dawn to ask Locrinos for fire with which to relight the one she had allowed to go out.

Now this Locrinos was a cruel monster who devoured everyone he came across, and especially enjoyed a chance of catching and eating any young girls. Our heroine obeyed with great sweetness, and without having been able to take leave of her lover she set off to go to Locrinos as to certain death. As she was crossing a wood a bird sang to her to pick up a shining pebble which she would find in a fountain close by, and to use it when needed. She took the bird's advice, and in due time arrived at the house of Locrinos. Luckily she only found his wife at home, who was much struck by the Princess's youth and beauty and sweet gentle manners, and still further impressed by the present of the shining pebble.

She readily let Fairer-than-a-Fairy have the fire, and in return for the stone she gave her another, which, she said, might prove useful some day. Then she sent her away without doing her any harm.

Lagree was as much surprised as displeased at the happy result of this expedition, and Fairer-than-a Fairy waited anxiously for an opportunity of meeting Prince Rainbow and telling him her adventures. She found, however, that he had already been told all about them by a Fairy who protected him, and to whom he was related.

The dread of fresh dangers to his beloved Princess made him devise some more convenient way of meeting than by the garden fountain, and Fairer-than-a-Fairy carried out his plan daily with entire success. Every morning she placed a large basin full of water on her window-sill, and as soon as the sun's rays fell on the water the Rainbow appeared as clearly as it had ever done in the fountain. By this means they were able to meet without losing sight of the fire or of the two bottles in which the old Fairy kept her eye and her tooth at night, and for some time the lovers enjoyed every hour of sunshine together.

One day Prince Rainbow appeared in the depths of woe. He had just heard that he was to be banished from this lovely spot, but he had no idea where he was to go. The poor young couple were in despair, and only parted with the last ray of sunshine, and in hopes of meeting next morning. Alas! next day was dark and gloomy, and it was only late in the afternoon that the sun broke through the clouds for a few minutes.

Fairer-than-a-Fairy eagerly ran to the window, but in her haste she upset the basin, and spilt all the water with which she had carefully filled it over-night. No other water was at hand except that in the two bottles. It was the only chance of seeing her lover before they were separated, and she did not hesitate to break the bottle and pour their contents into the basin, when the Rainbow appeared at once. Their farewells were full of tenderness; the Prince made the most ardent and sincere protestations, and promised to neglect nothing which might help to deliver his dear Fairer-than-a-Fairy from her captivity, and implored her to consent to their marriage as soon as they should both be free. The Princess, on her side, vowed to have no other husband, and declared herself willing to brave death itself in order to rejoin him.

They were not allowed much time for their adieus; the Rainbow vanished, and the Princess, resolved to run all risks, started off at once, taking nothing with her but her dog, her cat, a sprig of myrtle, and the stone which the wife of Locrinos gave her.

When Lagree became aware of her prisoner's flight she was furious, and set off at full speed in pursuit. She overtook her just as the poor girl, overcome by fatigue, had lain down to rest in a cave which the stone had formed itself into to shelter her. The little dog who was watching her mistress promptly flew at Lagree and bit her so severely that she stumbled against a corner of the cave and broke off her only tooth. Before she had recovered from the pain and rage this caused her, the Princess had time to escape, and was some way on her road. Fear gave her strength for some time, but at last she could go no further, and sank down to rest. As she did so, the sprig of myrtle she carried touched the ground, and immediately a green and shady bower sprang up round her, in which she hoped to sleep in peace.

But Lagree had not given up her pursuit, and arrived just as Fairer-than-a-Fairy had fallen fast asleep. This time she made sure of catching her victim, but the cat spied her out, and, springing from one of the boughs of the arbor she flew at Lagree's face and tore out her only eye, thus delivering the Princess for ever from her persecutor.

One might have thought that all would now be well, but no sooner had Lagree been put to fight than our heroine was overwhelmed with hunger and thirst. She felt as though she should certainly expire, and it was with some difficulty that she dragged herself as far as a pretty little green and white house, which stood at no great distance. Here she was received by a beautiful lady dressed in green and white to match the house, which apparently belonged to her, and of which she seemed the only inhabitant.

She greeted the fainting Princess most kindly, gave her an excellent supper, and after a long night's rest in a delightful bed told her that after many troubles she should finally attain her desire.

As the green and white lady took leave of the Princess she gave her a nut, desiring her only to open it in the most urgent need.

After a long and tiring journey Fairer-than-a-Fairy was once more received in a house, and by a lady exactly like the one she had quitted. Here again she received a present with the same injunctions, but instead of a nut this lady gave her a golden pomegranate. The mournful Princess had to continue her weary way, and after many troubles and hardships she again found rest and shelter in a third house exactly similar to the two others.

These houses belonged to three sisters, all endowed with fairy gifts, and all so alike in mind and person that they wished their houses and garments to be equally alike. Their occupation consisted in helping those in misfortune, and they were as gentle and benevolent as Lagree had been cruel and spiteful.

The third Fairy comforted the poor traveler, begged her not to lose heart, and assured her that her troubles should be rewarded.

She accompanied her advice by the gift of a crystal smelling-bottle, with strict orders only to open it in case of urgent need. Fairer-than-a-Fairy thanked her warmly, and resumed her way cheered by pleasant thoughts.

After a time her road led through a wood, full of soft airs and sweet odors, and before she had gone a hundred yards she saw a wonderful silver Castle suspended by strong silver chains to four of the largest trees. It was so perfectly hung that a gentle breeze rocked it sufficiently to send you pleasantly to sleep.

Fairer-than-a-Fairy felt a strong desire to enter this Castle, but besides being hung a little above the ground there seemed to be neither doors nor windows. She had no doubt (though really I cannot think why) that the moment had come in which to use the nut which had been given her. She opened it, and out came a diminutive hall porter at whose belt hung a tiny chain, at the end of which was a golden key half as long as the smallest pin you ever saw.

The Princess climbed up one of the silver chains, holding in her hand the little porter who, in spite of his minute size, opened a secret door with his golden key and let her in. She entered a magnificent room which appeared to

began to think it was time to go home. So they called to their daughters and called again, but no one answered them.

Frightened at the silence, they searched every corner of the garden, the house, and the neighboring wood, but no trace of the girls was to be found anywhere. The earth seemed to have swallowed them up. The poor parents were in despair. The queen wept all the way home, and for many days after, and the king issued a proclamation that whoever should bring back his lost daughters should have one of them to wife, and should, after his death, reign in his stead.

Now two young generals were at that time living at the court, and when they heard the king's declaration, they said one to the other: "Let us go in search of them; perhaps we shall be the lucky persons."

And they set out, each mounted on a strong horse, taking with them a change of raiment and some money.

But though they inquired at every village they rode through, they could hear nothing of the princesses, and by-and-by their money was all spent, and they were forced to sell their horses, or give up the search. Even this money only lasted a little while longer, and nothing but their clothes lay between them and starvation. They sold the spare garments that were bound on their saddles, and went in the coats they stood up in to the inn, to beg for some food, as they were really starving. When, however, they had to pay for what they had eaten and drank, they said to the host: "We have no money, and naught but the clothes we stand up in. Take these, and give us instead some old rags, and let us stay here and serve you." And the innkeeper was content with the bargain, and the generals remained, and were his servants.

All this time the king and queen remained in their palace hungering for their children, but not a word was heard of either of them or of the generals who had gone to seek for them.

Now there was living in the palace a faithful servant of the king's called Bensurdatu, who had served him for many years, and when Bensurdatu saw how grieved the king was, he lifted up his voice and said to him: "Your majesty, let me go and seek your daughters."

"No, no, Bensurdatu," replied the king. "Three daughters have I lost, and two generals, and shall I lose you also?"

But Bensurdatu said again: "Let me now go, your majesty; trust me, and I will bring you back your daughters."

Then the king gave way, and Bensurdatu set forth, and rode on till he came to the inn, where he dismounted and asked for food. It was brought by the two generals, whom he knew at once in spite of their miserable clothes, and, much astonished, asked them how in the world they came there.

They told him all their adventures, and he sent for the innkeeper, and said to him: "Give them back their garments, and I will pay everything that they owe you."

And the innkeeper did as he was bid, and when the two generals were dressed in their proper clothes, they declared they would join Bensurdatu, and with him seek for the king's daughters.

The three companions rode on for many miles, and at length they came to a wild place, without sign of a human being. It was getting dark, and fearing to be lost on this desolate spot they pushed on their horses, and at last saw a light in the window of a tiny hut.

"Who comes there?" asked a voice, as they knocked at the door.

"Oh! have pity on us, and give us a night's shelter," replied Bensurdatu; "we are three tired travelers who have lost our way."

Then the door was opened by a very old woman, who stood back, and beckoned them to enter. "Whence do you come, and whither do you go?" said she.

"Ah, good woman, we have a heavy task before us," answered Bensurdatu, "we are bound to carry the king's daughters back to the palace!"

"Oh, unhappy creatures," cried she, "you know not what you are doing! The king's daughters were covered by a thick cloud, and no one knows where they may now be."

"Oh, tell us, if you know, my good woman," entreated Bensurdatu, "for with them lies all our happiness."

"Even if I were to tell you," answered she, "you could not rescue them. To do that you would have to go to the very bottom of a deep river, and though certainly you would find the king's daughters there, yet the two eldest are guarded by two giants, and the youngest is watched by a serpent with seven heads."

The two generals, who stood by listening, were filled with terror at her words, and wished to return immediately; but Bensurdatu stood firm, and said: "Now we have got so far we must carry the thing through. Tell us where the river is, so that we may get there as soon as possible." And the old woman told them, and gave them some cheese, wine, and bread, so that they should not set forth starving; and when they had eaten and drunk they laid themselves down to sleep.

The sun had only just risen above the hills next morning before they all woke, and, taking leave of the wise woman who had helped them, they rode on till they came to the river.

"I am the eldest," said one of the generals, "and it is my right to go down first."

So the others fastened a cord round him, and gave him a little bell, and let him down into the water. But scarcely had the river closed above his head when such dreadful rushing sounds and peals of thunder came crashing round about him that he lost all his courage, and rang his bell, if perchance it might be heard amidst all this clamor. Great was his relief when the rope began slowly to pull him upwards.

Then the other general plunged in; but he fared no better than the first, and was soon on dry ground again.

"Well, you are a brave pair!" said Bensurdatu, as he tied the rope round his own waist; "let us see what will happen to me." And when he heard the thunder and clamor round about him he thought to himself, "Oh, make as much noise as you like, it won't hurt me!" When his feet touched the bottom he found himself in a large, brilliantly lighted hall, and in the middle sat the eldest princess, and in front of her lay a huge giant, fast asleep. Directly she saw Bensurdatu she nodded to him, and asked with her eyes how he had come there.

For answer he drew his sword, and was about to cut off the giant's head, when she stopped him quickly, and made signs to hide himself, as the giant was just beginning to wake. "I smell the flesh of a man!" murmured he, stretching his great arms.

"Why, how in the world could any man get down here?" replied she; "you had better go to sleep again."

So he turned over and went to sleep. Then the princess signed to Bensurdatu, who drew his sword and cut off the giant's head with such a blow that it flew into the corner. And the heart of the princess leapt within her, and she placed a golden crown on the head of Bensurdatu, and called him her deliverer.

"Now show me where your sisters are," he said, "that I may free them also."

So the princess opened a door, and led him into another hall, wherein sat her next sister, guarded by a giant who was fast asleep. When the second

183

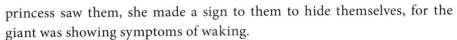

princess saw them, she made a sign to them to hide themselves, for the giant was showing symptoms of waking.

"I smell man's flesh!" murmured he, sleepily.

"Now, how could any man get down here?" asked she; "go to sleep again." And as soon as he closed his eyes, Bensurdatu stole out from his corner, and struck such a blow at his head that it flew far, far away. The princess could not find words to thank Bensurdatu for what he had done, and she too placed in his hand a golden crown.

"Now show me where your youngest sister is," said he, "that I may free her also."

"Ah! that I fear you will never be able to do," sighed they, "for she is in the power of a serpent with seven heads."

"Take me to him," replied Bensurdatu. "It will be a splendid fight."

Then the princess opened a door, and Bensurdatu passed through, and found himself in a hall that was even larger than the other two. And there stood the youngest sister, chained fast to the wall, and before her was stretched a serpent with seven heads, horrible to see. As Bensurdatu came forward it twisted all its seven heads in his direction, and then made a quick dart to snatch him within its grasp. But Bensurdatu drew his sword and laid about him, till the seven heads were rolling on the floor. Flinging down his sword he rushed to the princess and broke her chains, and she wept for joy, and embraced him, and took the golden crown from off her head, and placed it in his hand.

"Now we must go back to the upper world," said Bensurdatu, and led her to the bottom of the river. The other princesses were waiting there, and he tied the rope round the eldest, and rung his bell. And the generals above heard, and drew her gently up. They then unfastened the cord and threw it back into the river, and in a few moments the second princess stood beside her sister.

So now there were left only Bensurdatu and the youngest princess. "Dear Bensurdatu," said she, "do me a kindness, and let them draw you up before me. I dread the treachery of the generals."

"No, no," replied Bensurdatu, "I certainly will not leave you down here. There is nothing to fear from my comrades."

"If it is your wish I will go up then; but first I swear that if you do not follow to marry me, I shall stay single for the rest of my life." Then he bound the rope round her, and the generals drew her up.

But instead of lowering the rope again into the river, envy at the courage and success of Bensurdatu so filled the hearts of the two generals, that they turned away and left him to perish. And, more than that, they threatened the princesses, and forced them to promise to tell their parents that it was the two generals who had set them free. "And if they should ask you about Bensurdatu, you must say you have never seen him," they added; and the princesses, fearing for their lives, promised everything, and they rode back to court together.

The king and queen were beside themselves with joy when they saw their dear children once more. But when the generals had told their story, and the dangers they had run, the king declared that they had gained their reward, and that the two eldest princesses should become their wives.

And now we must see what poor Bensurdatu was doing.

He waited patiently a long, long time, but when the rope never came back he knew he had been wrong, and that his comrades had betrayed him. "Ah, now I shall never reach the world again," murmured he; but being a brave man, and knowing that moaning his fate would profit him nothing, he rose and began to search through the three halls, where, perhaps, he might find something to help him. In the last one stood a dish, covered with food, which reminded him that he was hungry, and he sat down and ate and drank.

Months passed away, when, one morning, as he was walking through the halls, he noticed a purse hanging on the wall, which had never been there before. He took it down to examine it, and nearly let it fall with surprise when a voice came from the purse saying: "What commands have you?"

"Oh, take me out of this horrible place, and up into the world again"; and in a moment he was, standing by the river bank, with the purse tightly grasped in his hand.

"Now let me have the most beautiful ship that ever was built, all manned and ready for sea." And there was the ship, with a flag floating from its mast on which were the words, "King with the three crowns." Then Bensurdatu climbed on board, and sailed away to the city where the three princesses dwelt; and when he reached the harbor he blew trumpets and beat drums, so that every one ran to the doors and windows. And the king heard too, and saw the beautiful vessel, and said to himself: "That must indeed be a mighty monarch, for he has three crowns while I have only one." So he hastened to greet the stranger, and invited him to his castle, for, thought he, "this will be a fine husband for my youngest daughter." Now, the youngest princess had never married, and had turned a deaf ear to all her wooers.

Such a long time had passed since Bensurdatu had left the palace, that the king never guessed for a moment that the splendidly clad stranger before him was the man whom he had so deeply mourned as dead. "Noble lord," said he, "let us feast and make merry together, and then, if it seem good to you, do me the honor to take my youngest daughter to wife."

And Bensurdatu was glad, and they all sat down to a great feast, and there were great rejoicings. But only the youngest daughter was sad, for her thoughts were with Bensurdatu. After they arose from the table the king said to her, "Dear child, this mighty lord does you the honor to ask your hand in marriage."

"Oh, father," answered she, "spare me, I pray you, for I desire to remain single."

Then Bensurdatu turned to her, and said: "And if I were Bensurdatu, would you give the same answer to me?"

And as she stood silently gazing at him, he added: "Yes, I am Bensurdatu; and this is my story."

The king and queen had their hearts stirred within them at the tale of his adventures, and when he had ended the king stretched out his hand, and said: "Dear Bensurdatu, my youngest daughter shall indeed be your wife; and when I die my crown shall be yours. As for the men who have betrayed you, they shall leave the country and you shall see them no more."

And the wedding feast was ordered, and rejoicings were held for three days over the marriage of Bensurdatu and the youngest princess.

Maiden Bright-eye

(FROM *THE PINK FAIRY BOOK*)

Once, upon a time there was a man and his wife who had two children, a boy and a girl. The wife died, and the man married again. His new wife had an only daughter, who was both ugly and untidy, whereas her step-daughter was a beautiful girl, and was known as Maiden Bright-eye. Her stepmother was very cruel to her on this account; she had always to do the hardest work, and got very little to eat, and no attention paid to her; but to her own daughter she was all that was good. She was spared from all the hardest of the housework, and had always the prettiest clothes to wear.

Maiden Bright-eye had also to watch the sheep, but of course it would never do to let her go idle and enjoy herself too much at this work, so she had to pull heather while she was out on the moors with them. Her stepmother gave her pancakes to take with her for her dinner, but she had mixed the flour with ashes, and made them just as bad as she could.

The little girl came out on the moor and began to pull heather on the side of a little mound, but next minute a little fellow with a red cap on his head popped up out of the mound and said:

"Who's that pulling the roof off my house?"

"Oh, it's me, a poor little girl," said she; "my mother sent me out here, and told me to pull heather. If you will be good to me I will give you a bit of my dinner."

The little fellow was quite willing, and she gave him the biggest share of her pancakes. They were not particularly good, but when one is hungry anything tastes well. After he had got them all eaten he said to her:

"Now, I shall give you three wishes, for you are a very nice little girl; but I will choose the wishes for you. You are beautiful, and much more beautiful shall you be; yes, so lovely that there will not be your like in the world. The next wish shall be that every time you open your mouth a gold coin shall fall out of it, and your voice shall be like the most beautiful music. The third wish shall be that you may be married to the young king, and become the queen of the country. At the same time I shall give you a cap, which you must carefully keep, for it can save you, if you ever are in danger of your life, if you just put it on your head.

Maiden Bright-eye thanked the little bergman ever so often, and drove home her sheep in the evening. By that time she had grown so beautiful that her people could scarcely recognize her. Her stepmother asked her how it had come about that she had grown so beautiful. She told the whole story—for she always told the truth—that a little man had come to her out on the moor and had given her all this beauty. She did not tell, however, that she had given him a share of her dinner.

The stepmother thought to herself, "If one can become so beautiful by going out there, my own daughter shall also be sent, for she can well stand being made a little prettier."

Next morning she baked for her the finest cakes, and dressed her prettily to go out with the sheep. But she was afraid to go away there without having a stick to defend herself with if anything should come near her.

She was not very much inclined for pulling the heather, as she never was in the habit of doing any work, but she was only a minute or so at it when up came the same little fellow with the red cap, and said:

"Who's that pulling the roof off my house?"

"What's that to you?" said she.

"Well, if you will give me a bit of your dinner I won't do you any mischief," said he.

"I will give you something else in place of my dinner," said she. "I can easily eat it myself; but if you *will* have something you can have a whack of my stick," and with that she raised it in the air and struck the bergman over the head with it.

"What a wicked little girl you are!" said he; "but you shall be none the better of this. I shall give you three wishes, and choose them for you. First, I shall say, 'Ugly are you, but you shall become so ugly that there will not be an uglier one on earth.' Next I shall wish that every time you open your mouth a big toad may fall out of it, and your voice shall be like the roaring of a bull. In the third place I shall wish for you a violent death."

The girl went home in the evening, and when her mother saw her she was as vexed as she could be, and with good reason, too; but it was still worse when she saw the toads fall out of her mouth and heard her voice.

Now we must hear something about the stepson. He had gone out into the world to look about him, and took service in the king's palace. About this time he got permission to go home and see his sister, and when he saw how lovely and beautiful she was, he was so pleased and delighted that when he came back to the king's palace everyone there wanted to know what he was always so happy about. He told them that it was because he had such a lovely sister at home.

At last it came to the ears of the king what the brother said about his sister, and, besides that, the report of her beauty spread far and wide, so that the youth was summoned before the king, who asked him if everything was true that was told about the girl. He said it was quite true, for he had seen her beauty with his own eyes, and had heard with his own ears how sweetly she could sing and what a lovely voice she had.

The king then took a great desire for her, and ordered her brother to go home and bring her back with him, for he trusted no one better to accomplish that errand. He got a ship, and everything else that he required, and sailed home for his sister. As soon as the stepmother heard what his errand was she at once said to herself, "This will never come about if I can do anything to hinder it. She must not be allowed to come to such honor."

She then got a dress made for her own daughter, like the finest robe for a queen, and she had a mask prepared and put upon her face, so that she looked quite pretty, and gave her strict orders not to take it off until the king had promised to wed her.

The brother now set sail with his two sisters, for the stepmother pretended that the ugly one wanted to see the other a bit on her way. But when they got out to sea, and Maiden Bright-eye came up on deck, the sister did as her mother had instructed her—she gave her a push and made her fall into the water. When the brother learned what had happened he was greatly distressed, and did not know what to do. He could not bring himself to tell the truth about what had happened, nor did he expect that the king would believe it. In the long run he decided to hold on his way, and let things go as they liked. What he had expected happened—the king received his sister and wedded her at once, but repented it after the first night, as he could scarcely put down his foot in the morning for all the toads that were about the room, and when he saw her real face he was so enraged against the brother that he had him thrown into a pit full of serpents. He was so angry, not merely because he had been deceived, but because he could not get rid of the ugly wretch that was now tied to him for life.

Now we shall hear a little about Maiden Bright-eye. When she fell into the water she was fortunate enough to get the bergman's cap put on her head, for now she was in danger of her life, and she was at once transformed into a duck. The duck swam away after the ship, and came to the king's palace on the next evening. There it waddled up the drain, and so into the kitchen, where her little dog lay on the hearth-stone; it could not bear to stay in the fine chambers along with the ugly sister, and had taken refuge down here. The duck hopped up till it could talk to the dog.

"Good evening," it said.

"Thanks, Maiden Bright-eye," said the dog.

"Where is my brother?"

"He is in the serpent-pit."

"Where is my wicked sister?"

"She is with the noble king."

"Alas! alas! I am here this evening, and shall be for two evenings yet, and then I shall never come again."

When it had said this the duck waddled off again. Several of the servant girls heard the conversation, and were greatly surprised at it, and thought that it would be worth while to catch the bird next evening and see into the matter a little more closely. They had heard it say that it would come again.

Next evening it appeared as it had said, and a great many were present to see it. It came waddling in by the drain, and went up to the dog, which was lying on the hearth-stone.

"Good evening," it said.

"Thanks, Maiden Bright-eye," said the dog.

"Where is my brother?"

"He is in the serpent-pit."

"Where is my wicked sister?"

"She is with the noble king."

"Alas! alas! I am here this evening, and shall be for one evening yet, and then I shall never come again."

After this it slipped out, and no one could get hold of it. But the king's cook thought to himself, "I shall see if I can't get hold of you to-morrow evening."

On the third evening the duck again came waddling in by the drain, and up to the dog on the hearth-stone.

"Good evening," it said.

"Thanks, Maiden Bright-eye," said the dog.

"Where is my brother?"

"He is in the serpent-pit."

"Where is my wicked sister?"

"She is with the noble king."

"Alas! alas! now I shall never come again."

With this it slipped out again, but in the meantime the cook had posted himself at the outer end of the drain with a net, which he threw over it as it came out. In this way he caught it, and came in to the others with the most beautiful duck they had ever seen—with so many golden feathers on it that everyone marveled. No one, however, knew what was to be done with it; but after what they had heard they knew that there was something uncommon about it, so they took good care of it.

At this time the brother in the serpent-pit dreamed that his right sister had come swimming to the king's palace in the shape of a duck, and that she could not regain her own form until her beak was cut off. He got this dream told to some one, so that the king at last came to hear of it, and had him taken up out of the pit and brought before him. The king then asked him if he could produce to him his sister as beautiful as he had formerly described her. The brother said he could if they would bring him the duck and a knife.

Both of them were brought to him, and he said, "I wonder how you would look if I were to cut the point off your beak."

With this he cut a piece off the beak, and there came a voice which said, "Oh, oh, you cut my little finger!"

Next moment Maiden Bright-eye stood there, as lovely and beautiful as he had seen her when he was home. This was his sister now, he said; and the whole story now came out of how the other had behaved to her. The wicked sister was put into a barrel with spikes round it which was dragged off by six wild horses, and so she came to her end. But the king was delighted with Maiden Bright-eye, and immediately made her his queen, while her brother became his prime minister.

The Story of Pretty Goldilocks

(FROM *THE BLUE FAIRY BOOK*)

Once upon a time there was a princess who was the prettiest creature in the world. And because she was so beautiful, and because her hair was like the finest gold, and waved and rippled nearly to the ground, she was called Pretty Goldilocks. She always wore a crown of flowers, and her dresses were embroidered with diamonds and pearls, and everybody who saw her fell in love with her.

Now one of her neighbors was a young king who was not married. He was very rich and handsome, and when he heard all that was said about Pretty Goldilocks, though he had never seen her, he fell so deeply in love with her that he could neither eat nor drink. So he resolved to send an ambassador to ask for her in marriage. He had a splendid carriage made for his ambassador, and gave him more than a hundred horses and a hundred servants, and told him to be sure and bring the Princess back with him. After he had started nothing else was talked of at Court, and the King felt so sure that the Princess would consent that he set his people to work at pretty dresses and splendid furniture, that they might be ready by the time she came. Meanwhile, the ambassador arrived at the Princess's palace and delivered his little message, but whether she happened to be cross that day, or whether the compliment did not please her, is not known. She only answered that she was very much obliged to the King, but she had no wish to be married. The ambassador set off sadly on his homeward way, bringing all the King's presents back with him, for the Princess was too well brought up to accept the pearls and diamonds when she would not accept the King, so she had only kept twenty-five English pins that he might not be vexed.

When the ambassador reached the city, where the King was waiting impatiently, everybody was very much annoyed with him for not bringing the Princess, and the King cried like a baby, and nobody could console him. Now there was at the Court a young man, who was more clever and handsome than anyone else. He was called Charming, and everyone loved him, excepting a few envious people who were angry at his being the King's favorite and knowing all the State secrets. He happened to one day be with some people who were speaking of the ambassador's return and saying that his going to the Princess had not done much good, when Charming said rashly:

"If the King had sent me to the Princess Goldilocks I am sure she would have come back with me."

His enemies at once went to the King and said:

"You will hardly believe, sire, what Charming has the audacity to say— that if *he* had been sent to the Princess Goldilocks she would certainly have come back with him. He seems to think that he is so much handsomer than you that the Princess would have fallen in love with him and followed him willingly." The King was very angry when he heard this.

"Ha, ha!" said he; "does he laugh at my unhappiness, and think himself more fascinating than I am? Go, and let him be shut up in my great tower to die of hunger."

So the King's guards went to fetch Charming, who had thought no more of his rash speech, and carried him off to prison with great cruelty. The poor prisoner had only a little straw for his bed, and but for a little stream of water which flowed through the tower he would have died of thirst.

One day when he was in despair he said to himself:

"How can I have offended the King? I am his most faithful subject, and have done nothing against him."

The King chanced to be passing the tower and recognized the voice of his former favorite. He stopped to listen in spite of Charming's enemies, who tried to persuade him to have nothing more to do with the traitor. But the King said:

"Be quiet, I wish to hear what he says."

And then he opened the tower door and called to Charming, who came very sadly and kissed the King's hand, saying:

"What have I done, sire, to deserve this cruel treatment?"

"You mocked me and my ambassador," said the King, "and you said that if I had sent you for the Princess Goldilocks you would certainly have brought her back."

"It is quite true, sire," replied Charming; "I should have drawn such a picture of you, and represented your good qualities in such a way, that I am certain the Princess would have found you irresistible. But I cannot see what there is in that to make you angry."

The King could not see any cause for anger either when the matter was presented to him in this light, and he began to frown very fiercely at the courtiers who had so misrepresented his favorite.

So he took Charming back to the palace with him, and after seeing that he had a very good supper he said to him:

"You know that I love Pretty Goldilocks as much as ever, her refusal has not made any difference to me; but I don't know how to make her change her mind; I really should like to send you, to see if you can persuade her to marry me."

Charming replied that he was perfectly willing to go, and would set out the very next day.

"But you must wait till I can get a grand escort for you," said the King. But Charming said that he only wanted a good horse to ride, and the King, who was delighted at his being ready to start so promptly, gave him letters to the Princess, and bade him good speed. It was on a Monday morning that he set out all alone upon his errand, thinking of nothing but how he could persuade the Princess Goldilocks to marry the King. He had a writing-book in his pocket, and whenever any happy thought struck him he dismounted from his horse and sat down under the trees to put it into the harangue which he was preparing for the Princess, before he forgot it.

One day when he had started at the very earliest dawn, and was riding over a great meadow, he suddenly had a capital idea, and, springing from his horse, he sat down under a willow tree which grew by a little river. When he had written it down he was looking round him, pleased to find himself in such a pretty place, when all at once he saw a great golden carp lying gasping and exhausted upon the grass. In leaping after little flies she had thrown herself high upon the bank, where she had lain till she was nearly dead. Charming had pity upon her, and, though he couldn't help thinking that she would have been very nice for dinner, he picked her up gently and put her back into the water. As soon as Dame Carp felt the refreshing coolness of the water she sank down joyfully to the bottom of the river, then, swimming up to the bank quite boldly, she said:

"I thank you, Charming, for the kindness you have done me. You have saved my life; one day I will repay you." So saying, she sank down into the water again, leaving Charming greatly astonished at her politeness.

Another day, as he journeyed on, he saw a raven in great distress. The poor bird was closely pursued by an eagle, which would soon have eaten it up, had not Charming quickly fitted an arrow to his bow and shot the eagle dead. The raven perched upon a tree very joyfully.

"Charming," said he, "it was very generous of you to rescue a poor raven; I am not ungrateful, some day I will repay you."

Charming thought it was very nice of the raven to say so, and went on his way.

Before the sun rose he found himself in a thick wood where it was too dark for him to see his path, and here he heard an owl crying as if it were in despair.

"Hark!" said he, "that must be an owl in great trouble, I am sure it has gone into a snare"; and he began to hunt about, and presently found a great net which some bird-catchers had spread the night before.

"What a pity it is that men do nothing but torment and persecute poor creatures which never do them any harm!" said he, and he took out his knife and cut the cords of the net, and the owl flitted away into the darkness, but then turning, with one flicker of her wings, she came back to Charming and said:

"It does not need many words to tell you how great a service you have done me. I was caught; in a few minutes the fowlers would have been here—without your help I should have been killed. I am grateful, and one day I will repay you."

These three adventures were the only ones of any consequence that befell Charming upon his journey, and he made all the haste he could to reach the palace of the Princess Goldilocks.

When he arrived he thought everything he saw delightful and magnificent. Diamonds were as plentiful as pebbles, and the gold and silver, the beautiful dresses, the sweetmeats and pretty things that were everywhere quite amazed him; he thought to himself: "If the Princess consents to leave all this, and come with me to marry the King, he may think himself lucky!"

Then he dressed himself carefully in rich brocade, with scarlet and white plumes, and threw a splendid embroidered scarf over his shoulder, and, looking as gay and as graceful as possible, he presented himself at the door of the palace, carrying in his arm a tiny pretty dog which he had bought on the way. The guards saluted him respectfully, and a messenger was sent to the Princess to announce the arrival of Charming as ambassador of her neighbor the King.

"Charming," said the Princess, "the name promises well; I have no doubt that he is good looking and fascinates everybody."

"Indeed he does, madam," said all her maids of honor in one breath. "We saw him from the window of the garret where we were spinning flax, and we could do nothing but look at him as long as he was in sight."

"Well to be sure," said the Princess, "that's how you amuse yourselves, is it? Looking at strangers out of the window! Be quick and give me my blue satin embroidered dress, and comb out my golden hair. Let somebody make me fresh garlands of flowers, and give me my high-heeled shoes and my fan, and tell them to sweep my great hall and my throne, for I want everyone to say I am really 'Pretty Goldilocks.' "

You can imagine how all her maids scurried this way and that to make the Princess ready, and how in their haste they knocked their heads together and hindered each other, till she thought they would never have done. However, at last they led her into the gallery of mirrors that she might assure herself that nothing was lacking in her appearance, and then she mounted her throne of gold, ebony, and ivory, while her ladies took their guitars and began to sing softly. Then Charming was led in, and was so struck with astonishment and admiration that at first not a word could he say. But presently he took courage and delivered his harangue, bravely ending by begging the Princess to spare him the disappointment of going back without her.

"Sir Charming," answered she, "all the reasons you have given me are very good ones, and I assure you that I should have more pleasure in obliging you than anyone else, but you must know that a month ago as I was walking by the river with my ladies I took off my glove, and as I did so a ring that I was wearing slipped off my finger and rolled into the water. As I valued it more than my kingdom, you may imagine how vexed I was at losing it, and I vowed to never listen to any proposal of marriage unless the ambassador first brought me back my ring. So now you know what is expected of you, for if you talked for fifteen days and fifteen nights you could not make me change my mind."

Charming was very much surprised by this answer, but he bowed low to the Princess, and begged her to accept the embroidered scarf and the tiny dog he had brought with him. But she answered that she did not want any presents, and that he was to remember what she had just told him. When he got back to his lodging he went to bed without eating any supper, and his little dog, who was called Frisk, couldn't eat any either, but came and lay down close to him. All night Charming sighed and lamented.

"How am I to find a ring that fell into the river a month ago?" said he. "It is useless to try; the Princess must have told me to do it on purpose, knowing it was impossible." And then he sighed again.

Frisk heard him and said:

"My dear master, don't despair; the luck may change, you are too good not to be happy. Let us go down to the river as soon as it is light."

But Charming only gave him two little pats and said nothing, and very soon he fell asleep.

At the first glimmer of dawn Frisk began to jump about, and when he had waked Charming they went out together, first into the garden, and then down to the river's brink, where they wandered up and down. Charming was thinking sadly of having to go back unsuccessful when he heard someone calling: "Charming, Charming!" He looked all about him and thought he must be dreaming, as he could not see anybody. Then he walked on and the voice called again: "Charming, Charming!"

"Who calls me?" said he. Frisk, who was very small and could look closely into the water, cried out: "I see a golden carp coming." And sure enough there was the great carp, who said to Charming:

"You saved my life in the meadow by the willow tree, and I promised that I would repay you. Take this, it is Princess Goldilock's ring." Charming took the ring out of Dame Carp's mouth, thanking her a thousand times, and he and tiny Frisk went straight to the palace, where someone told the Princess that he was asking to see her.

"Ah! poor fellow," said she, "he must have come to say good-by, finding it impossible to do as I asked."

So in came Charming, who presented her with the ring and said:

"Madam, I have done your bidding. Will it please you to marry my master?" When the Princess saw her ring brought back to her unhurt she was so astonished that she thought she must be dreaming.

"Truly, Charming," said she, "you must be the favorite of some fairy, or you could never have found it."

"Madam," answered he, "I was helped by nothing but my desire to obey your wishes."

"Since you are so kind," said she, "perhaps you will do me another service, for till it is done I will never be married. There is a prince not far from here whose name is Galifron, who once wanted to marry me, but when I refused he uttered the most terrible threats against me, and vowed that he would lay waste my country. But what could I do? I could not marry a frightful giant as tall as a tower, who eats up people as a monkey eats chestnuts, and who talks so loud that anybody who has to listen to him becomes quite deaf. Nevertheless, he does not cease to persecute me and to kill my subjects. So before I can listen to your proposal you must kill him and bring me his head."

Charming was rather dismayed at this command, but he answered:

"Very well, Princess, I will fight this Galifron; I believe that he will kill me, but at any rate I shall die in your defense."

Then the Princess was frightened and said everything she could think of to prevent Charming from fighting the giant, but it was of no use, and he went out to arm himself suitably, and then, taking little Frisk with him, he mounted his horse and set out for Galifron's country. Everyone he met told him what a terrible giant Galifron was, and that nobody dared go near him; and the more he heard, the more frightened he grew. Frisk tried to encourage him by saying: "While you are fighting the giant, dear master, I will go and bite his heels, and when he stoops down to look at me you can kill him."

Charming praised his little dog's plan, but knew that this help would not do much good.

At last he drew near the giant's castle, and saw to his horror that every path that led to it was strewn with bones. Before long he saw Galifron coming. His head was higher than the tallest trees, and he sang in a terrible voice:

> "Bring out your little boys and girls,
> Pray do not stay to do their curls,
> For I shall eat so very many,
> I shall not know if they have any."

Thereupon Charming sang out as loud as he could to the same tune:

> "Come out and meet the valiant Charming
> Who finds you not at all alarming;
> Although he is not very tall,
> He's big enough to make you fall."

The rhymes were not very correct, but you see he had made them up so quickly that it is a miracle that they were not worse; especially as he was horribly frightened all the time. When Galifron heard these words he looked all about him, and saw Charming standing, sword in hand; this put the giant into a terrible rage, and he aimed a blow at Charming with his huge iron club, which would certainly have killed him if it had reached him, but at that instant a raven perched upon the giant's head, and, pecking with its strong beak and beating with its great wings so confused and blinded him that all his blows fell harmlessly upon the air, and Charming, rushing in, gave him several strokes with his sharp sword so that he fell to the ground. Whereupon Charming cut off his head before he knew anything about it, and the raven from a tree close by croaked out:

"You see I have not forgotten the good turn you did me in killing the eagle. To-day I think I have fulfilled my promise of repaying you."

"Indeed, I owe you more gratitude than you ever owed me," replied Charming.

And then he mounted his horse and rode off with Galifron's head.

When he reached the city the people ran after him in crowds, crying:

"Behold the brave Charming, who has killed the giant!" And their shouts reached the Princess's ear, but she dared not ask what was happening, for fear she should hear that Charming had been killed. But very soon he arrived at the palace with the giant's head, of which she was still terrified, though it could no longer do her any harm.

"Princess," said Charming, "I have killed your enemy; I hope you will now consent to marry the King my master."

"Oh dear! no," said the Princess, "not until you have brought me some water from the Gloomy Cavern.

"Not far from here there is a deep cave, the entrance to which is guarded by two dragons with fiery eyes, who will not allow anyone to pass them. When you get into the cavern you will find an immense hole, which you must go down, and it is full of toads and snakes; at the bottom of this hole there is another little cave, in which rises the Fountain of Health and Beauty.

It is some of this water that I really must have: everything it touches becomes wonderful. The beautiful things will always remain beautiful, and the ugly things become lovely. If one is young one never grows old, and if one is old one becomes young. You see, Charming, I could not leave my kingdom without taking some of it with me."

"Princess," said he, "you at least can never need this water, but I am an unhappy ambassador, whose death you desire. Where you send me I will go, though I know I shall never return."

And, as the Princess Goldilocks showed no sign of relenting, he started with his little dog for the Gloomy Cavern. Everyone he met on the way said:

"What a pity that a handsome young man should throw away his life so carelessly! He is going to the cavern alone, though if he had a hundred men with him he could not succeed. Why does the Princess ask impossibilities?" Charming said nothing, but he was very sad. When he was near the top of a hill he dismounted to let his horse graze, while Frisk amused himself by chasing flies. Charming knew he could not be far from the Gloomy Cavern, and on looking about him he saw a black hideous rock from which came a thick smoke, followed in a moment by one of the dragons with fire blazing from his mouth and eyes. His body was yellow and green, and his claws scarlet, and his tail was so long that it lay in a hundred coils. Frisk was so terrified at the sight of it that he did not know where to hide. Charming, quite determined to get the water or die, now drew his sword, and, taking the crystal flask which Pretty Goldilocks had given him to fill, said to Frisk:

"I feel sure that I shall never come back from this expedition; when I am dead, go to the Princess and tell her that her errand has cost me my life. Then find the King my master, and relate all my adventures to him."

As he spoke he heard a voice calling: "Charming, Charming!"

"Who calls me?" said he; then he saw an owl sitting in a hollow tree, who said to him:

"You saved my life when I was caught in the net, now I can repay you. Trust me with the flask, for I know all the ways of the Gloomy Cavern, and can fill it from the Fountain of Beauty." Charming was only too glad to give her the flask, and she flitted into the cavern quite unnoticed by the dragon, and after some time returned with the flask, filled to the very brim with sparkling water. Charming thanked her with all his heart, and joyfully hastened back to the town.

He went straight to the palace and gave the flask to the Princess, who had no further objection to make. So she thanked Charming, and ordered that preparations should be made for her departure, and they soon set out together. The Princess found Charming such an agreeable companion that she sometimes said to him: "Why didn't we stay where we were? I could have made you king, and we should have been so happy!"

But Charming only answered:

"I could not have done anything that would have vexed my master so much, even for a kingdom, or to please you, though I think you are as beautiful as the sun."

At last they reached the King's great city, and he came out to meet the Princess, bringing magnificent presents, and the marriage was celebrated with great rejoicings. But Goldilocks was so fond of Charming that she could not be happy unless he was near her, and she was always singing his praises.

"If it hadn't been for Charming," she said to the King, "I should never have come here; you ought to be very much obliged to him, for he did the most impossible things and got me water from the Fountain of Beauty, so I can never grow old, and shall get prettier every year."

Then Charming's enemies said to the King:

"It is a wonder that you are not jealous, the Queen thinks there is nobody in the world like Charming. As if anybody you had sent could not have done just as much!"

"It is quite true, now I come to think of it," said the King. "Let him be chained hand and foot, and thrown into the tower."

So they took Charming, and as a reward for having served the King so faithfully he was shut up in the tower, where he only saw the jailer, who brought him a piece of black bread and a pitcher of water every day.

However, little Frisk came to console him, and told him all the news.

When Pretty Goldilocks heard what had happened she threw herself at the King's feet and begged him to set Charming free, but the more she cried, the more angry he was, and at last she saw that it was useless to say any more; but it made her very sad. Then the King took it into his head that perhaps he was not handsome enough to please the Princess Goldilocks, and he thought he would bathe his face with the water from the Fountain of Beauty, which was in the flask on a shelf in the Princess's room, where she had placed it that she might see it often. Now it happened that one of the

Princess's ladies in chasing a spider had knocked the flask off the shelf and broken it, and every drop of the water had been spilt. Not knowing what to do, she had hastily swept away the pieces of crystal, and then remembered that in the King's room she had seen a flask of exactly the same shape, also filled with sparkling water. So, without saying a word, she fetched it and stood it upon the Queen's shelf.

Now the water in this flask was what was used in the kingdom for getting rid of troublesome people. Instead of having their heads cut off in the usual way, their faces were bathed with the water, and they instantly fell asleep and never woke up any more. So, when the King, thinking to improve his beauty, took the flask and sprinkled the water upon his face, *he* fell asleep, and nobody could wake him.

Little Frisk was the first to hear the news, and he ran to tell Charming, who sent him to beg the Princess not to forget the poor prisoner. All the palace was in confusion on account of the King's death, but tiny Frisk made his way through the crowd to the Princess's side, and said:

"Madam, do not forget poor Charming!"

Then she remembered all he had done for her, and without saying a word to anyone went straight to the tower, and with her own hands took off Charming's chains. Then, putting a golden crown upon his head, and the royal mantle upon his shoulders, she said:

"Come, faithful Charming, I make you king, and will take you for my husband."

Charming, once more free and happy, fell at her feet and thanked her for her gracious words.

Everybody was delighted that he should be king, and the wedding, which took place at once, was the prettiest that can be imagined, and Prince Charming and Princess Goldilocks lived happily ever after.

The True Sweetheart

(From *Grimm's Complete Fairy Tales*)

There was once on a time a girl who was young and beautiful, but she had lost her mother when she was quite a child, and her step-mother did all she could to make the girl's life wretched. Whenever this woman gave her anything to do, she worked at it indefatigably, and did everything that lay in her power. Still she could not touch the heart of the wicked woman by that; she was never satisfied; it was never enough. The harder the girl worked, the more work was put upon her, and all that the woman thought of was how to weigh her down with still heavier burdens, and make her life still more miserable.

One day she said to her, "Here are twelve pounds of feathers which thou must pick, and if they are not done this evening, thou mayst expect a good beating. Dost thou imagine thou art to idle away the whole day?" The poor girl sat down to the work, but tears ran down her cheeks as she did so, for she saw plainly enough that it was quite impossible to finish the work in one day. Whenever she had a little heap of feathers lying before her, and she sighed or smote her hands together in her anguish, they flew away, and she had to pick them out again, and begin her work anew. Then she put her elbows on the table, laid her face in her two hands, and cried, "Is there no one, then, on God's earth to have pity on me?"

Then she heard a low voice which said, "Be comforted, my child, I have come to help thee." The maiden looked up, and an old woman was by her side. She took the girl kindly by the hand, and said, "Only tell me what is troubling thee." As she spoke so kindly, the girl told her of her miserable life, and how one burden after another was laid upon her, and she never could get to the end of the work which was given to her. "If I have not done these feathers by this evening, my step-mother will beat me; she has threatened she will, and I know she keeps her word." Her tears began to flow again, but the good old woman

203

said, "Do not be afraid, my child; rest a while, and in the meantime I will look to thy work." The girl lay down on her bed, and soon fell asleep.

The old woman seated herself at the table with the feathers, and how they did fly off the quills, which she scarcely touched with her withered hands! The twelve pounds were soon finished, and when the girl awoke, great snow-white heaps were lying, piled up, and everything in the room was neatly cleared away, but the old woman had vanished. The maiden thanked God, and sat still till evening came, when the step-mother came in and marveled to see the work completed. "Just look, you awkward creature," said she, "what can be done when people are industrious; and why couldst thou not set about something else? There thou sittest with thy hands crossed." When she went out she said, "The creature is worth more than her salt. I must give her some work that is still harder."

Next morning she called the girl, and said, "There is a spoon for thee; with that thou must empty out for me the great pond which is beside the garden, and if it is not done by night, thou knowest what will happen." The girl took the spoon, and saw that it was full of holes; but even if it had not been, she never could have emptied the pond with it. She set to work at once, knelt down by the water, into which her tears were falling, and began to empty it. But the good old woman appeared again, and when she learnt the cause of her grief, she said, "Be of good cheer, my child. Go into the thicket and lie down and sleep; I will soon do thy work."

As soon as the old woman was alone, she barely touched the pond, and a vapor rose up on high from the water, and mingled itself with the clouds. Gradually the pond was emptied, and when the maiden awoke before sunset and came thither, she saw nothing but the fishes which were struggling in the mud. She went to her step-mother, and showed her that the work was done. "It ought to have been done long before this," said she, and grew white with anger, but she meditated something new.

On the third morning she said to the girl, "Thou must build me a castle on the plain there, and it must be ready by the evening." The maiden was dismayed, and said, "How can I complete such a great work?" "I will endure no opposition," screamed the step-mother. "If thou canst empty a pond with a spoon that is full of holes, thou canst build a castle too. I will take possession of it this very day, and if anything is wanting, even if it be the most trifling thing in the kitchen or cellar, thou knowest what lies before thee!" She drove the girl out, and when she entered the valley, the rocks were there, piled up one above the other, and all her strength would not have enabled her even to move the very smallest of them. She sat down and wept, and still she hoped the old woman would help her. The old woman was not long in coming; she comforted her and said, "Lie down there in the shade and sleep, and I will soon build the castle for thee. If it would be a pleasure to thee, thou canst live in it thyself."

When the maiden had gone away, the old woman touched the gray rocks. They began to rise, and immediately moved together as if giants had built the walls; and on these the building arose, and it seemed as if countless hands were working invisibly, and placing one stone upon another. There was a dull heavy noise from the ground; pillars arose of their own accord on high, and placed themselves in order near each other. The tiles laid themselves in order on the roof, and when noon-day came, the great weather-cock was already turning itself on the summit of the tower, like a golden figure of the Virgin with fluttering garments. The inside of the castle was being finished while evening was drawing near. How the old woman managed it, I know not; but the walls of the rooms were hung with silk and velvet, embroidered chairs were there, and richly ornamented arm-chairs by marble tables; crystal chandeliers hung down from the ceilings, and mirrored themselves in the smooth pavement; green parrots were there in gilt cages, and so were strange birds which sang most beautifully, and there was on all sides as much magnificence as if a king were going to live there.

The sun was just setting when the girl awoke, and the brightness of a thousand lights flashed in her face. She hurried to the castle, and entered by the open door. The steps were spread with red cloth, and the golden balustrade beset with flowering trees. When she saw the splendor of the apartment, she stood as if turned to stone. Who knows how long she might have stood there if she had not remembered the step-mother? "Alas!" she said to herself, "if she could but be satisfied at last, and would give up making my life a misery to me." The girl went and told her that the castle was ready. "I will move into it at once," said she, and rose from her seat.

When they entered the castle, she was forced to hold her hand before her eyes, the brilliancy of everything was so dazzling. "Thou seest," said she to the girl, "how easy it has been for thee to do this; I ought to have given thee something harder." She went through all the rooms, and examined every corner to see if anything was wanting or defective; but she could discover nothing. "Now we will go down below," said she, looking at the girl with malicious eyes. "The kitchen and the cellar still have to be examined, and if thou hast forgotten anything thou shalt not escape thy punishment." But the fire was burning on the hearth, and the meat was cooking in the pans, the tongs and shovel were leaning against the wall, and the shining brazen utensils all arranged in sight. Nothing was wanting, not even a coal-box and water-pail. "Which is the way to the cellar?" she cried. "If that is not abundantly filled, it shall go ill with thee." She herself raised up the trap-door and descended; but she had hardly made two steps before the heavy trap-door which was only laid back, fell down. The girl heard a scream, lifted up the door very quickly to go to her aid, but she had fallen down, and the girl found her lying lifeless at the bottom.

And now the magnificent castle belonged to the girl alone. She at first did not know how to reconcile herself to her good fortune. Beautiful dresses were hanging in the wardrobes, the chests were filled with gold or silver, or with pearls and jewels, and she never felt a desire that she was not able to gratify. And soon the fame of the beauty and riches of the maiden went over all the world. Wooers presented themselves daily, but none pleased her. At length the son of the King came and he knew how to touch her heart, and she betrothed herself to him. In the garden of the castle was a lime-tree, under which they were one day sitting together, when he said to her, "I will go home and obtain my father's consent to our marriage. I entreat thee to wait for me here under this lime-tree, I shall be back with thee in a few hours." The maiden kissed him on his left cheek, and said, "Keep true to me, and never let any one else kiss thee on this cheek. I will wait here under the lime-tree until thou returnest."

The maid stayed beneath the lime-tree until sunset, but he did not return. She sat three days from morning till evening, waiting for him, but in vain. As he still was not there by the fourth day, she said, "Some accident has assuredly befallen him. I will go out and seek him, and will not come back until I have found him." She packed up three of her most beautiful dresses, one embroidered with bright stars, the second with silver moons, the third with golden suns, tied up a handful of jewels in her handkerchief, and set out. She inquired everywhere for her betrothed, but no one had seen him; no one knew anything about him. Far and wide did she wander through the world, but she found him not. At last she hired herself to a farmer as a cow-herd, and buried her dresses and jewels beneath a stone.

And now she lived as a herdswoman, guarded her herd, and was very sad and full of longing for her beloved one; she had a little calf which she taught to know her, and fed it out of her own hand, and when she said,

> "Little calf, little calf, kneel by my side,
> And do not forget thy shepherd-maid,
> As the prince forgot his betrothed bride,
> Who waited for him 'neath the lime-tree's shade."

the little calf knelt down, and she stroked it.

And when she had lived for a couple of years alone and full of grief, a report was spread over all the land that the King's daughter was about to celebrate her marriage. The road to the town passed through the village where the maiden was living, and it came to pass that once when the maiden was driving out her herd, her bridegroom traveled by. He was sitting proudly on his horse, and never looked round, but when she saw him she recognized her beloved, and it was just as if a sharp knife had pierced her heart. "Alas!" said she, "I believed him true to me, but he has forgotten me."

Next day he again came along the road. When he was near her she said to the little calf,

> "Little calf, little calf, kneel by my side,
> And do not forget thy shepherd-maid,
> As the prince forgot his betrothed bride,
> Who waited for him 'neath the lime-tree's shade."

When he was aware of the voice, he looked down and reined in his horse. He looked into the herd's face, and then put his hands before his eyes as if he were trying to remember something, but he soon rode onwards and was out of sight. "Alas!" said she, "he no longer knows me," and her grief was ever greater.

Soon after this a great festival three days long was to be held at the King's court, and the whole country was invited to it.

"Now will I try my last chance," thought the maiden, and when evening came she went to the stone under which she had buried her treasures. She took out the dress with the golden suns, put it on, and adorned herself with the jewels. She let down her hair, which she had concealed under a handkerchief, and it fell down in long curls about her, and thus she went into the town, and in the darkness was observed by no one. When she entered the brightly-lighted hall, every one started back in amazement, but no one knew who she was. The King's son went to meet her, but he did not recognize her. He led her out to dance, and was so enchanted with her beauty, that he thought no more of the other bride. When the feast was over, she vanished in the crowd, and hastened before daybreak to the village, where she once more put on her herd's dress.

Next evening she took out the dress with the silver moons, and put a half-moon made of precious stones in her hair. When she appeared at the festival, all eyes were turned upon her, but the King's son hastened to meet her, and filled with love for her, danced with her alone, and no longer so much as glanced at anyone else. Before she went away she was forced to promise him to come again to the festival on the last evening.

When she appeared for the third time, she wore the star-dress which sparkled at every step she took, and her hair-ribbon and girdle were starred with jewels. The prince had already been waiting for her for a long time, and forced his way up to her. "Do but tell who thou art," said he, "I feel just as if I had already known thee a long time." "Dost thou not know what I did when thou leftest me?" Then she stepped up to him, and kissed him on his left cheek, and in a moment it was as if scales fell from his eyes, and he recognized the true bride. "Come," said he to her, "here I stay no longer," gave her his hand, and led her down to the carriage. The horses hurried away to the magic castle as if the wind had been harnessed to the carriage. The illuminated windows already shone in the distance. When they drove past the lime-tree, countless glow-worms were swarming about it. It shook its branches, and sent forth their fragrance. On the steps flowers were blooming, and the room echoed with the song of strange birds, but in the hall the entire court was assembled, and the priest was waiting to marry the bridegroom to the true bride.

Rumpelstiltzkin

(FROM *THE BLUE FAIRY BOOK*)

There was once upon a time a poor miller who had a very beautiful daughter. Now it happened one day that he had an audience with the King, and in order to appear a person of some importance he told him that he had a daughter who could spin straw into gold. "Now that's a talent worth having," said the King to the miller; "if your daughter is as clever as you say, bring her to my palace to-morrow, and I'll put her to the test." When the girl was brought to him he led her into a room full of straw, gave her a spinning-wheel and spindle, and said: "Now set to work and spin all night till early dawn, and if by that time you haven't spun the straw into gold you shall die." Then he closed the door behind him and left her alone inside.

So the poor miller's daughter sat down, and didn't know what in the world she was to do. She hadn't the least idea of how to spin straw into gold, and became at last so miserable that she began to cry. Suddenly the door opened, and in stepped a tiny little man and said: "Good-evening, Miss Miller-maid; why are you crying so bitterly?" "Oh!" answered the girl, "I have to spin straw into gold, and haven't a notion how it's done." "What will you give me if I spin it for you?" asked the manikin. "My necklace," replied the girl. The little man took the necklace, sat himself down at the wheel, and whir, whir, whir, the wheel went round three times, and the bobbin was full. Then he put on another, and whir, whir, whir, the wheel went round three times, and the second too was full; and so it went on till the morning, when all the straw was spun away, and all the bobbins were full of gold. As soon as the sun rose the King came, and when he perceived the gold he was astonished and delighted, but his heart only lusted more than ever after the precious metal. He had the miller's daughter put into another room full of straw, much bigger than the first, and bade her, if she valued her life, spin it all into gold before the following morning. The girl didn't know what to do, and began to cry; then the door opened as before, and the tiny little man

209

appeared and said: "What'll you give me if I spin the straw into gold for you?" "The ring from my finger," answered the girl. The manikin took the ring, and whir! round went the spinning-wheel again, and when morning broke he had spun all the straw into glittering gold. The King was pleased beyond measure at the sights but his greed for gold was still not satisfied, and he had the miller's daughter brought into a yet bigger room full of straw, and said: "You must spin all this away in the night; but if you succeed this time you shall become my wife." "She's only a miller's daughter, it's true," he thought; "but I couldn't find a richer wife if I were to search the whole world over." When the girl was alone the little man appeared for the third time, and said: "What'll you give me if I spin the straw for you once again?" "I've nothing more to give," answered the girl. "Then promise me when you are Queen to give me your first child." "Who knows what may not happen before that?" thought the miller's daughter; and besides, she saw no other way out of it, so she promised the manikin what he demanded, and he set to work once more and spun the straw into gold. When the King came in the morning, and found everything as he had desired, he straightway made her his wife, and the miller's daughter became a queen.

When a year had passed a beautiful son was born to her, and she thought no more of the little man, till all of a sudden one day he stepped into her room and said: "Now give me what you promised." The Queen was in a great state, and offered the little man all the riches in her kingdom if he would only leave her the child. But the manikin said: "No, a living creature is dearer to me than all the treasures in the world." Then the Queen began to cry and sob so bitterly that the little man was sorry for her, and said: "I'll give you three days to guess my name, and if you find it out in that time you may keep your child."

Then the Queen pondered the whole night over all the names she had ever heard, and sent a messenger to scour the land, and to pick up far and near any names he could come across. When the little man arrived on the following day she began with Kasper, Melchior, Belshazzar, and all the other names she knew, in a string, but at each one the manikin called out: "That's not my name." The next day she sent to inquire the names of all the people in the neighborhood, and had a long list of the most uncommon and extraordinary for the little man when he made his appearance. "Is your name, perhaps, Sheepshanks Cruickshanks, Spindleshanks?" but he always replied: "That's not my name." On the third day the messenger returned and announced: "I have not been able to find any new names, but as I came upon a high hill round the corner of the wood, where the foxes and hares bid each other good-night, I saw a little house, and in front of the house burned a fire, and round the fire sprang the most grotesque little man, hopping on one leg and crying:

> "To-morrow I brew, to-day I bake,
> And then the child away I'll take;
> For little deems my royal dame
> That Rumpelstiltzkin is my name!"

You can imagine the Queen's delight at hearing the name, and when the little man stepped in shortly afterward and asked: "Now, my lady Queen, what's my name?" she asked first: "Is your name Conrad?" "No." "Is your name Harry?" "No." "Is your name, perhaps, Rumpelstiltzkin?" "Some demon has told you that! some demon has told you that!" screamed the little man, and in his rage drove his right foot so far into the ground that it sank in up to his waist; then in a passion he seized the left foot with both hands and tore himself in two.

Princess Minon-Minette

(FROM *THE PINK FAIRY BOOK*)

Once upon a time there lived a young king whose name was Souci, and he had been brought up, ever since he was a baby, by the fairy Inconstancy. Now the fairy Girouette had a kind heart, but she was a very trying person to live with, for she never knew her own mind for two minutes together, and as she was the sole ruler at Court till the prince grew up everything was always at sixes and sevens. At first she determined to follow the old custom of keeping the young king ignorant of the duties he would have to perform some day; then, quite suddenly, she resigned the reins of government into his hands; but, unluckily, it was too late to train him properly for the post. However, the fairy did not think of that, but, carried away by her new ideas, she hastily formed a Council, and named as Prime Minister the excellent "Ditto," so called because he had never been known to contradict anybody.

Young Prince Souci had a handsome face, and at the bottom a good deal of common sense; but he had never been taught good manners, and was shy and awkward; and had, besides, never learned how to use his brains.

Under these circumstances it is not surprising that the Council did not get through much work. Indeed, the affairs of the country fell into such disorder that at last the people broke out into open rebellion, and it was only the courage of the king, who continued to play the flute while swords and spears were flashing before the palace gate, that prevented civil war from being declared.

No sooner was the revolt put down than the Council turned their attention to the question of the young king's marriage. Various princesses were proposed to him, and the fairy, who was anxious to get the affair over before she left the Court for ever, gave it as her opinion that the Princess Diaphana would make the most suitable wife. Accordingly envoys were sent to bring back an exact report of the princess's looks and ways, and they returned saying that she was tall and well made, but so very light that the equerries who accompanied her in her walks had to be always watching her, lest she should suddenly be blown away. This had happened so often that her subjects lived in terror of losing her altogether, and tried everything they could think of to keep her to the ground. They even suggested that she should carry weights in her pockets, or have them tied to her ankles; but this idea was given up, as the princess found it so uncomfortable. At length it was decided that she was never to go out in a wind, and in order to make matters surer still the equerries each held the end of a string which was fastened to her waist.

The Council talked over this report for some days, and then the king made up his mind that he would judge for himself, and pretend to be his own ambassador. This plan was by no means new, but it had often succeeded, and, anyhow, they could think of nothing better.

Such a splendid embassy had never before been seen in any country. The kingdom was left in the charge of the Prime Minister, who answered "Ditto" to everything; but the choice was better than it seemed, for the worthy man was much beloved by the people, as he agreed with all they said, and they left him feeling very pleased with themselves and their own wisdom.

When the king arrived at Diaphana's Court he found a magnificent reception awaiting him, for, though they pretended not to know who he was, secrets like this are never hidden. Now the young king had a great dislike to long ceremonies, so he proposed that his second interview with the princess should take place in the garden. The princess made some difficulties, but, as the weather was lovely and very still, she at last consented to the king's wishes. But no sooner had they finished their first bows and curtseys than a slight breeze sprung up, and began to sway the princess, whose equerries had retired out of respect. The king went forward to steady her, but the wind that he caused only drove her further away from him. He rushed after her exclaiming, "O princess! are you really running away from me?"

"Good gracious, no!" she replied. "Run a little quicker and you will be able to stop me, and I shall be for ever grateful. That is what comes of talking in a garden," she added in disgust; "as if one wasn't much better in a room that was tightly closed all round."

The king ran as fast as he could, but the wind ran faster still, and in a moment the princess was whirled to the bottom of the garden, which was bounded by a ditch. She cleared it like a bird, and the king, who was obliged to stop short at the edge, saw the lovely Diaphana flying over the plain, sometimes driven to the right, sometimes to the left, till at last she vanished out of sight.

By this time the whole court were running over the plain, some on foot and some on horseback, all hurrying to the help of their princess, who really was in some danger, for the wind was rising to the force of a gale. The king looked on for a little, and then returned with his attendants to the palace, reflecting all the while on the extreme lightness of his proposed bride and the absurdity of having a wife that rose in the air better than any kite. He thought on the whole that it would be wiser not to wait longer, but to depart at once, and he started on horseback at the very moment when the princess had been found by her followers, wet to the skin, and blown against a rick. Souci met the carriage which was bringing her home, and stopped to congratulate her on her escape, and to advise her to put on dry clothes. Then he continued his journey.

It took a good while for the king to get home again, and he was rather cross at having had so much trouble for nothing. Besides which, his courtiers made fun at his adventure, and he did not like being laughed at, though of course they did not dare to do it before his face. And the end of it was that very soon he started on his travels again, only allowing one equerry to accompany him, and even this attendant he managed to lose the moment he had left his own kingdom behind him.

Now it was the custom in those days for princes and princesses to be brought up by fairies, who loved them as their own children, and did not mind what inconvenience they put other people to for their sakes, for all the world as if they had been real mothers. The fairy Aveline, who lived in a country that touched at one point the kingdom of King Souci, had under her care the lovely Princess Minon-Minette, and had made up her mind to marry her to the young king, who, in spite of his awkward manners, which could be improved, was really very much nicer than most of the young men she was likely to meet.

So Aveline made her preparations accordingly, and began by arranging that the equerry should lose himself in the forest, after which she took away the king's sword and his horse while he lay asleep under a tree. Her reason for this was that she felt persuaded that, finding himself suddenly alone and robbed of everything, the king would hide his real birth, and would have to fall back on his powers of pleasing, like other men, which would be much better for him.

When the king awoke and found that the tree to which he had tied his horse had its lowest branch broken, and that nothing living was in sight, he was much dismayed, and sought high and low for his lost treasure, but all in vain. After a time he began to get hungry, so he decided that he had better try to find his way out of the forest, and perhaps he might have a chance of getting something to eat. He had only gone a few steps when he met Aveline, who had taken the shape of an old woman with a heavy bundle of faggots on her back. She staggered along the path and almost fell at his feet, and Souci, afraid that she might have hurt herself, picked her up and set her on her feet again before passing on his way. But he was not to be let off so easy.

"What about my bundle?" cried the old woman. "Where is your politeness? Really, you seem to have been very nicely brought up! What have they taught you?"

"Taught me? Nothing," replied he.

"I can well believe it!" she said. "You don't know even how to pick up a bundle. Oh, you can come near; I am cleverer than you, and know how to pick up a bundle very well."

The king blushed at her words, which he felt had a great deal of truth in them, and took up the bundle meekly.

Aveline, delighted at the success of her first experiment, hobbled along after him, chattering all the while, as old women do.

"I wish," she said, "that all kings had done as much once in their lives. Then they would know what a lot of trouble it takes to get wood for their fires."

Souci felt this to be true, and was sorry for the old woman.

"Where are we going to?" asked he.

"To the castle of the White Demon; and if you are in want of work I will find you something to do."

"But I can't do anything," he said, "except carry a bundle, and I shan't earn much by that."

"Oh, you are learning," replied the old woman, "and it isn't bad for a first lesson." But the king was paying very little attention to her, for he was rather cross and very tired. Indeed, he felt that he really could not carry the bundle any further, and was about to lay it down when up came a young maiden more beautiful than the day, and covered with precious stones. She ran to them, exclaiming to the old woman,

"Oh, you poor thing! I was just coming after you to see if I could help you."

"Here is a young man," replied the old woman, "who will be quite ready to give you up the bundle. You see he does not look as if he enjoyed carrying it."

"Will you let me take it, sir?" she asked.

But the king felt ashamed of himself, and held on to it tightly, while the presence of the princess put him in a better temper.

So they all traveled together till they arrived at a very ordinary-looking house, which Aveline pointed out as the castle of the White Demon, and told the king that he might put down his bundle in the courtyard. The young man was terribly afraid of being recognized by someone in this strange position, and would have turned on his heel and gone away had it not been for the thought of Minon-Minette. Still, he felt very awkward and lonely, for both the princess and the old woman had entered the castle without taking the slightest notice of the young man, who remained where he was for some time, not quite knowing what he had better do. At length a servant arrived and led him up into a beautiful room filled with people, who were either playing on musical instruments or talking in a lively manner, which astonished the king, who stood silently listening, and not at all pleased at the want of attention paid him.

Matters went on this way for some time. Every day the king fell more and more in love with Minon-Minette, and every day the princess seemed more and more taken up with other people. At last, in despair, the prince sought out the old woman, to try to get some advice from her as to his conduct, or, anyway, to have the pleasure of talking about Minon-Minette.

He found her spinning in an underground chamber, but quite ready to tell him all he wanted to know. In answer to his questions he learned that in order to win the hand of the princess it was not enough to be born a prince, for she would marry nobody who had not proved himself faithful, and had, besides, all those talents and accomplishments which help to make people happy.

For a moment Souci was very much cast down on hearing this, but then he plucked up. "Tell me what I must do in order to win the heart of the princess, and no matter how hard it is I will do it. And show me how I can repay you for your kindness, and you shall have anything I can give you. Shall I bring in your bundle of faggots every day?"

"It is enough that you should have made the offer," replied the old woman; and she added, holding out a skein of thread, "Take this; one day you will be thankful for it, and when it becomes useless your difficulties will be past."

"Is it the skein of my life?" he asked.

"It is the skein of your love's ill-luck," she said.

And he took it and went away.

Now the fairy Girouette, who had brought up Souci, had an old friend called Grimace, the protectress of Prince Fluet. Grimace often talked over the young prince's affairs with Girouette, and, when she decided that he was old enough to govern his own kingdom, consulted Girouette as to a suitable wife. Girouette, who never stopped to think or to make inquiries, drew such a delightful picture of Minon-Minette that Grimace determined to spare no pains to bring about the marriage, and accordingly Fluet was presented at court. But though the young man was pleasant and handsome, the princess thought him rather womanish in some ways, and displayed her opinion so openly as to draw upon herself and Aveline the anger of the fairy, who declared that Minon-Minette should never know happiness till she had found a bridge without an arch and a bird without feathers. So saying, she also went away.

Before the king set out afresh on his travels Aveline had restored to him his horse and his sword, and though these were but small consolation for the absence of the princess, they were better than nothing, for he felt that somehow they might be the means of leading him back to her.

After crossing several deserts the king arrived at length in a country that seemed inhabited, but the instant he stepped over the border he was seized and flung into chains, and dragged at once to the capital. He asked his guards why he was treated like this, but the only answer he got was that he was in the territory of the Iron King, for in those days countries had no names of their own, but were called after their rulers.

The young man was led into the presence of the Iron King, who was seated on a black throne in a hall also hung with black, as a token of mourning for all the relations whom he had put to death.

"What are you doing in my country?" he cried fiercely.

"I came here by accident," replied Souci, "and if I ever escape from your clutches I will take warning by you and treat my subjects differently."

"Do you dare to insult me in my own court?" cried the king. "Away with him to Little Ease!"

Now Little Ease was an iron cage hung by four thick chains in the middle of a great vaulted hall, and the prisoner inside could neither sit, nor stand, nor lie; and, besides that, he was made to suffer by turns unbearable heat and cold, while a hundred heavy bolts kept everything safe. Girouette, whose business it was to see after Souci, had forgotten his existence in the excitement of some new idea, and he would not have been alive long to trouble anybody if Aveline had not come to the rescue and whispered in his ear, "And the skein of thread?" He took it up obediently, though he did not see how it would help him but he tied it round one of the iron bars of his cage, which seemed the only thing he could do, and gave a pull. To his surprise the bar gave way at once, and he found he could break it into a thousand pieces. After this it did not take him long to get out of his cage, or to treat the closely barred windows of the hall in the same manner. But even after he had done all this freedom appeared as far from him as ever, for between him and the open country was a high wall, and so smooth that not even a monkey could climb it. Then Souci's heart died within him. He saw nothing for it but to submit to some horrible death, but he determined that the Iron King should not profit more than he could help, and flung his precious thread into the air, saying, as he did so, "O fairy, my misfortunes are greater than your power. I am grateful for your goodwill, but take back your gift!" The fairy had pity on his youth and want of faith, and took care that one end of the thread remained in his hand. He suddenly felt a jerk, and saw that the thread must have caught on something, and this thought filled him with the daring that is born of despair. "Better," he said to himself, "trust to a thread than to the mercies of a king"; and, gliding down, he found himself safe on the other side of the wall. Then he rolled up the thread and put it carefully into his pocket, breathing silent thanks to the fairy.

Now Minon-Minette had been kept informed by Aveline of the prince's adventures, and when she heard of the way in which he had been treated by the Iron King she became furious, and began to prepare for war. She made her plans with all the secrecy she could, but when great armies are collected people are apt to suspect a storm is brewing, and of course it is very difficult to keep anything hidden from fairy godmothers. Anyway, Grimace soon heard of it, and as she had never forgiven Minon-Minette for refusing Prince Fluet, she felt that here was her chance of revenge.

Up to this time Aveline had been able to put a stop to many of Grimace's spiteful tricks, and to keep guard over Minon-Minette, but she had no power over anything that happened at a distance; and when the princess declared her intention of putting herself at the head of her army, and began to train herself to bear fatigue by hunting daily, the fairy entreated her to be careful never to cross the borders of her dominions without Aveline to protect her. The princess at once gave her promise, and all went well for some days. Unluckily one morning, as Minon-Minette was cantering slowly on her beautiful white horse, thinking a great deal about Souci and not at all of the boundaries of her kingdom (of which, indeed, she was very ignorant), she suddenly found herself in front of a house made entirely of dead leaves, which somehow brought all sorts of unpleasant things into her head. She remembered Aveline's warning, and tried to turn her horse, but it stood as still as if it had been marble. Then the princess felt that she was slowly, and against her will, being dragged to the ground. She shrieked, and clung tightly to the saddle, but it was all in vain; she longed to fly, but something outside herself proved too strong for her, and she was forced to take the path that led to the House of Dead Leaves.

Scarcely had her feet touched the threshold than Grimace appeared. "So here you are at last, Minon-Minette! I have been watching for you a long time, and my trap was ready for you from the beginning. Come here, my darling! I will teach you to make war on my friends! Things won't turn out exactly as you fancied. What you have got to do now is to go on your knees to the king and crave his pardon, and before he consents to a peace you will have to implore him to grant you the favor of becoming his wife. Meanwhile you will have to be my servant."

From that day the poor princess was put to the hardest and dirtiest work, and each morning something more disagreeable seemed to await her. Besides which, she had no food but a little black bread, and no bed but a little straw. Out of pure spite she was sent in the heat of the day to look after the geese, and would most likely have got a sunstroke if she had not happened to pick up in the fields a large fan, with which she sheltered her face. To be sure, a fan seems rather an odd possession for a goose-girl, but the princess did not think of that, and she forgot all her troubles when, on opening the fan to use it as a parasol, out tumbled a letter from her lover. Then she felt sure that the fairy had not forgotten her, and took heart.

When Grimace saw that Minon-Minette still managed to look as white as snow, instead of being burnt as brown as a berry, she wondered what could have happened, and began to watch her closely. The following day, when the sun was at its highest and hottest, she noticed her draw a fan from the folds of her dress and hold it before her eyes. The fairy, in a rage, tried to snatch it from her, but the princess would not let it go. "Give me that fan at once!" cried Grimace.

"Never while I live!" answered the princess, and, not knowing where it would be safest, placed it under her feet. In an instant she felt herself rising from the ground, with the fan always beneath her, and while Grimace was too much blinded by her fury to notice what was going on the princess was quickly soaring out of her reach.

All this time Souci had been wandering through the world with his precious thread carefully fastened round him, seeking every possible and impossible place where his beloved princess might chance to be. But though he sometimes found traces of her, or even messages scratched on a rock, or cut in the bark of a tree, she herself was nowhere to be found. "If she is not on the earth," said Souci to himself, "perhaps she is hiding somewhere in the air. It is there that I shall find her." So, by the help of his thread, he tried to mount upwards, but he could go such a little way, and hurt himself dreadfully when he tumbled back to earth again. Still he did not give up, and after many days of efforts and tumbles he found to his great joy that he could go a little higher and stay up a little longer than he had done at first, and by-and-bye he was able to live in the air altogether. But alas! the world of the air seemed as empty of her as the world below, and Souci was beginning to despair, and to think that he must go and search the world that lay in the sea. He was floating sadly along, not paying any heed to where he was going, when he saw in the distance a beautiful, bright sort of bird coming towards him. His heart beat fast—he did not know why—and as they both drew near the voice of the princess exclaimed, "Behold the bird without feathers and the bridge without an arch!"

So their first meeting took place in the air, but it was none the less happy for that; and the fan grew big enough to hold the king as well as Aveline, who had hastened to give them some good advice. She guided the fan above the spot where the two armies lay encamped before each other ready to give battle. The fight was long and bloody, but in the end the Iron King was obliged to give way and surrender to the princess, who set him to keep King Souci's sheep, first making him swear a solemn oath that he would treat them kindly.

Then the marriage took place, in the presence of Girouette, whom they had the greatest trouble to find, and who was much astonished to discover how much business had been got through in her absence.

An Impossible Enchantment

(From *The Gray Fairy Book*)

There once lived a king who was much loved by his people, and he, too, loved them warmly. He led a very happy life, but he had the greatest dislike to the idea of marrying, nor had he ever felt the slightest wish to fall in love. His subjects begged him to marry, and at last he promised to try to do so. But as, so far, he had never cared for any woman he had seen, he made up his mind to travel in hopes of meeting some lady he could love.

So he arranged all the affairs of state in an orderly manner, and set out, attended by only one equerry, who, though not very clever, had most excellent good sense. These people indeed generally make the best fellow-travelers.

The king explored several countries, doing all he could to fall in love, but in vain; and at the end of two years' journeys he turned his face towards home, with as free a heart as when he set out.

As he was riding along through a forest he suddenly heard the most awful miawing and shrieking of cats you can imagine. The noise drew nearer, and nearer, and at last they saw a hundred huge Spanish cats rush through the trees close to them. They were so closely packed together that you could easily have covered them with a large cloak, and all were following the same track. They were closely pursued by two enormous apes, dressed in purple suits, with the prettiest and best made boots you ever saw.

The apes were mounted on superb mastiffs, and spurred them on in hot haste, blowing shrill blasts on little toy trumpets all the time.

The king and his equerry stood still to watch this strange hunt, which was followed by twenty or more little dwarfs, some mounted on wolves, and leading relays, and others with cats in leash. The dwarfs were all dressed in purple silk liveries like the apes.

A moment later a beautiful young woman mounted on a tiger came in sight. She passed close to the king, riding at full speed, without taking any notice of him; but he was at once enchanted by her, and his heart was gone in a moment.

221

To his great joy he saw that one of the dwarfs had fallen behind the rest, and at once began to question him.

The dwarf told him that the lady he had just seen was the Princess Mutinosa, the daughter of the king in whose country they were at that moment. He added that the princess was very fond of hunting, and that she was now in pursuit of rabbits.

The king then asked the way to the court, and having been told it, hurried off, and reached the capital in a couple of hours.

As soon as he arrived, he presented himself to the king and queen, and on mentioning his own name and that of his country, was received with open arms. Not long after, the princess returned, and hearing that the hunt had been very successful, the king complimented her on it, but she would not answer a word.

Her silence rather surprised him, but he was still more astonished when he found that she never spoke once all through supper-time. Sometimes she seemed about to speak, but whenever this was the case her father or mother at once took up the conversation. However, this silence did not cool the king's affection, and when he retired to his rooms at night he confided his feelings to his faithful equerry. But the equerry was by no means delighted at his king's love affair, and took no pains to hide his disappointment.

"But why are you vexed?" asked the king. "Surely the princess is beautiful enough to please anyone?"

"She is certainly very handsome," replied the equerry, "but to be really happy in love something more than beauty is required. To tell the truth, sire," he added, "her expression seems to me hard."

"That is pride and dignity," said the king, "and nothing can be more becoming."

"Pride or hardness, as you will," said the equerry; "but to my mind the choice of so many fierce creatures for her amusements seems to tell of a fierce nature, and I also think there is something suspicious in the care taken to prevent her speaking."

The equerry's remarks were full of good sense; but as opposition is only apt to increase love in the hearts of men, and especially of kings who hate being contradicted, this king begged, the very next day, for the hand of the Princess Mutinosa. It was granted him on two conditions.

The first was that the wedding should take place the very next day; and the second, that he should not speak to the princess till she was his wife; to all of which the king agreed, in spite of his equerry's objections, so that the first word he heard his bride utter was the "Yes" she spoke at their marriage.

Once married, however, she no longer placed any check on herself, and her ladies-in-waiting came in for plenty of rude speeches—even the king did not escape scolding; but as he was a good-tempered man, and very much in love, he bore it patiently. A few days after the wedding the newly married pair set out for their kingdom without leaving many regrets behind.

The good equerry's fears proved only too true, as the king found out to his cost. The young queen made herself most disagreeable to all her court, her spite and bad temper knew no bounds, and before the end of a month she was known far and wide as a regular vixen.

One day, when riding out, she met a poor old woman walking along the road, who made a curtsy and was going on, when the queen had her stopped, and cried: "You are a very impertinent person; don't you know that I am the queen? And how dare you not make me a deeper curtsy?"

"Madam," said the old woman, "I have never learnt how to measure curtsies; but I had no wish to fail in proper respect."

"What!" screamed the queen; "she dares to answer! Tie her to my horse's tail and I'll just carry her at once to the best dancing-master in the town to learn how to curtsy."

The old woman shrieked for mercy, but the queen would not listen, and only mocked when she said she was protected by the fairies. At last the poor old thing submitted to be tied up, but when the queen urged her horse on he never stirred. In vain she spurred him, he seemed turned to bronze. At the same moment the cord with which the old woman was tied changed into wreaths of flowers, and she herself into a tall and stately lady.

Looking disdainfully at the queen, she said, "Bad woman, unworthy of your crown; I wished to judge for myself whether all I heard of you was true. I have now no doubt of it, and you shall see whether the fairies are to be laughed at."

So saying the fairy Placida (that was her name) blew a little gold whistle, and a chariot appeared drawn by six splendid ostriches. In it was seated the fairy queen, escorted by a dozen other fairies mounted on dragons.

All having dismounted, Placida told her adventures, and the fairy queen approved all she had done, and proposed turning Mutinosa into bronze like her horse. Placida, however, who was very kind and gentle, begged for a milder sentence, and at last it was settled that Mutinosa should become her slave for life unless she should have a child to take her place.

The king was told of his wife's fate and submitted to it, which, as he could do nothing to help it, was the only course open to him.

The fairies then all dispersed, Placida taking her slave with her, and on reaching her palace she said: "You ought by rights to be scullion, but as you have been delicately brought up the change might be too great for you. I shall therefore only order you to sweep my rooms carefully, and to wash and comb my little dog."

Mutinosa felt there was no use in disobeying, so she did as she was bid and said nothing.

After some time she gave birth to a most lovely little girl, and when she was well again the fairy gave her a good lecture on her past life, made her promise to behave better in future, and sent her back to the king, her husband.

Placida now gave herself up entirely to the little princess who was left in her charge. She anxiously thought over which of the fairies she would invite to be godmothers, so as to secure the best gift, for her adopted child.

At last she decided on two very kindly and cheerful fairies, and asked them to the christening feast. Directly it was over the baby was brought to them in a lovely crystal cradle hung with red silk curtains embroidered with gold.

The little thing smiled so sweetly at the fairies that they decided to do all they could for her. They began by naming her Graziella, and then Placida said: "You know, dear sisters, that the commonest form of spite or punishment among us consists of changing beauty to ugliness, cleverness to stupidity, and oftener still to change a person's form altogether. Now, as we can only each bestow one gift, I think the best plan will be for one of you to give her beauty, the other good understanding, whilst I will undertake that she shall never be changed into any other form."

The two godmothers quite agreed, and as soon as the little princess had received their gifts, they went home, and Placida gave herself up to the child's education. She succeeded so well with it, and little Graziella grew so lovely, that when she was still quite a child her fame was spread abroad only too much, and one day Placida was surprised by a visit from the Fairy Queen, who was attended by a very grave and severe-looking fairy.

The queen began at once: "I have been much surprised by your behavior to Mutinosa; she had insulted our whole race, and deserved punishment. You might forgive your own wrongs if you chose, but not those of others. You treated her very gently whilst she was with you, and I come now to avenge our wrongs on her daughter. You have ensured her being lovely and clever, and not subject to change of form, but I shall place her in an enchanted prison, which she shall never leave till she finds herself in the arms of a lover whom she herself loves. It will be my care to prevent anything of the kind happening."

The enchanted prison was a large high tower in the midst of the sea, built of shells of all shapes and colors. The lower floor was like a great bathroom, where the water was let in or off at will. The first floor contained the princess's apartments, beautifully furnished. On the second was a library, a large wardrobe-room filled with beautiful clothes and every kind of linen, a music room, a pantry with bins full of the best wines, and a store-room with all manner of preserves, bonbons, pastry and cakes, all of which remained as fresh as if just out of the oven.

The top of the tower was laid out like a garden, with beds of the loveliest flowers, fine fruit trees, and shady arbors and shrubs, where many birds sang among the branches.

The fairies escorted Graziella and her governess, Bonnetta, to the tower, and then mounted a dolphin which was waiting for them. At a little distance from the tower the queen waved her wand and summoned two thousand great fierce sharks, whom she ordered to keep close guard, and not to let a soul enter the tower.

The good governess took such pains with Graziella's education that when she was nearly grown up she was not only most accomplished, but a very sweet, good girl.

One day, as the princess was standing on a balcony, she saw the most extraordinary figure rise out of the sea. She quickly called Bonnetta to ask her what it could be. It looked like some kind of man, with a bluish face and long sea-green hair. He was swimming towards the tower, but the sharks took no notice of him.

"It must be a merman," said Bonnetta.

"A *man*, do you say?" cried Graziella; "let us hurry down to the door and see him nearer."

When they stood in the doorway the merman stopped to look at the princess and made many signs of admiration. His voice was very hoarse and husky, but when he found that he was not understood he took to signs. He carried a little basket made of osiers and filled with rare shells, which he presented to the princess.

She took it with signs of thanks; but as it was getting dusk she retired, and the merman plunged back into the sea.

When they were alone, Graziella said to her governess: "What a dreadful-looking creature that was! Why do those odious sharks let him come near the tower? I suppose all men are not like him?"

"No, indeed," replied Bonnetta. "I suppose the sharks look on him as a sort of relation, and so did not attack him."

A few days later the two ladies heard a strange sort of music, and looking out of the window, there was the merman, his head crowned with water plants, and blowing a great sea-shell with all his might.

They went down to the tower door, and Graziella politely accepted some coral and other marine curiosities he had brought her. After this he used to come every evening, and blow his shell, or dive and play antics under the princess's window. She contented herself with bowing to him from the balcony, but she would not go down to the door in spite of all his signs.

Some days later he came with a person of his own kind, but of another sex. Her hair was dressed with great taste, and she had a lovely voice. This new arrival induced the ladies to go down to the door. They were surprised to find that, after trying various languages, she at last spoke to them in their own, and paid Graziella a very pretty compliment on her beauty.

The mermaid noticed that the lower floor was full of water. "Why," cried she, "that is just the place for us, for we can't live quite out of water." So saying, she and her brother swam in and took up a position in the bathroom, the princess and her governess seating themselves on the steps which ran round the room.

"No doubt, madam," said the mermaid, "you have given up living on land so as to escape from crowds of lovers; but I fear that even here you cannot avoid them, for my brother is already dying of love for you, and I am sure that once you are seen in our city he will have many rivals."

She then went on to explain how grieved her brother was not to be able to make himself understood, adding: "I interpret for him, having been taught several languages by a fairy."

"Oh, then, you have fairies, too?" asked Graziella, with a sigh.

"Yes, we have," replied the mermaid; "but if I am not mistaken you have suffered from the fairies on earth."

The princess, on this, told her entire history to the mermaid, who assured her how sorry she felt for her, but begged her not to lose courage; adding, as she took her leave: "Perhaps, some day, you may find a way out of your difficulties."

The princess was delighted with this visit and with the hopes the mermaid held out. It was something to meet some one fresh to talk to.

"We will make acquaintance with several of these people," she said to her governess, "and I dare say they are not all as hideous as the first one we saw. Anyhow, we shan't be so dreadfully lonely."

"Dear me," said Bonnetta, "how hopeful young people are to be sure! As for me I feel afraid of these folk. But what do you think of the lover you have captivated?"

"Oh, I could never love him," cried the princess; "I can't bear him. But, perhaps, as his sister says they are related to the fairy Marina, they may be of some use to us."

The mermaid often returned, and each time she talked of her brother's love, and each time Graziella talked of her longing to escape from her prison, till at length the mermaid promised to bring the fairy Marina to see her, in hopes she might suggest something.

Next day the fairy came with the mermaid, and the princess received her with delight. After a little talk she begged Graziella to show her the inside of the tower and let her see the garden on the top, for with the help of crutches she could manage to move about, and being a fairy could live out of water for a long time, provided she wetted her forehead now and then.

Graziella gladly consented, and Bonnetta stayed below with the mermaid.

When they were in the garden the fairy said: "Let us lose no time, but tell me how I can be of use to you." Graziella then told all her story and Marina replied: "My dear princess, I can do nothing for you as regards dry land, for my power does not reach beyond my own element. I can only say that if you will honor my cousin by accepting his hand, you could then come and live among us. I could teach you in a moment to swim and dive with the best of us. I can harden your skin without spoiling its color. My cousin is one of the best matches in the sea, and I will bestow so many gifts on him that you will be quite happy."

The fairy talked so well and so long that the princess was rather impressed, and promised to think the matter over.

Just as they were going to leave the garden they saw a ship sailing nearer the tower than any other had done before. On the deck lay a young man under a splendid awning, gazing at the tower through a spy-glass; but before they could see anything clearly the ship moved away, and the two ladies parted, the fairy promising to return shortly.

As soon as she was gone Graziella told her governess what she had said. Bonnetta was not at all pleased at the turn matters were taking, for she did not fancy being turned into a mermaid in her old age. She thought the matter well over, and this was what she did. She was a very clever artist, and next morning she began to paint a picture of a handsome young man, with beautiful curly hair, a fine complexion, and lovely blue eyes. When it was finished she showed it to Graziella, hoping it would show her the difference there was between a fine young man and her marine suitor.

The princess was much struck by the picture, and asked anxiously whether there could be any man so good-looking in the world. Bonnetta assured her that there were plenty of them; indeed, many far handsomer.

"I can hardly believe that," cried the princess; "but, alas! if there are, I don't suppose I shall ever see them or they me, so what is the use? Oh, dear, how unhappy I am!"

She spent the rest of the day gazing at the picture, which certainly had the effect of spoiling all the merman's hopes or prospects.

After some days, the fairy Marina came back to hear what was decided; but Graziella hardly paid any attention to her, and showed such dislike to the idea of the proposed marriage that the fairy went off in a regular huff.

Without knowing it, the princess had made another conquest. On board the ship which had sailed so near was the handsomest prince in the world. He had heard of the enchanted tower, and determined to get as near it as he could. He had strong glasses on board, and whilst looking through them he saw the princess quite clearly, and fell desperately in love with her at once. He wanted to steer straight for the tower and to row off to it in a small boat, but his entire crew fell at his feet and begged him not to run such a risk. The captain, too, urged him not to attempt it. "You will only lead us all to certain death," he said. "Pray anchor nearer land, and I will then seek a kind fairy I know, who has always been most obliging to me, and who will, I am sure, try to help your Highness."

The prince rather unwillingly listened to reason. He landed at the nearest point, and sent off the captain in all haste to beg the fairy's advice and help. Meantime he had a tent pitched on the shore, and spent all his time gazing at the tower and looking for the princess through his spy-glass.

After a few days the captain came back, bringing the fairy with him. The prince was delighted to see her, and paid her great attention. "I have heard about this matter," she said; "and, to lose no time, I am going to send off a trusty pigeon to test the enchantment. If there is any weak spot he is sure to find it out and get in. I shall bid him bring a flower back as a sign of success, and if he does so I quite hope to get you in too."

"But," asked the prince, "could I not send a line by the pigeon to tell the princess of my love?"

"Certainly," replied the fairy, "it would be a very good plan."

So the prince wrote as follows:—

Lovely Princess,—I adore you, and beg you to accept my heart, and to believe there is nothing I will not do to end your misfortunes.—BLONDEL.

This note was tied round the pigeon's neck, and he flew off with it at once. He flew fast till he got near the tower, when a fierce wind blew so hard against him that he could not get on. But he was not to be beaten, but flew carefully round the top of the tower till he came to one spot which, by some mistake, had not been enchanted like the rest. He quickly slipped into the arbor and waited for the princess.

Before long Graziella appeared alone, and the pigeon at once fluttered to meet her, and seemed so tame that she stopped to caress the pretty creature. As she did so she saw it had a pink ribbon round its neck, and tied to the ribbon was a letter. She read it over several times and then wrote this answer:—

You say you love me; but I cannot promise to love you without seeing you. Send me your portrait by this faithful messenger. If I return it to you, you must give up hope; but if I keep it you will know that to help me will be to help yourself.—GRAZIELLA.

Before flying back the pigeon remembered about the flower, so, seeing one in the princess's dress, he stole it and flew away.

The prince was wild with joy at the pigeon's return with the note. After an hour's rest the trusty little bird was sent back again, carrying a miniature of the prince, which by good luck he had with him.

On reaching the tower the pigeon found the princess in the garden. She hastened to untie the ribbon, and on opening the miniature case what was her surprise and delight to find it very like the picture her governess had painted for her. She hastened to send the pigeon back, and you can fancy the prince's joy when he found she had kept his portrait.

"Now," said the fairy, "let us lose no more time. I can only make you happy by changing you into a bird, but I will take care to give you back your proper shape at the right time."

The prince was eager to start, so the fairy, touching him with her wand, turned him into the loveliest humming-bird you ever saw, at the same time letting him keep the power of speech. The pigeon was told to show him the way.

Graziella was much surprised to see a perfectly strange bird, and still more so when it flew to her saying, "Good-morning, sweet princess."

She was delighted with the pretty creature, and let him perch on her finger, when he said, "Kiss, kiss, little birdie," which she gladly did, petting and stroking him at the same time.

After a time the princess, who had been up very early, grew tired, and as the sun was hot she went to lie down on a mossy bank in the shade of the arbor. She held the pretty bird near her breast, and was just falling asleep, when the fairy contrived to restore the prince to his own shape, so that as Graziella opened her eyes she found herself in the arms of a lover whom she loved in return!

At the same moment her enchantment came to an end. The tower began to rock and to split. Bonnetta hurried up to the top so that she might at least perish with her dear princess. Just as she reached the garden, the kind fairy who had helped the prince arrived with the fairy Placida, in a car of Venetian glass drawn by six eagles.

"Come away quickly," they cried, "the tower is about to sink!" The prince, princess, and Bonnetta lost no time in stepping into the car, which rose in the air just as, with a terrible crash, the tower sank into the depths of the sea, for the fairy Marina and the mermen had destroyed its foundations to avenge themselves on Graziella. Luckily their wicked plans were defeated, and the good fairies took their way to the kingdom of Graziella's parents.

They found that Queen Mutinosa had died some years ago, but her kind husband lived on peaceably, ruling his country well and happily. He received his daughter with great delight, and there were universal rejoicings at the return of the lovely princess.

The wedding took place the very next day, and, for many days after, balls, dinners, tournaments, concerts and all sorts of amusements went on all day and all night.

All the fairies were carefully invited, and they came in great state, and promised the young couple their protection and all sorts of good gifts. Prince Blondel and Princess Graziella lived to a good old age, beloved by every one, and loving each other more and more as time went on.

Snow-White and the Seven Dwarfs

(FROM *GRIMM'S COMPLETE FAIRY TALES*)

Once upon a time in the middle of winter, when the flakes of snow were falling like feathers from the sky, a queen sat at a window sewing, and the frame of the window was made of black ebony. And whilst she was sewing and looking out of the window at the snow, she pricked her finger with the needle, and three drops of blood fell upon the snow. And the red looked pretty upon the white snow, and she thought to herself, "Would that I had a child as white as snow, as red as blood, and as black as the wood of the window-frame."

Soon after that she had a little daughter, who was as white as snow, and as red as blood, and her hair was as black as ebony; and she was therefore called Little Snow-White. And when the child was born, the Queen died.

After a year had passed the King took to himself another wife. She was a beautiful woman, but proud and haughty, and she could not bear that anyone else should surpass her in beauty. She had a wonderful looking-glass, and when she stood in front of it and looked at herself in it, and said—

"Looking-glass, Looking-glass, on the wall,
Who in this land is the fairest of all?"

the looking-glass answered—

"Thou, O Queen, art the fairest of all!"

Then she was satisfied, for she knew that the looking-glass spoke the truth.

But Snow-White was growing up, and grew more and more beautiful; and when she was seven years old she was as beautiful as the day, and more beautiful than the Queen herself. And once when the Queen asked her looking-glass—

"Looking-glass, Looking-glass, on the wall,
Who in this land is the fairest of all?"

it answered—

"Thou art fairer than all who are here, Lady Queen.
But more beautiful still is Snow-White, as I ween."

Then the Queen was shocked, and turned yellow and green with envy. From that hour, whenever she looked at Snow-White, her heart heaved in her breast, she hated the girl so much.

And envy and pride grew higher and higher in her heart like a weed, so that she had no peace day or night. She called a huntsman, and said, "Take the child away into the forest; I will no longer have her in my sight. Kill her, and bring me back her heart as a token."

The huntsman obeyed, and took her away; but when he had drawn his knife, and was about to pierce Snow-White's innocent heart, she began to weep, and said, "Ah dear huntsman, leave me my life! I will run away into the wild forest, and never come home again."

And as she was so beautiful the huntsman had pity on her and said, "Run away, then, you poor child." "The wild beasts will soon have devoured you," thought he, and yet it seemed as if a stone had been rolled from his heart since it was no longer needful for him to kill her. And as a young boar just then came running by he stabbed it, and cut out its heart and took it to the Queen as proof that the child was dead. The cook had to salt this, and the wicked Queen ate it, and thought she had eaten the heart of Snow-White.

But now the poor child was all alone in the great forest, and so terrified that she looked at every leaf of every tree, and did not know what to do. Then she began to run, and ran over sharp stones and through thorns, and the wild beasts ran past her, but did her no harm. She ran as long as her feet would go until it was almost evening; then she saw a little cottage and went into it to rest herself. Everything in the cottage was small, but neater and cleaner than can be told. There was a table on which was a white cover, and seven little plates, and on each plate a little spoon; moreover, there were seven little knives and forks, and seven little mugs. Against the wall stood seven little beds side by side, and covered with Snow-White counterpanes.

Little Snow-White was so hungry and thirsty that she ate some vegetables and bread from each plate and drank a drop of wine out of each mug, for she did not wish to take all from one only. Then, as she was so tired, she laid herself down on one of the little beds, but none of them suited her; one was too long, another too short, but at last she found that the seventh one was right, and so she remained in it, said a prayer and went to sleep.

When it was quite dark the owners of the cottage came back; they were seven dwarfs who dug and delved in the mountains for ore. They lit their seven candles, and as it was now light within the cottage they saw that someone had been there, for everything was not in the same order in which they had left it.

The first said, "Who has been sitting on my chair?"

The second, "Who has been eating off my plate?"

The third, "Who has been taking some of my bread?"

The fourth, "Who has been eating my vegetables?"

The fifth, "Who has been using my fork?"

The sixth, "Who has been cutting with my knife?"

The seventh, "Who has been drinking out of my mug?"

Then the first looked round and saw that there was a little hole on his bed, and he said, "Who has been getting into my bed?" The others came up and each called out, "Somebody has been lying in my bed too." But the seventh when he looked at his bed saw little Snow-White, who was lying asleep therein. And he called the others, who came running up, and they cried out with astonishment, and brought their seven little candles and let the light fall on little Snow-White.

"Oh, heavens! oh, heavens!" cried they, "what a lovely child!" and they were so glad that they did not wake her up, but let her sleep on in the bed. And the seventh dwarf slept with his companions, one hour with each, and so got through the night.

When it was morning little Snow-White awoke, and was frightened when she saw the seven dwarfs. But they were friendly and asked her what her name was. "My name is Snow-White," she answered. "How have you come to our house?" said the dwarfs. Then she told them that her step-mother had wished to have her killed, but that the huntsman had spared her life, and that she had run for the whole day, until at last she had found their dwelling.

The dwarfs said, "If you will take care of our house, cook, make the beds, wash, sew, and knit, and if you will keep everything neat and clean, you can stay with us and you shall want for nothing."

"Yes," said Snow-White, "with all my heart," and she stayed with them. She kept the house in order for them; in the mornings they went to the mountains and looked for copper and gold, in the evenings they came back, and then their supper had to be ready. The girl was alone the whole day, so the good dwarfs warned her and said, "Beware of your step-mother, she will soon know that you are here; be sure to let no one come in."

But the Queen, believing that she had eaten Snow-White's heart, could not but think that she was again the first and most beautiful of all; and she went to her looking-glass and said—

> "Looking-glass, Looking-glass, on the wall,
> Who in this land is the fairest of all?"

and the glass answered —

> "Oh, Queen, thou art fairest of all I see,
> But over the hills, where the seven dwarfs dwell,
> Snow-White is still alive and well,
> And none is so fair as she."

234

Then she was astounded, for she knew that the looking-glass never spoke falsely, and she knew that the huntsman had betrayed her, and that little Snow-White was still alive.

And so she thought and thought again how she might kill her, for so long as she was not the fairest in the whole land, envy let her have no rest. And when she had at last thought of something to do, she painted her face, and dressed herself like an old peddler-woman, and no one could have known her. In this disguise she went over the seven mountains to the seven dwarfs, and knocked at the door and cried, "Pretty things to sell, very cheap, very cheap."

Little Snow-White looked out of the window and called out, "Good-day my good woman, what have you to sell?"

"Good things, pretty things," she answered; "stay-laces of all colors," and she pulled out one which was woven of bright-colored silk.

"I may let the worthy old woman in," thought Snow-White, and she unbolted the door and bought the pretty laces.

"Child," said the old woman, "what a fright you look; come, I will lace you properly for once."

Snow-White had no suspicion, but stood before her, and let herself be laced with the new laces. But the old woman laced so quickly and so tightly that Snow-White lost her breath and fell down as if dead.

"Now I am the most beautiful," said the Queen to herself, and ran away.

Not long afterwards, in the evening, the seven dwarfs came home, but how shocked they were when they saw their dear little Snow-White lying on the ground, and that she neither stirred nor moved, and seemed to be dead. They lifted her up, and, as they saw that she was laced too tightly, they cut the laces; then she began to breathe a little, and after a while came to life again. When the dwarfs heard what had happened they said, "The old peddler-woman was no one else than the wicked Queen; take care and let no one come in when we are not with you."

But the wicked woman when she had reached home went in front of the glass and asked—

"Looking-glass, Looking-glass, on the wall,
Who in this land is the fairest of all?"

and it answered as before—

> "Oh, Queen, thou art fairest of all I see,
> But over the hills, where the seven dwarfs dwell,
> Snow-White is still alive and well,
> And none is so fair as she."

When she heard that, all her blood rushed to her heart with fear, for she saw plainly that little Snow-White was again alive. "But now," she said, "I will think of something that shall put an end to you," and by the help of witchcraft, which she understood, she made a poisonous comb. Then she disguised herself and took the shape of another old woman. So she went over the seven mountains to the seven dwarfs, knocked at the door, and cried, "Good things to sell, cheap, cheap!" Little Snow-White looked out and said, "Go away; I cannot let any one come in." "I suppose you can look," said the old woman, and pulled the poisonous comb out and held it up. It pleased the girl so well that she let herself be beguiled, and opened the door. When they had made a bargain the old woman said, "Now I will comb you properly for once." Poor little Snow-White had no suspicion, and let the old woman do as she pleased, but hardly had she put the comb in her hair than the poison in it took effect, and the girl fell down senseless. "You paragon of beauty," said the wicked woman, "you are done for now," and she went away.

But fortunately it was almost evening, when the seven dwarfs came home. When they saw Snow-White lying as if dead upon the ground they at once suspected the step-mother, and they looked and found the poisoned comb. Scarcely had they taken it out when Snow-White came to herself, and told them what had happened. Then they warned her once more to be upon her guard and to open the door to no one.

The Queen, at home, went in front of the glass and said—

> "Looking-glass, Looking-glass, on the wall,
> Who in this land is the fairest of all?"

then it answered as before—

"Oh, Queen, thou art fairest of all I see,
   But over the hills, where the seven dwarfs dwell,
   Snow-White is still alive and well,
   And none is so fair as she."

When she heard the glass speak thus she trembled and shook with rage. "Snow-White shall die," she cried, "even if it costs me my life!"

Thereupon she went into a quite secret, lonely room, where no one ever came, and there she made a very poisonous apple. Outside it looked pretty, white with a red cheek, so that everyone who saw it longed for it; but whoever ate a piece of it must surely die. When the apple was ready she painted her face, and dressed herself up as a country-woman, and so she went over the seven mountains to the seven dwarfs. She knocked at the door. Snow-White put her head out of the window and said, "I cannot let any one in; the seven dwarfs have forbidden me." "It is all the same to me," answered the woman, "I shall soon get rid of my apples. There, I will give you one."

"No," said Snow-White, "I dare not take anything." "Are you afraid of poison?" said the old woman; "look, I will cut the apple in two pieces; you eat the red cheek, and I will eat the white." The apple was so cunningly made that only the red cheek was poisoned. Snow-White longed for the fine apple, and when she saw that the woman ate part of it she could resist no longer, and stretched out her hand and took the poisonous half. But hardly had she a bit of it in her mouth than she fell down dead. Then the Queen looked at her with a dreadful look, and laughed aloud and said, "White as snow, red as blood, black as ebony-wood! this time the dwarfs cannot wake you up again."

And when she asked of the Looking-glass at home—

"Looking-glass, Looking-glass, on the wall,
   Who in this land is the fairest of all?"

it answered at last —

"Oh, Queen, in this land thou art fairest of all."

Then her envious heart had rest, so far as an envious heart can have rest.

The dwarfs, when they came home in the evening, found Snow-White lying upon the ground; she breathed no longer and was dead. They lifted her up, looked to see whether they could find anything poisonous, unlaced her, combed her hair, washed her with water and wine, but it was all of no use; the poor child was dead, and remained dead. They laid her upon a bier, and all seven of them sat round it and wept for her, and wept three days long.

Then they were going to bury her, but she still looked as if she were living, and still had her pretty red cheeks. They said, "We could not bury her in the dark ground," and they had a transparent coffin of glass made, so that she could be seen from all sides, and they laid her in it, and wrote her name upon it in golden letters, and that she was a king's daughter. Then they put the coffin out upon the mountain, and one of them always stayed by it and watched it. And birds came too, and wept for Snow-White; first an owl, then a raven, and last a dove.

And now Snow-White lay a long, long time in the coffin, and she did not change, but looked as if she were asleep; for she was as white as snow, as red as blood, and her hair was as black as ebony.

It happened, however, that a king's son came into the forest, and went to the dwarfs' house to spend the night. He saw the coffin on the mountain, and the beautiful Snow-White within it, and read what was written upon it in golden letters. Then he said to the dwarfs, "Let me have the coffin, I will give you whatever you want for it." But the dwarfs answered, "We will not part with it for all the gold in the world." Then he said, "Let me have it as a gift, for I cannot live without seeing Snow-White. I will honor and prize her as my dearest possession." As he spoke in this way the good dwarfs took pity upon him, and gave him the coffin.

And now the King's son had it carried away by his servants on their shoulders. And it happened that they stumbled over a tree-stump, and with the shock the poisonous piece of apple which Snow-White had bitten off came out of her throat. And before long she opened her eyes, lifted up the lid of the coffin, sat up, and was once more alive. "Oh, heavens, where am I?" she cried. The King's son, full of joy, said, "You are with me," and told her what had happened, and said, "I love you more than everything in the world; come with me to my father's palace, you shall be my wife."

And Snow-White was willing, and went with him, and their wedding was held with great show and splendor. But Snow-White's wicked step-mother was also bidden to the feast. When she had arrayed herself in beautiful clothes she went before the Looking-glass, and said—

> "Looking-glass, Looking-glass, on the wall,
> Who in this land is the fairest of all?"

the glass answered—

> "Oh, Queen, of all here the fairest art thou,
> But the young Queen is fairer by far as I trow."

Then the wicked woman uttered a curse, and was so wretched, so utterly wretched, that she knew not what to do. At first she would not go to the wedding at all, but she had no peace, and must go to see the young Queen. And when she went in she knew Snow-White; and she stood still with rage and fear, and could not stir. But iron slippers had already been put upon the fire, and they were brought in with tongs, and set before her. Then she was forced to put on the red-hot shoes, and dance until she dropped down dead.

The Little Green Frog

(FROM *THE YELLOW FAIRY BOOK*)

In a part of the world whose name I forget lived once upon a time two kings, called Peridor and Diamantino. They were cousins as well as neighbors, and both were under the protection of the fairies; though it is only fair to say that the fairies did not love them half so well as their wives did.

Now it often happens that as princes can generally manage to get their own way it is harder for them to be good than it is for common people. So it was with Peridor and Diamantino; but of the two, the fairies declared that Diamantino was much the worst; indeed, he behaved so badly to his wife Aglantino, that the fairies would not allow him to live any longer; and he died, leaving behind him a little daughter. As she was an only child, of course this little girl was the heiress of the kingdom, but, being still only a baby, her mother, the widow of Diamantino, was proclaimed regent. The Queen-dowager was wise and good, and tried her best to make her people happy. The only thing she had to vex her was the absence of her daughter; for the fairies, for reasons of their own, determined to bring up the little Princess Serpentine among themselves.

As to the other King, he was really fond of his wife, Queen Constance, but he often grieved her by his thoughtless ways, and in order to punish him for his carelessness, the fairies caused her to die quite suddenly. When she was gone the King felt how much he had loved her, and his grief was so great (though he never neglected his duties) that his subjects called him Peridor the Sorrowful. It seems hardly possible that any man should live like Peridor for fifteen years plunged in such depth of grief, and most likely he would have died too if it had not been for the fairies.

The one comfort the poor King had was his son, Prince Saphir, who was only three years old at the time of his mother's death, and great care was given to his education. By the time he was fifteen Saphir had learnt everything that a prince should know, and he was, besides, charming and agreeable.

It was about this time that the fairies suddenly took fright lest his love for his father should interfere with the plans they had made for the young prince. So, to prevent this, they placed in a pretty little room of which Saphir was very fond a little mirror in a black frame, such as were often brought from Venice. The Prince did not notice for some days that there was anything new in the room, but at last he perceived it, and went up to look at it more closely. What was his surprise to see reflected in the mirror, not his own face, but that of a young girl as lovely as the morning! And, better still, every movement of the girl, just growing out of childhood, was also reflected in the wonderful glass.

As might have been expected, the young Prince lost his heart completely to the beautiful image, and it was impossible to get him out of the room, so busy was he in watching the lovely unknown. Certainly it was very delightful to be able to see her whom he loved at any moment he chose, but his spirits sometimes sank when he wondered what was to be the end of this adventure.

The magic mirror had been for about a year in the Prince's possession, when one day a new subject of disquiet seized upon him. As usual, he was engaged in looking at the girl, when suddenly he thought he saw a second mirror reflected in the first, exactly like his own, and with the same power. And in this he was perfectly right. The young girl had only possessed it for a short time, and neglected all her duties for the sake of the mirror. Now it was not difficult for Saphir to guess the reason of the change in her, nor why the new mirror was consulted so often; but try as he would he could never see the face of the person who was reflected in it, for the young girl's figure always came between. All he knew was that the face was that of a man, and this was quite enough to make him madly jealous. This was the doing of the fairies, and we must suppose that they had their reasons for acting as they did.

When these things happened Saphir was about eighteen years old, and fifteen years had passed away since the death of his mother. King Peridor had grown more and more unhappy as time went on, and at last he fell so ill that it seemed as if his days were numbered. He was so much beloved by his subjects that this sad news was heard with despair by the nation, and more than all by the Prince.

During his whole illness the King never spoke of anything but the Queen, his sorrow at having grieved her, and his hope of one day seeing her again. All the doctors and all the water-cures in the kingdom had been tried, and nothing would do him any good. At last he persuaded them to let him lie quietly in his room, where no one came to trouble him.

Perhaps the worst pain he had to bear was a sort of weight on his chest, which made it very hard for him to breathe. So he commanded his servants to leave the windows open in order that he might get more air. One day, when he had been left alone for a few minutes, a bird with brilliant plumage came and fluttered round the window, and finally rested on the sill. His feathers were sky-blue and gold, his feet and his beak of such glittering rubies that no one could bear to look at them, his eyes made the brightest diamonds look dull, and on his head he wore a crown. I cannot tell you what the crown was made of, but I am quite certain that it was still more splendid than all the rest. As to his voice I can say nothing about that, for the bird never sang at all. In fact, he did nothing but gaze steadily at the King, and as he gazed, the King felt his strength come back to him. In a little while the bird flew into the room, still with his eyes fixed on the King, and at every glance the strength of the sick man became greater, till he was once more as well as he used to be before the Queen died. Filled with joy at his cure, he tried to seize the bird to whom he owed it all, but, swifter than a swallow, it managed to avoid him. In vain he described the bird to his attendants, who rushed at his first call; in vain they sought the wonderful creature both on horse and foot, and summoned the fowlers to their aid: the bird could nowhere be found. The love the people bore King Peridor was so strong, and the reward he promised was so large, that in the twinkling of an eye every man, woman, and child had fled into the fields, and the towns were quite empty.

All this bustle, however, ended in nothing but confusion, and, what was worse, the King soon fell back into the same condition as he was in before. Prince Saphir, who loved his father very dearly, was so unhappy at this that he persuaded himself that he might succeed where the others had failed, and at once prepared himself for a more distant search. In spite of the opposition he met with, he rode away, followed by his household, trusting to chance to help him. He had formed no plan, and there was no reason that he should choose one path more than another. His only idea was to make straight for those spots which were the favorite haunts of birds. But in vain he examined all the hedges and all the thickets; in vain he questioned everyone he met along the road. The more he sought the less he found.

At last he came to one of the largest forests in all the world, composed entirely of cedars. But in spite of the deep shadows cast by the wide-spreading branches of the trees, the grass underneath was soft and green, and covered with the rarest flowers. It seemed to Saphir that this was exactly the place where the birds would choose to live, and he determined not to quit the wood until he had examined it from end to end. And he did more. He ordered some nets to be prepared and painted of the same colors as the bird's plumage, thinking that we are all easily caught by what is like ourselves. In this he had to help him not only the fowlers by profession, but also his attendants, who excelled in this art. For a man is not a courtier unless he can do everything.

After searching as usual for nearly a whole day Prince Saphir began to feel overcome with thirst. He was too tired to go any farther, when happily he discovered a little way off a bubbling fountain of the clearest water. Being an experienced traveler, he drew from his pocket a little cup (without which no one should ever take a journey), and was just about to dip it in the water, when a lovely little green frog, much prettier than frogs generally are, jumped into the cup. Far from admiring its beauty, Saphir shook it impatiently off; but it was no good, for quick as lightning the frog jumped back again. Saphir, who was raging with thirst, was just about to shake it off anew, when the little creature fixed upon him the most beautiful eyes in the world, and said, "I am a friend of the bird you are seeking, and when you have quenched your thirst listen to me."

So the Prince drank his fill, and then, by the command of the Little Green Frog, he lay down on the grass to rest himself.

"Now," she began, "be sure you do exactly in every respect what I tell you. First you must call together your attendants, and order them to remain in a little hamlet close by until you want them. Then go, quite alone, down a road that you will find on your right hand, looking southwards. This road is planted all the way with cedars of Lebanon; and after going down it a long way you will come at last to a magnificent castle. And now," she went on, "attend carefully to what I am going to say. Take this tiny grain of sand, and put it into the ground as close as you can to the gate of the castle. It has the virtue both of opening the gate and also of sending to sleep all the inhabitants. Then go at once to the stable, and pay no heed to anything except what I tell you. Choose the handsomest of all the horses, leap quickly on its back, and come to me as fast as you can. Farewell, Prince; I wish you good luck," and with these words the Little Frog plunged into the water and disappeared.

The Prince, who felt more hopeful than he had done since he left home, did precisely as he had been ordered. He left his attendants in the hamlet, found the road the frog had described to him, and followed it all alone, and at last he arrived at the gate of the castle, which was even more splendid than he had expected, for it was built of crystal, and all its ornaments were of massive gold. However, he had no thoughts to spare for its beauty, and quickly buried his grain of sand in the earth. In one instant the gates flew open, and all the dwellers inside fell sound asleep. Saphir flew straight to the stable, and already had his hand on the finest horse it contained, when his eye was caught by a suit of magnificent harness hanging up close by. It occurred to him directly that the harness belonged to the horse, and without ever thinking of harm (for indeed he who steals a horse can hardly be blamed for taking his saddle), he hastily placed it on the animal's back. Suddenly the people in the castle became broad awake, and rushed to the stable. They flung themselves on the Prince, seized him, and dragged him before their lord; but, luckily for the Prince, who could only find very lame excuses for his conduct, the lord of the castle took a fancy to his face, and let him depart without further questions.

Very sad, and very much ashamed of himself poor Saphir crept back to the fountain, where the Frog was awaiting him with a good scolding.

"Whom do you take me for?" she exclaimed angrily. "Do you really believe that it was just for the pleasure of talking that I gave you the advice you have neglected so abominably?"

But the Prince was so deeply grieved, and apologized so very humbly, that after some time the heart of the good little Frog was softened, and she gave him another tiny little grain, but instead of being sand it was now a grain of gold. She directed him to do just as he had done before, with only this difference, that instead of going to the stable which had been the ruin of his hopes, he was to enter right into the castle itself, and to glide as fast as he could down the passages till he came to a room filled with perfume, where he would find a beautiful maiden asleep on a bed. He was to wake the maiden instantly and carry her off, and to be sure not to pay any heed to whatever resistance she might make.

The Prince obeyed the Frog's orders one by one, and all went well for this second time also. The gate opened, the inhabitants fell sound asleep, and he walked down the passage till he found the girl on her bed, exactly as he had been told he would. He woke her, and begged her firmly, but politely, to follow him quickly. After a little persuasion the maiden consented, but only on condition that she was allowed first to put on her dress. This sounded so reasonable and natural that it did not enter the Prince's head to refuse her request.

But the maiden's hand had hardly touched the dress when the palace suddenly awoke from its sleep, and the Prince was seized and bound. He was so vexed with his own folly, and so taken aback at the disaster, that he did not attempt to explain his conduct, and things would have gone badly with him if his friends the fairies had not softened the hearts of his captors, so that they once more allowed him to leave quietly. However, what troubled him most was the idea of having to meet the Frog who had been his benefactress. How was he ever to appear before her with this tale? Still, after a long struggle with himself, he made up his mind that there was nothing else to be done, and that he deserved whatever she might say to him. And she said a great deal, for she had worked herself into a terrible passion; but the Prince humbly implored her pardon, and ventured to point out that it would have been very hard to refuse the young lady's reasonable request. "You must learn to do as you are told," was all the Frog would reply.

But poor Saphir was so unhappy, and begged so hard for forgiveness, that at last the Frog's anger gave way, and she held up to him a tiny diamond stone. "Go back," she said, "to the castle, and bury this little diamond close to the door. But be careful not to return to the stable or to the bedroom; they have proved too fatal to you. Walk straight to the garden and enter through a portico, into a small green wood, in the midst of which is a tree with a trunk of gold and leaves of emeralds. Perched on this tree you will see the beautiful bird you have been seeking so long. You must cut the branch on which it is sitting, and bring it back to me without delay. But I warn you solemnly that if you disobey my directions, as you have done twice before, you have nothing more to expect either of me or anyone else."

With these words she jumped into the water, and the Prince, who had taken her threats much to heart, took his departure, firmly resolved not to deserve them. He found it all just as he had been told: the portico, the wood, the magnificent tree, and the beautiful bird, which was sleeping soundly on one of the branches. He speedily lopped off the branch, and though he noticed a splendid golden cage hanging close by, which would have been very useful for the bird to travel in, he left it alone, and came back to the fountain, holding his breath and walking on tip-toe all the way, for fear lest he should awake his prize. But what was his surprise, when instead of finding the fountain in the spot where he had left it, he saw in its place a little rustic palace built in the best taste, and standing in the doorway a charming maiden, at whose sight his mind seemed to give way.

"What! Madam!" he cried, hardly knowing what he said. "What! Is it you?"

The maiden blushed and answered: "Ah, my lord, it is long since I first beheld your face, but I did not think you had ever seen mine."

"Oh, madam," replied he, "you can never guess the days and the hours I have passed lost in admiration of you." And after these words they each related all the strange things that had happened, and the more they talked the more they felt convinced of the truth of the images they had seen in their mirrors. After some time spent in the most tender conversation, the Prince could not restrain himself from asking the lovely unknown by what lucky chance she was wandering in the forest; where the fountain had gone; and if she knew anything of the Frog to whom he owed all his happiness, and to whom he must give up the bird, which, somehow or other, was still sound asleep.

"Ah, my lord," she replied, with rather an awkward air, "as to the Frog, she stands before you. Let me tell you my story; it is not a long one. I know neither my country nor my parents, and the only thing I can say for certain is that I am called Serpentine. The fairies, who have taken care of me ever since I was born, wished me to be in ignorance as to my family, but they have looked after my education, and have bestowed on me endless kindness. I have always lived in seclusion, and for the last two years I have wished for nothing better. I had a mirror"—here shyness and embarrassment choked her words—but regaining her self-control, she added, "You know that fairies insist on being obeyed without questioning. It was they who changed the little house you saw before you into the fountain for which you are now asking, and, having turned me into a frog, they ordered me to say to the first person who came to the fountain exactly what I repeated to you. But, my lord, when you stood before me, it was agony to my heart, filled as it was with thoughts of you, to appear to your eyes under so monstrous a form. However, there was no help for it, and, painful as it was, I had to submit. I desired your success with all my soul, not only for your own sake, but also for my own, because I could not get back my proper shape till you had become master of the beautiful bird, though I am quite ignorant as to your reason for seeking it."

On this Saphir explained about the state of his father's health, and all that has been told before.

On hearing this story Serpentine grew very sad, and her lovely eyes filled with tears.

"Ah, my lord," she said, "you know nothing of me but what you have seen in the mirror; and I, who cannot even name my parents, learn that you are a king's son."

In vain Saphir declared that love made them equal; Serpentine would only reply: "I love you too much to allow you to marry beneath your rank. I shall be very unhappy, of course, but I shall never alter my mind. If I do not find from the fairies that my birth is worthy of you, then, whatever be my feelings, I will never accept your hand."

The conversation was at this point, and bid fair to last some time longer, when one of the fairies appeared in her ivory car, accompanied by a beautiful woman past her early youth. At this moment the bird suddenly awakened, and, flying on to Saphir's shoulder (which it never afterwards left), began fondling him as well as a bird can do. The fairy told Serpentine that she was quite satisfied with her conduct, and made herself very agreeable to Saphir, whom she presented to the lady she had brought with her, explaining that the lady was no other than his Aunt Aglantine, widow of Diamantino.

Then they all fell into each other's arms, till the fairy mounted her chariot, placed Aglantine by her side, and Saphir and Serpentine on the front seat. She also sent a message to the Prince's attendants that they might travel slowly back to the Court of King Peridor, and that the beautiful bird had really been found. This matter being comfortably arranged, she started off her chariot. But in spite of the swiftness with which they flew through the air, the time passed even quicker for Saphir and Serpentine, who had so much to think about.

They were still quite confused with the pleasure of seeing each other, when the chariot arrived at King Peridor's palace. He had had himself carried to a room on the roof, where his nurses thought that he would die at any moment. Directly the chariot drew within sight of the castle the beautiful bird took flight, and, making straight for the dying King, at once cured him of his sickness. Then she resumed her natural shape, and he found that the bird was no other than the Queen Constance, whom he had long believed to be dead. Peridor was rejoiced to embrace his wife and his son once more, and with the help of the fairies began to make preparations for the marriage of Saphir and Serpentine, who turned out to be the daughter of Aglantine and Diamantino, and as much a princess as he was a prince. The people of the kingdom were delighted, and everybody lived happy and contented to the end of their lives.

The Enchanted Knife

(FROM *THE VIOLET FAIRY BOOK*)

Once upon a time there lived a young man who vowed that he would never marry any girl who had not royal blood in her veins. One day he plucked up all his courage and went to the palace to ask the emperor for his daughter. The emperor was not much pleased at the thought of such a match for his only child, but being very polite, he only said:

"Very well, my son, if you can win the princess you shall have her, and the conditions are these. In eight days you must manage to tame and bring to me three horses that have never felt a master. The first is pure white, the second a foxy-red with a black head, the third coal black with a white head and feet. And besides that, you must also bring as a present to the empress, my wife, as much gold as the three horses can carry."

The young man listened in dismay to these words, but with an effort he thanked the emperor for his kindness and left the palace, wondering how he was to fulfill the task allotted to him. Luckily for him, the emperor's daughter had overheard everything her father had said, and peeping through a curtain had seen the youth, and thought him handsomer than anyone she had ever beheld.

So returning hastily to her own room, she wrote him a letter which she gave to a trusty servant to deliver, begging her wooer to come to her rooms early the next day, and to undertake nothing without her advice, if he ever wished her to be his wife.

That night, when her father was asleep, she crept softly into his chamber and took out an enchanted knife from the chest where he kept his treasures, and hid it carefully in a safe place before she went to bed.

The sun had hardly risen the following morning when the princess's nurse brought the young man to her apartments. Neither spoke for some minutes, but stood holding each other's hands for joy, till at last they both cried out that nothing but death should part them. Then the maiden said:

"Take my horse, and ride straight through the wood towards the sunset till you come to a hill with three peaks. When you get there, turn first to the right and then to the left, and you will find yourself in a sun meadow, where many horses are feeding. Out of these you must pick out the three described to you by my father. If they prove shy, and refuse to let you get near them, draw out your knife, and let the sun shine on it so that the whole meadow is lit up by its rays, and the horses will then approach you of their own accord, and will let you lead them away. When you have them safely, look about till you see a cypress tree, whose roots are of brass, whose boughs are of silver, and whose leaves are of gold. Go to it, and cut away the roots with your knife, and you will come to countless bags of gold. Load the horses with all they can carry, and return to my father, and tell him that you have done your task, and can claim me for your wife."

The princess had finished all she had to say, and now it depended on the young man to do his part. He hid the knife in the folds of his girdle, mounted his horse, and rode off in search of the meadow. This he found without much difficulty, but the horses were all so shy that they galloped away directly he approached them. Then he drew his knife, and held it up towards the sun, and directly there shone such a glory that the whole meadow was bathed in it. From all sides the horses rushed pressing round, and each one that passed him fell on its knees to do him honor. But he only chose from them all the three that the emperor had described. These he secured by a silken rope to his own horse, and then looked about for the cypress tree. It was standing by itself in one corner, and in a moment he was beside it, tearing away the earth with his knife. Deeper and deeper he dug, till far down, below the roots of brass, his knife struck upon the buried treasure, which lay heaped up in bags all around. With a great effort he lifted them from their hiding place, and laid them one by one on his horses' backs, and when they could carry no more he led them back to the emperor. And when the emperor saw him, he wondered, but never guessed how it was the young man had been too clever for him, till the betrothal ceremony was over. Then he asked his newly made son-in-law what dowry he would require with his bride. To which the bridegroom made answer, "Noble emperor! all I desire is that I may have your daughter for my wife, and enjoy for ever the use of your enchanted knife."

The Princess Mayblossom

(FROM *THE RED FAIRY BOOK*)

Once upon a time there lived a King and Queen whose children had all died, first one and then another, until at last only one little daughter remained, and the Queen was at her wits' end to know where to find a really good nurse who would take care of her, and bring her up. A herald was sent who blew a trumpet at every street corner, and commanded all the best nurses to appear before the Queen, that she might choose one for the little Princess. So on the appointed day the whole palace was crowded with nurses, who came from the four corners of the world to offer themselves, until the Queen declared that if she was ever to see the half of them, they must be brought out to her, one by one, as she sat in a shady wood near the palace.

This was accordingly done, and the nurses, after they had made their curtsey to the King and Queen, ranged themselves in a line before her that she might choose. Most of them were fair and fat and charming, but there was one who was dark-skinned and ugly, and spoke a strange language which nobody could understand. The Queen wondered how she dared offer herself, and she was told to go away, as she certainly would not do. Upon which she muttered something and passed on, but hid herself in a hollow tree, from which she could see all that happened. The Queen, without giving her another thought, chose a pretty rosy-faced nurse, but no sooner was her choice made than a snake, which was hidden in the grass, bit that very nurse on her foot, so that she fell down as if dead. The Queen was very much vexed by this accident, but she soon selected another, who was just stepping forward when an eagle flew by and dropped a large tortoise upon her head, which was cracked in pieces like an egg-shell. At this the Queen was much horrified; nevertheless, she chose a third time, but with no better fortune, for the nurse, moving quickly, ran into the branch of a tree and blinded herself with a thorn. Then the Queen in dismay cried that there must be some malignant influence at work, and that she would choose no more that day; and she had just risen to return to the palace when she heard peals of malicious laughter behind her, and turning round saw the ugly stranger whom she had dismissed, who was making very merry over the disasters and mocking everyone, but especially the Queen. This annoyed Her Majesty very much, and she was about to order that she should be arrested, when the witch—for she was a witch—with two blows from a wand summoned a chariot of fire drawn by winged dragons, and was whirled off through the air uttering threats and cries. When the King saw this he cried:

"Alas! now we are ruined indeed, for that was no other than the Fairy Carabosse, who has had a grudge against me ever since I was a boy and put sulfur into her porridge one day for fun."

Then the Queen began to cry.

"If I had only known who it was," she said, "I would have done my best to make friends with her; now I suppose all is lost."

The King was sorry to have frightened her so much, and proposed that they should go and hold a council as to what was best to be done to avert the misfortunes which Carabosse certainly meant to bring upon the little Princess.

So all the counselors were summoned to the palace, and when they had shut every door and window, and stuffed up every keyhole that they might not be overheard, they talked the affair over, and decided that every fairy for a thousand leagues round should be invited to the christening of the Princess, and that the time of the ceremony should be kept a profound secret, in case the Fairy Carabosse should take it into her head to attend it.

The Queen and her ladies set to work to prepare presents for the fairies who were invited: for each one a blue velvet cloak, a petticoat of apricot satin, a pair of high-heeled shoes, some sharp needles, and a pair of golden scissors. Of all the fairies the Queen knew, only five were able to come on the day appointed, but they began immediately to bestow gifts upon the Princess. One promised that she should be perfectly beautiful, the second that she should understand anything—no matter what—the first time it was explained to her, the third that she should sing like a nightingale, the fourth that she should succeed in everything she undertook, and the fifth was opening her mouth to speak when a tremendous rumbling was heard in the chimney, and Carabosse, all covered with soot, came rolling down, crying:

"I say that she shall be the unluckiest of the unlucky until she is twenty years old."

Then the Queen and all the fairies began to beg and beseech her to think better of it, and not be so unkind to the poor little Princess, who had never done her any harm. But the ugly old Fairy only grunted and made no answer. So the last Fairy, who had not yet given her gift, tried to mend matters by promising the Princess a long and happy life after the fatal time was over. At this Carabosse laughed maliciously, and climbed away up the chimney, leaving them all in great consternation, and especially the Queen. However, she entertained the fairies splendidly, and gave them beautiful ribbons, of which they are very fond, in addition to the other presents.

When they were going away the oldest Fairy said that they were of opinion that it would be best to shut the Princess up in some place, with her waiting-women, so that she might not see anyone else until she was twenty years old. So the King had a tower built on purpose. It had no windows, so it was lighted with wax candles, and the only way into it was by an underground passage, which had iron doors only twenty feet apart, and guards were posted everywhere.

The Princess had been named Mayblossom, because she was as fresh and blooming as Spring itself, and she grew up tall and beautiful, and everything she did and said was charming. Every time the King and Queen came to see her they were more delighted with her than before, but though she was weary of the tower, and often begged them to take her away from it, they always refused. The Princess's nurse, who had never left her, sometimes told her about the world outside the tower, and though the Princess had never seen anything for herself, yet she always understood exactly, thanks to the second Fairy's gift. Often the King said to the Queen:

"We were cleverer than Carabosse after all. Our Mayblossom will be happy in spite of her predictions."

And the Queen laughed until she was tired at the idea of having outwitted the old Fairy. They had caused the Princess's portrait to be painted and sent to all the neighboring Courts, for in four days she would have completed her twentieth year, and it was time to decide whom she should marry. All the town was rejoicing at the thought of the Princess's approaching freedom, and when the news came that King Merlin was sending his ambassador to ask her in marriage for his son, they were still more delighted. The nurse, who kept the Princess informed of everything that went forward in the town, did not fail to repeat the news that so nearly concerned her, and gave such a description of the splendor in which the ambassador Fanfaronade would enter the town, that the Princess was wild to see the procession for herself.

"What an unhappy creature I am," she cried, "to be shut up in this dismal tower as if I had committed some crime! I have never seen the sun, or the stars, or a horse, or a monkey, or a lion, except in pictures, and though the King and Queen tell me I am to be set free when I am twenty, I believe they only say it to keep me amused, when they never mean to let me out at all."

And then she began to cry, and her nurse, and the nurse's daughter, and the cradle-rocker, and the nursery-maid, who all loved her dearly, cried too for company, so that nothing could be heard but sobs and sighs. It was a scene of woe. When the Princess saw that they all pitied her she made up her mind to have her own way. So she declared that she would starve herself to death if they did not find some means of letting her see Fanfaronade's grand entry into the town.

"If you really love me," she said, "you will manage it, somehow or other, and the King and Queen need never know anything about it."

Then the nurse and all the others cried harder than ever, and said everything they could think of to turn the Princess from her idea. But the more they said the more determined she was, and at last they consented to make a tiny hole in the tower on the side that looked towards the city gates.

After scratching and scraping all day and all night, they presently made a hole through which they could, with great difficulty, push a very slender needle, and out of this the Princess looked at the daylight for the first time. She was so dazzled and delighted by what she saw, that there she stayed, never taking her eyes away from the peep-hole for a single minute, until presently the ambassador's procession appeared in sight.

At the head of it rode Fanfaronade himself upon a white horse, which pranced and caracoled to the sound of the trumpets. Nothing could have been more splendid than the ambassador's attire. His coat was nearly hidden under an embroidery of pearls and diamonds, his boots were solid gold, and from his helmet floated scarlet plumes. At the sight of him the Princess lost her wits entirely, and determined that Fanfaronade and nobody else would she marry.

"It is quite impossible," she said, "that his master should be half as handsome and delightful. I am not ambitious, and having spent all my life in this tedious tower, anything—even a house in the country—will seem a delightful change. I am sure that bread and water shared with Fanfaronade will please me far better than roast chicken and sweetmeats with anybody else."

And so she went on talk, talk, talking, until her waiting-women wondered where she got it all from. But when they tried to stop her, and represented that her high rank made it perfectly impossible that she should do any such thing, she would not listen, and ordered them to be silent.

As soon as the ambassador arrived at the palace, the Queen started to fetch her daughter.

All the streets were spread with carpets, and the windows were full of ladies who were waiting to see the Princess, and carried baskets of flowers and sweetmeats to shower upon her as she passed.

They had hardly begun to get the Princess ready when a dwarf arrived, mounted upon an elephant. He came from the five fairies, and brought for the Princess a crown, a scepter, and a robe of golden brocade, with a petticoat marvelously embroidered with butterflies' wings. They also sent a casket of jewels, so splendid that no one had ever seen anything like it before, and the Queen was perfectly dazzled when she opened it. But the Princess scarcely gave a glance to any of these treasures, for she thought of nothing but Fanfaronade. The Dwarf was rewarded with a gold piece, and decorated with so many ribbons that it was hardly possible to see him at all. The Princess sent to each of the fairies a new spinning-wheel with a distaff of cedar wood, and the Queen said she must look through her treasures and find something very charming to send them also.

When the Princess was arrayed in all the gorgeous things the Dwarf had brought, she was more beautiful than ever, and as she walked along the streets the people cried: "How pretty she is! How pretty she is!"

The procession consisted of the Queen, the Princess, five dozen other princesses, her cousins, and ten dozen who came from the neighboring kingdoms; and as they proceeded at a stately pace the sky began to grow dark, then suddenly the thunder growled, and rain and hail fell in torrents. The Queen put her royal mantle over her head, and all the princesses did the same with their trains. Mayblossom was just about to follow their example when a terrific croaking, as of an immense army of crows, rooks, ravens, screech-owls, and all birds of ill-omen was heard, and at the same instant a huge owl skimmed up to the Princess, and threw over her a scarf woven of spiders' webs and embroidered with bats' wings. And then peals of mocking laughter rang through the air, and they guessed that this was another of the Fairy Carabosse's unpleasant jokes.

The Queen was terrified at such an evil omen, and tried to pull the black scarf from the Princess's shoulders, but it really seemed as if it must be nailed on, it clung so closely.

"Ah!" cried the Queen, "can nothing appease this enemy of ours? What good was it that I sent her more than fifty pounds of sweetmeats, and as much again of the best sugar, not to mention two Westphalia hams? She is as angry as ever."

While she lamented in this way, and everybody was as wet as if they had been dragged through a river, the Princess still thought of nothing but the ambassador, and just at this moment he appeared before her, with the King, and there was a great blowing of trumpets, and all the people shouted louder than ever. Fanfaronade was not generally at a loss for something to say, but when he saw the Princess, she was so much more beautiful and majestic than he had expected that he could only stammer out a few words, and entirely forgot the harangue which he had been learning for months, and knew well enough to have repeated it in his sleep. To gain time to remember at least part of it, he made several low bows to the Princess, who on her side dropped half-a-dozen curtseys without stopping to think, and then said, to relieve his evident embarrassment:

"Sir Ambassador, I am sure that everything you intend to say is charming, since it is you who mean to say it; but let us make haste into the palace, as it is pouring cats and dogs, and the wicked Fairy Carabosse will be amused to see us all stand dripping here. When we are once under shelter we can laugh at her."

Upon this the Ambassador found his tongue, and replied gallantly that the Fairy had evidently foreseen the flames that would be kindled by the bright eyes of the Princess, and had sent this deluge to extinguish them. Then he offered his hand to conduct the Princess, and she said softly:

"As you could not possibly guess how much I like you, Sir Fanfaronade, I am obliged to tell you plainly that, since I saw you enter the town on your beautiful prancing horse, I have been sorry that you came to speak for another instead of for yourself. So, if you think about it as I do, I will marry you instead of your master. Of course I know you are not a prince, but I shall be just as fond of you as if you were, and we can go and live in some cozy little corner of the world, and be as happy as the days are long."

The Ambassador thought he must be dreaming, and could hardly believe what the lovely Princess said. He dared not answer, but only squeezed the Princess's hand until he really hurt her little finger, but she did not cry out. When they reached the palace the King kissed his daughter on both cheeks, and said:

"My little lambkin, are you willing to marry the great King Merlin's son, for this Ambassador has come on his behalf to fetch you?"

"If you please, sire," said the Princess, dropping a curtsey.

"I consent also," said the Queen; "so let the banquet be prepared."

This was done with all speed, and everybody feasted except Mayblossom and Fanfaronade, who looked at one another and forgot everything else.

After the banquet came a ball, and after that again a ballet, and at last they were all so tired that everyone fell asleep just where he sat. Only the lovers were as wide-awake as mice, and the Princess, seeing that there was nothing to fear, said to Fanfaronade:

"Let us be quick and run away, for we shall never have a better chance than this."

Then she took the King's dagger, which was in a diamond sheath, and the Queen's neck-handkerchief, and gave her hand to Fanfaronade, who carried a lantern, and they ran out together into the muddy street and down to the sea-shore. Here they got into a little boat in which the poor old boatman was sleeping, and when he woke up and saw the lovely Princess, with all her diamonds and her spiders'-web scarf, he did not know what to think, and obeyed her instantly when she commanded him to set out. They could see neither moon nor stars, but in the Queen's neck-handkerchief there was a carbuncle which glowed like fifty torches. Fanfaronade asked the Princess where she would like to go, but she only answered that she did not care where she went as long as he was with her.

"But, Princess," said he, "I dare not take you back to King Merlin's court. He would think hanging too good for me."

"Oh, in that case," she answered, "we had better go to Squirrel Island; it is lonely enough, and too far off for anyone to follow us there."

So she ordered the old boatman to steer for Squirrel Island.

Meanwhile the day was breaking, and the King and Queen and all the courtiers began to wake up and rub their eyes, and think it was time to finish the preparations for the wedding. And the Queen asked for her neck-handkerchief, that she might look smart. Then there was a scurrying hither and thither, and a hunting everywhere: they looked into every place, from the wardrobes to the stoves, and the Queen herself ran about from the garret to the cellar, but the handkerchief was nowhere to be found.

By this time the King had missed his dagger, and the search began all over again. They opened boxes and chests of which the keys had been lost for a hundred years, and found numbers of curious things, but not the dagger, and the King tore his beard, and the Queen tore her hair, for the handkerchief and the dagger were the most valuable things in the kingdom.

When the King saw that the search was hopeless he said:

"Never mind, let us make haste and get the wedding over before anything else is lost." And then he asked where the Princess was. Upon this her nurse came forward and said:

"Sire, I have been seeking her these two hours, but she is nowhere to be found." This was more than the Queen could bear. She gave a shriek of alarm and fainted away, and they had to pour two barrels of eau-de-cologne over her before she recovered. When she came to herself everybody was looking for the Princess in the greatest terror and confusion, but as she did not appear, the King said to his page:

"Go and find the Ambassador Fanfaronade, who is doubtless asleep in some corner, and tell him the sad news."

So the page hunted hither and thither, but Fanfaronade was no more to be found than the Princess, the dagger, or the neck-handkerchief!

Then the King summoned his counselors and his guards, and, accompanied by the Queen, went into his great hall. As he had not had time to prepare his speech beforehand, the King ordered that silence should be kept for three hours, and at the end of that time he spoke as follows:

"Listen, great and small! My dear daughter Mayblossom is lost: whether she has been stolen away or has simply disappeared I cannot tell. The Queen's neck-handkerchief and my sword, which are worth their weight in gold, are also missing, and, what is worst of all, the Ambassador Fanfaronade is nowhere to be found. I greatly fear that the King, his master, when he receives no tidings from him, will come to seek him among us, and will accuse us of having made mince-meat of him. Perhaps I could bear even that if I had any money, but I assure you that the expenses of the wedding have completely ruined me. Advise me, then, my dear subjects, what had I better do to recover my daughter, Fanfaronade, and the other things."

This was the most eloquent speech the King had been known to make, and when everybody had done admiring it the Prime Minister made answer:

"Sire, we are all very sorry to see you so sorry. We would give everything we value in the world to take away the cause of your sorrow, but this seems to be another of the tricks of the Fairy Carabosse. The Princess's twenty unlucky years were not quite over, and really, if the truth must be told, I noticed that Fanfaronade and the Princess appeared to admire one another greatly. Perhaps this may give some clue to the mystery of their disappearance."

Here the Queen interrupted him, saying, "Take care what you say, sir. Believe me, the Princess Mayblossom was far too well brought up to think of falling in love with an Ambassador."

At this the nurse came forward, and, falling on her knees, confessed how they had made the little needle-hole in the tower, and how the Princess had declared when she saw the Ambassador that she would marry him and nobody else. Then the Queen was very angry, and gave the nurse, and the cradle-rocker, and the nursery-maid such a scolding that they shook in their shoes. But the Admiral Cocked-Hat interrupted her, crying:

"Let us be off after this good-for-nothing Fanfaronade, for with out a doubt he has run away with our Princess."

Then there was a great clapping of hands, and everybody shouted, "By all means let us be after him."

So while some embarked upon the sea, the others ran from kingdom to kingdom beating drums and blowing trumpets, and wherever a crowd collected they cried:

"Whoever wants a beautiful doll, sweetmeats of all kinds, a little pair of scissors, a golden robe, and a satin cap has only to say where Fanfaronade has hidden the Princess Mayblossom."

But the answer everywhere was, "You must go farther, we have not seen them."

However, those who went by sea were more fortunate, for after sailing about for some time they noticed a light before them which burned at night like a great fire. At first they dared not go near it, not knowing what it might be, but by-and-by it remained stationary over Squirrel Island, for, as you have guessed already, the light was the glowing of the carbuncle. The Princess and Fanfaronade on landing upon the island had given the boatman a hundred gold pieces, and made him promise solemnly to tell no one where he had taken them; but the first thing that happened was that, as he rowed away, he got into the midst of the fleet, and before he could escape the Admiral had seen him and sent a boat after him.

When he was searched they found the gold pieces in his pocket, and as they were quite new coins, struck in honor of the Princess's wedding, the Admiral felt certain that the boatman must have been paid by the Princess to aid her in her flight. But he would not answer any questions, and pretended to be deaf and dumb.

Then the Admiral said: "Oh! deaf and dumb is he? Lash him to the mast and give him a taste of the cat-o'-nine-tails. I don't know anything better than that for curing the deaf and dumb!"

And when the old boatman saw that he was in earnest, he told all he knew about the cavalier and the lady whom he had landed upon Squirrel Island, and the Admiral knew it must be the Princess and Fanfaronade; so he gave the order for the fleet to surround the island.

Meanwhile the Princess Mayblossom, who was by this time terribly sleepy, had found a grassy bank in the shade, and throwing herself down had already fallen into a profound slumber, when Fanfaronade, who happened to be hungry and not sleepy, came and woke her up, saying, very crossly:

"Pray, madam, how long do you mean to stay here? I see nothing to eat, and though you may be very charming, the sight of you does not prevent me from famishing."

"What! Fanfaronade," said the Princess, sitting up and rubbing her eyes, "is it possible that when I am here with you you can want anything else? You ought to be thinking all the time how happy you are."

"Happy!" cried he; "say rather unhappy. I wish with all my heart that you were back in your dark tower again."

"Darling, don't be cross," said the Princess. "I will go and see if I can find some wild fruit for you."

"I wish you might find a wolf to eat you up," growled Fanfaronade.

The Princess, in great dismay, ran hither and thither all about the wood, tearing her dress, and hurting her pretty white hands with the thorns and brambles, but she could find nothing good to eat, and at last she had to go back sorrowfully to Fanfaronade. When he saw that she came empty-handed he got up and left her, grumbling to himself.

The next day they searched again, but with no better success.

"Alas!" said the Princess, "if only I could find something for you to eat, I should not mind being hungry myself."

"No, I should not mind that either," answered Fanfaronade.

"Is it possible," said she, "that you would not care if I died of hunger? Oh, Fanfaronade, you said you loved me!"

"That was when we were in quite another place and I was not hungry," said he. "It makes a great difference in one's ideas to be dying of hunger and thirst on a desert island."

At this the Princess was dreadfully vexed, and she sat down under a white rose bush and began to cry bitterly.

"Happy roses," she thought to herself, "they have only to blossom in the sunshine and be admired, and there is nobody to be unkind to them." And the tears ran down her cheeks and splashed on to the rose-tree roots. Presently she was surprised to see the whole bush rustling and shaking, and a soft little voice from the prettiest rosebud said:

"Poor Princess! look in the trunk of that tree, and you will find a honeycomb, but don't be foolish enough to share it with Fanfaronade."

Mayblossom ran to the tree, and sure enough there was the honey. Without losing a moment she ran with it to Fanfaronade, crying gaily:

"See, here is a honeycomb that I have found. I might have eaten it up all by myself, but I had rather share it with you."

But without looking at her or thanking her he snatched the honey comb out of her hands and ate it all up—every bit, without offering her a morsel. Indeed, when she humbly asked for some he said mockingly that it was too sweet for her, and would spoil her teeth.

Mayblossom, more downcast than ever, went sadly away and sat down under an oak tree, and her tears and sighs were so piteous that the oak fanned her with his rustling leaves, and said:

"Take courage, pretty Princess, all is not lost yet. Take this pitcher of milk and drink it up, and whatever you do, don't leave a drop for Fanfaronade."

The Princess, quite astonished, looked round, and saw a big pitcher full of milk, but before she could raise it to her lips the thought of how thirsty Fanfaronade must be, after eating at least fifteen pounds of honey, made her run back to him and say:

"Here is a pitcher of milk; drink some, for you must be thirsty I am sure; but pray save a little for me, as I am dying of hunger and thirst."

But he seized the pitcher and drank all it contained at a single draught, and then broke it to atoms on the nearest stone, saying with a malicious smile: "As you have not eaten anything you cannot be thirsty."

"Ah!" cried the Princess, "I am well punished for disappointing the King and Queen, and running away with this Ambassador about whom I knew nothing."

And so saying she wandered away into the thickest part of the wood, and sat down under a thorn tree, where a nightingale was singing. Presently she heard him say: "Search under the bush Princess; you will find some sugar, almonds, and some tarts there But don't be silly enough to offer Fanfaronade any." And this time the Princess, who was fainting with hunger, took the nightingale's advice, and ate what she found all by herself. But Fanfaronade, seeing that she had found something good, and was not going to share it with him, ran after her in such a fury that she hastily drew out the Queen's carbuncle, which had the property of rendering people invisible if they were in danger, and when she was safely hidden from him she reproached him gently for his unkindness.

Meanwhile Admiral Cocked-Hat had dispatched Jack-the-Chatterer-of-the-Straw-Boots, Courier in Ordinary to the Prime Minister, to tell the King that the Princess and the Ambassador had landed on Squirrel Island, but that not knowing the country he had not pursued them, for fear of being captured by concealed enemies. Their Majesties were overjoyed at the news, and the King sent for a great book, each leaf of which was eight ells long. It was the work of a very clever Fairy, and contained a description of the whole earth. He very soon found that Squirrel Island was uninhabited.

"Go," said he, to Jack-the-Chatterer, "tell the Admiral from me to land at once. I am surprised at his not having done so sooner." As soon as this message reached the fleet, every preparation was made for war, and the noise was so great that it reached the ears of the Princess, who at once flew to protect her lover. As he was not very brave he accepted her aid gladly.

"You stand behind me," said she, "and I will hold the carbuncle which will make us invisible, and with the King's dagger I can protect you from the enemy." So when the soldiers landed they could see nothing, but the Princess touched them one after another with the dagger, and they fell insensible upon the sand, so that at last the Admiral, seeing that there was some enchantment, hastily gave orders for a retreat to be sounded, and got his men back into their boats in great confusion.

Fanfaronade, being once more left with the Princess, began to think that if he could get rid of her, and possess himself of the carbuncle and the dagger, he would be able to make his escape. So as they walked back over the cliffs he gave the Princess a great push, hoping she would fall into the sea; but she stepped aside so quickly that he only succeeded in overbalancing himself, and over he went, and sank to the bottom of the sea like a lump of lead, and was never heard of any more. While the Princess was still looking after him in horror, her attention was attracted by a rushing noise over her head, and looking up she saw two chariots approaching rapidly from opposite directions. One was bright and glittering, and drawn by swans and peacocks, while the Fairy who sat in it was beautiful as a sunbeam; but the other was drawn by bats and ravens, and contained a frightful little Dwarf, who was dressed in a snake's skin, and wore a great toad upon her head for a hood. The chariots met with a frightful crash in mid-air, and the Princess looked on in breathless anxiety while a furious battle took place between the lovely Fairy with her golden lance, and the hideous little Dwarf and her rusty pike. But very soon it was evident that the Beauty had the best of it, and the Dwarf turned her bats' heads and flickered away in great confusion, while the Fairy came down to where the Princess stood, and said, smiling, "You see Princess, I have completely routed that malicious old Carabosse. Will you believe it! she actually wanted to claim authority over you for ever, because you came out of the tower four days before the twenty years were ended. However, I think I have settled her pretensions, and I hope you will be very happy and enjoy the freedom I have won for you."

The Princess thanked her heartily, and then the Fairy dispatched one of her peacocks to her palace to bring a gorgeous robe for Mayblossom, who certainly needed it, for her own was torn to shreds by the thorns and briars. Another peacock was sent to the Admiral to tell him that he could now land in perfect safety, which he at once did, bringing all his men with him, even to Jack-the-Chatterer, who, happening to pass the spit upon which the Admiral's dinner was roasting, snatched it up and brought it with him.

Admiral Cocked-Hat was immensely surprised when he came upon the golden chariot, and still more so to see two lovely ladies walking under the trees a little farther away. When he reached them, of course he recognized the Princess, and he went down on his knees and kissed her hand quite joyfully. Then she presented him to the Fairy, and told him how Carabosse had been finally routed, and he thanked and congratulated the Fairy, who was most gracious to him. While they were talking she cried suddenly:

"I declare I smell a savory dinner."

"Why yes, Madam, here it is," said Jack-the-Chatterer, holding up the spit, where all the pheasants and partridges were frizzling. "Will your Highness please to taste any of them?"

"By all means," said the Fairy, "especially as the Princess will certainly be glad of a good meal."

So the Admiral sent back to his ship for everything that was needful, and they feasted merrily under the trees. By the time they had finished the peacock had come back with a robe for the Princess, in which the Fairy arrayed her. It was of green and gold brocade, embroidered with pearls and rubies, and her long golden hair was tied back with strings of diamonds and emeralds, and crowned with flowers. The Fairy made her mount beside her in the golden chariot, and took her on board the Admiral's ship, where she bade her farewell, sending many messages of friendship to the Queen, and bidding the Princess tell her that she was the fifth Fairy who had attended the christening. Then salutes were fired, the fleet weighed anchor, and very soon they reached the port. Here the King and Queen were waiting, and they received the Princess with such joy and kindness that she could not get a word in edgewise, to say how sorry she was for having run away with such a very poor spirited Ambassador. But, after all, it must have been all Carabosse's fault. Just at this lucky moment who should arrive but King Merlin's son, who had become uneasy at not receiving any news from his Ambassador, and so had started himself with a magnificent escort of a thousand horsemen, and thirty body-guards in gold and scarlet uniforms, to see what could have happened. As he was a hundred times handsomer and braver than the Ambassador, the Princess found she could like him very much. So the wedding was held at once, with so much splendor and rejoicing that all the previous misfortunes were quite forgotten.

The Two Caskets

(FROM *THE ORANGE FAIRY BOOK*)

Far, far away, in the midst of a pine forest, there lived a woman who had both a daughter and a stepdaughter. Ever since her own daughter was born the mother had given her all that she cried for, so she grew up to be as cross and disagreeable as she was ugly. Her stepsister, on the other hand, had spent her childhood in working hard to keep house for her father, who died soon after his second marriage; and she was as much beloved by the neighbors for her goodness and industry as she was for her beauty.

As the years went on, the difference between the two girls grew more marked, and the old woman treated her stepdaughter worse than ever, and was always on the watch for some pretext for beating her, or depriving her of her food. Anything, however foolish, was good enough for this, and one day, when she could think of nothing better, she set both the girls to spin while sitting on the low wall of the well.

"And you had better mind what you do," said she, "for the one whose thread breaks first shall be thrown to the bottom."

But of course she took good care that her own daughter's flax was fine and strong, while the stepsister had only some coarse stuff, which no one would have thought of using. As might be expected, in a very little while the poor girl's thread snapped, and the old woman, who had been watching from behind a door, seized her stepdaughter by her shoulders, and threw her into the well.

"That is an end of you!" she said. But she was wrong, for it was only the beginning.

Down, down, down went the girl—it seemed as if the well must reach to the very middle of the earth; but at last her feet touched the ground, and she found herself in a field more beautiful than even the summer pastures of her native mountains. Trees waved in the soft breeze, and flowers of the brightest colors danced in the grass. And though she was quite alone, the girl's heart danced too, for she felt happier than she had since her father died. So she

walked on through the meadow till she came to an old tumbledown fence—
so old that it was a wonder it managed to stand up at all, and it looked as if it
depended for support on the old man's beard that climbed all over it.

The girl paused for a moment as she came up, and gazed about for a place
where she might safely cross. But before she could move a voice cried from
the fence:

"Do not hurt me, little maiden; I am so old, so old, I have not much longer
to live."

And the maiden answered:

"No, I will not hurt you; fear nothing." And then seeing a spot where the
clematis grew less thickly than in other places, she jumped lightly over.

"May all go well with thee," said the fence, as the girl walked on.

She soon left the meadow and turned into a path which ran between two
flowery hedges. Right in front of her stood an oven, and through its open
door she could see a pile of white loaves.

"Eat as many loaves as you like, but do me no harm, little maiden,"
cried the oven. And the maiden told her to fear nothing, for she never hurt
anything, and was very grateful for the oven's kindness in giving her such a
beautiful white loaf. When she had finished it, down to the last crumb, she
shut the oven door and said: "Good-morning."

"May all go well with thee," said the oven, as the girl walked on.

By-and-by she became very thirsty, and seeing a cow with a milk-pail
hanging on her horn, turned towards her.

"Milk me and drink as much as you will, little maiden," cried the cow,
"but be sure you spill none on the ground; and do me no harm, for I have
never harmed anyone."

"Nor I," answered the girl; "fear nothing." So she sat down and milked till the
pail was nearly full. Then she drank it all up except a little drop at the bottom.

"Now throw any that is left over my hoofs, and hang the pail on my horns
again," said the cow. And the girl did as she was bid, and kissed the cow on
her forehead and went her way.

Many hours had now passed since the girl had fallen down the well, and
the sun was setting.

"Where shall I spend the night?" thought she. And suddenly she saw
before her a gate which she had not noticed before, and a very old woman
leaning against it.

"Good evening," said the girl politely; and the old woman answered:

"Good evening, my child. Would that everyone was as polite as you. Are you in search of anything?"

"I am in search of a place," replied the girl; and the woman smiled and said:

"Then stop a little while and comb my hair, and you shall tell me all the things you can do."

"Willingly, mother," answered the girl. And she began combing out the old woman's hair, which was long and white.

Half an hour passed in this way, and then the old woman said:

"As you did not think yourself too good to comb me, I will show you where you may take service. Be prudent and patient and all will go well."

So the girl thanked her, and set out for a farm at a little distance, where she was engaged to milk the cows and sift the corn.

As soon as it was light next morning the girl got up and went into the cow-house. "I'm sure you must be hungry," said she, patting each in turn. And then she fetched hay from the barn, and while they were eating it, she swept out the cow-house, and strewed clean straw upon the floor. The cows were so pleased with the care she took of them that they stood quite still while she milked them, and did not play any of the tricks on her that they had played on other dairymaids who were rough and rude. And when she had done, and was going to get up from her stool, she found sitting round her a whole circle of cats, black and white, tabby and tortoise-shell, who all cried with one voice:

"We are very thirsty, please give us some milk!"

"My poor little pussies," said she, "of course you shall have some." And she went into the dairy, followed by all the cats, and gave each one a little red saucerful. But before they drank they all rubbed themselves against her knees and purred by way of thanks.

The next thing the girl had to do was to go to the storehouse, and to sift the corn through a sieve. While she was busy rubbing the corn she heard a whirr of wings, and a flock of sparrows flew in at the window.

"We are hungry; give us some corn! give us some corn!" cried they; and the girl answered:

"You poor little birds, of course you shall have some!" and scattered a fine handful over the floor. When they had finished they flew on her shoulders and flapped their wings by way of thanks.

Time went by, and no cows in the whole country-side were so fat and well tended as hers, and no dairy had so much milk to show. The farmer's wife was so well satisfied that she gave her higher wages, and treated her like her own daughter. At length, one day, the girl was bidden by her mistress to come into the kitchen, and when there, the old woman said to her: "I know you can tend cows and keep a diary; now let me see what you can do besides. Take this sieve to the well, and fill it with water, and bring it home to me without spilling one drop by the way."

The girl's heart sank at this order; for how was it possible for her to do her mistress's bidding? However, she was silent, and taking the sieve went down to the well with it. Stopping over the side, she filled it to the brim, but as soon as she lifted it the water all ran out of the holes. Again and again she tried, but not a drop would remaining in the sieve, and she was just turning away in despair when a flock of sparrows flew down from the sky.

"Ashes! ashes!" they twittered; and the girl looked at them and said:

"Well, I can't be in a worse plight than I am already, so I will take your advice." And she ran back to the kitchen and filled her sieve with ashes. Then once more she dipped the sieve into the well, and, behold, this time not a drop of water disappeared!

"Here is the sieve, mistress," cried the girl, going to the room where the old woman was sitting.

"You are cleverer than I expected," answered she; "or else someone helped you who is skilled in magic." But the girl kept silence, and the old woman asked her no more questions.

Many days passed during which the girl went about her work as usual, but at length one day the old woman called her and said:

"I have something more for you to do. There are here two yarns, the one white, the other black. What you must do is to wash them in the river till the black one becomes white and the white black." And the girl took them to the river and washed hard for several hours, but wash as she would they never changed one whit.

"This is worse than the sieve," thought she, and was about to give up in despair when there came a rush of wings through the air, and on every twig of the birch trees which grew by the bank was perched a sparrow.

"The black to the east, the white to the west!" they sang, all at once; and the girl dried her tears and felt brave again. Picking up the black yarn, she stood facing the east and dipped it in the river, and in an instant it grew white as snow, then turning to the west, she held the white yarn in the water, and it became as black as a crow's wing. She looked back at the sparrows and smiled and nodded to them, and flapping their wings in reply they flew swiftly away.

At the sight of the yarn the old woman was struck dumb; but when at length she found her voice she asked the girl what magician had helped her to do what no one had done before. But she got no answer, for the maiden was afraid of bringing trouble on her little friends.

For many weeks the mistress shut herself up in her room, and the girl went about her work as usual. She hoped that there was an end to the difficult tasks which had been set her; but in this she was mistaken, for one day the old woman appeared suddenly in the kitchen, and said to her:

"There is one more trial to which I must put you, and if you do not fail in that you will be left in peace for evermore. Here are the yarns which you washed. Take them and weave them into a web that is as smooth as a king's robe, and see that it is spun by the time that the sun sets."

"This is the easiest thing I have been set to do," thought the girl, who was a good spinner. But when she began she found that the skein tangled and broke every moment.

"Oh, I can never do it!" she cried at last, and leaned her head against the loom and wept; but at that instant the door opened, and there entered, one behind another, a procession of cats.

"What is the matter, fair maiden?" asked they. And the girl answered:

"My mistress has given me this yarn to weave into a piece of cloth, which must be finished by sunset, and I have not even begun yet, for the yarn breaks whenever I touch it."

"If that is all, dry your eyes," said the cats; "we will manage it for you." And they jumped on the loom, and wove so fast and so skillfully that in a very short time the cloth was ready and was as fine as any king ever wore. The girl was so delighted at the sight of it that she gave each cat a kiss on his forehead as they left the room behind one the other as they had come.

"Who has taught you this wisdom?" asked the old woman, after she had passed her hands twice or thrice over the cloth and could find no roughness anywhere. But the girl only smiled and did not answer. She had learned early the value of silence.

After a few weeks the old woman sent for her maid and told her that as her year of service was now up, she was free to return home, but that, for her part, the girl had served her so well that she hoped she might stay with her. But at these words the maid shook her head, and answered gently:

"I have been happy here, Madam, and I thank you for your goodness to me; but I have left behind me a stepsister and a stepmother, and I am fain to be with them once more." The old woman looked at her for a moment, and then she said:

"Well, that must be as you like; but as you have worked faithfully for me I will give you a reward. Go now into the loft above the store house and there you will find many caskets. Choose the one which pleases you best, but be careful not to open it till you have set it in the place where you wish it to remain."

The girl left the room to go to the loft, and as soon as she got outside, she found all the cats waiting for her. Walking in procession, as was their custom, they followed her into the loft, which was filled with caskets big and little, plain and splendid. She lifted up one and looked at it, and then put it down to examine another yet more beautiful. Which should she choose, the yellow or the blue, the red or the green, the gold or the silver? She hesitated long, and went first to one and then to another, when she heard the cats' voices calling: "Take the black! take the black!"

The words make her look round—she had seen no black casket, but as the cats continued their cry she peered into several corners that had remained unnoticed, and at length discovered a little black box, so small and so black, that it might easily have been passed over.

"This is the casket that pleases me best, mistress," said the girl, carrying it into the house. And the old woman smiled and nodded, and bade her go her way. So the girl set forth, after bidding farewell to the cows and the cats and the sparrows, who all wept as they said good-bye.

She walked on and on and on, till she reached the flowery meadow, and there, suddenly, something happened, she never knew what, but she was sitting on the wall of the well in her stepmother's yard. Then she got up and entered the house.

The woman and her daughter stared as if they had been turned into stone; but at length the stepmother gasped out:

"So you are alive after all! Well, luck was ever against me! And where have you been this year past?" Then the girl told how she had taken service in the under-world, and, beside her wages, had brought home with her a little casket, which she would like to set up in her room.

"Give me the money, and take the ugly little box off to the outhouse," cried the woman, beside herself with rage, and the girl, quite frightened at her violence, hastened away, with her precious box clasped to her bosom.

The outhouse was in a very dirty state, as no one had been near it since the girl had fallen down the well; but she scrubbed and swept till everything was clean again, and then she placed the little casket on a small shelf in the corner.

"Now I may open it," she said to herself; and unlocking it with the key which hung to its handle, she raised the lid, but started back as she did so, almost blinded by the light that burst upon her. No one would ever have guessed that that little black box could have held such a quantity of beautiful things! Rings, crowns, girdles, necklaces—all made of wonderful stones; and they shone with such brilliance that not only the stepmother and her daughter but all the people round came running to see if the house was on fire. Of course the woman felt quite ill with greed and envy, and she would have certainly taken all the jewels for herself had she not feared the wrath of the neighbors, who loved her stepdaughter as much as they hated her.

But if she could not steal the casket and its contents for herself, at least she could get another like it, and perhaps a still richer one. So she bade her own daughter sit on the edge of the well, and threw her into the water, exactly as she had done to the other girl; and, exactly as before, the flowery meadow lay at the bottom.

Every inch of the way she trod the path which her stepsister had trodden, and saw the things which she had seen; but there the likeness ended. When the fence prayed her to do it no harm, she laughed rudely, and tore up some of the stakes so that she might get over the more easily; when the oven offered her bread, she scattered the loaves onto the ground and stamped on them; and after she had milked the cow, and drunk as much as she wanted, she threw the rest on the grass, and kicked the pail to bits, and never heard them say, as they looked after her: "You shall not have done this to me for nothing!"

Towards evening she reached the spot where the old woman was leaning against the gate-post, but she passed her by without a word.

"Have you no manners in your country?" asked the crone.

"I can't stop and talk; I am in a hurry," answered the girl. "It is getting late, and I have to find a place."

"Stop and comb my hair for a little," said the old woman, "and I will help you to get a place."

"Comb your hair, indeed! I have something better to do than that!" And slamming the gate in the crone's face she went her way. And she never heard the words that followed her: "You shall not have done this to me for nothing!"

By-and-by the girl arrived at the farm, and she was engaged to look after the cows and sift the corn as her stepsister had been. But it was only when someone was watching her that she did her work; at other times the cow-house was dirty, and the cows ill-fed and beaten, so that they kicked over the pail, and tried to butt her; and everyone said they had never seen such thin cows or such poor milk. As for the cats, she chased them away, and ill-treated them, so that they had not even the spirit to chase the rats and mice, which nowadays ran about everywhere. And when the sparrows came to beg for some corn, they fared no better than the cows and the cats, for the girl threw her shoes at them, till they flew in a fright to the woods, and took shelter among the trees.

Months passed in this manner, when, one day, the mistress called the girl to her.

"All that I have given you to do you have done ill," said she, "yet will I give you another chance. For though you cannot tend cows, or divide the grain from the chaff, there may be other things that you can do better. Therefore take this sieve to the well, and fill it with water, and see that you bring it back without spilling a drop."

The girl took the sieve and carried it to the well as her sister had done; but no little birds came to help her, and after dipping it in the well two or three times she brought it back empty.

"I thought as much," said the old woman angrily; "she that is useless in one thing is useless in another."

Perhaps the mistress may have thought that the girl had learnt a lesson, but, if she did, she was quite mistaken, as the work was no better done than before. By-and-by she sent for her again, and gave her maid the black and white yarn to wash in the river; but there was no one to tell her the secret by which the black would turn white, and the white black; so she brought them back as they were. This time the old woman only looked at her grimly but the girl was too well pleased with herself to care what anyone thought about her.

After some weeks her third trial came, and the yarn was given her to spin, as it had been given to her stepsister before her.

But no procession of cats entered the room to weave a web of fine cloth, and at sunset she only brought back to her mistress an armful of dirty, tangled wool.

"There seems nothing in the world you can do," said the old woman, and left her to herself.

Soon after this the year was up, and the girl went to her mistress to tell her that she wished to go home.

"Little desire have I to keep you," answered the old woman, "for no one thing have you done as you ought. Still, I will give you some payment, therefore go up into the loft, and choose for yourself one of the caskets that lies there. But see that you do not open it till you place it where you wish it to stay."

This was what the girl had been hoping for, and so rejoiced was she, that, without even stopping to thank the old woman, she ran as fast as she could to the loft. There were the caskets, blue and red, green and yellow, silver and gold; and there in the corner stood a little black casket just like the one her stepsister had brought home.

"If there are so many jewels in that little black thing, this big red one will hold twice the number," she said to herself; and snatching it up she set off on her road home without even going to bid farewell to her mistress.

"See, mother, see what I have brought!" cried she, as she entered the cottage holding the casket in both hands.

"Ah! you have got something very different from that little black box," answered the old woman with delight. But the girl was so busy finding a place for it to stand that she took little notice of her mother.

"It will look best here—no, here," she said, setting it first on one piece of furniture and then on another. "No, after all it is to fine to live in a kitchen, let us place it in the guest chamber."

So mother and daughter carried it proudly upstairs and put it on a shelf over the fireplace; then, untying the key from the handle, they opened the box. As before, a bright light leapt out directly the lid was raised, but it did not spring from the luster of jewels, but from hot flames, which darted along the walls and burnt up the cottage and all that was in it and the mother and daughter as well.

As they had done when the stepdaughter came home, the neighbors all hurried to see what was the matter; but they were too late. Only the hen-house was left standing; and, in spite of her riches, there the stepdaughter lived happily to the end of her days.

Little One-eye, Little Two-eyes, and Little Three-eyes

(FROM *THE GREEN FAIRY BOOK*)

There was once a woman who had three daughters, of whom the eldest was called Little One-eye, because she had only one eye in the middle of her forehead; and the second, Little Two-eyes, because she had two eyes like other people; and the youngest, Little Three-eyes, because she had three eyes, and *her* third eye was also in the middle of her forehead. But because Little Two-eyes did not look any different from other children, her sisters and mother could not bear her. They would say to her, "You with your two eyes are no better than common folk; you don't belong to us." They pushed her here, and threw her wretched clothes there, and gave her to eat only what they left, and they were as unkind to her as ever they could be.

It happened one day that Little Two-eyes had to go out into the fields to take care of the goat, but she was still quite hungry because her sisters had given her so little to eat. So she sat down in the meadow and began to cry, and she cried so much that two little brooks ran out of her eyes. But when she looked up once in her grief there stood a woman beside her who asked, "Little Two-eyes, what are you crying for?" Little Two-eyes answered, "Have I not reason to cry? Because I have two eyes like other people, my sisters and my mother cannot bear me; they push me out of one corner into another, and give me nothing to eat except what they leave. To-day they have given me so little that I am still quite hungry." Then the wise woman said, "Little Two-eyes, dry your eyes, and I will tell you something so that you need never be hungry again. Only say to your goat,

'Little goat, bleat,
Little table, appear,'

and a beautifully spread table will stand before you, with the most delicious food on it, so that you can eat as much as you want. And when you have had enough and don't want the little table any more, you have only to say,

'Little goat, bleat,
Little table, away,'

and then it will vanish." Then the wise woman went away.

But Little Two-eyes thought, "I must try at once if what she has told me is true, for I am more hungry than ever"; and she said,

"Little goat, bleat,
Little table, appear,"

and scarcely had she uttered the words, when there stood a little table before her covered with a white cloth, on which were arranged a plate, with a knife and fork and a silver spoon, and the most beautiful dishes, which were smoking hot, as if they had just come out of the kitchen. Then Little Two-eyes said the shortest grace she knew, and set to work and made a good dinner. And when she had had enough, she said, as the wise woman had told her,

"Little goat, bleat,
Little table, away,"

and immediately the table and all that was on it disappeared again. "That is a splendid way of housekeeping," thought Little Two-eyes, and she was quite happy and contented.

In the evening, when she went home with her goat, she found a little earthenware dish with the food that her sisters had thrown to her, but she did not touch it. The next day she went out again with her goat, and left the few scraps which were given her. The first and second times her sisters did not notice this, but when it happened continually, they remarked it and said, "Something is the matter with Little Two-eyes, for she always leaves her food now, and she used to gobble up all that was given her. She must have found other means of getting food." So in order to get at the truth, Little One-eye was told to go out with Little Two-eyes when she drove the goat to pasture, and to notice particularly what she got there, and whether anyone brought her food and drink.

Now when Little Two-eyes was setting out, Little One-eye came up to her and said, "I will go into the field with you and see if you take good care of the goat, and if you drive him properly to get grass." But Little Two-eyes saw what Little One-eye had in her mind, and she drove the goat into the long grass and said, "Come, Little One-eye, we will sit down here, and I will sing you something."

Little One-eye sat down, and as she was very much tired by the long walk to which she was not used, and by the hot day, and as Little Two-eyes went on singing

> "Little One-eye, are you awake?
> Little One-eye, are you asleep?"

she shut her one eye and fell asleep. When Little Two-eyes saw that Little One-eye was asleep and could find out nothing, she said,

> "Little goat, bleat,
> Little table, appear,"

and sat down at her table and ate and drank as much as she wanted. Then she said again,

> "Little goat, bleat,
> Little table, away,"

and in the twinkling of an eye all had vanished.

Little Two-eyes then woke Little One-eye and said, "Little One-eye, you meant to watch, and, instead, you went to sleep; in the meantime the goat might have run far and wide. Come, we will go home." So they went home, and Little Two-eyes again left her little dish untouched, and Little One-eye could not tell her mother why she would not eat, and said as an excuse, "I was so sleepy out-of-doors."

The next day the mother said to Little Three-eyes, "This time you shall go with Little Two-eyes and watch whether she eats anything out in the fields, and whether anyone brings her food and drink, for eat and drink she must secretly." So Little Three-eyes went to Little Two-eyes and said, "I will go with you and see if you take good care of the goat, and if you drive him properly to get grass." But little Two-eyes knew what Little Three-eyes had in her mind, and she drove the goat out into the tall grass and said, "We will sit down here, Little Three-eyes, and I will sing you something." Little Three-eyes sat down; she was tired by the walk and the hot day, and Little Two-eyes sang the same little song again:

"Little Three-eyes, are you awake?"

but instead of singing as she ought to have done,

"Little Three-eyes, are you asleep?"

she sang, without thinking,

"Little *Two-eyes*, are you asleep?"

She went on singing,
"Little Three-eyes, are you awake?
Little *Two-eyes*, are you asleep?"

so that the two eyes of Little Three-eyes fell asleep, but the third, which was not spoken to in the little rhyme, did not fall asleep. Of course Little Three-eyes shut that eye also out of cunning, to look as if she were asleep, but it was blinking and could see everything quite well.

And when Little Two-eyes thought that Little Three-eyes was sound asleep, she said her rhyme,

"Little goat, bleat,
Little table, appear,"

and ate and drank to her heart's content, and then made the table go away again, by saying,

> "Little goat, bleat,
> Little table, away."

But Little Three-eyes had seen everything. Then Little Two-eyes came to her, and woke her and said, "Well, Little Three-eyes, have you been asleep? You watch well! Come, we will go home." When they reached home, Little Two-eyes did not eat again, and Little Three-eyes said to the mother, "I know now why that proud thing eats nothing. When she says to the goat in the field,

> 'Little goat, bleat,
> Little table, appear,'

a table stands before her, spread with the best food, much better than we have; and when she has had enough, she says,

> 'Little goat, bleat,
> Little table, away,'

and everything disappears again. I saw it all exactly. She made two of my eyes go to sleep with a little rhyme, but the one in my forehead remained awake, luckily!"

Then the envious mother cried out, "Will you fare better than we do? you shall not have the chance to do so again!" and she fetched a knife, and killed the goat.

When Little Two-eyes saw this, she went out full of grief, and sat down in the meadow and wept bitter tears. Then again the wise woman stood before her, and said, "Little Two-eyes, what are you crying for?" "Have I not reason to cry?" she answered, "the goat, which when I said the little rhyme, spread the table so beautifully, my mother has killed, and now I must suffer hunger and want again." The wise woman said, "Little Two-eyes, I will give you a good piece of advice. Ask your sisters to give you the heart of the dead goat, and bury it in the earth before the house-door; that will bring you good luck." Then she disappeared, and Little Two-eyes went home, and said to her sisters, "Dear sisters, do give me something of my goat; I ask nothing better than its heart." Then they laughed and said, "You can have that if you want nothing more." And Little Two-eyes took the heart and buried it in the evening when all was quiet, as the wise woman had told her, before the house-door. The next morning when they all awoke and came to the house-door, there stood a most wonderful tree, which had leaves of silver and fruit of gold growing on it—you never saw anything more lovely and gorgeous in your life! But they did not know how the tree had grown up in the night; only Little Two-eyes knew that it had sprung from the heart of the goat, for it was standing just where she had buried it in the ground. Then the mother said to Little One-eye, "Climb up, my child, and break us off the fruit from the tree." Little One-eye climbed up, but just when she was going to take hold of one of the golden apples the bough sprang out of her hands; and this happened every time, so that she could not break off a single apple, however hard she tried. Then the mother said, "Little Three-eyes, do you climb up; you with your three eyes can see round better than Little One-eye." So Little One-eye slid down, and Little Three-eyes climbed up; but she was not any more successful; look round as she might, the golden apples bent themselves back. At last the mother got impatient and climbed up herself, but she was even less successful than Little One-eye and Little Three-eyes in catching hold of the fruit, and only grasped at the empty air. Then Little Two-eyes said, "I will just try once, perhaps I shall succeed better." The sisters called out, "You with your two eyes will no doubt succeed!" But Little Two-eyes climbed up, and the golden apples did not jump away from her, but behaved quite properly, so that she could pluck them off, one after the other, and brought a whole apron-full down with her. The mother took them from her, and, instead of behaving better to poor Little Two-eyes, as they ought to have done, they were jealous that she only could reach the fruit and behaved still more unkindly to her.

It happened one day that when they were all standing together by the tree that a young knight came riding along. "Be quick, Little Two-eyes," cried the two sisters, "creep under this, so that you shall not disgrace us," and they put over poor Little Two-eyes as quickly as possible an empty cask, which was standing close to the tree, and they pushed the golden apples which she had broken off under with her. When the knight, who was a very handsome young man, rode up, he wondered to see the marvelous tree of gold and silver, and said to the two sisters, "Whose is this beautiful tree? Whoever will give me a twig of it shall have whatever she wants." Then Little One-eye and Little Three-eyes answered that the tree belonged to them, and that they would certainly break him off a twig. They gave themselves a great deal of trouble, but in vain; the twigs and fruit bent back every time from their hands. Then the knight said, "It is very strange that the tree should belong to you, and yet that you have not the power to break anything from it!" But they would have that the tree was theirs; and while they were saying this, Little Two-eyes rolled a couple of golden apples from under the cask, so that they lay at the knight's feet, for she was angry with Little One-eye and Little Three-eyes for not speaking the truth. When the knight saw the apples he was astonished, and asked where they came from. Little One-eye and Little Three-eyes answered that they had another sister, but she could not be seen because she had only two eyes, like ordinary people. But the knight demanded to see her, and called out, "Little Two-eyes, come forth." Then Little Two-eyes came out from under the cask quite happily, and the knight was astonished at her great beauty, and said, "Little Two-eyes, I am sure you can break me off a twig from the tree." "Yes," answered Little Two-eyes, "I can, for the tree is mine." So she climbed up and broke off a small branch with its silver leaves and golden fruit without any trouble, and gave it to the knight. Then he said, "Little Two-eyes, what shall I give you for this?" "Ah," answered Little Two-eyes, "I suffer hunger and thirst, want and sorrow, from early morning till late in the evening; if you would take me with you, and free me from this, I should be happy!" Then the knight lifted Little Two-eyes on his horse, and took her home to his father's castle. There he gave her beautiful clothes, and food and drink, and because he loved her so much he married her, and the wedding was celebrated with great joy.

When the handsome knight carried Little Two-eyes away with him, the two sisters envied her good luck at first. "But the wonderful tree is still with us, after all," they thought, "and although we cannot break any fruit from it, everyone will stop and look at it, and will come to us and praise it; who knows whether *we* may not reap a harvest from it?" But the next morning the tree had flown, and their hopes with it; and when Little Two-eyes looked out of her window there it stood underneath, to her great delight. Little Two-eyes lived happily for a long time. Once two poor women came to the castle to beg alms. Then Little Two-eyes looked at them and recognized both her sisters, Little One-eye and Little Three-eyes, who had become so poor that they came to beg bread at her door. But Little Two-eyes bade them welcome, and was so good to them that they both repented from their hearts of having been so unkind to their sister.

Long, Broad, and Quickeye

(FROM *THE GRAY FAIRY BOOK*)

Once upon a time there lived a king who had an only son whom he loved dearly. Now one day the king sent for his son and said to him:

"My dearest child, my hair is grey and I am old, and soon I shall feel no more the warmth of the sun, or look upon the trees and flowers. But before I die I should like to see you with a good wife; therefore marry, my son, as speedily as possible."

"My father," replied the prince, "now and always, I ask nothing better than to do your bidding, but I know of no daughter-in-law that I could give you."

On hearing these words the old king drew from his pocket a key of gold, and gave it to his son, saying:

"Go up the staircase, right up to the top of the tower. Look carefully round you, and then come and tell me which you like best of all that you see."

So the young man went up. He had never before been in the tower, and had no idea what it might contain.

The staircase wound round and round and round, till the prince was almost giddy, and every now and then he caught sight of a large room that opened out from the side. But he had been told to go to the top, and to the top he went. Then he found himself in a hall, which had an iron door at one end. This door he unlocked with his golden key, and he passed through into a vast chamber which had a roof of blue sprinkled with golden stars, and a carpet of green silk soft as turf. Twelve windows framed in gold let in the light of the sun, and on every window was painted the figure of a young girl, each more beautiful than the last. While the prince gazed at them in surprise, not knowing which he liked best, the girls began to lift their eyes and smile at him. He waited, expecting them to speak, but no sound came.

Suddenly he noticed that one of the windows was covered by a curtain of white silk.

He lifted it, and saw before him the image of a maiden beautiful as the day and sad as the tomb, clothed in a white robe, having a girdle of silver and a crown of pearls. The prince stood and gazed at her, as if he had been turned into stone, but as he looked the sadness which, was on her face seemed to pass into his heart, and he cried out:

"This one shall be my wife. This one and no other."

As he said the words the young girl blushed and hung her head, and all the other figures vanished.

The young prince went quickly back to his father, and told him all he had seen and which wife he had chosen. The old man listened to him full of sorrow, and then he spoke:

"You have done ill, my son, to search out that which was hidden, and you are running to meet a great danger. This young girl has fallen into the power of a wicked sorcerer, who lives in an iron castle. Many young men have tried to deliver her, and none have ever come back. But what is done is done! You have given your word, and it cannot be broken. Go, dare your fate, and return to me safe and sound."

So the prince embraced his father, mounted his horse, and set forth to seek his bride. He rode on gaily for several hours, till he found himself in a wood where he had never been before, and soon lost his way among its winding paths and deep valleys. He tried in vain to see where he was: the thick trees shut out the sun, and he could not tell which was north and which was south, so that he might know what direction to make for. He felt in despair, and had quite given up all hope of getting out of this horrible place, when he heard a voice calling to him.

"Hey! hey! stop a minute!"

The prince turned round and saw behind him a very tall man, running as fast as his legs would carry him.

"Wait for me," he panted, "and take me into your service. If you do, you will never be sorry."

"Who are you?" asked the prince, "and what can you do?"

"Long is my name, and I can lengthen my body at will. Do you see that nest up there on the top of that pine-tree? Well, I can get it for you without taking the trouble of climbing the tree," and Long stretched himself up and up and up, till he was very soon as tall as the pine itself. He put the nest in his pocket, and before you could wink your eyelid he had made himself small again, and stood before the prince.

"Yes; you know your business," said he, "but birds' nests are no use to me. I am too old for them. Now if you were only able to get me out of this wood, you would indeed be good for something."

"Oh, there's no difficulty about that," replied Long, and he stretched himself up and up and up till he was three times as tall as the tallest tree in the forest. Then he looked all round and said, "We must go in this direction in order to get out of the wood," and shortening himself again, he took the prince's horse by the bridle, and led him along. Very soon they got clear of the forest, and saw before them a wide plain ending in a pile of high rocks, covered here and there with trees, and very much like the fortifications of a town.

As they left the wood behind, Long turned to the prince and said, "My lord, here comes my comrade. You should take him into your service too, as you will find him a great help."

"Well, call him then, so that I can see what sort of a man he is."

"He is a little too far off for that," replied Long. "He would hardly hear my voice, and he couldn't be here for some time yet, as he has so much to carry. I think I had better go and bring him myself," and this time he stretched himself to such a height that his head was lost in the clouds. He made two or three strides, took his friend on his back, and set him down before the prince. The new-comer was a very fat man, and as round as a barrel.

"Who are you?" asked the prince, "and what can you do?"

"Your worship, Broad is my name, and I can make myself as wide as I please."

"Let me see how you manage it."

"Run, my lord, as fast as you can, and hide yourself in the wood," cried Broad, and he began to swell himself out.

The prince did not understand why he should run to the wood, but when he saw Long flying towards it, he thought he had better follow his example. He was only just in time, for Broad had so suddenly inflated himself that he very nearly knocked over the prince and his horse too. He covered all the space for acres round. You would have thought he was a mountain!

At length Broad ceased to expand, drew a deep breath that made the whole forest tremble, and shrank into his usual size.

"You have made me run away," said the prince. "But it is not every day one meets with a man of your sort. I will take you into my service."

So the three companions continued their journey, and when they were drawing near the rocks they met a man whose eyes were covered by a bandage.

"Your excellency," said Long, "this is our third comrade. You will do well to take him into your service, and, I assure you, you will find him worth his salt."

"Who are you?" asked the prince. "And why are your eyes bandaged? You can never see your way!"

"It is just the contrary, my lord! It is because I see only too well that I am forced to bandage my eyes. Even so I see as well as people who have no bandage. When I take it off my eyes pierce through everything. Everything I look at catches fire, or, if it cannot catch fire, it falls into a thousand pieces. They call me Quickeye."

And so saying he took off his bandage and turned towards the rock. As he fixed his eyes upon it a crack was heard, and in a few moments it was nothing but a heap of sand. In the sand something might be detected glittering brightly. Quickeye picked it up and brought it to the prince. It turned out to be a lump of pure gold.

"You are a wonderful creature," said the prince, "and I should be a fool not to take you into my service. But since your eyes are so good, tell me if I am very far from the Iron Castle, and what is happening there just now."

"If you were traveling alone," replied Quickeye, "it would take you at least a year to get to it; but as we are with you, we shall arrive there to-night. Just now they are preparing supper."

"There is a princess in the castle. Do you see her?"

"A wizard keeps her in a high tower, guarded by iron bars."

"Ah, help me to deliver her!" cried the prince.

And they promised they would.

Then they all set out through the grey rocks, by the breach made by the eyes of Quickeye, and passed over great mountains and through deep woods. And every time they met with any obstacle the three friends contrived somehow to put it aside. As the sun was setting, the prince beheld the towers of the Iron Castle, and before it sank beneath the horizon he was crossing the iron bridge which led to the gates. He was only just in time, for no sooner had the sun disappeared altogether, than the bridge drew itself up and the gates shut themselves.

There was no turning back now!

The prince put up his horse in the stable, where everything looked as if a guest was expected, and then the whole party marched straight up to the castle. In the court, in the stables, and all over the great halls, they saw a number of men richly dressed, but every one turned into stone. They crossed an endless set of rooms, all opening into each other, till they reached the dining-hall. It was brilliantly lighted; the table was covered with wine and fruit, and was laid for four. They waited a few minutes expecting someone to come, but as nobody did, they sat down and began to eat and drink, for they were very hungry.

When they had done their supper they looked about for some place to sleep. But suddenly the door burst open, and the wizard entered the hall. He was old and hump-backed, with a bald head and a grey beard that fell to his knees. He wore a black robe, and instead of a belt three iron circlets clasped his waist. He led by the hand a lady of wonderful beauty, dressed in white, with a girdle of silver and a crown of pearls, but her face was pale and sad as death itself.

The prince knew her in an instant, and moved eagerly forward; but the wizard gave him no time to speak, and said:

"I know why you are here. Very good; you may have her if for three nights following you can prevent her making her escape. If you fail in this, you and your servants will all be turned into stone, like those who have come before you." And offering the princess a chair, he left the hall.

The prince could not take his eyes from the princess, she was so lovely! He began to talk to her, but she neither answered nor smiled, and sat as if she were made of marble. He seated himself by her, and determined not to close his eyes that night, for fear she should escape him. And in order that she should be doubly guarded, Long stretched himself like a strap all round the room, Broad took his stand by the door and puffed himself out, so that not even a mouse could slip by, and Quickeye leant against a pillar which stood in the middle of the floor and supported the roof. But in half a second they were all sound asleep, and they slept sound the whole night long.

In the morning, at the first peep of dawn, the prince awoke with a start. But the princess was gone. He aroused his servants and implored them to tell him what he must do.

"Calm yourself, my lord," said Quickeye. "I have found her already. A hundred miles from here there is a forest. In the middle of the forest, an old oak, and on the top of the oak, an acorn. This acorn is the princess. If Long will take me on his shoulders, we shall soon bring her back." And sure enough, in less time than it takes to walk round a cottage, they had returned from the forest, and Long presented the acorn to the prince.

"Now, your excellency, throw it on the ground."

The prince obeyed, and was enchanted to see the princess appear at his side. But when the sun peeped for the first time over the mountains, the door burst open as before, and the wizard entered with a loud laugh. Suddenly he caught sight of the princess; his face darkened, he uttered a low growl, and one of the iron circlets gave way with a crash. He seized the young girl by the hand and bore her away with him.

All that day the prince wandered about the castle, studying the curious treasures it contained, but everything looked as if life had suddenly come to a standstill. In one place he saw a prince who had been turned into stone in the act of brandishing a sword round which his two hands were clasped. In another, the same doom had fallen upon a knight in the act of running away. In a third, a serving man was standing eternally trying to convey a piece of beef to his mouth, and all around them were others, still preserving for evermore the attitudes they were in when the wizard had commanded "From henceforth be turned into marble." In the castle, and round the castle all was dismal and desolate. Trees there were, but without leaves; fields there were, but no grass grew on them. There was one river, but it never flowed and no fish lived in it. No flowers blossomed, and no birds sang.

Three times during the day food appeared, as if by magic, for the prince and his servants. And it was not until supper was ended that the wizard appeared, as on the previous evening, and delivered the princess into the care of the prince.

All four determined that this time they would keep awake at any cost. But it was no use. Off they went as they had done before, and when the prince awoke the next morning the room was again empty.

With a pang of shame, he rushed to find Quickeye. "Awake! Awake! Quickeye! Do you know what has become of the princess?"

Quickeye rubbed his eyes and answered: "Yes, I see her. Two hundred miles from here there is a mountain. In this mountain is a rock. In the rock, a precious stone. This stone is the princess. Long shall take me there, and we will be back before you can turn round."

So Long took him on his shoulders and they set out. At every stride they covered twenty miles, and as they drew near Quickeye fixed his burning eyes on the mountain; in an instant it split into a thousand pieces, and in one of these sparkled the precious stone. They picked it up and brought it to the prince, who flung it hastily down, and as the stone touched the floor the princess stood before him. When the wizard came, his eyes shot forth flames of fury. Cric-crac was heard, and another of his iron bands broke and fell. He seized the princess by the hand and led her off, growling louder than ever.

All that day things went on exactly as they had done the day before. After supper the wizard brought back the princess, and looking him straight in the eyes he said, "We shall see which of us two will gain the prize after all!"

That night they struggled their very hardest to keep awake, and even walked about instead of sitting down. But it was quite useless. One after another they had to give in, and for the third time the princess slipped through their fingers.

When morning came, it was as usual the prince who awoke the first, and as usual, the princess being gone, he rushed to Quickeye.

"Get up, get up, Quickeye, and tell me where is the princess?"

Quickeye looked about for some time without answering. "Oh, my lord, she is far, very far. Three hundred miles away there lies a black sea. In the middle of this sea there is a little shell, and in the middle of the shell is fixed a gold ring. That gold ring is the princess. But do not vex your soul; we will get her. Only to-day, Long must take Broad with him. He will be wanted badly."

So Long took Quickeye on one shoulder, and Broad on the other, and they set out. At each stride they left thirty miles behind them. When they reached the black sea, Quickeye showed them the spot where they must seek the shell. But though Long stretched down his hand as far as it would go, he could not find the shell, for it lay at the bottom of the sea.

"Wait a moment, comrades, it will be all right. I will help you," said Broad.

Then he swelled himself out so that you would have thought the world could hardly have held him, and stooping down he drank. He drank so much at every mouthful, that only a minute or so passed before the water had sunk enough for Long to put his hand to the bottom. He soon found the shell, and pulled the ring out. But time had been lost, and Long had a double burden to carry. The dawn was breaking fast before they got back to the castle, where the prince was waiting for them in an agony of fear.

Soon the first rays of the sun were seen peeping over the tops of the mountains. The door burst open, and finding the prince standing alone the wizard broke into peals of wicked laughter. But as he laughed a loud crash was heard, the window fell into a thousand pieces, a gold ring glittered in the air, and the princess stood before the enchanter. For Quickeye, who was watching from afar, had told Long of the terrible danger now threatening the prince, and Long, summoning all his strength for one gigantic effort, had thrown the ring right through the window.

The wizard shrieked and howled with rage, till the whole castle trembled to its foundations. Then a crash was heard, the third band split in two, and a crow flew out of the window.

Then the princess at length broke the enchanted silence, and blushing like a rose, gave the prince her thanks for her unlooked-for deliverance.

But it was not only the princess who was restored to life by the flight of the wicked black crow. The marble figures became men once more, and took up their occupations just as they had left them off. The horses neighed in the stables, the flowers blossomed in the garden, the birds flew in the air, the fish darted in the water. Everywhere you looked, all was life, all was joy!

And the knights who had been turned into stone came in a body to offer their homage to the prince who had set them free.

"Do not thank me," he said, "for I have done nothing. Without my faithful servants, Long, Broad, and Quickeye, I should even have been as one of you."

With these words he bade them farewell, and departed with the princess and his faithful companions for the kingdom of his father.

The old king, who had long since given up all hope, wept for joy at the sight of his son, and insisted that the wedding should take place as soon as possible.

All the knights who had been enchanted in the Iron Castle were invited to the ceremony, and after it had taken place, Long, Broad, and Quickeye took leave of the young couple, saying that they were going to look for more work.

The prince offered them all their hearts could desire if they would only remain with him, but they replied that an idle life would not please them, and that they could never be happy unless they were busy, so they went away to seek their fortunes, and for all I know are seeking still.

Maid Maleen

(FROM *GRIMM'S COMPLETE FAIRY TALES*)

There was once a King who had a son who asked in marriage the daughter of a mighty King; she was called Maid Maleen, and was very beautiful. As her father wished to give her to another, the prince was rejected; but as they both loved each other with all their hearts, they would not give each other up, and Maid Maleen said to her father, "I can and will take no other for my husband."

Then the King flew into a passion, and ordered a dark tower to be built, into which no ray of sunlight or moonlight should enter. When it was finished, he said, "Therein shalt thou be imprisoned for seven years, and then I will come and see if thy perverse spirit is broken." Meat and drink for the seven years were carried into the tower, and then she and her waiting-woman were led into it and walled up, and thus cut off from the sky and from the earth. There they sat in the darkness, and knew not when day or night began. The King's son often went round and round the tower, and called their names, but no sound from without pierced through the thick walls. What else could they do but lament and complain?

Meanwhile the time passed, and by the diminution of the food and drink they knew that the seven years were coming to an end. They thought the moment of their deliverance was come; but no stroke of the hammer was heard, no stone fell out of the wall, and it seemed to Maid Maleen that her father had forgotten her. As they only had food for a short time longer, and saw a miserable death awaiting them, Maid Maleen said, "We must try our last chance, and see if we can break through the wall." She took the bread-knife, and picked and bored at the mortar of a stone, and when she was tired, the waiting-maid took her turn. With great labor they succeeded in getting out one stone, and then a second, and a third, and when three days were over the first ray of light fell on their darkness, and at last the opening was so large that they could look out.

The sky was blue, and a fresh breeze played on their faces; but how melancholy everything looked all around! Her father's castle lay in ruins, the town and the villages were, so far as could be seen, destroyed by fire, the fields far and wide laid to waste, and no human being was visible. When the opening in the wall was large enough for them to slip through, the waiting-maid sprang down first, and then Maid Maleen followed. But where were they to go? The enemy had ravaged the whole kingdom, driven away the King, and slain all the inhabitants. They wandered forth to seek another country, but nowhere did they find a shelter, or a human being to give them a mouthful of bread, and their need was so great that they were forced to appease their hunger with nettles. When, after long journeying, they came into another country, they tried to get work everywhere; but wherever they knocked they were turned away, and no one would have pity on them. At last they arrived in a large city and went to the royal palace. There also they were ordered to go away, but at last the cook said that they might stay in the kitchen and be scullions.

The son of the King in whose kingdom they were, was, however, the very man who had been betrothed to Maid Maleen. His father had chosen another bride for him, whose face was as ugly as her heart was wicked. The wedding was fixed, and the maiden had already arrived; but because of her great ugliness, however, she shut herself in her room, and allowed no one to see her, and Maid Maleen had to take her her meals from the kitchen. When the day came for the bride and the bridegroom to go to church, she was ashamed of her ugliness, and afraid that if she showed herself in the streets, she would be mocked and laughed at by the people. Then said she to Maid Maleen, "A great piece of luck has befallen thee. I have sprained my foot, and cannot well walk through the streets; thou shalt put on my wedding-clothes and take my place; a greater honor than that thou canst not have!" Maid Maleen, however, refused it, and said, "I wish for no honor which is not suitable for me." It was in vain, too, that the bride offered her gold. At last she said angrily,

"If thou dost not obey me, it shall cost thee thy life. I have but to speak the word, and thy head will lie at thy feet." Then she was forced to obey, and put on the bride's magnificent clothes and all her jewels. When she entered the royal hall, every one was amazed at her great beauty, and the King said to his son, "This is the bride whom I have chosen for thee, and whom thou must lead to church." The bridegroom was astonished, and thought, "She is like my Maid Maleen, and I should believe that it was she herself, but she has long been shut up in the tower, or dead." He took her by the hand and led her to church. On the way was a nettle-plant, and she said,

> "Oh, nettle-plant,
> Little nettle-plant,
> What dost thou here alone?
> I have known the time
> When I ate thee unboiled,
> When I ate thee unroasted."

"What art thou saying?" asked the King's son. "Nothing," she replied, "I was only thinking of Maid Maleen." He was surprised that she knew about her, but kept silence. When they came to the foot-plank into the churchyard, she said,

> "Foot-bridge, do not break,
> I am not the true bride."

"What art thou saying there?" asked the King's son. "Nothing," she replied, "I was only thinking of Maid Maleen." "Dost thou know Maid Maleen?" "No," she answered, "how should I know her; I have only heard of her." When they came to the church-door, she said once more,

> "Church-door, break not,
> I am not the true bride."

"What art thou saying there?" asked he. "Ah," she answered, "I was only thinking of Maid Maleen." Then he took out a precious chain, put it round her neck, and fastened the clasp. Thereupon they entered the church, and the priest joined their hands together before the altar, and married them. He led her home, but she did not speak a single word the whole way. When they got back to the royal palace, she hurried into the bride's chamber, put off the magnificent clothes and the jewels, dressed herself in her gray gown, and kept nothing but the jewel on her neck, which she had received from the bridegroom.

When the night came, and the bride was to be led into the prince's apartment, she let her veil fall over her face, that he might not observe the deception. As soon as every one had gone away, he said to her, "What didst thou say to the nettle-plant which was growing by the wayside?" "To which nettle-plant?" asked she; "I don't talk to nettle-plants." "If thou didst not do it, then thou art not the true bride," said he. So she bethought herself, and said,

> "I must go out unto my maid,
> Who keeps my thoughts for me."

She went out and sought Maid Maleen. "Girl, what hast thou been saying to the nettle?"

"I said nothing but,

> 'Oh, nettle-plant,
> Little nettle-plant,
> What dost thou here alone?
> I have known the time
> When I ate thee unboiled,
> When I ate thee unroasted.'"

The bride ran back into the chamber, and said, "I know now what I said to the nettle," and she repeated the words which she had just heard. "But what didst thou say to the foot-bridge when we went over it?" asked the King's son. "To the foot-bridge?" she answered. "I don't talk to foot-bridges." "Then thou art not the true bride." She again said,

> "I must go out unto my maid,
> Who keeps my thoughts for me."

And ran out and found Maid Maleen, "Girl, what didst thou say to the foot-bridge?"

"I said nothing but,

> 'Foot-bridge, do not break,
> I am not the true bride.'"

"That costs thee thy life!" cried the bride, but she hurried into the room, and said, "I know now what I said to the foot-bridge," and she repeated the words. "But what didst thou say to the church-door?" "To the church-door?" she replied; "I don't talk to church-doors." "Then thou art not the true bride."

She went out and found Maid Maleen, and said, "Girl, what didst thou say to the church-door?"

"I said nothing but,

> 'Church-door, break not,
> I am not the true bride.'"

"That will break thy neck for thee!" cried the bride, and flew into a terrible passion, but she hastened back into the room, and said, "I know now what I said to the church-door," and she repeated the words. "But where hast thou the jewel which I gave thee at the church-door?" "What jewel?" she answered; "thou didst not give me any jewel." "I myself put it round thy neck, and I myself fastened it; if thou dost not know that, thou art not the true bride." He drew the veil from her face, and when he saw her immeasurable ugliness, he sprang back terrified, and said, "How comest thou here? Who art thou?" "I am thy betrothed bride, but because I feared lest the people should mock me when they saw me out of doors, I commanded the scullery-maid to dress herself in my clothes, and to go to church instead of me." "Where is the girl?" said he; "I want to see her, go and bring her here." She went out and told the servants that the scullery-maid was an impostor, and that they must take her out into the court-yard and strike off her head. The servants laid hold of Maid Maleen and wanted to drag her out, but she screamed so loudly for help, that the King's son heard her voice, hurried out of his chamber and ordered them to set the maiden free instantly.

Lights were brought, and then he saw on her neck the gold chain which he had given her at the church-door. "Thou art the true bride," said he, "who went with me to the church; come with me now to my room." When they were both alone, he said, "On the way to church thou didst name Maid Maleen, who was my betrothed bride; if I could believe it possible, I should think she was standing before me thou art like her in every respect." She answered, "I am Maid Maleen, who for thy sake was imprisoned seven years in the darkness, who suffered hunger and thirst, and has lived so long in want and poverty. To-day, however, the sun is shining on me once more. I was married to thee in the church, and I am thy lawful wife." Then they kissed each other, and were happy all the days of their lives. The false bride was rewarded for what she had done by having her head cut off.

The tower in which Maid Maleen had been imprisoned remained standing for a long time, and when the children passed by it they sang,

> "Kling, klang, gloria.
> Who sits within this tower?
> A King's daughter, she sits within,
> A sight of her I cannot win,
> The wall it will not break,
> The stone cannot be pierced.
> Little Hans, with your coat so gay,
> Follow me, follow me, fast as you may."

Prince Vivien and the Princess Placida

(FROM *THE GREEN FAIRY BOOK*)

O nce upon a time there lived a King and Queen who loved one another dearly. Indeed the Queen, whose name was Santorina, was so pretty and so kind-hearted that it would have been a wonder if her husband had not been fond of her, while King Gridelin himself was a perfect bundle of good qualities, for the Fairy who presided at his christening had summoned the shades of all his ancestors, and taken something good from each of them to form his character. Unfortunately, though, she had given him rather too much kindness of heart, which is a thing that generally gets its possessor into trouble, but so far all things had prospered with King Gridelin. However, it was not to be expected such good fortune could last, and before very long the Queen had a lovely little daughter who was named Placida. Now the King, who thought that if she resembled her mother in face and mind she would need no other gift, never troubled to ask any of the Fairies to her christening, and this offended them mortally, so that they resolved to punish him severely for thus depriving them of their rights. So, to the despair of King Gridelin, the Queen first of all became very ill, and then disappeared altogether. If it had not been for the little Princess there is no saying what would have become of him, he was so miserable, but there she was to be brought up, and luckily the good Fairy Lolotte, in spite of all that had passed, was willing to come and take charge of her, and of her little cousin Prince Vivien, who was an orphan and had been placed under the care of his uncle, King Gridelin, when he was quite a baby. Although she neglected nothing that could possibly have been done for them, their characters, as they grew up, plainly proved that education only softens down natural defects, but cannot entirely do away with them; for Placida, who was perfectly lovely, and with a capacity and intelligence which enabled her to learn and understand anything that presented itself, was at the same time as lazy and indifferent as it is possible for anyone to be, while Vivien on the contrary was only too lively, and was for ever taking up some new thing and as promptly tiring of it, and flying off to something else which held his fickle fancy an equally short time. As these two children would possibly inherit the kingdom, it was natural that their people should take a great interest in them, and it fell out that all the tranquil and peace-loving citizens desired that Placida should one day be their Queen, while the rash and quarrelsome hoped great things for Vivien. Such a division of ideas seemed to promise civil wars and all kinds of troubles to the State, and even in the Palace the two parties frequently came into collision. As for the children themselves, though they were too well brought up to quarrel, still the difference in all their tastes and feelings made it impossible for them to like one another, so there seemed no chance of their ever consenting to be married, which was a pity, since that was the only thing that would have satisfied both parties. Prince Vivien was fully aware of the feeling in his favor, but being too honorable to wish to injure his pretty cousin, and perhaps too impatient and volatile to care to think seriously about anything, he suddenly took it into his head that he would go off by himself in search of adventure. Luckily this idea occurred to him when he was on horseback, for he would certainly have set out on foot rather than lose an instant. As it was, he simply turned his horse's head, without another thought than that of getting out of the kingdom as soon as possible. This abrupt departure was a great blow to the State, especially as no one had any idea what had become of the Prince. Even King Gridelin, who had never cared for anything since the disappearance of Queen Santorina, was roused by this new loss, and though he could not so much as look at the Princess Placida without shedding floods of tears, he resolved to see for himself what talents and capabilities she showed. He very soon found out that in addition to her natural indolence, she was being as much indulged and spoilt day by day as if the Fairy had been her grandmother, and was obliged to remonstrate very seriously upon the subject. Lolotte took his reproaches meekly, and promised faithfully that she would not encourage the Princess in her idleness and indifference any more. From this moment poor Placida's troubles began! She was actually expected to choose her own dresses, to take care of her jewels, and to find her own amusements; but rather than take so much trouble she wore the same old frock from morning till night, and never appeared in public if she could possibly avoid it. However, this was not all, King Gridelin insisted that the affairs of the kingdom should be explained to her, and that she should attend all the councils and give her opinion upon the matter in hand whenever it was asked of her, and this made her life such a burden to her that she implored Lolotte to take her away from a country where too much was required of an unhappy Princess.

The Fairy refused at first with a great show of firmness, but who could resist the tears and entreaties of anyone so pretty as Placida? It came to this in the end, that she transported the Princess just as she was, cozily tucked up upon her favorite couch, to her own Grotto, and this new disappearance left all the people in despair, and Gridelin went about looking more distracted than ever. But now let us return to Prince Vivien, and see what his restless spirit has brought him to. Though Placida's kingdom was a large one; his horse had carried him gallantly to the limit of it, but it could go no further, and the Prince was obliged to dismount and continue his journey on foot, though this slow mode of progress tired his patience severely.

After what seemed to him a very long time, he found himself all alone in a vast forest, so dark and gloomy that he secretly shuddered; however, he chose the most promising looking path he could find, and marched along it courageously at his best speed, but in spite of all his efforts, night fell before he reached the edge of the wood.

For some time he stumbled along, keeping to the path as well as he could in the darkness, and just as he was almost wearied out he saw before him a gleam of light.

This sight revived his drooping spirits, and he made sure that he was now close to the shelter and supper he needed so much, but the more he walked towards the light the further away it seemed; sometimes he even lost sight of it altogether, and you may imagine how provoked and impatient he was by the time he finally arrived at the miserable cottage from which the light proceeded. He gave a loud knock at the door, and an old woman's voice answered from within, but as she did not seem to be hurrying herself to open it he redoubled his blows, and demanded to be let in imperiously, quite forgetting that he was no longer in his own kingdom. But all this had no effect upon the old woman, who only noticed all the uproar he was making by saying gently:

"You must have patience."

He could hear that she really was coming to open the door to him, only she was so very long about it. First she chased away her cat, lest it should run away when the door was opened, then he heard her talking to herself and made out that her lamp wanted trimming, that she might see better who it was that knocked, and then that it lacked fresh oil, and she must refill it. So what with one thing and another she was an immense time trotting to and fro, and all the while she now and again bade the Prince have patience. When at last he stood within the little hut he saw with despair that it was a picture of poverty, and that not a crumb of anything eatable was to be seen, and when he explained to the old woman that he was dying of hunger and fatigue she only answered tranquilly that he must have patience. However, she presently showed him a bundle of straw on which he could sleep.

"But what can I have to eat?" cried Prince Vivien sharply.

"Wait a little, wait a little," she replied. "If you will only have patience I am just going out into the garden to gather some peas: we will shell them at our leisure, then I will light a fire and cook them, and when they are thoroughly done, we can enjoy them peaceably; there is no hurry."

"I shall have died of starvation by the time all that is done," said the Prince ruefully.

"Patience, patience," said the old woman looking at him with her slow gentle smile, "I can't be hurried. 'All things come at last to him who waits'; you must have heard that often."

Prince Vivien was wild with aggravation, but there was nothing to be done.

"Come then," said the old woman, "you shall hold the lamp to light me while I pick the peas."

The Prince in his haste snatched it up so quickly that it went out, and it took him a long time to light it again with two little bits of glowing charcoal which he had to dig out from the pile of ashes upon the hearth. However, at last the peas were gathered and shelled, and the fire lighted, but then they had to be carefully counted, since the old woman declared that she would cook fifty-four, and no more. In vain did the Prince represent to her that he was famished—that fifty-four peas would go no way towards satisfying his hunger—that a few peas, more or less, surely could not matter. It was quite useless, in the end he had to count out the fifty-four, and worse than that, because he dropped one or two in his hurry, he had to begin again from the very first, to be sure the number was complete. As soon as they were cooked the old dame took a pair of scales and a morsel of bread from the cupboard, and was just about to divide it when Prince Vivien, who really could wait no longer, seized the whole piece and ate it up, saying in his turn, "Patience."

"You mean that for a joke," said the old woman, as gently as ever, "but that is really my name, and some day you will know more about me."

Then they each ate their twenty-seven peas, and the Prince was surprised to find that he wanted nothing more, and he slept as sweetly upon his bed of straw as he had ever done in his palace.

In the morning the old woman gave him milk and bread for his breakfast, which he ate contentedly, rejoicing that there was nothing to be gathered, or counted, or cooked, and when he had finished he begged her to tell him who she was.

"That I will, with pleasure," she replied. "But it will be a long story."

"Oh! if it's long, I can't listen," cried the Prince.

"But," said she, "at your age, you should attend to what old people say, and learn to have patience."

"But, but," said the Prince, in his most impatient tone, "old people should not be so long-winded! Tell me what country I have got into, and nothing else."

"With all my heart," said she. "You are in the Forest of the Black Bird; it is here that he utters his oracles."

"An Oracle," cried the Prince. "Oh! I must go and consult him." Thereupon he drew a handful of gold from his pocket, and offered it to the old woman, and when she would not take it, he threw it down upon the table and was off like a flash of lightning, without even staying to ask the way. He took the first path that presented itself and followed it at the top of his speed, often losing his way, or stumbling over some stone, or running up against a tree, and leaving behind him without regret the cottage which had been as little to his taste as the character of its possessor. After some time he saw in the distance a huge black castle which commanded a view of the whole forest. The Prince felt certain that this must be the abode of the Oracle, and just as the sun was setting he reached its outermost gates. The whole castle was surrounded by a deep moat, and the drawbridge and the gates, and even the water in the moat, were all of the same somber hue as the walls and towers. Upon the gate hung a huge bell, upon which was written in red letters:

"Mortal, if thou art curious to know thy fate, strike this bell, and submit to what shall befall thee."

The Prince, without the smallest hesitation, snatched up a great stone, and hammered vigorously upon the bell, which gave forth a deep and terrible sound, the gate flew open, and closed again with a thundering clang the moment the Prince had passed through it, while from every tower and battlement rose a wheeling, screaming crowd of bats which darkened the whole sky with their multitudes. Anyone but Prince Vivien would have been terrified by such an uncanny sight, but he strode stoutly forward till he reached the second gate, which was opened to him by sixty black slaves covered from head to foot in long mantles.

He wished to speak to them, but soon discovered that they spoke an utterly unknown language, and did not seem to understand a word he said. This was a great aggravation to the Prince, who was not accustomed to keep his ideas to himself, and he positively found himself wishing for his old friend Patience. However, he had to follow his guides in silence, and they led him into a magnificent hall; the floor was of ebony, the walls of jet, and all the hangings were of black velvet, but the Prince looked round it in vain for something to eat, and then made signs that he was hungry. In the same manner he was respectfully given to understand that he must wait, and after several hours the sixty hooded and shrouded figures re-appeared, and conducted him with great ceremony, and also very very slowly, to a banqueting hall, where they all placed themselves at a long table. The dishes were arranged down the center of it, and with his usual impetuosity the Prince seized the one that stood in front of him to draw it nearer, but soon found that it was firmly fixed in its place. Then he looked at his solemn and lugubrious neighbors, and saw that each one was supplied with a long hollow reed through which he slowly sucked up his portion, and the Prince was obliged to do the same, though he found it a frightfully tedious process. After supper, they returned as they had come to the ebony room, where he was compelled to look on while his companions played interminable games of chess, and not until he was nearly dying of weariness did they, slowly and ceremoniously as before, conduct him to his sleeping apartment. The hope of consulting the Oracle woke him very early the next morning, and his first demand was to be allowed to present himself before it, but, without replying, his attendants conducted him to a huge marble bath, very shallow at one end, and quite deep at the other, and gave him to understand that he was to go into it. The Prince, nothing loth, was for springing at once into deep water, but he was gently but forcibly held back and only allowed to stand where it was about an inch deep, and he was nearly wild with impatience when he found that this process was to be repeated every day in spite of all he could say or do, the water rising higher and higher by inches, so that for sixty days he had to live in perpetual silence, ceremoniously conducted to and fro, supping all his meals through the long reed, and looking on at innumerable games of chess, the game of all others which he detested most. But at last the water rose as high as his chin, and his bath was complete. And that day the slaves in their black robes, and each having a large bat perched upon his head, marched in slow procession with the Prince in their midst, chanting a melancholy song, to the iron gate that led into a kind of Temple. At the sound of their chanting, another band of slaves appeared, and took possession of the unhappy Vivien.

They looked to him exactly like the ones he had left, except that they moved more slowly still, and each one held a raven upon his wrist, and their harsh croakings re-echoed through the dismal place. Holding the Prince by the arms, not so much to do him honor as to restrain his impatience, they proceeded by slow degrees up the steps of the Temple, and when they at last reached the top he thought his long waiting must be at an end. But on the contrary, after slowly enshrouding him in a long black robe like their own, they led him into the Temple itself, where he was forced to witness numbers of lengthy rites and ceremonies. By this time Vivien's active impatience had subsided into passive weariness, his yawns were continual and scandalous, but nobody heeded him, he stared hopelessly at the thick black curtain which hung down straight in front of him, and could hardly believe his eyes when it presently began to slide back, and he saw before him the Black Bird. It was of enormous size, and was perched upon a thick bar of iron which ran across from one side of the Temple to the other. At the sight of it all the slaves fell upon their knees and hid their faces, and when it had three times flapped its mighty wings it uttered distinctly in Prince Vivien's own language the words:

"Prince, your only chance of happiness depends upon that which is most opposed to your own nature."

Then the curtain fell before it once more, and the Prince, after many ceremonies, was presented with a raven which perched upon his wrist, and was conducted slowly back to the iron gate. Here the raven left him and he was handed over once more to the care of the first band of slaves, while a large bat flickered down and settled upon his head of its own accord, and so he was taken back to the marble bath, and had to go through the whole process again, only this time he began in deep water which receded daily inch by inch. When this was over the slaves escorted him to the outer gate, and took leave of him with every mark of esteem and politeness, to which it is to be feared he responded but indifferently, since the gate was no sooner opened than he took to his heels, and fled away with all his might, his one idea being to put as much space as possible between himself and the dreary place into which he had ventured so rashly, just to consult a tedious Oracle who after all had told him nothing. He actually reflected for about five seconds on his folly, and came to the conclusion that it might sometimes be advisable to think before one acted.

After wandering about for several days until he was weary and hungry, he at last succeeded in finding a way out of the forest, and soon came to a wide and rapid river, which he followed, hoping to find some means of crossing it, and it happened that as the sun rose the next morning he saw something of a dazzling whiteness moored out in the middle of the stream. Upon looking more attentively at it he found that it was one of the prettiest little ships he had ever seen, and the boat that belonged to it was made fast to the bank quite close to him. The Prince was immediately seized with the most ardent desire to go on board the ship, and shouted loudly to attract the notice of her crew, but no one answered. So he sprang into the little boat and rowed away without finding it at all hard work, for the boat was made all of white paper and was as light as a rose leaf. The ship was made of white paper too, as the Prince presently discovered when he reached it. He found not a soul on board, but there was a very cozy little bed in the cabin, and an ample supply of all sorts of good things to eat and drink, which he made up his mind to enjoy until something new happened. Having been thoroughly well brought up at the court of King Gridelin, of course he understood the art of navigation, but when once he had started, the current carried the vessel down at such a pace that before he knew where he was the Prince found himself out at sea, and a wind springing up behind him just at this moment soon drove him out of sight of land. By this time he was somewhat alarmed, and did his best to put the ship about and get back to the river, but wind and tide were too strong for him, and he began to think of the number of times, from his childhood up, that he had been warned not to meddle with water. But it was too late now to do anything but wish vainly that he had stayed on shore, and to grow heartily weary of the boat and the sea and everything connected with it. These two things, however, he did most thoroughly. To put the finishing touch to his misfortunes he presently found himself becalmed in mid-ocean, a state of affairs which would be considered trying by the most patient of men, so you may imagine how it affected Prince Vivien! He even came to wishing himself back at the Castle of the Black Bird, for there at least he saw some living beings, whereas on board the white-paper ship he was absolutely alone, and could not imagine how he was ever to get away from his wearisome prison. However, after a very long time, he did see land, and his impatience to be on shore was so great that he at once flung himself over the ship's side that he might reach it sooner by swimming. But this was quite useless, for spring as far as he might from the vessel, it was always under his feet again before he reached the water, and he had to resign himself to his fate, and wait with what patience he could muster until the winds and waves carried the ship into a kind of natural harbor which ran far into the land. After his long imprisonment at sea the Prince was delighted with the sight of the great trees which grew down to the very edge of the water, and leaping lightly on shore he speedily lost himself in the thick forest. When he had wandered a long way he stopped to rest beside a clear spring of water, but scarcely had he thrown himself down upon the mossy bank when there was a great rustling in the bushes close by, and out sprang a pretty little gazelle panting and exhausted, which fell at his feet gasping out—

"Oh! Vivien, save me!"

The Prince in great astonishment leapt to his feet, and had just time to draw his sword before he found himself face to face with a large green lion which had been hotly pursuing the poor little gazelle. Prince Vivien attacked it gallantly and a fierce combat ensued, which, however, ended before long in the Prince's dealing his adversary a terrific blow which felled him to the earth. As he fell the lion whistled loudly three times with such force that the forest rang again, and the sound must have been heard for more than two leagues round, after which having apparently nothing more to do in the world he rolled over on his side and died. The Prince without paying any further heed to him or to his whistling returned to the pretty gazelle, saying:

"Well! are you satisfied now? Since you can talk, pray tell me instantly what all this is about, and how you happen to know my name."

"Oh, I must rest for a long time before I can talk," she replied, "and beside, I very much doubt if you will have leisure to listen, for the affair is by no means finished. In fact," she continued in the same languid tone, "you had better look behind you now."

The Prince turned sharply round and to his horror saw a huge Giant approaching with mighty strides, crying fiercely—

"Who has made my lion whistle I should like to know?"

"I have," replied Prince Vivien boldly, "but I can answer for it that he will not do it again!"

At these words the Giant began to howl and lament.

"Alas, my poor Tiny, my sweet little pet," he cried, "but at least I can avenge thy death."

Thereupon he rushed at the Prince, brandishing an immense serpent which was coiled about his wrist. Vivien, without losing his coolness, aimed a terrific blow at it with his sword, but no sooner did he touch the snake than it changed into a Giant and the Giant into a snake, with such rapidity that the Prince felt perfectly giddy, and this happened at least half-a-dozen times, until at last with a fortunate stroke he cut the serpent in halves, and picking up one morsel flung it with all his force at the nose of the Giant, who fell insensible on top of the lion, and in an instant a thick black cloud rolled up which hid them from view, and when it cleared away they had all disappeared.

Then the Prince, without even waiting to sheathe his sword, rushed back to the gazelle, crying:

"Now you have had plenty of time to recover your wits, and you have nothing more to fear, so tell me who you are, and what this horrible Giant, with his lion and his serpent, have to do with you and for pity's sake be quick about it."

"I will tell you with pleasure," she answered, "but where is the hurry? I want you to come back with me to the Green Castle, but I don't want to walk there, it is so far, and walking is so fatiguing."

"Let us set out at once then," replied the Prince severely, "or else really I shall have to leave you where you are. Surely a young and active gazelle like you ought to be ashamed of not being able to walk a few steps. The further off this castle is the faster we ought to walk, but as you don't appear to enjoy that, I will promise that we will go gently, and we can talk by the way."

"It would be better still if you would carry me," said she sweetly, "but as I don't like to see people giving themselves trouble, you may carry me, and make that snail carry you." So saying, she pointed languidly with one tiny foot at what the Prince had taken for a block of stone, but now he saw that it was a huge snail.

"What! I ride a snail!" cried the Prince; "you are laughing at me, and beside we should not get there for a year."

"Oh! well then don't do it," replied the gazelle, "I am quite willing to stay here. The grass is green, and the water clear. But if I were you I should take the advice that was given me and ride the snail."

So, though it did not please him at all, the Prince took the gazelle in his arms, and mounted upon the back of the snail, which glided along very peaceably, entirely declining to be hurried by frequent blows from the Prince's heels. In vain did the gazelle represent to him that she was enjoying herself very much, and that this was the easiest mode of conveyance she had ever discovered. Prince Vivien was wild with impatience, and thought that the Green Castle would never be reached. However, at last, they did get there, and everyone who was in it ran to see the Prince dismount from his singular steed.

But what was his surprise, when having at her request set the gazelle gently down upon the steps which led up to the castle, he saw her suddenly change into a charming Princess, and recognized in her his pretty cousin Placida, who greeted him with her usual tranquil sweetness. His delight knew no bounds, and he followed her eagerly up into the castle, impatient to know what strange events had brought her there. But after all he had to wait for the Princess's story, for the inhabitants of the Green Lands, hearing that the Giant was dead, ran to offer the kingdom to his vanquisher, and Prince Vivien had to listen to various complimentary harangues, which took a great deal of time, though he cut them as short as politeness allowed—if not shorter. But at last he was free to rejoin Placida, who at once began the story of her adventures.

"After you had gone away," said she, "they tried to make me learn how to govern the kingdom, which wearied me to death, so that I begged and prayed Lolotte to take me away with her, and this she presently did, but very reluctantly. However, having been transported to her grotto upon my favorite couch, I spent several delicious days, soothed by the soft green light, which was like a beech wood in the spring, and by the murmuring of bees and the tinkle of falling water. But alas! Lolotte was forced to go away to a general assembly of the Fairies, and she came back in great dismay, telling me that her indulgence to me had cost her dear, for she had been severely reprimanded and ordered to hand me over to the Fairy Mirlifiche, who was already taking charge of you, and who had been much commended for her management of you."

"Fine management, indeed," interrupted the Prince, "if it is to her I owe all the adventures I have met with! But go on with your story, my cousin. I can tell you all about my doings afterwards, and then you can judge for yourself."

"At first I was grieved to see Lolotte cry," resumed the Princess, "but I soon found that grieving was very troublesome, so I thought it better to be calm, and very soon afterwards I saw the Fairy Mirlifiche arrive, mounted upon her great unicorn. She stopped before the grotto and bade Lolotte bring me out to her, at which she cried worse than ever, and kissed me a dozen times, but she dared not refuse. I was lifted up on to the unicorn, behind Mirlifiche, who said to me—

"'Hold on tight, little girl, if you don't want to break your neck.'

"And, indeed, I had to hold on with all my might, for her horrible steed trotted so violently that it positively took my breath away. However, at last we stopped at a large farm, and the farmer and his wife ran out as soon as they saw the Fairy, and helped us to dismount.

"I knew that they were really a King and Queen, whom the Fairies were punishing for their ignorance and idleness. You may imagine that I was by this time half dead with fatigue, but Mirlifiche insisted upon my feeding her unicorn before I did anything else. To accomplish this I had to climb up a long ladder into the hayloft, and bring down, one after another, twenty-four handfuls of hay. Never, never before, did I have such a wearisome task! It makes me shudder to think of it now, and that was not all. In the same way I had to carry the twenty-four handfuls of hay to the stable, and then it was supper time, and I had to wait upon all the others. After that I really thought I should be allowed to go peaceably to my little bed, but, oh dear no! First of all I had to make it, for it was all in confusion, and then I had to make one for the Fairy, and tuck her in, and draw the curtains round her, beside rendering her a dozen little services which I was not at all accustomed to. Finally, when I was perfectly exhausted by all this toil, I was free to go to bed myself, but as I had never before undressed myself, and really did not know how to begin, I lay down as I was. Unfortunately, the Fairy found this out, and just as I was falling into a sweet slumber, she made me get up once more, but even then I managed to escape her vigilance, and only took off my upper robe. Indeed, I may tell you in confidence, that I always find disobedience answer very well. One is often scolded, it is true, but then one has been saved some trouble.

"At the earliest dawn of day Mirlifiche woke me, and made me take many journeys to the stable to bring her word how her unicorn had slept, and how much hay he had eaten, and then to find out what time it was, and if it was a fine day. I was so slow, and did my errands so badly, that before she left she called the King and Queen and said to them:

" 'I am much more pleased with you this year. Continue to make the best of your farm, if you wish to get back to your kingdom, and also take care of this little Princess for me, and teach her to be useful, that when I come I may find her cured of her faults. If she is not—'

"Here she broke off with a significant look, and mounting my enemy the unicorn, speedily disappeared.

"Then the King and Queen, turning to me, asked me what I could do.

" 'Nothing at all, I assure you,' I replied in a tone which really ought to have convinced them, but they went on to describe various employments, and tried to discover which of them would be most to my taste. However, at last I persuaded them that to do nothing whatever would be the only thing that would suit me, and that if they really wanted to be kind to me, they would let me go to bed and to sleep, and not tease me about doing anything. To my great joy, they not only permitted this, but actually, when they had their own meals, the Queen brought my portion up to me. But early the next morning she appeared at my bedside, saying, with an apologetic air:

" 'My pretty child, I am afraid you must really make up your mind to get up to-day. I know quite well how delightful it is to be thoroughly idle, for when my husband and I were King and Queen we did nothing at all from morning to night, and I sincerely hope that it will not be long before those happy days will come again for us. But at present we have not reached them, nor have you, and you know from what the Fairy said that perhaps worse things may happen to us if she is not obeyed. Make haste, I beg of you, and come down to breakfast, for I have put by some delicious cream for you.'

"It was really very tiresome, but as there was no help for it I went down!

"But the instant breakfast was over they began again their cuckoo-cry of 'What will you do?' In vain did I answer—

"'Nothing at all, if it please you, madam.'

"The Queen at last gave me a spindle and about four pounds of hemp upon a distaff, and sent me out to keep the sheep, assuring me that there could not be a pleasanter occupation, and that I could take my ease as much as I pleased. I was forced to set out, very unwillingly, as you may imagine, but I had not walked far before I came to a shady bank in what seemed to me a charming place. I stretched myself cozily upon the soft grass, and with the bundle of hemp for a pillow slept as tranquilly as if there were no such things as sheep in the world, while they for their part wandered hither and thither at their own sweet will, as if there were no such thing as a shepherdess, invading every field, and browsing upon every kind of forbidden dainty, until the peasants, alarmed by the havoc they were making, raised a clamor, which at last reached the ears of the King and Queen, who ran out, and seeing the cause of the commotion, hastily collected their flock. And, indeed, the sooner the better, since they had to pay for all the damage they had done. As for me I lay still and watched them run, for I was very comfortable, and there I might be still if they had not come up, all panting and breathless, and compelled me to get up and follow them; they also reproached me bitterly, but I need hardly tell you that they did not again entrust me with the flock.

"But whatever they found for me to do it was always the same thing, I spoilt and mismanaged it all, and was so successful in provoking even the most patient people, that one day I ran away from the farm, for I was really afraid the Queen would be obliged to beat me. When I came to the little river in which the King used to fish, I found the boat tied to a tree, and stepping in I unfastened it, and floated gently down with the current. The gliding of the boat was so soothing that I did not trouble myself in the least when the Queen caught sight of me and ran along the bank, crying—

"'My boat, my boat! Husband, come and catch the little Princess who is running away with my boat!'

"The current soon carried me out of hearing of her cries, and I dreamed to the song of the ripples and the whisper of the trees, until the boat suddenly stopped, and I found it was stuck fast beside a fresh green meadow, and that the sun was rising. In the distance I saw some little houses which seemed to be built in a most singular fashion, but as I was by this time very hungry I set out towards them, but before I had walked many steps, I saw that the air was full of shining objects which seemed to be fixed, and yet I could not see what they hung from.

"I went nearer, and saw a silken cord hanging down to the ground, and pulled it just because it was so close to my hand. Instantly the whole meadow resounded to the melodious chiming of a peal of silver bells, and they sounded so pretty that I sat down to listen, and to watch them as they swung shining in the sunbeams. Before they ceased to sound, came a great flight of birds, and each one perching upon a bell added its charming song to the concert. As they ended, I looked up and saw a tall and stately dame advancing towards me, surrounded and followed by a vast flock of every kind of bird.

"'Who are you, little girl,' said she, 'who dares to come where I allow no mortal to live, lest my birds should be disturbed? Still, if you are clever at anything,' she added, 'I might be able to put up with your presence.'

"'Madam,' I answered, rising, 'you may be very sure that I shall not do anything to alarm your birds. I only beg you, for pity's sake, to give me something to eat.'

"'I will do that,' she replied, 'before I send you where you deserve to go.'

"And thereupon she dispatched six jays, who were her pages, to fetch me all sorts of biscuits, while some of the other birds brought ripe fruits. In fact, I had a delicious breakfast, though I do not like to be waited upon so quickly. It is so disagreeable to be hurried. I began to think I should like very well to stay in this pleasant country, and I said so to the stately lady, but she answered with the greatest disdain:

"'Do you think I would keep you here? You! Why what do you suppose would be the good of you in this country, where everybody is wide-awake and busy? No, no, I have shown you all the hospitality you will get from me.'

"With these words she turned and gave a vigorous pull to the silken rope which I mentioned before, but instead of a melodious chime, there arose a hideous clanging which quite terrified me, and in an instant a huge Black Bird appeared, which alighted at the Fairy's feet, saying in a frightful voice—

"'What do you want of me, my sister?'

" 'I wish you to take this little Princess to my cousin, the Giant of the Green Castle, at once,' she replied, 'and beg him from me to make her work day and night upon his beautiful tapestry.'

"At these words the great Bird snatched me up, regardless of my cries, and flew off at a terrific pace—"

"Oh! you are joking, cousin," interrupted Prince Vivien; "you mean as slowly as possible. I know that horrible Black Bird, and the lengthiness of all his proceedings and surroundings."

"Have it your own way," replied Placida, tranquilly. "I cannot bear arguing. Perhaps, this was not even the same bird. At any rate, he carried me off at a prodigious speed, and set me gently down in this very castle of which you are now the master. We entered by one of the windows, and when the Bird had handed me over to the Giant from whom you have been good enough to deliver me, and given the Fairy's message, it departed.

"Then the Giant turned to me, saying,

" 'So you are an idler! Ah! well, we must teach you to work. You won't be the first we have cured of laziness. See how busy all my guests are.'

"I looked up as he spoke, and saw that an immense gallery ran all round the hall, in which were tapestry frames, spindles, skeins of wool, patterns, and all necessary things. Before each frame about a dozen people were sitting, hard at work, at which terrible sight I fainted away, and as soon as I recovered they began to ask me what I could do.

"It was in vain that I replied as before, and with the strongest desire to be taken at my word, 'Nothing at all.'

"The Giant only said,

" 'Then you must learn to do something; in this world there is enough work for everybody.'

"It appeared that they were working into the tapestry all the stories the Fairies liked best, and they began to try and teach me to help them, but from the first class, where they tried me to begin with, I sank lower and lower, and not even the most simple stitches could I learn.

"In vain they punished me by all the usual methods. In vain the Giant showed me his menagerie, which was entirely composed of children who would not work! Nothing did me any good, and at last I was reduced to drawing water for the dyeing of the wools, and even over that I was so slow that this morning the Giant flew into a rage and changed me into a gazelle. He was just putting me into the menagerie when I happened to catch sight of a dog, and was seized with such terror that I fled away at my utmost speed, and escaped through the outer court of the castle. The Giant, fearing that I should be lost altogether, sent his green lion after me, with orders to bring me back, cost what it might, and I should certainly have let myself be caught, or eaten up, or anything, rather than run any further, if I had not luckily met you by the fountain. And oh!" concluded the Princess, "how delightful it is once more to be able to sit still in peace. I was so tired of trying to learn things."

Prince Vivien said that, for his part, he had been kept a great deal too still, and had not found it at all amusing, and then he recounted all his adventures with breathless rapidity. How he had taken shelter with Dame Patience, and consulted the Oracle, and voyaged in the paper ship. Then they went hand in hand to release all the prisoners in the castle, and all the Princes and Princesses who were in cages in the menagerie, for the instant the Green Giant was dead they had resumed their natural forms. As you may imagine, they were all very grateful, and Princess Placida entreated them never, never to do another stitch of work so long as they lived, and they promptly made a great bonfire in the courtyard, and solemnly burnt all the embroidery frames and spinning wheels. Then the Princess gave them splendid presents, or rather sat by while Prince Vivien gave them, and there were great rejoicings in the Green Castle, and everyone did his best to please the Prince and Princess. But with all their good intentions, they often made mistakes, for Vivien and Placida were never of one mind about their plans, so it was very confusing, and they frequently found themselves obeying the Prince's orders, very, very slowly, and rushing off with lightning speed to do something that the Princess did not wish to have done at all, until, by-and-by, the two cousins took to consulting with, and consoling one another in all these little vexations, and at last came to be so fond of each other that for Placida's sake Vivien became quite patient, and for Vivien's sake Placida made the most unheard-of exertions. But now the Fairies who had been watching all these proceedings with interest, thought it was time to interfere, and ascertain by further trials if this improvement was likely to continue, and if they really loved one another. So they caused Placida to seem to have a violent fever, and Vivien to languish and grow dull, and made each of them very uneasy about the other, and then, finding a moment when they were apart, the Fairy Mirlifiche suddenly appeared to Placida, and said—

"I have just seen Prince Vivien, and he seemed to me to be very ill."

"Alas! yes, madam," she answered, "and if you will but cure him, you may take me back to the farm, or bring the Green Giant to life again, and you shall see how obedient I will be."

"If you really wish him to recover," said the Fairy, "you have only to catch the Trotting Mouse and the Chaffinch-on-the-Wing and bring them to me. Only remember that time presses!"

She had hardly finished speaking before the Princess was rushing headlong out of the castle gate, and the Fairy after watching her till she was lost to sight, gave a little chuckle and went in search of the Prince, who begged her earnestly to send him back to the Black Castle, or to the paper boat if she would but save Placida's life. The Fairy shook her head, and looked very grave. She quite agreed with him, the Princess was in a bad way—"But," said she, "if you can find the Rosy Mole, and give him to her she will recover." So now it was the Prince's turn to set off in a vast hurry, only as soon as he left the Castle he happened to go in exactly the opposite direction to the one Placida had taken. Now you can imagine these two devoted lovers hunting night and day. The Princess in the woods, always running, always listening, pursuing hotly after two creatures which seemed to her very hard to catch, which she yet never ceased from pursuing. The Prince on the other hand wandering continually across the meadows, his eyes fixed upon the ground, attentive to every movement among the moles. He was forced to walk slowly—slowly upon tip-toe, hardly venturing to breathe. Often he stood for hours motionless as a statue, and if the desire to succeed could have helped him he would soon have possessed the Rosy Mole. But alas! all that he caught were black and ordinary, though strange to say he never grew impatient, but always seemed ready to begin the tedious hunt again. But this changing of character is one of the most ordinary miracles which love works. Neither the Prince nor the Princess gave a thought to anything but their quest. It never even occurred to them to wonder what country they had reached. So you may guess how astonished they were one day, when having at last been successful after their long and weary chase, they cried aloud at the same instant: "At last I have saved my beloved," and then recognizing each other's voice looked up, and rushed to meet one another with the wildest joy.

Surprise kept them silent while for one delicious moment they gazed into each other's eyes, and just then who should come up but King Gridelin, for it was into his kingdom they had accidentally strayed. He recognized them in his turn and greeted them joyfully, but when they turned afterwards to look for the Rosy Mole, the Chaffinch, and the Trotting-Mouse, they had vanished, and in their places stood a lovely lady whom they did not know, the Black Bird, and the Green Giant. King Gridelin had no sooner set eyes upon the lady than with a cry of joy he clasped her in his arms, for it was no other than his long-lost wife, Santorina, about whose imprisonment in Fairyland you may perhaps read some day.

Then the Black Bird and the Green Giant resumed their natural form, for they were enchanters, and up flew Lolotte and Mirlifiche in their chariots, and then there was a great kissing and congratulating, for everybody had regained someone he loved, including the enchanters, who loved their natural forms dearly. After this they repaired to the Palace, and the wedding of Prince Vivien and Princess Placida was held at once with all the splendor imaginable.

King Gridelin and Queen Santorina, after all their experiences had no further desire to reign, so they retired happily to a peaceful place, leaving their kingdom to the Prince and Princess, who were beloved by all their subjects, and found their greatest happiness all their lives long in making other people happy.

The Green Knight

(FROM *THE OLIVE FAIRY BOOK*)

There lived once a king and queen who had an only daughter, a charming and beautiful girl, dearer to them than anything else in the world. When the princess was twelve years old the queen fell sick, and nothing that could be done for her was of any use. All the doctors in the kingdom did their best to cure her, but in spite of their efforts she grew worse and worse. As she was about to die, she sent for the king and said to him:

"Promise me that whatever our daughter asks, you will do, no matter whether you wish to or not."

The king at first hesitated, but as she added:

"Unless you promise this I cannot die in peace," he at length did as she desired, and gave the promise, after which she became quite happy and died.

It happened that near the king's palace lived a noble lady, whose little girl was of about the same age as the princess, and the two children were always together. After the queen's death the princess begged that this lady should come to live with her in the palace. The king was not quite pleased with this arrangement, for he distrusted the lady; but the princess wished so much for it that he did not like to refuse.

"I am lonely, father," she said, "and all the beautiful presents you give me cannot make up to me for the loss of my mother. If this lady comes to live here I shall almost feel as if the queen had come back to me."

So a magnificent suite of rooms was prepared and set aside for the new-comers, and the little princess was wild with joy at the thought of having her friends so near her. The lady and her daughter arrived, and for a long time all went well. They were very kind to the motherless princess, and she almost began to forget how dull she had been before they came. Then, one day, as she and the other girl were playing together in the gardens of the palace, the lady came to them, dressed for a journey, and kissed the princess tenderly, saying:

"Farewell, my child; my daughter and I must leave you and go far away."

The poor princess began to cry bitterly. "Oh! you must not leave me!" she sobbed. "What shall I do without you? Please, oh! please stay."

The lady shook her head.

"It almost breaks my heart to go, dear child," she said, "but, alas! it must be."

"Is there nothing that can keep you here?" asked the princess.

"Only one thing," answered the lady, "and as that is impossible, we will not speak of it."

"Nothing is impossible," persisted the princess. "Tell me what it is, and it shall be done."

So at last her friend told her.

"If the king, your father, would make me his queen I would stay," she said; "but that he would never do."

"Oh, yes! *that* is easy enough!" cried the princess, delighted to think that, after all, they need not be parted. And she ran off to find her father, and beg him to marry the lady at once. He had done everything she asked, and she was quite certain he would do it.

"What is it, my daughter?" he asked, when he saw her. "You have been crying—are you not happy?"

"Father," she said, "I have come to ask you to marry the countess"—(for that was the lady's real title)—"if you do not she will leave us, and then I shall be as lonely as before. You have never refused me what I have asked before, do not refuse me now."

The king turned quite pale when he heard this. He did not like the countess, and so, of course, he did not wish to marry her; besides, he still loved his dead wife.

"No, that I cannot do, my child," he said at last.

At these words the princess began to cry once more, and the tears ran down her cheeks so fast, and she sobbed so bitterly, that her father felt quite miserable too. He remembered the promise he had given always to do what his daughter asked him and in the end he gave way, and promised to marry the countess. The princess at once was all smiles, and ran away to tell the good news.

Soon after, the wedding was celebrated with great festivities, and the countess became queen; but, in spite of all the joy and merriment that filled the palace, the king looked pale and sad, for he was certain that ill would come of the marriage. Sure enough, in a very short time the queen's manner towards the princess began to change. She was jealous of her because she, instead of her own daughter, was heir to the throne, and very soon she could no longer hide her thoughts. Instead of speaking kindly and lovingly as before, her words became rough and cruel, and once or twice she even slapped the princess's face.

The king was very unhappy at seeing his dearly loved daughter suffer, and at last she became so wretched that he could no longer bear it. Calling her to him one day he said:

"My daughter, you are no longer merry as you should be, and I fear that it is the fault of your step-mother. It will be better for you to live with her no longer; therefore I have built you a castle on the island in the lake, and that is to be your home in future. There you can do just as you like, and your step-mother will never enter it."

The princess was delighted to hear this, and still more pleased when she saw the castle, which was full of beautiful things, and had a great number of windows looking out on the lovely blue water. There was a boat in which she might row herself about, and a garden where she could walk whenever she wished without fear of meeting the unkind queen; and the king promised to visit her every day.

For a long time she dwelt in peace, and grew more and more beautiful every day. Everyone who saw her said "The princess is the loveliest lady in the land." And this was told to the queen, who hated her step-daughter still more because her own daughter was ugly and stupid.

One day it was announced that a great meeting of knights and nobles was to be held in a neighboring kingdom distant about two days' journey. There were to be all kinds of festivities, and a tournament was to be fought and a banquet held, in honor of the coming of age of the prince of the country.

The princess's father was among those invited, but before he set out he went to take leave of his daughter. Although she had such a beautiful home, and was no longer scolded by the queen, the poor princess was dreadfully lonely, and she told her father that it would be better if she were dead. He did his best to comfort her and promised that he would soon return. Was there anything he could do to help her?

"Yes," she said. "You may greet the Green Knight from me."

Now the king wondered a little at these words, for he had never heard of the Green Knight; but there was no time to ask questions, therefore he gave the promise, and rode off on his journey. When he came to the palace where the festivities were to take place, the first thing he did was to ask:

"Can anyone tell me where I may find the Green Knight?"

No, they were very sorry; but none had ever heard of such a person either—certainly he was not to be found there. At this the king grew troubled, and not even the banquet or the tournament could make him feel happier. He inquired of everyone he saw, "Do you know the Green Knight?" but the only answer he got was:

"No, your majesty, we have never heard of him."

At length he began to believe that the princess was mistaken, and that there was no such person; and he started on his homeward journey sorrowfully enough, for this was the first time for many months that the princess had asked him to do anything for her and he could not do it. He thought so much about it that he did not notice the direction his horse was taking, and presently he found himself in the midst of a dense forest where he had never been before. He rode on and on, looking for the path, but as the sun began to set he realized that he was lost. At last, to his delight, he saw a man driving some pigs, and riding up to him, he said:

"I have lost my way. Can you tell me where I am?"

"You are in the Green Knight's forest," answered the man, "and these are his pigs."

At that the king's heart grew light. "Where does the Green Knight live?" he asked.

"It is a very long way from here," said the swineherd; "but I will show you the path." So he went a little farther with the king and put him on the right road, and the king bade him farewell.

Presently he came to a second forest, and there he met another swineherd driving pigs.

"Whose beasts are those, my man?" he asked.

"They are the Green Knight's," said the man.

"And where does he live?" inquired the king.

"Oh, not far from here," was the reply.

Then the king rode on, and about midday he reached a beautiful castle standing in the midst of the loveliest garden you can possibly imagine, where fountains played in marble basins, and peacocks walked on the smooth lawns. On the edge of a marble basin sat a young and handsome man, who was dressed from head to foot in a suit of green armor, and was feeding the goldfish which swam in the clear water.

"This must be the Green Knight," thought the king; and going up to the young man he said courteously:

"I have come, sir, to give you my daughter's greeting. But I have wandered far, and lost my way in your forest."

The knight looked at him for a moment as though puzzled.

"I have never met either you or your daughter," he said at last; "but you are very welcome all the same." And he waved his hand towards the castle. However, the king took no notice, and told him that his daughter had sent a message to the Green Knight, and as he was the only Green Knight in the kingdom this message must be for him.

"You must pass the night with me here," said the knight; and as the sun was already set, the king was thankful to accept the invitation. They sat down in the castle hall to a magnificent banquet, and although he had traveled much and visited many monarchs in their palaces, the king had never fared better than at the table of the Green Knight, whilst his host himself was so clever and agreeable, that he was delighted, and thought "what a charming son-in-law this knight would make!"

Next morning, when he was about to set forth on his journey home, the Green Knight put into his hand a jeweled casket, saying:

"Will your highness graciously condescend to carry this gift to the princess, your daughter? It contains my portrait, that when I come she may know me; for I feel certain that she is the lady I have seen night after night in a dream, and I must win her for my bride."

The king gave the knight his blessing, and promised to take the gift to his daughter. With that he set off, and ere long reached his own country.

The princess was awaiting him anxiously when he arrived, and ran to his arms in her joy at seeing her dear father again.

"And did you see the Green Knight?" she asked.

"Yes," answered the king, drawing out the casket the knight had sent, "and he begged me to give you this that you may know him when he arrives and not mistake him for somebody else."

When the princess saw the portrait she was delighted, and exclaimed: "It is indeed the man whom I have seen in my dreams! Now I shall be happy, for he and no other shall be my husband."

Very soon after the Green Knight arrived, and he looked so handsome in his green armor, with a long green plume in his helmet, that the princess fell still more in love with him than before, and when he saw her, and recognized her as the lady whom he had so often dreamt of, he immediately asked her to be his bride. The princess looked down and smiled as she answered him:

"We must keep the secret from my step-mother until the wedding-day," said she, "for otherwise she will find a way to do us some evil."

"As you please," replied the prince; "but I must visit you daily, for I can live no longer without you! I will come early in the morning and not leave until it is dark; thus the queen will not see me row across the lake."

For a long time, the Green Knight visited the princess every day, and spent many hours wandering with her through the beautiful gardens where they knew the queen could not see them. But secrets, as you know, are dangerous things, and at last, one morning, a girl who was in service at the palace happened to be walking by the lake early in the morning and beheld a wonderfully handsome young man, in a beautiful suit of green satin, come down to the edge of the lake. Not guessing that he was watched, he got into a little boat that lay moored to the bank, rowed himself over to the island where the princess's castle stood. The girl went home wondering who the knight could be; and as she was brushing the queen's hair, she said to her:

"Does your majesty know that the princess has a suitor?"

"Nonsense!" replied the queen crossly. But she was dreadfully vexed at the mere idea, as her own daughter was still unmarried, and was likely to remain so, because she was so ill-tempered and stupid that no one wanted her.

"It is true," persisted the girl. "He is dressed all in green, and is very handsome. I saw him myself, though he did not see me, and he got into a boat and rowed over to the island, and the princess was waiting for him at the castle door."

"I must find out what this means," thought the queen. But she bade her maid of honor cease chattering and mind her own business.

Early next morning the queen got up and went down to the shore of the lake, where she hid herself behind a tree. Sure enough there came a handsome knight dressed in green, just as the maid of honor had said, and he got into a boat and rowed over to the island where the princess awaited him. The angry queen remained by the lake all day, but it was not until the evening that the knight returned, and leaping on shore, he tied the boat to its moorings and went away through the forest.

"I have caught my step-daughter nicely," thought the queen. "But she shall not be married before my own sweet girl. I must find a way to put a stop to this."

Accordingly she took a poisoned nail and stuck it in the handle of the oar in such a way that the knight would be sure to scratch his hand when he picked up the oar. Then she went home laughing, very much pleased with her cleverness.

The next day the Green Knight went to visit the princess as usual; but directly he took up the oars to row over to the island he felt a sharp scratch on his hand.

"Oof!" he said, dropping the oars from pain, "what can have scratched so?" But, look as he might, only a tiny mark was to be seen.

"Well, it's strange how a nail could have come here since yesterday," he thought. "Still, it is not very serious, though it hurts a good deal."

And, indeed, it seemed such a little thing that he did not mention it to the princess. However, when he reached home in the evening, he felt so ill he was obliged to go to bed, with no one to attend on him except his old nurse. But of this, of course, the princess knew nothing; and the poor girl, fearing lest some evil should have befallen him, or some other maiden more beautiful than she should have stolen his heart from her, grew almost sick with waiting. Lonely, indeed, she was, for her father, who would have helped her, was traveling in a foreign country, and she knew not how to obtain news of her lover.

In this manner time passed away, and one day, as she sat by the open window crying and feeling very sad, a little bird came and perched on the branch of a tree that stood just underneath. It began to sing, and so beautifully that the princess was obliged to stop crying and listen to it, and very soon she found out that the bird was trying to attract her attention.

"*Tu-whit, tu-whit!* your lover is sick!" it sang.

"Alas!" cried the princess. "What can I do?"

"*Tu-whit, tu-whit!* you must go to your father's palace!"

"And what shall I do there?" she asked.

"*Tu-whit!* there you will find a snake with nine young ones."

"Ugh!" answered the princess with a shiver, for she did not like snakes. But the little bird paid no heed.

"Put them in a basket and go to the Green Knight's palace," said she.

"And what am I to do with them when I get there?" she cried, blushing all over, though there was no one to see her but the bird.

"Dress yourself as a kitchen-maid and ask for a place. *Tu-whit!* Then you must make soup out of the snakes. Give it three times to the knight and he will be cured. *Tu-whit!*"

"But what has made him ill?" asked the princess. The bird, however, had flown away, and there was nothing for it but to go to her father's palace and look for the snakes. When she came there she found the mother snake with the nine little snakes all curled up so that you could hardly tell their heads from their tails. The princess did not like having to touch them, but when the old snake had wriggled out of the nest to bask a little in the sun, she picked up the young ones and put them in a basket as the bird had told her, and ran off to find the Green Knight's castle. All day she walked along, sometimes stopping to pick the wild berries, or to gather a nosegay; but though she rested now and

319

then, she would not lie down to sleep before she reached the castle. At last she came in sight of it, and just then she met a girl driving a flock of geese.

"Good-day!" said the princess; "can you tell me if this is the castle of the Green Knight?"

"Yes, that it is," answered the goose-girl, "for I am driving his geese. But the Green Knight is very ill, and they say that unless he can be cured within three days he will surely die."

At this news the princess grew as white as death. The ground seemed to spin round, and she closed her hand tight on a bush that was standing beside her. By-and-by, with a great effort, she recovered herself and said to the goose-girl:

"Would you like to have a fine silk dress to wear?"

The goose-girl's eyes glistened.

"Yes, that I would!" answered she.

"Then take off your dress and give it to me, and I will give you mine," said the princess.

The girl could scarcely believe her ears, but the princess was already unfastening her beautiful silk dress, and taking off her silk stockings and pretty red shoes; and the goose-girl lost no time in slipping out of her rough linen skirt and tunic. Then the princess put on the other's rags and let down her hair, and went to the kitchen to ask for a place.

"Do you want a kitchen-maid?" she said.

"Yes, we do," answered the cook, who was too busy to ask the new-comer many questions.

The following day, after a good night's rest, the princess set about her new duties. The other servants were speaking of their master, and saying to each other how ill he was, and that unless he could be cured within three days he would surely die.

The princess thought of the snakes, and the bird's advice, and lifting her head from the pots and pans she was scouring, she said: "I know how to make a soup that has such a wonderful power that whoever tastes it is sure to be cured, whatever his illness may be. As the doctors cannot cure your master shall I try?"

At first they all laughed at her.

"What! a scullion cure the knight when the best physicians in the kingdom have failed?"

But at last, just because all the physicians *had* failed, they decided that it would do no harm to try; and she ran off joyfully to fetch her basket of snakes and make them into broth. When this was ready she carried some to the knight's room and entered it boldly, pushing aside all the learned doctors who stood beside his bed. The poor knight was too ill to know her, besides, she was so ragged and dirty that he would not have been likely to do so had he been well; but when he had taken the soup he was so much better that he was able to sit up.

The next day he had some more, and then he was able to dress himself.

"That is certainly wonderful soup!" said the cook.

The third day, after he had eaten his soup, the knight was quite well again.

"Who are you?" he asked the girl; "was it you who made this soup that has cured me?"

"Yes," answered the princess.

"Choose, then, whatever you wish as a reward," said the knight, "and you shall have it."

"I would be your bride!" said the princess.

The knight frowned in surprise at such boldness, and shook his head.

"That is the one thing I cannot grant," he said, "for I am pledged to marry the most beautiful princess in the world. Choose again."

Then the princess ran away and washed herself and mended her rags, and when she returned the Green Knight recognized her at once.

You can think what a joyful meeting that was!

Soon after, they were married with great splendor. All the knights and princes in the kingdom were summoned to the wedding, and the princess wore a dress that shone like the sun, so that no one had ever beheld a more gorgeous sight. The princess's father, of course, was present, but the wicked queen and her daughter were driven out of the country, and as nobody has seen them since, very likely they were eaten by wild beasts in the forest. But the bride and bridegroom were so happy that they forgot all about them, and they lived with the old king till he died, when they succeeded him.

The Iron Stove

(FROM *THE YELLOW FAIRY BOOK*)

Once upon a time when wishes came true there was a kings son who was enchanted by an old witch, so that he was obliged to sit in a large iron stove in a wood. There he lived for many years, and no one could free him. At last a kings daughter came into the wood; she had lost her way, and could not find her father's kingdom again. She had been wandering round and round for nine days, and she came at last to the iron case. A voice came from within and asked her, "Where do you come from, and where do you want to go?" She answered, "I have lost my way to my father's kingdom, and I shall never get home again." Then the voice from the iron stove said, "I will help you to find your home again, and that in a very short time, if you will promise to do what I ask you. I am a greater prince than you are a princess, and I will marry you." Then she grew frightened, and thought, "What can a young lassie do with an iron stove?" But as she wanted very much to go home to her father, she promised to do what he wished. He said, "You must come again, and bring a knife with you to scrape a hole in the iron."

Then he gave her someone for a guide, who walked near her and said nothing, but he brought her in two hours to her house. There was great joy in the castle when the Princess came back, and the old King fell on her neck and kissed her. But she was very much troubled, and said, "Dear father, listen to what has befallen me! I should never have come home again out of the great wild wood if I had not come to an iron stove, to whom I have had to promise that I will go back to free him and marry him!" The old King was so frightened that he nearly fainted, for she was his only daughter. So they consulted together, and determined that the miller's daughter, who was very beautiful, should take her place. They took her there, gave her a knife, and said she must scrape at the iron stove. She scraped for twenty-four hours, but did not make the least impression. When the day broke, a voice called from the iron stove,

"It seems to me that it is day outside." Then she answered, "It seems so to me; I think I hear my father's mill rattling."

"So you are a miller's daughter! Then go away at once, and tell the King's daughter to come."

Then she went away, and told the old King that the thing inside the iron stove would not have her, but wanted the Princess. The old King was frightened, and his daughter wept. But they had a swineherd's daughter who was even more beautiful than the miller's daughter, and they gave her a piece of gold to go to the iron stove instead of the Princess. Then she was taken out, and had to scrape for four-and-twenty hours, but she could make no impression. As soon as the day broke the voice from the stove called out, "It seems to be daylight outside." Then she answered, "It seems so to me too; I think I hear my father blowing his horn." "So you are a swineherd's daughter! Go away at once, and let the King's daughter come. And say to her that what I foretell shall come to pass, and if she does not come everything in the kingdom shall fall into ruin, and not one stone shall be left upon another." When the Princess heard this she began to cry, but it was no good; she had to keep her word. She took leave of her father, put a knife in her belt, and went to the iron stove in the wood. As soon as she reached it she began to scrape, and the iron gave way and before two hours had passed she had made a little hole. Then she peeped in and saw such a beautiful youth all shining with gold and precious stones that she fell in love with him on the spot. So she scraped away harder than ever, and made the hole so large that he could get out. Then he said, "You are mine, and I am thine; you are my bride and have set me free!" He wanted to take her with him to his kingdom, but she begged him just to let her go once more to her father; and the Prince let her go, but told her not to say more than three words to her father, then to come back again. So she went home, but alas! she said *more than three words*; and immediately the iron stove vanished and went away over a mountain of glass and sharp swords. But the Prince was free, and was no longer shut up in it. Then she said good-bye to her father, and took a little money with her, and went again into the great wood to look for the iron stove; but she could not find it. She sought it for nine days, and then her hunger became so great that she did not know how she could live any longer. And when it was evening she climbed a little tree and wished that the night would not come, because she was afraid of the wild beasts. When midnight came she saw afar off a little light, and thought, "Ah! if only I could reach that!" Then she got down from the tree and went towards the light. She came to a little old house with a great deal of grass growing round, and stood in front of a little heap of wood. She thought, "Alas! what am I coming to?" and peeped through the window; but she saw nothing inside except big and little toads, and a table beautifully spread with roast meats and wine, and all the dishes and drinking-cups were of silver. Then she took heart and knocked. Then a fat toad called out:

> "Little green toad with leg like crook,
>   Open wide the door, and look
>   Who it was the latch that shook."

And a little toad came forward and let her in. When she entered they all bid her welcome, and made her sit down. They asked her how she came there and what she wanted. Then she told everything that had happened to her, and how, because she had exceeded her permission only to speak three words, the stove had disappeared with the Prince; and how she had searched a very long time, and must wander over mountain and valley till she found him.

Then the old toad said:

> "Little green toad whose leg doth twist,
>   Go to the corner of which you wist,
>   And bring to me the large old kist."

And the little toad went and brought out a great chest. Then they gave her food and drink, and led her to a beautifully made bed of silk and samite, on which she lay down and slept soundly. When the day dawned she arose, and the old toad gave her three things out of the huge chest to take with her. She would have need of them, for she had to cross a high glass mountain, three cutting swords, and a great lake. When she had passed these she would find her lover again. So she was given three large needles, a plough-wheel, and three nuts, which she was to take great care of. She set out with these things, and when she came to the glass mountain which was so slippery she stuck the three needles behind her feet and then in front, and so got over it, and when she was on the other side put them carefully away.

Then she reached the three cutting swords, and got on her plough-wheel and rolled over them. At last she came to a great lake, and, when she had crossed that, arrived at a beautiful castle. She went in and gave herself out as a servant, a poor maid who would gladly be engaged. But she knew that the Prince whom she had freed from the iron stove in the great wood was in the castle. So she was taken on as a kitchen-maid for very small wages. Now the Prince was about to marry another princess, for he thought she was dead long ago.

In the evening, when she had washed up and was ready, she felt in her pocket and found the three nuts which the old toad had given her. She cracked one and was going to eat the kernel, when behold! there was a beautiful royal dress inside it! When the bride heard of this, she came and begged for the dress, and wanted to buy it, saying that it was not a dress for a serving-maid. Then she said she would not sell it unless she was granted one favor—namely, to sleep by the Prince's door. The bride granted her this, because the dress was so beautiful and she had so few like it. When it was evening she said to her bridegroom, "That stupid maid wants to sleep by your door."

"If you are contented, I am," he said. But she gave him a glass of wine in which she had poured a sleeping-draught. Then they both went to his room, but he slept so soundly that she could not wake him. The maid wept all night long, and said, "I freed you in the wild wood out of the iron stove; I have sought you, and have crossed a glassy mountain, three sharp swords, and a great lake before I found you, and will you not hear me now?" The servants outside heard how she cried the whole night, and they told their master in the morning.

When she had washed up the next evening she bit the second nut, and there was a still more beautiful dress inside. When the bride saw it she wanted to buy it also. But the maid did not want money, and asked that she should sleep again by the Prince's door. The bride, however, gave him a sleeping-draught, and he slept so soundly that he heard nothing. But the kitchen-maid wept the whole night long, and said, "I have freed you in a wood and from an iron stove; I sought you and have crossed a glassy mountain, three sharp swords, and a great lake to find you, and now you will not hear me!" The servants outside heard how she cried the whole night, and in the morning they told their master.

And when she had washed up on the third night she bit the third nut, and there was a still more beautiful dress inside that was made of pure gold. When the bride saw it she wanted to have it, but the maid would only give it her on condition that she should sleep for the third time by the Prince's door. But the Prince took care not to drink the sleeping-draught. When she began to weep and to say, "Dearest sweetheart, I freed you in the horrible wild wood, and from an iron stove," he jumped up and said, "You are right. You are mine, and I am thine." Though it was still night, he got into a carriage with her, and they took the false bride's clothes away, so that she could not follow them. When they came to the great lake they rowed across, and when they reached the three sharp swords they sat on the plough-wheel, and on the glassy mountain they stuck the three needles in. So they arrived at last at the little old house, but when they stepped inside it turned into a large castle. The toads were all freed, and were beautiful King's children, running about for joy. There they were married, and they remained in the castle, which was much larger than that of the Princess's father's. But because the old man did not like being left alone, they went and fetched him. So they had two kingdoms and lived in great wealth.

A mouse has run,
My story's done.

The Sleeping Beauty in the Wood

(FROM *THE BLUE FAIRY BOOK*)

There were formerly a king and a queen, who were so sorry that they had no children; so sorry that it cannot be expressed. They went to all the waters in the world; vows, pilgrimages, all ways were tried, and all to no purpose.

At last, however, the Queen had a daughter. There was a very fine christening; and the Princess had for her god-mothers all the fairies they could find in the whole kingdom (they found seven), that every one of them might give her a gift, as was the custom of fairies in those days. By this means the Princess had all the perfections imaginable.

After the ceremonies of the christening were over, all the company returned to the King's palace, where was prepared a great feast for the fairies. There was placed before every one of them a magnificent cover with a case of massive gold, wherein were a spoon, knife, and fork, all of pure gold set with diamonds and rubies. But as they were all sitting down at table they saw come into the hall a very old fairy, whom they had not invited, because it was above fifty years since she had been out of a certain tower, and she was believed to be either dead or enchanted.

The King ordered her a cover, but could not furnish her with a case of gold as the others, because they had only seven made for the seven fairies. The old Fairy fancied she was slighted, and muttered some threats between her teeth. One of the young fairies who sat by her overheard how she grumbled; and, judging that she might give the little Princess some unlucky gift, went, as soon as they rose from table, and hid herself behind the hangings, that she might speak last, and repair, as much as she could, the evil which the old Fairy might intend.

In the meanwhile all the fairies began to give their gifts to the Princess. The youngest gave her the gift that she should be the most beautiful person in the world; the next, that she should have the wit of an angel; the third, that she should have a wonderful grace in everything she did; the fourth, that she should dance perfectly well; the fifth, that she should sing like a nightingale; and the sixth, that she should play all kinds of music to the utmost perfection.

The old Fairy's turn coming next, with a head shaking more with spite than age, she said that the Princess should have her hand pierced with a spindle and die of the wound. This terrible gift made the whole company tremble, and everybody fell a-crying.

At this very instant the young Fairy came out from behind the hangings, and spake these words aloud:

"Assure yourselves, O King and Queen, that your daughter shall not die of this disaster. It is true, I have no power to undo entirely what my elder has done. The Princess shall indeed pierce her hand with a spindle; but, instead of dying, she shall only fall into a profound sleep, which shall last a hundred years, at the expiration of which a king's son shall come and awake her."

The King, to avoid the misfortune foretold by the old Fairy, caused immediately proclamation to be made, whereby everybody was forbidden, on pain of death, to spin with a distaff and spindle, or to have so much as any spindle in their houses. About fifteen or sixteen years after, the King and Queen being gone to one of their houses of pleasure, the young Princess happened one day to divert herself in running up and down the palace; when going up from one apartment to another, she came into a little room on the top of the tower, where a good old woman, alone, was spinning with her spindle. This good woman had never heard of the King's proclamation against spindles.

"What are you doing there, goody?" said the Princess.

"I am spinning, my pretty child," said the old woman, who did not know who she was.

"Ha!" said the Princess, "this is very pretty; how do you do it? Give it to me, that I may see if I can do so."

She had no sooner taken it into her hand than, whether being very hasty at it, somewhat unhandy, or that the decree of the Fairy had so ordained it, it ran into her hand, and she fell down in a swoon.

The good old woman, not knowing very well what to do in this affair, cried out for help. People came in from every quarter in great numbers; they threw water upon the Princess's face, unlaced her, struck her on the palms of her hands, and rubbed her temples with Hungary-water; but nothing would bring her to herself.

And now the King, who came up at the noise, bethought himself of the prediction of the fairies, and, judging very well that this must necessarily come to pass, since the fairies had said it, caused the Princess to be carried into the finest apartment in his palace, and to be laid upon a bed all embroidered with gold and silver.

One would have taken her for a little angel, she was so very beautiful; for her swooning away had not diminished one bit of her complexion; her cheeks were carnation, and her lips were coral; indeed, her eyes were shut, but she was heard to breathe softly, which satisfied those about her that she was not dead. The King commanded that they should not disturb her, but let her sleep quietly till her hour of awaking was come.

The good Fairy who had saved her life by condemning her to sleep a hundred years was in the kingdom of Matakin, twelve thousand leagues off, when this accident befell the Princess; but she was instantly informed of it by a little dwarf, who had boots of seven leagues, that is, boots with which he could tread over seven leagues of ground in one stride. The Fairy came away immediately, and she arrived, about an hour after, in a fiery chariot drawn by dragons.

The King handed her out of the chariot, and she approved everything he had done, but as she had very great foresight, she thought when the Princess should awake she might not know what to do with herself, being all alone in this old palace; and this was what she did: she touched with her wand everything in the palace (except the King and Queen)—governesses, maids of honor, ladies of the bedchamber, gentlemen, officers, stewards, cooks, undercooks, scullions, guards, with their beefeaters, pages, footmen; she likewise touched all the horses which were in the stables, pads as well as others, the great dogs in the outward court and pretty little Mopsey too, the Princess's little spaniel, which lay by her on the bed.

Immediately upon her touching them they all fell asleep, that they might not awake before their mistress and that they might be ready to wait upon her when she wanted them. The very spits at the fire, as full as they could hold of partridges and pheasants, did fall asleep also. All this was done in a moment. Fairies are not long in doing their business.

And now the King and the Queen, having kissed their dear child without waking her, went out of the palace and put forth a proclamation that nobody should dare to come near it.

This, however, was not necessary, for in a quarter of an hour's time there grew up all round about the park such a vast number of trees, great and small, bushes and brambles, twining one within another, that neither man nor beast could pass through; so that nothing could be seen but the very top of the towers of the palace; and that, too, not unless it was a good way off. Nobody; doubted but the Fairy gave herein a very extraordinary sample of her art, that the Princess, while she continued sleeping, might have nothing to fear from any curious people.

When a hundred years were gone and passed the son of the King then reigning, and who was of another family from that of the sleeping Princess, being gone a-hunting on that side of the country, asked:

What those towers were which he saw in the middle of a great thick wood?

Everyone answered according as they had heard. Some said:

That it was a ruinous old castle, haunted by spirits.

Others, That all the sorcerers and witches of the country kept there their sabbath or night's meeting.

The common opinion was: That an ogre lived there, and that he carried thither all the little children he could catch, that he might eat them up at his leisure, without anybody being able to follow him, as having himself only the power to pass through the wood.

The Prince was at a stand, not knowing what to believe, when a very good countryman spake to him thus:

"May it please your royal highness, it is now about fifty years since I heard from my father, who heard my grandfather say, that there was then in this castle a princess, the most beautiful was ever seen; that she must sleep there a hundred years, and should be waked by a king's son, for whom she was reserved."

The young Prince was all on fire at these words, believing, without weighing the matter, that he could put an end to this rare adventure; and, pushed on by love and honor, resolved that moment to look into it.

Scarce had he advanced toward the wood when all the great trees, the bushes, and brambles gave way of themselves to let him pass through; he walked up to the castle which he saw at the end of a large avenue which he went into; and what a little surprised him was that he saw none of his people could follow him, because the trees closed again as soon as he had passed through them. However, he did not cease from continuing his way; a young and amorous prince is always valiant.

He came into a spacious outward court, where everything he saw might have frozen the most fearless person with horror. There reigned all over a most frightful silence; the image of death everywhere showed itself, and there was nothing to be seen but stretched-out bodies of men and animals, all seeming to be dead. He, however, very well knew, by the ruby faces and pimpled noses of the beefeaters, that they were only asleep; and their goblets, wherein still remained some drops of wine, showed plainly that they fell asleep in their cups.

He then crossed a court paved with marble, went up the stairs and came into the guard chamber, where guards were standing in their ranks, with their muskets upon their shoulders, and snoring as loud as they could. After that he went through several rooms full of gentlemen and ladies, all asleep, some standing, others sitting. At last he came into a chamber all gilded with gold, where he saw upon a bed, the curtains of which were all open, the finest sight was ever beheld—a princess, who appeared to be about fifteen or sixteen years of age, and whose bright and, in a manner, resplendent beauty, had somewhat in it divine. He approached with trembling and admiration, and fell down before her upon his knees.

And now, as the enchantment was at an end, the Princess awaked, and looking on him with eyes more tender than the first view might seem to admit of:

"Is it you, my Prince?" said she to him. "You have waited a long while."

The Prince, charmed with these words, and much more with the manner in which they were spoken, knew not how to show his joy and gratitude; he assured her that he loved her better than he did himself; their discourse was not well connected, they did weep more than talk—little eloquence, a great deal of love. He was more at a loss than she, and we need not wonder at it; she had time to think on what to say to him; for it is very probable (though history mentions nothing of it) that the good Fairy, during so long a sleep, had given her very agreeable dreams. In short, they talked four hours together, and yet they said not half what they had to say.

In the meanwhile all the palace awaked; everyone thought upon their particular business, and as all of them were not in love they were ready to die for hunger. The chief lady of honor, being as sharp set as other folks, grew very impatient, and told the Princess aloud that supper was served up. The Prince helped the Princess to rise; she was entirely dressed, and very magnificently, but his royal highness took care not to tell her that she was dressed like his great-grandmother, and had a point band peeping over a high collar; she looked not a bit less charming and beautiful for all that.

They went into the great hall of looking-glasses, where they supped, and were served by the Princess's officers, the violins and hautboys played old tunes, but very excellent, though it was now above a hundred years since they had played; and after supper, without losing any time, the lord almoner married them in the chapel of the castle, and the chief lady of honor drew the curtains. They had but very little sleep—the Princess had no occasion; and the Prince left her next morning to return to the city, where his father must needs have been in pain for him. The Prince told him:

That he lost his way in the forest as he was hunting, and that he had lain in the cottage of a charcoal-burner, who gave him cheese and brown bread.

The King, his father, who was a good man, believed him; but his mother could not be persuaded it was true; and seeing that he went almost every day a-hunting, and that he always had some excuse ready for so doing, though he had lain out three or four nights together, she began to suspect that he was married, for he lived with the Princess above two whole years, and had by her two children, the eldest of which, who was a daughter, was named *Morning*, and the youngest, who was a son, they called *Day*, because he was a great deal handsomer and more beautiful than his sister.

The Queen spoke several times to her son, to inform herself after what manner he did pass his time, and that in this he ought in duty to satisfy her. But he never dared to trust her with his secret; he feared her, though he loved her, for she was of the race of the Ogres, and the King would never have married her had it not been for her vast riches; it was even whispered about the Court that she had Ogreish inclinations, and that, whenever she saw little children passing by, she had all the difficulty in the world to avoid falling upon them. And so the Prince would never tell her one word.

But when the King was dead, which happened about two years afterward, and he saw himself lord and master, he openly declared his marriage; and he went in great ceremony to conduct his Queen to the palace. They made a magnificent entry into the capital city, she riding between her two children.

Soon after the King went to make war with the Emperor Contalabutte, his neighbor. He left the government of the kingdom to the Queen his mother, and earnestly recommended to her care his wife and children. He was obliged to continue his expedition all the summer, and as soon as he departed the Queen-mother sent her daughter-in-law to a country house among the woods, that she might with the more ease gratify her horrible longing.

Some few days afterward she went thither herself, and said to her clerk of the kitchen:

"I have a mind to eat little Morning for my dinner to-morrow."

"Ah! madam," cried the clerk of the kitchen.

"I will have it so," replied the Queen (and this she spoke in the tone of an Ogress who had a strong desire to eat fresh meat), "and will eat her with a *sauce Robert*."

The poor man, knowing very well that he must not play tricks with Ogresses, took his great knife and went up into little Morning's chamber.

She was then four years old, and came up to him jumping and laughing, to take him about the neck, and ask him for some sugar-candy. Upon which he began to weep, the great knife fell out of his hand, and he went into the back yard, and killed a little lamb, and dressed it with such good sauce that his mistress assured him that she had never eaten anything so good in her life. He had at the same time taken up little Morning, and carried her to his wife, to conceal her in the lodging he had at the bottom of the courtyard.

About eight days afterward the wicked Queen said to the clerk of the kitchen, "I will sup on little Day."

He answered not a word, being resolved to cheat her as he had done before. He went to find out little Day, and saw him with a little foil in his hand, with which he was fencing with a great monkey, the child being then only three years of age. He took him up in his arms and carried him to his wife, that she might conceal him in her chamber along with his sister, and in the room of little Day cooked up a young kid, very tender, which the Ogress found to be wonderfully good.

This was hitherto all mighty well; but one evening this wicked Queen said to her clerk of the kitchen:

"I will eat the Queen with the same sauce I had with her children."

It was now that the poor clerk of the kitchen despaired of being able to deceive her. The young Queen was turned of twenty, not reckoning the hundred years she had been asleep; and how to find in the yard a beast so firm was what puzzled him. He took then a resolution, that he might save his own life, to cut the Queen's throat; and going up into her chamber, with intent to do it at once, he put himself into as great fury as he could possibly, and came into the young Queen's room with his dagger in his hand. He would not, however, surprise her, but told her, with a great deal of respect, the orders he had received from the Queen-mother.

"Do it; do it" (said she, stretching out her neck). "Execute your orders, and then I shall go and see my children, my poor children, whom I so much and so tenderly loved."

For she thought them dead ever since they had been taken away without her knowledge.

"No, no, madam" (cried the poor clerk of the kitchen, all in tears); "you shall not die, and yet you shall see your children again; but then you must go home with me to my lodgings, where I have concealed them, and I shall deceive the Queen once more, by giving her in your stead a young hind."

Upon this he forthwith conducted her to his chamber, where, leaving her to embrace her children, and cry along with them, he went and dressed a young hind, which the Queen had for her supper, and devoured it with the same appetite as if it had been the young Queen. Exceedingly was she delighted with her cruelty, and she had invented a story to tell the King, at his return, how the mad wolves had eaten up the Queen his wife and her two children.

One evening, as she was, according to her custom, rambling round about the courts and yards of the palace to see if she could smell any fresh meat, she heard, in a ground room, little Day crying, for his mamma was going to whip him, because he had been naughty; and she heard, at the same time, little Morning begging pardon for her brother.

The Ogress presently knew the voice of the Queen and her children, and being quite mad that she had been thus deceived, she commanded next morning, by break of day (with a most horrible voice, which made everybody tremble), that they should bring into the middle of the great court a large tub, which she caused to be filled with toads, vipers, snakes, and all sorts of serpents, in order to have thrown into it the Queen and her children, the clerk of the kitchen, his wife and maid; all whom she had given orders should be brought thither with their hands tied behind them.

They were brought out accordingly, and the executioners were just going to throw them into the tub, when the King (who was not so soon expected) entered the court on horseback (for he came post) and asked, with the utmost astonishment, what was the meaning of that horrible spectacle.

No one dared to tell him, when the Ogress, all enraged to see what had happened, threw herself head foremost into the tub, and was instantly devoured by the ugly creatures she had ordered to be thrown into it for others. The King could not but be very sorry, for she was his mother; but he soon comforted himself with his beautiful wife and his pretty children.

Cannetella

(FROM *THE GRAY FAIRY BOOK*)

There was once upon a time a king who reigned over a country called "Bello Puojo." He was very rich and powerful, and had everything in the world he could desire except a child. But at last, after he had been married for many years, and was quite an old man, his wife Renzolla presented him with a fine daughter, whom they called Cannetella.

She grew up into a beautiful girl, and was as tall and straight as a young fir-tree. When she was eighteen years old her father called her to him and said: "You are of an age now, my daughter, to marry and settle down; but as I love you more than anything else in the world, and desire nothing but your happiness, I am determined to leave the choice of a husband to yourself. Choose a man after your own heart, and you are sure to satisfy me." Cannetella thanked her father very much for his kindness and consideration, but told him that she had not the slightest wish to marry, and was quite determined to remain single.

The king, who felt himself growing old and feeble, and longed to see an heir to the throne before he died, was very unhappy at her words, and begged her earnestly not to disappoint him.

When Cannetella saw that the king had set his heart on her marriage, she said: "Very well, dear father, I will marry to please you, for I do not wish to appear ungrateful for all your love and kindness; but you must find me a husband handsomer, cleverer, and more charming than anyone else in the world."

The king was overjoyed by her words, and from early in the morning till late at night he sat at the window and looked carefully at all the passers-by, in the hopes of finding a son-in-law among them.

One day, seeing a very good-looking man crossing the street, the king called his daughter and said: "Come quickly, dear Cannetella, and look at this man, for I think he might suit you as a husband."

335

They called the young man into the palace, and set a sumptuous feast before him, with every sort of delicacy you can imagine. In the middle of the meal the youth let an almond fall out of his mouth, which, however, he picked up again very quickly and hid under the table-cloth.

When the feast was over the stranger went away, and the king asked Cannetella: "Well, what did you think of the youth?"

"I think he was a clumsy wretch," replied Cannetella. "Fancy a man of his age letting an almond fall out of his mouth!"

When the king heard her answer he returned to his watch at the window, and shortly afterwards a very handsome young man passed by. The king instantly called his daughter to come and see what she thought of the new comer.

"Call him in," said Cannetella, "that we may see him close."

Another splendid feast was prepared, and when the stranger had eaten and drunk as much as he was able, and had taken his departure, the king asked Cannetella how she liked him.

"Not at all," replied his daughter; "what could you do with a man who requires at least two servants to help him on with his cloak, because he is too awkward to put it on properly himself?"

"If that's all you have against him," said the king, "I see how the land lies. You are determined not to have a husband at all; but marry someone you shall, for I do not mean my name and house to die out."

"Well, then, my dear parent," said Cannetella, "I must tell you at once that you had better not count upon me, for I never mean to marry unless I can find a man with a gold head and gold teeth."

The king was very angry at finding his daughter so obstinate; but as he always gave the girl her own way in everything, he issued a proclamation to the effect that any man with a gold head and gold teeth might come forward and claim the princess as his bride, and the kingdom of Bello Puojo as a wedding gift.

Now the king had a deadly enemy called Scioravante, who was a very powerful magician. No sooner had this man heard of the proclamation than he summoned his attendant spirits and commanded them to gild his head and teeth. The spirits said, at first, that the task was beyond their powers, and suggested that a pair of golden horns attached to his forehead would both be easier to make and more comfortable to wear; but Scioravante would allow no compromise, and insisted on having a head and teeth made of the finest gold. When it was fixed on his shoulders he went for a stroll in front of the palace. And the king, seeing the very man he was in search of, called his daughter, and said: "Just look out of the window, and you will find exactly what you want."

Then, as Scioravante was hurrying past, the king shouted out to him: "Just stop a minute, brother, and don't be in such desperate haste. If you will step in here you shall have my daughter for a wife, and I will send attendants with her, and as many horses and servants as you wish."

"A thousand thanks," returned Scioravante; "I shall be delighted to marry your daughter, but it is quite unnecessary to send anyone to accompany her. Give me a horse and I will carry off the princess in front of my saddle, and will bring her to my own kingdom, where there is no lack of courtiers or servants, or, indeed, of anything your daughter can desire."

At first the king was very much against Cannetella's departing in this fashion; but finally Scioravante got his way, and placing the princess before him on his horse, he set out for his own country.

Towards evening he dismounted, and entering a stable he placed Cannetella in the same stall as his horse, and said to her: "Now listen to what I have to say. I am going to my home now, and that is a seven years' journey from here; you must wait for me in this stable, and never move from the spot, or let yourself be seen by a living soul. If you disobey my commands, it will be the worse for you."

The princess answered meekly: "Sir, I am your servant, and will do exactly as you bid me; but I should like to know what I am to live on till you come back?"

"You can take what the horses leave," was Scioravante's reply.

When the magician had left her Cannetella felt very miserable, and bitterly cursed the day she was born. She spent all her time weeping and bemoaning the cruel fate that had driven her from a palace into a stable, from soft down cushions to a bed of straw, and from the dainties of her father's table to the food that the horses left.

She led this wretched life for a few months, and during that time she never saw who fed and watered the horses, for it was all done by invisible hands.

One day, when she was more than usually unhappy, she perceived a little crack in the wall, through which she could see a beautiful garden, with all manner of delicious fruits and flowers growing in it. The sight and smell of such delicacies were too much for poor Cannetella, and she said to herself, "I will slip quietly out, and pick a few oranges and grapes, and I don't care what happens. Who is there to tell my husband what I do? and even if he should hear of my disobedience, he cannot make my life more miserable than it is already."

So she slipped out and refreshed her poor, starved body with the fruit she plucked in the garden.

But a short time afterwards her husband returned unexpectedly, and one of the horses instantly told him that Cannetella had gone into the garden, in his absence, and had stolen some oranges and grapes.

Scioravante was furious when he heard this, and seizing a huge knife from his pocket he threatened to kill his wife for her disobedience. But Cannetella threw herself at his feet and implored him to spare her life, saying that hunger drove even the wolf from the wood. At last she succeeded in so far softening her husband's heart that he said, "I will forgive you this time, and spare your life; but if you disobey me again, and I hear, on my return, that you have as much as moved out of the stall, I will certainly kill you. So, beware; for I am going away once more, and shall be absent for seven years."

With these words he took his departure, and Cannetella burst into a flood of tears, and, wringing her hands, she moaned: "Why was I ever born to such a hard fate? Oh! father, how miserable you have made your poor daughter! But, why should I blame my father? for I have only myself to thank for all my sufferings. I got the cursed head of gold, and it has brought all this misery on me. I am indeed punished for not doing as my father wished!"

When a year had gone by, it chanced, one day, that the king's cooper passed the stables where Cannetella was kept prisoner. She recognized the man, and called him to come in. At first he did not know the poor princess, and could not make out who it was that called him by name. But when he heard Cannetella's tale of woe, he hid her in a big empty barrel he had with him, partly because he was sorry for the poor girl, and, even more, because he wished to gain the king's favor. Then he slung the barrel on a mule's back, and in this way the princess was carried to her own home. They arrived at the palace about four o'clock in the morning, and the cooper knocked loudly at the door. When the servants came in haste and saw only the cooper standing at the gate, they were very indignant, and scolded him soundly for coming at such an hour and waking them all out of their sleep.

The king hearing the noise and the cause of it, sent for the cooper, for he felt certain the man must have some important business, to have come and disturbed the whole palace at such an early hour.

The cooper asked permission to unload his mule, and Cannetella crept out of the barrel. At first the king refused to believe that it was really his daughter, for she had changed so terribly in a few years, and had grown so thin and pale, that it was pitiful to see her. At last the princess showed her father a mole she had on her right arm, and then he saw that the poor girl was indeed his long-lost Cannetella. He kissed her a thousand times, and instantly had the choicest food and drink set before her.

After she had satisfied her hunger, the king said to her: "Who would have thought, my dear daughter, to have found you in such a state? What, may I ask, has brought you to this pass?"

Cannetella replied: "That wicked man with the gold head and teeth treated me worse than a dog, and many a time, since I left you, have I longed to die. But I couldn't tell you all that I have suffered, for you would never believe me. It is enough that I am once more with you, and I shall never leave you again, for I would rather be a slave in your house than queen in any other."

In the meantime Scioravante had returned to the stables, and one of the horses told him that Cannetella had been taken away by a cooper in a barrel.

When the wicked magician heard this he was beside himself with rage, and, hastening to the kingdom of Bello Puojo, he went straight to an old woman who lived exactly opposite the royal palace, and said to her: "If you will let me see the king's daughter, I will give you whatever reward you like to ask for."

The woman demanded a hundred ducats of gold, and Scioravante counted them out of his purse and gave them to her without a murmur. Then the old woman led him to the roof of the house, where he could see Cannetella combing out her long hair in a room in the top story of the palace.

The princess happened to look out of the window, and when she saw her husband gazing at her, she got such a fright that she flew downstairs to the king, and said: "My lord and father, unless you shut me up instantly in a room with seven iron doors, I am lost."

"If that's all," said the king, "it shall be done at once." And he gave orders for the doors to be closed on the spot.

When Scioravante saw this he returned to the old woman, and said: "I will give you whatever you like if you will go into the palace, hide under the princess's bed, and slip this little piece of paper beneath her pillow, saying, as you do so: 'May everyone in the palace, except the princess, fall into a sound sleep.'"

The old woman demanded another hundred golden ducats, and then proceeded to carry out the magician's wishes. No sooner had she slipped the piece of paper under Cannetella's pillow, than all the people in the palace fell fast asleep, and only the princess remained awake.

Then Scioravante hurried to the seven doors and opened them one after the other. Cannetella screamed with terror when she saw her husband, but no one came to her help, for all in the palace lay as if they were dead. The magician seized her in the bed on which she lay, and was going to carry her off with him, when the little piece of paper which the old woman had placed under her pillow fell on the floor.

In an instant all the people in the palace woke up, and as Cannetella was still screaming for help, they rushed to her rescue. They seized Scioravante and put him to death; so he was caught in the trap which he had laid for the princess—and, as is so often the case in this world, the biter himself was bit.

How the Hermit Helped to Win the King's Daughter

(FROM *THE PINK FAIRY BOOK*)

Long ago there lived a very rich man who had three sons. When he felt himself to be dying he divided his property between them, making them share alike, both in money and lands. Soon after he died the king set forth a proclamation through the whole country that whoever could build a ship that should float both on land and sea should have his daughter to wife.

The eldest brother, when he heard it, said to the other, "I think I will spend some of my money in trying to build that ship, as I should like to have the king for my father-in-law." So he called together all the shipbuilders in the land, and gave them orders to begin the ship without delay. And trees were cut down, and great preparations made, and in a few days everybody knew what it was all for; and there was a crowd of old people pressing round the gates of the yard, where the young man spent the most of his day.

"Ah, master, give us work," they said, "so that we may earn our bread."

But he only gave them hard words, and spoke roughly to them. "You are old, and have lost your strength; of what use are you?" And he drove them away. Then came some boys and prayed him, "master, give us work," but he answered them, "Of what use can you be, weaklings as you are! Get you gone!" And if any presented themselves that were not skilled workmen he would have none of them.

At last there knocked at the gate a little old man with a long white beard, and said, "Will you give me work, so that I may earn my bread?" But he was only driven away like the rest.

The ship took a long while to build, and cost a great deal of money, and when it was launched a sudden squall rose, and it fell to pieces, and with it all the young man's hopes of winning the princess. By this time he had not a penny left, so he went back to his two brothers and told his tale. And the second brother said to himself as he listened, "Certainly he has managed very badly, but I should like to see if I can't do better, and win the princess for my own self." So he called together all the shipbuilders throughout the country, and gave them orders to build a ship which should float on the land as well as on the sea. But his heart was no softer than his brother's, and every man that was not a skilled workman was chased away with hard words. Last came the white-bearded man, but he fared no better than the rest.

When the ship was finished the launch took place, and everything seemed going smoothly when a gale sprang up, and the vessel was dashed to pieces on the rocks. The young man had spent his whole fortune on it, and now it was all swallowed up, was forced to beg shelter from his youngest brother. When he told his story the youngest said to himself, "I am not rich enough to support us all three. I had better take my turn, and if I manage to win the princess there will be her fortune as well as my own for us to live on." So he called together all the shipbuilders in the kingdom, and gave orders that a new ship should be built. Then all the old people came and asked for work, and he answered cheerfully, "Oh, yes, there is plenty for everybody"; and when the boys begged to be allowed to help he found something that they could do. And when the old man with the long white beard stood before him, praying that he might earn his bread, he replied, "Oh, father, I could not suffer you to work, but you shall be overseer, and look after the rest."

Now the old man was a holy hermit, and when he saw how kind-hearted the youth was he determined to do all he could for him to gain the wish of his heart.

By-and-bye, when the ship was finished, the hermit said to his young friend, "Now you can go and claim the king's daughter, for the ship will float both by land and sea."

"Oh, good father," cried the young man, "you will not forsake me? Stay with me, I pray you, and lead me to the king!"

"If you wish it, I will," said the hermit, "on condition that you will give me half of anything you get."

"Oh, if that is all," answered he, "it is easily promised!" And they set out together on the ship.

After they had gone some distance they saw a man standing in a thick fog, which he was trying to put into a sack.

"Oh, good father," exclaimed the youth, "what can he be doing?"

"Ask him," said the old man.

"What are you doing, my fine fellow?"

"I am putting the fog into my sack. That is my business."

"Ask him if he will come with us," whispered the hermit.

And the man answered: "If you will give me enough to eat and drink I will gladly stay with you."

So they took him on their ship, and the youth said, as they started off again, "Good father, before we were two, and now we are three!"

After they had traveled a little further they met a man who had torn up half the forest, and was carrying all the trees on his shoulders.

"Good father," exclaimed the youth, "only look! What can he have done that for?"

"Ask him why he has torn up all those trees."

And the man replied, "Why, I've merely been gathering a handful of brushwood."

"Beg him to come with us," whispered the hermit.

And the strong man answered: "Willingly, as long as you give me enough to eat and drink." And he came on the ship.

And the youth said to the hermit, "Good father, before we were three, and now we are four."

The ship traveled on again, and some miles further on they saw a man drinking out of a stream till he had nearly drunk it dry.

"Good father," said the youth, "just look at that man! Did you ever see anybody drink like that?"

"Ask him why he does it," answered the hermit.

"Why, there is nothing very odd in taking a mouthful of water!" replied the man, standing up.

"Beg him to come with us." And the youth did so.

"With pleasure, as long as you give me enough to eat and drink."

And the youth whispered to the hermit, "Good father, before we were four, and now we are five."

A little way along they noticed another man in the middle of a stream, who was shooting into the water.

"Good father," said the youth, "what can he be shooting at?"

"Ask him," answered the hermit.

"Hush, hush!" cried the man; "now you have frightened it away. In the Underworld sits a quail on a tree, and I wanted to shoot it. That is my business. I hit everything I aim at."

"Ask him if he will come with us."

And the man replied, "With all my heart, as long as I get enough to eat and drink."

So they took him into the ship, and the young man whispered, "Good father, before we were five, and now we are six."

Off they went again, and before they had gone far they met a man striding towards them whose steps were so long that while one foot was on the north of the island the other was right down in the south.

"Good father, look at him! What long steps he takes!"

"Ask him why he does it," replied the hermit.

"Oh, I am only going out for a little walk," answered he.

"Ask him if he will come with us."

"Gladly, if you will give me as much as I want to eat and drink," said he, climbing up into the ship.

And the young man whispered, "Good father, before we were six, and now we are seven." But the hermit knew what he was about, and why he gathered these strange people into the ship.

After many days, at last they reached the town where lived the king and his daughter. They stopped the vessel right in front of the palace, and the young man went in and bowed low before the king.

"O Majesty, I have done your bidding, and now is the ship built that can travel over land and sea. Give me my reward, and let me have your daughter to wife."

But the king said to himself, "What! am I to wed my daughter to a man of whom I know nothing. Not even whether he be rich or poor—a knight or a beggar."

And aloud he spake: It is not enough that you have managed to build the ship. You must find a runner who shall take this letter to the ruler of the Underworld, and bring me the answer back in an hour."

"That is not in the bond," answered the young man.

"Well, do as you like," replied the king, "only you will not get my daughter."

The young man went out, sorely troubled, to tell his old friend what had happened.

"Silly boy!" cried the hermit, "Accept his terms at once. And send off the long-legged man with the letter. He will take it in no time at all."

So the youth's heard leapt for joy, and he returned to the king. "Majesty, I accept your terms. Here is the messenger who will do what you wish."

The king had no choice but to give the man the letter, and he strode off, making short work of the distance that lay between the palace and the Underworld. He soon found the ruler, who looked at the letter, and said to him, "Wait a little while I write the answer"; but the man was so tired with his quick walk that he went sound asleep and forgot all about his errand.

All this time the youth was anxiously counting the minutes till he could get back, and stood with his eyes fixed on the road down which his messenger must come.

"What can be keeping him," he said to the hermit when the hour was nearly up. Then the hermit sent for the man who could hit everything he aimed at, and said to him, "Just see why the messenger stays so long."

"Oh, he is sound asleep in the palace of the Underworld. However, I can wake him."

Then he drew his bow, and shot an arrow straight into the man's knee. The messenger awoke with such a start, and when he saw that the hour had almost run out he snatched up the answer and rushed back with such speed that the clock had not yet struck when he entered the palace.

Now the young man thought he was sure of his bride, but the king said, "Still you have not done enough. Before I give you my daughter you must find a man who can drink half the contents of my cellar in one day."

"That is not in the bond," complained the poor youth.

"Well, do as you like, only you will not get my daughter."

The young man went sadly out, and asked the hermit what he was to do.

"Silly boy!" said he. "Why, tell the man to do it who drinks up everything."

So they sent for the man and said, "Do you think you are able to drink half the royal cellar in one day?"

"Dear me, yes, and as much more as you want," answered he. "I am never satisfied."

The king was not pleased at the young man agreeing so readily, but he had no choice, and ordered the servant to be taken downstairs. Oh, how he enjoyed himself! All day long he drank, and drank, and drank, till instead of half the cellar, he had drunk the whole, and there was not a cask but what stood empty. And when the king saw this he said to the youth, "You have conquered, and I can no longer withhold my daughter. But, as her dowry, I shall only give so much as one man can carry away."

"But," answered he, "let a man be ever so strong, he cannot carry more than a hundredweight, and what is that for a king's daughter?"

"Well, do as you like; I have said my say. It is your affair—not mine."

The young man was puzzled, and did not know what to reply, for, though he would gladly have married the princess without a sixpence, he had spent all his money in building the ship, and knew he could not give her all she wanted. So he went to the hermit and said to him, "The king will only give for her dowry as much as a man can carry. I have no money of my own left, and my brothers have none either."

"Silly boy! Why, you have only got to fetch the man who carried half the forest on his shoulders."

And the youth was glad, and called the strong man, and told him what he must do. "Take everything you can, till you are bent double. Never mind if you leave the palace bare."

The strong man promised, and nobly kept his word. He piled all he could see on his back—chairs, tables, wardrobes, chests of gold and silver—till there was nothing left to pile. At last he took the king's crown, and put it on the top. He carried his burden to the ship and stowed his treasures away, and the youth followed, leading the king's daughter. But the king was left raging in his empty palace, and he called together his army, and got ready his ships of war, in order that he might go after the vessel and bring back what had been taken away.

And the king's ships sailed very fast, and soon caught up the little vessel, and the sailors all shouted for joy. Then the hermit looked out and saw how near they were, and he said to the youth, "Do you see that?"

The youth shrieked and cried, "Ah, good father, it is a fleet of ships, and they are chasing us, and in a few moments they will be upon us."

But the hermit bade him call the man who had the fog in his sack, and the sack was opened and the fog flew out, and hung right round the king's ships, so that they could see nothing. So they sailed back to the palace, and told the king what strange things had happened. Meanwhile the young man's vessel reached home in safety.

"Well, here you are once more" said the hermit; "and now you can fulfill the promise you made me to give me the half of all you had."

"That will I do with all my heart," answered the youth, and began to divide all his treasures, putting part on one side for himself and setting aside the other for his friend. "Good father, it is finished," said he at length; "there is nothing more left to divide."

"Nothing more left!" cried the hermit. "Why, you have forgotten the best thing of all!"

"What can that be?" asked he. "We have divided everything."

"And the king's daughter?" said the hermit.

Then the young man's heart stood still, for he loved her dearly. But he answered, "It is well; I have sworn, and I will keep my word," and drew his sword to cut her in pieces. When the hermit saw that he held his honor dearer than his wife he lifted his hand and cried, "Hold! she is yours, and all the treasures too. I gave you my help because you had pity on those that were in need. And when you are in need yourself, call upon me, and I will come to you."

As he spoke he softly touched their heads and vanished.

The next day the wedding took place, and the two brothers came to the house, and they all lived happily together, but they never forgot the holy man who had been such a good friend.

Cinderella, or, the Little Glass Slipper

(FROM *THE BLUE FAIRY BOOK*)

Once there was a gentleman who married, for his second wife, the proudest and most haughty woman that was ever seen. She had, by a former husband, two daughters of her own humor, who were, indeed, exactly like her in all things. He had likewise, by another wife, a young daughter, but of unparalleled goodness and sweetness of temper, which she took from her mother, who was the best creature in the world.

No sooner were the ceremonies of the wedding over but the mother-in-law began to show herself in her true colors. She could not bear the good qualities of this pretty girl, and the less because they made her own daughters appear the more odious. She employed her in the meanest work of the house: she scoured the dishes, tables, etc., and scrubbed madam's chamber, and those of misses, her daughters; she lay up in a sorry garret, upon a wretched straw bed, while her sisters lay in fine rooms, with floors all inlaid, upon beds of the very newest fashion, and where they had looking-glasses so large that they might see themselves at their full length from head to foot.

The poor girl bore all patiently, and dared not tell her father, who would have rattled her off; for his wife governed him entirely. When she had done her work, she used to go into the chimney-corner, and sit down among cinders and ashes, which made her commonly be called Cinderwench; but the youngest, who was not so rude and uncivil as the eldest, called her Cinderella. However, Cinderella, notwithstanding her mean apparel, was a hundred times handsomer than her sisters, though they were always dressed very richly.

It happened that the King's son gave a ball, and invited all persons of fashion to it. Our young misses were also invited, for they cut a very grand figure among the quality. They were mightily delighted at this invitation, and wonderfully busy in choosing out such gowns, petticoats, and head-clothes as might become them. This was a new trouble to Cinderella; for it was she who ironed her sisters' linen, and plaited their ruffles; they talked all day long of nothing but how they should be dressed.

"For my part," said the eldest, "I will wear my red velvet suit with French trimming."

"And I," said the youngest, "shall have my usual petticoat; but then, to make amends for that, I will put on my gold-flowered manteau, and my diamond stomacher, which is far from being the most ordinary one in the world."

They sent for the best tire-woman they could get to make up their head-dresses and adjust their double pinners, and they had their red brushes and patches from Mademoiselle de la Poche.

Cinderella was likewise called up to them to be consulted in all these matters, for she had excellent notions, and advised them always for the best, nay, and offered her services to dress their heads, which they were very willing she should do. As she was doing this, they said to her:

"Cinderella, would you not be glad to go to the ball?"

"Alas!" said she, "you only jeer me; it is not for such as I am to go thither."

"Thou art in the right of it," replied they; "it would make the people laugh to see a Cinderwench at a ball."

Anyone but Cinderella would have dressed their heads awry, but she was very good, and dressed them perfectly well. They were almost two days without eating, so much were they transported with joy. They broke above a dozen laces in trying to be laced up close, that they might have a fine slender shape, and they were continually at their looking-glass. At last the happy day came; they went to Court, and Cinderella followed them with her eyes as long as she could, and when she had lost sight of them, she fell a-crying.

Her godmother, who saw her all in tears, asked her what was the matter.

"I wish I could—I wish I could—"; she was not able to speak the rest, being interrupted by her tears and sobbing.

This godmother of hers, who was a fairy, said to her, "Thou wishest thou couldst go to the ball; is it not so?"

"Y—es," cried Cinderella, with a great sigh.

"Well," said her godmother, "be but a good girl, and I will contrive that thou shalt go." Then she took her into her chamber, and said to her, "Run into the garden, and bring me a pumpkin."

Cinderella went immediately to gather the finest she could get, and brought it to her godmother, not being able to imagine how this pumpkin could make her go to the ball. Her godmother scooped out all the inside of it, having left nothing but the rind; which done, she struck it with her wand, and the pumpkin was instantly turned into a fine coach, gilded all over with gold.

She then went to look into her mouse-trap, where she found six mice, all alive, and ordered Cinderella to lift up a little the trapdoor, when, giving each mouse, as it went out, a little tap with her wand, the mouse was that moment turned into a fine horse, which altogether made a very fine set of six horses of a beautiful mouse-colored dapple-gray. Being at a loss for a coachman, "I will go and see," says Cinderella, "if there is never a rat in the rat-trap— we may make a coachman of him."

"Thou art in the right," replied her godmother; "go and look."

Cinderella brought the trap to her, and in it there were three huge rats. The fairy made choice of one of the three which had the largest beard, and, having touched him with her wand, he was turned into a fat, jolly coachman, who had the smartest whiskers eyes ever beheld. After that, she said to her:

"Go again into the garden, and you will find six lizards behind the watering-pot, bring them to me."

She had no sooner done so but her godmother turned them into six footmen, who skipped up immediately behind the coach, with their liveries all bedaubed with gold and silver, and clung as close behind each other as if they had done nothing else their whole lives. The Fairy then said to Cinderella:

"Well, you see here an equipage fit to go to the ball with; are you not pleased with it?"

"Oh! yes," cried she; "but must I go thither as I am, in these nasty rags?"

Her godmother only just touched her with her wand, and, at the same instant, her clothes were turned into cloth of gold and silver, all beset with jewels. This done, she gave her a pair of glass slippers, the prettiest in the whole world. Being thus decked out, she got up into her coach; but her godmother, above all things, commanded her not to stay till after midnight, telling her, at the same time, that if she stayed one moment longer, the coach would be a pumpkin again, her horses mice, her coachman a rat, her footmen lizards, and her clothes become just as they were before.

She promised her godmother she would not fail of leaving the ball before midnight; and then away she drives, scarce able to contain herself for joy. The King's son who was told that a great princess, whom nobody knew, was come, ran out to receive her; he gave her his hand as she alighted out of the coach, and led her into the ball, among all the company. There was immediately a profound silence, they left off dancing, and the violins ceased to play, so attentive was everyone to contemplate the singular beauties of the unknown new-comer. Nothing was then heard but a confused noise of:

"Ha! how handsome she is! Ha! how handsome she is!"

The King himself, old as he was, could not help watching her, and telling the Queen softly that it was a long time since he had seen so beautiful and lovely a creature.

All the ladies were busied in considering her clothes and headdress, that they might have some made next day after the same pattern, provided they could meet with such fine material and as able hands to make them.

The King's son conducted her to the most honorable seat, and afterward took her out to dance with him; she danced so very gracefully that they all more and more admired her. A fine collation was served up, whereof the young prince ate not a morsel, so intently was he busied in gazing on her.

She went and sat down by her sisters, showing them a thousand civilities, giving them part of the oranges and citrons which the Prince had presented her with, which very much surprised them, for they did not know her. While Cinderella was thus amusing her sisters, she heard the clock strike eleven and three-quarters, whereupon she immediately made a courtesy to the company and hasted away as fast as she could.

Being got home she ran to seek out her godmother, and, after having thanked her, she said she could not but heartily wish she might go next day to the ball, because the King's son had desired her.

As she was eagerly telling her godmother whatever had passed at the ball, her two sisters knocked at the door, which Cinderella ran and opened.

"How long you have stayed!" cried she, gaping, rubbing her eyes and stretching herself as if she had been just waked out of her sleep; she had not, however, any manner of inclination to sleep since they went from home.

"If thou hadst been at the ball," said one of her sisters, "thou wouldst not have been tired with it. There came thither the finest princess, the most beautiful ever was seen with mortal eyes; she showed us a thousand civilities, and gave us oranges and citrons."

Cinderella seemed very indifferent in the matter; indeed, she asked them the name of that princess; but they told her they did not know it, and that the King's son was very uneasy on her account and would give all the world to know who she was. At this Cinderella, smiling, replied:

"She must, then, be very beautiful indeed; how happy you have been! Could not I see her? Ah! dear Miss Charlotte, do lend me your yellow suit of clothes which you wear every day."

"Ay, to be sure!" cried Miss Charlotte; "lend my clothes to such a dirty Cinderwench as thou art! I should be a fool."

Cinderella, indeed, expected well such answer, and was very glad of the refusal; for she would have been sadly put to it if her sister had lent her what she asked for jestingly.

The next day the two sisters were at the ball, and so was Cinderella, but dressed more magnificently than before. The King's son was always by her, and never ceased his compliments and kind speeches to her; to whom all this was so far from being tiresome that she quite forgot what her godmother had recommended to her; so that she, at last, counted the clock striking twelve when she took it to be no more than eleven; she then rose up and fled, as nimble as a deer. The Prince followed, but could not overtake her. She left behind one of her glass slippers, which the Prince took up most carefully. She got home but quite out of breath, and in her nasty old clothes, having nothing left her of all her finery but one of the little slippers, fellow to that she dropped. The guards at the palace gate were asked:

If they had not seen a princess go out.

Who said: They had seen nobody go out but a young girl, very meanly dressed, and who had more the air of a poor country wench than a gentlewoman.

When the two sisters returned from the ball Cinderella asked them: If they had been well diverted, and if the fine lady had been there.

They told her: Yes, but that she hurried away immediately when it struck twelve, and with so much haste that she dropped one of her little glass slippers, the prettiest in the world, which the King's son had taken up; that he had done nothing but look at her all the time at the ball, and that most certainly he was very much in love with the beautiful person who owned the glass slipper.

What they said was very true; for a few days after the King's son caused it to be proclaimed, by sound of trumpet, that he would marry her whose foot the slipper would just fit. They whom he employed began to try it upon the princesses, then the duchesses and all the Court, but in vain; it was brought to the two sisters, who did all they possibly could to thrust their foot into the slipper, but they could not effect it. Cinderella, who saw all this, and knew her slipper, said to them, laughing:

"Let me see if it will not fit me."

Her sisters burst out a-laughing, and began to banter her. The gentleman who was sent to try the slipper looked earnestly at Cinderella, and, finding her very handsome, said:

It was but just that she should try, and that he had orders to let everyone make trial.

He obliged Cinderella to sit down, and, putting the slipper to her foot, he found it went on very easily, and fitted her as if it had been made of wax. The astonishment her two sisters were in was excessively great, but still abundantly greater when Cinderella pulled out of her pocket the other slipper, and put it on her foot. Thereupon, in came her godmother, who, having touched with her wand Cinderella's clothes, made them richer and more magnificent than any of those she had before.

And now her two sisters found her to be that fine, beautiful lady whom they had seen at the ball. They threw themselves at her feet to beg pardon for all the ill-treatment they had made her undergo. Cinderella took them up, and, as she embraced them, cried:

That she forgave them with all her heart, and desired them always to love her.

She was conducted to the young prince, dressed as she was; he thought her more charming than ever, and, a few days after, married her. Cinderella, who was no less good than beautiful, gave her two sisters lodgings in the palace, and that very same day matched them with two great lords of the Court.

The Grateful Prince

(FROM *The Violet Fairy Book*)

Once upon a time the king of the Goldland lost himself in a forest, and try as he would he could not find the way out. As he was wandering down one path which had looked at first more hopeful than the rest he saw a man coming towards him.

"What are you doing here, friend?" asked the stranger; "darkness is falling fast, and soon the wild beasts will come from their lairs to seek for food."

"I have lost myself," answered the king, "and am trying to get home."

"Then promise me that you will give me the first thing that comes out of your house, and I will show you the way," said the stranger.

The king did not answer directly, but after awhile he spoke: "Why should I give away my *best* sporting dog. I can surely find my way out of the forest as well as this man."

So the stranger left him, but the king followed path after path for three whole days, with no better success than before. He was almost in despair, when the stranger suddenly appeared, blocking up his way.

"Promise you will give me the first thing that comes out of your house to meet you?"

But still the king was stiff-necked and would promise nothing.

For some days longer he wandered up and down the forest, trying first one path, then another, but his courage at last gave way, and he sank wearily on the ground under a tree, feeling sure his last hour had come. Then for the third time the stranger stood before the king, and said:

"Why are you such a fool? What can a dog be to you, that you should give your life for him like this? Just promise me the reward I want, and I will guide you out of the forest."

"Well, my life is worth more than a thousand dogs," answered the king, "the welfare of my kingdom depends on me. I accept your terms, so take me to my palace." Scarcely had he uttered the words than he found himself at the edge of the wood, with the palace in the dim distance. He made all the haste he could, and just as he reached the great gates out came the nurse with the royal baby, who stretched out his arms to his father. The king shrank back, and ordered the nurse to take the baby away at once. Then his great boarhound bounded up to him, but his caresses were only answered by a violent push.

When the king's anger was spent, and he was able to think what was best to be done, he exchanged his baby, a beautiful boy, for the daughter of a peasant, and the prince lived roughly as the son of poor people, while the little girl slept in a golden cradle, under silken sheets. At the end of a year, the stranger arrived to claim his property, and took away the little girl, believing her to be the true child of the king. The king was so delighted with the success of his plan that he ordered a great feast to be got ready, and gave splendid presents to the foster parents of his son, so that he might lack nothing. But he did not dare to bring back the baby, lest the trick should be found out. The peasants were quite contented with this arrangement, which gave them food and money in abundance.

By-and-by the boy grew big and tall, and seemed to lead a happy life in the house of his foster parents. But a shadow hung over him which really poisoned most of his pleasure, and that was the thought of the poor innocent girl who had suffered in his stead, for his foster father had told him in secret, that he was the king's son. And the prince determined that when he grew old enough he would travel all over the world, and never rest till he had set her free. To become king at the cost of a maiden's life was too heavy a price to pay. So one day he put on the dress of a farm servant, threw a sack of peas on his back, and marched straight into the forest where eighteen years before his father had lost himself. After he had walked some way he began to cry loudly: "Oh, how unlucky I am! Where can I be? Is there no one to show me the way out of the wood?"

Then appeared a strange man with a long grey beard, with a leather bag hanging from his girdle. He nodded cheerfully to the prince, and said: "I know this place well, and can lead you out of it, if you will promise me a good reward."

"What can a beggar such as I promise you?" answered the prince. "I have nothing to give you save my life; even the coat on my back belongs to my master, whom I serve for my keep and my clothes."

The stranger looked at the sack of peas, and said, "But you must possess something; you are carrying this sack, which seems to be very heavy."

"It is full of peas," was the reply. "My old aunt died last night, without leaving money enough to buy peas to give the watchers, as is the custom throughout the country. I have borrowed these peas from my master, and thought to take a short cut across the forest; but I have lost myself, as you see."

"Then you are an orphan?" asked the stranger. "Why should you not enter my service? I want a sharp fellow in the house, and you please me."

"Why not, indeed, if we can strike a bargain?" said the other. "I was born a peasant, and strange bread is always bitter, so it is the same to me whom I serve! What wages will you give me?"

"Every day fresh food, meat twice a week, butter and vegetables, your summer and winter clothes, and a portion of land for your own use."

"I shall be satisfied with that," said the youth. "Somebody else will have to bury my aunt. I will go with you!"

Now this bargain seemed to please the old fellow so much that he spun round like a top, and sang so loud that the whole wood rang with his voice. Then he set out with his companion, and chattered so fast that he never noticed that his new servant kept dropping peas out of the sack. At night they slept under a fig tree, and when the sun rose started on their way. About noon they came to a large stone, and here the old fellow stopped, looked carefully round, gave a sharp whistle, and stamped three times on the ground with his left foot. Suddenly there appeared under the stone a secret door, which led to what looked like the mouth of a cave. The old fellow seized the youth by the arm, and said roughly, "Follow me!"

Thick darkness surrounded them, yet it seemed to the prince as if their path led into still deeper depths. After a long while he thought he saw a glimmer of light, but the light was neither that of the sun nor of the moon. He looked eagerly at it, but found it was only a kind of pale cloud, which was all the light this strange underworld could boast. Earth and water, trees and plants, birds and beasts, each was different from those he had seen before; but what most struck terror into his heart was the absolute stillness that reigned everywhere. Not a rustle or a sound could be heard. Here and there he noticed a bird sitting on a branch, with head erect and swelling throat, but his ear caught nothing. The dogs opened their mouths as if to bark, the toiling oxen seemed about to bellow, but neither bark nor bellow reached the prince. The water flowed noiselessly over the pebbles, the wind bowed the tops of the trees, flies and chafers darted about, without breaking the silence. The old greybeard uttered no word, and when his companion tried to ask him the meaning of it all he felt that his voice died in his throat.

How long this fearful stillness lasted I do not know, but the prince gradually felt his heart turning to ice, his hair stood up like bristles, and a cold chill was creeping down his spine, when at last—oh, ecstasy!—a faint noise broke on his straining ears, and this life of shadows suddenly became real. It sounded as if a troop of horses were plowing their way over a moor.

Then the greybeard opened his mouth, and said: "The kettle is boiling; we are expected at home."

They walked on a little further, till the prince thought he heard the grinding of a saw-mill, as if dozens of saws were working together, but his guide observed, "The grandmother is sleeping soundly; listen how she snores."

When they had climbed a hill which lay before them the prince saw in the distance the house of his master, but it was so surrounded with buildings of all kinds that the place looked more like a village or even a small town. They reached it at last, and found an empty kennel standing in front of the gate. "Creep inside this," said the master, "and wait while I go in and see my grandmother. Like all very old people, she is very obstinate, and cannot bear fresh faces about her."

The prince crept tremblingly into the kennel, and began to regret the daring which had brought him into this scrape.

By-and-by the master came back, and called him from his hiding-place. Something had put out his temper, for with a frown he said, "Watch carefully our ways in the house, and beware of making any mistake, or it will go ill with you. Keep your eyes and ears open, and your mouth shut, obey without questions. Be grateful if you will, but never speak unless you are spoken to."

When the prince stepped over the threshold he caught sight of a maiden of wonderful beauty, with brown eyes and fair curly hair. "Well!" the young man said to himself, "if the old fellow has many daughters like that I should not mind being his son-in-law. This one is just what I admire"; and he watched her lay the table, bring in the food, and take her seat by the fire as if she had never noticed that a strange man was present. Then she took out a needle and thread, and began to darn her stockings. The master sat at table alone, and invited neither his new servant nor the maid to eat with him. Neither was the old grandmother anywhere to be seen. His appetite was tremendous: he soon cleared all the dishes, and ate enough to satisfy a dozen men. When at last he could eat no more he said to the girl, "Now you can pick up the pieces, and take what is left in the iron pot for your own dinner, but give the bones to the dog."

The prince did not at all like the idea of dining off scraps, which he helped the girl to pick up, but, after all, he found that there was plenty to eat, and that the food was very good. During the meal he stole many glances at the maiden, and would even have spoken to her, but she gave him no encouragement. Every time he opened his mouth for the purpose she looked at him sternly, as if to say, "Silence," so he could only let his eyes speak for him. Besides, the master was stretched on a bench by the oven after his huge meal, and would have heard everything.

After supper that night, the old man said to the prince, "For two days you may rest from the fatigues of the journey, and look about the house. But the day after to-morrow you must come with me, and I will point out the work you have to do. The maid will show you where you are to sleep."

The prince thought, from this, he had leave to speak, but his master turned on him with a face of thunder and exclaimed:

"You dog of a servant! If you disobey the laws of the house you will soon find yourself a head shorter! Hold your tongue, and leave me in peace."

The girl made a sign to him to follow her, and, throwing open a door, nodded to him to go in. He would have lingered a moment, for he thought she looked sad, but dared not do so, for fear of the old man's anger.

"It is impossible that she can be his daughter!" he said to himself, "for she has a kind heart. I am quite sure she must be the same girl who was brought here instead of me, so I am bound to risk my head in this mad adventure." He got into bed, but it was long before he fell asleep, and even then his dreams gave him no rest. He seemed to be surrounded by dangers, and it was only the power of the maiden who helped him through it all.

When he woke his first thoughts were for the girl, whom he found hard at work. He drew water from the well and carried it to the house for her, kindled the fire under the iron pot, and, in fact, did everything that came into his head that could be of any use to her. In the afternoon he went out, in order to learn something of his new home, and wondered greatly not to come across the old grandmother. In his rambles he came to the farmyard, where a beautiful white horse had a stall to itself; in another was a black cow with two white-faced calves, while the clucking of geese, ducks, and hens reached him from a distance.

Breakfast, dinner, and supper were as savory as before, and the prince would have been quite content with his quarters had it not been for the difficulty of keeping silence in the presence of the maiden. On the evening of the second day he went, as he had been told, to receive his orders for the following morning.

"I am going to set you something very easy to do to-morrow," said the old man when his servant entered. "Take this scythe and cut as much grass as the white horse will want for its day's feed, and clean out its stall. If I come back and find the manger empty it will go ill with you. So beware!"

The prince left the room, rejoicing in his heart, and saying to himself, "Well, I shall soon get through that! If I have never yet handled either the plough or the scythe, at least I have often watched the country people work them, and know how easy it is."

He was just going to open his door, when the maiden glided softly past and whispered in his ear: "What task has he set you?"

"For to-morrow," answered the prince, "it is really nothing at all! Just to cut hay for the horse, and to clean out his stall!"

"Oh, luckless being!" sighed the girl; "how will you ever get through with it. The white horse, who is our master's grandmother, is always hungry: it takes twenty men always mowing to keep it in food for one day, and another twenty to clean out its stall. How, then, do you expect to do it all by yourself? But listen to me, and do what I tell you. It is your only chance. When you have filled the manger as full as it will hold you must weave a strong plait of the rushes which grow among the meadow hay, and cut a thick peg of stout wood, and be sure that the horse sees what you are doing. Then it will ask you what it is for, and you will say, 'With this plait I intend to bind up your mouth so that you cannot eat any more, and with this peg I am going to keep you still in one spot, so that you cannot scatter your corn and water all over the place!'" After these words the maiden went away as softly as she had come.

Early the next morning he set to work. His scythe danced through the grass much more easily than he had hoped, and soon he had enough to fill the manger. He put it in the crib, and returned with a second supply, when to his horror he found the crib empty. Then he knew that without the maiden's advice he would certainly have been lost, and began to put it into practice. He took out the rushes which had somehow got mixed up with the hay, and plaited them quickly.

"My son, what are you doing?" asked the horse wonderingly.

"Oh, nothing!" replied he. "Just weaving a chin strap to bind your jaws together, in case you might wish to eat any more!"

The white horse sighed deeply when it heard this, and made up its mind to be content with what it had eaten.

The youth next began to clean out the stall, and the horse knew it had found a master; and by mid-day there was still fodder in the manger, and the place was as clean as a new pin. He had barely finished when in walked the old man, who stood astonished at the door.

"Is it really you who have been clever enough to do that?" he asked. "Or has some one else given you a hint?"

"Oh, I have had no help," replied the prince, "except what my poor weak head could give me."

The old man frowned, and went away, and the prince rejoiced that everything had turned out so well.

In the evening his master said, "To-morrow I have no special task to set you, but as the girl has a great deal to do in the house you must milk the black cow for her. But take care you milk her dry, or it may be the worse for you."

"Well," thought the prince as he went away, "unless there is some trick behind, this does not sound very hard. I have never milked a cow before, but I have good strong fingers."

He was very sleepy, and was just going toward his room, when the maiden came to him and asked: "What is your task to-morrow?"

"I am to help you," he answered, "and have nothing to do all day, except to milk the black cow dry."

"Oh, you *are* unlucky," cried she. "If you were to try from morning till night you couldn't do it. There is only one way of escaping the danger, and that is, when you go to milk her, take with you a pan of burning coals and a pair of tongs. Place the pan on the floor of the stall, and the tongs on the fire, and blow with all your might, till the coals burn brightly. The black cow will ask you what is the meaning of all this, and you must answer what I will whisper to you." And she stood on tip-toe and whispered something in his ear, and then went away.

The dawn had scarcely reddened the sky when the prince jumped out of bed, and, with the pan of coals in one hand and the milk pail in the other, went straight to the cow's stall, and began to do exactly as the maiden had told him the evening before.

The black cow watched him with surprise for some time, and then said: "What are you doing, sonny?"

"Oh, nothing," answered he; "I am only heating a pair of tongs in case you may not feel inclined to give as much milk as I want."

The cow sighed deeply, and looked at the milkman with fear, but he took no notice, and milked briskly into the pail, till the cow ran dry.

Just at that moment the old man entered the stable, and sat down to milk the cow himself, but not a drop of milk could he get. "Have you really managed it all yourself, or did somebody help you?"

"I have nobody to help me," answered the prince, "but my own poor head." The old man got up from his seat and went away.

That night, when the prince went to his master to hear what his next day's work was to be, the old man said: "I have a little hay-stack out in the meadow which must be brought in to dry. To-morrow you will have to stack it all in the shed, and, as you value your life, be careful not to leave the smallest strand behind." The prince was overjoyed to hear he had nothing worse to do.

"To carry a little hay-rick requires no great skill," thought he, "and it will give me no trouble, for the horse will have to draw it in. I am certainly not going to spare the old grandmother."

By-and-by the maiden stole up to ask what task he had for the next day.

The young man laughed, and said: "It appears that I have got to learn all kinds of farmer's work. To-morrow I have to carry a hay-rick, and leave not a stalk in the meadow, and that is my whole day's work!"

"Oh, you unlucky creature!" cried she; "and how do you think you are to do it. If you had all the men in the world to help you, you could not clear off this one little hay-rick in a week. The instant you have thrown down the hay at the top, it will take root again from below. But listen to what I say. You must steal out at daybreak to-morrow and bring out the white horse and some good strong ropes. Then get on the hay-stack, put the ropes round it, and harness the horse to the ropes. When you are ready, climb up the hay-stack and begin to count one, two, three. The horse will ask you what you are counting, and you must be sure to answer what I whisper to you."

So the maiden whispered something in his ear, and left the room. And the prince knew nothing better to do than to get into bed.

He slept soundly, and it was still almost dark when he got up and proceeded to carry out the instructions given him by the girl. First he chose some stout ropes, and then he led the horse out of the stable and rode it to the hay-stack, which was made up of fifty cartloads, so that it could hardly be called "a little one." The prince did all that the maiden had told him, and when at last he was seated on top of the rick, and had counted up to twenty, he heard the horse ask in amazement: "What are you counting up there, my son?"

"Oh, nothing," said he, "I was just amusing myself with counting the packs of wolves in the forest, but there are really so many of them that I don't think I should ever be done."

The word "wolf" was hardly out of his mouth than the white horse was off like the wind, so that in the twinkling of an eye it had reached the shed, dragging the hay-stack behind it. The master was dumb with surprise as he came in after breakfast and found his man's day's work quite done.

"Was it really you who were so clever?" asked he. "Or did some one give you good advice?"

"Oh, I have only myself to take counsel with," said the prince, and the old man went away, shaking his head.

Late in the evening the prince went to his master to learn what he was to do next day.

"To-morrow," said the old man, "you must bring the white-headed calf to the meadow, and, as you value your life, take care it does not escape from you."

The prince answered nothing, but thought, "Well, most peasants of nineteen have got a whole herd to look after, so surely I can manage one." And he went towards his room, where the maiden met him.

"To morrow I have got an idiot's work," said he; "nothing but to take the white-headed calf to the meadow."

"Oh, you unlucky being!" sighed she. "Do you know that this calf is so swift that in a single day he can run three times round the world? Take heed to what I tell you. Bind one end of this silk thread to the left fore-leg of the calf, and the other end to the little toe of your left foot, so that the calf will never be able to leave your side, whether you walk, stand, or lie." After this the prince went to bed and slept soundly.

The next morning he did exactly what the maiden had told him, and led the calf with the silken thread to the meadow, where it stuck to his side like a faithful dog.

By sunset, it was back again in its stall, and then came the master and said, with a frown, "Were you really so clever yourself, or did somebody tell you what to do?"

"Oh, I have only my own poor head," answered the prince, and the old man went away growling, "I don't believe a word of it! I am sure you have found some clever friend!"

In the evening he called the prince and said: "To-morrow I have no work for you, but when I wake you must come before my bed, and give me your hand in greeting."

The young man wondered at this strange freak, and went laughing in search of the maiden.

"Ah, it is no laughing matter," sighed she. "He means to eat you, and there is only one way in which I can help you. You must heat an iron shovel red hot, and hold it out to him instead of your hand."

So next morning he wakened very early, and had heated the shovel before the old man was awake. At length he heard him calling, "You lazy fellow, where are you? Come and wish me good morning."

But when the prince entered with the red-hot shovel his master only said, "I am very ill to-day, and too weak even to touch your hand. You must return this evening, when I may be better."

The prince loitered about all day, and in the evening went back to the old man's room. He was received in the most; friendly manner, and, to his surprise, his master exclaimed, "I am very well satisfied with you. Come to me at dawn and bring the maiden with you. I know you have long loved each other, and I wish to make you man and wife."

The young man nearly jumped into the air for joy, but, remembering the rules of the house, he managed to keep still. When he told the maiden, he saw to his astonishment that she had become as white as a sheet, and she was quite dumb.

"The old man has found out who was your counselor," she said when she could speak, "and he means to destroy us both. We must escape somehow, or else we shall be lost. Take an axe, and cut off the head of the calf with one blow.

With a second, split its head in two, and in its brain you will see a bright red ball. Bring that to me. Meanwhile, I will do what is needful here."

And the prince thought to himself, "Better kill the calf than be killed ourselves. If we can once escape, we will go back home. The peas which I strewed about must have sprouted, so that we shall not miss the way."

Then he went into the stall, and with one blow of the axe killed the calf, and with the second split its brain. In an instant the place was filled with light, as the red ball fell from the brain of the calf. The prince picked it up, and, wrapping it round with a thick cloth, hid it in his bosom. Mercifully, the cow slept through it all, or by her cries she would have awakened the master.

He looked round, and at the door stood the maiden, holding a little bundle in her arms.

"Where is the ball?" she asked.

"Here," answered he.

"We must lose no time in escaping," she went on, and uncovered a tiny bit of the shining ball, to light them on their way.

As the prince had expected the peas had taken root, and grown into a little hedge, so that they were sure they would not lose the path. As they fled, the girl told him that she had overheard a conversation between the old man and his grandmother, saying that she was a king's daughter, whom the old fellow had obtained by cunning from her parents. The prince, who knew all about the affair, was silent, though he was glad from his heart that it had fallen to his lot to set her free. So they went on till the day began to dawn.

The old man slept very late that morning, and rubbed his eyes till he was properly awake. Then he remembered that very soon the couple were to present themselves before him. After waiting and waiting till quite a long time had passed, he said to himself, with a grin, "Well, they are not in much hurry to be married," and waited again.

At last he grew a little uneasy, and cried loudly, "Man and maid! what has become of you?"

After repeating this many times, he became quite frightened, but, call as he would, neither man nor maid appeared. At last he jumped angrily out of bed to go in search of the culprits, but only found an empty house, and beds that had never been slept in. Then he went straight to the stable, where the sight of the dead calf told him all. Swearing loudly, he opened the door of the third stall quickly, and cried to his goblin servants to go and chase the fugitives. "Bring them to me, however you may find them, for have them I must!" he said. So spake the old man, and the servants fled like the wind.

The runaways were crossing a great plain, when the maiden stopped. "Something has happened!" she said. "The ball moves in my hand, and I'm sure we are being followed!" and behind them they saw a black cloud flying before the wind. Then the maiden turned the ball thrice in her hand, and cried,

"Listen to me, my ball, my ball.
Be quick and change me into a brook,
And my lover into a little fish."

And in an instant there was a brook with a fish swimming in it. The goblins arrived just after, but, seeing nobody, waited for a little, then hurried home, leaving the brook and the fish undisturbed. When they were quite out of sight, the brook and the fish returned to their usual shapes and proceeded on their journey.

When the goblins, tired and with empty hands, returned, their master inquired what they had seen, and if nothing strange had befallen them.

"Nothing," said they; "the plain was quite empty, save for a brook and a fish swimming in it."

"Idiots!" roared the master; "of course it was they!" And dashing open the door of the fifth stall, he told the goblins inside that they must go and drink up the brook, and catch the fish. And the goblins jumped up, and flew like the wind.

The young pair had almost reached the edge of the wood, when the maiden stopped again. "Something has happened," said she. "The ball is moving in my hand," and looking round she beheld a cloud flying towards them, large and blacker than the first, and striped with red. "Those are our pursuers," cried she, and turning the ball three times in her hand she spoke to it thus:

"Listen to me, my ball, my ball.
Be quick and change us both.
Me into a wild rose bush,
And him into a rose on my stem."

And in the twinkling of an eye it was done. Only just in time too, for the goblins were close at hand, and looked round eagerly for the stream and the fish. But neither stream nor fish was to be seen; nothing but a rose bush. So they went sorrowing home, and when they were out of sight the rose bush and rose returned to their proper shapes and walked all the faster for the little rest they had had.

"Well, did you find them?" asked the old man when his goblins came back.

"No," replied the leader of the goblins, "we found neither brook nor fish in the desert."

"And did you find nothing else at all?"

"Oh, nothing but a rose tree on the edge of a wood, with a rose hanging on it."

"Idiots!" cried he. "Why, that was they." And he threw open the door of the seventh stall, where his mightiest goblins were locked in. "Bring them to me, however you find them, dead or alive!" thundered he, "for I will have them! Tear up the rose tree and the roots too, and don't leave anything behind, however strange it may be!"

The fugitives were resting in the shade of a wood, and were refreshing themselves with food and drink. Suddenly the maiden looked up. "Something has happened," said she. "The ball has nearly jumped out of my bosom! Some one is certainly following us, and the danger is near, but the trees hide our enemies from us."

As she spoke she took the ball in her hand, and said:

> "Listen to me, my ball, my ball.
> Be quick and change me into a breeze,
> And make my lover into a midge."

An instant, and the girl was dissolved into thin air, while the prince darted about like a midge. The next moment a crowd of goblins rushed up, and looked about in search of something strange, for neither a rose bush nor anything else was to be seen. But they had hardly turned their backs to go home empty-handed when the prince and the maiden stood on the earth again.

"We must make all the haste we can," said she, "before the old man himself comes to seek us, for he will know us under any disguise."

They ran on till they reached such a dark part of the forest that, if it had not been for the light shed by the ball, they could not have made their way at all. Worn out and breathless, they came at length to a large stone, and here the ball began to move restlessly. The maiden, seeing this, exclaimed:

> "Listen to me, my ball, my ball.
> Roll the stone quickly to one side,
> That we may find a door."

And in a moment the stone had rolled away, and they had passed through the door to the world again.

"Now we are safe," cried she. "Here the old wizard has no more power over us, and we can guard ourselves from his spells. But, my friend, we have to part! You will return to your parents, and I must go in search of mine."

"No! no!" exclaimed the prince. "I will never part from you. You must come with me and be my wife. We have gone through many troubles together, and now we will share our joys." The maiden resisted his words for some time, but at last she went with him.

In the forest they met a woodcutter, who told them that in the palace, as well as in all the land, there had been great sorrow over the loss of the prince, and many years had now passed away during which they had found no traces of him. So, by the help of the magic ball, the maiden managed that he should put on the same clothes that he had been wearing at the time he had vanished, so that his father might know him more quickly. She herself stayed behind in a peasant's hut, so that father and son might meet alone.

But the father was no longer there, for the loss of his son had killed him; and on his deathbed he confessed to his people how he had contrived that the old wizard should carry away a peasant's child instead of the prince, wherefore this punishment had fallen upon him.

The prince wept bitterly when he heard this news, for he had loved his father well, and for three days he ate and drank nothing. But on the fourth day he stood in the presence of his people as their new king, and, calling his councilors, he told them all the strange things that had befallen him, and how the maiden had borne him safe through all.

And the councilors cried with one voice, "Let her be your wife, and our liege lady."

And that is the end of the story.

The Dirty Shepherdess

(From *The Green Fairy Book*)

Once upon a time there lived a King who had two daughters, and he loved them with all his heart. When they grew up, he was suddenly seized with a wish to know if they, on their part, truly loved him, and he made up his mind that he would give his kingdom to whichever best proved her devotion.

So he called the elder Princess and said to her, "How much do you love me?"

"As the apple of my eye!" answered she.

"Ah!" exclaimed the King, kissing her tenderly as he spoke, "you are indeed a good daughter."

Then he sent for the younger, and asked her how much she loved him.

"I look upon you, my father," she answered, "as I look upon salt in my food."

But the King did not like her words, and ordered her to quit the court, and never again to appear before him. The poor Princess went sadly up to her room and began to cry, but when she was reminded of her father's commands, she dried her eyes, and made a bundle of her jewels and her best dresses and hurriedly left the castle where she was born.

She walked straight along the road in front of her, without knowing very well where she was going or what was to become of her, for she had never been shown how to work, and all she had learnt consisted of a few household rules, and receipts of dishes which her mother had taught her long ago. And as she was afraid that no housewife would want to engage a girl with such a pretty face, she determined to make herself as ugly as she could.

She therefore took off the dress that she was wearing and put on some horrible old rags belonging to a beggar, all torn and covered with mud. After that she smeared mud all over her hands and face, and shook her hair into a great tangle. Having thus changed her appearance, she went about offering herself as a goose-girl or shepherdess. But the farmers' wives would have nothing to say to such a dirty maiden, and sent her away with a morsel of bread for charity's sake.

After walking for a great many days without being able to find any work, she came to a large farm where they were in want of a shepherdess, and engaged her gladly.

One day when she was keeping her sheep in a lonely tract of land, she suddenly felt a wish to dress herself in her robes of splendor. She washed herself carefully in the stream, and as she always carried her bundle with her, it was easy to shake off her rags, and transform herself in a few moments into a great lady.

The King's son, who had lost his way out hunting, perceived this lovely damsel a long way off, and wished to look at her closer. But as soon as the girl saw what he was at, she fled into the wood as swiftly as a bird. The Prince ran after her, but as he was running he caught his foot in the root of a tree and fell, and when he got up again, she was nowhere to be seen.

When she was quite safe, she put on her rags again, and smeared over her face and hands. However the young Prince, who was both hot and thirsty, found his way to the farm, to ask for a drink of cider, and he inquired the name of the beautiful lady that kept the sheep. At this everyone began to laugh, for they said that the shepherdess was one of the ugliest and dirtiest creatures under the sun.

The Prince thought some witchcraft must be at work, and he hastened away before the return of the shepherdess, who became that evening the butt of everybody's jests.

But the King's son thought often of the lovely maiden whom he had only seen for a moment, though she seemed to him much more fascinating than any lady of the Court. At last he dreamed of nothing else, and grew thinner day by day till his parents inquired what was the matter, promising to do all they could to make him as happy as he once was. He dared not tell them the truth, lest they should laugh at him, so he only said that he should like some bread baked by the kitchen girl in the distant farm.

Although the wish appeared rather odd, they hastened to fulfill it, and the farmer was told the request of the King's son. The maiden showed no surprise at receiving such an order, but merely asked for some flour, salt, and water, and also that she might be left alone in a little room adjoining the oven, where the kneading-trough stood. Before beginning her work she washed herself carefully, and even put on her rings; but, while she was baking, one of her rings slid into the dough. When she had finished she dirtied herself again, and let the lumps of the dough stick to her fingers, so that she became as ugly as before.

The loaf, which was a very little one, was brought to the King's son, who ate it with pleasure. But in cutting it he found the ring of the Princess, and declared to his parents that he would marry the girl whom that ring fitted.

So the King made a proclamation through his whole kingdom and ladies came from afar to lay claim to the honor. But the ring was so tiny that even those who had the smallest hands could only get it on their little fingers. In a short time all the maidens of the kingdom, including the peasant girls, had tried on the ring, and the King was just about to announce that their efforts had been in vain, when the Prince observed that he had not yet seen the shepherdess.

They sent to fetch her, and she arrived covered with rags, but with her hands cleaner than usual, so that she could easily slip on the ring. The King's son declared that he would fulfill his promise, and when his parents mildly remarked that the girl was only a keeper of sheep, and a very ugly one too, the maiden boldly said that she was born a princess, and that, if they would only give her some water and leave her alone in a room for a few minutes, she would show that she could look as well as anyone in fine clothes.

They did what she asked, and when she entered in a magnificent dress, she looked so beautiful that all saw she must be a princess in disguise. The King's son recognized the charming damsel of whom he had once caught a glimpse, and, flinging himself at her feet, asked if she would marry him. The Princess then told her story, and said that it would be necessary to send an ambassador to her father to ask his consent and to invite him to the wedding.

The Princess's father, who had never ceased to repent his harshness towards his daughter, had sought her through the land, but as no one could tell him anything of her, he supposed her dead. Therefore it was with great joy he heard that she was living and that a king's son asked her in marriage, and he quitted his kingdom with his elder daughter so as to be present at the ceremony.

By the orders of the bride, they only served her father at the wedding breakfast bread without salt, and meat without seasoning. Seeing him make faces, and eat very little, his daughter, who sat beside him, inquired if his dinner was not to his taste.

"No," he replied, "the dishes are carefully cooked and sent up, but they are all so dreadfully tasteless."

"Did not I tell you, my father, that salt was the best thing in life? And yet, when I compared you to salt, to show how much I loved you, you thought slightingly of me and you chased me from your presence."

The King embraced his daughter, and allowed that he had been wrong to misinterpret her words. Then, for the rest of the wedding feast they gave him bread made with salt, and dishes with seasoning, and he said they were the very best he had ever eaten.

The King Who Would Have a Beautiful Wife

(FROM THE PINK FAIRY BOOK)

Fifty years ago there lived a king who was very anxious to get married; but, as he was quite determined that his wife should be as beautiful as the sun, the thing was not so easy as it seemed, for no maiden came up to his standard. Then he commanded a trusty servant to search through the length and breadth of the land till he found a girl fair enough to be queen, and if he had the good luck to discover one he was to bring her back with him.

The servant set out at once on his journey, and sought high and low—in castles and cottages; but though pretty maidens were plentiful as blackberries, he felt sure that none of them would please the king.

One day he had wandered far and wide, and was feeling very tired and thirsty. By the roadside stood a tiny little house, and here he knocked and asked for a cup of water. Now in this house dwelt two sisters, and one was eighty and the other ninety years old. They were very poor, and earned their living by spinning. This had kept their hands very soft and white, like the hands of a girl, and when the water was passed through the lattice, and the servant saw the small, delicate fingers, he said to himself: "A maiden must indeed be lovely if she has a hand like that." And he made haste back, and told the king.

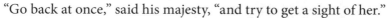

"Go back at once," said his majesty, "and try to get a sight of her."

The faithful servant departed on his errand without losing any time, and again he knocked at the door of the little house and begged for some water. As before, the old woman did not open the door, but passed the water through the lattice.

"Do you live here alone?" asked the man.

"No," replied she, "my sister lives with me. We are poor girls, and have to work for our bread."

"How old are you?"

"I am fifteen, and she is twenty."

Then the servant went back to the king, and told him all he knew. And his majesty answered: "I will have the fifteen-year-old one. Go and bring her here."

The servant returned a third time to the little house and knocked at the door. In reply to his knock the lattice window was pushed open, and a voice inquired what it was he wanted.

"The king has desired me to bring back the youngest of you to become his queen," he replied.

"Tell his majesty I am ready to do his bidding, but since my birth no ray of light has fallen upon my face. If it should ever do so I shall instantly grow black. Therefore beg, I pray you, his most gracious majesty to send this evening a shut carriage, and I will return in it to the castle."

When the king heard this he ordered his great golden carriage to be prepared, and in it to be placed some magnificent robes; and the old woman wrapped herself in a thick veil, and was driven to the castle.

The king was eagerly awaiting her, and when she arrived he begged her politely to raise her veil and let him see her face.

But she answered: "Here the tapers are too bright and the light too strong. Would you have me turn black under your very eyes?"

And the king believed her words, and the marriage took place without the veil being once lifted. Afterwards, when they were alone, he raised the corner, and knew for the first time that he had wedded a wrinkled old woman. And, in a furious burst of anger, he dashed open the window and flung her out. But, luckily for her, her clothes caught on a nail in the wall, and kept her hanging between heaven and earth.

While she was thus suspended, expecting every moment to be dashed to the ground, four fairies happened to pass by.

"Look, sisters," cried one, "surely that is the old woman that the king sent for. Shall we wish that her clothes may give way, and that she should be dashed to the ground?"

"Oh no! no!" exclaimed another. "Let us wish her something good. I myself will wish her youth."

"And I beauty."

"And I wisdom."

"And I a tender heart."

So spake the fairies, and went their way, leaving the most beautiful maiden in the world behind them.

The next morning when the king looked from his window he saw this lovely creature hanging on the nail. "Ah! what have I done? Surely I must have been blind last night!"

And he ordered long ladders to be brought and the maiden to be rescued. Then he fell on his knees before her, and prayed her to forgive him, and a great feast was made in her honor.

Some days after came the ninety-year-old sister to the palace and asked for the queen.

"Who is that hideous old witch?" said the king.

"Oh, an old neighbor of mine, who is half silly," she replied.

But the old woman looked at her steadily, and knew her again, and said: "How have you managed to grow so young and beautiful? I should like to be young and beautiful too."

This question she repeated the whole day long, till at length the queen lost patience and said: "I had my old head cut off, and this new head grew in its place."

Then the old woman went to a barber, and spoke to him, saying, "I will give you all you ask if you will only cut off my head, so that I may become young and lovely."

"But, my good woman, if I do that you will die!"

But the old woman would listen to nothing; and at last the barber took out his knife and struck the first blow at her neck.

"Ah!" she shrieked as she felt the pain.

"*Il faut souffrir pour etre belle*," said the barber, who had been in France.

And at the second blow her head rolled off, and the old woman was dead for good and all.

Prince Featherhead and the Princess Celandine

(FROM *THE GREEN FAIRY BOOK*)

Once upon a time there lived a King and Queen, who were the best creatures in the world, and so kind-hearted that they could not bear to see their subjects want for anything. The consequence was that they gradually gave away all their treasures, till they positively had nothing left to live upon; and this coming to the ears of their neighbor, King Bruin, he promptly raised a large army and marched into their country. The poor King, having no means of defending his kingdom, was forced to disguise himself with a false beard, and carrying his only son, the little Prince Featherhead, in his arms, and accompanied only by the Queen, to make the best of his way into the wild country. They were lucky enough to escape the soldiers of King Bruin, and at last, after unheard-of fatigues and adventures, they found themselves in a charming green valley, through which flowed a stream clear as crystal and overshadowed by beautiful trees. As they looked round them with delight, a voice said suddenly: "Fish, and see what you will catch." Now the King had always loved fishing, and never went anywhere without a fish-hook or two in his pocket, so he drew one out hastily, and the Queen lent him her girdle to fasten it to, and it had hardly touched the water before it caught a big fish, which made them an excellent meal—and not before they needed it, for they had found nothing until then but a few wild berries and roots. They thought that for the present they could not do better than stay in this delightful place, and the King set to work, and soon built a bower of branches to shelter them; and when it was finished the Queen was so charmed with it that she declared nothing was lacking to complete her happiness but a flock of sheep, which she and the little Prince might tend while the King fished. They soon found that the fish were not only abundant and easily caught, but also very beautiful, with glittering scales of every imaginable hue; and before long the King discovered that he could teach them to talk and whistle better than any parrot. Then he determined to carry some to the nearest town and try to sell them; and as no one had ever before seen any like them the people flocked about him eagerly and bought all he had caught, so that presently not a house in the city was considered complete without a crystal bowl full of fish, and the King's customers were very particular about having them to match the rest of the furniture, and gave him a vast amount of trouble in choosing them. However, the money he obtained in this way enabled him to buy the Queen her flock of sheep, as well as many of the other things which go to make life pleasant, so that they never once regretted their lost kingdom. Now it happened that the Fairy of the Beech-Woods lived in the lovely valley to which chance had led the poor fugitives, and it was she who had, in pity for their forlorn condition, sent the King such good luck to his fishing, and generally taken them under her protection. This she was all the more inclined to do as she loved children, and little Prince Featherhead, who never cried and grew prettier day by day, quite won her heart. She made the acquaintance of the King and the Queen without at first letting them know that she was a fairy, and they soon took a great fancy to her, and even trusted her with the precious Prince, whom she carried off to her palace, where she regaled him with cakes and tarts and every other good thing. This was the way she chose of making him fond of her; but afterwards, as he grew older, she spared no pains in educating and training him as a prince should be trained. But unfortunately, in spite of all her care, he grew so vain and frivolous that he quitted his peaceful country life in disgust, and rushed eagerly after all the foolish gaieties of the neighboring town, where his handsome face and charming manners speedily made him popular. The King and Queen deeply regretted this alteration in their son, but did not know how to mend matters, since the good old Fairy had made him so self-willed.

Just at this time the Fairy of the Beech-Woods received a visit from an old friend of hers called Saradine, who rushed into her house so breathless with rage that she could hardly speak.

"Dear, dear! what is the matter?" said the Fairy of the Beech-Woods soothingly.

"The matter!" cried Saradine. "You shall soon hear all about it. You know that, not content with endowing Celandine, Princess of the Summer Islands, with everything she could desire to make her charming, I actually took the trouble to bring her up myself; and now what does she do but come to me with more coaxings and caresses than usual to beg a favor. And what do you suppose this favor turns out to be—when I have been cajoled into promising to grant it? Nothing more nor less than a request that I will take back all my gifts—'since,' says my young madam, 'if I have the good fortune to please you, how am I to know that it is really I, myself? And that's how it will be all my life long, whenever I meet anybody. You see what a weariness my life will be to me under these circumstances, and yet I assure you I am not ungrateful to you for all your kindness!' I did all I could," continued Saradine, "to make her think better of it, but in vain; so after going through the usual ceremony for taking back my gifts, I'm come to you for a little peace and quietness. But, after all, I have not taken anything of consequence from this provoking Celandine. Nature had already made her so pretty, and given her such a ready wit of her own, that she will do perfectly well without me. However, I thought she deserved a little lesson, so to begin with I have whisked her off into the desert, and there left her!"

"What! all alone, and without any means of existence?" cried the kind-hearted old Fairy. "You had better hand her over to me. I don't think so very badly of her after all. I'll just cure her vanity by making her love someone better than herself. Really, when I come to consider of it, I declare the little minx has shown more spirit and originality in the matter than one expects of a princess."

Saradine willingly consented to this arrangement, and the old Fairy's first care was to smooth away all the difficulties which surrounded the Princess, and lead her by the mossy path overhung with trees to the bower of the King and Queen, who still pursued their peaceful life in the valley.

They were immensely surprised at her appearance, but her charming face, and the deplorably ragged condition to which the thorns and briers had reduced her once elegant attire, speedily won their compassion; they recognized her as a companion in misfortune, and the Queen welcomed her heartily, and begged her to share their simple repast. Celandine gracefully accepted their hospitality, and soon told them what had happened to her. The King was charmed with her spirit, while the Queen thought she had indeed been daring thus to go against the Fairy's wishes.

"Since it has ended in my meeting you," said the Princess, "I cannot regret the step I have taken, and if you will let me stay with you, I shall be perfectly happy."

The King and Queen were only too delighted to have this charming Princess to supply the place of Prince Featherhead, whom they saw but seldom, since the Fairy had provided him with a palace in the neighboring town, where he lived in the greatest luxury, and did nothing but amuse himself from morning to night. So Celandine stayed, and helped the Queen to keep house, and very soon they loved her dearly. When the Fairy of the Beech-Woods came to them, they presented the Princess to her, and told her story, little thinking that the Fairy knew more about Celandine than they did. The old Fairy was equally delighted with her, and often invited her to visit her Leafy Palace, which was the most enchanting place that could be imagined, and full of treasures. Often she would say to the Princess, when showing her some wonderful thing:

"This will do for a wedding gift some day." And Celandine could not help thinking that it was to her that the Fairy meant to give the two blue wax-torches which burned without ever getting smaller, or the diamond from which more diamonds were continually growing, or the boat that sailed under water, or whatever beautiful or wonderful thing they might happen to be looking at. It is true that she never said so positively, but she certainly allowed the Princess to believe it, because she thought a little disappointment would be good for her. But the person she really relied upon for curing Celandine of her vanity was Prince Featherhead. The old Fairy was not at all pleased with the way he had been going on for some time, but her heart was so soft towards him that she was unwilling to take him away from the pleasures he loved, except by offering him something better, which is not the most effectual mode of correction, though it is without doubt the most agreeable.

However, she did not even hint to the Princess that Featherhead was anything but absolutely perfect, and talked of him so much that when at last she announced that he was coming to visit her, Celandine made up her mind that this delightful Prince would be certain to fall in love with her at once, and was quite pleased at the idea. The old Fairy thought so too, but as this was not at all what she wished, she took care to throw such an enchantment over the Princess that she appeared to Featherhead quite ugly and awkward, though to every one else she looked just as usual. So when he arrived at the Leafy Palace, more handsome and fascinating even than ever she had been led to expect, he hardly so much as glanced at the Princess, but bestowed all his attention upon the old Fairy, to whom he seemed to have a hundred things to say. The Princess was immensely astonished at his indifference, and put on a cold and offended air, which, however, he did not seem to observe. Then as a last resource she exerted all her wit and gaiety to amuse him, but with no better success, for he was of an age to be more attracted by beauty than by anything else, and though he responded politely enough, it was evident that his thoughts were elsewhere. Celandine was deeply mortified, since for her part the Prince pleased her very well, and for the first time she bitterly regretted the fairy gifts she had been anxious to get rid of. Prince Featherhead was almost equally puzzled, for he had heard nothing from the King and Queen but the praises of this charming Princess, and the fact that they had spoken of her as so very beautiful only confirmed his opinion that people who live in the country have no taste. He talked to them of his charming acquaintances in the town, the beauties he had admired, did admire, or thought he was going to admire, until Celandine, who heard it all, was ready to cry with vexation. The Fairy, too, was quite shocked at his conceit, and hit upon a plan for curing him of it. She sent to him by an unknown messenger a portrait of Princess Celandine as she really was, with this inscription: "All this beauty and sweetness, with a loving heart and a great kingdom, might have been yours but for your well-known fickleness."

This message made a great impression upon the Prince, but not so much as the portrait. He positively could not tear his eyes away from it, and exclaimed aloud that never, never had he seen anything so lovely and so graceful. Then he began to think that it was too absurd that he, the fascinating Featherhead, should fall in love with a portrait; and, to drive away the recollections of its haunting eyes, he rushed back to the town; but somehow everything seemed changed. The beauties no longer pleased him, their witty speeches had ceased to amuse; and indeed, for their parts, they found the Prince far less amiable than of yore, and were not sorry when he declared that, after all, a country life suited him best, and went back to the Leafy Palace. Meanwhile, the Princess Celandine had been finding the time pass but slowly with the King and Queen, and was only too pleased when Featherhead reappeared. She at once noticed the change in him, and was deeply curious to find the reason of it. Far from avoiding her, he now sought her company and seemed to take pleasure in talking to her, and yet the Princess did not for a moment flatter herself with the idea that he was in love with her, though it did not take her long to decide that he certainly loved someone. But one day the Princess, wandering sadly by the river, spied Prince Featherhead fast asleep in the shade of a tree, and stole nearer to enjoy the delight of gazing at his dear face unobserved. Judge of her astonishment when she saw that he was holding in his hand a portrait of herself! In vain did she puzzle over the apparent contradictoriness of his behavior. Why did he cherish her portrait while he was so fatally indifferent to herself? At last she found an opportunity of asking him the name of the Princess whose picture he carried about with him always.

"Alas! how can I tell you?" replied he.

"Why should you not?" said the Princess timidly. "Surely there is nothing to prevent you."

"Nothing to prevent me!" repeated he, "when my utmost efforts have failed to discover the lovely original. Should I be so sad if I could but find her? But I do not even know her name."

More surprised than ever, the Princess asked to be allowed to see the portrait, and after examining it for a few minutes returned it, remarking shyly that at least the original had every cause to be satisfied with it.

"That means that you consider it flattered," said the Prince severely. "Really, Celandine, I thought better of you, and should have expected you to be above such contemptible jealousy. But all women are alike!"

"Indeed, I meant only that it was a good likeness," said the Princess meekly.

"Then you know the original," cried the Prince, throwing himself on his knees beside her. "Pray tell me at once who it is, and don't keep me in suspense!"

"Oh! don't you see that it is meant for me?" cried Celandine.

The Prince sprang to his feet, hardly able to refrain from telling her that she must be blinded by vanity to suppose she resembled the lovely portrait even in the slightest degree; and after gazing at her for an instant with icy surprise, turned and left her without another word, and in a few hours quitted the Leafy Palace altogether.

Now the Princess was indeed unhappy, and could no longer bear to stay in a place where she had been so cruelly disdained. So, without even bidding farewell to the King and Queen, she left the valley behind her, and wandered sadly away, not caring whither. After walking until she was weary, she saw before her a tiny house, and turned her slow steps towards it. The nearer she approached the more miserable it appeared, and at length she saw a little old woman sitting upon the door-step, who said grimly:

"Here comes one of these fine beggars who are too idle to do anything but run about the country!"

"Alas! madam," said Celandine, with tears in her pretty eyes, "a sad fate forces me to ask you for shelter."

"Didn't I tell you what it would be?" growled the old hag. "From shelter we shall proceed to demand supper, and from supper money to take us on our way. Upon my word, if I could be sure of finding some one every day whose head was as soft as his heart, I wouldn't wish for a more agreeable life myself! But I have worked hard to build my house and secure a morsel to eat, and I suppose you think that I am to give away everything to the first passer-by who chooses to ask for it. Not at all! I wager that a fine lady like you has more money than I have. I must search her, and see if it is not so," she added, hobbling towards Celandine with the aid of her stick.

"Alas! madam," replied the Princess, "I only wish I had. I would give it to you with all the pleasure in life."

"But you are very smartly dressed for the kind of life you lead," continued the old woman.

"What!" cried the Princess, "do you think I am come to beg of you?"

"I don't know about that," answered she; "but at any rate you don't seem to have come to bring me anything. But what is it that you do want? Shelter? Well, that does not cost much; but after that comes supper, and that I can't hear of. Oh dear no! Why, at your age one is always ready to eat; and now you have been walking, and I suppose you are ravenous?"

"Indeed no, madam," answered the poor Princess, "I am too sad to be hungry."

"Oh, well! if you will promise to go on being sad, you may stay for the night," said the old woman mockingly.

Thereupon she made the Princess sit down beside her, and began fingering her silken robe, while she muttered "Lace on top, lace underneath! This must have cost you a pretty penny! It would have been better to save enough to feed yourself, and not come begging to those who want all they have for themselves. Pray, what may you have paid for these fine clothes?"

"Alas! madam," answered the Princess, "I did not buy them, and I know nothing about money."

"What do you know, if I may ask?" said the old dame.

"Not much; but indeed I am very unhappy," cried Celandine, bursting into tears, "and if my services are any good to you—"

"Services!" interrupted the hag crossly. "One has to pay for services, and I am not above doing my own work."

"Madam, I will serve you for nothing," said the poor Princess, whose spirits were sinking lower and lower. "I will do anything you please; all I wish is to live quietly in this lonely spot."

"Oh! I know you are only trying to take me in," answered she; "and if I do let you serve me, is it fitting that you should be so much better dressed than I am? If I keep you, will you give me your clothes and wear some that I will provide you with? It is true that I am getting old and may want someone to take care of me some day."

"Oh! for pity's sake, do what you please with my clothes," cried poor Celandine miserably.

And the old woman hobbled off with great alacrity, and fetched a little bundle containing a wretched dress, such as the Princess had never even seen before, and nimbly skipped round, helping her to put it on instead of her own rich robe, with many exclamations of:

"Saints!—what a magnificent lining! And the width of it! It will make me four dresses at least. Why, child, I wonder you could walk under such a weight, and certainly in my house you would not have had room to turn round."

So saying, she folded up the robe, and put it by with great care, while she remarked to Celandine:

"That dress of mine certainly suits you to a marvel; be sure you take great care of it."

When supper-time came she went into the house, declining all the Princess's offers of assistance, and shortly afterwards brought out a very small dish, saying:

"Now let us sup."

Whereupon she handed Celandine a small piece of black bread and uncovered the dish, which contained two dried plums.

"We will have one between us," continued the old dame; "and as you are the visitor, you shall have the half which contains the stone; but be very careful that you don't swallow it, for I keep them against the winter, and you have no idea what a good fire they make. Now, you take my advice—which won't cost you anything—and remember that it is always more economical to buy fruit with stones on this account."

Celandine, absorbed in her own sad thoughts, did not even hear this prudent counsel, and quite forgot to eat her share of the plum, which delighted the old woman, who put it by carefully for her breakfast, saying:

"I am very much pleased with you, and if you go on as you have begun, we shall do very well, and I can teach you many useful things which people don't generally know. For instance, look at my house! It is built entirely of the seeds of all the pears I have eaten in my life. Now, most people throw them away, and that only shows what a number of things are wasted for want of a little patience and ingenuity."

But Celandine did not find it possible to be interested in this and similar pieces of advice. And the old woman soon sent her to bed, for fear the night air might give her an appetite. She passed a sleepless night; but in the morning the old dame remarked:

"I heard how well you slept. After such a night you cannot want any breakfast; so while I do my household tasks you had better stay in bed, since the more one sleeps the less one need eat; and as it is market-day I will go to town and buy a pennyworth of bread for the week's eating."

And so she chattered on, but poor Celandine did not hear or heed her; she wandered out into the desolate country to think over her sad fate. However, the good Fairy of the Beech-Woods did not want her to be starved, so she sent her an unlooked-for relief in the shape of a beautiful white cow, which followed her back to the tiny house. When the old woman saw it her joy knew no bounds.

"Now we can have milk and cheese and butter!" cried she. "Ah! how good milk is! What a pity it is so ruinously expensive!" So they made a little shelter of branches for the beautiful creature which was quite gentle, and followed Celandine about like a dog when she took it out every day to graze. One morning as she sat by a little brook, thinking sadly, she suddenly saw a young stranger approaching, and got up quickly, intending to avoid him. But Prince Featherhead, for it was he, perceiving her at the same moment, rushed towards her with every demonstration of joy: for he had recognized her, not as the Celandine whom he had slighted, but as the lovely Princess whom he had sought vainly for so long. The fact was that the Fairy of the Beech-Woods, thinking she had been punished enough, had withdrawn the enchantment from her, and transferred it to Featherhead, thereby in an instant depriving him of the good looks which had done so much towards making him the fickle creature he was. Throwing himself down at the Princess's feet, he implored her to stay, and at least speak to him, and she at last consented, but only because he seemed to wish it so very much. After that he came every day in the hope of meeting her again, and often expressed his delight at being with her. But one day, when he had been begging Celandine to love him, she confided to him that it was quite impossible, since her heart was already entirely occupied by another.

"I have," said she, "the unhappiness of loving a Prince who is fickle, frivolous, proud, incapable of caring for anyone but himself, who has been spoilt by flattery, and, to crown all, who does not love me."

"But," cried Prince Featherhead, "surely you cannot care for so contemptible and worthless a creature as that."

"Alas! but I do care," answered the Princess, weeping.

"But where can his eyes be," said the Prince, "that your beauty makes no impression upon him? As for me, since I have possessed your portrait I have wandered over the whole world to find you, and, now we have met, I see that you are ten times lovelier than I could have imagined, and I would give all I own to win your love."

"My portrait?" cried Celandine with sudden interest. "Is it possible that Prince Featherhead can have parted with it?"

"He would part with his life sooner, lovely Princess," answered he; "I can assure you of that, for I am Prince Featherhead."

At the same moment the Fairy of the Beech-Woods took away the enchantment, and the happy Princess recognized her lover, now truly hers, for the trials they had both undergone had so changed and improved them that they were capable of a real love for each other. You may imagine how perfectly happy they were, and how much they had to hear and to tell. But at length it was time to go back to the little house, and as they went along Celandine remembered for the first time what a ragged old dress she was wearing, and what an odd appearance she must present. But the Prince declared that it became her vastly, and that he thought it most picturesque. When they reached the house the old woman received them very crossly.

"I declare," said she, "that it's perfectly true: wherever there is a girl you may be sure that a young man will appear before long! But don't imagine that I'm going to have you here—not a bit of it, be off with you, my fine fellow!"

Prince Featherhead was inclined to be angry at this uncivil reception, but he was really too happy to care much, so he only demanded, on Celandine's behalf, that the old dame should give her back her own attire, that she might go away suitably dressed.

This request roused her to fury, since she had counted upon the Princess's fine robes to clothe her for the rest of her life, so that it was some time before the Prince could make himself heard to explain that he was willing to pay for them. The sight of a handful of gold pieces somewhat mollified her, however, and after making them both promise faithfully that on no consideration would they ask for the gold back again, she took the Princess into the house and grudgingly doled out to her just enough of her gay attire to make her presentable, while the rest she pretended to have lost. After this they found that they were very hungry, for one cannot live on love, any more than on air, and then the old woman's lamentations were louder than before. "What!" she cried, "feed people who were as happy as all that! Why, it was simply ruinous!"

But as the Prince began to look angry, she, with many sighs and mutterings, brought out a morsel of bread, a bowl of milk, and six plums, with which the lovers were well content: for as long as they could look at one another they really did not know what they were eating. It seemed as if they would go on for ever with their reminiscences, the Prince telling how he had wandered all over the world from beauty to beauty, always to be disappointed when he found that no one resembled the portrait; the Princess wondering how it was he could have been so long with her and yet never have recognized her, and over and over again pardoning him for his cold and haughty behavior to her.

"For," she said, "you see, Featherhead, I love you, and love makes everything right! But we cannot stay here," she added; "what are we to do?"

The Prince thought they had better find their way to the Fairy of the Beech-Woods and put themselves once more under her protection, and they had hardly agreed upon this course when two little chariots wreathed with jasmine and honeysuckle suddenly appeared, and, stepping into them, they were whirled away to the Leafy Palace. Just before they lost sight of the little house they heard loud cries and lamentations from the miserly old dame, and, looking round, perceived that the beautiful cow was vanishing in spite of her frantic efforts to hold it fast. And they afterwards heard that she spent the rest of her life in trying to put the handful of gold the Prince had thrown to her into her money-bag. For the Fairy, as a punishment for her avarice, caused it to slip out again as fast as she dropped it in.

The Fairy of the Beech-Woods ran to welcome the Prince and Princess with open arms, only too delighted to find them so much improved that she could, with a clear conscience, begin to spoil them again. Very soon the Fairy Saradine also arrived, bringing the King and Queen with her. Princess Celandine implored her pardon, which she graciously gave; indeed the Princess was so charming she could refuse her nothing. She also restored to her the Summer Islands, and promised her protection in all things. The Fairy of the Beech-Woods then informed the King and Queen that their subjects had chased King Bruin from the throne, and were waiting to welcome them back again; but they at once abdicated in favor of Prince Featherhead, declaring that nothing could induce them to forsake their peaceful life, and the Fairies undertook to see the Prince and Princess established in their beautiful kingdoms. Their marriage took place the next day, and they lived happily ever afterwards, for Celandine was never vain and Featherhead was never fickle any more.

Catherine and Her Destiny

(From *The Pink Fairy Book*)

Long ago there lived a rich merchant who, besides possessing more treasures than any king in the world, had in his great hall three chairs, one of silver, one of gold, and one of diamonds. But his greatest treasure of all was his only daughter, who was called Catherine.

One day Catherine was sitting in her own room when suddenly the door flew open, and in came a tall and beautiful woman holding in her hands a little wheel.

"Catherine," she said, going up to the girl, "which would you rather have—a happy youth or a happy old age?"

Catherine was so taken by surprise that she did not know what to answer, and the lady repeated again, "Which would you rather have—a happy youth or a happy old age?"

Then Catherine thought to herself, "If I say a happy youth, then I shall have to suffer all the rest of my life. No, I would bear trouble now, and have something better to look forward to." So she looked up and replied, "Give me a happy old age."

"So be it," said the lady, and turned her wheel as she spoke, vanishing the next moment as suddenly as she had come.

Now this beautiful lady was the Destiny of poor Catherine.

Only a few days after this the merchant heard the news that all his finest ships, laden with the richest merchandise, had been sunk in a storm, and he was left a beggar. The shock was too much for him. He took to his bed, and in a short time he was dead of his disappointment.

So poor Catherine was left alone in the world without a penny or a creature to help her. But she was a brave girl and full of spirit, and soon made up her mind that the best thing she could do was to go to the nearest town and become a servant. She lost no time in getting herself ready, and did not take long over her journey; and as she was passing down the chief street of the town a noble lady saw her out of the window, and, struck by her sad face, said to her: "Where are you going all alone, my pretty girl?"

"Ah, my lady, I am very poor, and must go to service to earn my bread."

"I will take you into my service," said she; and Catherine served her well.

Some time after her mistress said to Catherine, "I am obliged to go out for a long while, and must lock the house door, so that no thieves shall get in."

So she went away, and Catherine took her work and sat down at the window. Suddenly the door burst open, and in came her Destiny.

"Oh! so here you are, Catherine! Did you really think I was going to leave you in peace?" And as she spoke she walked to the linen press where Catherine's mistress kept all her finest sheets and underclothes, tore everything in pieces, and flung them on the floor. Poor Catherine wrung her hands and wept, for she thought to herself, "When my lady comes back and sees all this ruin she will think it is my fault," and starting up, she fled through the open door. Then Destiny took all the pieces and made them whole again, and put them back in the press, and when everything was tidy she too left the house.

When the mistress reached home she called Catherine, but no Catherine was there. "Can she have robbed me?" thought the old lady, and looked hastily round the house; but nothing was missing. She wondered why Catherine should have disappeared like this, but she heard no more of her, and in a few days she filled her place.

Meanwhile Catherine wandered on and on, without knowing very well where she was going, till at last she came to another town. Just as before, a noble lady happened to see her passing her window, and called out to her, "Where are you going all alone, my pretty girl?"

And Catherine answered, "Ah, my lady, I am very poor, and must go to service to earn my bread."

"I will take you into my service," said the lady; and Catherine served her well, and hoped she might now be left in peace. But, exactly as before, one day that Catherine was left in the house alone her Destiny came again and spoke to her with hard words: "What! are you here now?" And in a passion she tore up everything she saw, till in sheer misery poor Catherine rushed out of the house. And so it befell for seven years, and directly Catherine found a fresh place her Destiny came and forced her to leave it.

After seven years, however, Destiny seemed to get tired of persecuting her, and a time of peace set in for Catherine. When she had been chased away from her last house by Destiny's wicked pranks she had taken service with another lady, who told her that it would be part of her daily work to walk to a mountain that overshadowed the town, and, climbing up to the top, she was to lay on the ground some loaves of freshly baked bread, and cry with a loud voice, "O Destiny, my mistress," three times. Then her lady's Destiny would come and take away the offering. "That will I gladly do," said Catherine.

So the years went by, and Catherine was still there, and every day she climbed the mountain with her basket of bread on her arm. She was happier than she had been, but sometimes, when no one saw her, she would weep as she thought over her old life, and how different it was to the one she was now leading. One day her lady saw her, and said, "Catherine, what is it? Why are you always weeping?" And then Catherine told her story.

"I have got an idea," exclaimed the lady. "To-morrow, when you take the bread to the mountain, you shall pray my Destiny to speak to yours, and entreat her to leave you in peace. Perhaps something may come of it!"

At these words Catherine dried her eyes, and next morning, when she climbed the mountain, she told all she had suffered, and cried, "O Destiny, my mistress, pray, I entreat you, of my Destiny that she may leave me in peace."

And Destiny answered, "Oh, my poor girl, know you not your Destiny lies buried under seven coverlids, and can hear nothing? But if you will come to-morrow I will bring her with me."

And after Catherine had gone her way her lady's Destiny went to find her sister, and said to her, "Dear sister, has not Catherine suffered enough? It is surely time for her good days to begin?"

And the sister answered, "To-morrow you shall bring her to me, and I will give her something that may help her out of her need."

The next morning Catherine set out earlier than usual for the mountain, and her lady's Destiny took the girl by the hand and led her to her sister, who lay under the seven coverlids. And her Destiny held out to Catherine a ball of silk, saying, "Keep this—it may be useful some day"; then pulled the coverings over her head again.

But Catherine walked sadly down the hill, and went straight to her lady and showed her the silken ball, which was the end of all her high hopes.

"What shall I do with it?" she asked. "It is not worth sixpence, and it is no good to me!"

"Take care of it," replied her mistress. "Who can tell how useful it may be?"

A little while after this grand preparations were made for the king's marriage, and all the tailors in the town were busy embroidering fine clothes. The wedding garment was so beautiful nothing like it had ever been seen before, but when it was almost finished the tailor found that he had no more silk. The color was very rare, and none could be found like it, and the king made a proclamation that if anyone happened to possess any they should bring it to the court, and he would give them a large sum.

"Catherine!" exclaimed the lady, who had been to the tailors and seen the wedding garment, "your ball of silk is exactly the right color. Bring it to the king, and you can ask what you like for it."

Then Catherine put on her best clothes and went to the court, and looked more beautiful than any woman there.

"May it please your majesty," she said, "I have brought you a ball of silk of the color you asked for, as no one else has any in the town."

"Your majesty," asked one of the courtiers, "shall I give the maiden its weight in gold?"

The king agreed, and a pair of scales were brought; and a handful of gold was placed in one scale and the silken ball in the other. But lo! let the king lay in the scales as many gold pieces as he would, the silk was always heavier still. Then the king took some larger scales, and heaped up all his treasures on one side, but the silk on the other outweighed them all. At last there was only one thing left that had not been put in, and that was his golden crown. And he took it from his head and set it on top of all, and at last the scale moved and the ball had founds its balance.

"Where got you this silk?" asked the king.

"It was given me, royal majesty, by my mistress," replied Catherine.

"That is not true," said the king, "and if you do not tell me the truth I will have your head cut off this instant."

So Catherine told him the whole story, and how she had once been as rich as he.

Now there lived at the court a wise woman, and she said to Catherine, "You have suffered much, my poor girl, but at length your luck has turned, and I know by the weighing of the scales through the crown that you will die a queen."

"So she shall," cried the king, who overheard these words; "she shall die my queen, for she is more beautiful than all the ladies of the court, and I will marry no one else."

And so it fell out. The king sent back the bride he had promised to wed to her own country, and the same Catherine was queen at the marriage feast instead, and lived happy and contented to the end of her life.

The Story of Three Wonderful Beggars

(FROM *THE VIOLET FAIRY BOOK*)

There once lived a merchant whose name was Mark, and whom people called "Mark the Rich." He was a very hard-hearted man, for he could not bear poor people, and if he caught sight of a beggar anywhere near his house, he would order the servants to drive him away, or would set the dogs at him.

One day three very poor old men came begging to the door, and just as he was going to let the fierce dogs loose on them, his little daughter, Anastasia, crept close up to him and said:

"Dear daddy, let the poor old men sleep here to-night, do—to please me."

Her father could not bear to refuse her, and the three beggars were allowed to sleep in a loft, and at night, when everyone in the house was fast asleep, little Anastasia got up, climbed up to the loft, and peeped in.

The three old men stood in the middle of the loft, leaning on their sticks, with their long gray beards flowing down over their hands, and were talking together in low voices.

"What news is there?" asked the eldest.

"In the next village the peasant Ivan has just had his seventh son. What shall we name him, and what fortune shall we give him?" said the second.

The third whispered, "Call him Vassili, and give him all the property of the hard-hearted man in whose loft we stand, and who wanted to drive us from his door."

After a little more talk the three made themselves ready and crept softly away.

Anastasia, who had heard every word, ran straight to her father, and told him all.

Mark was very much surprised; he thought, and thought, and in the morning he drove to the next village to try and find out if such a child really had been born. He went first to the priest, and asked him about the children in his parish.

"Yesterday," said the priest, "a boy was born in the poorest house in the village. I named the unlucky little thing 'Vassili.' He is the seventh son, and the eldest is only seven years old, and they hardly have a mouthful among them all. Who can be got to stand godfather to such a little beggar boy?"

The merchant's heart beat fast, and his mind was full of bad thoughts about that poor little baby. He would be godfather himself, he said, and he ordered a fine christening feast; so the child was brought and christened, and Mark was very friendly to its father. After the ceremony was over he took Ivan aside and said:

"Look here, my friend, you are a poor man. How can you afford to bring up the boy? Give him to me and I'll make something of him, and I'll give you a present of a thousand crowns. Is that a bargain?"

Ivan scratched his head, and thought, and thought, and then he agreed. Mark counted out the money, wrapped the baby up in a fox skin, laid it in the sledge beside him, and drove back towards home. When he had driven some miles he drew up, carried the child to the edge of a steep precipice and threw it over, muttering, "There, now try to take my property!"

Very soon after this some foreign merchants traveled along that same road on the way to see Mark and to pay the twelve thousand crowns which they owed him.

As they were passing near the precipice they heard a sound of crying, and on looking over they saw a little green meadow wedged in between two great heaps of snow, and on the meadow lay a baby among the flowers.

The merchants picked up the child, wrapped it up carefully, and drove on. When they saw Mark they told him what a strange thing they had found. Mark guessed at once that the child must be his godson, asked to see him, and said:

"That's a nice little fellow; I should like to keep him. If you will make him over to me, I will let you off your debt."

The merchants were very pleased to make so good a bargain, left the child with Mark, and drove off.

At night Mark took the child, put it in a barrel, fastened the lid tight down, and threw it into the sea. The barrel floated away to a great distance, and at last it floated close up to a monastery. The monks were just spreading out their nets to dry on the shore, when they heard the sound of crying. It seemed to come from the barrel which was bobbing about near the water's edge. They drew it to land and opened it, and there was a little child! When the abbot heard the news, he decided to bring up the boy, and named him "Vassili."

The boy lived on with the monks, and grew up to be a clever, gentle, and handsome young man. No one could read, write, or sing better than he, and he did everything so well that the abbot made him wardrobe keeper.

Now, it happened about this time that the merchant, Mark, came to the monastery in the course of a journey. The monks were very polite to him and showed him their house and church and all they had. When he went into the church the choir was singing, and one voice was so clear and beautiful, that he asked who it belonged to. Then the abbot told him of the wonderful way in which Vassili had come to them, and Mark saw clearly that this must be his godson whom he had twice tried to kill.

He said to the abbot: "I can't tell you how much I enjoy that young man's singing. If he could only come to me I would make him overseer of all my business. As you say, he is so good and clever. Do spare him to me. I will make his fortune, and will present your monastery with twenty thousand crowns."

The abbot hesitated a good deal, but he consulted all the other monks, and at last they decided that they ought not to stand in the way of Vassili's good fortune.

Then Mark wrote a letter to his wife and gave it to Vassili to take to her, and this was what was in the letter: "When the bearer of this arrives, take him into the soap factory, and when you pass near the great boiler, push him in. If you don't obey my orders I shall be very angry, for this young man is a bad fellow who is sure to ruin us all if he lives."

Vassili had a good voyage, and on landing set off on foot for Mark's home. On the way he met three beggars, who asked him: "Where are you going, Vassili?"

"I am going to the house of Mark the Merchant, and have a letter for his wife," replied Vassili.

"Show us the letter."

Vassili handed them the letter. They blew on it and gave it back to him, saying: "Now go and give the letter to Mark's wife. You will not be forsaken."

Vassili reached the house and gave the letter. When the mistress read it she could hardly believe her eyes and called for her daughter. In the letter was written, quite plainly: "When you receive this letter, get ready for a wedding, and let the bearer be married next day to my daughter, Anastasia. If you don't obey my orders I shall be very angry."

Anastasia saw the bearer of the letter and he pleased her very much. They dressed Vassili in fine clothes and next day he was married to Anastasia.

In due time, Mark returned from his travels. His wife, daughter, and son-in-law all went out to meet him. When Mark saw Vassili he flew into a terrible rage with his wife. "How dared you marry my daughter without my consent?" he asked.

"I only carried out your orders," said she. "Here is your letter."

Mark read it. It certainly was his handwriting, but by no means his wishes.

"Well," thought he, "you've escaped me three times, but I think I shall get the better of you now." And he waited a month and was very kind and pleasant to his daughter and her husband.

At the end of that time he said to Vassili one day, "I want you to go for me to my friend the Serpent King, in his beautiful country at the world's end. Twelve years ago he built a castle on some land of mine. I want you to ask for the rent for those twelve years and also to find out from him what has become of my twelve ships which sailed for his country three years ago."

Vassili dared not disobey. He said good-bye to his young wife, who cried bitterly at parting, hung a bag of biscuits over his shoulders, and set out.

I really cannot tell you whether the journey was long or short. As he tramped along he suddenly heard a voice saying: "Vassili! where are you going?"

Vassili looked about him, and, seeing no one, called out: "Who spoke to me?"

"I did; this old wide-spreading oak. Tell me where you are going."

"I am going to the Serpent King to receive twelve years' rent from him."

"When the time comes, remember me and ask the king: 'Rotten to the roots, half dead but still green, stands the old oak. Is it to stand much longer on the earth?'"

Vassili went on further. He came to a river and got into the ferryboat. The old ferryman asked: "Are you going far, my friend?"

"I am going to the Serpent King."

"Then think of me and say to the king: 'For thirty years the ferryman has rowed to and fro. Will the tired old man have to row much longer?'"

"Very well," said Vassili; "I'll ask him."

And he walked on. In time he came to a narrow strait of the sea and across it lay a great whale over whose back people walked and drove as if it had been a bridge or a road. As he stepped on it the whale said, "Do tell me where you are going."

"I am going to the Serpent King."

And the whale begged: "Think of me and say to the king: 'The poor whale has been lying three years across the strait, and men and horses have nearly trampled his back into his ribs. Is he to lie there much longer?'"

"I will remember," said Vassili, and he went on.

He walked, and walked, and walked, till he came to a great green meadow. In the meadow stood a large and splendid castle. Its white marble walls sparkled in the light, the roof was covered with mother o' pearl, which shone like a rainbow, and the sun glowed like fire on the crystal windows. Vassili walked in, and went from one room to another astonished at all the splendor he saw.

When he reached the last room of all, he found a beautiful girl sitting on a bed.

As soon as she saw him she said: "Oh, Vassili, what brings you to this accursed place?"

Vassili told her why he had come, and all he had seen and heard on the way.

The girl said: "You have not been sent here to collect rents, but for your own destruction, and that the serpent may devour you."

She had not time to say more, when the whole castle shook, and a rustling, hissing, groaning sound was heard. The girl quickly pushed Vassili into a chest under the bed, locked it and whispered: "Listen to what the serpent and I talk about."

Then she rose up to receive the Serpent King.

The monster rushed into the room, and threw itself panting on the bed, crying: "I've flown half over the world. I'm tired, *very* tired, and want to sleep—scratch my head."

The beautiful girl sat down near him, stroking his hideous head, and said in a sweet coaxing voice: "You know everything in the world. After you left, I had such a wonderful dream. Will you tell me what it means?"

"Out with it then, quick! What was it?"

"I dreamt I was walking on a wide road, and an oak tree said to me: 'Ask the king this: Rotten at the roots, half dead, and yet green stands the old oak. Is it to stand much longer on the earth?'"

"It must stand till some one comes and pushes it down with his foot. Then it will fall, and under its roots will be found more gold and silver than even Mark the Rich has got."

"Then I dreamt I came to a river, and the old ferryman said to me: 'For thirty years the ferryman has rowed to and fro. Will the tired old man have to row much longer?'"

"That depends on himself. If some one gets into the boat to be ferried across, the old man has only to push the boat off, and go his way without looking back. The man in the boat will then have to take his place."

"And at last I dreamt that I was walking over a bridge made of a whale's back, and the living bridge spoke to me and said: 'Here have I been stretched out these three years, and men and horses have trampled my back down into my ribs. Must I lie here much longer?'"

"He will have to lie there till he has thrown up the twelve ships of Mark the Rich which he swallowed. Then he may plunge back into the sea and heal his back."

And the Serpent King closed his eyes, turned round on his other side, and began to snore so loud that the windows rattled.

In all haste the lovely girl helped Vassili out of the chest, and showed him part of his way back. He thanked her very politely, and hurried off.

When he reached the strait the whale asked: "Have you thought of me?"

"Yes, as soon as I am on the other side I will tell you what you want to know."

When he was on the other side Vassili said to the whale: "Throw up those twelve ships of Mark's which you swallowed three years ago."

The great fish heaved itself up and threw up all the twelve ships and their crews. Then he shook himself for joy, and plunged into the sea.

Vassili went on further till he reached the ferry, where the old man asked: "Did you think of me?"

"Yes, and as soon as you have ferried me across I will tell you what you want to know."

When they had crossed over, Vassili said: "Let the next man who comes stay in the boat, but do you step on shore, push the boat off, and you will be free, and the other man must take your place."

Then Vassili went on further still, and soon came to the old oak tree, pushed it with his foot, and it fell over. There, at the roots, was more gold and silver than even Mark the Rich had.

And now the twelve ships which the whale had thrown up came sailing along and anchored close by. On the deck of the first ship stood the three beggars whom Vassili had met formerly, and they said: "Heaven has blessed you, Vassili." Then they vanished away and he never saw them again.

The sailors carried all the gold and silver into the ship, and then they set sail for home with Vassili on board.

Mark was more furious than ever. He had his horses harnessed and drove off himself to see the Serpent King and to complain of the way in which he had been betrayed. When he reached the river he sprang into the ferryboat. The ferryman, however, did not get in but pushed the boat off. . . .

Vassili led a good and happy life with his dear wife, and his kind mother-in-law lived with them. He helped the poor and fed and clothed the hungry and naked and all Mark's riches became his.

For many years Mark has been ferrying people across the river. His face is wrinkled, his hair and beard are snow white, and his eyes are dim; but still he rows on.

Prince Narcissus and the Princess Potentilla

(FROM *THE GREEN FAIRY BOOK*)

Once upon a time there lived a King and Queen who, though it is a very long while since they died, were much the same in their tastes and pursuits as people nowadays. The King, who was called Cloverleaf, liked hunting better than anything else; but he nevertheless bestowed as much care upon his kingdom as he felt equal to—that is to say, he never made an end of folding and unfolding the State documents. As to the Queen, she had once been very pretty, and she liked to believe that she was so still, which is, of course, always made quite easy for queens. Her name was Frivola, and her one occupation in life was the pursuit of amusement. Balls, masquerades, and picnics followed one another in rapid succession, as fast as she could arrange them, and you may imagine that under these circumstances the kingdom was somewhat neglected. As a matter of fact, if anyone had a fancy for a town, or a province, he helped himself to it; but as long as the King had his horses and dogs, and the Queen her musicians and her actors, they did not trouble themselves about the matter. King Cloverleaf and Queen Frivola had but one child, and this Princess had from her very babyhood been so beautiful, that by the time she was four years old the Queen was desperately jealous of her, and so fearful that when she was grown up she would be more admired than herself, that she resolved to keep her hidden away out of sight. To this end she caused a little house to be built not far beyond the Palace gardens, on the bank of a river. This was surrounded by a high wall, and in it the charming Potentilla was imprisoned. Her nurse, who was dumb, took care of her, and the necessaries of life were conveyed to her through a little window in the wall, while guards were always pacing to and fro outside, with orders to cut off the head of anyone who tried to approach, which they would certainly have done without thinking twice about it. The Queen told everyone, with much pretended sorrow, that the Princess was so ugly, and so troublesome, and altogether so impossible to love, that to keep her out of sight was the only thing that could be done for her. And this tale she repeated so often, that at last the whole court believed it.

Things were in this state, and the Princess was about fifteen years old, when Prince Narcissus, attracted by the report of Queen Frivola's gay doings, presented himself at the court. He was not much older than the Princess, and was as handsome a Prince as you would see in a day's journey, and really, for his age, not so very scatter-brained. His parents were a King and Queen, whose story you will perhaps read some day. They died almost at the same time, leaving their kingdom to the eldest of their children, and commending their youngest son, Prince Narcissus, to the care of the Fairy Melinette. In this they did very well for him, for the Fairy was as kind as she was powerful, and she spared no pains in teaching the little Prince everything it was good for him to know, and even imparted to him some of her own Fairy lore. But as soon as he was grown up she sent him out to see the world for himself, though all the time she was secretly keeping watch over him, ready to help in any time of need. Before he started she gave him a ring which would render him invisible when he put it on his finger. These rings seem to be quite common; you must often have heard of them, even if you have never seen one. It was in the course of the Prince's wanderings, in search of experience of men and things, that he came to the court of Queen Frivola, where he was extremely well received. The Queen was delighted with him, so were all her ladies; and the King was very polite to him, though he did not quite see why the whole court was making such a fuss over him.

Prince Narcissus enjoyed all that went on, and found the time passed very pleasantly. Before long, of course, he heard the story about the Princess Potentilla, and, as it had by that time been repeated many times, and had been added to here and there, she was represented as such a monster of ugliness that he was really quite curious to see her, and resolved to avail himself of the magic power of his ring to accomplish his design. So he made himself invisible, and passed the guard without their so much as suspecting that anyone was near. Climbing the wall was rather a difficulty, but when he at length found himself inside it he was charmed with the peaceful beauty of the little domain it enclosed, and still more delighted when he perceived a slender, lovely maiden wandering among the flowers. It was not until he had sought vainly for the imaginary monster that he realized that this was the Princess herself, and by that time he was deeply in love with her, for indeed it would have been hard to find anyone prettier than Potentilla, as she sat by the brook, weaving a garland of blue forget-me-nots to crown her waving golden locks, or to imagine anything more gentle than the way she tended all the birds and beasts who inhabited her small kingdom, and who all loved and followed her. Prince Narcissus watched her every movement, and hovered near her in a dream of delight, not daring as yet to appear to her, so humble had he suddenly become in her presence. And when evening came, and the nurse fetched the Princess into her little house, he felt obliged to go back to Frivola's palace, for fear his absence should be noticed and someone should discover his new treasure. But he forgot that to go back absent, and dreamy, and indifferent, when he had before been gay and ardent about everything, was the surest way of awakening suspicion; and when, in response to the jesting questions which were put to him upon the subject, he only blushed and returned evasive answers, all the ladies were certain that he had lost his heart, and did their utmost to discover who was the happy possessor of it.

As to the Prince, he was becoming day by day more attached to Potentilla, and his one thought was to attend her, always invisible, and help her in everything she did, and provide her with everything that could possibly amuse or please her. And the Princess, who had learnt to find diversion in very small things in her quiet life, was in a continual state of delight over the treasures which the Prince constantly laid where she must find them. Then Narcissus implored his faithful friend Melinette to send the Princess such dreams of him as should make her recognize him as a friend when he actually appeared before her eyes; and this device was so successful that the Princess quite dreaded the cessation of these amusing dreams, in which a certain Prince Narcissus was such a delightful lover and companion. After that he went a step further and began to have long talks with the Princess— still, however, keeping himself invisible, until she begged him so earnestly to appear to her that he could no longer resist, and after making her promise that, no matter what he was like, she would still love him, he drew the ring from his finger, and the Princess saw with delight that he was as handsome as he was agreeable.

Now, indeed, they were perfectly happy, and they passed the whole long summer day in Potentilla's favorite place by the brook, and when at last Prince Narcissus had to leave her it seemed to them both that the hours had gone by with the most amazing swiftness. The Princess stayed where she was, dreaming of her delightful Prince, and nothing could have been further from her thoughts than any trouble or misfortune, when suddenly, in a cloud of dust and shavings, by came the enchanter Grumedan, and unluckily he chanced to catch sight of Potentilla. Down he came straightway and alighted at her feet, and one look at her charming blue eyes and smiling lips quite decided him that he must appear to her at once, though he was rather annoyed to remember that he had on only his second-best cloak. The Princess sprang to her feet with a cry of terror at this sudden apparition, for really the Enchanter was no beauty. To begin with, he was very big and clumsy, then he had but one eye, and his teeth were long, and he stammered badly; nevertheless, he had an excellent opinion of himself, and mistook the Princess's cry of terror for an exclamation of delighted surprise. After pausing a moment to give her time to admire him, the Enchanter made her the most complimentary speech he could invent, which, however, did not please her at all, though he was extremely delighted with it himself. Poor Potentilla only shuddered and cried:

"Oh! where is my Narcissus?"

To which he replied with a self-satisfied chuckle: "You want a narcissus, madam? Well, they are not rare; you shall have as many as you like."

Whereupon he waved his wand, and the Princess found herself surrounded and half buried in the fragrant flowers. She would certainly have betrayed that this was not the kind of narcissus she wanted, but for the Fairy Melinette, who had been anxiously watching the interview, and now thought it quite time to interfere. Assuming the Prince's voice, she whispered in Potentilla's ear:

"We are menaced by a great danger, but my only fear is for you, my Princess. Therefore I beg you to hide what you really feel, and we will hope that some way out of the difficulty may present itself."

The Princess was much agitated by this speech, and feared lest the Enchanter should have overheard it; but he had been loudly calling her attention to the flowers, and chuckling over his own smartness in getting them for her; and it was rather a blow to him when she said very coldly that they were not the sort she preferred, and she would be glad if he would send them all away. This he did, but afterwards wished to kiss the Princess's hand as a reward for having been so obliging; but the Fairy Melinette was not going to allow anything of that kind. She appeared suddenly, in all her splendor, and cried:

"Stay, Grumedan; this Princess is under my protection, and the smallest impertinence will cost you a thousand years of captivity. If you can win Potentilla's heart by the ordinary methods I cannot oppose you, but I warn you that I will not put up with any of your usual tricks."

This declaration was not at all to the Enchanter's taste; but he knew that there was no help for it, and that he would have to behave well, and pay the Princess all the delicate attentions he could think of; though they were not at all the sort of thing he was used to. However, he decided that to win such a beauty it was quite worth while; and Melinette, feeling that she could now leave the Princess in safety, hurried off to tell Prince Narcissus what was going forward. Of course, at the very mention of the Enchanter as a rival he was furious, and I don't know what foolish things he would not have done if Melinette had not been there to calm him down. She represented to him what a powerful enchanter Grumedan was, and how, if he were provoked, he might avenge himself upon the Princess, since he was the most unjust and churlish of all the enchanters, and had often before had to be punished by the Fairy Queen for some of his ill-deeds. Once he had been imprisoned in a tree, and was only released when it was blown down by a furious wind; another time he was condemned to stay under a big stone at the bottom of a river, until by some chance the stone should be turned over; but nothing could ever really improve him. The Fairy finally made Narcissus promise that he would remain invisible when he was with the Princess, since she felt sure that this would make things easier for all of them. Then began a struggle between Grumedan and the Prince, the latter under the name of Melinette, as to which could best delight and divert the Princess and win her approbation. Prince Narcissus first made friends with all the birds in Potentilla's little domain, and taught them to sing her name and her praises, with all their sweetest trills and most touching melodies, and all day long to tell her how dearly he loved her. Grumedan, thereupon, declared that there was nothing new about that, since the birds had sung since the world began, and all lovers had imagined that they sang for them alone. Therefore he said he would himself write an opera that should be absolutely a novelty and something worth hearing. When the time came for the performance (which lasted five weary hours) the Princess found to her dismay that the "opera" consisted of this more than indifferent verse, chanted with all their might by ten thousand frogs:

> "Admirable Potentilla,
> Do you think it kind or wise
> In this sudden way to kill a
> Poor Enchanter with your eyes?"

Really, if Narcissus had not been there to whisper in her ear and divert her attention, I don't know what would have become of poor Potentilla, for though the first repetition of this absurdity amused her faintly, she nearly died of weariness before the time was over. Luckily Grumedan did not perceive this, as he was too much occupied in whipping up the frogs, many of whom perished miserably from fatigue, since he did not allow them to rest for a moment. The Prince's next idea for Potentilla's amusement was to cause a fleet of boats exactly like those of Cleopatra, of which you have doubtless read in history, to come up the little river, and upon the most gorgeously decorated of these reclined the great Queen herself, who, as soon as she reached the place where Potentilla sat in rapt attention, stepped majestically on shore and presented the Princess with that celebrated pearl of which you have heard so much, saying:

"You are more beautiful than I ever was. Let my example warn you to make a better use of your beauty!"

And then the little fleet sailed on, until it was lost to view in the windings of the river. Grumedan was also looking on at the spectacle, and said very contemptuously:

"I cannot say I think these marionettes amusing. What a to-do to make over a single pearl! But if you like pearls, madam, why, I will soon gratify you."

So saying, he drew a whistle from his pocket, and no sooner had he blown it than the Princess saw the water of the river bubble and grow muddy, and in another instant up came hundreds of thousands of great oysters, who climbed slowly and laboriously towards her and laid at her feet all the pearls they contained.

"Those are what I call pearls," cried Grumedan in high glee. And truly there were enough of them to pave every path in Potentilla's garden and leave some to spare! The next day Prince Narcissus had prepared for the Princess's pleasure a charming arbor of leafy branches, with couches of moss and grassy floor and garlands everywhere, with her name written in different colored blossoms. Here he caused a dainty little banquet to be set forth, while hidden musicians played softly, and the silvery fountains plashed down into their marble basins, and when presently the music stopped a single nightingale broke the stillness with his delicious chant.

"Ah!" cried the Princess, recognizing the voice of one of her favorites, "Philomel, my sweet one, who taught you that new song?"

And he answered: "Love, my Princess."

Meanwhile the Enchanter was very ill-pleased with the entertainment, which he declared was dullness itself.

"You don't seem to have any idea in these parts beyond little squeaking birds!" said he. "And fancy giving a banquet without so much as an ounce of plate!"

So the next day, when the Princess went out into her garden, there stood a summer-house built of solid gold, decorated within and without with her initials and the Enchanter's combined. And in it was spread an enormous repast, while the table so glittered with golden cups and plates, flagons and dishes, candlesticks and a hundred other things beside, that it was hardly possible to look steadily at it. The Enchanter ate like six ogres, but the Princess could not touch a morsel. Presently Grumedan remarked with a grin:

"I have provided neither musicians nor singers; but as you seem fond of music I will sing to you myself."

Whereupon he began, with a voice like a screech-owl's, to chant the words of his "opera," only this time happily not at such a length, and without the frog accompaniment. After this the Prince again asked the aid of his friends the birds, and when they had assembled from all the country round he tied about the neck of each one a tiny lamp of some brilliant color, and when darkness fell he made them go through a hundred pretty tricks before the delighted Potentilla, who clapped her little hands with delight when she saw her own name traced in points of light against the dark trees, or when the whole flock of sparks grouped themselves into bouquets of different colors, like living flowers. Grumedan, leaning back in his arm-chair, with one knee crossed over the other and his nose in the air, looked on disdainfully.

"Oh! if you like fireworks, Princess," said he; and the next night all the will-o'-the-wisps in the country came and danced on the plain, which could be seen from the Princess's windows, and as she was looking out, and rather enjoying the sight, up sprang a frightful volcano, pouring out smoke and flames which terrified her greatly, to the intense amusement of the Enchanter, who laughed like a pack of wolves quarreling. After this, as many of the will-o'-the-wisps as could get in crowded into Potentilla's garden, and by their light the tall yew-trees danced minuets until the Princess was weary and begged to be excused from looking at anything more that night. But, in spite of Potentilla's efforts to behave politely to the tiresome old Enchanter, whom she detested, he could not help seeing that he failed to please her, and then he began to suspect very strongly that she must love someone else, and that somebody besides Melinette was responsible for all the festivities he had witnessed. So after much consideration he devised a plan for finding out the truth. He went to the Princess suddenly, and announced that he was most unwillingly forced to leave her, and had come to bid her farewell. Potentilla could scarcely hide her delight when she heard this, and his back was hardly turned before she was entreating Prince Narcissus to make himself visible once more. The poor Prince had been getting quite thin with anxiety and annoyance, and was only too delighted to comply with her request. They greeted one another rapturously, and were just sitting down to talk over everything cosily, and enjoy the Enchanter's discomfiture together, when out he burst in a fury from behind a bush. With his huge club he aimed a terrific blow at Narcissus, which must certainly have killed him but for the adroitness of the Fairy Melinette, who arrived upon the scene just in time to snatch him up and carry him off at lightning speed to her castle in the air. Poor Potentilla, however, had not the comfort of knowing this, for at the sight of the Enchanter threatening her beloved Prince she had given one shriek and fallen back insensible. When she recovered her senses she was more than ever convinced that he was dead, since even Melinette was no longer near her, and no one was left to defend her from the odious old Enchanter.

To make matters worse, he seemed to be in a very bad temper, and came blustering and raging at the poor Princess.

"I tell you what it is, madam," said he: "whether you love this whipper-snapper Prince or not doesn't matter in the least. You are going to marry me, so you may as well make up your mind to it; and I am going away this very minute to make all the arrangements. But in case you should get into mischief in my absence, I think I had better put you to sleep."

So saying, he waved his wand over her, and in spite of her utmost efforts to keep awake she sank into a profound and dreamless slumber.

As he wished to make what he considered a suitable entry into the King's palace, he stepped outside the Princess's little domain, and mounted upon an immense chariot with great solid wheels, and shafts like the trunk of an oak-tree, but all of solid gold. This was drawn with great difficulty by forty-eight strong oxen; and the Enchanter reclined at his ease, leaning upon his huge club, and holding carelessly upon his knee a tawny African lion, as if it had been a little lapdog. It was about seven o'clock in the morning when this extraordinary chariot reached the palace gates; the King was already astir, and about to set off on a hunting expedition; as for the Queen, she had only just gone off into her first sleep, and it would have been a bold person indeed who ventured to wake her.

The King was greatly annoyed at having to stay and see a visitor at such a time, and pulled off his hunting boots again with many grimaces. Meantime the Enchanter was stumping about in the hall, crying:

"Where is this King? Let him be told that I must see him and his wife also."

The King, who was listening at the top of the staircase, thought this was not very polite; however, he took counsel with his favorite huntsman, and, following his advice, presently went down to see what was wanted of him. He was struck with astonishment at the sight of the chariot, and was gazing at it, when the Enchanter strode up to him, exclaiming:

"Shake hands, Cloverleaf, old fellow! Don't you know me?"

"No, I can't say I do," replied the King, somewhat embarrassed.

"Why, I am Grumedan, the Enchanter," said he, "and I am come to make your fortune. Let us come in and talk things over a bit."

Thereupon he ordered the oxen to go about their business, and they bounded off like stags, and were out of sight in a moment. Then, with one blow of his club, he changed the massive chariot into a perfect mountain of gold pieces.

"Those are for your lackeys," said he to the King, "that they may drink my health."

Naturally a great scramble ensued, and at last the laughter and shouting awoke the Queen, who rang for her maids to ask the reason of such an unwonted hurry-burly. When they said that a visitor was asking for her, and then proceeded each one to tell breathlessly a different tale of wonder, in which she could only distinguish the words, "oxen," "gold," "club," "giant," "lion," she thought they were all out of their minds. Meanwhile the King was asking the Enchanter to what he was indebted for the honor of this visit, and on his replying that he would not say until the Queen was also present, messenger after messenger was dispatched to her to beg her immediate attendance. But Frivola was in a very bad humor at having been so unceremoniously awakened, and declared that she had a pain in her little finger, and that nothing should induce her to come.

When the Enchanter heard this he insisted that she must come.

"Take my club to her Majesty," said he, "and tell her that if she smells the end of it she will find it wonderfully reviving."

So four of the King's strongest men-at-arms staggered off with it; and after some persuasion the Queen consented to try this novel remedy. She had hardly smelt it for an instant when she declared herself to be perfectly restored; but whether that was due to the scent of the wood or to the fact that as soon as she touched it out fell a perfect shower of magnificent jewels, I leave you to decide. At any rate, she was now all eagerness to see the mysterious stranger, and hastily throwing on her royal mantle, popped her second-best diamond crown over her night-cap, put a liberal dab of rouge upon each cheek, and holding up her largest fan before her nose—for she was not used to appearing in broad daylight—she went mincing into the great hall. The Enchanter waited until the King and Queen had seated themselves upon their throne, and then, taking his place between them, he began solemnly:

"My name is Grumedan. I am an extremely well-connected Enchanter; my power is immense. In spite of all this, the charms of your daughter Potentilla have so fascinated me that I cannot live without her. She fancies that she loves a certain contemptible puppy called Narcissus; but I have made very short work with him. I really do not care whether you consent to my marriage with your daughter or not, but I am bound to ask your consent, on account of a certain meddling Fairy called Melinette, with whom I have reason for wishing to keep on good terms."

The King and Queen were somewhat embarrassed to know what answer to make to this terrible suitor, but at last they asked for time to talk over the matter: since, they said, their subjects might think that the heir to the throne should not be married with as little consideration as a dairymaid.

"Oh! take a day or two if you like," said the Enchanter; "but in the meantime, I am going to send for your daughter. Perhaps you will be able to induce her to be reasonable."

So saying, he drew out his favorite whistle, and blew one ear-piercing note—whereupon the great lion, who had been dozing in the sunny courtyard, come bounding in on his soft, heavy feet. "Orion," said the Enchanter, "go and fetch me the Princess, and bring her here at once. Be gentle now!"

At these words Orion went off at a great pace, and was soon at the other end of the King's gardens. Scattering the guards right and left, he cleared the wall at a bound, and seizing the sleeping Princess, he threw her on to his back, where he kept her by holding her robe in his teeth. Then he trotted gently back, and in less than five minutes stood in the great hall before the astonished King and Queen.

The Enchanter held his club close to the Princess's charming little nose, whereupon she woke up and shrieked with terror at finding herself in a strange place with the detested Grumedan. Frivola, who had stood by, stiff with displeasure at the sight of the lovely Princess, now stepped forward, and with much pretended concern proposed to carry off Potentilla to her own apartments that she might enjoy the quiet she seemed to need. Really her one idea was to let the Princess be seen by as few people as possible; so, throwing a veil over her head, she led her away and locked her up securely. All this time Prince Narcissus, gloomy and despairing, was kept a prisoner by Melinette in her castle in the air, and in spite of all the splendor by which he was surrounded, and all the pleasures which he might have enjoyed, his one thought was to get back to Potentilla. The Fairy, however, left him there, promising to do her very best for him, and commanding all her swallows and butterflies to wait upon him and do his bidding. One day, as he paced sadly to and fro, he thought he heard a voice he knew calling to him, and sure enough there was the faithful Philomel, Potentilla's favorite, who told him all that had passed, and how the sleeping Princess had been carried off by the Lion to the great grief of all her four-footed and feathered subjects, and how, not knowing what to do, he had wandered about until he heard the swallows telling one another of the Prince who was in their airy castle and had come to see if it could be Narcissus. The Prince was more distracted than ever, and tried vainly to escape from the castle, by leaping from the roof into the clouds; but every time they caught him, and rolling softly up, brought him back to the place from which he started, so at last he gave up the attempt and waited with desperate patience for the return of Melinette. Meanwhile matters were advancing rapidly in the court of King Cloverleaf, for the Queen quite made up her mind that such a beauty as Potentilla must be got out of the way as quickly as possible. So she sent for the Enchanter secretly, and after making him promise that he would never turn herself and King Cloverleaf out of their kingdom, and that he would take Potentilla far away, so that never again might she set eyes upon her, she arranged the wedding for the next day but one.

You may imagine how Potentilla lamented her sad fate, and entreated to be spared. All the comfort she could get out of Frivola was, that if she preferred a cup of poison to a rich husband, she would certainly provide her with one.

When, then, the fatal day came the unhappy Potentilla was led into the great hall between the King and Queen, the latter wild with envy at the murmurs of admiration which rose on all sides at the loveliness of the Princess. An instant later in came Grumedan by the opposite door. His hair stood on end, and he wore a huge bag-purse and a cravat tied in a bow, his mantle was made of a shower of silver coins with a lining of rose color, and his delight in his own appearance knew no bounds. That any Princess could prefer a cup of poison to himself never for an instant occurred to him. Nevertheless, that was what did happen, for when Queen Frivola in jest held out the fatal cup to the Princess, she took it eagerly, crying:

"Ah! beloved Narcissus, I come to thee!" and was just raising it to her lips when the window of the great hall burst open, and the Fairy Melinette floated in upon a glowing sunset cloud, followed by the Prince himself.

All the court looked on in dazzled surprise, while Potentilla, catching sight of her lover, dropped the cup and ran joyfully to meet him.

The Enchanter's first thought was to defend himself when he saw Melinette appear, but she slipped round his blind side, and catching him by the eyelashes dragged him off to the ceiling of the hall, where she held him kicking for a while just to give him a lesson, and then touching him with her wand she imprisoned him for a thousand years in a crystal ball which hung from the roof. "Let this teach you to mind what I tell you another time," she remarked severely. Then turning to the King and Queen, she begged them to proceed with the wedding, since she had provided a much more suitable bridegroom. She also deprived them of their kingdom, for they had really shown themselves unfit to manage it, and bestowed it upon the Prince and Princess, who, though they were unwilling to take it, had no choice but to obey the Fairy. However, they took care that the King and Queen were always supplied with everything they could wish for.

Prince Narcissus and Princess Potentilla lived long and happily, beloved by all their subjects. As for the Enchanter, I don't believe he has been let out yet.

The Twelve Dancing Princesses

(FROM *THE RED FAIRY BOOK*)

I

ONCE UPON A TIME THERE LIVED IN THE VILLAGE OF MONTIGNIES-SUR-ROC a little cow-boy, without either father or mother. His real name was Michael, but he was always called the Star Gazer, because when he drove his cows over the commons to seek for pasture, he went along with his head in the air, gaping at nothing.

As he had a white skin, blue eyes, and hair that curled all over his head, the village girls used to cry after him, "Well, Star Gazer, what are you doing?" and Michael would answer, "Oh, nothing," and go on his way without even turning to look at them.

The fact was he thought them very ugly, with their sun-burnt necks, their great red hands, their coarse petticoats and their wooden shoes. He had heard that somewhere in the world there were girls whose necks were white and whose hands were small, who were always dressed in the finest silks and laces, and were called princesses, and while his companions round the fire saw nothing in the flames but common everyday fancies, he dreamed that he had the happiness to marry a princess.

II

One morning about the middle of August, just at mid-day when the sun was hottest, Michael ate his dinner of a piece of dry bread, and went to sleep under an oak. And while he slept he dreamt that there appeared before him a beautiful lady, dressed in a robe of cloth of gold, who said to him: "Go to the castle of Belœil, and there you shall marry a princess."

That evening the little cow-boy, who had been thinking a great deal about the advice of the lady in the golden dress, told his dream to the farm people. But, as was natural, they only laughed at the Star Gazer.

The next day at the same hour he went to sleep again under the same tree. The lady appeared to him a second time, and said: "Go to the castle of Belœil, and you shall marry a princess."

In the evening Michael told his friends that he had dreamed the same dream again, but they only laughed at him more than before. "Never mind," he thought to himself; "if the lady appears to me a third time, I will do as she tells me."

The following day, to the great astonishment of all the village, about two o'clock in the afternoon a voice was heard singing:

> "Raleô, raleô,
> How the cattle go!"

It was the little cow-boy driving his herd back to the byre.

The farmer began to scold him furiously, but he answered quietly, "I am going away," made his clothes into a bundle, said good-bye to all his friends, and boldly set out to seek his fortunes.

There was great excitement through all the village, and on the top of the hill the people stood holding their sides with laughing, as they watched the Star Gazer trudging bravely along the valley with his bundle at the end of his stick.

It was enough to make anyone laugh, certainly.

III

It was well known for full twenty miles round that there lived in the castle of Beloeil twelve princesses of wonderful beauty, and as proud as they were beautiful, and who were besides so very sensitive and of such truly royal blood, that they would have felt at once the presence of a pea in their beds, even if the mattresses had been laid over it.

It was whispered about that they led exactly the lives that princesses ought to lead, sleeping far into the morning, and never getting up till mid-day. They had twelve beds all in the same room, but what was very extraordinary was the fact that though they were locked in by triple bolts, every morning their satin shoes were found worn into holes.

When they were asked what they had been doing all night, they always answered that they had been asleep; and, indeed, no noise was ever heard in the room, yet the shoes could not wear themselves out alone!

At last the Duke of Belœil ordered the trumpet to be sounded, and a proclamation to be made that whoever could discover how his daughters wore out their shoes should choose one of them for his wife.

On hearing the proclamation a number of princes arrived at the castle to try their luck. They watched all night behind the open door of the princesses, but when the morning came they had all disappeared, and no one could tell what had become of them.

IV

When he reached the castle, Michael went straight to the gardener and offered his services. Now it happened that the garden boy had just been sent away, and though the Star Gazer did not look very sturdy, the gardener agreed to take him, as he thought that his pretty face and golden curls would please the princesses.

The first thing he was told was that when the princesses got up he was to present each one with a bouquet, and Michael thought that if he had nothing more unpleasant to do than that he should get on very well.

Accordingly he placed himself behind the door of the princesses' room, with the twelve bouquets in a basket. He gave one to each of the sisters, and they took them without even deigning to look at the lad, except Lina the youngest, who fixed her large black eyes as soft as velvet on him, and exclaimed, "Oh, how pretty he is—our new flower boy!" The rest all burst out laughing, and the eldest pointed out that a princess ought never to lower herself by looking at a garden boy.

Now Michael knew quite well what had happened to all the princes, but notwithstanding, the beautiful eyes of the Princess Lina inspired him with a violent longing to try his fate. Unhappily he did not dare to come forward, being afraid that he should only be jeered at, or even turned away from the castle on account of his impudence.

V

Nevertheless, the Star Gazer had another dream. The lady in the golden dress appeared to him once more, holding in one hand two young laurel trees, a cherry laurel and a rose laurel, and in the other hand a little golden rake, a little golden bucket, and a silken towel. She thus addressed him:

"Plant these two laurels in two large pots, rake them over with the rake, water them with the bucket, and wipe them with the towel. When they have grown as tall as a girl of fifteen, say to each of them, 'My beautiful laurel, with the golden rake I have raked you, with the golden bucket I have watered you, with the silken towel I have wiped you.' Then after that ask anything you choose, and the laurels will give it to you."

Michael thanked the lady in the golden dress, and when he woke he found the two laurel bushes beside him. So he carefully obeyed the orders he had been given by the lady.

The trees grew very fast, and when they were as tall as a girl of fifteen he said to the cherry laurel, "My lovely cherry laurel, with the golden rake I have raked thee, with the golden bucket I have watered thee, with the silken towel I have wiped thee. Teach me how to become invisible." Then there instantly appeared on the laurel a pretty white flower, which Michael gathered and stuck into his button-hole.

VI

That evening, when the princesses went upstairs to bed, he followed them barefoot, so that he might make no noise, and hid himself under one of the twelve beds, so as not to take up much room.

The princesses began at once to open their wardrobes and boxes. They took out of them the most magnificent dresses, which they put on before their mirrors, and when they had finished, turned themselves all round to admire their appearances.

Michael could see nothing from his hiding-place, but he could hear everything, and he listened to the princesses laughing and jumping with pleasure. At last the eldest said, "Be quick, my sisters, our partners will be impatient." At the end of an hour, when the Star Gazer heard no more noise, he peeped out and saw the twelve sisters in splendid garments, with their satin shoes on their feet, and in their hands the bouquets he had brought them.

"Are you ready?" asked the eldest.

"Yes," replied the other eleven in chorus, and they took their places one by one behind her.

Then the eldest Princess clapped her hands three times and a trap door opened. All the princesses disappeared down a secret staircase, and Michael hastily followed them.

As he was following on the steps of the Princess Lina, he carelessly trod on her dress.

"There is somebody behind me," cried the Princess; "they are holding my dress."

"You foolish thing," said her eldest sister, "you are always afraid of something. It is only a nail which caught you."

VII

They went down, down, down, till at last they came to a passage with a door at one end, which was only fastened with a latch. The eldest Princess opened it, and they found themselves immediately in a lovely little wood, where the leaves were spangled with drops of silver which shone in the brilliant light of the moon.

They next crossed another wood where the leaves were sprinkled with gold, and after that another still, where the leaves glittered with diamonds.

At last the Star Gazer perceived a large lake, and on the shores of the lake twelve little boats with awnings, in which were seated twelve princes, who, grasping their oars, awaited the princesses.

Each princess entered one of the boats, and Michael slipped into that which held the youngest. The boats glided along rapidly, but Lina's, from being heavier, was always behind the rest. "We never went so slowly before," said the Princess; "what can be the reason?"

"I don't know," answered the Prince. "I assure you I am rowing as hard as I can."

On the other side of the lake the garden boy saw a beautiful castle splendidly illuminated, whence came the lively music of fiddles, kettle-drums, and trumpets.

In a moment they touched land, and the company jumped out of the boats; and the princes, after having securely fastened their barks, gave their arms to the princesses and conducted them to the castle.

VIII

Michael followed, and entered the ball-room in their train. Everywhere were mirrors, lights, flowers, and damask hangings.

The Star Gazer was quite bewildered at the magnificence of the sight.

He placed himself out of the way in a corner, admiring the grace and beauty of the princesses. Their loveliness was of every kind. Some were fair and some were dark; some had chestnut hair, or curls darker still, and some had golden locks. Never were so many beautiful princesses seen together at one time, but the one whom the cow-boy thought the most beautiful and the most fascinating was the little Princess with the velvet eyes.

With what eagerness she danced! leaning on her partner's shoulder she swept by like a whirlwind. Her cheeks flushed, her eyes sparkled, and it was plain that she loved dancing better than anything else.

The poor boy envied those handsome young men with whom she danced so gracefully, but he did not know how little reason he had to be jealous of them.

The young men were really the princes who, to the number of fifty at least, had tried to steal the princesses' secret. The princesses had made them drink something of a philter, which froze the heart and left nothing but the love of dancing.

IX

They danced on till the shoes of the princesses were worn into holes. When the cock crowed the third time the fiddles stopped, and a delicious supper was served by negro boys, consisting of sugared orange flowers, crystallized rose leaves, powdered violets, cracknels, wafers, and other dishes, which are, as everyone knows, the favorite food of princesses. After supper, the dancers all went back to their boats, and this time the Star Gazer entered that of the eldest Princess. They crossed again the wood with the diamond-spangled leaves, the wood with gold-sprinkled leaves, and the wood whose leaves glittered with drops of silver, and as a proof of what he had seen, the boy broke a small branch from a tree in the last wood. Lina turned as she heard the noise made by the breaking of the branch.

"What was that noise?" she said.

"It was nothing," replied her eldest sister; "it was only the screech of the barn-owl that roosts in one of the turrets of the castle."

While she was speaking Michael managed to slip in front, and running up the staircase, he reached the princesses' room first. He flung open the window, and sliding down the vine which climbed up the wall, found himself in the garden just as the sun was beginning to rise, and it was time for him to set to his work.

X

That day, when he made up the bouquets, Michael hid the branch with the silver drops in the nosegay intended for the youngest Princess.

When Lina discovered it she was much surprised. However, she said nothing to her sisters, but as she met the boy by accident while she was walking under the shade of the elms, she suddenly stopped as if to speak to him; then, altering her mind, went on her way.

The same evening the twelve sisters went again to the ball, and the Star Gazer again followed them and crossed the lake in Lina's boat. This time it was the Prince who complained that the boat seemed very heavy.

"It is the heat," replied the Princess. "I, too, have been feeling very warm."

During the ball she looked everywhere for the gardener's boy, but she never saw him.

As they came back, Michael gathered a branch from the wood with the gold-spangled leaves, and now it was the eldest Princess who heard the noise that it made in breaking.

"It is nothing," said Lina; "only the cry of the owl which roosts in the turrets of the castle."

XI

As soon as she got up she found the branch in her bouquet. When the sisters went down she stayed a little behind and said to the cow-boy: "Where does this branch come from?"

"Your Royal Highness knows well enough," answered Michael.

"So you have followed us?"

"Yes, Princess."

"How did you manage it? we never saw you."

"I hid myself," replied the Star Gazer quietly.

The Princess was silent a moment, and then said:

"You know our secret!—keep it. Here is the reward of your discretion." And she flung the boy a purse of gold.

"I do not sell my silence," answered Michael, and he went away without picking up the purse.

For three nights Lina neither saw nor heard anything extraordinary; on the fourth she heard a rustling among the diamond-spangled leaves of the wood. That day there was a branch of the trees in her bouquet.

She took the Star Gazer aside, and said to him in a harsh voice:

"You know what price my father has promised to pay for our secret?"

"I know, Princess," answered Michael.

"Don't you mean to tell him?"

"That is not my intention."

"Are you afraid?"

"No, Princess."

"What makes you so discreet, then?"

But Michael was silent.

XII

Lina's sisters had seen her talking to the little garden boy, and jeered at her for it.

"What prevents your marrying him?" asked the eldest, "you would become a gardener too; it is a charming profession. You could live in a cottage at the end of the park, and help your husband to draw up water from the well, and when we get up you could bring us our bouquets."

The Princess Lina was very angry, and when the Star Gazer presented her bouquet, she received it in a disdainful manner.

Michael behaved most respectfully. He never raised his eyes to her, but nearly all day she felt him at her side without ever seeing him.

One day she made up her mind to tell everything to her eldest sister.

"What!" said she, "this rogue knows our secret, and you never told me! I must lose no time in getting rid of him."

"But how?"

"Why, by having him taken to the tower with the dungeons, of course."

For this was the way that in old times beautiful princesses got rid of people who knew too much.

But the astonishing part of it was that the youngest sister did not seem at all to relish this method of stopping the mouth of the gardener's boy, who, after all, had said nothing to their father.

XIII

It was agreed that the question should be submitted to the other ten sisters. All were on the side of the eldest. Then the youngest sister declared that if they laid a finger on the little garden boy, she would herself go and tell their father the secret of the holes in their shoes.

At last it was decided that Michael should be put to the test; that they would take him to the ball, and at the end of supper would give him the philter which was to enchant him like the rest.

They sent for the Star Gazer, and asked him how he had contrived to learn their secret; but still he remained silent.

Then, in commanding tones, the eldest sister gave him the order they had agreed upon.

He only answered:

"I will obey."

He had really been present, invisible, at the council of princesses, and had heard all; but he had made up his mind to drink of the philter, and sacrifice himself to the happiness of her he loved.

Not wishing, however, to cut a poor figure at the ball by the side of the other dancers, he went at once to the laurels, and said:

"My lovely rose laurel, with the golden rake I have raked thee, with the golden bucket I have watered thee, with a silken towel I have dried thee. Dress me like a prince."

A beautiful pink flower appeared. Michael gathered it, and found himself in a moment clothed in velvet, which was as black as the eyes of the little Princess, with a cap to match, a diamond aigrette, and a blossom of the rose laurel in his button-hole.

Thus dressed, he presented himself that evening before the Duke of Belœil, and obtained leave to try and discover his daughters' secret. He looked so distinguished that hardly anyone would have known who he was.

XIV

The twelve princesses went upstairs to bed. Michael followed them, and waited behind the open door till they gave the signal for departure.

This time he did not cross in Lina's boat. He gave his arm to the eldest sister, danced with each in turn, and was so graceful that everyone was delighted with him. At last the time came for him to dance with the little Princess. She found him the best partner in the world, but he did not dare to speak a single word to her.

When he was taking her back to her place she said to him in a mocking voice:

"Here you are at the summit of your wishes: you are being treated like a prince."

"Don't be afraid," replied the Star Gazer gently. "You shall never be a gardener's wife."

The little Princess stared at him with a frightened face, and he left her without waiting for an answer.

When the satin slippers were worn through the fiddles stopped, and the negro boys set the table. Michael was placed next to the eldest sister, and opposite to the youngest.

They gave him the most exquisite dishes to eat, and the most delicate wines to drink; and in order to turn his head more completely, compliments and flattery were heaped on him from every side.

But he took care not to be intoxicated, either by the wine or the compliments.

XV

At last the eldest sister made a sign, and one of the black pages brought in a large golden cup.

"The enchanted castle has no more secrets for you," she said to the Star Gazer. "Let us drink to your triumph."

He cast a lingering glance at the little Princess, and without hesitation lifted the cup.

"Don't drink!" suddenly cried out the little Princess; "I would rather marry a gardener."

And she burst into tears.

Michael flung the contents of the cup behind him, sprang over the table, and fell at Lina's feet. The rest of the princes fell likewise at the knees of the princesses, each of whom chose a husband and raised him to her side. The charm was broken.

The twelve couples embarked in the boats, which crossed back many times in order to carry over the other princes. Then they all went through the three woods, and when they had passed the door of the underground passage a great noise was heard, as if the enchanted castle was crumbling to the earth.

They went straight to the room of the Duke of Belœil, who had just awoke. Michael held in his hand the golden cup, and he revealed the secret of the holes in the shoes.

"Choose, then," said the Duke, "whichever you prefer."

"My choice is already made," replied the garden boy, and he offered his hand to the youngest Princess, who blushed and lowered her eyes.

XVI

The Princess Lina did not become a gardener's wife; on the contrary, it was the Star Gazer who became a Prince: but before the marriage ceremony the Princess insisted that her lover should tell her how he came to discover the secret.

So he showed her the two laurels which had helped him, and she, like a prudent girl, thinking they gave him too much advantage over his wife, cut them off at the root and threw them in the fire. And this is why the country girls go about singing:

"Nous n'irons plus au bois,
Les lauriers sont coupes,"

and dancing in summer by the light of the moon.

BEASTS

The Dragon of the North

(FROM *THE YELLOW FAIRY BOOK*)

Very long ago, as old people have told me, there lived a terrible monster, who came out of the North, and laid waste whole tracts of country, devouring both men and beasts; and this monster was so destructive that it was feared that unless help came no living creature would be left on the face of the earth. It had a body like an ox, and legs like a frog, two short fore-legs, and two long ones behind, and besides that it had a tail like a serpent, ten fathoms in length. When it moved it jumped like a frog, and with every spring it covered half a mile of ground. Fortunately, its habit was to remain for several years in the same place, and not to move on till the whole neighborhood was eaten up. Nothing could hunt it, because its whole body was covered with scales, which were harder than stone or metal; its two great eyes shone by night, and even by day, like the brightest lamps, and anyone who had the ill luck to look into those eyes became as it were bewitched, and was obliged to rush of his own accord into the monster's jaws. In this way the Dragon was able to feed upon both men and beasts without the least trouble to itself, as it needed not to move from the spot where it was lying. All the neighboring kings had offered rich rewards to anyone who should be able to destroy the monster, either by force or enchantment, and many had tried their luck, but all had miserably failed. Once a great forest in which the Dragon lay had been set on fire; the forest was burnt down, but the fire did not do the monster the least harm. However, there was a tradition among the wise men of the country that the Dragon might be overcome by one who possessed King Solomon's signet-ring, upon which a secret writing was engraved. This inscription would enable anyone who was wise enough to interpret it to find out how the Dragon could be destroyed. Only no one knew where the ring was hidden, nor was there any sorcerer or learned man to be found who would be able to explain the inscription.

At last a young man, with a good heart and plenty of courage, set out to search for the ring. He took his way towards the sun rising, because he knew that all the wisdom of old time comes from the East. After some years he met with a famous Eastern magician, and asked for his advice in the matter. The magician answered:

"Mortal men have but little wisdom, and can give you no help, but the birds of the air would be better guides to you if you could learn their language. I can help you to understand it if you will stay with me a few days."

The youth thankfully accepted the magician's offer, and said, "I cannot now offer you any reward for your kindness, but should my undertaking succeed your trouble shall be richly repaid."

Then the magician brewed a powerful potion out of nine sorts of herbs which he had gathered himself all alone by moonlight, and he gave the youth nine spoonfuls of it daily for three days, which made him able to understand the language of birds.

At parting the magician said to him. "If you ever find Solomon's ring and get possession of it, then come back to me, that I may explain the inscription on the ring to you, for there is no one else in the world who can do this."

From that time the youth never felt lonely as he walked along; he always had company, because he understood the language of birds; and in this way he learned many things which mere human knowledge could never have taught him. But time went on, and he heard nothing about the ring. It happened one evening, when he was hot and tired with walking, and had sat down under a tree in a forest to eat his supper, that he saw two gaily-plumaged birds, that were strange to him, sitting at the top of the tree talking to one another about him. The first bird said:

"I know that wandering fool under the tree there, who has come so far without finding what he seeks. He is trying to find King Solomon's lost ring."

The other bird answered, "He will have to seek help from the *Witch-maiden*, who will doubtless be able to put him on the right track. If she has not got the ring herself, she knows well enough who has it."

"But where is he to find the Witch-maiden?" said the first bird. "She has no settled dwelling, but is here to-day and gone to-morrow. He might as well try to catch the wind."

The other replied, "I do not know, certainly, where she is at present, but in three nights from now she will come to the spring to wash her face, as she does every month when the moon is full, in order that she may never grow old nor wrinkled, but may always keep the bloom of youth."

"Well," said the first bird, "the spring is not far from here. Shall we go and see how it is she does it?"

"Willingly, if you like," said the other.

The youth immediately resolved to follow the birds to the spring. Only two things made him uneasy: first, lest he might be asleep when the birds went, and secondly, lest he might lose sight of them, since he had not wings to carry him along so swiftly. He was too tired to keep awake all night, yet his anxiety prevented him from sleeping soundly, and when with the earliest dawn he looked up to the tree-top, he was glad to see his feathered companions still asleep with their heads under their wings. He ate his breakfast, and waited until the birds should start, but they did not leave the place all day. They hopped about from one tree to another looking for food, all day long until the evening, when they went back to their old perch to sleep. The next day the same thing happened, but on the third morning one bird said to the other, "To-day we must go to the spring to see the Witch-maiden wash her face." They remained on the tree till noon; then they flew away and went towards the south. The young man's heart beat with anxiety lest he should lose sight of his guides, but he managed to keep the birds in view until they again perched upon a tree. The young man ran after them until he was quite exhausted and out of breath, and after three short rests the birds at length reached a small open space in the forest, on the edge of which they placed themselves on the top of a high tree. When the youth had overtaken them, he saw that there was a clear spring in the middle of the space. He sat down at the foot of the tree upon which the birds were perched, and listened attentively to what they were saying to each other.

"The sun is not down yet," said the first bird; "we must wait yet awhile till the moon rises and the maiden comes to the spring. Do you think she will see that young man sitting under the tree?"

"Nothing is likely to escape her eyes, certainly not a young man", said the other bird. "Will the youth have the sense not to let himself be caught in her toils?"

"We will wait," said the first bird, "and see how they get on together."

The evening light had quite faded, and the full moon was already shining down upon the forest, when the young man heard a slight rustling sound.

After a few moments there came out of the forest a maiden, gliding over the grass so lightly that her feet seemed scarcely to touch the ground, and stood beside the spring. The youth could not turn away his eyes from the maiden, for he had never in his life seen a woman so beautiful. Without seeming to notice anything, she went to the spring, looked up to the full moon, then knelt down and bathed her face nine times, then looked up to the moon again and walked nine times round the well, and as she walked she sang this song:

> "Full-faced moon with light unshaded,
> Let my beauty ne'er be faded.
> Never let my cheek grow pale!
> While the moon is waning nightly,
> May the maiden bloom more brightly,
> May her freshness never fail!"

Then she dried her face with her long hair, and was about to go away, when her eye suddenly fell upon the spot where the young man was sitting, and she turned towards the tree. The youth rose and stood waiting. Then the maiden said, "You ought to have a heavy punishment because you have presumed to watch my secret doings in the moonlight. But I will forgive you this time, because you are a stranger and knew no better. But you must tell me truly who you are and how you came to this place, where no mortal has ever set foot before."

The youth answered humbly: "Forgive me, beautiful maiden, if I have unintentionally offended you. I chanced to come here after long wandering, and found a good place to sleep under this tree. At your coming I did not know what to do, but stayed where I was, because I thought my silent watching could not offend you."

The maiden answered kindly, "Come and spend this night with us. You will sleep better on a pillow than on damp moss."

The youth hesitated for a little, but presently he heard the birds saying from the top of the tree, "Go where she calls you, but take care to give no blood, or you will sell your soul." So the youth went with her, and soon they reached a beautiful garden, where stood a splendid house, which glittered in the moonlight as if it was all built out of gold and silver. When the youth entered he found many splendid chambers, each one finer than the last. Hundreds of tapers burnt upon golden candlesticks, and shed a light like the brightest day. At length they reached a chamber where a table was spread with the most costly dishes. At the table were placed two chairs, one of silver, the other of gold. The maiden seated herself upon the golden chair, and offered the silver one to her companion. They were served by maidens dressed in white, whose feet made no sound as they moved about, and not a word was spoken during the meal. Afterwards the youth and the Witch-maiden conversed pleasantly together, until a woman, dressed in red, came in to remind them that it was bedtime. The youth was now shown into another room, containing a silken bed with down cushions, where he slept delightfully, yet he seemed to hear a voice near his bed which repeated to him, "Remember to give no blood!"

The next morning the maiden asked him whether he would not like to stay with her always in this beautiful place, and as he did not answer immediately, she continued: "You see how I always remain young and beautiful, and I am under no one's orders, but can do just what I like, so that I have never thought of marrying before. But from the moment I saw you I took a fancy to you, so if you agree, we might be married and might live together like princes, because I have great riches."

The youth could not but be tempted with the beautiful maiden's offer, but he remembered how the birds had called her the witch, and their warning always sounded in his ears. Therefore he answered cautiously, "Do not be angry, dear maiden, if I do not decide immediately on this important matter. Give me a few days to consider before we come to an understanding."

"Why not?" answered the maiden. "Take some weeks to consider if you like, and take counsel with your own heart." And to make the time pass pleasantly, she took the youth over every part of her beautiful dwelling, and showed him all her splendid treasures. But these treasures were all produced by enchantment, for the maiden could make anything she wished appear by the help of King Solomon's signet ring; only none of these things remained fixed; they passed away like the wind without leaving a trace behind. But the youth did not know this; he thought they were all real.

One day the maiden took him into a secret chamber, where a little gold box was standing on a silver table. Pointing to the box, she said, "Here is my greatest treasure, whose like is not to be found in the whole world. It is a precious gold ring. When you marry me, I will give you this ring as a marriage gift, and it will make you the happiest of mortal men. But in order that our love may last for ever, you must give me for the ring three drops of blood from the little finger of your left hand."

When the youth heard these words a cold shudder ran over him, for he remembered that his soul was at stake. He was cunning enough, however, to conceal his feelings and to make no direct answer, but he only asked the maiden, as if carelessly, what was remarkable about the ring?

She answered, "No mortal is able entirely to understand the power of this ring, because no one thoroughly understands the secret signs engraved upon it. But even with my half-knowledge I can work great wonders. If I put the ring upon the little finger of my left hand, then I can fly like a bird through the air wherever I wish to go. If I put it on the third finger of my left hand I am invisible, and I can see everything that passes around me, though no one can see me. If I put the ring upon the middle finger of my left hand, then neither fire nor water nor any sharp weapon can hurt me. If I put it on the forefinger of my left hand, then I can with its help produce whatever I wish. I can in a single moment build houses or anything I desire. Finally, as long as I wear the ring on the thumb of my left hand, that hand is so strong that it can break down rocks and walls. Besides these, the ring has other secret signs which, as I said, no one can understand. No doubt it contains secrets of great importance. The ring formerly belonged to King Solomon, the wisest of kings, during whose reign the wisest men lived. But it is not known whether this ring was ever made by mortal hands: it is supposed that an angel gave it to the wise King."

When the youth heard all this he determined to try and get possession of the ring, though he did not quite believe in all its wonderful gifts. He wished the maiden would let him have it in his hand, but he did not quite like to ask her to do so, and after a while she put it back into the box. A few days after they were again speaking of the magic ring, and the youth said, "I do not think it possible that the ring can have all the power you say it has."

Then the maiden opened the box and took the ring out, and it glittered as she held it like the clearest sunbeam. She put it on the middle finger of her left hand, and told the youth to take a knife and try as hard as he could to cut her with it, for he would not be able to hurt her. He was unwilling at first, but the maiden insisted. Then he tried, at first only in play, and then seriously, to strike her with the knife, but an invisible wall of iron seemed to be between them, and the maiden stood before him laughing and unhurt. Then she put the ring on her third finger, and in an instant she had vanished from his eyes. Presently she was beside him again laughing, and holding the ring between her fingers.

"Do let me try," said the youth, "whether I can do these wonderful things."

The maiden, suspecting no treachery, gave him the magic ring.

The youth pretended to have forgotten what to do, and asked what finger he must put the ring on so that no sharp weapon could hurt him?

"Oh, the middle finger of your left hand," the maiden answered, laughing.

She took the knife and tried to strike the youth, and he even tried to cut himself with it, but found it impossible. Then he asked the maiden to show him how to split stones and rocks with the help of the ring. So she led him into a courtyard where stood a great boulder-stone. "Now," she said, "put the ring upon the thumb of your left hand, and you will see how strong that hand has become." The youth did so, and found to his astonishment that with a single blow of his fist the stone flew into a thousand pieces. Then the youth bethought him that he who does not use his luck when he has it is a fool, and that this was a chance which once lost might never return. So while they stood laughing at the shattered stone he placed the ring, as if in play, upon the third finger of his left hand.

"Now," said the maiden, "you are invisible to me until you take the ring off again."

But the youth had no mind to do that; on the contrary, he went farther off, then put the ring on the little finger of his left hand, and soared into the air like a bird.

When the maiden saw him flying away she thought at first that he was still in play, and cried, "Come back, friend, for now you see I have told you the truth." But the young man never came back.

Then the maiden saw she was deceived, and bitterly repented that she had ever trusted him with the ring.

The young man never halted in his flight until he reached the dwelling of the wise magician who had taught him the speech of birds. The magician was delighted to find that his search had been successful, and at once set to work to interpret the secret signs engraved upon the ring, but it took him seven weeks to make them out clearly. Then he gave the youth the following instructions how to overcome the Dragon of the North: "You must have an iron horse cast, which must have little wheels under each foot. You must also be armed with a spear two fathoms long, which you will be able to wield by means of the magic ring upon your left thumb. The spear must be as thick in the middle as a large tree, and both its ends must be sharp. In the middle of the spear you must have two strong chains ten fathoms in length. As soon as the Dragon has made himself fast to the spear, which you must thrust through his jaws, you must spring quickly from the iron horse and fasten the ends of the chains firmly to the ground with iron stakes, so that he cannot get away from them. After two or three days the monster's strength will be so far exhausted that you will be able to come near him. Then you can put Solomon's ring upon your left thumb and give him the finishing stroke, but keep the ring on your third finger until you have come close to him, so that the monster cannot see you, else he might strike you dead with his long tail. But when all is done, take care you do not lose the ring, and that no one takes it from you by cunning."

The young man thanked the magician for his directions, and promised, should they succeed, to reward him. But the magician answered, "I have profited so much by the wisdom the ring has taught me that I desire no other reward." Then they parted, and the youth quickly flew home through the air. After remaining in his own home for some weeks, he heard people say that the terrible Dragon of the North was not far off, and might shortly be expected in the country. The King announced publicly that he would give his daughter in marriage, as well as a large part of his kingdom, to whosoever should free the country from the monster. The youth then went to the King and told him that he had good hopes of subduing the Dragon, if the King would grant him all he desired for the purpose. The King willingly agreed, and the iron horse, the great spear, and the chains were all prepared as the youth requested. When all was ready, it was found that the iron horse was so heavy that a hundred men could not move it from the spot, so the youth found there was nothing for it but to move it with his own strength by means of the magic ring. The Dragon was now so near that in a couple of springs he would be over the frontier. The youth now began to consider how he should act, for if he had to push the iron horse from behind he could not ride upon it as the sorcerer had said he must. But a raven unexpectedly gave him this advice: "Ride upon the horse, and push the spear against the ground, as if you were pushing off a boat from the land." The youth did so, and found that in this way he could easily move forwards. The Dragon had his monstrous jaws wide open, all ready for his expected prey. A few paces nearer, and man and horse would have been swallowed up by them! The youth trembled with horror, and his blood ran cold, yet he did not lose his courage; but, holding the iron spear upright in his hand, he brought it down with all his might right through the monster's lower jaw. Then quick as lightning he sprang from his horse before the Dragon had time to shut his mouth. A fearful clap like thunder, which could be heard for miles around, now warned him that the Dragon's jaws had closed upon the spear. When the youth turned round he saw the point of the spear sticking up high above the Dragon's upper jaw, and knew that the other end must be fastened firmly to the ground; but the Dragon had got his teeth fixed in the iron horse, which was now useless. The youth now hastened to fasten down the chains to the ground by means of the enormous iron pegs which he had provided. The death struggle of the monster lasted three days and three nights; in his writhing he beat his tail so violently against the ground, that at ten miles' distance the earth trembled as if with an earthquake. When he at length lost power to move his tail, the youth with the help of the ring took up a stone which twenty ordinary men could not have moved, and beat the Dragon so hard about the head with it that very soon the monster lay lifeless before him.

You can fancy how great was the rejoicing when the news was spread abroad that the terrible monster was dead. His conqueror was received into the city with as much pomp as if he had been the mightiest of kings. The old King did not need to urge his daughter to marry the slayer of the Dragon; he found her already willing to bestow her hand upon this hero, who had done all alone what whole armies had tried in vain to do. In a few days a magnificent wedding was celebrated, at which the rejoicings lasted four whole weeks, for all the neighboring kings had met together to thank the man who had freed the world from their common enemy. But everyone forgot amid the general joy that they ought to have buried the Dragon's monstrous body, for it began now to have such a bad smell that no one could live in the neighborhood, and before long the whole air was poisoned, and a pestilence broke out which destroyed many hundreds of people. In this distress, the King's son-in-law resolved to seek help once more from the Eastern magician, to whom he at once traveled through the air like a bird by the help of the ring. But there is a proverb which says that ill-gotten gains never prosper, and the Prince found that the stolen ring brought him ill-luck after all. The Witch-maiden had never rested night nor day until she had found out where the ring was. As soon as she had discovered by means of magical arts that the Prince in the form of a bird was on his way to the Eastern magician, she changed herself into an eagle and watched in the air until the bird she was waiting for came in sight, for she knew him at once by the ring which was hung round his neck by a ribbon. Then the eagle pounced upon the bird, and the moment she seized him in her talons she tore the ring from his neck before the man in bird's shape had time to prevent her. Then the eagle flew down to the earth with her prey, and the two stood face to face once more in human form.

"Now, villain, you are in my power!" cried the Witch-maiden. "I favored you with my love, and you repaid me with treachery and theft. You stole my most precious jewel from me, and do you expect to live happily as the King's son-in-law? Now the tables are turned; you are in my power, and I will be revenged on you for your crimes."

"Forgive me! forgive me!" cried the Prince; "I know too well how deeply I have wronged you, and most heartily do I repent it."

The maiden answered, "Your prayers and your repentance come too late, and if I were to spare you everyone would think me a fool. You have doubly wronged me; first you scorned my love, and then you stole my ring, and you must bear the punishment."

With these words she put the ring upon her left thumb, lifted the young man with one hand, and walked away with him under her arm. This time she did not take him to a splendid palace, but to a deep cave in a rock, where there were chains hanging from the wall. The maiden now chained the young man's hands and feet so that he could not escape; then she said in an angry voice, "Here you shall remain chained up until you die. I will bring you every day enough food to prevent you dying of hunger, but you need never hope for freedom any more." With these words she left him.

The old King and his daughter waited anxiously for many weeks for the Prince's return, but no news of him arrived. The King's daughter often dreamed that her husband was going through some great suffering: she therefore begged her father to summon all the enchanters and magicians, that they might try to find out where the Prince was and how he could be set free. But the magicians, with all their arts, could find out nothing, except that he was still living and undergoing great suffering; but none could tell where he was to be found. At last a celebrated magician from Finland was brought before the King, who had found out that the King's son-in-law was imprisoned in the East, not by men, but by some more powerful being. The King now sent messengers to the East to look for his son-in-law, and they by good luck met with the old magician who had interpreted the signs on King Solomon's ring, and thus was possessed of more wisdom than anyone else in the world. The magician soon found out what he wished to know, and pointed out the place where the Prince was imprisoned, but said: "He is kept there by enchantment, and cannot be set free without my help. I will therefore go with you myself."

So they all set out, guided by birds, and after some days came to the cave where the unfortunate Prince had been chained up for nearly seven years. He recognized the magician immediately, but the old man did not know him, he had grown so thin. However, he undid the chains by the help of magic, and took care of the Prince until he recovered and became strong enough to travel. When he reached home he found that the old King had died that morning, so that he was now raised to the throne. And now after his long suffering came prosperity, which lasted to the end of his life; but he never got back the magic ring, nor has it ever again been seen by mortal eyes.

Now, if *you* had been the Prince, would you not rather have stayed with the pretty witch-maiden?

The White Cat

(FROM *THE BLUE FAIRY BOOK*)

Once upon a time there was a King who had three sons, who were all so clever and brave that he began to be afraid that they would want to reign over the kingdom before he was dead. Now the King, though he felt that he was growing old, did not at all wish to give up the government of his kingdom while he could still manage it very well, so he thought the best way to live in peace would be to divert the minds of his sons by promises which he could always get out of when the time came for keeping them.

So he sent for them all, and, after speaking to them kindly, he added:

"You will quite agree with me, my dear children, that my great age makes it impossible for me to look after my affairs of state as carefully as I once did.

I begin to fear that this may affect the welfare of my subjects, therefore I wish that one of you should succeed to my crown; but in return for such a gift as this it is only right that you should do something for me. Now, as I think of retiring into the country, it seems to me that a pretty, lively, faithful little dog would be very good company for me; so, without any regard for your ages, I promise that the one who brings me the most beautiful little dog shall succeed me at once."

The three Princes were greatly surprised by their father's sudden fancy for a little dog, but as it gave the two younger ones a chance they would not otherwise have had of being king, and as the eldest was too polite to make any objection, they accepted the commission with pleasure. They bade farewell to the King, who gave them presents of silver and precious stones, and appointed to meet them at the same hour, in the same place, after a year had passed, to see the little dogs they had brought for him.

Then they went together to a castle which was about a league from the city, accompanied by all their particular friends, to whom they gave a grand banquet, and the three brothers promised to be friends always, to share whatever good fortune befell them, and not to be parted by any envy or jealousy; and so they set out, agreeing to meet at the same castle at the appointed time, to present themselves before the King together. Each one took a different road, and the two eldest met with many adventures; but it is about the youngest that you are going to hear. He was young, and gay, and handsome, and knew everything that a prince ought to know; and as for his courage, there was simply no end to it.

Hardly a day passed without his buying several dogs—big and little, greyhounds, mastiffs, spaniels, and lapdogs. As soon as he had bought a pretty one he was sure to see a still prettier, and then he had to get rid of all the others and buy that one, as, being alone, he found it impossible to take thirty or forty thousand dogs about with him. He journeyed from day to day, not knowing where he was going, until at last, just at nightfall, he reached a great, gloomy forest. He did not know his way, and, to make matters worse, it began to thunder, and the rain poured down. He took the first path he could find, and after walking for a long time he fancied he saw a faint light, and began to hope that he was coming to some cottage where he might find shelter for the night. At length, guided by the light, he reached the door of the most splendid castle he could have imagined. This door was of gold covered with carbuncles, and it was the pure red light which shone from them that had shown him the way through the forest. The walls were of the finest porcelain in all the most delicate colors, and the Prince saw that all the stories he had ever read were pictured upon them; but as he was terribly wet, and the rain still fell in torrents, he could not stay to look about any more, but came back to the golden door. There he saw a deer's foot hanging by a chain of diamonds, and he began to wonder who could live in this magnificent castle.

"They must feel very secure against robbers," he said to himself. "What is to hinder anyone from cutting off that chain and digging out those carbuncles, and making himself rich for life?"

He pulled the deer's foot, and immediately a silver bell sounded and the door flew open, but the Prince could see nothing but numbers of hands in the air, each holding a torch. He was so much surprised that he stood quite still, until he felt himself pushed forward by other hands, so that, though he was somewhat uneasy, he could not help going on. With his hand on his sword, to be prepared for whatever might happen, he entered a hall paved with lapis-lazuli, while two lovely voices sang:

> "The hands you see floating above
> Will swiftly your bidding obey;
> If your heart dreads not conquering Love,
> In this place you may fearlessly stay."

The Prince could not believe that any danger threatened him when he was welcomed in this way, so, guided by the mysterious hands, he went toward a door of coral, which opened of its own accord, and he found himself in a vast hall of mother-of-pearl, out of which opened a number of other rooms, glittering with thousands of lights, and full of such beautiful pictures and precious things that the Prince felt quite bewildered. After passing through sixty rooms the hands that conducted him stopped, and the Prince saw a most comfortable-looking arm-chair drawn up close to the chimney-corner; at the same moment the fire lighted itself, and the pretty, soft, clever hands took off the Prince's wet, muddy clothes, and presented him with fresh ones made of the richest stuffs, all embroidered with gold and emeralds. He could not help admiring everything he saw, and the deft way in which the hands waited on him, though they sometimes appeared so suddenly that they made him jump.

When he was quite ready—and I can assure you that he looked very different from the wet and weary Prince who had stood outside in the rain, and pulled the deer's foot—the hands led him to a splendid room, upon the walls of which were painted the histories of Puss in Boots and a number of other famous cats. The table was laid for supper with two golden plates, and golden spoons and forks, and the sideboard was covered with dishes and glasses of crystal set with precious stones. The Prince was wondering who the second place could be for, when suddenly in came about a dozen cats carrying guitars and rolls of music, who took their places at one end of the room, and under the direction of a cat who beat time with a roll of paper began to mew in every imaginable key, and to draw their claws across the strings of the guitars, making the strangest kind of music that could be heard. The Prince hastily stopped up his ears, but even then the sight of these comical musicians sent him into fits of laughter.

"What funny thing shall I see next?" he said to himself, and instantly the door opened, and in came a tiny figure covered by a long black veil. It was conducted by two cats wearing black mantles and carrying swords, and a large party of cats followed, who brought in cages full of rats and mice.

The Prince was so much astonished that he thought he must be dreaming, but the little figure came up to him and threw back its veil, and he saw that it was the loveliest little white cat it is possible to imagine. She looked very young and very sad, and in a sweet little voice that went straight to his heart she said to the Prince:

"King's son, you are welcome; the Queen of the Cats is glad to see you."

"Lady Cat," replied the Prince, "I thank you for receiving me so kindly, but surely you are no ordinary pussy-cat? Indeed, the way you speak and the magnificence of your castle prove it plainly."

"King's son," said the White Cat, "I beg you to spare me these compliments, for I am not used to them. But now," she added, "let supper be served, and let the musicians be silent, as the Prince does not understand what they are saying."

So the mysterious hands began to bring in the supper, and first they put on the table two dishes, one containing stewed pigeons and the other a fricassee of fat mice. The sight of the latter made the Prince feel as if he could not enjoy his supper at all; but the White Cat, seeing this, assured him that the dishes intended for him were prepared in a separate kitchen, and he might be quite certain that they contained neither rats nor mice; and the Prince felt so sure that she would not deceive him that he had no more hesitation in beginning. Presently he noticed that on the little paw that was next him the White Cat wore a bracelet containing a portrait, and he begged to be allowed to look at it. To his great surprise he found it represented an extremely handsome young man, who was so like himself that it might have been his own portrait! The White Cat sighed as he looked at it, and seemed sadder than ever, and the Prince dared not ask any questions for fear of displeasing her; so he began to talk about other things, and found that she was interested in all the subjects he cared for himself, and seemed to know quite well what was going on in the world. After supper they went into another room, which was fitted up as a theater, and the cats acted and danced for their amusement, and then the White Cat said good-night to him, and the hands conducted him into a room he had not seen before, hung with tapestry worked with butterflies' wings of every color; there were mirrors that reached from the ceiling to the floor, and a little white bed with curtains of gauze tied up with ribbons. The Prince went to bed in silence, as he did not quite know how to begin a conversation with the hands that waited on him, and in the morning he was awakened by a noise and confusion outside of his window, and the hands came and quickly dressed him in hunting costume. When he looked out all the cats were assembled in the courtyard, some leading greyhounds, some blowing horns, for the White Cat was going out hunting. The hands led a wooden horse up to the Prince, and seemed to expect him to mount it, at which he was very indignant; but it was no use for him to object, for he speedily found himself upon its back, and it pranced gaily off with him.

The White Cat herself was riding a monkey, which climbed even up to the eagles' nests when she had a fancy for the young eaglets. Never was there a pleasanter hunting party, and when they returned to the castle the Prince and the White Cat supped together as before, but when they had finished she offered him a crystal goblet, which must have contained a magic draught, for, as soon as he had swallowed its contents, he forgot everything, even the little dog that he was seeking for the King, and only thought how happy he was to be with the White Cat! And so the days passed, in every kind of amusement, until the year was nearly gone. The Prince had forgotten all about meeting his brothers: he did not even know what country he belonged to; but the White Cat knew when he ought to go back, and one day she said to him:

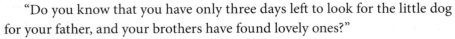

"Do you know that you have only three days left to look for the little dog for your father, and your brothers have found lovely ones?"

Then the Prince suddenly recovered his memory, and cried:

"What can have made me forget such an important thing? My whole fortune depends upon it; and even if I could in such a short time find a dog pretty enough to gain me a kingdom, where should I find a horse who would carry me all that way in three days?" And he began to be very vexed. But the White Cat said to him: "King's son, do not trouble yourself; I am your friend, and will make everything easy for you. You can still stay here for a day, as the good wooden horse can take you to your country in twelve hours."

"I thank you, beautiful Cat," said the Prince; "but what good will it do me to get back if I have not a dog to take to my father?"

"See here," answered the White Cat, holding up an acorn; "there is a prettier one in this than in the Dogstar!"

"Oh! White Cat dear," said the Prince, "how unkind you are to laugh at me now!"

"Only listen," she said, holding the acorn to his ear.

And inside it he distinctly heard a tiny voice say: "Bow-wow!"

The Prince was delighted, for a dog that can be shut up in an acorn must be very small indeed. He wanted to take it out and look at it, but the White Cat said it would be better not to open the acorn till he was before the King, in case the tiny dog should be cold on the journey. He thanked her a thousand times, and said good-bye quite sadly when the time came for him to set out.

"The days have passed so quickly with you," he said, "I only wish I could take you with me now."

But the White Cat shook her head and sighed deeply in answer.

After all the Prince was the first to arrive at the castle where he had agreed to meet his brothers, but they came soon after, and stared in amazement when they saw the wooden horse in the courtyard jumping like a hunter.

The Prince met them joyfully, and they began to tell him all their adventures; but he managed to hide from them what he had been doing, and even led them to think that a turnspit dog which he had with him was the one he was bringing for the King. Fond as they all were of one another, the two eldest could not help being glad to think that their dogs certainly had a better chance. The next morning they started in the same chariot. The elder brothers carried in baskets two such tiny, fragile dogs that they

438

hardly dared to touch them. As for the turnspit, he ran after the chariot, and got so covered with mud that one could hardly see what he was like at all. When they reached the palace everyone crowded round to welcome them as they went into the King's great hall; and when the two brothers presented their little dogs nobody could decide which was the prettier. They were already arranging between themselves to share the kingdom equally, when the youngest stepped forward, drawing from his pocket the acorn the White Cat had given him. He opened it quickly, and there upon a white cushion they saw a dog so small that it could easily have been put through a ring. The Prince laid it upon the ground, and it got up at once and began to dance. The King did not know what to say, for it was impossible that anything could be prettier than this little creature. Nevertheless, as he was in no hurry to part with his crown, he told his sons that, as they had been so successful the first time, he would ask them to go once again, and seek by land and sea for a piece of muslin so fine that it could be drawn through the eye of a needle. The brothers were not very willing to set out again, but the two eldest consented because it gave them another chance, and they started as before. The youngest again mounted the wooden horse, and rode back at full speed to his beloved White Cat. Every door of the castle stood wide open, and every window and turret was illuminated, so it looked more wonderful than before. The hands hastened to meet him, and led the wooden horse off to the stable, while he hurried in to find the White Cat. She was asleep in a little basket on a white satin cushion, but she very soon started up when she heard the Prince, and was overjoyed at seeing him once more.

"How could I hope that you would come back to me King's son?" she said. And then he stroked and petted her, and told her of his successful journey, and how he had come back to ask her help, as he believed that it was impossible to find what the King demanded. The White Cat looked serious, and said she must think what was to be done, but that, luckily, there were some cats in the castle who could spin very well, and if anybody could manage it they could, and she would set them the task herself.

And then the hands appeared carrying torches, and conducted the Prince and the White Cat to a long gallery which overlooked the river, from the windows of which they saw a magnificent display of fireworks of all sorts; after which they had supper, which the Prince liked even better than the fireworks, for it was very late, and he was hungry after his long ride.

And so the days passed quickly as before; it was impossible to feel dull with the White Cat, and she had quite a talent for inventing new amusements— indeed, she was cleverer than a cat has any right to be. But when the Prince asked her how it was that she was so wise, she only said:

"King's son, do not ask me; guess what you please. I may not tell you anything."

The Prince was so happy that he did not trouble himself at all about the time, but presently the White Cat told him that the year was gone, and that he need not be at all anxious about the piece of muslin, as they had made it very well.

"This time," she added, "I can give you a suitable escort"; and on looking out into the courtyard the Prince saw a superb chariot of burnished gold, enameled in flame color with a thousand different devices. It was drawn by twelve snow-white horses, harnessed four abreast; their trappings were flame-colored velvet, embroidered with diamonds. A hundred chariots followed, each drawn by eight horses, and filled with officers in splendid uniforms, and a thousand guards surrounded the procession. "Go!" said the White Cat, "and when you appear before the King in such state he surely will not refuse you the crown which you deserve. Take this walnut, but do not open it until you are before him, then you will find in it the piece of stuff you asked me for."

"Lovely Blanchette," said the Prince, "how can I thank you properly for all your kindness to me? Only tell me that you wish it, and I will give up for ever all thought of being king, and will stay here with you always."

"King's son," she replied, "it shows the goodness of your heart that you should care so much for a little white cat, who is good for nothing but to catch mice; but you must not stay."

So the Prince kissed her little paw and set out. You can imagine how fast he traveled when I tell you that they reached the King's palace in just half the time it had taken the wooden horse to get there. This time the Prince was so late that he did not try to meet his brothers at their castle, so they thought he could not be coming, and were rather glad of it, and displayed their pieces of muslin to the King proudly, feeling sure of success. And indeed the stuff was very fine, and would go through the eye of a very large needle; but the King, who was only too glad to make a difficulty, sent for a particular needle, which was kept among the Crown jewels, and had such a small eye that everybody saw at once that it was impossible that the muslin should pass through it. The Princes were angry, and were beginning to complain that it was a trick, when suddenly the trumpets sounded and the youngest Prince came in. His father and brothers were quite astonished at his magnificence, and after he had greeted them he took the walnut from his pocket and opened it, fully expecting to find the piece of muslin, but instead there was only a hazel-nut. He cracked it, and there lay a cherry-stone. Everybody was looking on, and the King was chuckling to himself at the idea of finding the piece of muslin in a nutshell.

However, the Prince cracked the cherry-stone, but everyone laughed when he saw it contained only its own kernel. He opened that and found a grain of wheat, and in that was a millet seed. Then he himself began to wonder, and muttered softly:

"White Cat, White Cat, are you making fun of me?"

In an instant he felt a cat's claw give his hand quite a sharp scratch, and hoping that it was meant as an encouragement he opened the millet seed, and drew out of it a piece of muslin four hundred ells long, woven with the loveliest colors and most wonderful patterns; and when the needle was brought it went through the eye six times with the greatest ease! The King turned pale, and the other Princes stood silent and sorrowful, for nobody could deny that this was the most marvelous piece of muslin that was to be found in the world.

Presently the King turned to his sons, and said, with a deep sigh:

"Nothing could console me more in my old age than to realize your willingness to gratify my wishes. Go then once more, and whoever at the end of a year can bring back the loveliest princess shall be married to her, and shall, without further delay, receive the crown, for my successor must certainly be married." The Prince considered that he had earned the kingdom fairly twice over but still he was too well bred to argue about it, so he just went back to his gorgeous chariot, and, surrounded by his escort, returned to the White Cat faster than he had come. This time she was expecting him, the path was strewn with flowers, and a thousand braziers were burning scented woods which perfumed the air. Seated in a gallery from which she could see his arrival, the White Cat waited for him. "Well, King's son," she said, "here you are once more, without a crown." "Madam," said he, "thanks to your generosity I have earned one twice over; but the fact is that my father is so loth to part with it that it would be no pleasure to me to take it."

"Never mind," she answered, "it's just as well to try and deserve it. As you must take back a lovely princess with you next time I will be on the look-out for one for you. In the meantime let us enjoy ourselves; to-night I have ordered a battle between my cats and the river rats on purpose to amuse you." So this year slipped away even more pleasantly than the preceding ones. Sometimes the Prince could not help asking the White Cat how it was she could talk.

"Perhaps you are a fairy," he said. "Or has some enchanter changed you into a cat?"

But she only gave him answers that told him nothing. Days go by so quickly when one is very happy that it is certain the Prince would never have thought of its being time to go back, when one evening as they sat together the White Cat said to him that if he wanted to take a lovely princess home with him the next day he must be prepared to do what she told him.

"Take this sword," she said, "and cut off my head!"

"I!" cried the Prince, "I cut off your head! Blanchette darling, how could I do it?"

"I entreat you to do as I tell you, King's son," she replied.

The tears came into the Prince's eyes as he begged her to ask him anything but that—to set him any task she pleased as a proof of his devotion, but to spare him the grief of killing his dear Pussy. But nothing he could say altered her determination, and at last he drew his sword, and desperately, with a trembling hand, cut off the little white head. But imagine his astonishment and delight when suddenly a lovely princess stood before him, and, while he was still speechless with amazement, the door opened and a goodly company of knights and ladies entered, each carrying a cat's skin! They hastened with every sign of joy to the Princess, kissing her hand and congratulating her on being once more restored to her natural shape. She received them graciously, but after a few minutes begged that they would leave her alone with the Prince, to whom she said:

"You see, Prince, that you were right in supposing me to be no ordinary cat. My father reigned over six kingdoms. The Queen, my mother, whom he loved dearly, had a passion for traveling and exploring, and when I was only a few weeks old she obtained his permission to visit a certain mountain of which she had heard many marvelous tales, and set out, taking with her a number of her attendants. On the way they had to pass near an old castle belonging to the fairies. Nobody had ever been into it, but it was reported to be full of the most wonderful things, and my mother remembered to have heard that the fairies had in their garden such fruits as were to be seen and tasted nowhere else. She began to wish to try them for herself, and turned her steps in the direction of the garden. On arriving at the door, which blazed with gold and jewels, she ordered her servants to knock loudly, but it was useless; it seemed as if all the inhabitants of the castle must be asleep or dead. Now the more difficult it became to obtain the fruit, the more the Queen was determined that have it she would. So she ordered that they should bring ladders, and get over the wall into the garden; but though the wall did not look very high, and they tied the ladders together to make them very long, it was quite impossible to get to the top.

"The Queen was in despair, but as night was coming on she ordered that they should encamp just where they were, and went to bed herself, feeling quite ill, she was so disappointed. In the middle of the night she was suddenly awakened, and saw to her surprise a tiny, ugly old woman seated by her bedside, who said to her:

" 'I must say that we consider it somewhat troublesome of your Majesty to insist upon tasting our fruit; but to save you annoyance, my sisters and I will consent to give you as much as you can carry away, on one condition—that is, that you shall give us your little daughter to bring up as our own.'

" 'Ah! my dear madam,' cried the Queen, 'is there nothing else that you will take for the fruit? I will give you my kingdoms willingly.'

" 'No,' replied the old fairy, 'we will have nothing but your little daughter. She shall be as happy as the day is long, and we will give her everything that is worth having in fairy-land, but you must not see her again until she is married.'

" 'Though it is a hard condition,' said the Queen, 'I consent, for I shall certainly die if I do not taste the fruit, and so I should lose my little daughter either way.'

"So the old fairy led her into the castle, and, though it was still the middle of the night, the Queen could see plainly that it was far more beautiful than she had been told, which you can easily believe, Prince," said the White Cat, "when I tell you that it was this castle that we are now in. 'Will you gather the fruit yourself, Queen?' said the old fairy, 'or shall I call it to come to you?'

" 'I beg you to let me see it come when it is called,' cried the Queen; 'that will be something quite new.' The old fairy whistled twice, then she cried:

" 'Apricots, peaches, nectarines, cherries, plums, pears, melons, grapes, apples, oranges, lemons, gooseberries, strawberries, raspberries, come!'

"And in an instant they came tumbling in one over another, and yet they were neither dusty nor spoilt, and the Queen found them quite as good as she had fancied them. You see they grew upon fairy trees.

"The old fairy gave her golden baskets in which to take the fruit away, and it was as much as four hundred mules could carry. Then she reminded the Queen of her agreement, and led her back to the camp, and next morning she went back to her kingdom, but before she had gone very far she began to repent of her bargain, and when the King came out to meet her she looked so sad that he guessed that something had happened, and asked what was the matter. At first the Queen was afraid to tell him, but when, as soon as they reached the palace, five frightful little dwarfs were sent by the fairies to fetch me, she was obliged to confess what she had promised. The King was very angry, and had the Queen and myself shut up in a great tower and safely guarded, and drove the little dwarfs out of his kingdom; but the fairies sent a great dragon who ate up all the people he met, and whose breath burnt up everything as he passed through the country; and at last, after trying in vain to rid himself of this monster, the King, to save his subjects, was obliged to consent that I should be given up to the fairies. This time they came themselves to fetch me, in a chariot of pearl drawn by sea-horses, followed by the dragon, who was led with chains of diamonds. My cradle was placed between the old fairies, who loaded me with caresses, and away we whirled through the air to a tower which they had built on purpose for me. There I grew up surrounded with everything that was beautiful and rare, and learning everything that is ever taught to a princess, but without any companions but a parrot and a little dog, who could both talk; and receiving every day a visit from one of the old fairies, who came mounted upon the dragon. One day, however, as I sat at my window I saw a handsome young prince, who seemed to have been hunting in the forest which surrounded my prison, and who was standing and looking up at me. When he saw that I observed him he saluted me with great deference. You can imagine that I was delighted to have some one new to talk to, and in spite of the height of my window our conversation was prolonged till night fell, then my prince reluctantly bade me farewell. But after that he came again many times and at last I consented to marry him, but the question was how was I to escape from my tower. The fairies always supplied me with flax for my spinning, and by great diligence I made enough cord for a ladder that would reach to the foot of the tower; but, alas! just as my prince was helping me to descend it, the crossest and ugliest of the old fairies flew in. Before he had time to defend himself my unhappy lover was swallowed up by the dragon. As for me, the fairies, furious at having their plans defeated, for they intended me to marry the king of the dwarfs, and I utterly refused, changed me into a white cat. When they brought me here I found all the lords and ladies of my father's court awaiting me under the same enchantment, while the people of lesser rank had been made invisible, all but their hands.

"As they laid me under the enchantment the fairies told me all my history, for until then I had quite believed that I was their child, and warned me that my only chance of regaining my natural form was to win the love of a prince who resembled in every way my unfortunate lover."

"And you have won it, lovely Princess," interrupted the Prince.

"You are indeed wonderfully like him," resumed the Princess—"in voice, in features, and everything; and if you really love me all my troubles will be at an end."

"And mine too," cried the Prince, throwing himself at her feet, "if you will consent to marry me."

"I love you already better than anyone in the world," she said; "but now it is time to go back to your father, and we shall hear what he says about it."

So the Prince gave her his hand and led her out, and they mounted the chariot together; it was even more splendid than before, and so was the whole company. Even the horses' shoes were of rubies with diamond nails, and I suppose that is the first time such a thing was ever seen.

As the Princess was as kind and clever as she was beautiful, you may imagine what a delightful journey the Prince found it, for everything the Princess said seemed to him quite charming.

When they came near the castle where the brothers were to meet, the Princess got into a chair carried by four of the guards; it was hewn out of one splendid crystal, and had silken curtains, which she drew round her that she might not be seen.

The Prince saw his brothers walking upon the terrace, each with a lovely princess, and they came to meet him, asking if he had also found a wife. He said that he had found something much rarer—a little white cat! At which they laughed very much, and asked him if he was afraid of being eaten up by mice in the palace. And then they set out together for the town. Each prince and princess rode in a splendid carriage; the horses were decked with plumes of feathers, and glittered with gold. After them came the youngest prince, and last of all the crystal chair, at which everybody looked with admiration and curiosity. When the courtiers saw them coming they hastened to tell the King.

"Are the ladies beautiful?" he asked anxiously.

And when they answered that nobody had ever before seen such lovely princesses he seemed quite annoyed.

However, he received them graciously, but found it impossible to choose between them.

Then turning to his youngest son he said:

"Have you come back alone, after all?"

"Your Majesty," replied the Prince, "will find in that crystal chair a little white cat, which has such soft paws, and mews so prettily, that I am sure you will be charmed with it."

The King smiled, and went to draw back the curtains himself, but at a touch from the Princess the crystal shivered into a thousand splinters, and there she stood in all her beauty; her fair hair floated over her shoulders and was crowned with flowers, and her softly falling robe was of the purest white. She saluted the King gracefully, while a murmur of admiration rose from all around.

"Sire," she said, "I am not come to deprive you of the throne you fill so worthily. I have already six kingdoms, permit me to bestow one upon you, and upon each of your sons. I ask nothing but your friendship, and your consent to my marriage with your youngest son; we shall still have three kingdoms left for ourselves."

The King and all the courtiers could not conceal their joy and astonishment, and the marriage of the three Princes was celebrated at once. The festivities lasted several months, and then each king and queen departed to their own kingdom and lived happily ever after.

I Know What I Have Learned

(FROM *THE PINK FAIRY BOOK*)

There was once a man who had three daughters, and they were all married to trolls, who lived underground. One day the man thought that he would pay them a visit, and his wife gave him some dry bread to eat by the way. After he had walked some distance he grew both tired and hungry, so he sat down on the east side of a mound and began to eat his dry bread. The mound then opened, and his youngest daughter came out of it, and said, "Why, father! why are you not coming in to see me?"

"Oh," said he, "if I had known that you lived here, and had seen any entrance, I would have come in."

Then he entered the mound along with her.

The troll came home soon after this, and his wife told him that her father was come, and asked him to go and buy some beef to make broth with.

"We can get it easier than that!" said the troll.

He fixed an iron spike into one of the beams of the roof, and ran his head against this till he had knocked several large pieces off his head. He was just as well as ever after doing this, and they got their broth without further trouble.

The troll then gave the old man a sackful of money, and laden with this he betook himself homewards. When he came near his home he remembered that he had a cow about to calve, so he laid down the money on the ground, ran home as fast as he could, and asked his wife whether the cow had calved yet.

"What kind of a hurry is this to come home in?" said she. "No, the cow has not calved yet."

"Then you must come out and help me in with a sackful of money," said the man.

"A sackful of money?" cried his wife.

447

"Yes, a sackful of money," said he. "Is that so very wonderful?"

His wife did not believe very much what he told her, but she humored him, and went out with him.

When they came to the spot where he had left it there was no money there; a thief had come along and stolen it. His wife then grew angry and scolded him heartily.

"Well, well!" said he, "hang the money! I know what I have learned."

"What have you learned?" said she.

"Ah! I know that," said the man.

After some time had passed the man had a mind to visit his second eldest daughter. His wife again gave him some dry bread to eat, and when he grew tired and hungry he sat down on the east side of a mound and began to eat it. As he sat there his daughter came up out of the mound, and invited him to come inside, which he did very willingly.

Soon after this the troll came home. It was dark by that time, and his wife bade him go and buy some candles.

"Oh, we shall soon get a light," said the troll. With that he dipped his fingers into the fire, and they then gave light without being burned in the least.

The old man got two sacks of money here, and plodded away homewards with these. When he was very nearly home he again thought of the cow that was with calf, so he laid down the money, ran home, and asked his wife whether the cow had calved yet.

"Whatever is the matter with you?" said she. "You come hurrying as if the whole house was about to fall. You may set your mind at rest: the cow has not calved yet."

The man now asked her to come and help him home with the two sacks of money. She did not believe him very much, but he continued to assure her that it was quite true, till at last she gave in and went with him. When they came to the spot there had again been a thief there and taken the money. It was no wonder that the woman was angry about this, but the man only said, "Ah, if you only knew what I have learned."

A third time the man set out—to visit his eldest daughter. When he came to a mound he sat down on the east side of it and ate the dry bread which his wife had given him to take with him. The daughter then came out of the mound and invited her father to come inside.

In a little the troll came home, and his wife asked him to go and buy some fish.

"We can get them much more easily than that," said the troll. "Give me your dough trough and your ladle."

They seated themselves in the trough, and rowed out on the lake which was beside the mound. When they had got out a little way the troll said to his wife, "Are my eyes green?"

"No, not yet," said she.

He rowed on a little further and asked again, "Are my eyes not green yet?"

"Yes," said his wife, "they are green now."

Then the troll sprang into the water and ladled up so many fish that in a short time the trough could hold no more. They then rowed home again, and had a good meal off the fish.

The old man now got three sacks full of money, and set off home with them. When he was almost home the cow again came into his head, and he laid down the money. This time, however, he took his wooden shoes and laid them above the money, thinking that no one would take it after that. Then he ran home and asked his wife whether the cow had calved. It had not, and she scolded him again for behaving in this way, but in the end he persuaded her to go with him to help him with the three sacks of money.

When they came to the spot they found only the wooden shoes, for a thief had come along in the meantime and taken all the money. The woman was very angry, and broke out upon her husband; but he took it all very quietly, and only said, "Hang the money! I know what I have learned."

"What have you learned I should like to know?" said his wife.

"You will see that yet," said the man.

One day his wife took a fancy for broth, and said to him, "Oh, go to the village, and buy a piece of beef to make broth."

"There's no need of that," said he; "we can get it an easier way." With that he drove a spike into a beam, and ran his head against it, and in consequence had to lie in bed for a long time afterwards.

After he had recovered from this his wife asked him one day to go and buy candles, as they had none.

"No," he said, "there's no need for that"; and he stuck his hand into the fire. This also made him take to bed for a good while.

When he had got better again his wife one day wanted fish, and asked him to go and buy some. The man, however, wished again to show what he had learned, so he asked her to come along with him and bring her dough trough and a ladle. They both seated themselves in this, and rowed upon the lake. When they had got out a little way the man said, "Are my eyes green?"

"No," said his wife; "why should they be?"

They rowed a little further out, and he asked again, "Are my eyes not green yet?"

"What nonsense is this?" said she; "why should they be green?"

"Oh, my dear," said he, "can't you just say that they are green?"

"Very well," said she, "they are green."

As soon as he heard this he sprang out into the water with the ladle for the fishes, but he just got leave to stay there with them!

Alphege, or the Green Monkey

(FROM *THE YELLOW FAIRY BOOK*)

Many years ago there lived a King, who was twice married. His first wife, a good and beautiful woman, died at the birth of her little son, and the King her husband was so overwhelmed with grief at her loss that his only comfort was in the sight of his heir.

When the time for the young Prince's christening came the King chose as godmother a neighboring Princess, so celebrated for her wisdom and goodness that she was commonly called "the Good Queen." She named the baby Alphege, and from that moment took him to her heart.

Time wipes away the greatest griefs, and after two or three years the King married again. His second wife was a Princess of undeniable beauty, but by no means of so amiable a disposition as the first Queen. In due time a second Prince was born, and the Queen was devoured with rage at the thought that Prince Alphege came between her son and the throne. She took care however to conceal her jealous feelings from the King.

At length she could control herself no longer, so she sent a trusty servant to her old and faithful friend the Fairy of the Mountain, to beg her to devise some means by which she might get rid of her stepson.

The Fairy replied that, much as she desired to be agreeable to the Queen in every way, it was impossible for her to attempt anything against the young Prince, who was under the protection of some greater Power than her own.

The "Good Queen" on her side watched carefully over her godson. She was obliged to do so from a distance, her own country being a remote one, but she was well informed of all that went on and knew all about the Queen's wicked designs. She therefore sent the Prince a large and splendid ruby, with injunctions to wear it night and day as it would protect him from all attacks, but added that the talisman only retained its power as long as the Prince remained within his father's dominions. The Wicked Queen knowing this made every attempt to get the Prince out of the country, but her efforts failed, till one day accident did what she was unable to accomplish.

The King had an only sister who was deeply attached to him, and who was married to the sovereign of a distant country. She had always kept up a close correspondence with her brother, and the accounts she heard of Prince Alphege made her long to become acquainted with so charming a nephew. She entreated the King to allow the Prince to visit her, and after some hesitation which was overruled by his wife, he finally consented.

Prince Alphege was at this time fourteen years old, and the handsomest and most engaging youth imaginable. In his infancy he had been placed in the charge of one of the great ladies of the Court, who, according to the prevailing custom, acted first as his head nurse and then as his governess. When he outgrew her care her husband was appointed as his tutor and governor, so that he had never been separated from this excellent couple, who loved him as tenderly as they did their only daughter Zayda, and were warmly loved by him in return.

When the Prince set forth on his travels it was but natural that this devoted couple should accompany him, and accordingly he started with them and attended by a numerous retinue.

For some time he traveled through his father's dominions and all went well; but soon after passing the frontier they had to cross a desert plain under a burning sun. They were glad to take shelter under a group of trees near, and here the Prince complained of burning thirst. Luckily a tiny stream ran close by and some water was soon procured, but no sooner had he tasted it than he sprang from his carriage and disappeared in a moment. In vain did his anxious followers seek for him, he was nowhere to be found.

As they were hunting and shouting through the trees a black monkey suddenly appeared on a point of rock and said: "Poor sorrowing people, you are seeking your Prince in vain. Return to your own country and know that he will not be restored to you till you have for some time failed to recognize him."

With these words he vanished, leaving the courtiers sadly perplexed; but as all their efforts to find the Prince were useless they had no choice but to go home, bringing with them the sad news, which so greatly distressed the King that he fell ill and died not long after.

The Queen, whose ambition was boundless, was delighted to see the crown on her son's head and to have the power in her own hands. Her hard rule made her very unpopular, and it was commonly believed that she had made away with Prince Alphege. Indeed, had the King her son not been deservedly beloved a revolution would certainly have arisen.

Meantime the former governess of the unfortunate Alphege, who had lost her husband soon after the King's death, retired to her own house with her daughter, who grew up a lovely and most loveable girl, and both continued to mourn the loss of their dear Prince.

The young King was devoted to hunting, and often indulged in his favorite pastime, attended by the noblest youths in his kingdom.

One day, after a long morning's chase, he stopped to rest near a brook in the shade of a little wood, where a splendid tent had been prepared for him. Whilst at luncheon he suddenly spied a little monkey of the brightest green sitting on a tree and gazing so tenderly at him that he felt quite moved. He forbade his courtiers to frighten it, and the monkey, noticing how much attention was being paid him, sprang from bough to bough, and at length gradually approached the King, who offered him some food. The monkey took it very daintily and finally came to the table. The King took him on his knees, and, delighted with his capture, brought him home with him. He would trust no one else with its care, and the whole Court soon talked of nothing but the pretty green monkey.

One morning, as Prince Alphege's governess and her daughter were alone together, the little monkey sprang in through an open window. He had escaped from the palace, and his manners were so gentle and caressing that Zayda and her mother soon got over the first fright he had given them. He had spent some time with them and quite won their hearts by his insinuating ways, when the King discovered where he was and sent to fetch him back. But the monkey made such piteous cries, and seemed so unhappy when anyone attempted to catch him, that the two ladies begged the King to leave him a little longer with them, to which he consented.

One evening, as they sat by the fountain in the garden, the little monkey kept gazing at Zayda with such sad and loving eyes that she and her mother could not think what to make of it, and they were still more surprised when they saw big tears rolling down his cheeks.

Next day both mother and daughter were sitting in a jessamine bower in the garden, and they began to talk of the green monkey and his strange ways. The mother said, "My dear child, I can no longer hide my feelings from you. I cannot get the thought out of my mind that the green monkey is no other than our beloved Prince Alphege, transformed in this strange fashion. I know the idea sounds wild, but I cannot get it out of my heart, and it leaves me no peace."

As she spoke she glanced up, and there sat the little monkey, whose tears and gestures seemed to confirm her words.

The following night the elder lady dreamt that she saw the Good Queen, who said, "Do not weep any longer but follow my directions. Go into your garden and lift up the little marble slab at the foot of the great myrtle tree. You will find beneath it a crystal vase filled with a bright green liquid. Take it with you and place the thing which is at present most in your thoughts into a bath filled with roses and rub it well with the green liquid."

At these words the sleeper awoke, and lost no time in rising and hurrying to the garden, where she found all as the Good Queen had described. Then she hastened to rouse her daughter and together they prepared the bath, for they would not let their women know what they were about. Zayda gathered quantities of roses, and when all was ready they put the monkey into a large jasper bath, where the mother rubbed him all over with the green liquid.

Their suspense was not long, for suddenly the monkey skin dropped off, and there stood Prince Alphege, the handsomest and most charming of men. The joy of such a meeting was beyond words. After a time the ladies begged the Prince to relate his adventures, and he told them of all his sufferings in the desert when he was first transformed. His only comfort had been in visits from the Good Queen, who had at length put him in the way of meeting his brother.

Several days were spent in these interesting conversations, but at length Zayda's mother began to think of the best means for placing the Prince on the throne, which was his by right.

The Queen on her side was feeling very anxious. She had felt sure from the first that her son's pet monkey was no other than Prince Alphege, and she longed to put an end to him. Her suspicions were confirmed by the Fairy of the Mountain, and she hastened in tears to the King, her son.

"I am informed," she cried, "that some ill-disposed people have raised up an impostor in the hopes of dethroning you. You must at once have him put to death."

The King, who was very brave, assured the Queen that he would soon punish the conspirators. He made careful inquiries into the matter, and thought it hardly probable that a quiet widow and a young girl would think of attempting anything of the nature of a revolution.

He determined to go and see them, and to find out the truth for himself; so one night, without saying anything to the Queen or his ministers, he set out for the palace where the two ladies lived, attended only by a small band of followers.

The two ladies were at the moment deep in conversation with Prince Alphege, and hearing a knocking so late at night begged him to keep out of sight for a time. What was their surprise when the door was opened to see the King and his suite.

"I know," said the King, "that you are plotting against my crown and person, and I have come to have an explanation with you."

As she was about to answer Prince Alphege, who had heard all, came forward and said, "It is from me you must ask an explanation, brother." He spoke with such grace and dignity that everyone gazed at him with mute surprise.

At length the King, recovering from his astonishment at recognizing the brother who had been lost some years before, exclaimed, "Yes, you are indeed my brother, and now that I have found you, take the throne to which I have no longer a right." So saying, he respectfully kissed the Prince's hand.

Alphege threw himself into his arms, and the brothers hastened to the royal palace, where in the presence of the entire court he received the crown from his brother's hand. To clear away any possible doubt, he showed the ruby which the Good Queen had given him in his childhood. As they were gazing at it, it suddenly split with a loud noise, and at the same moment the Wicked Queen expired.

King Alphege lost no time in marrying his dear and lovely Zayda, and his joy was complete when the Good Queen appeared at his wedding. She assured him that the Fairy of the Mountain had henceforth lost all power over him, and after spending some time with the young couple, and bestowing the most costly presents on them, she retired to her own country.

King Alphege insisted on his brother sharing his throne, and they all lived to a good old age, universally beloved and admired.

The Colony of Cats

(FROM *THE CRIMSON FAIRY BOOK*)

Long, long ago, as far back as the time when animals spoke, there lived a community of cats in a deserted house they had taken possession of not far from a large town. They had everything they could possibly desire for their comfort, they were well fed and well lodged, and if by any chance an unlucky mouse was stupid enough to venture in their way, they caught it, not to eat it, but for the pure pleasure of catching it. The old people of the town related how they had heard their parents speak of a time when the whole country was so overrun with rats and mice that there was not so much as a grain of corn nor an ear of maize to be gathered in the fields; and it might be out of gratitude to the cats who had rid the country of these plagues that their descendants were allowed to live in peace. No one knows where they got the money to pay for everything, nor who paid it, for all this happened so very long ago. But one thing is certain, they were rich enough to keep a servant; for though they lived very happily together, and did not scratch nor fight more than human beings would have done, they were not clever enough to do the housework themselves, and preferred at all events to have some one to cook their meat, which they would have scorned to eat raw.

Not only were they very difficult to please about the housework, but most women quickly tired of living alone with only cats for companions, consequently they never kept a servant long; and it had become a saying in the town, when anyone found herself reduced to her last penny: "I will go and live with the cats," and so many a poor woman actually did.

Now Lizina was not happy at home, for her mother, who was a widow, was much fonder of her elder daughter; so that often the younger one fared very badly, and had not enough to eat, while the elder could have everything she desired, and if Lizina dared to complain she was certain to have a good beating.

At last the day came when she was at the end of her courage and patience, and exclaimed to her mother and sister:

"As you hate me so much you will be glad to be rid of me, so I am going to live with the cats!"

"Be off with you!" cried her mother, seizing an old broom-handle from behind the door. Poor Lizina did not wait to be told twice, but ran off at once and never stopped till she reached the door of the cats' house. Their cook had left them that very morning, with her face all scratched, the result of such a quarrel with the head of the house that he had very nearly scratched out her eyes. Lizina therefore was warmly welcomed, and she set to work at once to prepare the dinner, not without many misgivings as to the tastes of the cats, and whether she would be able to satisfy them.

Going to and fro about her work, she found herself frequently hindered by a constant succession of cats who appeared one after another in the kitchen to inspect the new servant; she had one in front of her feet, another perched on the back of her chair while she peeled the vegetables, a third sat on the table beside her, and five or six others prowled about among the pots and pans on the shelves against the wall. The air resounded with their purring, which meant that they were pleased with their new maid, but Lizina had not yet learned to understand their language, and often she did not know what they wanted her to do. However, as she was a good, kindhearted girl, she set to work to pick up the little kittens which tumbled about on the floor, she patched up quarrels, and nursed on her lap a big tabby—the oldest of the community—which had a lame paw. All these kindnesses could hardly fail to make a favorable impression on the cats, and it was even better after a while, when she had had time to grow accustomed to their strange ways. Never had the house been kept so clean, the meats so well served, nor the sick cats so well cared for. After a time they had a visit from an old cat, whom they called their father, who lived by himself in a barn at the top of the hill, and came down from time to time to inspect the little colony. He too was much taken with Lizina, and inquired, on first seeing her: "Are you well served by this nice, black-eyed little person?" and the cats answered with one voice: "Oh, yes, Father Gatto, we have never had so good a servant!"

At each of his visits the answer was always the same; but after a time the old cat, who was very observant, noticed that the little maid had grown to look sadder and sadder. "What is the matter, my child has any one been unkind to you?" he asked one day, when he found her crying in her kitchen. She burst into tears and answered between her sobs: "Oh, no! they are all very good to me; but I long for news from home, and I pine to see my mother and my sister."

Old Gatto, being a sensible old cat, understood the little servant's feelings. "You shall go home," he said, "and you shall not come back here unless you please. But first you must be rewarded for all your kind services to my children. Follow me down into the inner cellar, where you have never yet been, for I always keep it locked and carry the key away with me."

Lizina looked round her in astonishment as they went down into the great vaulted cellar underneath the kitchen. Before her stood the big earthenware water jars, one of which contained oil, the other a liquid shining like gold. "In which of these jars shall I dip you?" asked Father Gatto, with a grin that showed all his sharp white teeth, while his moustaches stood out straight on either side of his face. The little maid looked at the two jars from under her long dark lashes: "In the oil jar!" she answered timidly, thinking to herself: "I could not ask to be bathed in gold."

But Father Gatto replied: "No, no; you have deserved something better than that." And seizing her in his strong paws he plunged her into the liquid gold. Wonder of wonders! when Lizina came out of the jar she shone from head to foot like the sun in the heavens on a fine summer's day. Her pretty pink cheeks and long black hair alone kept their natural color, otherwise she had become like a statue of pure gold. Father Gatto purred loudly with satisfaction. "Go home," he said, "and see your mother and sisters; but take care if you hear the cock crow to turn towards it; if on the contrary the ass brays, you must look the other way."

The little maid, having gratefully kissed the white paw of the old cat, set off for home; but just as she got near her mother's house the cock crowed, and quickly she turned towards it. Immediately a beautiful golden star appeared on her forehead, crowning her glossy black hair. At the same time the ass began to bray, but Lizina took care not to look over the fence into the field where the donkey was feeding. Her mother and sister, who were in front of their house, uttered cries of admiration and astonishment when they saw her, and their cries became still louder when Lizina, taking her handkerchief from her pocket, drew out also a handful of gold.

For some days the mother and her two daughters lived very happily together, for Lizina had given them everything she had brought away except her golden clothing, for that would not come off, in spite of all the efforts of her sister, who was madly jealous of her good fortune. The golden star, too, could not be removed from her forehead. But all the gold pieces she drew from her pockets had found their way to her mother and sister.

"I will go now and see what *I* can get out of the pussies," said Peppina, the elder girl, one morning, as she took Lizina's basket and fastened her pockets into her own skirt. "I should like some of the cats' gold for myself," she thought, as she left her mother's house before the sun rose.

The cat colony had not yet taken another servant, for they knew they could never get one to replace Lizina, whose loss they had not yet ceased to mourn. When they heard that Peppina was her sister, they all ran to meet her. "She is not the least like her," the kittens whispered among themselves.

"Hush, be quiet!" the older cats said; "all servants cannot be pretty."

No, decidedly she was not at all like Lizina. Even the most reasonable and large-minded of the cats soon acknowledged that.

The very first day she shut the kitchen door in the face of the tom-cats who used to enjoy watching Lizina at her work, and a young and mischievous cat who jumped in by the open kitchen window and alighted on the table got such a blow with the rolling-pin that he squalled for an hour.

With every day that passed the household became more and more aware of its misfortune.

The work was as badly done as the servant was surly and disagreeable; in the corners of the rooms there were collected heaps of dust; spiders' webs hung from the ceilings and in front of the window-panes; the beds were hardly ever made, and the feather beds, so beloved by the old and feeble cats, had never once been shaken since Lizina left the house. At Father Gatto's next visit he found the whole colony in a state of uproar.

"Caesar has one paw so badly swollen that it looks as if it were broken," said one. "Peppina kicked him with her great wooden shoes on. Hector has an abscess in his back where a wooden chair was flung at him; and Agrippina's three little kittens have died of hunger beside their mother, because Peppina forgot them in their basket up in the attic. There is no putting up with the creature—do send her away, Father Gatto! Lizina herself would not be angry with us; she must know very well what her sister is like."

"Come here," said Father Gatto, in his most severe tones to Peppina. And he took her down into the cellar and showed her the same two great jars that he had showed Lizina. "In which of these shall I dip you?" he asked; and she made haste to answer: "In the liquid gold," for she was no more modest than she was good and kind.

Father Gatto's yellow eyes darted fire. "You have not deserved it," he uttered, in a voice like thunder, and seizing her he flung her into the jar of oil, where she was nearly suffocated. When she came to the surface screaming and struggling, the vengeful cat seized her again and rolled her in the ash-heap on the floor; then when she rose, dirty, blinded, and disgusting to behold, he thrust her from the door, saying: "Begone, and when you meet a braying ass be careful to turn your head towards it."

Stumbling and raging, Peppina set off for home, thinking herself fortunate to find a stick by the wayside with which to support herself. She was within sight of her mother's house when she heard in the meadow on the right, the voice of a donkey loudly braying. Quickly she turned her head towards it, and at the same time put her hand up to her forehead, where, waving like a plume, was a donkey's tail. She ran home to her mother at the top of her speed, yelling with rage and despair; and it took Lizina two hours with a big basin of hot water and two cakes of soap to get rid of the layer of ashes with which Father Gatto had adorned her. As for the donkey's tail, it was impossible to get rid of that; it was as firmly fixed on her forehead as was the golden star on Lizina's. Their mother was furious. She first beat Lizina unmercifully with the broom, then she took her to the mouth of the well and lowered her into it, leaving her at the bottom weeping and crying for help.

Before this happened, however, the king's son in passing the mother's house had seen Lizina sitting sewing in the parlor, and had been dazzled by her beauty. After coming back two or three times, he at last ventured to approach the window and to whisper in the softest voice: "Lovely maiden, will you be my bride?" and she had answered: "I will."

Next morning, when the prince arrived to claim his bride, he found her wrapped in a large white veil. "It is so that maidens are received from their parents' hands," said the mother, who hoped to make the king's son marry Peppina in place of her sister, and had fastened the donkey's tail round her head like a lock of hair under the veil. The prince was young and a little timid, so he made no objections, and seated Peppina in the carriage beside him.

Their way led past the old house inhabited by the cats, who were all at the window, for the report had got about that the prince was going to marry the most beautiful maiden in the world, on whose forehead shone a golden star, and they knew that this could only be their adored Lizina. As the carriage slowly passed in front of the old house, where cats from all parts of world seemed to be gathered a song burst from every throat:

> "Mew, mew, mew!
> Prince, look quick behind you!
> In the well is fair Lizina,
> And you've got nothing but Peppina."

When he heard this the coachman, who understood the cat's language better than the prince, his master, stopped his horses and asked:

"Does your highness know what the grimalkins are saying?" and the song broke forth again louder than ever.

With a turn of his hand the prince threw back the veil, and discovered the puffed-up, swollen face of Peppina, with the donkey's tail twisted round her head. "Ah, traitress!" he exclaimed, and ordering the horses to be turned round, he drove the elder daughter, quivering with rage, to the old woman who had sought to deceive him. With his hand on the hilt of his sword he demanded Lizina in so terrific a voice that the mother hastened to the well to draw her prisoner out. Lizina's clothing and her star shone so brilliantly that when the prince led her home to the king, his father, the whole palace was lit up. Next day they were married, and lived happy ever after; and all the cats, headed by old Father Gatto, were present at the wedding.

The Three Dogs

(FROM *THE GREEN FAIRY BOOK*)

There was once upon a time a shepherd who had two children, a son and a daughter. When he was on his death-bed he turned to them and said, "I have nothing to leave you but three sheep and a small house; divide them between you, as you like, but don't quarrel over them whatever you do."

When the shepherd was dead, the brother asked his sister which she would like best, the sheep or the little house; and when she had chosen the house he said, "Then I'll take the sheep and go out to seek my fortune in the wide world. I don't see why I shouldn't be as lucky as many another who has set out on the same search, and it wasn't for nothing that I was born on a Sunday."

And so he started on his travels, driving his three sheep in front of him, and for a long time it seemed as if fortune didn't mean to favor him at all. One day he was sitting disconsolately at a cross road, when a man suddenly appeared before him with three black dogs, each one bigger than the other.

"Hullo, my fine fellow," said the man, "I see you have three fat sheep. I'll tell you what; if you'll give them to me, I'll give you my three dogs."

In spite of his sadness, the youth smiled and replied, "What would I do with your dogs? My sheep at least feed themselves, but I should have to find food for the dogs."

"My dogs are not like other dogs," said the stranger; "they will feed you instead of you them, and will make your fortune. The smallest one is called 'Salt,' and will bring you food whenever you wish; the second is called 'Pepper,' and will tear anyone to pieces who offers to hurt you; and the great big strong one is called 'Mustard,' and is so powerful that it will break iron or steel with its teeth."

The shepherd at last let himself be persuaded, and gave the stranger his sheep. In order to test the truth of his statement about the dogs, he said at once, "Salt, I am hungry," and before the words were out of his mouth the dog had disappeared, and returned in a few minutes with a large basket full of the most delicious food. Then the youth congratulated himself on the bargain he had made, and continued his journey in the best of spirits.

One day he met a carriage and pair, all draped in black; even the horses were covered with black trappings, and the coachman was clothed in crape from top to toe. Inside the carriage sat a beautiful girl in a black dress crying bitterly. The horses advanced slowly and mournfully, with their heads bent on the ground.

"Coachman, what's the meaning of all this grief?" asked the shepherd.

At first the coachman wouldn't say anything, but when the youth pressed him he told him that a huge dragon dwelt in the neighborhood, and required yearly the sacrifice of a beautiful maiden. This year the lot had fallen on the King's daughter, and the whole country was filled with woe and lamentation in consequence.

The shepherd felt very sorry for the lovely maiden, and determined to follow the carriage. In a little it halted at the foot of a high mountain. The girl got out, and walked slowly and sadly to meet her terrible fate. The coachman perceived that the shepherd wished to follow her, and warned him not to do so if he valued his life; but the shepherd wouldn't listen to his advice. When they had climbed about half-way up the hill they saw a terrible-looking monster with the body of a snake, and with huge wings and claws, coming towards them, breathing forth flames of fire, and preparing to seize its victim. Then the shepherd called, "Pepper, come to the rescue," and the second dog set upon the dragon, and after a fierce struggle bit it so sharply in the neck that the monster rolled over, and in a few moments breathed its last. Then the dog ate up the body, all except its two front teeth, which the shepherd picked up and put in his pocket.

The Princess was quite overcome with terror and joy, and fell fainting at the feet of her deliverer. When she recovered her consciousness she begged the shepherd to return with her to her father, who would reward him richly. But the youth answered that he wanted to see something of the world, and that he would return again in three years, and nothing would make him change this resolve. The Princess seated herself once more in her carriage, and, bidding each other farewell, she and the shepherd separated, she to return home, and he to see the world.

But while the Princess was driving over a bridge the carriage suddenly stood still, and the coachman turned round to her and said, "Your deliverer has gone, and doesn't thank you for your gratitude. It would be nice of you to make a poor fellow happy; therefore you may tell your father that it was I who slew the dragon, and if you refuse to, I will throw you into the river, and no one will be any the wiser, for they will think the dragon has devoured you."

The maiden was in a dreadful state when she heard these words; but there was nothing for her to do but to swear that she would give out the coachman as her deliverer, and not to divulge the secret to anyone. So they returned to the capital, and everyone was delighted when they saw the Princess had returned unharmed; the black flags were taken down from all the palace towers, and gay-colored ones put up in their place, and the King embraced his daughter and her supposed rescuer with tears of joy, and, turning to the coachman, he said, "You have not only saved the life of my child, but you have also freed the country from a terrible scourge; therefore, it is only fitting that you should be richly rewarded. Take, therefore, my daughter for your wife; but as she is still so young, do not let the marriage be celebrated for another year."

The coachman thanked the King for his graciousness, and was then led away to be richly dressed and instructed in all the arts and graces that befitted his new position. But the poor Princess wept bitterly, though she did not dare to confide her grief to anyone. When the year was over, she begged so hard for another year's respite that it was granted to her. But this year passed also, and she threw herself at her father's feet, and begged so piteously for one more year that the King's heart was melted, and he yielded to her request, much to the Princess's joy, for she knew that her real deliverer would appear at the end of the third year. And so the year passed away like the other two, and the wedding-day was fixed, and all the people were prepared to feast and make merry.

But on the wedding-day it happened that a stranger came to the town with three black dogs. He asked what the meaning of all the feasting and fuss was, and they told him that the King's daughter was just going to be married to the man who had slain the terrible dragon. The stranger at once denounced the coachman as a liar; but no one would listen to him, and he was seized and thrown into a cell with iron doors.

While he was lying on his straw pallet, pondering mournfully on his fate, he thought he heard the low whining of his dogs outside; then an idea dawned on him, and he called out as loudly as he could, "Mustard, come to my help," and in a second he saw the paws of his biggest dog at the window of his cell, and before he could count two the creature had bitten through the iron bars and stood beside him. Then they both let themselves out of the prison by the window, and the poor youth was free once more, though he felt very sad when he thought that another was to enjoy the reward that rightfully belonged to him. He felt hungry too, so he called his dog "Salt," and asked him to bring home some food. The faithful creature trotted off, and soon returned with a table-napkin full of the most delicious food, and the napkin itself was embroidered with a kingly crown.

The King had just seated himself at the wedding-feast with all his Court, when the dog appeared and licked the Princess's hand in an appealing manner. With a joyful start she recognized the beast, and bound her own table-napkin round his neck. Then she plucked up her courage and told her father the whole story. The King at once sent a servant to follow the dog, and in a short time the stranger was led into the King's presence. The former coachman grew as white as a sheet when he saw the shepherd, and, falling on his knees, begged for mercy and pardon. The Princess recognized her deliverer at once, and did not need the proof of the two dragon's teeth which he drew from his pocket. The coachman was thrown into a dark dungeon, and the shepherd took his place at the Princess's side, and this time, you may be sure, she did not beg for the wedding to be put off.

The young couple lived for some time in great peace and happiness, when suddenly one day the former shepherd bethought himself of his poor sister and expressed a wish to see her again, and to let her share in his good fortune. So they sent a carriage to fetch her, and soon she arrived at the court, and found herself once more in her brother's arms. Then one of the dogs spoke and said, "Our task is done; you have no more need of us. We only waited to see that you did not forget your sister in your prosperity." And with these words the three dogs became three birds and flew away into the heavens.

Jackal or Tiger?

(FROM *THE OLIVE FAIRY BOOK*)

One hot night, in Hindustan, a king and queen lay awake in the palace in the midst of the city. Every now and then a faint air blew through the lattice, and they hoped they were going to sleep, but they never did. Presently they became more broad awake than ever at the sound of a howl outside the palace.

"Listen to that tiger!" remarked the king.

"Tiger?" replied the queen. "How should there be a tiger inside the city? It was only a jackal."

"I tell you it was a tiger," said the king.

"And I tell you that you were dreaming if you thought it was anything but a jackal," answered the queen.

"I say it was a tiger," cried the king; "don't contradict me."

"Nonsense!" snapped the queen. "It was a jackal." And the dispute waxed so warm that the king said at last:

"Very well, we'll call the guard and ask; and if it was a jackal I'll leave this kingdom to you and go away; and if it was a tiger then you shall go, and I will marry a new wife."

"As you like," answered the queen, "there isn't any doubt which it was."

So the king called the two soldiers who were on guard outside and put the question to them. But, whilst the dispute was going on, the king and queen had got so excited and talked so loud that the guards had heard nearly all they said, and one man observed to the other:

"Mind you declare that the king is right. It certainly was a jackal, but, if we say so, the king will probably not keep his word about going away, and we shall get into trouble, so we had better take his side."

To this the other agreed; therefore, when the king asked them what animal they had seen, both the guards said it was certainly a tiger, and that the king

465

was right of course, as he always was. The king made no remark, but sent for a palanquin, and ordered the queen to be placed in it, bidding the four bearers of the palanquin to take her a long way off into the forest and there leave her. In spite of her tears, she was forced to obey, and away the bearers went for three days and three nights until they came to a dense wood. There they set down the palanquin with the queen in it, and started home again.

Now the queen thought to herself that the king could not mean to send her away for good, and that as soon as he had got over his fit of temper he would summon her back; so she stayed quite still for a long time, listening with all her ears for approaching footsteps, but heard none. After a while she grew nervous, for she was all alone, and put her head out of the palanquin and looked about her. Day was just breaking, and birds and insects were beginning to stir; the leaves rustled in a warm breeze; but, although the queen's eyes wandered in all directions, there was no sign of any human being. Then her spirit gave way, and she began to cry.

It so happened that close to the spot where the queen's palanquin had been set down, there dwelt a man who had a tiny farm in the midst of the forest, where he and his wife lived alone far from any neighbors. As it was hot weather the farmer had been sleeping on the flat roof of his house, but was awakened by the sound of weeping. He jumped up and ran downstairs as fast as he could, and into the forest towards the place the sound came from, and there he found the palanquin.

"Oh, poor soul that weeps," cried the farmer, standing a little way off, "who are you?" At this salutation from a stranger the queen grew silent, dreading she knew not what.

"Oh, you that weep," repeated the farmer, "fear not to speak to me, for you are to me as a daughter. Tell me, who are you?"

His voice was so kind that the queen gathered up her courage and spoke. And when she had told her story, the farmer called his wife, who led her to their house, and gave her food to eat, and a bed to lie on. And in the farm, a few days later, a little prince was born, and by his mother's wish named Ameer Ali.

Years passed without a sign from the king. His wife might have been dead for all he seemed to care, though the queen still lived with the farmer, and the little prince had by this time grown up into a strong, handsome, and healthy youth. Out in the forest they seemed far from the world; very few ever came near them, and the prince was continually begging his mother and the farmer to be allowed to go away and seek adventures and to make his own living. But she and the wise farmer always counseled him to wait, until, at last, when he was eighteen years of age, they had not the heart to forbid him any longer. So he started off one early morning, with a sword by his side, a big brass pot to hold water, a few pieces of silver, and a galail or two-stringed bow in his hand, with which to shoot birds as he traveled.

Many a weary mile he tramped day after day, until, one morning, he saw before him just such a forest as that in which he had been born and bred, and he stepped joyfully into it, like one who goes to meet an old friend. Presently, as he made his way through a thicket, he saw a pigeon which he thought would make a good dinner, so he fired a pellet at it from his galail, but missed the pigeon which fluttered away with a startled clatter. At the same instant he heard a great clamor from beyond the thicket, and, on reaching the spot, he found an ugly old woman streaming wet and crying loudly as she lifted from her head an earthen vessel with a hole in it from which the water was pouring. When she saw the prince with his galail in his hand, she called out:

"Oh, wretched one! why must you choose an old woman like me to play your pranks upon? Where am I to get a fresh pitcher instead of this one that you have broken with your foolish tricks? And how am I to go so far for water twice when one journey wearies me?"

"But, mother," replied the prince, "I played no trick upon you! I did but shoot at a pigeon that should have served me for dinner, and as my pellet missed it, it must have broken your pitcher. But, in exchange, you shall have my brass pot, and that will not break easily; and as for getting water, tell me where to find it, and I'll fetch it while you dry your garments in the sun, and carry it whither you will."

At this the old woman's face brightened. She showed him where to seek the water, and when he returned a few minutes later with his pot filled to the brim, she led the way without a word, and he followed. In a short while they came to a hut in the forest, and as they drew near it Ameer Ali beheld in the doorway the loveliest damsel his eyes had ever looked on. At the sight of a stranger she drew her veil about her and stepped into the hut, and much as he wished to see her again Ameer Ali could think of no excuse by which to bring her back, and so, with a heavy heart, he made his salutation, and bade the old woman farewell. But when he had gone a little way she called after him:

"If ever you are in trouble or danger, come to where you now stand and cry: "'Fairy of the Forest! Fairy of the forest, help me now!'" And I will listen to you."

The prince thanked her and continued his journey, but he thought little of the old woman's saying, and much of the lovely damsel. Shortly afterwards he arrived at a city; and, as he was now in great straits, having come to the end of his money, he walked straight to the palace of the king and asked for employment. The king said he had plenty of servants and wanted no more; but the young man pleaded so hard that at last the rajah was sorry for him, and promised that he should enter his bodyguard on the condition that he would undertake any service which was especially difficult or dangerous. This was just what Ameer Ali wanted, and he agreed to do whatever the king might wish.

Soon after this, on a dark and stormy night, when the river roared beneath the palace walls, the sound of a woman weeping and wailing was heard above the storm. The king ordered a servant to go and see what was the matter; but the servant, falling on his knees in terror, begged that he might not be sent on such an errand, particularly on a night so wild, when evil spirits and witches were sure to be abroad. Indeed, so frightened was he, that the king, who was very kind-hearted, bade another to go in his stead, but each one showed the same strange fear. Then Ameer Ali stepped forward:

"This is my duty, your majesty," he said, "I will go."

The king nodded, and off he went. The night was as dark as pitch, and the wind blew furiously and drove the rain in sheets into his face; but he made his way down to the ford under the palace walls and stepped into the flooded water. Inch by inch, and foot by foot he fought his way across, now nearly swept off his feet by some sudden swirl or eddy, now narrowly escaping being caught in the branches of some floating tree that came tossing and swinging down the stream. At length he emerged, panting and dripping wet, on the other side. Close by the bank stood a gallows, and on the gallows hung the body of some evildoer, whilst from the foot of it came the sound of sobbing that the king had heard.

Ameer Ali was so grieved for the one who wept there that he thought nothing of the wildness of the night or of the roaring river. As for ghosts and witches, they had never troubled him, so he walked up towards the gallows where crouched the figure of the woman.

"What ails you?" he said.

Now the woman was not really a woman at all, but a horrid kind of witch who really lived in Witchland, and had no business on earth. If ever a man strayed into Witchland the ogresses used to eat him up, and this old witch thought she would like to catch a man for supper, and that is why she had been sobbing and crying in hopes that someone out of pity might come to her rescue.

So when Ameer Ali questioned her, she replied:

"Ah, kind sir, it is my poor son who hangs upon that gallows; help me to get him down and I will bless you for ever."

Ameer Ali thought that her voice sounded rather eager than sorrowful, and he suspected that she was not telling the truth, so he determined to be very cautious.

"That will be rather difficult," he said, "for the gallows is high, and we have no ladder."

"Ah, but if you will just stoop down and let me climb upon your shoulders," answered the old witch, "I think I could reach him." And her voice now sounded so cruel that Ameer Ali was sure that she intended some evil. But he only said:

"Very well, we will try." With that he drew his sword, pretending that he needed it to lean upon, and bent so that the old woman could clamber on to his back, which she did very nimbly. Then, suddenly, he felt a noose slipped over his neck, and the old witch sprang from his shoulders on to the gallows, crying:

"Now, foolish one, I have got you, and will kill you for my supper."

But Ameer Ali gave a sweep upwards with his sharp sword to cut the rope that she had slipped round his neck, and not only cut the cord but cut also the old woman's foot as it dangled above him; and with a yell of pain and anger she vanished into the darkness.

Ameer Ali then sat down to collect himself a little, and felt upon the ground by his side an anklet that had evidently fallen off the old witch's foot. This he put into his pocket, and as the storm had by this time passed over he made his way back to the palace. When he had finished his story, he took the anklet out of his pocket and handed it to the king, who, like everyone else, was amazed at the glory of the jewels which composed it. Indeed, Ameer Ali himself was astonished, for he had slipped the anklet into his pocket in the dark and had not looked at it since. The king was delighted at its beauty, and having praised and rewarded Ameer Ali, he gave the anklet to his daughter, a proud and spoiled princess.

Now in the women's apartments in the palace there hung two cages, in one of which was a parrot and in the other a starling, and these two birds could talk as well as human beings. They were both pets of the princess who always fed them herself, and the next day, as she was walking grandly about with her treasure tied round her ankle, she heard the starling say to the parrot:

"Oh, Toté" (that was the parrot's name), "how do you think the princess looks in her new jewel?"

"Think?" snapped the parrot, who was cross because they hadn't given him his bath that morning, "I think she looks like a washerwoman's daughter, with one shoe on and the other off! Why doesn't she wear two of them, instead of going about with one leg adorned and the other empty?"

When the princess heard this she burst into tears; and sending for her father she declared that he must get her another such an anklet to wear on the other leg, or she would die of shame. So the king sent for Ameer Ali and told him that he must get a second anklet exactly like the first within a month, or he should be hanged, for the princess would certainly die of disappointment.

Poor Ameer Ali was greatly troubled at the king's command, but he thought to himself that he had, at any rate, a month in which to lay his plans. He left the palace at once, and inquired of everyone where the finest jewels were to be got; but though he sought night and day he never found one to compare with the anklet. At last only a week remained, and he was in sore difficulty, when he remembered the Fairy of the forest, and determined to go without loss of time and seek her. Therefore away he went, and after a day's traveling he reached the cottage in the forest, and, standing where he had stood when the old woman called to him, he cried:

"Fairy of the forest! Fairy of the forest! Help me! help me!"

Then there appeared in the doorway the beautiful girl he had seen before, whom in all his wanderings he had never forgotten.

"What is the matter?" she asked, in a voice so soft that he listened like one struck dumb, and she had to repeat the question before he could answer. Then he told her his story, and she went within the cottage and came back with two wands, and a pot of boiling water. The two wands she planted in the ground about six feet apart, and then, turning to him, she said:

"I am going to lie down between these two wands. You must then draw your sword and cut off my foot, and, as soon as you have done that, you must seize it and hold it over the cauldron, and every drop of blood that falls from it into the water will become a jewel. Next you must change the wands so that the one that stood at my head is at my feet, and the one at my feet stands at my head, and place the severed foot against the wound and it will heal, and I shall become quite well again as before."

At first Ameer Ali declared that he would sooner be hanged twenty times over than treat her so roughly; but at length she persuaded him to do her bidding. He nearly fainted himself with horror when he found that, after the cruel blow which lopped her foot off, she lay as one lifeless; but he held the severed foot over the cauldron, and, as drops of blood fell from it, and he saw each turn in the water into shining gems, his heart took courage. Very soon there were plenty of jewels in the cauldron, and he quickly changed the wands, placed the severed foot against the wound, and immediately the two parts became one as before. Then the maiden opened her eyes, sprang to her feet, and drawing her veil about her, ran into the hut, and would not come out or speak to him any more. For a long while he waited, but, as she did not appear, he gathered up the precious stones and returned to the palace. He easily got some one to set the jewels, and found that there were enough to make, not only one, but three rare and beautiful anklets, and these he duly presented to the king on the very day that his month of grace was over.

The king embraced him warmly, and made him rich gifts; and the next day the vain princess put two anklets on each foot, and strutted up and down in them admiring herself in the mirrors that lined her room.

"Oh, Toté," asked the starling, "how do you think our princess looks now in these fine jewels?"

"Ugh!" growled the parrot, who was really always cross in the mornings, and never recovered his temper until after lunch, "she's got all her beauty at one end of her now; if she had a few of those fine gew-gaws round her neck and wrists she would look better; but now, to my mind, she looks more than ever like the washerwoman's daughter dressed up."

Poor princess! she wept and stormed and raved until she made herself quite ill; and then she declared to her father that, unless she had bracelets and necklace to match the anklets she would die.

Again the king sent for Ameer Ali, and ordered him to get a necklace and bracelets to match those anklets within a month, or be put to a cruel death.

And again Ameer Ali spent nearly the whole month searching for the jewels, but all in vain. At length he made his way to the hut in the forest, and stood and cried:

"Fairy of the forest! Fairy of the forest! Help me! help me!"

Once more the beautiful maiden appeared at his summons and asked what he wanted, and when he had told her she said he must do exactly as he had done the first time, except that now he must cut off both her hands and her head. Her words turned Ameer Ali pale with horror; but she reminded him that no harm had come to her before, and at last he consented to do as she bade him. From her severed hands and head there fell into the cauldron bracelets and chains of rubies and diamonds, emeralds and pearls that surpassed any that ever were seen. Then the head and hands were joined on to the body, and left neither sign nor scar. Full of gratitude, Ameer Ali tried to speak to her, but she ran into the house and would not come back, and he was forced to leave her and go away laden with the jewels.

When, on the day appointed, Ameer Ali produced a necklace and bracelets each more beautiful and priceless than the last, the king's astonishment knew no bounds, and as for his daughter she was nearly mad with joy. The very next morning she put on all her finery, and thought that now, at least, that disagreeable parrot could find no fault with her appearance, and she listened eagerly when she heard the starling say:

"Oh, Toté, how do you think our princess is looking *now*?"

"Very fine, no doubt," grumbled the parrot; "but what is the use of dressing up like that for oneself only? She ought to have a husband—why doesn't she marry the man who got her all these splendid things?"

Then the princess sent for her father and told him that she wished to marry Ameer Ali.

"My dear child," said her father, "you really are very difficult to please, and want something new every day. It certainly is time you married someone, and if you choose this man, of course he shall marry you."

So the king sent for Ameer Ali, and told him that within a month he proposed to do him the honor of marrying him to the princess, and making him heir to the throne.

On hearing this speech Ameer Ali bowed low and answered that he had done and would do the king all the service that lay in his power, save only this one thing. The king, who considered his daughter's hand a prize for any man, flew into a passion, and the princess was more furious still. Ameer Ali was instantly thrown into the most dismal prison that they could find, and ordered to be kept there until the king had time to think in what way he should be put to death.

Meanwhile the king determined that the princess ought in any case to be married without delay, so he sent forth heralds throughout the neighboring countries, proclaiming that on a certain day any person fitted for a bridegroom and heir to the throne should present himself at the palace.

When the day came, all the court were gathered together, and a great crowd assembled of men, young and old, who thought that they had as good a chance as anyone else to gain both the throne and the princess. As soon as the king was seated, he called upon an usher to summon the first claimant. But, just then, a farmer who stood in front of the crowd cried out that he had a petition to offer.

"Well, hasten then," said the king; "I have no time to waste."

"Your majesty," said the farmer, "has now lived and administered justice long in this city, and will know that the tiger who is king of beasts hunts only in the forest, whilst jackals hunt in every place where there is something to be picked up."

"What is all this? what is all this?" asked the king. "The man must be mad!"

"No, your majesty," answered the farmer, "I would only remind your majesty that there are plenty of jackals gathered to-day to try and claim your daughter and kingdom: every city has sent them, and they wait hungry and eager; but do not, O king, mistake or pretend again to mistake the howl of a jackal for the hunting cry of a tiger."

The king turned first red and then pale.

"There is," continued the farmer, "a royal tiger bred in the forest who has the first and only true claim to your throne."

"Where? what do you mean?" stammered the king, growing pale as he listened.

"In prison," replied the farmer; "if your majesty will clear this court of the jackals I will explain."

"Clear the court!" commanded the king; and, very unwillingly, the visitors left the palace.

"Now tell me what riddle this is," said he.

Then the farmer told the king and his ministers how he had rescued the queen and brought up Ameer Ali; and he fetched the old queen herself, whom he had left outside. At the sight of her the king was filled with shame and self-reproach, and wished he could have lived his life over again, and not have married the mother of the proud princess, who caused him endless trouble until her death.

"My day is past," said he. And he gave up his crown to his son Ameer Ali, who went once more and called to the forest fairy to provide him with a queen to share his throne.

"There is only one person I will marry," said he. And this time the maiden did not run away, but agreed to be his wife. So the two were married without delay, and lived long and reigned happily.

As for the old woman whose pitcher Ameer Ali had broken, she was the forest maiden's fairy godmother, and when she was no longer needed to look after the girl she gladly returned to fairyland.

The old king has never been heard to contradict his wife any more. If he even looks as if he does not agree with her, she smiles at him and says:

"Is it the tiger, then? or the jackal?" And he has not another word to say.

The Lion and the Cat

(FROM *THE BROWN FAIRY BOOK*)

Far away on the other side of the world there lived, long ago, a lion and his younger brother, the wild cat, who were so fond of each other that they shared the same hut. The lion was much the bigger and stronger of the two—indeed, he was much bigger and stronger than any of the beasts that dwelt in the forest; and, besides, he could jump farther and run faster than all the rest. If strength and swiftness could gain him a dinner he was sure never to be without one, but when it came to cunning, both the grizzly bear and the serpent could get the better of him, and he was forced to call in the help of the wild cat.

Now the young wild cat had a lovely golden ball, so beautiful that you could hardly look at it except through a piece of smoked glass, and he kept it hidden in the thick fur muff that went round his neck. A very large old animal, since dead, had given it to him when he was hardly more than a baby, and had told him never to part with it, for as long as he kept it no harm could ever come near him.

In general the wild cat did not need to use his ball, for the lion was fond of hunting, and could kill all the food that they needed; but now and then his life would have been in danger had it not been for the golden ball.

One day the two brothers started to hunt at daybreak, but as the cat could not run nearly as fast as the lion, he had quite a long start. At least he *thought* it was a long one, but in a very few bounds and springs the lion reached his side.

"There is a bear sitting on that tree," he whispered softly. "He is only waiting for us to pass, to drop down on my back."

"Ah, you are so big that he does not see I am behind you," answered the wild cat. And, touching the ball, he just said: "Bear, die!" And the bear tumbled dead out of the tree, and rolled over just in front of them.

For some time they trotted on without any adventures, till just as they were about to cross a strip of long grass on the edge of the forest, the lion's quick ears detected a faint rustling noise.

"That is a snake," he cried, stopping short, for he was much more afraid of snakes than of bears.

"Oh, it is all right," answered the cat. "Snake, die!" And the snake died, and the two brothers skinned it. They then folded the skin up into a very small parcel, and the cat tucked it into his mane, for snakes' skins can do all sorts of wonderful things, if you are lucky enough to have one of them.

All this time they had had no dinner, for the snake's flesh was not nice, and the lion did not like eating bear—perhaps because he never felt sure that the bear was *really* dead, and would not jump up alive when his enemy went near him. Most people are afraid of *some* thing, and bears and serpents were the only creatures that caused the lion's heart to tremble. So the two brothers set off again and soon reached the side of a hill where some fine deer were grazing.

"Kill one of those deer for your own dinner," said the boy-brother, "but catch me another alive. I want him."

The lion at once sprang towards them with a loud roar, but the deer bounded away, and they were all three soon lost to sight. The cat waited for a long while, but finding that the lion did not return, went back to the house where they lived.

It was quite dark when the lion came home, where his brother was sitting curled up in one corner.

"Did you catch the deer for me?" asked the boy-brother, springing up.

"Well, no," replied the man-brother. "The fact is, that I did not get up to them till we had run half way across the world and left the wind far behind us. Think what a trouble it would have been to drag it here! So—I just ate them both."

The cat said nothing, but he did not feel that he loved his big brother. He had thought a great deal about that deer, and had meant to get on his back to ride him as a horse, and go to see all the wonderful places the lion talked to him about when he was in a good temper. The more he thought of it the more sulky he grew, and in the morning, when the lion said that it was time for them to start to hunt, the cat told him that he might kill the bear and snake by himself, as *he* had a headache, and would rather stay at home. The little fellow knew quite well that the lion would not dare to go out without him and his ball for fear of meeting a bear or a snake.

The quarrel went on, and for many days neither of the brothers spoke to each other, and what made them still more cross was, that they could get very little to eat, and we know that people are often cross when they are hungry. At last it occurred to the lion that if he could only steal the magic ball he could kill bears and snakes for himself, and then the cat might be as sulky as he liked for anything that it would matter. But how was the stealing to be done? The cat had the ball hung round his neck day and night, and he was such a light sleeper that it was useless to think of taking it while he slept. No! the only thing was to get him to lend it of his own accord, and after some days the lion (who was not at all clever) hit upon a plan that he thought would do.

"Dear me, how dull it is here!" said the lion one afternoon, when the rain was pouring down in such torrents that, however sharp your eyes or your nose might be, you could not spy a single bird or beast among the bushes. "Dear me, how dull, how dreadfully dull I am. Couldn't we have a game of catch with that golden ball of yours?"

"I don't care about playing catch, it does not amuse me," answered the cat, who was as cross as ever; for no cat, even to this day, ever forgets an injury done to him.

"Well, then, lend me the ball for a little, and I will play by myself," replied the lion, stretching out a paw as he spoke.

"You can't play in the rain, and if you did, you would only lose it in the bushes," said the cat.

"Oh, no, I won't; I will play in here. Don't be so ill-natured." And with a very bad grace the cat untied the string and threw the golden ball into the lion's lap, and composed himself to sleep again.

For a long while the lion tossed it up and down gaily, feeling that, however sound asleep the boy-brother might *look*, he was sure to have one eye open; but gradually he began to edge closer to the opening, and at last gave such a toss that the ball went up high into the air, and he could not see what became of it.

"Oh, how stupid of me!" he cried, as the cat sprang up angrily, "let us go at once and search for it. It can't really have fallen very far." But though they searched that day and the next, and the next after that, they never found it, because it never came down.

After the loss of his ball the cat refused to live with the lion any longer, but wandered away to the north, always hoping he might meet with his ball again. But months passed, and years passed, and though he traveled over hundreds of miles, he never saw any traces of it.

At length, when he was getting quite old, he came to a place unlike any that he had ever seen before, where a big river rolled right to the foot of some high mountains. The ground all about the river bank was damp and marshy, and as no cat likes to wet its feet, this one climbed a tree that rose high above the water, and thought sadly of his lost ball, which would have helped him out of this horrible place. Suddenly he saw a beautiful ball, for all the world like his own, dangling from a branch of the tree he was on. He longed to get at it; but was the branch strong enough to bear his weight? It was no use, after all he had done, getting drowned in the water. However, it could do no harm, if he was to go a little way; he could always manage to get back somehow.

So he stretched himself at full length upon the branch, and wriggled his body cautiously along. To his delight it seemed thick and stout. Another movement, and, by stretching out his paw, he would be able to draw the string towards him, when the branch gave a loud crack, and the cat made haste to wriggle himself back the way he had come.

But when cats make up their minds to do anything they generally *do* it; and this cat began to look about to see if there was really no way of getting at his ball. Yes! there was, and it was much surer than the other, though rather more difficult. Above the bough where the ball was hung was another bough much thicker, which he knew could not break with his weight; and by holding on tight to this with all his four paws, he could just manage to touch the ball with his tail. He would thus be able to whisk the ball to and fro till, by-and-by, the string would become quite loose, and it would fall to the ground. It might take some time, but the lion's little brother was patient, like most cats.

Well, it all happened just as the cat intended it should, and when the ball dropped on the ground the cat ran down the tree like lightning, and, picking it up, tucked it away in the snake's skin round his neck. Then he began jumping along the shore of the Big Water from one place to another, trying to find a boat, or even a log of wood, that would take him across. But there was nothing; only, on the other side, he saw two girls cooking, and though he shouted to them at the top of his voice, they were too far off to hear what he said. And, what was worse, the ball suddenly fell out of its snake's skin bag right into the river.

Now, it is not at all an uncommon thing for balls to tumble into rivers, but in that case they generally either fall to the bottom and stay there, or else bob about on the top of the water close to where they first touched it. But this ball, instead of doing either of these things, went straight across to the other side, and there one of the girls saw it when she stooped to dip some water into her pail.

"Oh! what a lovely ball!" cried she, and tried to catch it in her pail; but the ball always kept bobbing just out of her reach.

"Come and help me!" she called to her sister, and after a long while they had the ball safe inside the pail. They were delighted with their new toy, and one or the other held it in her hand till bedtime came, and then it was a long time before they could make up their minds where it would be safest for the night. At last they locked it in a cupboard in one corner of their room, and as there was no hole anywhere the ball could not possibly get out. After that they went to sleep.

In the morning the first thing they both did was to run to the cupboard and unlock it, but when the door opened they started back, for, instead of the ball, there stood a handsome young man.

"Ladies," he said, "how can I thank you for what you have done for me? Long, long ago, I was enchanted by a wicked fairy, and condemned to keep the shape of a ball till I should meet with two maidens, who would take me to their own home. But where was I to meet them? For hundreds of years I have lived in the depths of the forest, where nothing but wild beasts ever came, and it was only when the lion threw me into the sky that I was able to fall to earth near this river. Where there is a river, sooner or later people will come; so, hanging myself on a tree, I watched and waited. For a moment I lost heart when I fell once more into the hands of my old master the wild cat, but my hopes rose again as I saw he was making for the river bank opposite where you were standing. That was my chance, and I took it. And now, ladies, I have only to say that, if ever I can do anything to help you, go to the top of that high mountain and knock three times at the iron door at the north side, and I will come to you."

So, with a low bow, he vanished from before them, leaving the maidens weeping at having lost in one moment both the ball and the prince.

Geirlaug the King's Daughter

(FROM *THE OLIVE FAIRY BOOK*)

One day a powerful king and his beautiful wife were sitting in the gardens of their capital city, talking earnestly about the future life of their little son, who was sleeping by their side in his beautiful golden cradle. They had been married for many years without children, so when this baby came they thought themselves the happiest couple in the whole world. He was a fine sturdy little boy, who loved to kick and to strike out with his fists; but even if he had been weak and small they would still have thought him the most wonderful creature upon earth, and so absorbed were they in making plans for him, that they never noticed a huge dark shadow creeping up, till a horrible head with gleaming teeth stretched over them, and in an instant their beloved baby was snatched away.

For a while the king and queen remained where they were, speechless with horror. Then the king rose slowly, and holding out his hand to his wife, led her weeping into the palace, and for many days their subjects saw no more of them.

Meanwhile the dragon soared high into the air, holding the cradle between his teeth, and the baby still slept on. He flew so fast that he soon crossed the borders of another kingdom, and again he beheld the king and queen of the country seated in the garden with a little girl lying in a wonderful cradle of white satin and lace. Swooping down from behind as he had done before, he was just about to seize the cradle, when the king jumped up and dealt him such a blow with his golden staff that the dragon not only started back, but in his pain let fall the boy, as he spread his wings and soared into the air away from all danger.

"That was a narrow escape," said the king, turning to his wife, who sat pale with fright, and clasping her baby tightly in her arms. "Frightful," murmured the queen; "but look, what is that glittering object that is lying out there?" The king walked in the direction of her finger, and to his astonishment beheld another cradle and another baby.

"Ah! the monster must have stolen this as he sought to steal Geirlaug," cried he. And stooping lower, he read some words that were written on the fine linen that was wound round the boy. "This is Grethari, son of Grethari the king!" Unfortunately it happened that the two neighboring monarchs had had a serious quarrel, and for some years had ceased holding communication with each other. So, instead of sending a messenger at once to Grethari to tell him of the safety of his son, the king contented himself with adopting the baby, which was brought up with Geirlaug the princess.

For a while things went well with the children, who were as happy as the day was long, but at last there came a time when the queen could no more run races or play at hide-and-seek with them in the garden as she was so fond of doing, but lay and watched them from a pile of soft cushions. By-and-by she gave up doing even that, and people in the palace spoke with low voices, and even Geirlaug and Grethari trod gently and moved quietly when they drew near her room. At length, one morning, they were sent for by the king himself, who, his eyes red with weeping, told them that the queen was dead.

Great was the sorrow of the two children, for they had loved the queen very dearly, and life seemed dull without her. But the lady-in-waiting who took care of them in the tower which had been built for them while they were still babies, was kind and good, and when the king was busy or away in other parts of his kingdom she made them quite happy, and saw that they were taught everything that a prince and princess ought to know. Thus two or three years passed, when, one day, as the children were anxiously awaiting their father's return from a distant city, there rode post haste into the courtyard of the palace a herald whom the king had sent before him, to say that he was bringing back a new wife.

Now, in itself, there was nothing very strange or dreadful in the fact that the king should marry again, but, as the old lady-in-waiting soon guessed, the queen, in spite of her beauty, was a witch, and as it was easy to see that she was jealous of everyone who might gain power over her husband, it boded ill for Geirlaug and Grethari. The faithful woman could not sleep for thinking about her charges, and her soul sank when, a few months after the marriage, war broke out with a country across the seas, and the king rode away at the head of his troops. Then there happened what she had so long expected. One night, when, unlike her usual habit, she was sleeping soundly—afterwards she felt sure that a drug had been put into her food—the witch came to the tower. Exactly what she did there no one knew, but, when the sun rose, the beds of Grethari and Geirlaug were empty. At dawn the queen summoned some of her guards, and told them that she had been warned in a dream that some evil fate would befall her through a wild beast, and bade them go out and kill every animal within two miles of the palace. But the only beasts they found were two black foals of wondrous beauty, fitted for the king's riding; it seemed a pity to kill them, for what harm could two little foals do anyone? So they let them run away, frisking over the plain, and returned to the palace.

"Did you see *nothing*, really *nothing*?" asked the queen, when they again appeared before her.

"Nothing, your majesty," they replied. But the queen did not believe them, and when they were gone, she gave orders to her steward that at supper the guards should be well plied with strong drink so that their tongues should be loosened, and, further, that he was to give heed to their babble, and report to her, whatever they might let fall.

"Your majesty's commands have been obeyed," said the steward when, late in the evening, he begged admittance to the royal apartments; "but, after all, the men have told you the truth. I listened to their talk from beginning to end, and nothing did they see save two black foals." He might have added more, but the look in the queen's blazing eyes terrified him, and, bowing hastily, he backed quickly out of her presence.

In a week's time the king came home, and right glad were all the courtiers to see him.

"Now, perhaps, she will find some one else to scream at," whispered they among themselves. "She" was the queen, who had vented her rage on her attendants during these days, though what had happened to make her so angry nobody knew. But whatever might be the meaning of it, things would be sure to improve with the king to rule in the palace instead of his wife. Unfortunately, their joy only lasted a short while; for the very first night after the king's arrival the queen related the evil dream she had dreamt in his absence, and begged him to go out the next morning and kill every living creature he saw within two miles of the city. The king, who always believed everything the queen said, promised to do as she wished. But before he had ridden through the lovely gardens that surrounded the palace, he was attracted by the singing of two little blue birds perched on a scarlet-berried holly, which made him think of everything beautiful that he had ever heard of or imagined. Hour after hour passed by, and still the birds sang, and still the king listened, though of course he never guessed that it was Geirlaug and Grethari whose notes filled him with enchantment. At length darkness fell; the birds' voices were hushed, and the king awoke with a start to find that for that day his promise to the queen could not be kept.

"Well! did you see anything?" she asked eagerly, when the king entered her apartments.

"Ah, my dear, I am almost ashamed to confess to you. But the fact is that before I rode as far as the western gate the singing of two strange little blue birds made me forget all else in the world. And you will hardly believe it—but not until it grew dark did I remember where I was and what I should have been doing. However, to-morrow nothing shall hinder me from fulfilling your desires."

"There will be no to-morrow," muttered the queen, as she turned away with a curious glitter in her eyes. But the king did not hear her.

That night the king gave a great supper in the palace in honor of the victory he had gained over the enemy. The three men whom the queen had sent forth to slay the wild beasts held positions of trust in the household, for to them was committed the custody of the queen's person. And on the occasion of a feast their places were always next that of the king, so it was easy for the queen to scatter a slow but fatal poison in their cups without anyone being the wiser. Before dawn the palace was roused by the news that the king was dead, and that the three officers of the guards were dying also. Of course nobody's cries and laments were as loud as those of the queen. But when once the splendid funeral was over, she gave out that she was going to shut herself up in a distant castle till the year of her mourning was over, and after appointing a regent of the kingdom, she set out attended only by a maid who knew all her secrets. Once she had left the palace she quickly began to work her spells, to discover under what form Geirlaug and Grethari lay hidden. Happily, the princess had studied magic under a former governess, so was able to fathom her stepmother's wicked plot, and hastily changed herself into a whale, and her foster-brother into its fin. Then the queen took the shape of a shark and gave chase.

For several hours a fierce battle raged between the whale and the shark, and the sea around was red with blood; first one of the combatants got the better, and then the other, but at length it became plain to the crowd of little fishes gathered round to watch, that the victory would be to the whale. And so it was. But when, after a mighty struggle, the shark floated dead and harmless on the surface of the water, the whale was so exhausted that she had only strength enough to drag her wounded body into a quiet little bay, and for three days she remained there as still and motionless as if she had been dead herself. At the end of the three days her wounds were healed, and she began to think what it was best to do.

"Let us go back to your father's kingdom," she said to Grethari, when they had both resumed their proper shapes, and were sitting on a high cliff above the sea.

"How clever you are! I never should have thought of that!" answered Grethari, who, in truth, was not clever at all. But Geirlaug took a small box of white powder from her dress, and sprinkled some over him and some over herself, and, quicker than lightning, they found themselves in the palace grounds from which Grethari had been carried off by the dragon so many years before.

"Now take up the band with the golden letters and bind it about your forehead," said Geirlaug, "and go boldly up to the castle. And, remember, however great may be your thirst, you must drink nothing till you have first spoken to your father. If you do, ill will befall us both."

"*Why* should I be thirsty?" replied Grethari, staring at her in astonishment. "It will not take me five minutes to reach the castle gate." Geirlaug held her peace, but her eyes had in them a sad look. "Good-bye," she said at last, and she turned and kissed him.

Grethari had spoken truly when he declared that he could easily get to the castle in five minutes. At least, no one would have dreamed that it could possibly take any longer. Yet, to his surprise, the door which stood so widely open that he could see the color of the hangings within never appeared to grow any nearer, while each moment the sun burned more hotly, and his tongue was parched with thirst.

"I don't understand! What *can* be the matter with me—and why haven't I reached the castle long ago?" he murmured to himself, as his knees began to knock under him with fatigue, and his head to swim. For a few more paces he staggered on blindly, when, suddenly, the sound of rushing water smote upon his ears; and in a little wood that bordered the path he beheld a stream falling over a rock. At this sight his promise to Geirlaug was forgotten. Fighting his way through the brambles that tore his clothes, he cast himself down beside the fountain, and seizing the golden cup that hung from a tree, he drank a deep draught.

When he rose up the remembrance of Geirlaug and of his past life had vanished, and, instead, something stirred dimly within him at the vision of the white-haired man and woman who stood in the open door with outstretched hands.

"Grethari! Grethari! So you have come home at last," cried they.

For three hours Geirlaug waited in the spot where Grethari had left her, and then she began to understand what had happened. Her heart was heavy, but she soon made up her mind what to do, and pushing her way out of the wood, she skirted the high wall that enclosed the royal park and gardens, till she reached a small house where the forester lived with his two daughters.

"Do you want a girl to sweep, and to milk the cows?" asked she, when one of the sisters answered her knock.

"Yes, we do, very badly; and as you look strong and clean, we will take you for a servant if you like to come," replied the young woman.

"But, first, what is your name?"

"Lauphertha," said Geirlaug quickly, for she did not wish anyone to know who she was; and following her new mistress into the house, she begged to be taught her work without delay. And so clever was she, that, by-and-by, it began to be noised abroad that the strange girl who had come to live in the forester's house had not her equal in the whole kingdom for skill as well as beauty. Thus the years slipped away, during which Geirlaug grew to be a woman. Now and then she caught glimpses of Grethari as he rode out to hunt in the forest, but when she saw him coming she hid herself behind the great trees, for her heart was still sore at his forgetfulness. One day, however, when she was gathering herbs, he came upon her suddenly, before she had time to escape, though as she had stained her face and hands brown, and covered her beautiful hair with a scarlet cap, he did not guess her to be his foster-sister.

"What is your name, pretty maiden?" asked he.

"Lauphertha," answered the girl with a low curtsy.

"Ah! it is you, then, of whom I have heard so much," said he; "you are too beautiful to spend your life serving the forester's daughters. Come with me to the palace, and my mother the queen will make you one of her ladies in waiting."

"Truly, that would be a great fortune," replied the maiden. "And, if you really mean it, I will go with you. But how shall I know that you are not jesting?"

"Give me something to do for you, and I will do it, whatever it is," cried the young man eagerly. And she cast down her eyes, and answered:

"Go to the stable, and bind the calf that is there so that it shall not break loose in the night and wander away, for the forester and his daughters have treated me well, and I would not leave them with aught of my work still undone."

So Grethari set out for the stable where the calf stood, and wound the rope about its horns. But when he had made it fast to the wall, he found that a coil of the rope had twisted itself round his wrist, and, pull as he might, he could not get free. All night he wriggled and struggled till he was half dead with fatigue. But when the sun rose the rope suddenly fell away from him, and, very angry with the maiden he dragged himself back to the palace. "She is a witch," he muttered crossly to himself, "and I will have no more to do with her." And he flung himself on his bed and slept all day.

Not long after this adventure the king and queen sent their beloved son on an embassy to a neighboring country to seek a bride from among the seven princesses. The most beautiful of all was, of course, the one chosen, and the young pair took ship without delay for the kingdom of the prince's parents. The wind was fair and the vessel so swift that, in less time than could have been expected, the harbor nearest the castle was reached. A splendid carriage had been left in readiness close to the beach, but no horses were to be found, for every one had been carried off to take part in a great review which the king was to hold that day in honor of his son's marriage.

"I can't stay here all day," said the princess, crossly, when Grethari told her of the plight they were in. "I am perfectly worn out as it is, and you will have to find something to draw the carriage, if it is only a donkey. If you don't, I will sail back straight to my father."

Poor Grethari was much troubled by the words of the princess. Not that he felt so very much in love with her, for during the voyage she had shown him several times how vain and bad tempered she was; but as a prince and a bridegroom, he could not, of course, bear to think that any slight had been put upon her. So he hastily bade his attendants to go in search of some animal, and bring it at once to the place at which they were waiting.

During the long pause the princess sat in the beautiful golden coach, her blue velvet mantle powdered with silver bees drawn closely round her, so that not even the tip of her nose could be seen. At length a girl appeared driving a young ox in front of her, followed by one of the prince's messengers, who was talking eagerly.

"Will you lend me your ox, fair maiden?" asked Grethari, jumping up and going to meet them. "You shall fix your own price, and it shall be paid ungrudgingly, for never before was king's son in such a plight."

"My price is seats for me and my two friends behind you and your bride at the wedding feast," answered she. And to this Grethari joyfully consented.

Six horses would not have drawn the coach at the speed of this one ox. Trees and fields flew by so fast that the bride became quite giddy, and expected, besides, that they would be upset every moment. But, in spite of her fears, nothing happened, and they drew up in safety at the door of the palace, to the great surprise of the king and queen. The marriage preparations were hurried on, and by the end of the week everything was ready. It was, perhaps, fortunate that the princess was too busy with her clothes and her jewels during this period to pay much heed to Grethari, so that by the time the wedding day came round he had almost forgotten how cross and rude she had been on the journey.

The oldest men and women in the town agreed that nothing so splendid had ever been seen as the bridal procession to the great hall, where the banquet was to be held, before the ceremony was celebrated in the palace. The princess was in high good humor, feeling that all eyes were upon her, and bowed and smiled right and left. Taking the prince's hand, she sailed proudly down the room, where the guests were already assembled, to her place at the head of the table by the side of the bridegroom. As she did so, three strange ladies in shining dresses of blue, green, and red, glided in and seated themselves on a vacant bench immediately behind the young couple. The red lady was Geirlaug, who had brought with her the forester's daughters, and in one hand she held a wand of birch bark, and in the other a closed basket.

Silently they sat as the feast proceeded; hardly anyone noticed their presence, or, if they did, supposed them to be attendants of their future queen. Suddenly, when the merriment was at its height, Geirlaug opened the basket, and out flew a cock and hen. To the astonishment of everyone, the birds circled about in front of the royal pair, the cock plucking the feathers out of the tail of the hen, who tried in vain to escape from him.

"Will you treat me as badly as Grethari treated Geirlaug?" cried the hen at last. And Grethari heard, and started up wildly. In an instant all the past rushed back to him; the princess by his side was forgotten, and he only saw the face of the child with whom he had played long years ago.

"Where is Geirlaug?" he exclaimed, looking round the hall; and his eyes fell upon the strange lady. With a smile she held out a ring which he had given her on her twelfth birthday, when they were still children, without a thought of the future. "You and none other shall be my wife," he said, taking her hand, and leading her into the middle of the company.

It is not easy to describe the scene that followed. Of course, nobody understood what had occurred, and the king and queen imagined that their son had suddenly gone mad. As for the princess her rage and fury were beyond belief. The guests left the hall as quickly as they could, so that the royal family might arrange their own affairs, and in the end it was settled that half the kingdom must be given to the despised princess, instead of a husband. She sailed back at once to her country, where she was soon betrothed to a young noble, whom, in reality, she liked much better than Grethari. That evening Grethari was married to Geirlaug, and they lived happily till they died, and made all their people happy also.

The White Doe

(FROM *THE ORANGE FAIRY BOOK*)

Once upon a time there lived a king and queen who loved each other dearly, and would have been perfectly happy if they had only had a little son or daughter to play with. They never talked about it, and always pretended that there was nothing in the world to wish for; but, sometimes when they looked at other people's children, their faces grew sad, and their courtiers and attendants knew the reason why.

One day the queen was sitting alone by the side of a waterfall which sprung from some rocks in the large park adjoining the castle. She was feeling more than usually miserable, and had sent away her ladies so that no one might witness her grief. Suddenly she heard a rustling movement in the pool below the waterfall, and, on glancing up, she saw a large crab climbing on to a stone beside her.

"Great queen," said the crab, "I am here to tell you that the desire of your heart will soon be granted. But first you must permit me to lead you to the palace of the fairies, which, though hard by, has never been seen by mortal eyes because of the thick clouds that surround it. When there you will know more; that is, if you will trust yourself to me."

The queen had never before heard an animal speak, and was struck dumb with surprise. However, she was so enchanted at the words of the crab that she smiled sweetly and held out her hand; it was taken, not by the crab, which had stood there only a moment before, but by a little old woman smartly dressed in white and crimson with green ribbons in her gray hair. And, wonderful to say, not a drop of water fell from her clothes.

The old woman ran lightly down a path along which the queen had been a hundred times before, but it seemed so different she could hardly believe it was the same. Instead of having to push her way through nettles and brambles, roses and jasmine hung about her head, while under her feet the ground was sweet with violets. The orange trees were so tall and thick that, even at mid-day, the sun was never too hot, and at the end of the path was a glimmer of something so dazzling that the queen had to shade her eyes, and peep at it only between her fingers.

"What can it be?" she asked, turning to her guide; who answered:

"Oh, that is the fairies' palace, and here are some of them coming to meet us."

As she spoke the gates swung back and six fairies approached, each bearing in her hand a flower made of precious stones, but so like a real one that it was only by touching you could tell the difference.

"Madam," they said, "we know not how to thank you for this mark of your confidence, but have the happiness to tell you that in a short time you will have a little daughter."

The queen was so enchanted at this news that she nearly fainted with joy; but when she was able to speak, she poured out all her gratitude to the fairies for their promised gift.

"And now," she said, "I ought not to stay any longer, for my husband will think that I have run away, or that some evil beast has devoured me."

In a little while it happened just as the fairies had foretold, and a baby girl was born in the palace. Of course both the king and queen were delighted, and the child was called Désirée, which means "desired," for she had been "desired" for five years before her birth.

At first the queen could think of nothing but her new plaything, but then she remembered the fairies who had sent it to her. Bidding her ladies bring her the posy of jeweled flowers which had been given her at the palace, she took each flower in her hand and called it by name, and, in turn, each fairy appeared before her. But, as unluckily often happens, the one to whom she owed the most, the crab-fairy, was forgotten, and by this, as in the case of other babies you have read about, much mischief was wrought.

However, for the moment all was gaiety in the palace, and everybody inside ran to the windows to watch the fairies' carriages, for no two were alike. One had a car of ebony, drawn by white pigeons, another was lying back in her ivory chariot, driving ten black crows, while the rest had chosen rare woods or many-colored sea-shells, with scarlet and blue macaws, long-tailed peacocks, or green love-birds for horses. These carriages were only used on occasions of state, for when they went to war flying dragons, fiery serpents, lions or leopards, took the place of the beautiful birds.

The fairies entered the queen's chamber followed by little dwarfs who carried their presents and looked much prouder than their mistresses. One by one their burdens were spread upon the ground, and no one had ever seen such lovely things. Everything that a baby could possibly wear or play with was there, and besides, they had other and more precious gifts to give her, which only children who have fairies for godmothers can ever hope to possess.

They were all gathered round the heap of pink cushions on which the baby lay asleep, when a shadow seemed to fall between them and the sun, while a cold wind blew through the room. Everybody looked up, and there was the crab-fairy, who had grown as tall as the ceiling in her anger.

"So I am forgotten!" cried she, in a voice so loud that the queen trembled as she heard it. "Who was it soothed you in your trouble? Who was it led you to the fairies? Who was it brought you back in safety to your home again? Yet I—I—am overlooked, while *these* who have done nothing in comparison, are petted and thanked."

The queen, almost dumb with terror, in vain tried to think of some explanation or apology; but there was none, and she could only confess her fault and implore forgiveness. The fairies also did their best to soften the wrath of their sister, and knowing that, like many plain people who are *not* fairies, she was very vain, they entreated her to drop her crab's disguise, and to become once more the charming person they were accustomed to see.

For some time the enraged fairy would listen to nothing; but at length the flatteries began to take effect. The crab's shell fell from her, she shrank into her usual size, and lost some of her fierce expression.

"Well," she said, "I will not cause the princess's death, as I had meant to do, but at the same time she will have to bear the punishment of her mother's fault, as many other children have done before her. The sentence I pass upon her is, that if she is allowed to see one ray of daylight before her fifteenth birthday she will rue it bitterly, and it may perhaps cost her her life." And with these words she vanished by the window through which she came, while the fairies comforted the weeping queen and took counsel how best the princess might be kept safe during her childhood.

At the end of half an hour they had made up their minds what to do, and at the command of the fairies, a beautiful palace sprang up, close to that of the king and queen, but different from every palace in the world in having no windows, and only a door right under the earth. However, once within, daylight was hardly missed, so brilliant were the multitudes of tapers that were burning on the walls.

Now up to this time the princess's history has been like the history of many a princess that you have read about; but, when the period of her imprisonment was nearly over, her fortunes took another turn. For almost fifteen years the fairies had taken care of her, and amused her and taught her, so that when she came into the world she might be no whit behind the daughters of other kings in all that makes a princess charming and accomplished. They all loved her dearly, but the fairy Tulip loved her most of all; and as the princess's fifteenth birthday drew near, the fairy began to tremble lest something terrible should happen—some accident which had not been foreseen. "Do not let her out of your sight," said Tulip to the queen, "and meanwhile, let her portrait be painted and carried to the neighboring Courts, as is the custom in order that the kings may see how far her beauty exceeds that of every other princess, and that they may demand her in marriage for their sons."

And so it was done; and as the fairy had prophesied, all the young princes fell in love with the picture; but the last one to whom it was shown could think of nothing else, and refused to let it be removed from his chamber, where he spent whole days gazing at it.

The king his father was much surprised at the change which had come over his son, who generally passed all his time in hunting or hawking, and his anxiety was increased by a conversation he overheard between two of his courtiers that they feared the prince must be going out of his mind, so moody had he become. Without losing a moment the king went to visit his son, and no sooner had he entered the room than the young man flung himself at his father's feet.

"You have betrothed me already to a bride I can never love!" cried he; "but if you will not consent to break off the match, and ask for the hand of the princess Désirée, I shall die of misery, thankful to be alive no longer."

These words much displeased the king, who felt that, in breaking off the marriage already arranged he would almost certainly be bringing on his subjects a long and bloody war; so, without answering, he turned away, hoping that a few days might bring his son to reason. But the prince's condition grew rapidly so much worse that the king, in despair, promised to send an embassy at once to Désirée's father.

This news cured the young man in an instant of all his ills; and he began to plan out every detail of dress and of horses and carriages which were necessary to make the train of the envoy, whose name was Becasigue, as splendid as possible. He longed to form part of the embassy himself, if only in the disguise of a page; but this the king would not allow, and so the prince had to content himself with searching the kingdom for everything that was rare and beautiful to send to the princess. Indeed, he arrived, just as the embassy was starting, with his portrait, which had been painted in secret by the court painter.

The king and queen wished for nothing better than that their daughter marry into such a great and powerful family, and received the ambassador with every sign of welcome. They even wished him to see the princess Désirée, but this was prevented by the fairy Tulip, who feared some ill might come of it.

"And be sure you tell him," added she, "that the marriage cannot be celebrated till she is fifteen years old, or else some terrible misfortune will happen to the child."

So when Becasigue, surround by his train, made a formal request that the princess Désirée might be given in marriage to his master's son, the king replied that he was much honored, and would gladly give his consent; but that no one could even see the princess till her fifteenth birthday, as the spell laid upon her in her cradle by a spiteful fairy would not cease to work till that was past. The ambassador was greatly surprised and disappointed, but he knew too much about fairies to venture to disobey them, therefore he had to content himself with presenting the prince's portrait to the queen, who lost no time in carrying it to the princess. As the girl took it in her hands it suddenly spoke, as it had been taught to do, and uttered a compliment of the most delicate and charming sort, which made the princess flush with pleasure.

"How would you like to have a husband like that?" asked the queen, laughing.

"As if I knew anything about husbands!" replied Désirée, who had long ago guessed the business of the ambassador.

"Well, he will be your husband in three months," answered the queen, ordering the prince's presents to be brought in. The princess was very pleased with them, and admired them greatly, but the queen noticed that all the while her eyes constantly strayed from the softest silks and most brilliant jewels to the portrait of the prince.

The ambassador, finding that there was no hope of his being allowed to see the princess, took his leave, and returned to his own court; but here a new difficulty appeared. The prince, though transported with joy at the thought that Désirée was indeed to be his bride, was bitterly disappointed that she had not been allowed to return with Becasigue, as he had foolishly expected; and never having been taught to deny himself anything or to control his feelings, he fell as ill as he had done before. He would eat nothing nor take pleasure in anything, but lay all day on a heap of cushions, gazing at the picture of the princess.

"If I have to wait three months before I can marry the princess I shall die!" was all this spoilt boy would say; and at length the king, in despair, resolved to send a fresh embassy to Désirée's father to implore him to permit the marriage to be celebrated at once. "I would have presented my prayer in person", he added in his letter, "but my great age and infirmities do not suffer me to travel; however my envoy has orders to agree to any arrangement that you may propose."

On his arrival at the palace Becasigue pleaded his young master's cause as fervently as the king his father could have done, and entreated that the princess might be consulted in the matter. The queen hastened to the marble tower, and told her daughter of the sad state of the prince. Désirée sank down fainting at the news but soon came to herself again, and set about inventing a plan which would enable her to go to the prince without risking the doom pronounced over her by the wicked fairy.

"I see!" she exclaimed joyfully at last. "Let a carriage be built through which no light can come, and let it be brought into my room. I will then get into it, and we can travel swiftly during the night and arrive before dawn at the palace of the prince. Once there, I can remain in some underground chamber, where no light can come."

"Ah, how clever you are," cried the queen, clasping her in her arms. And she hurried away to tell the king.

"What a wife our prince will have!" said Becasigue bowing low; "but I must hasten back with the tidings, and to prepare the underground chamber for the princess." And so he took his leave.

In a few days the carriage commanded by the princess was ready. It was of green velvet, scattered over with large golden thistles, and lined inside with silver brocade embroidered with pink roses. It had no windows, of course; but the fairy Tulip, whose counsel had been asked, had managed to light it up with a soft glow that came no one knew whither.

It was carried straight up into the great hall of the tower, and the princess stepped into it, followed by her faithful maid of honor, Eglantine, and by her lady in waiting Cérisette, who also had fallen in love with the prince's portrait and was bitterly jealous of her mistress. The fourth place in the carriage was filled by Cérisette's mother, who had been sent by the queen to look after the three young people.

Now the Fairy of the Fountain was the godmother of the princess Nera, to whom the prince had been betrothed before the picture of Désirée had made him faithless. She was very angry at the slight put upon her godchild, and from that moment kept careful watch on the princess. In this journey she saw her chance, and it was she who, invisible, sat by Cérisette, and put bad thoughts into the minds of both her and her mother.

The way to the city where the prince lived ran for the most part through a thick forest, and every night when there was no moon, and not a single star could be seen through the trees, the guards who traveled with the princess opened the carriage to give it an airing. This went on for several days, till only twelve hours journey lay between them and the palace. The Cérisette persuaded her mother to cut a great hole in the side of the carriage with a sharp knife which she herself had brought for the purpose. In the forest the darkness was so intense that no one perceived what she had done, but when they left the last trees behind them, and emerged into the open country, the sun was up, and for the first time since her babyhood, Désirée found herself in the light of day.

She looked up in surprise at the dazzling brilliance that streamed through the hole; then gave a sigh which seemed to come from her heart. The carriage door swung back, as if by magic, and a white doe sprang out, and in a moment was lost to sight in the forest. But, quick as she was, Eglantine, her maid of honor, had time to see where she went, and jumped from the carriage in pursuit of her, followed at a distance by the guards.

Cérisette and her mother looked at each other in surprise and joy. They could hardly believe in their good fortune, for everything had happened exactly as they wished. The first thing to be done was to conceal the hole which had been cut, and when this was managed (with the help of the angry fairy, though they did not know it), Cérisette hastened to take off her own clothes, and put on those of the princess, placing the crown of diamonds on her head. She found this heavier than she expected; but then, she had never been accustomed to wear crowns, which makes all the difference.

At the gates of the city the carriage was stopped by a guard of honor sent by the king as an escort to his son's bride. Though Cérisette and her mother could of course see nothing of what was going on outside, they heard plainly the shouts of welcome from the crowds along the streets.

The carriage stopped at length in the vast hall which Becasigue had prepared for the reception of the princess. The grand chamberlain and the lord high steward were awaiting her, and when the false bride stepped into the brilliantly lighted room, they bowed low, and said they had orders to inform his highness the moment she arrived. The prince, whom the strict etiquette of the court had prevented from being present in the underground hall, was burning with impatience in his own apartments.

"So she had come!" cried he, throwing down the bow he had been pretending to mend. "Well, was I not right? Is she not a miracle of beauty and grace? And has she her equal in the whole world?" The ministers looked at each other, and made no reply; till at length the chamberlain, who was the bolder of the two, observed:

"My lord, as to her beauty, you can judge of that for yourself. No doubt it is as great as you say; but at present it seems to have suffered, as is natural, from the fatigues of the journey."

This was certainly not what the prince had expected to hear. Could the portrait have flattered her? He had known of such things before, and a cold shiver ran through him; but with an effort he kept silent from further questioning, and only said:

"Has the king been told that the princess is in the palace?"

"Yes, highness; and he has probably already joined her."

"Then I will go too," said the prince.

Weak as he was from his long illness, the prince descended the staircase, supported by the ministers, and entered the room just in time to hear his father's loud cry of astonishment and disgust at the sight of Cérisette.

"There was been treachery at work," he exclaimed, while the prince leant, dumb with horror, against the doorpost. But the lady in waiting, who had been prepared for something of the sort, advanced, holding in her hand the letters which the king and queen had entrusted to her.

"This is the princess Désirée," said she, pretending to have heard nothing, "and I have the honor to present to you these letters from my liege lord and lady, together with the casket containing the princess' jewels."

The king did not move or answer her; so the prince, leaning on the arm of Becasigue, approached a little closer to the false princess, hoping against hope that his eyes had deceived him. But the longer he looked the more he agreed with his father that there was treason somewhere, for in no single respect did the portrait resemble the woman before him. Cérisette was so tall that the dress of the princess did not reach her ankles, and so thin that her bones showed through the stuff. Besides that her nose was hooked, and her teeth black and ugly.

In his turn, the prince stood rooted to the spot. At last he spoke, and his words were addressed to his father, and not to the bride who had come so far to marry him.

"We have been deceived," he said, "and it will cost me my life." And he leaned so heavily on the envoy that Becasigue feared he was going to faint, and hastily laid him on the floor. For some minutes no one could attend to anybody but the prince; but as soon as he revived the lady in waiting made herself heard.

"Oh, my lovely princess, why did we ever leave home?" cried she. "But the king your father will avenge the insults that have been heaped on you when we tell him how you have been treated."

"I will tell him myself," replied the king in wrath; "he promised me a wonder of beauty, he has sent me a skeleton! I am not surprised that he has kept her for fifteen years hidden away from the eyes of the world. Take them both away," he continued, turning to his guards, "and lodge them in the state prison. There is something more I have to learn of this matter."

His orders were obeyed, and the prince, loudly bewailing his sad fate, was led back to bed, where for many days he lay in a high fever. At length he slowly began to gain strength, but his sorrow was still so great that he could not bear the sight of a strange face, and shuddered at the notion of taking his proper part in the court ceremonies. Unknown to the king, or to anybody but Becasigue, he planned that, as soon as he was able, he would make his escape and pass the rest of his life alone in some solitary place. It was some weeks before he had regained his health sufficiently to carry out his design; but finally, one beautiful starlight night, the two friends stole away, and when the king woke next morning he found a letter lying by his bed, saying that his son had gone, he knew not whither. He wept bitter tears at the news, for he loved the prince dearly; but he felt that perhaps the young man had done wisely, and he trusted to time and Becasigue's influence to bring the wanderer home.

And while these things were happening, what had become of the white doe? Though when she sprang from the carriage she was aware that some unkind fate had changed her into an animal, yet, till she saw herself in a stream, she had no idea what it was.

"Is it really, I, Désirée?" she said to herself, weeping. "What wicked fairy can have treated me so; and shall I never, never take my own shape again? My only comfort that, in this great forest, full of lions and serpents, my life will be a short one."

Now the fairy Tulip was as much grieved at the sad fate of the princess as Désirée's own mother could have been if she had known of it. Still, she could not help feeling that if the king and queen had listened to her advice the girl would by this time be safely in the walls of her new home. However, she loved Désirée too much to let her suffer more than could be helped, and it was she who guided Eglantine to the place where the white doe was standing, cropping the grass which was her dinner.

At the sound of footsteps the pretty creature lifted her head, and when she saw her faithful companion approaching she bounded towards her, and rubbed her head on Eglantine's shoulder. The maid of honor was surprised; but she was fond of animals, and stroked the white doe tenderly, speaking gently to her all the while. Suddenly the beautiful creature lifted her head, and looked up into Eglantine's face, with tears streaming from her eyes. A thought flashed through her mind, and quick as lightning the girl flung herself on her knees, and lifting the animal's feet kissed them one by one. "My princess! O my dear princess!" cried she; and again the white doe rubbed her head against her, for thought the spiteful fairy had taken away her power of speech, she had not deprived her of her reason!

All day long the two remained together, and when Eglantine grew hungry she was led by the white doe to a part of the forest where pears and peaches grew in abundance; but, as night came on, the maid of honor was filled with the terrors of wild beasts which had beset the princess during her first night in the forest.

"Is there no hut or cave we could go into?" asked she. But the doe only shook her head; and the two sat down and wept with fright.

The fairy Tulip, who, in spite of her anger, was very soft-hearted, was touched at their distress, and flew quickly to their help.

"I cannot take away the spell altogether," she said, "for the Fairy of the Fountain is stronger than I; but I can shorten the time of your punishment, and am able to make it less hard, for as soon as darkness falls you shall resume your own shape."

To think that by-and-by she would cease to be a white doe—indeed, that she would at once cease to be one during the night—was for the present joy enough for Désirée, and she skipped about on the grass in the prettiest manner.

"Go straight down the path in front of you," continued the fairy, smiling as she watched her; "go straight down the path and you will soon reach a little hut where you will find shelter." And with these words she vanished, leaving her hearers happier than they ever thought they could be again.

An old woman was standing at the door of the hut when Eglantine drew near, with the white doe trotting by her side.

"Good evening!" she said; "could you give me a night's lodging for myself and my doe?"

"Certainly I can," replied the old woman. And she led them into a room with two little white beds, so clean and comfortable that it made you sleepy even to look at them.

The door had hardly closed behind the old woman when the sun sank below the horizon, and Désirée became a girl again.

"Oh, Eglantine! what should I have done if you had not followed me," she cried. And she flung herself into her friend's arms in a transport of delight.

Early in the morning Eglantine was awakened by the sound of someone scratching at the door, and on opening her eyes she saw the white doe struggling to get out. The little creature looked up and into her face, and nodded her head as the maid of honor unfastened the latch, but bounded away into the woods, and was lost to sight in a moment.

Meanwhile, the prince and Becasigue were wandering through the wood, till at last the prince grew so tired, that he lay down under a tree, and told Becasigue that he had better go in search of food, and of some place where they could sleep. Becasigue had not gone very far, when a turn of the path brought him face to face with the old woman who was feeding her doves before her cottage.

"Could you give me some milk and fruit?" asked he. "I am very hungry myself, and, besides, I have left a friend behind me who is still weak from illness."

"Certainly I can," answered the old woman. "But come and sit down in my kitchen while I catch the goat and milk it."

Becasigue was glad enough to do as he was bid, and in a few minutes the old woman returned with a basket brimming over with oranges and grapes.

"If your friend has been ill he should not pass the night in the forest," said she. "I have room in my hut—tiny enough, it is true; but better than nothing, and to that you are both heartily welcome."

Becasigue thanked her warmly, and as by this time it was almost sunset, he set out to fetch the prince. It was while he was absent that Eglantine and the white doe entered the hut, and having, of course, no idea that in the very next room was the man whose childish impatience had been the cause of all their troubles.

In spite of his fatigue, the prince slept badly, and directly it was light he rose, and bidding Becasigue remain where he was, as he wished to be alone, he strolled out into the forest. He walked on slowly, just as his fancy led him, till, suddenly, he came to a wide open space, and in the middle was the white doe quietly eating her breakfast. She bounded off at the sight of a man, but not before the prince, who had fastened on his bow without thinking, had let fly several arrows, which the fairy Tulip took care should do her no harm. But, quickly as she ran, she soon felt her strength failing her, for fifteen years of life in a tower had not taught her how to exercise her limbs.

Luckily, the prince was too weak to follow her far, and a turn of a path brought her close to the hut, where Eglantine was awaiting her. Panting for breath, she entered their room, and flung herself down on the floor.

When it was dark again, and she was once more the princess Désirée, she told Eglantine what had befallen her.

"I feared the Fairy of the Fountain, and the cruel beasts," said she; "but somehow I never thought of the dangers that I ran from men. I do not know now what saved me."

"You must stay quietly here till the time of your punishment is over," answered Eglantine. But when the morning dawned, and the girl turned into a doe, the longing for the forest came over her, and she sprang away as before.

As soon as the prince was awake he hastened to the place where, only the day before, he had found the white doe feeding; but of course she had taken care to go in the opposite direction. Much disappointed, he tried first one green path and then another, and at last, wearied with walking, he threw himself down and went fast asleep.

Just at this moment the white doe sprang out of a thicket near by, and started back trembling when she beheld her enemy lying there. Yet, instead of turning to fly, something bade her go and look at him unseen. As she gazed a thrill ran through her, for she felt that, worn and wasted though he was by illness, it was the face of her destined husband. Gently stooping over him she kissed his forehead, and at her touch he awoke.

For a minute they looked at each other, and to his amazement he recognized the white doe which had escaped him the previous day. But in an instant the animal was aroused to a sense of her danger, and she fled with all her strength into the thickest part of the forest. Quick as lightning the prince was on her track, but this time it was with no wish to kill or even wound the beautiful creature.

"Pretty doe! pretty doe! stop! I won't hurt you," cried he, but his words were carried away by the wind.

At length the doe could run no more, and when the prince reached her, she was lying stretched out on the grass, waiting for her death blow. But instead the prince knelt at her side, and stroked her, and bade her fear nothing, as he would take care of her. So he fetched a little water from the stream in his horn hunting cup, then, cutting some branches from the trees, he twisted them into a litter which he covered with moss, and laid the white doe gently on it.

For a long time they remained thus, but when Désirée saw by the way that the light struck the trees, that the sun must be near its setting, she was filled with alarm lest the darkness should fall, and the prince should behold her in her human shape.

"No, he must not see me for the first time here," she thought, and instantly began to plan how to get rid of him. Then she opened her mouth and let her tongue hang out, as if she were dying of thirst, and the prince, as she expected, hastened to the stream to get her some more water.

When he returned, the white doe was gone.

That night Désirée confessed to Eglantine that her pursuer was no other than the prince, and that far from flattering him, the portrait had never done him justice.

"Is it not hard to meet him in this shape," wept she, "when we both love each other so much?" But Eglantine comforted her, and reminded her that in a short time all would be well.

The prince was very angry at the flight of the white doe, for whom he had taken so much trouble, and returning to the cottage he poured out his adventures and his wrath to Becasigue, who could not help smiling.

"She shall not escape me again," cried the prince. "If I hunt her every day for a year, I will have her at last." And in this frame of mind he went to bed.

When the white doe entered the forest next morning, she had not made up her mind whether she would go and meet the prince, or whether she would shun him, and hide in thickets of which he knew nothing. She decided that the last plan was the best; and so it would have been if the prince had not taken the very same direction in search of her.

Quite by accident he caught sight of her white skin shining through the bushes, and at the same instant she heard a twig snap under his feet. In a moment she was up and away, but the prince, not knowing how else to capture her, aimed an arrow at her leg, which brought her to the ground.

The young man felt like a murderer as he ran hastily up to where the white doe lay, and did his best to soothe the pain she felt, which, in reality, was the last part of the punishment sent by the Fairy of the Fountain. First he brought her some water, and then he fetched some healing herbs, and having crushed them in his hand, laid them on the wound.

"Ah! what a wretch I was to have hurt you," cried he, resting her head upon his knees; "and now you will hate me and fly from me for ever!"

For some time the doe lay quietly where she was, but, as before, she remembered that the hour of her transformation was near. She struggled to her feet, but the prince would not hear of her walking, and thinking the old woman might be able to dress her wound better than he could, he took her in his arms to carry her back to the hut. But, small as she was, she made herself so heavy that, after staggering a few steps under her weight, he laid her down, and tied her fast to a tree with some of the ribbons of his hat. This done he went away to get help.

Meanwhile Eglantine had grown very uneasy at the long absence of her mistress, and had come out to look for her. Just as the prince passed out of sight the fluttering ribbons dance before her eyes, and she descried her beautiful princess bound to a tree. With all her might she worked at the knots, but not a single one could she undo, though all appeared so easy. She was still busy with them when a voice behind her said:

"Pardon me, fair lady, but it is *my* doe you are trying to steal!"

"Excuse me, good knight" answered Eglantine, hardly glancing at him, "but it is *my* doe that is tied up here! And if you wish for a proof of it, you can see if she knows me or not. Touch my heart, my little one," she continued, dropping on her knees. And the doe lifted up its fore-foot and laid it on her side. "Now put your arms round my neck, and sigh." And again the doe did as she was bid.

"You are right," said the prince; "but it is with sorrow I give her up to you, for though I have wounded her yet I love her deeply."

To this Eglantine answered nothing; but carefully raising up the doe, she led her slowly to the hut.

Now both the prince and Becasigue were quite unaware that the old woman had any guests besides themselves, and, following afar, were much surprised to behold Eglantine and her charge enter the cottage. They lost no time in questioning the old woman, who replied that she knew nothing about the lady and her white doe, who slept next the chamber occupied by the prince and his friend, but that they were very quiet, and paid her well. Then she went back to her kitchen.

"Do you know," said Becasigue, when they were alone, "I am certain that the lady we saw is the maid of honor to the Princess Désirée, whom I met at the palace. And, as her room is next to this, it will be easy to make a small hole through which I can satisfy myself whether I am right or not."

So, taking a knife out of his pocket, he began to saw away the wood-work. The girls heard the grating noise, but fancying it was a mouse, paid no attention, and Becasigue was left in peace to pursue his work. At length the hole was large enough for him to peep through, and the sight was one to strike him dumb with amazement. He had guessed truly: the tall lady was Eglantine herself; but the other—where had he seen her? Ah! now he knew— it was the lady of the portrait!

Désirée, in a flowing dress of green silk, was lying stretched out upon cushions, and as Eglantine bent over her to bathe the wounded leg, she began to talk:

"Oh! let me die," cried she, "rather than go on leading this life. You cannot tell the misery of being a beast all the day, and unable to speak to the man I love, to whose impatience I owe my cruel fate. Yet, even so, I cannot bring myself to hate him."

These words, low though they were spoken, reached Becasigue, who could hardly believe his ears. He stood silent for a moment; then, crossing to the window out of which the prince was gazing, he took his arm and led him across the room. A single glance was sufficient to show the prince that it was indeed Désirée; and how another had come to the palace bearing her name, at that instant he neither knew nor cared. Stealing on tip-toe from the room, he knocked at the next door, which was opened by Eglantine, who thought it was the old woman bearing their supper.

She started back at the sight of the prince, whom this time she also recognized. But he thrust her aside, and flung himself at the feet of Désirée, to whom he poured out all his heart!

Dawn found them still conversing; and the sun was high in the heavens before the princess perceived that she retained her human form. Ah! how happy she was when she knew that the days of her punishment were over; and with a glad voice she told the prince the tale of her enchantment.

So the story ended well after all; and the fairy Tulip, who turned out to be the old woman of the hut, made the young couple such a wedding feast as had never been seen since the world began. And everybody was delighted, except Cérisette and her mother, who were put in a boat and carried to a small island, where they had to work hard for their living.

The Golden Lion

(FROM *THE PINK FAIRY BOOK*)

There was once a rich merchant who had three sons, and when they were grown up the eldest said to him, "Father, I wish to travel and see the world. I pray you let me."

So the father ordered a beautiful ship to be fitted up, and the young man sailed away in it. After some weeks the vessel cast anchor before a large town, and the merchant's son went on shore.

The first thing he saw was a large notice written on a board saying that if any man could find the king's daughter within eight days he should have her to wife, but that if he tried and failed his head must be the forfeit.

"Well," thought the youth as he read this proclamation, "that ought not to be a very difficult matter"; and he asked an audience of the king, and told him that he wished to seek for the princess.

"Certainly," replied the king. "You have the whole palace to search in; but remember, if you fail it will cost you your head."

So saying, he commanded the doors to be thrown open, and food and drink to be set before the young man, who, after he had eaten, began to look for the princess. But though he visited every corner and chest and cupboard, she was not in any of them, and after eight days he gave it up and his head was cut off.

All this time his father and brothers had had no news of him, and were very anxious. At last the second son could bear it no longer, and said, "Dear father, give me, I pray you, a large ship and some money, and let me go and seek for my brother."

So another ship was fitted out, and the young man sailed away, and was blown by the wind into the same harbor where his brother had landed.

Now when he saw the first ship lying at anchor his heart beat high, and he said to himself, "My brother cannot surely be far off," and he ordered a boat and was put on shore.

As he jumped on to the pier his eye caught the notice about the princess, and he thought, "He has undertaken to find her, and has certainly lost his head. I must try myself, and seek him as well as her. It cannot be such a very difficult matter." But he fared no better than his brother, and in eight days his head was cut off.

So now there was only the youngest at home, and when the other two never came he also begged for a ship that he might go in search of his lost brothers. And when the vessel started a high wind arose, and blew him straight to the harbor where the notice was set.

"Oho!" said he, as he read, "whoever can find the kings daughter shall have her to wife. It is quite clear now what has befallen my brothers. But in spite of that I think I must try my luck," and he took the road to the castle.

On the way he met an old woman, who stopped and begged.

"Leave me in peace, old woman," replied he.

"Oh, do not send me away empty," she said. "You are such a handsome young man you will surely not refuse an old woman a few pence."

"I tell you, old woman, leave me alone."

"You are in some trouble?" she asked. "Tell me what it is, and perhaps I can help you."

Then he told her how he had set his heart on finding the king's daughter.

"I can easily manage that for you as long as you have enough money."

"Oh, as to that, I have plenty," answered he.

"Well, you must take it to a goldsmith and get him to make it into a golden lion, with eyes of crystal; and inside it must have something that will enable it to play tunes. When it is ready bring it to me."

The young man did as he was bid, and when the lion was made the old woman hid the youth in it, and brought it to the king, who was so delighted with it that he wanted to buy it. But she replied, "It does not belong to me, and my master will not part from it at any price."

"At any rate, leave it with me for a few days," said he; "I should like to show it to my daughter."

"Yes, I can do that," answered the old woman; "but to-morrow I must have it back again." And she went away.

The king watched her till she was quite out of sight, so as to make sure that she was not spying upon him; then he took the golden lion into his room and lifted some loose boards from the floor. Below the floor there was a staircase, which he went down till he reached a door at the foot. This he unlocked, and found himself in a narrow passage closed by another door, which he also opened. The young man, hidden in the golden lion, kept count of everything, and marked that there were in all seven doors. After they had all been unlocked the king entered a lovely hall, where the princess was amusing herself with eleven friends. All twelve girls wore the same clothes, and were as like each other as two peas.

"What bad luck!" thought the youth. "Even supposing that I managed to find my way here again, I don't see how I could ever tell which was the princess."

And he stared hard at the princess as she clapped her hands with joy and ran up to them, crying, " Oh, do let us keep that delicious beast for to-night; it will make such a nice plaything."

The king did not stay long, and when he left he handed over the lion to the maidens, who amused themselves with it for some time, till they got sleepy, and thought it was time to go to bed. But the princess took the lion into her own room and laid it on the floor.

She was just beginning to doze when she heard a voice quite close to her, which made her jump. "O lovely princess, if you only knew what I have gone through to find you!" The princess jumped out of bed screaming, "The lion! the lion!" but her friends thought it was a nightmare, and did not trouble themselves to get up.

"O lovely princess!" continued the voice, "fear nothing! I am the son of a rich merchant, and desire above all things to have you for my wife. And in order to get to you I have hidden myself in this golden lion."

"What use is that?" she asked. "For if you cannot pick me out from among my companions you will still lose your head."

"I look to you to help me," he said. "I have done so much for you that you might do this one thing for me."

"Then listen to me. On the eighth day I will tie a white sash round my waist, and by that you will know me."

The next morning the king came very early to fetch the lion, as the old woman was already at the palace asking for it. When they were safe from view she let the young man out, and he returned to the king and told him that he wished to find the princess.

"Very good," said the king, who by this time was almost tired of repeating the same words; "but if you fail your head will be the forfeit."

So the youth remained quietly in the castle, eating and looking at all the beautiful things around him, and every now and then pretending to be searching busily in all the closets and corners. On the eighth day he entered the room where the king was sitting. "Take up the floor in this place," he said. The king gave a cry, but stopped himself, and asked, "What do you want the floor up for? There is nothing there."

But as all his courtiers were watching him he did not like to make any more objections, and ordered the floor to be taken up, as the young man desired. The youth then want straight down the staircase till he reached the door; then he turned and demanded that the key should be brought. So the king was forced to unlock the door, and the next and the next and the next, till all seven were open, and they entered into the hall where the twelve maidens were standing all in a row, so like that none might tell them apart. But as he looked one of them silently drew a white sash from her pocket and slipped it round her waist, and the young man sprang to her and said, "This is the princess, and I claim her for my wife." And the king owned himself beaten, and commanded that the wedding feast should be held.

After eight days the bridal pair said farewell to the king, and set sail for the youth's own country, taking with them a whole shipload of treasures as the princess's dowry. But they did not forget the old woman who had brought about all their happiness, and they gave her enough money to make her comfortable to the end of her days.

The Story of Sigurd

(FROM *THE RED FAIRY BOOK*)

Once upon a time there was a King in the North who had won many wars, but now he was old. Yet he took a new wife, and then another Prince, who wanted to have married her, came up against him with a great army. The old King went out and fought bravely, but at last his sword broke, and he was wounded and his men fled. But in the night, when the battle was over, his young wife came out and searched for him among the slain, and at last she found him, and asked whether he might be healed. But he said "No," his luck was gone, his sword was broken, and he must die. And he told her that she would have a son, and that son would be a great warrior, and would avenge him on the other King, his enemy. And he bade her keep the broken pieces of the sword, to make a new sword for his son, and that blade should be called *Gram*.

Then he died. And his wife called her maid to her and said, "Let us change clothes, and you shall be called by my name, and I by yours, lest the enemy finds us."

So this was done, and they hid in a wood, but there some strangers met them and carried them off in a ship to Denmark. And when they were brought before the King, he thought the maid looked like a Queen, and the Queen like a maid. So he asked the Queen, "How do you know in the dark of night whether the hours are wearing to the morning?"

And she said:

"I know because, when I was younger, I used to have to rise and light the fires, and still I waken at the same time."

"A strange Queen to light the fires," thought the King.

Then he asked the Queen, who was dressed like a maid, "How do you know in the dark of night whether the hours are wearing near the dawn?"

"My father gave me a gold ring," said she, "and always, ere the dawning, it grows cold on my finger."

"A rich house where the maids wore gold," said the King. "Truly you are no maid, but a King's daughter."

So he treated her royally, and as time went on she had a son called Sigurd, a beautiful boy and very strong. He had a tutor to be with him, and once the tutor bade him go to the King and ask for a horse.

"Choose a horse for yourself," said the King; and Sigurd went to the wood, and there he met an old man with a white beard, and said, "Come! help me in horse-choosing."

Then the old man said, "Drive all the horses into the river, and choose the one that swims across."

So Sigurd drove them, and only one swam across. Sigurd chose him: his name was Grani, and he came of Sleipnir's breed, and was the best horse in the world. For Sleipnir was the horse of Odin, the God of the North, and was as swift as the wind.

But a day or two later his tutor said to Sigurd, "There is a great treasure of gold hidden not far from here, and it would become you to win it."

But Sigurd answered, "I have heard stories of that treasure, and I know that the dragon Fafnir guards it, and he is so huge and wicked that no man dares to go near him."

"He is no bigger than other dragons," said the tutor, "and if you were as brave as your father you would not fear him."

"I am no coward," says Sigurd; "why do you want me to fight with this dragon?"

Then his tutor, whose name was Regin, told him that all this great hoard of red gold had once belonged to his own father. And his father had three sons—the first was Fafnir, the Dragon; the next was Otter, who could put on the shape of an otter when he liked; and the next was himself, Regin, and he was a great smith and maker of swords.

Now there was at that time a dwarf called Andvari, who lived in a pool beneath a waterfall, and there he had hidden a great hoard of gold. And one day Otter had been fishing there, and had killed a salmon and eaten it, and was sleeping, like an otter, on a stone. Then someone came by, and threw a stone at the otter and killed it, and flayed off the skin, and took it to the house of Otter's father. Then he knew his son was dead, and to punish the person who had killed him he said he must have the Otter's skin filled with gold, and covered all over with red gold, or it should go worse with him. Then the person who had killed Otter went down and caught the Dwarf who owned all the treasure and took it from him.

Only one ring was left, which the Dwarf wore, and even that was taken from him.

Then the poor Dwarf was very angry, and he prayed that the gold might never bring any but bad luck to all the men who might own it, for ever.

Then the otter skin was filled with gold and covered with gold, all but one hair, and that was covered with the poor Dwarf's last ring.

But it brought good luck to nobody. First Fafnir, the Dragon, killed his own father, and then he went and wallowed on the gold, and would let his brother have none, and no man dared go near it.

When Sigurd heard the story he said to Regin:

"Make me a good sword that I may kill this Dragon."

So Regin made a sword, and Sigurd tried it with a blow on a lump of iron, and the sword broke.

Another sword he made, and Sigurd broke that too.

Then Sigurd went to his mother, and asked for the broken pieces of his father's blade, and gave them to Regin. And he hammered and wrought them into a new sword, so sharp that fire seemed to burn along its edges.

Sigurd tried this blade on the lump of iron, and it did not break, but split the iron in two. Then he threw a lock of wool into the river, and when it floated down against the sword it was cut into two pieces. So Sigurd said that sword would do. But before he went against the Dragon he led an army to fight the men who had killed his father, and he slew their King, and took all his wealth, and went home.

When he had been at home a few days, he rode out with Regin one morning to the heath where the Dragon used to lie. Then he saw the track which the Dragon made when he went to a cliff to drink, and the track was as if a great river had rolled along and left a deep valley.

Then Sigurd went down into that deep place, and dug many pits in it, and in one of the pits he lay hidden with his sword drawn. There he waited, and presently the earth began to shake with the weight of the Dragon as he crawled to the water. And a cloud of venom flew before him as he snorted and roared, so that it would have been death to stand before him.

But Sigurd waited till half of him had crawled over the pit, and then he thrust the sword Gram right into his very heart.

Then the Dragon lashed with his tail till stones broke and trees crashed about him.

Then he spoke, as he died, and said:

"Whoever thou art that hast slain me this gold shall be thy ruin, and the ruin of all who own it."

Sigurd said:

"I would touch none of it if by losing it I should never die. But all men die, and no brave man lets death frighten him from his desire. Die thou, Fafnir," and then Fafnir died.

And after that Sigurd was called Fafnir's Bane, and Dragonslayer.

Then Sigurd rode back, and met Regin, and Regin asked him to roast Fafnir's heart and let him taste of it.

So Sigurd put the heart of Fafnir on a stake, and roasted it. But it chanced that he touched it with his finger, and it burned him. Then he put his finger in his mouth, and so tasted the heart of Fafnir.

Then immediately he understood the language of birds, and he heard the Woodpeckers say:

"There is Sigurd roasting Fafnir's heart for another, when he should taste of it himself and learn all wisdom."

The next bird said:

"There lies Regin, ready to betray Sigurd, who trusts him."

The third bird said:

"Let him cut off Regin's head, and keep all the gold to himself."

The fourth bird said:

"That let him do, and then ride over Hindfell, to the place where Brynhild sleeps."

When Sigurd heard all this, and how Regin was plotting to betray him, he cut off Regin's head with one blow of the sword Gram.

Then all the birds broke out singing:

> "We know a fair maid,
> A fair maiden sleeping;
> Sigurd, be not afraid,
> Sigurd, win thou the maid
> Fortune is keeping.

> "High over Hindfell
> Red fire is flaming,
> There doth the maiden dwell
> She that should love thee well,
> Meet for thy taming.

> "There must she sleep till thou
> Comest for her waking
> Rise up and ride, for now
> Sure she will swear the vow
> Fearless of breaking."

Then Sigurd remembered how the story went that somewhere, far away, there was a beautiful lady enchanted. She was under a spell, so that she must always sleep in a castle surrounded by flaming fire; there she must sleep for ever till there came a knight who would ride through the fire and waken her. There he determined to go, but first he rode right down the horrible trail of Fafnir. And Fafnir had lived in a cave with iron doors, a cave dug deep down in the earth, and full of gold bracelets, and crowns, and rings; and there, too, Sigurd found the Helm of Dread, a golden helmet, and whoever wears it is invisible. All these he piled on the back of the good horse Grani, and then he rode south to Hindfell.

Now it was night, and on the crest of the hill Sigurd saw a red fire blazing up into the sky, and within the flame a castle, and a banner on the topmost tower. Then he set the horse Grani at the fire, and he leaped through it lightly, as if it had been through the heather. So Sigurd went within the castle door, and there he saw someone sleeping, clad all in armor. Then he took the helmet off the head of the sleeper, and behold, she was a most beautiful lady. And she wakened and said, "Ah! is it Sigurd, Sigmund's son, who has broken the curse, and comes here to waken me at last?"

This curse came upon her when the thorn of the tree of sleep ran into her hand long ago as a punishment because she had displeased Odin the God. Long ago, too, she had vowed never to marry a man who knew fear, and dared not ride through the fence of flaming fire. For she was a warrior maid herself, and went armed into the battle like a man. But now she and Sigurd loved each other, and promised to be true to each other, and he gave her a ring, and it was the last ring taken from the dwarf Andvari. Then Sigurd rode away, and he came to the house of a King who had a fair daughter. Her name was Gudrun, and her mother was a witch. Now Gudrun fell in love with Sigurd, but he was always talking of Brynhild, how beautiful she was and how dear. So one day Gudrun's witch mother put poppy and forgetful drugs in a magical cup, and bade Sigurd drink to her health, and he drank, and instantly he forgot poor Brynhild, and he loved Gudrun, and they were married with great rejoicings.

Now the witch, the mother of Gudrun, wanted her son Gunnar to marry Brynhild, and she bade him ride out with Sigurd and go and woo her. So forth they rode to her father's house, for Brynhild had quite gone out of

Sigurd's mind by reason of the witch's wine; but she remembered him and loved him still. Then Brynhild's father told Gunnar that she would marry none but him who could ride the flame in front of her enchanted tower, and thither they rode; and Gunnar set his horse at the flame, but he would not face it. Then Gunnar tried Sigurd's horse Grani, but he would not move with Gunnar on his back. Then Gunnar remembered witchcraft that his mother had taught him, and by his magic he made Sigurd look exactly like himself, and he looked exactly like Gunnar. Then Sigurd, in the shape of Gunnar and in his mail, mounted on Grani, and Grani leaped the fence of fire, and Sigurd went in and found Brynhild, but he did not remember her yet, because of the forgetful medicine in the cup of the witch's wine.

Now Brynhild had no help but to promise she would be his wife, the wife of Gunnar as she supposed, for Sigurd wore Gunnar's shape, and she had sworn to wed whoever should ride the flames. And he gave her a ring, and she gave him back the ring he had given her before in his own shape as Sigurd, and it was the last ring of that poor dwarf Andvari. Then he rode out again, and he and Gunnar changed shapes, and each was himself again, and they went home to the witch Queen's, and Sigurd gave the dwarf's ring to his wife, Gudrun. And Brynhild went to her father, and said that a King had come called Gunnar, and had ridden the fire, and she must marry him. "Yet I thought," she said, "that no man could have done this deed but Sigurd, Fafnir's bane, who was my true love. But he has forgotten me, and my promise I must keep."

So Gunnar and Brynhild were married, though it was not Gunnar but Sigurd in Gunnar's shape, that had ridden the fire.

And when the wedding was over and all the feast, then the magic of the witch's wine went out of Sigurd's brain, and he remembered all. He remembered how he had freed Brynhild from the spell, and how she was his own true love, and how he had forgotten and had married another woman, and won Brynhild to be the wife of another man.

But he was brave, and he spoke not a word of it to the others to make them unhappy. Still he could not keep away the curse which was to come on every one who owned the treasure of the dwarf Andvari, and his fatal golden ring.

And the curse soon came upon all of them. For one day, when Brynhild and Gudrun were bathing, Brynhild waded farthest out into the river, and said she did that to show she was Gudrun's superior. For her husband, she said, had ridden through the flame when no other man dared face it.

Then Gudrun was very angry, and said that it was Sigurd, not Gunnar, who had ridden the flame, and had received from Brynhild that fatal ring, the ring of the dwarf Andvari.

Then Brynhild saw the ring which Sigurd had given to Gudrun, and she knew it and knew all, and she turned as pale as a dead woman, and went home. All that evening she never spoke. Next day she told Gunnar, her husband, that he was a coward and a liar, for he had never ridden the flame, but had sent Sigurd to do it for him, and pretended that he had done it himself. And she said he would never see her glad in his hall, never drinking wine, never playing chess, never embroidering with the golden thread, never speaking words of kindness. Then she rent all her needlework asunder and wept aloud, so that everyone in the house heard her. For her heart was broken, and her pride was broken in the same hour. She had lost her true love, Sigurd, the slayer of Fafnir, and she was married to a man who was a liar.

Then Sigurd came and tried to comfort her, but she would not listen, and said she wished the sword stood fast in his heart.

"Not long to wait," he said, "till the bitter sword stands fast in my heart, and thou will not live long when I am dead. But, dear Brynhild, live and be comforted, and love Gunnar thy husband, and I will give thee all the gold, the treasure of the dragon Fafnir."

Brynhild said:

"It is too late."

Then Sigurd was so grieved and his heart so swelled in his breast that it burst the steel rings of his shirt of mail.

Sigurd went out and Brynhild determined to slay him. She mixed serpent's venom and wolf's flesh, and gave them in one dish to her husband's younger brother, and when he had tasted them he was mad, and he went into Sigurd's chamber while he slept and pinned him to the bed with a sword. But Sigurd woke, and caught the sword Gram into his hand, and threw it at the man as he fled, and the sword cut him in twain. Thus died Sigurd, Fafnir's bane, whom no ten men could have slain in fair fight. Then Gudrun wakened and saw him dead, and she moaned aloud, and Brynhild heard her and laughed; but the kind horse Grani lay down and died of very grief. And then Brynhild fell a-weeping till her heart broke. So they attired Sigurd in all his golden armor, and built a great pile of wood on board his ship, and at night laid on it the dead Sigurd and the dead Brynhild, and the good horse, Grani, and set fire to it, and launched the ship. And the wind bore it blazing out to sea, flaming into the dark. So there were Sigurd and Brynhild burned together, and the curse of the dwarf Andvari was fulfilled.

Stan Bolovan

(FROM *THE VIOLET FAIRY BOOK*)

Once upon a time what happened did happen, and if it had not happened this story would never have been told.

On the outskirts of a village just where the oxen were turned out to pasture, and the pigs roamed about burrowing with their noses among the roots of the trees, there stood a small house. In the house lived a man who had a wife, and the wife was sad all day long.

"Dear wife, what is wrong with you that you hang your head like a drooping rosebud?" asked her husband one morning. "You have everything you want; why cannot you be merry like other women?"

"Leave me alone, and do not seek to know the reason," replied she, bursting into tears, and the man thought that it was no time to question her, and went away to his work.

He could not, however, forget all about it, and a few days after he inquired again the reason of her sadness, but only got the same reply. At length he felt he could bear it no longer, and tried a third time, and then his wife turned and answered him.

"Good gracious!" cried she, "why cannot you let things be as they are? If I were to tell you, you would become just as wretched as myself. If you would only believe, it is far better for you to know nothing."

But no man yet was ever content with such an answer. The more you beg him not to inquire, the greater is his curiosity to learn the whole.

"Well, if you *must* know," said the wife at last, "I will tell you. There is no luck in this house—no luck at all!"

"Is not your cow the best milker in all the village? Are not your trees as full of fruit as your hives are full of bees? Has anyone cornfields like ours? Really you talk nonsense when you say things like that!"

"Yes, all that you say is true, but we have no children."

Then Stan understood, and when a man once understands and has his eyes opened it is no longer well with him. From that day the little house in the outskirts contained an unhappy man as well as an unhappy woman. And at the sight of her husband's misery the woman became more wretched than ever.

And so matters went on for some time.

Some weeks had passed, and Stan thought he would consult a wise man who lived a day's journey from his own house. The wise man was sitting before his door when he came up, and Stan fell on his knees before him. "Give me children, my lord, give me children."

"Take care what you are asking," replied the wise man. "Will not children be a burden to you? Are you rich enough to feed and clothe them?"

"Only give them to me, my lord, and I will manage somehow!" and at a sign from the wise man Stan went his way.

He reached home that evening tired and dusty, but with hope in his heart. As he drew near his house a sound of voices struck upon his ear, and he looked up to see the whole place full of children. Children in the garden, children in the yard, children looking out of every window—it seemed to the man as if all the children in the world must be gathered there. And none was bigger than the other, but each was smaller than the other, and every one was more noisy and more impudent and more daring than the rest, and Stan gazed and grew cold with horror as he realized that they all belonged to him.

"Good gracious! how many there are! how many!" he muttered to himself.

"Oh, but not one too many," smiled his wife, coming up with a crowd more children clinging to her skirts.

But even she found that it was not so easy to look after a hundred children, and when a few days had passed and they had eaten up all the food there was in the house, they began to cry, "Father! I am hungry—I am hungry," till Stan scratched his head and wondered what he was to do next. It was not that he thought there were too many children, for his life had seemed more full of joy since they appeared, but now it came to the point he did not know how he was to feed them. The cow had ceased to give milk, and it was too early for the fruit trees to ripen.

"Do you know, old woman!" said he one day to his wife, "I must go out into the world and try to bring back food somehow, though I cannot tell where it is to come from."

To the hungry man any road is long, and then there was always the thought that he had to satisfy a hundred greedy children as well as himself.

Stan wandered, and wandered, and wandered, till he reached to the end of the world, where that which is, is mingled with that which is not, and there he saw, a little way off, a sheepfold, with seven sheep in it. In the shadow of some trees lay the rest of the flock.

Stan crept up, hoping that he might manage to decoy some of them away quietly, and drive them home for food for his family, but he soon found this could not be. For at midnight he heard a rushing noise, and through the air flew a dragon, who drove apart a ram, a sheep, and a lamb, and three fine cattle that were lying down close by. And besides these he took the milk of seventy-seven sheep, and carried it home to his old mother, that she might bathe in it and grow young again. And this happened every night.

The shepherd bewailed himself in vain: the dragon only laughed, and Stan saw that this was not the place to get food for his family.

But though he quite understood that it was almost hopeless to fight against such a powerful monster, yet the thought of the hungry children at home clung to him like a burr, and would not be shaken off, and at last he said to the shepherd, "What will you give me if I rid you of the dragon?"

"One of every three rams, one of every three sheep, one of every three lambs," answered the herd.

"It is a bargain," replied Stan, though at the moment he did not know how, supposing he *did* come off the victor, he would ever be able to drive so large a flock home.

However, that matter could be settled later. At present night was not far off, and he must consider how best to fight with the dragon.

Just at midnight, a horrible feeling that was new and strange to him came over Stan—a feeling that he could not put into words even to himself, but which almost forced him to give up the battle and take the shortest road home again. He half turned; then he remembered the children, and turned back.

"You or I," said Stan to himself, and took up his position on the edge of the flock.

"Stop!" he suddenly cried, as the air was filled with a rushing noise, and the dragon came dashing past.

"Dear me!" exclaimed the dragon, looking round. "Who are you, and where do you come from?"

"I am Stan Bolovan, who eats rocks all night, and in the day feeds on the flowers of the mountain; and if you meddle with those sheep I will carve a cross on your back."

When the dragon heard these words he stood quite still in the middle of the road, for he knew he had met with his match.

"But you will have to fight me first," he said in a trembling voice, for when you faced him properly he was not brave at all.

"I fight you?" replied Stan, "why I could slay you with one breath!" Then, stooping to pick up a large cheese which lay at his feet, he added, "Go and get a stone like this out of the river, so that we may lose no time in seeing who is the best man."

The dragon did as Stan bade him, and brought back a stone out of the brook.

"Can you get buttermilk out of your stone?" asked Stan.

The dragon picked up his stone with one hand, and squeezed it till it fell into powder, but no buttermilk flowed from it. "Of course I can't!" he said, half angrily.

"Well, if you can't, I can," answered Stan, and he pressed the cheese till buttermilk flowed through his fingers.

When the dragon saw that, he thought it was time he made the best of his way home again, but Stan stood in his path.

"We have still some accounts to settle," said he, "about what you have been doing here," and the poor dragon was too frightened to stir, lest Stan should slay him at one breath and bury him among the flowers in the mountain pastures.

"Listen to me," he said at last. "I see you are a very useful person, and my mother has need of a fellow like you. Suppose you enter her service for three days, which are as long as one of your years, and she will pay you each day seven sacks full of ducats."

Three times seven sacks full of ducats! The offer was very tempting, and Stan could not resist it. He did not waste words, but nodded to the dragon, and they started along the road.

It was a long, long way, but when they came to the end they found the dragon's mother, who was as old as time itself, expecting them. Stan saw her eyes shining like lamps from afar, and when they entered the house they beheld a huge kettle standing on the fire, filled with milk. When the old mother found that her son had arrived empty-handed she grew very angry, and fire and flame darted from her nostrils, but before she could speak the dragon turned to Stan.

"Stay here," said he, "and wait for me; I am going to explain things to my mother."

Stan was already repenting bitterly that he had ever come to such a place, but, since he was there, there was nothing for it but to take everything quietly, and not show that he was afraid.

"Listen, mother," said the dragon as soon as they were alone, "I have brought this man in order to get rid of him. He is a terrific fellow who eats rocks, and can press buttermilk out of a stone," and he told her all that had happened the night before.

"Oh, just leave him to me!" she said. "I have never yet let a man slip through my fingers." So Stan had to stay and do the old mother service.

The next day she told him that he and her son should try which was the strongest, and she took down a huge club, bound seven times with iron.

The dragon picked it up as if it had been a feather, and, after whirling it round his head, flung it lightly three miles away, telling Stan to beat that if he could.

They walked to the spot where the club lay. Stan stooped and felt it; then a great fear came over him, for he knew that he and all his children together would never lift that club from the ground.

"What are you doing?" asked the dragon.

"I was thinking what a beautiful club it was, and what a pity it is that it should cause your death."

"How do you mean—my death?" asked the dragon.

"Only that I am afraid that if I throw it you will never see another dawn. You don't know how strong I am!"

"Oh, never mind that be quick and throw."

"If you are really in earnest, let us go and feast for three days: that will at any rate give you three extra days of life."

Stan spoke so calmly that this time the dragon began to get a little frightened, though he did not quite believe that things would be as bad as Stan said.

They returned to the house, took all the food that could be found in the old mother's larder, and carried it back to the place where the club was lying. Then Stan seated himself on the sack of provisions, and remained quietly watching the setting moon.

"What are you doing?" asked the dragon.

"Waiting till the moon gets out of my way."

"What do you mean? I don't understand."

"Don't you see that the moon is exactly in my way? But of course, if you like, I will throw the club into the moon."

At these words the dragon grew uncomfortable for the second time.

He prized the club, which had been left him by his grandfather, very highly, and had no desire that it should be lost in the moon.

"I'll tell you what," he said, after thinking a little. "Don't throw the club at all. I will throw it a second time, and that will do just as well."

"No, certainly not!" replied Stan. "Just wait till the moon sets."

But the dragon, in dread lest Stan should fulfill his threats, tried what bribes could do, and in the end had to promise Stan seven sacks of ducats before he was suffered to throw back the club himself.

"Oh, dear me, that is indeed a strong man," said the dragon, turning to his mother. "Would you believe that I have had the greatest difficulty in preventing him from throwing the club into the moon?"

Then the old woman grew uncomfortable too! Only to think of it! It was no joke to throw things into the moon! So no more was heard of the club, and the next day they had all something else to think about.

"Go and fetch me water!" said the mother, when the morning broke, and gave them twelve buffalo skins with the order to keep filling them till night.

They set out at once for the brook, and in the twinkling of an eye the dragon had filled the whole twelve, carried them into the house, and brought them back to Stan. Stan was tired: he could scarcely lift the buckets when they were empty, and he shuddered to think of what would happen when they were full. But he only took an old knife out of his pocket and began to scratch up the earth near the brook.

"What are you doing there? How are you going to carry the water into the house?" asked the dragon.

"How? Dear me, that is easy enough! I shall just take the brook!"

At these words the dragon's jaw dropped. This was the last thing that had ever entered his head, for the brook had been as it was since the days of his grandfather.

"I'll tell you what!" he said. "Let me carry your skins for you."

"Most certainly not," answered Stan, going on with his digging, and the dragon, in dread lest he should fulfill his threat, tried what bribes would do, and in the end had again to promise seven sacks of ducats before Stan would agree to leave the brook alone and let him carry the water into the house.

On the third day the old mother sent Stan into the forest for wood, and, as usual, the dragon went with him.

Before you could count three he had pulled up more trees than Stan could have cut down in a lifetime, and had arranged them neatly in rows. When the dragon had finished, Stan began to look about him, and, choosing the biggest of the trees, he climbed up it, and, breaking off a long rope of wild vine, bound the top of the tree to the one next it. And so he did to a whole line of trees.

"What are you doing there?" asked the dragon.

"You can see for yourself," answered Stan, going quietly on with his work.

"Why are you tying the trees together?"

"Not to give myself unnecessary work; when I pull up one, all the others will come up too."

"But how will you carry them home?"

"Dear me! Don't you understand that I am going to take the whole forest back with me?" said Stan, tying two other trees as he spoke.

"I'll tell you what," cried the dragon, trembling with fear at the thought of such a thing; "let me carry the wood for you, and you shall have seven times seven sacks full of ducats."

"You are a good fellow, and I agree to your proposal," answered Stan, and the dragon carried the wood.

Now the three days' service which were to be reckoned as a year were over, and the only thing that disturbed Stan was, how to get all those ducats back to his home!

In the evening the dragon and his mother had a long talk, but Stan heard every word through a crack in the ceiling.

"Woe be to us, mother," said the dragon; "this man will soon get us into his power. Give him his money, and let us be rid of him."

But the old mother was fond of money, and did not like this.

"Listen to me," said she; "you must murder him this very night."

"I am afraid," answered he.

"There is nothing to fear," replied the old mother. "When he is asleep take the club, and hit him on the head with it. It is easily done."

And so it would have been, had not Stan heard all about it. And when the dragon and his mother had put out their lights, he took the pigs' trough and filled it with earth, and placed it in his bed, and covered it with clothes. Then he hid himself underneath, and began to snore loudly.

Very soon the dragon stole softly into the room, and gave a tremendous blow on the spot where Stan's head should have been. Stan groaned loudly from under the bed, and the dragon went away as softly as he had come. Directly he had closed the door, Stan lifted out the pigs' trough, and lay down himself, after making everything clean and tidy, but he was wise enough not to shut his eyes that night.

The next morning he came into the room when the dragon and his mother were having their breakfast.

"Good morning," said he.

"Good morning. How did you sleep?"

"Oh, very well, but I dreamed that a flea had bitten me, and I seem to feel it still."

The dragon and his mother looked at each other. "Do you hear that?" whispered he. "He talks of a flea. I broke my club on his head."

This time the mother grew as frightened as her son. There was nothing to be done with a man like this, and she made all haste to fill the sacks with ducats, so as to get rid of Stan as soon as possible. But on his side Stan was trembling like an aspen, as he could not lift even one sack from the ground. So he stood still and looked at them.

"What are you standing there for?" asked the dragon.

"Oh, I was standing here because it has just occurred to me that I should like to stay in your service for another year. I am ashamed that when I get home they should see I have brought back so little. I know that they will cry out, 'Just look at Stan Bolovan, who in one year has grown as weak as a dragon.'"

Here a shriek of dismay was heard both from the dragon and his mother, who declared they would give him seven or even seven times seven the number of sacks if he would only go away.

"I'll tell you what!" said Stan at last. "I see you don't want me to stay, and I should be very sorry to make myself disagreeable. I will go at once, but only on condition that you shall carry the money home yourself, so that I may not be put to shame before my friends."

The words were hardly out of his mouth before the dragon had snatched up the sacks and piled them on his back. Then he and Stan set forth.

The way, though really not far, was yet too long for Stan, but at length he heard his children's voices, and stopped short. He did not wish the dragon to know where he lived, lest some day he should come to take back his treasure. Was there nothing he could say to get rid of the monster? Suddenly an idea came into Stan's head, and he turned round.

"I hardly know what to do," said he. "I have a hundred children, and I am afraid they may do you harm, as they are always ready for a fight. However, I will do my best to protect you."

A hundred children! That was indeed no joke! The dragon let fall the sacks from terror, and then picked them up again. But the children, who had had nothing to eat since their father had left them, came rushing towards him, waving knives in their right hands and forks in their left, and crying, "Give us dragon's flesh; we will have dragon's flesh."

At this dreadful sight the dragon waited no longer: he flung down his sacks where he stood and took flight as fast as he could, so terrified at the fate that awaited him that from that day he has never dared to show his face in the world again.

How Brave Walter Hunted Wolves

(FROM *THE LILAC FAIRY BOOK*)

A little back from the high road there stands a house which is called "Hemgard." Perhaps you remember the two beautiful mountain ash trees by the reddish-brown palings, and the high gate, and the garden with the beautiful barberry bushes which are always the first to become grown in spring, and which in summer are weighed down with their beautiful berries.

Behind the garden there is a hedge with tall aspens which rustle in the morning wind, behind the hedge is a road, behind the road is a wood, and behind the wood the wide world.

But on the other side of the garden there is a lake, and beyond the lake is a village, and all around stretch meadows and fields, now yellow, now green.

In the pretty house, which has white window-frames, a neat porch and clean steps, which are always strewn with finely-cut juniper leaves, Walter's parents live. His brother Frederick, his sister Lotta, old Lena, Jonah, Caro and Bravo, Putte and Murre, and Kuckeliku.

Caro lives in the dog house, Bravo in the stable, Putte with the stableman, Murre a little here and a little there, and Kuckeliku lives in the hen house, that is his kingdom.

Walter is six years old, and he must soon begin to go to school. He cannot read yet, but he can do many other things. He can turn cartwheels, stand on his head, ride see-saw, throw snowballs, play ball, crow like a cock, eat bread and butter and drink sour milk, tear his trousers, wear holes in his elbows, break the crockery in pieces, throw balls through the windowpanes, draw old men on important papers, walk over the flower-beds, eat himself sick with gooseberries, and be well after a whipping. For the rest he has a good heart but a bad memory, and forgets his father's and his mother's admonitions, and so often gets into trouble and meets with adventures, as you shall hear, but first of all I must tell you how brave he was and how he hunted wolves.

Once in the spring, a little before Midsummer, Walter heard that there were a great many wolves in the wood, and that pleased him. He was wonderfully brave when he was in the midst of his companions or at home with his brothers and sister, then he used often to say "One wolf is nothing, there ought to be at least *four.*"

When he wrestled with Klas Bogenstrom or Frithiof Waderfelt and struck them in the back, he would say "That is what I shall do to a wolf!" and when he shot arrows at Jonas and they rattled against his sheepskin coat he would say: "That is how I should shoot you if you were a wolf!"

Indeed, some thought that the brave boy boasted a little; but one must indeed believe him since he said so himself. So Jonas and Lena used to say of him "Look, there goes Walter, who shoots the wolves." And other boys and girls would say "Look, there goes brave Walter, who is brave enough to fight with four."

There was no one so fully convinced of this as Walter himself, and one day he prepared himself for a real wolf hunt. He took with him his drum, which had holes in one end since the time he had climbed up on it to reach a cluster of rowan berries, and his tin sabre, which was a little broken, because he had with incredible courage fought his way through a whole unfriendly army of gooseberry bushes.

He did not forget to arm himself quite to the teeth with his pop-gun, his bow, and his air-pistol. He had a burnt cork in his pocket to blacken his moustache, and a red cock's feather to put in his cap to make himself look fierce. He had besides in his trouser pocket a clasp knife with a bone handle, to cut off the ears of the wolves as soon as he had killed them, for he thought it would be cruel to do that while they were still living.

It was such a good thing that Jonas was going with corn to the mill, for Walter got a seat on the load, while Caro ran barking beside them. As soon as they came to the wood Walter looked cautiously around him to see perchance if there was a wolf in the bushes, and he did not omit to ask Jonas if wolves were afraid of a drum. "Of course they are" (that is understood) said Jonas. Thereupon Walter began to beat his drum with all his might while they were going through the wood.

When they came to the mill Walter immediately asked if there had been any wolves in the neighborhood lately.

"Alas! yes," said the miller, "last night the wolves have eaten our fattest ram there by the kiln not far from here."

"Ah!" said Walter, "do you think that there were many?"

"We don't know," answered the miller.

"Oh, it is all the same," said Walter. "I only asked so that I should know if I should take Jonas with me.

"I could manage very well alone with *three*, but if there were more, I might not have time to kill them all before they ran away."

"In Walter's place I should go quite alone, it is more manly," said Jonas.

"No, it is better for you to come too," said Walter. "Perhaps there are many."

"No, I have not time," said Jonas, "and besides, there are sure not to be more than three. Walter can manage them very well alone."

"Yes," said Walter, "certainly I could; but, you see, Jonas, it might happen that one of them might bite me in the back, and I should have more trouble in killing them. If I only knew that there were not more than two I should not mind, for them I should take one in each hand and give them a good shaking, like Susanna once shook me."

"I certainly think that there will not be more than two," said Jonas, "there are never more than two when they slay children and rams; Walter can very well shake them without me."

"But, you see, Jonas," said Walter, "if there are two, it might still happen that one of them escapes and bites me in the leg, for you see I am not so strong in the left hand as in the right. You can very well come with me, and take a good stick in case there are really two. Look, if there is only one, I shall take him so with both my hands and thrown him living on to his back, and he can kick as much as he likes, I shall hold him fast."

"Now, when I really think over the thing," said Jonas, "I am almost sure there will not be more than one. What would two do with one ram? There will certainly not be more than one."

"But you should come with me all the same, Jonas," said Walter. "You see I can very well manage one, but I am not quite accustomed to wolves yet, and he might tear holes in my new trousers."

"Well, just listen," said Jonas, "I am beginning to think that Walter is not so brave as people say. First of all Walter would fight against four, and then against three, then two, and then one, and now Walter wants help with one. Such a thing must never be; what would people say? Perhaps they would think that Walter is a coward?"

"That's a lie," said Walter, "I am not at all frightened, but it is more amusing when there are two. I only want someone who will see how I strike the wolf and how the dust flies out of his skin."

"Well, then, Walter can take the miller's little Lisa with him. She can sit on a stone and look on," said Jonas.

"No, she would certainly be frightened," said Walter, "and how would it do for a girl to go wolf-hunting? Come with me, Jonas, and you shall have the skin, and I will be content with the ears and the tail."

"No, thank you," said Jonas, "Walter can keep the skin for himself. Now I see quite well that he is frightened. Fie, shame on him!"

This touched Walter's pride very near. "I shall show that I am not frightened," he said; and so he took his drum, sabre, cock's feather, clasp-knife, pop-gun and air-pistol, and went off quite alone to the wood to hunt wolves.

It was a beautiful evening, and the birds were singing in all the branches. Walter went very slowly and cautiously. At every step he looked all round him to see if perchance there was anything lurking behind the stones. He quite thought something moved away there in the ditch. Perhaps it was a wolf. "It is better for me to beat the drum a little before I go there," thought Walter.

Br-r-r, so he began to beat his drum. Then something moved again. Caw! caw! a crow flew up from the ditch. Walter immediately regained courage. "It was well I took my drum with me," he thought, and went straight on with courageous steps. Very soon he came quite close to the kiln, where the wolves had killed the ram. But the nearer he came the more dreadful he thought the kiln looked. It was so gray and old. Who knew how many wolves there might be hidden there? Perhaps the very ones which killed the ram were still sitting there in a corner. Yes, it was not at all safe here, and there were no other people to be seen in the neighborhood. It would be horrible to be eaten up here in the daylight, thought Walter to himself; and the more he thought about it the uglier and grayer the old kiln looked, and the more horrible and dreadful it seemed to become the food of wolves.

"Shall I go back and say that I struck one wolf and it escaped?" thought Walter. "Fie!" said his conscience, "Do you not remember that a lie is one of the worst sins, both in the sight of God and man? If you tell a lie to-day and say you struck a wolf, to-morrow surely it will eat you up."

"No, I will go to the kiln," thought Walter, and so he went. But he did not go quite near. He went only so near that he could see the ram's blood which colored the grass red, and some tufts of wool which the wolves had torn from the back of the poor animal.

It looked so dreadful.

"I wonder what the ram thought when they ate him up," thought Walter to himself; and just then a cold shiver ran through him from his collar right down to his boots.

"It is better for me to beat the drum," he thought to himself again, and so he began to beat it. But it sounded horrid, and an echo came out from the kiln that seemed almost like the howl of a wolf. The drumsticks stiffened in Walter's hands, and he thought now they are coming...!

Yes, sure enough, just then a shaggy, reddish-brown wolf's head looked out from under the kiln!

What did Walter do now? Yes, the brave Walter who alone could manage four, threw his drum far away, took to his heels and ran, and ran as fast as he could back to the mill.

But, alas! the wolf ran after him. Walter looked back; the wolf was quicker than he and only a few steps behind him. Then Walter ran faster. But fear got the better of him, he neither heard nor saw anything more. He ran over sticks, stones and ditches; he lost drum-sticks, saber, bow, and air-pistol, and in his terrible hurry he tripped over a tuft of grass. There he lay, and the wolf jumped on to him. . . .

It was a gruesome tale! Now you may well believe that it was all over with Walter and all his adventures. That would have been a pity. But do not be surprised if it was not quite so bad as that, for the wolf was quite a friendly one. He certainly jumped on to Walter, but he only shook his coat and rubbed his nose against his face; and Walter shrieked. Yes, he shrieked terribly!

Happily Jonas heard his cry of distress, for Walter was quite near the mill now, and he ran and helped him up.

"What has happened?" he asked. "Why did Walter scream so terribly?"

"A wolf! A wolf!" cried Walter, and that was all he could say.

"Where is the wolf?" said Jonas. "I don't see any wolf."

"Take care, he is here, he has bitten me to death," groaned Walter.

Then Jonas began to laugh; yes, he laughed so that he nearly burst his skin belt.

Well, well, was that the wolf? Was that the wolf which Walter was to take by the neck and shake and throw down on its back, no matter how much it struggled? Just look a little closer at him: he is your old friend, your own good old Caro. I quite expect he found a leg of the ram in the kiln. When Walter beat his drum, Caro crept out, and when Walter ran away, Caro ran after him, as he so often does when Walter wants to romp and play.

"Down, Caro! you ought to be rather ashamed to have put such a great hero to flight!"

Walter got up feeling very foolish.

"Down, Caro!" he said, both relieved and annoyed.

"It was only a dog, then if it had been a wolf I certainly should have killed him. . . ."

"If Walter would listen to my advice, and boast a little less, and do a little more," said Jonas, consolingly. "Walter is not a coward, is he?"

"I! You shall see, Jonas, when we next meet a bear. You see I like so much better to fight with bears."

"Indeed!" laughed Jonas. "Are you at it again?"

"Dear Walter, remember that it is only cowards who boast; a really brave man never talks of his bravery."

Laughing Eye and Weeping Eye, or the Limping Fox

(FROM *THE GRAY FAIRY BOOK*)

Once upon a time there lived a man whose right eye always smiled, and whose left eye always cried; and this man had three sons, two of them very clever, and the third very stupid. Now these three sons were very curious about the peculiarity of their father's eyes, and as they could not puzzle out the reason for themselves, they determined to ask their father why he did not have eyes like other people.

So the eldest of the three went one day into his father's room and put the question straight out; but, instead of answering, the man flew into a fearful rage, and sprang at him with a knife. The young fellow ran away in a terrible fright, and took refuge with his brothers, who were awaiting anxiously the result of the interview.

"You had better go yourselves," was all the reply they got, "and see if you will fare any better."

Upon hearing this, the second son entered his father's room, only to be treated in the same manner as his brother; and back he came telling the youngest, the fool of the family, that it was his turn to try his luck.

Then the youngest son marched boldly up to his father and said to him, "My brothers would not let me know what answer you had given to their question. But now, do tell me why your right eye always laughs and your left eye always weeps."

As before, the father grew purple with fury, and rushed forwards with his knife. But the simpleton did not stir a step; he knew that he had really nothing to fear from his father.

"Ah, now I see who is my true son," exclaimed the old man; "the others are mere cowards. And as you have shown me that you are brave, I will satisfy your curiosity. My right eye laughs because I am glad to have a son like you; my left eye weeps because a precious treasure has been stolen from me. I had in my garden a vine that yielded a tun of wine every hour—someone has managed to steal it, so I weep its loss."

The simpleton returned to his brothers and told them of their father's loss, and they all made up their minds to set out at once in search of the vine. They traveled together till they came to some cross roads, and there they parted, the two elder ones taking one road, and the simpleton the other.

"Thank goodness we have got rid of that idiot," exclaimed the two elder. "Now let us have some breakfast." And they sat down by the roadside and began to eat.

They had only half finished, when a lame fox came out of a wood and begged them to give him something to eat. But they jumped up and chased him off with their sticks, and the poor fox limped away on his three pads. As he ran he reached the spot where the youngest son was getting out the food he had brought with him, and the fox asked him for a crust of bread.

The simpleton had not very much for himself, but he gladly gave half of his meal to the hungry fox.

"Where are you going, brother?" said the fox, when he had finished his share of the bread; and the young man told him the story of his father and the wonderful vine.

"Dear me, how lucky!" said the fox. "I know what has become of it. Follow me!" So they went on till they came to the gate of a large garden.

"You will find here the vine that you are seeking, but it will not be at all easy to get it. You must listen carefully to what I am going to say. Before you reach the vine you will have to pass twelve outposts, each consisting of two guards. If you see these guards looking straight at you, go on without fear, for they are asleep. But if their eyes are shut then beware, for they are wide awake. If you once get to the vine, you will find two shovels, one of wood and the other of iron. Be sure not to take the iron one; it will make a noise and rouse the guards, and then you are lost."

The young man got safely through the garden without any adventures till he came to the vine which yielded a tun of wine an hour. But he thought he should find it impossible to dig the hard earth with only a wooden shovel, so picked up the iron one instead. The noise it made soon awakened the guards. They seized the poor simpleton and carried him to their master.

"Why do you try to steal my vine?" demanded he; "and how did you manage to get past the guards?"

"The vine is not yours; it belongs to my father, and if you will not give it to me now, I will return and get it somehow."

"You shall have the vine if you will bring me in exchange an apple off the golden apple-tree that flowers every twenty-four hours, and bears fruit of gold." So saying, he gave orders that the simpleton should be released, and this done, the youth hurried off to consult the fox.

"Now you see," observed the fox, "this comes of not following my advice. However, I will help you to get the golden apple. It grows in a garden that you will easily recognize from my description. Near the apple-tree are two poles, one of gold, the other of wood. Take the wooden pole, and you will be able to reach the apple."

Master Simpleton listened carefully to all that was told him, and after crossing the garden, and escaping as before from the men who were watching it, soon arrived at the apple-tree. But he was so dazzled by the sight of the beautiful golden fruit, that he quite forgot all that the fox had said. He seized the golden pole, and struck the branch a sounding blow. The guards at once awoke, and conducted him to their master. Then the simpleton had to tell his story.

"I will give you the golden apple," said the owner of the garden, "if you will bring me in exchange a horse which can go round the world in four-and-twenty hours." And the young man departed, and went to find the fox.

This time the fox was really angry, and no wonder.

"If you had listened to me, you would have been home with your father by this time. However I am willing to help you once more. Go into the forest, and you will find the horse with two halters round his neck. One is of gold, the other of hemp. Lead him by the hempen halter, or else the horse will begin to neigh, and will waken the guards. Then all is over with you."

So Master Simpleton searched till he found the horse, and was struck dumb at its beauty.

"What!" he said to himself, "put the hempen halter on an animal like that? Not I, indeed!"

Then the horse neighed loudly; the guards seized our young friend and conducted him before their master.

"I will give you the golden horse," said he, "if you will bring me in exchange a golden maiden who has never yet seen either sun or moon."

"But if I am to bring you the golden maiden you must lend me first the golden steed with which to seek for her."

"Ah," replied the owner of the golden horse, "but who will undertake that you will ever come back?"

"I swear on the head of my father," answered the young man, "that I will bring back either the maiden or the horse." And he went away to consult the fox.

Now, the fox who was always patient and charitable to other people's faults, led him to the entrance of a deep grotto, where stood a maiden all of gold, and beautiful as the day. He placed her on his horse and prepared to mount.

"Are you not sorry," said the fox, "to give such a lovely maiden in exchange for a horse? Yet you are bound to do it, for you have sworn by the head of your father. But perhaps I could manage to take her place." So saying, the fox transformed himself into another golden maiden, so like the first that hardly anyone could tell the difference between them.

The simpleton took her straight to the owner of the horse, who was enchanted with her.

And the young man got back his father's vine and married the *real* golden maiden into the bargain.

The Little Hare

(FROM *THE PINK FAIRY BOOK*)

Along, long way off, in a land where water is very scarce, there lived a man and his wife and several children. One day the wife said to her husband, "I am pining to have the liver of a *nyamatsané* for my dinner. If you love me as much as you say you do, you will go out and hunt for a *nyamatsané*, and will kill it and get its liver. If not, I shall know that your love is not worth having."

"Bake some bread," was all her husband answered, "then take the crust and put it in this little bag."

The wife did as she was told, and when she had finished she said to her husband, "The bag is all ready and quite full."

"Very well," said he, "and now good-bye; I am going after the *nyamatsané*."

But the *nyamatsané* was not so easy to find as the woman had hoped. The husband walked on and on and on without ever seeing one, and every now and then he felt so hungry that he was obliged to eat one of the crusts of bread out of his bag. At last, when he was ready to drop from fatigue, he found himself on the edge of a great marsh, which bordered on one side the country of the *nyamatsanés*. But there were no more *nyamatsanés* here than anywhere else. They had all gone on a hunting expedition, as their larder was empty, and the only person left at home was their grandmother, who was so feeble she never went out of the house. Our friend looked on this as a great piece of luck, and made haste to kill her before the others returned, and to take out her liver, after which he dressed himself in her skin as well as he could. He had scarcely done this when he heard the noise of the *nyamatsanés* coming back to their grandmother, for they were very fond of her, and never stayed away from her longer than they could help. They rushed clattering into the hut, exclaiming, "We smell human flesh! Some man is here," and began to look about for him; but they only saw their old grandmother, who answered, in a trembling voice, "No, my children, no! What should any man be doing here?" The *nyamatsanés* paid no attention to her, and began to open all the cupboards, and peep under all the beds, crying out all the while, "A man is here! a man is here!" but they could find nobody, and at length, tired out with their long day's hunting, they curled themselves up and fell asleep.

Next morning they woke up quite refreshed, and made ready to start on another expedition; but as they did not feel happy about their grandmother they said to her, "Grandmother, won't you come to-day and feed with us?" And they led their grandmother outside, and all of them began hungrily to eat pebbles. Our friend pretended to do the same, but in reality he slipped the stones into his pouch, and swallowed the crusts of bread instead. However, as the *nyamatsanés* did not see this they had no idea that he was not really their grandmother. When they had eaten a great many pebbles they thought they had done enough for that day, and all went home together and curled themselves up to sleep. Next morning when they woke they said, "Let us go and amuse ourselves by jumping over the ditch," and every time they cleared it with a bound. Then they begged their grandmother to jump over it too, end with a tremendous effort she managed to spring right over to the other side. After this they had no doubt at all of its being their true grandmother, and went off to their hunting, leaving our friend at home in the hut.

As soon as they had gone out of sight our hero made haste to take the liver from the place where he had hid it, threw off the skin of the old *nyamatsané*, and ran away as hard as he could, only stopping to pick up a very brilliant and polished little stone, which he put in his bag by the side of the liver.

Towards evening the *nyamatsanés* came back to the hut full of anxiety to know how their grandmother had got on during their absence. The first thing they saw on entering the door was her skin lying on the floor, and then they knew that they had been deceived, and they said to each other, "So we were right, after all, and it was human flesh we smelt." Then they stooped down to find traces of the man's footsteps, and when they had got them instantly set out in hot pursuit.

Meanwhile our friend had journeyed many miles, and was beginning to feel quite safe and comfortable, when, happening to look round, he saw in the distance a thick cloud of dust moving rapidly. His heart stood still within him, and he said to himself, "I am lost. It is the *nyamatsanés*, and they will tear me in pieces," and indeed the cloud of dust was drawing near with amazing quickness, and the *nyamatsanés* almost felt as if they were already devouring him. Then as a last hope the man took the little stone that he had picked up out of his bag and flung it on the ground. The moment it touched the soil it became a huge rock, whose steep sides were smooth as glass, and on the top of it our hero hastily seated himself. It was in vain that the *nyamatsanés* tried to climb up and reach him; they slid down again much faster than they had gone up; and by sunset they were quite worn out, and fell asleep at the foot of the rock.

No sooner had the *nyamatsanés* tumbled off to sleep than the man stole softly down and fled away as fast as his legs would carry him, and by the time his enemies were awake he was a very long way off. They sprang quickly to their feet and began to sniff the soil round the rock, in order to discover traces of his footsteps, and they galloped after him with terrific speed. The chase continued for several days and nights; several times the *nyamatsanés* almost reached him, and each time he was saved by his little pebble.

Between his fright and his hurry he was almost dead of exhaustion when he reached his own village, where the *nyamatsanés* could not follow him, because of their enemies the dogs, which swarmed over all the roads. So they returned home.

Then our friend staggered into his own hut and called to his wife: "Ichou! how tired I am! Quick, give me something to drink. Then go and get fuel and light a fire."

So she did what she was bid, and then her husband took the *nyamatsané's* liver from his pouch and said to her, "There, I have brought you what you wanted, and now you know that I love you truly."

And the wife answered, "It is well. Now go and take out the children, so that I may remain alone in the hut," and as she spoke she lifted down an old stone pot and put on the liver to cook. Her husband watched her for a moment, and then said, "Be sure you eat it all yourself. Do not give a scrap to any of the children, but eat every morsel up." So the woman took the liver and ate it all herself.

Directly the last mouthful had disappeared she was seized with such violent thirst that she caught up a great pot full of water and drank it at a single draught. Then, having no more in the house, she ran in next door and said, "Neighbor, give me, I pray you, something to drink." The neighbor gave her a large vessel quite full, and the woman drank it off at a single draught, and held it out for more.

But the neighbor pushed her away, saying, "No, I shall have none left for my children."

So the woman went into another house, and drank all the water she could find; but the more she drank the more thirsty she became. She wandered in this manner through the whole village till she had drunk every water-pot dry. Then she rushed off to the nearest spring, and swallowed that, and when she had finished all the springs and wells about she drank up first the river and then a lake. But by this time she had drunk so much that she could not rise from the ground.

In the evening, when it was time for the animals to have their drink before going to bed, they found the lake quite dry, and they had to make up their minds to be thirsty till the water flowed again and the streams were full. Even then, for some time, the lake was very dirty, and the lion, as king of the beasts, commanded that no one should drink till it was quite clear again.

But the little hare, who was fond of having his own way, and was very thirsty besides, stole quietly off when all the rest were asleep in their dens, and crept down to the margin of the lake and drank his fill. Then he smeared the dirty water all over the rabbit's face and paws, so that it might look as if it were he who had been disobeying Big Lion's orders.

The next day, as soon as it was light, Big Lion marched straight for the lake, and all the other beasts followed him. He saw at once that the water had been troubled again, and was very angry.

"Who has been drinking my water?" said he; and the little hare gave a jump, and, pointing to the rabbit, he answered, "Look there! it must be he! Why, there is mud all over his face and paws!"

The rabbit, frightened out of his wits, tried to deny the fact, exclaiming, "Oh, no, indeed I never did"; but Big Lion would not listen, and commanded them to cane him with a birch rod.

Now the little hare was very much pleased with his cleverness in causing the rabbit to be beaten instead of himself, and went about boasting of it.

At last one of the other animals overheard him, and called out, "Little hare, little hare! what is that you are saying?"

But the little hare hastily replied, "I only asked you to pass me my stick."

An hour or two later, thinking that no one was near him, he said to himself again, "It was really I who drank up the water, but I made them think it was the rabbit."

But one of the beasts whose ears were longer than the rest caught the words, and went to tell Big Lion about it. "Do you hear what the little hare is saying?"

So Big Lion sent for the little hare, and asked him what he meant by talking like that.

The little hare saw that there was no use trying to hide it, so he answered pertly, "It was I who drank the water, but I made them think it was the rabbit." Then he turned and ran as fast as he could, with all the other beasts pursuing him.

They were almost up to him when he dashed into a very narrow cleft in the rock, much too small for them to follow; but in his hurry he had left one of his long ears sticking out, which they just managed to seize. But pull as hard as they might they could not drag him out of the hole, and at last they gave it up and left him, with his ear very much torn and scratched.

When the last tail was out of sight the little hare crept cautiously out, and the first person he met was the rabbit. He had plenty of impudence, so he put a bold face on the matter, and said, "Well, my good rabbit, you see I have had a beating as well as you."

But the rabbit was still sore and sulky, and he did not care to talk, so he answered, coldly, "You have treated me very badly. It was really you who drank that water, and you accused me of having done it."

"Oh, my good rabbit, never mind that! I've got such a wonderful secret to tell you! Do you know what to do so as to escape death?"

"No, I don't."

"Well, we must begin by digging a hole."

So they dug a hole, and then the little hare said, "The next thing is to make a fire in the hole," and they set to work to collect wood, and lit quite a large fire.

When it was burning brightly the little hare said to the rabbit, "Rabbit, my friend, throw me into the fire, and when you hear my fur crackling, and I call 'Itchi, Itchi,' then be quick and pull me out."

The rabbit did as he was told, and threw the little hare into the fire; but no sooner did the little hare begin to feel the heat of the flames than he took some green bay leaves he had plucked for the purpose and held them in the middle of the fire, where they crackled and made a great noise. Then he called loudly "Itchi, Itchi! Rabbit, my friend, be quick, be quick! Don't you hear how my skin is crackling?"

And the rabbit came in a great hurry and pulled him out.

Then the little hare said, "Now it is your turn!" and he threw the rabbit in the fire. The moment the rabbit felt the flames he cried out "Itchi, Itchi, I am burning; pull me out quick, my friend!"

But the little hare only laughed, and said, "No, you may stay there! It is your own fault. Why were you such a fool as to let yourself be thrown in? Didn't you know that fire burns?" And in a very few minutes nothing was left of the rabbit but a few bones.

When the fire was quite out the little hare went and picked up one of these bones, and made a flute out of it, and sang this song:

> "Pii, pii, O flute that I love,
> Pii, pii, rabbits are but little boys.
> Pii, pii, he would have burned me if he could;
> Pii, pii, but I burned him, and he crackled finely."

When he got tired of going through the world singing this the little hare went back to his friends and entered the service of Big Lion. One day he said to his master, "Grandfather, shall I show you a splendid way to kill game?"

"What is it?" asked Big Lion.

"We must dig a ditch, and then you must lie in it and pretend to be dead."

Big Lion did as he was told, and when he had lain down the little hare got up on a wall blew a trumpet and shouted—

> "Pii, pii, all you animals come and see,
> Big Lion is dead, and now peace will be."

Directly they heard this they all came running. The little hare received them and said, "Pass on, this way to the lion." So they all entered into the Animal Kingdom. Last of all came the monkey with her baby on her back.

She approached the ditch, and took a blade of grass and tickled Big Lion's nose, and his nostrils moved in spite of his efforts to keep them still. Then the monkey cried, "Come, my baby, climb on my back and let us go. What sort of a dead body is it that can still feel when it is tickled?" And she and her baby went away in a fright. Then the little hare said to the other beasts, "Now, shut the gate of the Animal Kingdom." And it was shut, and great stones were rolled against it. When everything was tight closed the little hare turned to Big Lion and said "*Now!*" and Big Lion bounded out of the ditch and tore the other animals in pieces.

But Big Lion kept all the choice bits for himself, and only gave away the little scraps that he did not care about eating; and the little hare grew very angry, and determined to have his revenge. He had long ago found out that Big Lion was very easily taken in; so he laid his plans accordingly. He said to him, as if the idea had just come into his head, "Grandfather, let us build a hut," and Big Lion consented. And when they had driven the stakes into the ground, and had made the walls of the hut, the little hare told Big Lion to climb upon the top while he stayed inside. When he was ready he called out, "Now, grandfather, begin," and Big Lion passed his rod through the reeds with which the roofs are always covered in that country. The little hare took it and cried, "Now it is my turn to pierce them," and as he spoke he passed the rod back through the reeds and gave Big Lion's tail a sharp poke.

"What is pricking me so?" asked Big Lion.

"Oh, just a little branch sticking out. I am going to break it," answered the little hare; but of course he had done it on purpose, as he wanted to fix Big Lion's tail so firmly to the hut that he would not be able to move. In a little while he gave another prick, and Big Lion called again, "What is pricking me so?"

This time the little hare said to himself, "He will find out what I am at. I must try some other plan." So he called out, "Grandfather, you had better put your tongue here, so that the branches shall not touch you." Big Lion did as he was bid, and the little hare tied it tightly to the stakes of the wall. Then he went outside and shouted, "Grandfather, you can come down now," and Big Lion tried, but he could not move an inch.

Then the little hare began quietly to eat Big Lion's dinner right before his eyes, and paying no attention at all to his growls of rage. When he had quite done he climbed up on the hut, and, blowing his flute, he chanted "Pii, pii, fall rain and hail," and directly the sky was full of clouds, the thunder roared, and huge hailstones whitened the roof of the hut. The little hare, who had taken refuge within, called out again, "Big Lion, be quick and come down and dine with me." But there was no answer, not even a growl, for the hailstones had killed Big Lion.

The little hare enjoyed himself vastly for some time, living comfortably in the hut, with plenty of food to eat and no trouble at all in getting it. But one day a great wind arose, and flung down the Big Lion's half-dried skin from the roof of the hut. The little hare bounded with terror at the noise, for he thought Big Lion must have come to life again; but on discovering what had happened he set about cleaning the skin, and propped the mouth open with sticks so that he could get through. So, dressed in Big Lion's skin, the little hare started on his travels.

The first visit he paid was to the hyænas, who trembled at the sight of him, and whispered to each other, "How shall we escape from this terrible beast?" Meanwhile the little hare did not trouble himself about them, but just asked where the king of the hyænas lived, and made himself quite at home there. Every morning each hyæna thought to himself, "To-day he is certain to eat me"; but several days went by, and they were all still alive. At length, one evening, the little hare, looking round for something to amuse him, noticed a great pot full of boiling water, so he strolled up to one of the hyænas and said, "Go and get in." The hyæna dared not disobey, and in a few minutes was scalded to death. Then the little hare went the round of the village, saying to every hyæna he met, "Go and get into the boiling water," so that in a little while there was hardly a male left in the village.

One day all the hyænas that remained alive went out very early into the fields, leaving only one little daughter at home. The little hare, thinking he was all alone, came into the enclosure, and, wishing to feel what it was like to be a hare again, threw off Big Lion's skin, and began to jump and dance, singing—

"I am just the little hare, the little hare, the little hare;
I am just the little hare who killed the great hyænas."

The little hyæna gazed at him in surprise, saying to herself, "What! was it really this tiny beast who put to death all our best people?" when suddenly a gust of wind rustled the reeds that surrounded the enclosure, and the little hare, in a fright, hastily sprang back into Big Lion's skin.

When the hyænas returned to their homes the little hyæna said to her father: "Father, our tribe has very nearly been swept away, and all this has been the work of a tiny creature dressed in the lion's skin."

But her father answered, "Oh, my dear child, you don't know what you are talking about."

She replied, "Yes, father, it is quite true. I saw it with my own eyes."

The father did not know what to think, and told one of his friends, who said, "To-morrow we had better keep watch ourselves."

And the next day they hid themselves and waited till the little hare came out of the royal hut. He walked gaily towards the enclosure, threw off Big Lion's skin, and sang and danced as before—

"I am just the little hare, the little hare, the little hare;
I am just the little hare, who killed the great hyænas."

That night the two hyænas told all the rest, saying, "Do you know that we have allowed ourselves to be trampled on by a wretched creature with nothing of the lion about him but his skin?"

When supper was being cooked that evening, before they all went to bed, the little hare, looking fierce and terrible in Big Lion's skin, said as usual to one of the hyænas, "Go and get into the boiling water." But the hyæna never stirred. There was silence for a moment; then a hyæna took a stone, and flung it with all his force against the lion's skin. The little hare jumped out through the mouth with a single spring, and fled away like lightning, all the hyænas in full pursuit uttering great cries. As he turned a corner the little hare cut off both his ears, so that they should not know him, and pretended to be working at a grindstone which lay there.

The hyænas soon came up to him and said, "Tell me, friend, have you seen the little hare go by?"

"No, I have seen no one."

"Where can he be?" said the hyænas one to another. "Of course, this creature is quite different, and not at all like the little hare." Then they went on their way, but, finding no traces of the little hare, they returned sadly to their village, saying, "To think we should have allowed ourselves to be swept away by a wretched creature like that!"

Kisa the Cat

(FROM *THE BROWN FAIRY BOOK*)

Once upon a time there lived a queen who had a beautiful cat, the color of smoke, with china-blue eyes, which she was very fond of. The cat was constantly with her, and ran after her wherever she went, and even sat up proudly by her side when she drove out in her fine glass coach.

"Oh, pussy," said the queen one day, "you are happier than I am! For you have a dear kitten just like yourself, and I have nobody to play with but you."

"Don't cry," answered the cat, laying her paw on her mistress's arm. "Crying never does any good. I will see what can be done."

The cat was as good as her word. As soon as she returned from her drive she trotted off to the forest to consult a fairy who dwelt there, and very soon after the queen had a little girl, who seemed made out of snow and sunbeams. The queen was delighted, and soon the baby began to take notice of the kitten as she jumped about the room, and would not go to sleep at all unless the kitten lay curled up beside her.

Two or three months went by, and though the baby was still a baby, the kitten was fast becoming a cat, and one evening when, as usual, the nurse came to look for her, to put her in the baby's cot, she was nowhere to be found. What a hunt there was for that kitten, to be sure! The servants, each anxious to find her, as the queen was certain to reward the lucky man, searched in the most impossible places. Boxes were opened that would hardly have held the kitten's paw; books were taken from bookshelves, lest the kitten should have got behind them, drawers were pulled out, for perhaps the kitten might have got shut in. But it was all no use. The kitten had plainly run away, and nobody could tell if it would ever choose to come back.

Years passed away, and one day, when the princess was playing ball in the garden, she happened to throw her ball farther than usual, and it fell into a clump of rose-bushes. The princess of course ran after it at once, and she was stooping down to feel if it was hidden in the long grass, when she heard a voice calling her:

"Ingibjörg! Ingibjörg!" it said, "have you forgotten me? I am Kisa, your sister!"

"But I never *had* a sister," answered Ingibjörg, very much puzzled; for she knew nothing of what had taken place so long ago.

"Don't you remember how I always slept in your cot beside you, and how you cried till I came? But girls have no memories at all! Why, I could find my way straight up to that cot this moment, if I was once inside the palace."

"Why did you go away then?" asked the princess. But before Kisa could answer, Ingibjörg's attendants arrived breathless on the scene, and were so horrified at the sight of a strange cat, that Kisa plunged into the bushes and went back to the forest.

The princess was very much vexed with her ladies-in-waiting for frightening away her old playfellow, and told the queen who came to her room every evening to bid her good-night.

"Yes, it is quite true what Kisa said," answered the queen; "I should have liked to see her again. Perhaps, some day, she will return, and then you must bring her to me."

Next morning it was very hot, and the princess declared that she must go and play in the forest, where it was always cool, under the big shady trees. As usual, her attendants let her do anything she pleased, and sitting down on a mossy bank where a little stream tinkled by, soon fell sound asleep. The princess saw with delight that they would pay no heed to her, and wandered on and on, expecting every moment to see some fairies dancing round a ring, or some little brown elves peeping at her from behind a tree. But, alas! she met none of these; instead, a horrible giant came out of his cave and ordered her to follow him. The princess felt much afraid, as he was so big and ugly, and began to be sorry that she had not stayed within reach of help; but as there was no use in disobeying the giant, she walked meekly behind.

They went a long way, and Ingibjörg grew very tired, and at length began to cry.

"I don't like girls who make horrid noises," said the giant, turning round. "But if you *want* to cry, I will give you something to cry for." And drawing an axe from his belt, he cut off both her feet, which he picked up and put in his pocket. Then he went away.

Poor Ingibjörg lay on the grass in terrible pain, and wondering if she should stay there till she died, as no one would know where to look for her. How long it was since she had set out in the morning she could not tell—

it seemed years to her, of course; but the sun was still high in the heavens when she heard the sound of wheels, and then, with a great effort, for her throat was parched with fright and pain, she gave a shout.

"I am coming!" was the answer; and in another moment a cart made its way through the trees, driven by Kisa, who used her tail as a whip to urge the horse to go faster. Directly Kisa saw Ingibjörg lying there, she jumped quickly down, and lifting the girl carefully in her two front paws, laid her upon some soft hay, and drove back to her own little hut.

In the corner of the room was a pile of cushions, and these Kisa arranged as a bed. Ingibjörg, who by this time was nearly fainting from all she had gone through, drank greedily some milk, and then sank back on the cushions while Kisa fetched some dried herbs from a cupboard, soaked them in warm water and tied them on the bleeding legs. The pain vanished at once, and Ingibjörg looked up and smiled at Kisa.

"You will go to sleep now," said the cat, "and you will not mind if I leave you for a little while. I will lock the door, and no one can hurt you." But before she had finished the princess was asleep. Then Kisa got into the cart, which was standing at the door, and catching up the reins, drove straight to the giant's cave.

Leaving her cart behind some trees, Kisa crept gently up to the open door, and, crouching down, listened to what the giant was telling his wife, who was at supper with him.

"The first day that I can spare I shall just go back and kill her," he said; "it would never do for people in the forest to know that a mere girl can defy me!" And he and his wife were so busy calling Ingibjörg all sorts of names for her bad behavior, that they never noticed Kisa stealing into a dark corner, and upsetting a whole bag of salt into the great pot before the fire.

"Dear me, how thirsty I am!" cried the giant by-and-by.

"So am I," answered the wife. "I do wish I had not taken that last spoonful of broth; I am sure something was wrong with it."

"If I don't get some water I shall die," went on the giant. And rushing out of the cave, followed by his wife, he ran down the path which led to the river.

Then Kisa entered the hut, and lost no time in searching every hole till she came upon some grass, under which Ingibjörg's feet were hidden, and putting them in her cart, drove back again to her own hut.

Ingibjörg was thankful to see her, for she had lain, too frightened to sleep, trembling at every noise.

"Oh, is it you?" she cried joyfully, as Kisa turned the key. And the cat came in, holding up the two neat little feet in their silver slippers.

"In two minutes they shall be as tight as they ever were!" said Kisa. And taking some strings of the magic grass which the giant had carelessly heaped on them, she bound the feet on to the legs above.

"Of course you won't be able to walk for some time; you must not expect *that*," she continued. "But if you are very good, perhaps, in about a week, I may carry you home again."

And so she did; and when the cat drove the cart up to the palace gate, lashing the horse furiously with her tail, and the king and queen saw their lost daughter sitting beside her, they declared that no reward could be too great for the person who had brought her out of the giant's hands.

"We will talk about that by-and-by," said the cat, as she made her best bow, and turned her horse's head.

The princess was very unhappy when Kisa left her without even bidding her farewell. She would neither eat nor drink, nor take any notice of all the beautiful dresses her parents bought for her.

"She will die, unless we can make her laugh," one whispered to the other. "Is there anything in the world that we have left untried?"

"Nothing except marriage," answered the king. And he invited all the handsomest young men he could think of to the palace, and bade the princess choose a husband from among them.

It took her some time to decide which she admired the most, but at last she fixed upon a young prince, whose eyes were like the pools in the forest, and his hair of bright gold. The king and the queen were greatly pleased, as the young man was the son of a neighboring king, and they gave orders that a splendid feast should be got ready.

When the marriage was over, Kisa suddenly stood before them, and Ingibjörg rushed forward and clasped her in her arms.

"I have come to claim my reward," said the cat. "Let me sleep for this night at the foot of your bed."

"Is that *all*?" asked Ingibjörg, much disappointed.

"It is enough," answered the cat. And when the morning dawned, it was no cat that lay upon the bed, but a beautiful princess.

"My mother and I were both enchanted by a spiteful fairy," said she, "and we could not free ourselves till we had done some kindly deed that had never

545

been wrought before. My mother died without ever finding a chance of doing anything new, but I took advantage of the evil act of the giant to make you as whole as ever."

Then they were all more delighted than before, and the princess lived in the court until she, too, married, and went away to govern one of her own.

The Flower Queen's Daughter

(FROM *THE YELLOW FAIRY BOOK*)

A young Prince was riding one day through a meadow that stretched for miles in front of him, when he came to a deep open ditch. He was turning aside to avoid it, when he heard the sound of someone crying in the ditch. He dismounted from his horse, and stepped along in the direction the sound came from. To his astonishment he found an old woman, who begged him to help her out of the ditch. The Prince bent down and lifted her out of her living grave, asking her at the same time how she had managed to get there.

"My son," answered the old woman, "I am a very poor woman, and soon after midnight I set out for the neighboring town in order to sell my eggs in the market on the following morning; but I lost my way in the dark, and fell into this deep ditch, where I might have remained for ever but for your kindness."

Then the Prince said to her, "You can hardly walk; I will put you on my horse and lead you home. Where do you live?"

"Over there, at the edge of the forest in the little hut you see in the distance," replied the old woman.

The Prince lifted her on to his horse, and soon they reached the hut, where the old woman got down, and turning to the Prince said, "Just wait a moment, and I will give you something." And she disappeared into her hut, but returned very soon and said, "You are a mighty Prince, but at the same time you have a kind heart, which deserves to be rewarded. Would you like to have the most beautiful woman in the world for your wife?"

"Most certainly I would," replied the Prince.

So the old woman continued, "The most beautiful woman in the whole world is the daughter of the Queen of the Flowers, who has been captured by a dragon. If you wish to marry her, you must first set her free, and this I will help you to do. I will give you this little bell: if you ring it once, the King of the Eagles will appear; if you ring it twice, the King of the Foxes will come to you; and if you ring it three times, you will see the King of the Fishes by your side. These will help you if you are in any difficulty. Now farewell, and heaven prosper your undertaking." She handed him the little bell, and there disappeared hut and all, as though the earth had swallowed her up.

Then it dawned on the Prince that he had been speaking to a good fairy, and putting the little bell carefully in his pocket, he rode home and told his father that he meant to set the daughter of the Flower Queen free, and intended setting out on the following day into the wide world in search of the maid.

So the next morning the Prince mounted his fine horse and left his home. He had roamed round the world for a whole year, and his horse had died of exhaustion, while he himself had suffered much from want and misery, but still he had come on no trace of her he was in search of. At last one day he came to a hut, in front of which sat a very old man. The Prince asked him, "Do you not know where the Dragon lives who keeps the daughter of the Flower Queen prisoner?"

"No, I do not," answered the old man. "But if you go straight along this road for a year, you will reach a hut where my father lives, and possibly he may be able to tell you."

The Prince thanked him for his information, and continued his journey for a whole year along the same road, and at the end of it came to the little hut, where he found a very old man. He asked him the same question, and the old man answered, "No, I do not know where the Dragon lives. But go straight along this road for another year, and you will come to a hut in which my father lives. I know he can tell you."

And so the Prince wandered on for another year, always on the same road, and at last reached the hut where he found the third old man. He put the same question to him as he had put to his son and grandson; but this time the old man answered, "The Dragon lives up there on the mountain, and he has just begun his year of sleep. For one whole year he is always awake, and the next he sleeps. But if you wish to see the Flower Queen's daughter go up the second mountain: the Dragon's old mother lives there, and she has a ball every night, to which the Flower Queen's daughter goes regularly."

So the Prince went up the second mountain, where he found a castle all made of gold with diamond windows. He opened the big gate leading into the courtyard, and was just going to walk in, when seven dragons rushed on him and asked him what he wanted?

The Prince replied, "I have heard so much of the beauty and kindness of the Dragon's Mother, and would like to enter her service."

This flattering speech pleased the dragons, and the eldest of them said, "Well, you may come with me, and I will take you to the Mother Dragon."

They entered the castle and walked through twelve splendid halls, all made of gold and diamonds. In the twelfth room they found the Mother Dragon seated on a diamond throne. She was the ugliest woman under the sun, and, added to it all, she had three heads. Her appearance was a great shock to the Prince, and so was her voice, which was like the croaking of many ravens. She asked him, "Why have you come here?"

The Prince answered at once, "I have heard so much of your beauty and kindness, that I would very much like to enter your service."

"Very well," said the Mother Dragon; "but if you wish to enter my service, you must first lead my mare out to the meadow and look after her for three days; but if you don't bring her home safely every evening, we will eat you up."

The Prince undertook the task and led the mare out to the meadow. But no sooner had they reached the grass than she vanished. The Prince sought for her in vain, and at last in despair sat down on a big stone and contemplated his sad fate. As he sat thus lost in thought, he noticed an eagle flying over his head. Then he suddenly bethought him of his little bell, and taking it out of his pocket he rang it once. In a moment he heard a rustling sound in the air beside him, and the King of the Eagles sank at his feet.

"I know what you want of me," the bird said. "You are looking for the Mother Dragon's mare who is galloping about among the clouds. I will summon all the eagles of the air together, and order them to catch the mare and bring her to you." And with these words the King of the Eagles flew away. Towards evening the Prince heard a mighty rushing sound in the air, and when he looked up he saw thousands of eagles driving the mare before them. They sank at his feet on to the ground and gave the mare over to him. Then the Prince rode home to the old Mother Dragon, who was full of wonder when she saw him, and said, "You have succeeded to-day in looking after my mare, and as a reward you shall come to my ball to-night." She gave him at the same time a cloak made of copper, and led him to a big room where several young he-dragons and she-dragons were dancing together. Here, too, was the Flower Queen's beautiful daughter. Her dress was woven out of the most lovely flowers in the world, and her complexion was like lilies and roses. As the Prince was dancing with her he managed to whisper in her ear, "I have come to set you free!"

Then the beautiful girl said to him, "If you succeed in bringing the mare back safely the third day, ask the Mother Dragon to give you a foal of the mare as a reward."

The ball came to an end at midnight, and early next morning the Prince again led the Mother Dragon's mare out into the meadow. But again she vanished before his eyes. Then he took out his little bell and rang it twice.

In a moment the King of the Foxes stood before him and said: "I know already what you want, and will summon all the foxes of the world together to find the mare who has hidden herself in a hill."

With these words the King of the Foxes disappeared, and in the evening many thousand foxes brought the mare to the Prince.

Then he rode home to the Mother-Dragon, from whom he received this time a cloak made of silver, and again she led him to the ball-room.

The Flower Queen's daughter was delighted to see him safe and sound, and when they were dancing together she whispered in his ear: "If you succeed again to-morrow, wait for me with the foal in the meadow. After the ball we will fly away together."

On the third day the Prince led the mare to the meadow again; but once more she vanished before his eyes. Then the Prince took out his little bell and rang it three times.

In a moment the King of the Fishes appeared, and said to him: "I know quite well what you want me to do, and I will summon all the fishes of the sea together, and tell them to bring you back the mare, who is hiding herself in a river."

Towards evening the mare was returned to him, and when he led her home to the Mother Dragon she said to him:

"You are a brave youth, and I will make you my body-servant. But what shall I give you as a reward to begin with?"

The Prince begged for a foal of the mare, which the Mother Dragon at once gave him, and over and above, a cloak made of gold, for she had fallen in love with him because he had praised her beauty.

So in the evening he appeared at the ball in his golden cloak; but before the entertainment was over he slipped away, and went straight to the stables, where he mounted his foal and rode out into the meadow to wait for the Flower Queen's daughter. Towards midnight the beautiful girl appeared, and placing her in front of him on his horse, the Prince and she flew like the wind till they reached the Flower Queen's dwelling. But the dragons had noticed their flight, and woke their brother out of his year's sleep. He flew into a terrible rage when he heard what had happened, and determined to lay siege to the Flower Queen's palace; but the Queen caused a forest of flowers as high as the sky to grow up round her dwelling, through which no one could force a way.

When the Flower Queen heard that her daughter wanted to marry the Prince, she said to him: "I will give my consent to your marriage gladly, but my daughter can only stay with you in summer. In winter, when everything is dead and the ground covered with snow, she must come and live with me in my palace underground." The Prince consented to this, and led his beautiful bride home, where the wedding was held with great pomp and magnificence. The young couple lived happily together till winter came, when the Flower Queen's daughter departed and went home to her mother. In summer she returned to her husband, and their life of joy and happiness began again, and lasted till the approach of winter, when the Flower Queen's daughter went back again to her mother. This coming and going continued all her life long, and in spite of it they always lived happily together.

How the Wicked Tanuki Was Punished

(FROM *THE CRIMSON FAIRY BOOK*)

The hunters had hunted the wood for so many years that no wild animal was any more to be found in it. You might walk from one end to the other without ever seeing a hare, or a deer, or a boar, or hearing the cooing of the doves in their nest. If they were not dead, they had flown elsewhere. Only three creatures remained alive, and they had hidden themselves in the thickest part of the forest, high up the mountain. These were a gray-furred, long-tailed tanuki, his wife the fox, who was one of his own family, and their little son.

The fox and the tanuki were very clever, prudent beasts, and they also were skilled in magic, and by this means had escaped the fate of their unfortunate friends. If they heard the twang of an arrow or saw the glitter of a spear, ever so far off, they lay very still, and were not to be tempted from their hiding-place, if their hunger was ever so great, or the game ever so delicious. "We are not so foolish as to risk our lives," they said to each other proudly. But at length there came a day when, in spite of their prudence, they seemed likely to die of starvation, for no more food was to be had. Something had to be done, but they did not know what.

Suddenly a bright thought struck the tanuki. "I have got a plan," he cried joyfully to his wife. "I will pretend to be dead, and you must change yourself into a man, and take me to the village for sale. It will be easy to find a buyer, tanukis' skins are always wanted; then buy some food with the money and come home again. I will manage to escape somehow, so do not worry about me."

The fox laughed with delight, and rubbed her paws together with satisfaction. "Well, next time I will go," she said, "and you can sell me." And then she changed herself into a man, and picking up the stiff body of the tanuki, set off towards the village. She found him rather heavy, but it would never have done to let him walk through the wood and risk his being seen by somebody."

As the tanuki had foretold, buyers were many, and the fox handed him over to the person who offered the largest price, and hurried to get some food with the money. The buyer took the tanuki back to his house, and throwing him into a corner went out. Directly the tanuki found he was alone, he crept cautiously through a chink of the window, thinking, as he did so, how lucky it was that he was not a fox, and was able to climb. Once outside, he hid himself in a ditch till it grew dusk, and then galloped away into the forest.

While the food lasted they were all three as happy as kings; but there soon arrived a day when the larder was as empty as ever. "It is my turn now to pretend to be dead," cried the fox. So the tanuki changed himself into a peasant, and started for the village, with his wife's body hanging over his shoulder. A buyer was not long in coming forward, and while they were making the bargain a wicked thought darted into the tanuki's head, that if he got rid of the fox there would be more food for him and his son. So as he put the money in his pocket he whispered softly to the buyer that the fox was not really dead, and that if he did not take care she might run away from him. The man did not need twice telling. He gave the poor fox a blow on the head, which put an end to her, and the wicked tanuki went smiling to the nearest shop.

In former times he had been very fond of his little son; but since he had betrayed his wife he seemed to have changed all in a moment, for he would not give him as much as a bite, and the poor little fellow would have starved had he not found some nuts and berries to eat, and he waited on, always hoping that his mother would come back.

At length some notion of the truth began to dawn on him; but he was careful to let the old tanuki see nothing, though in his own mind he turned over plans from morning till night, wondering how best he might avenge his mother.

One morning, as the little tanuki was sitting with his father, he remembered, with a start, that his mother had taught him all she knew of magic, and that he could work spells as well as his father, or perhaps better. "I am as good a wizard as you," he said suddenly, and a cold chill ran through the tanuki as he heard him, though he laughed, and pretended to think it a joke. But the little tanuki stuck to his point, and at last the father proposed they should have a wager.

"Change yourself into any shape you like," said he, "and I will undertake to know you. I will go and wait on the bridge which leads over the river to the village, and you shall transform yourself into anything you please, but I will know you through any disguise." The little tanuki agreed, and went down the road which his father had pointed out. But instead of transforming himself into a different shape, he just hid himself in a corner of the bridge, where he could see without being seen.

He had not been there long when his father arrived and took up his place near the middle of the bridge, and soon after the king came by, followed by a troop of guards and all his court.

"Ah! he thinks that now he has changed himself into a king I shall not know him," thought the old tanuki, and as the king passed in his splendid carriage, borne by his servants, he jumped upon it crying: "I have won my wager; you cannot deceive me." But in reality it was he who had deceived himself. The soldiers, conceiving that their king was being attacked, seized the tanuki by the legs and flung him over into the river, and the water closed over him.

And the little tanuki saw it all, and rejoiced that his mother's death had been avenged. Then he went back to the forest, and if he has not found it too lonely, he is probably living there still.

The War of the Wolf and the Fox

(FROM *THE GREEN FAIRY BOOK*)

There was once upon a time a man and his wife who had an old cat and an old dog. One day the man, whose name was Simon, said to his wife, whose name was Susan, "Why should we keep our old cat any longer? She never catches any mice now-a-days, and is so useless that I have made up my mind to drown her."

But his wife replied, "Don't do that, for I'm sure she could still catch mice."

"Rubbish," said Simon. "The mice might dance on her and she would never catch one. I've quite made up my mind that the next time I see her, I shall put her in the water."

Susan was very unhappy when she heard this, and so was the cat, who had been listening to the conversation behind the stove. When Simon went off to his work, the poor cat miawed so pitifully, and looked up so pathetically into Susan's face, that the woman quickly opened the door and said, "Fly for your life, my poor little beast, and get well away from here before your master returns."

The cat took her advice, and ran as quickly as her poor old legs would carry her into the wood, and when Simon came home, his wife told him that the cat had vanished.

"So much the better for her," said Simon. "And now we have got rid of her, we must consider what we are to do with the old dog. He is quite deaf and blind, and invariably barks when there is no need, and makes no sound when there is. I think the best thing I can do with him is to hang him."

But soft-hearted Susan replied, "Please don't do so; he's surely not so useless as all that."

"Don't be foolish," said her husband. "The courtyard might be full of thieves and he'd never discover it. No, the first time I see him, It's all up with him, I can tell you."

Susan was very unhappy at his words, and so was the dog, who was lying in the corner of the room and had heard everything. As soon as Simon had gone to his work, he stood up and howled so touchingly that Susan quickly opened the door, and said "Fly for your life, poor beast, before your master gets home." And the dog ran into the wood with his tail between his legs.

When her husband returned, his wife told him that the dog had disappeared.

"That's lucky for him," said Simon, but Susan sighed, for she had been very fond of the poor creature.

Now it happened that the cat and dog met each other on their travels, and though they had not been the best of friends at home, they were quite glad to meet among strangers. They sat down under a holly tree and both poured forth their woes.

Presently a fox passed by, and seeing the pair sitting together in a disconsolate fashion, he asked them why they sat there, and what they were grumbling about.

The cat replied, "I have caught many a mouse in my day, but now that I am old and past work, my master wants to drown me."

And the dog said, "Many a night have I watched and guarded my master's house, and now that I am old and deaf, he wants to hang me."

The fox answered, "That's the way of the world. But I'll help you to get back into your master's favor, only you must first help me in my own troubles."

They promised to do their best, and the fox continued, "The wolf has declared war against me, and is at this moment marching to meet me in company with the bear and the wild boar, and to-morrow there will be a fierce battle between us."

"All right," said the dog and the cat, "we will stand by you, and if we are killed, it is at any rate better to die on the field of battle than to perish ignobly at home," and they shook paws and concluded the bargain. The fox sent word to the wolf to meet him at a certain place, and the three set forth to encounter him and his friends.

The wolf, the bear, and the wild boar arrived on the spot first, and when they had waited some time for the fox, the dog, and the cat, the bear said, "I'll climb up into the oak tree, and look if I can see them coming."

The first time he looked round he said, "I can see nothing," and the second time he looked round he said, "I can still see nothing." But the third time he said, "I see a mighty army in the distance, and one of the warriors has the biggest lance you ever saw!"

This was the cat, who was marching along with her tail erect.

And so they laughed and jeered, and it was so hot that the bear said, "The enemy won't be here at this rate for many hours to come, so I'll just curl myself up in the fork of the tree and have a little sleep."

And the wolf lay down under the oak, and the wild boar buried himself in some straw, so that nothing was seen of him but one ear.

And while they were lying there, the fox, the cat and the dog arrived. When the cat saw the wild boar's ear, she pounced upon it, thinking it was a mouse in the straw.

The wild boar got up in a dreadful fright, gave one loud grunt and disappeared into the wood. But the cat was even more startled than the boar, and, spitting with terror, she scrambled up into the fork of the tree, and as it happened right into the bear's face. Now it was the bear's turn to be alarmed, and with a mighty growl he jumped down from the oak and fell right on the top of the wolf and killed him as dead as a stone.

On their way home from the war the fox caught score of mice, and when they reached Simon's cottage he put them all on the stove and said to the cat, "Now go and fetch one mouse after the other, and lay them down before your master."

"All right," said the cat, and did exactly as the fox told her.

When Susan saw this she said to her husband, "Just look, here is our old cat back again, and see what a lot of mice she has caught."

"Wonders will never cease," cried Simon. "I certainly never thought the old cat would ever catch another mouse."

But Susan answered, "There, you see, I always said our cat was a most excellent creature—but you men always think you know best."

In the meantime the fox said to the dog, "Our friend Simon has just killed a pig; when it gets a little darker, you must go into the courtyard and bark with all your might."

"All right," said the dog, and as soon as it grew dusk he began to bark loudly.

Susan, who heard him first, said to her husband, "Our dog must have come back, for I hear him barking lustily. Do go out and see what's the matter; perhaps thieves may be stealing our sausages."

But Simon answered, "The foolish brute is as deaf as a post and is always barking at nothing," and he refused to get up.

The next morning Susan got up early to go to church at the neighboring town, and she thought she would take some sausages to her aunt who lived there. But when she went to her larder, she found all the sausages gone, and a great hole in the floor. She called out to her husband, "I was perfectly right. Thieves have been here last night, and they have not left a single sausage. Oh! if you had only got up when I asked you to!"

Then Simon scratched his head and said, "I can't understand it at all. I certainly never believed the old dog was so quick at hearing."

But Susan replied, "I always told you our old dog was the best dog in the world—but as usual you thought you knew so much better. Men are the same all the world over."

And the fox scored a point too, for he had carried away the sausages himself!

The Rover of the Plain

(FROM *THE ORANGE FAIRY BOOK*)

A long way off, near the sea coast of the east of Africa, there dwelt, once upon a time, a man and his wife. They had two children, a son and a daughter, whom they loved very much, and, like parents in other countries, they often talked of the fine marriages the young people would make some day. Out there both boys and girls marry early, and very soon, it seemed to the mother, a message was sent by a rich man on the other side of the great hills offering a fat herd of oxen in exchange for the girl. Everyone in the house and in the village rejoiced, and the maiden was dispatched to her new home. When all was quiet again the father said to his son:

"Now that we own such a splendid troop of oxen you had better hasten and get yourself a wife, lest some illness should overtake them. Already we have seen in the villages round about one or two damsels whose parents would gladly part with them for less than half the herd. Therefore tell us which you like best, and we will buy her for you."

But the son answered:

"Not so; the maidens I have seen do not please me. If, indeed, I must marry, let me travel and find a wife for myself."

"It shall be as you wish," said the parents; "but if by-and-by trouble should come of it, it will be your fault and not ours."

The youth, however, would not listen; and bidding his father and mother farewell, set out on his search. Far, far away he wandered, over mountains and across rivers, till he reached a village where the people were quite different from those of his own race. He glanced about him and noticed that the girls were fair to look upon, as they pounded maize or stewed something that smelt very nice in earthen pots—especially if you were hot and tired; and when one of the maidens turned round and offered the stranger some dinner, he made up his mind that he would wed her and nobody else.

So he sent a message to her parents asking their leave to take her for his wife, and they came next day to bring their answer.

"We will give you our daughter," said they, "if you can pay a good price for her. Never was there so hardworking a girl; and how we shall do without her we cannot tell! Still—no doubt your father and mother will come themselves and bring the price?"

"No; I have the price with me," replied the young man; laying down a handful of gold pieces. "Here it is—take it."

The old couple's eyes glittered greedily; but custom forbade them to touch the price before all was arranged.

"At least," said they, after a moment's pause, "we may expect them to fetch your wife to her new home?"

"No; they are not used to traveling," answered the bridegroom. "Let the ceremony be performed without delay, and we will set forth at once. It is a long journey."

Then the parents called in the girl, who was lying in the sun outside the hut, and, in the presence of all the village, a goat was killed, the sacred dance took place, and a blessing was said over the heads of the young people. After that the bride was led aside by her father, whose duty it was to bestow on her some parting advice as to her conduct in her married life.

"Be good to your husband's parents," added he, "and always do the will of your husband." And the girl nodded her head obediently. Next it was the mother's turn; and, as was the custom of the tribe, she spoke to her daughter:

"Will you choose which of your sisters shall go with you to cut your wood and carry your water?"

"I do not want any of them," answered she; "they are no use. They will drop the wood and spill the water."

"Then will you have any of the other children? There are enough to spare," asked the mother again. But the bride said quickly:

"I will have none of them! You must give me our buffalo, the Rover of the Plain; he alone shall serve me."

"What folly you talk!" cried the parents. "Give you our buffalo, the Rover of the Plain? Why, you know that our life depends on him. Here he is well fed and lies on soft grass; but how can you tell what will befall him in another country? The food may be bad, he will die of hunger; and, if he dies we die also."

"No, no," said the bride; "I can look after him as well as you. Get him ready, for the sun is sinking and it is time we set forth."

So she went away and put together a small pot filled with healing herms, a horn that she used in tending sick people, a little knife, and a calabash containing deer fat; and, hiding these about her, she took leave of her father and mother and started across the mountains by the side of her husband.

But the young man did not see the buffalo that followed them, which had left his home to be the servant of his wife.

No one ever knew how the news spread to the kraal that the young man was coming back, bringing a wife with him; but, somehow or other, when the two entered the village, every man and woman was standing in the road uttering shouts of welcome.

"Ah, you are not dead after all," cried they; "and have found a wife to your liking, though you would have none of our girls. Well, well, you have chosen your own path; and if ill comes of it beware lest you grumble."

Next day the husband took his wife to the fields and showed her which were his, and which belonged to his mother. The girl listened carefully to all he told her, and walked with him back to the hut; but close to the door she stopped, and said:

"I have dropped my necklace of beads in the field, and I must go and look for it." But in truth she had done nothing of the sort, and it was only an excuse to go and seek the buffalo.

The beast was crouching under a tree when she came up, and snorted with pleasure at the sight of her.

"You can roam about this field, and this, and this," she said, "for they belong to my husband; and that is his wood, where you may hide yourself. But the other fields are his mother's, so beware lest you touch them."

"I will beware," answered the buffalo; and, patting his head, the girl left him.

Oh, how much better a servant he was than any of the little girls the bride had refused to bring with her! If she wanted water, she had only to cross the patch of maize behind the hut and seek out the place where the buffalo lay hidden, and put down her pail beside him. Then she would sit at her ease while he went to the lake and brought the bucket back brimming over. If she wanted wood, he would break the branches off the trees and lay them at her feet. And the villagers watched her return laden, and said to each other:

"Surely the girls of her country are stronger than our girls, for none of *them* could cut so quickly or carry so much!" But then, nobody knew that she had a buffalo for a servant.

Only, all this time she never gave the poor buffalo anything to eat, because she had just one dish, out of which she and her husband ate; while in her old home there was a dish put aside expressly for the Rover of the Plain. The buffalo bore it as long as he could; but, one day, when his mistress bade him go to the lake and fetch water, his knees almost gave way from hunger. He kept silence, however, till the evening, when he said to his mistress:

"I am nearly starved; I have not touched food since I came here. I can work no more."

"Alas!" answered she, "what can I do? I have only one dish in the house. You will have to steal some beans from the fields. Take a few here and a few there; but be sure not to take too many from one place, or the owner may notice it."

Now the buffalo had always lived an honest life, but if his mistress did not feed him, he must get food for himself. So that night, when all the village was asleep, he came out from the wood and ate a few beans here and a few there, as his mistress had bidden him. And when at last his hunger was satisfied, he crept back to his lair. But a buffalo is not a fairy, and the next morning, when the women arrived to work in the fields, they stood still with astonishment, and said to each other:

"Just look at this; a savage beast has been destroying our crops, and we can see the traces of his feet!" And they hurried to their homes to tell their tale.

In the evening the girl crept out to the buffalo's hiding-place, and said to him:

"They perceived what happened, of course; so to-night you had better seek your supper further off." And the buffalo nodded his head and followed her counsel; but in the morning, when these women also went out to work, the traces of hoofs were plainly to be seen, and they hastened to tell their husbands, and begged them to bring their guns, and to watch for the robber.

It happened that the stranger girl's husband was the best marksman in all the village, and he hid himself behind the trunk of a tree and waited.

The buffalo, thinking that they would probably make a search for him in the fields he had laid waste the evening before, returned to the bean patch belonging to his mistress.

The young man saw him coming with amazement.

"Why, it is a buffalo!" cried he; "I never have beheld one in this country before!" And raising his gun, he aimed just behind the ear.

The buffalo gave a leap into the air, and then fell dead.

"It was a good shot," said the young man. And he ran to the village to tell them that the thief was punished.

When he entered his hut he found his wife, who had somehow heard the news, twisting herself to and fro and shedding tears.

"Are you ill?" asked he. And she answered: "Yes; I have pains all over my body." But she was not ill at all, only very unhappy at the death of the buffalo which had served her so well. Her husband felt anxious, and sent for the medicine man; but though she pretended to listen to him, she threw all his medicine out of the door directly he had gone away.

With the first rays of light the whole village was awake, and the women set forth armed with baskets and the men with knives in order to cut up the buffalo. Only the girl remained in her hut; and after a while she too went to join them, groaning and weeping as she walked along.

"What are you doing here?" asked her husband when he saw her. "If you are ill you are better at home."

"Oh! I could not stay alone in the village," said she. And her mother-in-law left off her work to come and scold her, and to tell her that she would kill herself if she did such foolish things. But the girl would not listen and sat down and looked on.

When they had divided the buffalo's flesh, and each woman had the family portion in her basket, the stranger wife got up and said:

"Let me have the head."

"You could never carry anything so heavy," answered the men, "and now you are ill besides."

"You do not know how strong I am," answered she. And at last they gave it her.

She did not walk to the village with the others, but lingered behind, and, instead of entering her hut, she slipped into the little shed where the pots for cooking and storing maize were kept. Then she laid down the buffalo's head and sat beside it. Her husband came to seek her, and begged her to leave the shed and go to bed, as she must be tired out; but the girl would not stir, neither would she attend to the words of her mother-in-law.

"I wish you would leave me alone!" she answered crossly. "It is impossible to sleep if somebody is always coming in." And she turned her back on them, and would not even eat the food they had brought. So they went away, and the young man soon stretched himself out on his mat; but his wife's odd conduct made him anxious, and he lay wake all night, listening.

When all was still the girl made a fire and boiled some water in a pot. As soon as it was quite hot she shook in the medicine that she had brought from home, and then, taking the buffalo's head, she made incisions with her little knife behind the ear, and close to the temple where the shot had struck him. Next she applied the horn to the spot and blew with all her force till, at length, the blood began to move. After that she spread some of the deer fat out of the calabash over the wound, which she held in the steam of the hot water. Last of all, she sang in a low voice a dirge over the Rover of the Plain.

As she chanted the final words the head moved, and the limbs came back. The buffalo began to feel alive again and shook his horns, and stood up and stretched himself. Unluckily it was just at this moment that the husband said to himself:

"I wonder if she is crying still, and what is the matter with her! Perhaps I had better go and see." And he got up and, calling her by name, went out to the shed.

"Go away! I don't want you!" she cried angrily. But it was too late. The buffalo had fallen to the ground, dead, and with the wound in his head as before.

The young man who, unlike most of his tribe, was afraid of his wife, returned to his bed without having seen anything, but wondering very much what she could be doing all this time. After waiting a few minutes, she began her task over again, and at the end the buffalo stood on his feet as before. But just as the girl was rejoicing that her work was completed, in came the husband once more to see what his wife was doing; and this time he sat himself down in the hut, and said that he wished to watch whatever was going on. Then the girl took up the pitcher and all her other things and left the shed, trying for the third time to bring the buffalo back to life.

She was too late; the dawn was already breaking, and the head fell to the ground, dead and corrupt as it was before.

The girl entered the hut, where her husband and his mother were getting ready to go out.

"I want to go down to the lake, and bathe," said she.

"But you could never walk so far," answered they. "You are so tired, as it is, that you can hardly stand!"

However, in spite of their warnings, the girl left the hut in the direction of the lake. Very soon she came back weeping, and sobbed out:

"I met some one in the village who lives in my country, and he told me that my mother is very, very ill, and if I do not go to her at once she will be dead before I arrive. I will return as soon as I can, and now farewell." And she set forth in the direction of the mountains. But this story was not true; she knew nothing about her mother, only she wanted an excuse to go home and tell her family that their prophecies had come true, and that the buffalo was dead.

Balancing her basket on her head, she walked along, and directly she had left the village behind her she broke out into the song of the Rover of the Plain, and at last, at the end of the day, she came to the group of huts where her parents lived. Her friends all ran to meet her, and, weeping, she told them that the buffalo was dead.

This sad news spread like lightning through the country, and the people flocked from far and near to bewail the loss of the beast who had been their pride.

"If you had only listened to us," they cried, "he would be alive now. But you refused all the little girls we offered you, and would have nothing but the buffalo. And remember what the medicine-man said: "If the buffalo dies you die also!"

So they bewailed their fate, one to the other, and for a while they did not perceive that the girl's husband was sitting in their midst, leaning his gun against a tree. Then one man, turning, beheld him, and bowed mockingly.

"Hail, murderer! hail! you have slain us all!"

The young man stared, not knowing what he meant, and answered, wonderingly:

"I shot a buffalo; is that why you call me a murderer?"

"A buffalo—yes; but the servant of your wife! It was he who carried the wood and drew the water. Did you not know it?"

"No; I did not know it," replied the husband in surprise. "Why did no one tell me? Of course I should not have shot him!"

"Well, he is dead," answered they, "and we must die too."

At this the girl took a cup in which some poisonous herbs had been crushed, and holding it in her hands, she wailed: "O my father, Rover of the Plain!" Then drinking a deep draught from it, fell back dead. One by one her parents, her brothers and her sisters, drank also and died, singing a dirge to the memory of the buffalo.

The girl's husband looked on with horror; and returned sadly home across the mountains, and, entering his hut, threw himself on the ground. At first he was too tired to speak; but at length he raised his head and told all the story to his father and mother, who sat watching him. When he had finished they shook their heads and said:

"Now you see that we spoke no idle words when we told you that ill would come of your marriage! We offered you a good and hard-working wife, and you would have none of her. And it is not only your wife you have lost, but your fortune also. For who will give you back your money if they are all dead?"

"It is true, O my father," answered the young man. But in his heart he thought more of the loss of his wife than of the money he had given for her.

The Seven Foals

(FROM THE RED FAIRY BOOK)

There was once upon a time a couple of poor folks who lived in a wretched hut, far away from everyone else, in a wood. They only just managed to live from hand to mouth, and had great difficulty in doing even so much as that, but they had three sons, and the youngest of them was called Cinderlad, for he did nothing else but lie and poke about among the ashes.

One day the eldest lad said that he would go out to earn his living; he soon got leave to do that, and set out on his way into the world. He walked on and on for the whole day, and when night was beginning to fall he came to a royal palace. The King was standing outside on the steps, and asked where he was going.

"Oh, I am going about seeking a place, my father," said the youth.

"Wilt thou serve me, and watch my seven foals?" asked the King. "If thou canst watch them for a whole day and tell me at night what they eat and drink, thou shalt have the Princess and half my kingdom, but if thou canst not, I will cut three red stripes on thy back."

The youth thought that it was very easy work to watch the foals, and that he could do it well enough.

Next morning, when day was beginning to dawn, the King's Master of the Horse let out the seven foals; and they ran away, and the youth after them just as it chanced, over hill and dale, through woods end bogs. When the youth had run thus for a long time he began to be tired, and when he had held on a little longer he was heartily weary of watching at all, and at the same moment he came to a cleft in a rock where an old woman was sitting spinning with her distaff in her hand.

As soon as she caught sight of the youth, who was running after the foals till the perspiration streamed down his face, she cried:

"Come hither, come hither, my handsome son, and let me comb your hair for you."

The lad was willing enough, so he sat down in the cleft of the rock beside the old hag, and laid his head on her knees, and she combed his hair all day while he lay there and gave himself up to idleness.

When evening was drawing near, the youth wanted to go.

"I may just as well go straight home again," said he, "for it is no use to go to the King's palace."

"Wait till it is dusk," said the old hag, "and then the King's foals will pass by this place again, and you can run home with them; no one will ever know that you have been lying here all day instead of watching the foals."

So when they came she gave the lad a bottle of water and a bit of moss, and told him to show these to the King and say that this was what his seven foals ate and drank.

"Hast thou watched faithfully and well the whole day long?" said the King, when the lad came into his presence in the evening.

"Yes, that I have!" said the youth.

"Then you are able to tell me what it is that my seven foals eat and drink," said the King.

So the youth produced the bottle of water and the bit of moss which he had got from the old woman, saying:

"Here you see their meat, and here you see their drink."

Then the King knew how his watching had been done, and fell into such a rage that he ordered his people to chase the youth back to his own home at once; but first they were to cut three red stripes in his back, and rub salt into them.

When the youth reached home again, anyone can imagine what a state of mind he was in. He had gone out once to seek a place, he said, but never would he do such a thing again.

Next day the second son said that he would now go out into the world to seek his fortune. His father and mother said "No," and bade him look at his brother's back, but the youth would not give up his design, and stuck to it, and after a long, long time he got leave to go, and set forth on his way. When he had walked all day he too came to the King's palace, and the King was standing outside on the steps, and asked where he was going; and when the youth replied that he was going about in search of a place, the King said that he might enter into his service and watch his seven foals. Then the King promised him the same punishment and the same reward that he had promised his brother.

The youth at once consented to this and entered into the King's service, for he thought he could easily watch the foals and inform the King what they ate and drank.

In the gray light of dawn the Master of the Horse let out the seven foals, and off they went again over hill and dale, and off went the lad after them. But all went with him as it had gone with his brother. When he had run after the foals for a long, long time and was hot and tired, he passed by a cleft in the rock where an old woman was sitting spinning with a distaff, and she called to him:

"Come hither, come hither, my handsome son, and let me comb your hair."

The youth liked the thought of this, let the foals run where they chose, and seated himself in the cleft of the rock by the side of the old hag. So there he sat with his head on her lap, taking his ease the livelong day.

The foals came back in the evening, and then he too got a bit of moss and a bottle of water from the old hag, which things he was to show to the King. But when the King asked the youth: "Canst thou tell me what my seven foals eat and drink?" and the youth showed him the bit of moss and the bottle of water, and said: "Yes here may you behold their meat, and here their drink," the King once more became wroth, and commanded that three red stripes should be cut on the lad's back, that salt should be strewn upon them, and that he should then be instantly chased back to his own home. So when the youth got home again he too related all that had happened to him, and he too said that he had gone out in search of a place once, but that never would he do it again.

On the third day Cinderlad wanted to set out. He had a fancy to try to watch the seven foals himself, he said.

The two others laughed at him, and mocked him. "What! when all went so ill with us, do you suppose that you are going to succeed? You look like succeeding—you who have never done anything else but lie and poke about among the ashes!" said they.

"Yes, I will go too," said Cinderlad, "for I have taken it into my head."

The two brothers laughed at him, and his father and mother begged him not to go, but all to no purpose, and Cinderlad set out on his way. So when he had walked the whole day, he too came to the King's palace as darkness began to fall.

There stood the King outside on the steps, and he asked whither he was bound.

"I am walking about in search of a place," said Cinderlad.

"From whence do you come, then?" inquired the King, for by this time he wanted to know a little more about the men before he took any of them into his service.

So Cinderlad told him whence he came, and that he was brother to the two who had watched the seven foals for the King, and then he inquired if he might be allowed to try to watch them on the following day.

"Oh, shame on them!" said the King, for it enraged him even to think of them. "If thou art brother to those two, thou too art not good for much. I have had enough of such fellows."

"Well, but as I have come here, you might just give me leave to make the attempt," said Cinderlad.

"Oh, very well, if thou art absolutely determined to have thy back flayed, thou may'st have thine own way if thou wilt," said the King.

"I would much rather have the Princess," said Cinderlad.

Next morning, in the gray light of dawn, the Master of the Horse let out the seven foals again, and off they set over hill and dale, through woods and bogs, and off went Cinderlad after them. When he had run thus for a long time, he too came to the cleft in the rock. There the old hag was once more sitting spinning from her distaff, and she cried to Cinderlad;

"Come hither, come hither, my handsome son, and let me comb your hair for you."

"Come to me, then; come to me!" said Cinderlad, as he passed by jumping and running, and keeping tight hold of one of the foals' tails.

When he had got safely past the cleft in the rock, the youngest foal said:

"Get on my back, for we have still a long way to go." So the lad did this.

And thus they journeyed onwards a long, long way.

"Dost thou see anything now?" said the Foal.

"No," said Cinderlad.

So they journeyed onwards a good bit farther.

"Dost thou see anything now?" asked the Foal.

"Oh, no," said the lad.

When they had gone thus for a long, long way, the Foal again asked:

"Dost thou see anything now?"

"Yes, now I see something that is white," said Cinderlad. "It looks like the trunk of a great thick birch tree."

"Yes, that is where we are to go in," said the Foal.

When they got to the trunk, the eldest foal broke it down on one side, and then they saw a door where the trunk had been standing, and inside this there was a small room, and in the room there was scarcely anything but a small fire-place and a couple of benches, but behind the door hung a great rusty sword and a small pitcher.

"Canst thou wield that sword?" asked the Foal.

Cinderlad tried, but could not do it; so he had to take a draught from the pitcher, and then one more, and after that still another, and then he was able to wield the sword with perfect ease.

"Good," said the Foal; "and now thou must take the sword away with thee, and with it shalt thou cut off the heads of all seven of us on thy wedding-day, and then we shall become princes again as we were before. For we are brothers of the Princess whom thou art to have when thou canst tell the King what we eat and drink, but there is a mighty Troll who has cast a spell over us. When thou hast cut off our heads, thou must take the greatest care to lay each head at the tail of the body to which it belonged before, and then the spell which the Troll has cast upon us will lose all its power."

Cinderlad promised to do this, and then they went on farther.

When they had traveled a long, long way, the Foal said:

"Dost thou see anything?"

"No," said Cinderlad.

So they went on a great distance farther.

"And now?" inquired the Foal, "seest thou nothing now?"

"Alas! no," said Cinderlad.

So they traveled onwards again, for many and many a mile, over hill and dale.

"Now, then," said the Foal, "dost thou not see anything now?"

"Yes," said Cinderlad; "now I see something like a bluish streak, far, far away."

"That is a river," said the Foal, "and we have to cross it."

There was a long, handsome bridge over the river, and when they had got to the other side of it they again traveled on a long, long way, and then once more the Foal inquired if Cinderlad saw anything. Yes, this time he saw something that looked black, far, far away, and was rather like a church tower.

"Yes," said the Foal, "we shall go into that."

When the Foals got into the churchyard they turned into men and looked like the sons of a king, and their clothes were so magnificent that they shone with splendor, and they went into the church and received bread and wine from the priest, who was standing before the altar, and Cinderlad went in too. But when the priest had laid his hands on the princes and read the blessing, they went out of the church again, and Cinderlad went out too, but he took with him a flask of wine and some consecrated bread. No sooner had the seven princes come out into the churchyard than they became foals again, and Cinderlad got upon the back of the youngest, and they returned by the way they had come, only they went much, much faster.

First they went over the bridge, and then past the trunk of the birch tree, and then past the old hag who sat in the cleft of the rock spinning, and they went by so fast that Cinderlad could not hear what the old hag screeched after him, but just heard enough to understand that she was terribly enraged.

It was all but dark when they got back to the King at nightfall, and he himself was standing in the courtyard waiting for them.

"Hast thou watched well and faithfully the whole day?" said the King to Cinderlad.

"I have done my best," replied Cinderlad.

"Then thou canst tell me what my seven foals eat and drink?" asked the King.

So Cinderlad pulled out the consecrated bread and the flask of wine, and showed them to the King. "Here may you behold their meat, and here their drink," said he.

"Yes, diligently and faithfully hast thou watched," said the King, "and thou shalt have the Princess and half the kingdom."

So all was made ready for the wedding, and the King said that it was to be so stately and magnificent that everyone should hear of it, and everyone inquire about it.

But when they sat down to the marriage-feast, the bridegroom arose and went down to the stable, for he said that he had forgotten something which he must go and look to. When he got there, he did what the foals had bidden him, and cut off the heads of all the seven. First the eldest, and then the second, and so on according to their age, and he was extremely careful to lay each head at the tail of the foal to which it had belonged, and when that was done, all the foals became princes again. When he returned to the marriage-feast with the seven princes, the King was so joyful that he both kissed Cinderlad and clapped him on the back, and his bride was still more delighted with him than she had been before.

"Half my kingdom is thine already," said the King, "and the other half shall be thine after my death, for my sons can get countries and kingdoms for themselves now that they have become princes again."

Therefore, as all may well believe, there was joy and merriment at that wedding.

The Story of a Gazelle

(From *The Violet Fairy Book*)

Once upon a time there lived a man who wasted all his money, and grew so poor that his only food was a few grains of corn, which he scratched like a fowl from out of a dust-heap.

One day he was scratching as usual among a dust-heap in the street, hoping to find something for breakfast, when his eye fell upon a small silver coin, called an eighth, which he greedily snatched up. "Now I can have a proper meal," he thought, and after drinking some water at a well he lay down and slept so long that it was sunrise before he woke again. Then he jumped up and returned to the dust-heap. "For who knows," he said to himself, "whether I may not have some good luck again."

As he was walking down the road, he saw a man coming towards him, carrying a cage made of twigs. "Hi! you fellow!" called he, "what have you got inside there?"

"Gazelles," replied the man.

"Bring them here, for I should like to see them."

As he spoke, some men who were standing by began to laugh, saying to the man with the cage: "You had better take care how you bargain with him, for he has nothing at all except what he picks up from a dust-heap, and if he can't feed himself, will he be able to feed a gazelle?"

But the man with the cage made answer: "Since I started from my home in the country, fifty people at the least have called me to show them my gazelles, and was there one among them who cared to buy? It is the custom for a trader in merchandise to be summoned hither and thither, and who knows where one may find a buyer?" And he took up his cage and went towards the scratcher of dust-heaps, and the men went with him.

"What do you ask for your gazelles?" said the beggar. "Will you let me have one for an eighth?"

571

And the man with the cage took out a gazelle, and held it out, saying, "Take this one, master!"

And the beggar took it and carried it to the dust-heap, where he scratched carefully till he found a few grains of corn, which he divided with his gazelle. This he did night and morning, till five days went by.

Then, as he slept, the gazelle woke him, saying, "Master."

And the man answered, "How is it that I see a wonder?"

"What wonder?" asked the gazelle.

"Why, that you, a gazelle, should be able to speak, for, from the beginning, my father and mother and all the people that are in the world have never told me of a talking gazelle."

"Never mind that," said the gazelle, "but listen to what I say! First, I took you for my master. Second, you gave for me all you had in the world. I cannot run away from you, but give me, I pray you, leave to go every morning and seek food for myself, and every evening I will come back to you. What you find in the dust-heaps is not enough for both of us."

"Go, then," answered the master; and the gazelle went.

When the sun had set, the gazelle came back, and the poor man was very glad, and they lay down and slept side by side.

In the morning it said to him, "I am going away to feed."

And the man replied, "Go, my son," but he felt very lonely without his gazelle, and set out sooner than usual for the dust-heap where he generally found most corn. And glad he was when the evening came, and he could return home. He lay on the grass chewing tobacco, when the gazelle trotted up.

"Good evening, my master; how have you fared all day? I have been resting in the shade in a place where there is sweet grass when I am hungry, and fresh water when I am thirsty, and a soft breeze to fan me in the heat. It is far away in the forest, and no one knows of it but me, and to-morrow I shall go again."

So for five days the gazelle set off at daybreak for this cool spot, but on the fifth day it came to a place where the grass was bitter, and it did not like it, and scratched, hoping to tear away the bad blades. But, instead, it saw something lying in the earth, which turned out to be a diamond, very large and bright. "Oh, ho!" said the gazelle to itself, "perhaps now I can do something for my master who bought me with all the money he had; but I must be careful or they will say he has stolen it. I had better take it myself to some great rich man, and see what it will do for me."

Directly the gazelle had come to this conclusion, it picked up the diamond in its mouth, and went on and on and on through the forest, but found no place where a rich man was likely to dwell. For two more days it ran, from dawn to dark, till at last early one morning it caught sight of a large town, which gave it fresh courage.

The people were standing about the streets doing their marketing, when the gazelle bounded past, the diamond flashing as it ran. They called after it, but it took no notice till it reached the palace, where the sultan was sitting, enjoying the cool air. And the gazelle galloped up to him, and laid the diamond at his feet.

The sultan looked first at the diamond and next at the gazelle; then he ordered his attendants to bring cushions and a carpet, that the gazelle might rest itself after its long journey. And he likewise ordered milk to be brought, and rice, that it might eat and drink and be refreshed.

And when the gazelle was rested, the sultan said to it: "Give me the news you have come with."

And the gazelle answered: "I am come with this diamond, which is a pledge from my master the Sultan Darai. He has heard you have a daughter, and sends you this small token, and begs you will give her to him to wife."

And the sultan said: "I am content. The wife is his wife, the family is his family, the slave is his slave. Let him come to me empty-handed, I am content."

When the sultan had ended, the gazelle rose, and said: "Master, farewell; I go back to our town, and in eight days, or it may be in eleven days, we shall arrive as your guests."

And the sultan answered: "So let it be."

All this time the poor man far away had been mourning and weeping for his gazelle, which he thought had run away from him for ever. And when it came in at the door he rushed to embrace it with such joy that he would not allow it a chance to speak.

"Be still, master, and don't cry," said the gazelle at last; "let us sleep now, and in the morning, when I go, follow me."

With the first ray of dawn they got up and went into the forest, and on the fifth day, as they were resting near a stream, the gazelle gave its master a sound beating, and then bade him stay where he was till it returned. And the gazelle ran off, and about ten o'clock it came near the sultan's palace, where the road was all lined with soldiers who were there to do honor to

Sultan Darai. And directly they caught sight of the gazelle in the distance one of the soldiers ran on and said, "Sultan Darai is coming: I have seen the gazelle."

Then the sultan rose up, and called his whole court to follow him, and went out to meet the gazelle, who, bounding up to him, gave him greeting. The sultan answered politely, and inquired where it had left its master, whom it had promised to bring back.

"Alas!" replied the gazelle, "he is lying in the forest, for on our way here we were met by robbers, who, after beating and robbing him, took away all his clothes. And he is now hiding under a bush, lest a passing stranger might see him."

The sultan, on hearing what had happened to his future son-in-law, turned his horse and rode to the palace, and bade a groom to harness the best horse in the stable and order a woman slave to bring a bag of clothes, such as a man might want, out of the chest; and he chose out a tunic and a turban and a sash for the waist, and fetched himself a gold-hilted sword, and a dagger and a pair of sandals, and a stick of sweet-smelling wood.

"Now," said he to the gazelle, "take these things with the soldiers to the sultan, that he may be able to come."

And the gazelle answered: "Can I take those soldiers to go and put my master to shame as he lies there naked? I am enough by myself, my lord."

"How will you be enough," asked the sultan, "to manage this horse and all these clothes?"

"Oh, that is easily done," replied the gazelle. "Fasten the horse to my neck and tie the clothes to the back of the horse, and be sure they are fixed firmly, as I shall go faster than he does."

Everything was carried out as the gazelle had ordered, and when all was ready it said to the sultan: "Farewell, my lord, I am going."

"Farewell, gazelle," answered the sultan; "when shall we see you again?"

"To-morrow about five," replied the gazelle, and, giving a tug to the horse's rein, they set off at a gallop.

The sultan watched them till they were out of sight: then he said to his attendants, "That gazelle comes from gentle hands, from the house of a sultan, and that is what makes it so different from other gazelles." And in the eyes of the sultan the gazelle became a person of consequence.

Meanwhile the gazelle ran on till it came to the place where its master was seated, and his heart laughed when he saw the gazelle.

And the gazelle said to him, "Get up, my master, and bathe in the stream!" and when the man had bathed it said again, "Now rub yourself well with earth, and rub your teeth well with sand to make them bright and shining." And when this was done it said, "The sun has gone down behind the hills; it is time for us to go": so it went and brought the clothes from the back of the horse, and the man put them on and was well pleased.

"Master!" said the gazelle when the man was ready, "be sure that where we are going you keep silence, except for giving greetings and asking for news. Leave all the talking to me. I have provided you with a wife, and have made her presents of clothes and turbans and rare and precious things, so it is needless for you to speak."

"Very good, I will be silent," replied the man as he mounted the horse. "You have given all this; it is you who are the master, and I who am the slave, and I will obey you in all things."

"So they went their way, and they went and went till the gazelle saw in the distance the palace of the sultan. Then it said, "Master, that is the house we are going to, and you are not a poor man any longer: even your name is new."

"What *is* my name, eh, my father?" asked the man.

"Sultan Darai," said the gazelle.

Very soon some soldiers came to meet them, while others ran off to tell the sultan of their approach. And the sultan set off at once, and the viziers and the emirs, and the judges, and the rich men of the city, all followed him.

Directly the gazelle saw them coming, it said to its master: "Your father-in-law is coming to meet you; that is he in the middle, wearing a mantle of sky-blue. Get off your horse and go to greet him."

And Sultan Darai leapt from his horse, and so did the other sultan, and they gave their hands to one another and kissed each other, and went together into the palace.

The next morning the gazelle went to the rooms of the sultan, and said to him: "My lord, we want you to marry us our wife, for the soul of Sultan Darai is eager."

"The wife is ready, so call the priest," answered he, and when the ceremony was over a cannon was fired and music was played, and within the palace there was feasting.

"Master," said the gazelle the following morning, "I am setting out on a journey, and I shall not be back for seven days, and perhaps not then. But be careful not to leave the house till I come."

And the master answered, "I will not leave the house."

And it went to the sultan of the country and said to him: "My lord, Sultan Darai has sent me to his town to get the house in order. It will take me seven days, and if I am not back in seven days he will not leave the palace till I return."

"Very good," said the sultan.

And it went and it went through the forest and wilderness, till it arrived at a town full of fine houses. At the end of the chief road was a great house, beautiful exceedingly, built of sapphire and turquoise and marbles. "That," thought the gazelle, "is the house for my master, and I will call up my courage and go and look at the people who are in it, if any people there are. For in this town have I as yet seen no people. If I die, I die, and if I live, I live. Here can I think of no plan, so if anything is to kill me, it will kill me."

Then it knocked twice at the door, and cried "Open," but no one answered. And it cried again, and a voice replied:

"Who are you that are crying 'Open'?"

And the gazelle said, "It is I, great mistress, your grandchild."

"If you are my grandchild," returned the voice, "go back whence you came. Don't come and die here, and bring me to my death as well."

"Open, mistress, I entreat, I have something to say to you."

"Grandchild," replied she, "I fear to put your life in danger, and my own too."

"Oh, mistress, my life will not be lost, nor yours either; open, I pray you." So she opened the door.

"What is the news where you come from, my grandson," asked she.

"Great lady, where I come from it is well, and with you it is well."

"Ah, my son, here it is not well at all. If you seek a way to die, or if you have not yet seen death, then is to-day the day for you to know what dying is."

"If I am to know it, I shall know it," replied the gazelle; "but tell me, who is the lord of this house?"

And she said: "Ah, father! in this house is much wealth, and much people, and much food, and many horses. And the lord of it all is an exceeding great and wonderful snake."

"Oh!" cried the gazelle when he heard this; "tell me how I can get at the snake to kill him?"

"My son," returned the old woman, "do not say words like these; you risk both our lives. He has put me here all by myself, and I have to cook his food. When the great snake is coming there springs up a wind, and blows the dust about, and this goes on till the great snake glides into the courtyard and calls for his dinner, which must always be ready for him in those big pots. He eats till he has had enough, and then drinks a whole tankful of water. After that he goes away. Every second day he comes, when the sun is over the house. And he has seven heads. How then can you be a match for him, my son?"

"Mind your own business, mother," answered the gazelle, "and don't mind other people's! Has this snake a sword?"

"He has a sword, and a sharp one too. It cuts like a dash of lightning."

"Give it to me, mother!" said the gazelle, and she unhooked the sword from the wall, as she was bidden. "You must be quick," she said, "for he may be here at any moment. Hark! is not that the wind rising? He has come!"

They were silent, but the old woman peeped from behind a curtain, and saw the snake busy at the pots which she had placed ready for him in the courtyard. And after he had done eating and drinking he came to the door:

"You old body!" he cried; "what smell is that I smell inside that is not the smell of every day?"

"Oh, master!" answered she, "I am alone, as I always am! But to-day, after many days, I have sprinkled fresh scent all over me, and it is that which you smell. What else could it be, master?"

All this time the gazelle had been standing close to the door, holding the sword in one of its front paws. And as the snake put one of his heads through the hole that he had made so as to get in and out comfortably, it cut it of so clean that the snake really did not feel it. The second blow was not quite so straight, for the snake said to himself, "Who is that who is trying to scratch me?" and stretched out his third head to see; but no sooner was the neck through the hole than the head went rolling to join the rest.

When six of his heads were gone the snake lashed his tail with such fury that the gazelle and the old woman could not see each other for the dust he made. And the gazelle said to him, "You have climbed all sorts of trees, but this you can't climb," and as the seventh head came darting through it went rolling to join the rest.

Then the sword fell rattling on the ground, for the gazelle had fainted.

The old woman shrieked with delight when she saw her enemy was dead, and ran to bring water to the gazelle, and fanned it, and put it where the wind could blow on it, till it grew better and gave a sneeze. And the heart of the old woman was glad, and she gave it more water, till by-and-by the gazelle got up.

"Show me this house," it said, "from beginning to end, from top to bottom, from inside to out."

So she arose and showed the gazelle rooms full of gold and precious things, and other rooms full of slaves. "They are all yours, goods and slaves," said she.

But the gazelle answered, "You must keep them safe till I call my master."

For two days it lay and rested in the house, and fed on milk and rice, and on the third day it bade the old woman farewell and started back to its master.

And when he heard that the gazelle was at the door he felt like a man who has found the time when all prayers are granted, and he rose and kissed it, saying: "My father, you have been a long time; you have left sorrow with me. I cannot eat, I cannot drink, I cannot laugh; my heart felt no smile at anything, because of thinking of you."

And the gazelle answered: "I am well, and where I come from it is well, and I wish that after four days you would take your wife and go home."

And he said: "It is for you to speak. Where you go, I will follow."

"Then I shall go to your father-in-law and tell him this news."

"Go, my son."

So the gazelle went to the father-in-law and said: "I am sent by my master to come and tell you that after four days he will go away with his wife to his own home."

"Must he really go so quickly? We have not yet sat much together, I and Sultan Darai, nor have we yet talked much together, nor have we yet ridden out together, nor have we eaten together; yet it is fourteen days since he came."

But the gazelle replied: "My lord, you cannot help it, for he wishes to go home, and nothing will stop him."

"Very good," said the sultan, and he called all the people who were in the town, and commanded that the day his daughter left the palace ladies and guards were to attend her on her way.

And at the end of four days a great company of ladies and slaves and horses went forth to escort the wife of Sultan Darai to her new home. They rode all day, and when the sun sank behind the hills they rested, and ate of the food the gazelle gave them, and lay down to sleep. And they journeyed on for many days, and they all, nobles and slaves, loved the gazelle with a great love—more than they loved the Sultan Darai.

At last one day signs of houses appeared, far, far off. And those who saw cried out, "Gazelle!"

And it answered, "Ah, my mistresses, that is the house of Sultan Darai."

At this news the women rejoiced much, and the slaves rejoiced much, and in the space of two hours they came to the gates, and the gazelle bade them all stay behind, and it went on to the house with Sultan Darai.

When the old woman saw them coming through the courtyard she jumped and shouted for joy, and as the gazelle drew near she seized it in her arms, and kissed it. The gazelle did not like this, and said to her: "Old woman, leave me alone; the one to be carried is my master, and the one to be kissed is my master."

And she answered, "Forgive me, my son. I did not know this was our master," and she threw open all the doors so that the master might see everything that the rooms and storehouses contained. Sultan Darai looked about him, and at length he said:

"Unfasten those horses that are tied up, and let loose those people that are bound. And let some sweep, and some spread the beds, and some cook, and some draw water, and some come out and receive the mistress."

And when the sultana and her ladies and her slaves entered the house, and saw the rich stuffs it was hung with, and the beautiful rice that was prepared for them to eat, they cried: "Ah, you gazelle, we have seen great houses, we have seen people, we have heard of things. But this house, and you, such as you are, we have never seen or heard of."

After a few days, the ladies said they wished to go home again. The gazelle begged them hard to stay, but finding they would not, it brought many gifts, and gave some to the ladies and some to their slaves. And they all thought the gazelle greater a thousand times than its master, Sultan Darai.

The gazelle and its master remained in the house many weeks, and one day it said to the old woman, "I came with my master to this place, and I have done many things for my master, good things, and till to-day he has never asked me: 'Well, my gazelle, how did you get this house? Who is the owner of it? And this town, were there no people in it?' All good things I have done for the master, and he has not one day done me any good thing. But people say, 'If you want to do any one good, don't do him good only, do him evil also, and there will be peace between you.' So, mother, I have done: I want to see the favors I have done to my master, that he may do me the like."

"Good," replied the old woman, and they went to bed.

In the morning, when light came, the gazelle was sick in its stomach and feverish, and its legs ached. And it said "Mother!"

And she answered, "Here, my son?"

And it said, "Go and tell my master upstairs the gazelle is very ill."

"Very good, my son; and if he should ask me what is the matter, what am I to say?"

"Tell him all my body aches badly; I have no single part without pain."

The old woman went upstairs, and she found the mistress and master sitting on a couch of marble spread with soft cushions, and they asked her, "Well, old woman, what do you want?"

"To tell the master the gazelle is ill," said she.

"What is the matter?" asked the wife.

"All its body pains; there is no part without pain."

"Well, what can I do? Make some gruel of red millet, and give to it."

But his wife stared and said: "Oh, master, do you tell her to make the gazelle gruel out of red millet, which a horse would not eat? Eh, master, that is not well."

But he answered, "Oh, you are mad! Rice is only kept for people."

"Eh, master, this is not like a gazelle. It is the apple of your eye. If sand got into that, it would trouble you."

"My wife, your tongue is long," and he left the room.

The old woman saw she had spoken vainly, and went back weeping to the gazelle. And when the gazelle saw her it said, "Mother, what is it, and why do you cry? If it be good, give me the answer; and if it be bad, give me the answer."

But still the old woman would not speak, and the gazelle prayed her to let it know the words of the master. At last she said: "I went upstairs and found the mistress and the master sitting on a couch, and he asked me what I wanted, and I told him that you, his slave, were ill. And his wife asked what was the matter, and I told her that there was not a part of your body without pain. And the master told me to take some red millet and make you gruel, but the mistress said, 'Eh, master, the gazelle is the apple of your eye; you have no child, this gazelle is like your child; so this gazelle is not one to be done evil to. This is a gazelle in form, but not a gazelle in heart; he is in all things better than a gentleman, be he who he may.'

"And he answered her, 'Silly chatterer, your words are many. I know its price; I bought it for an eighth. What loss will it be to me?'"

The gazelle kept silence for a few moments. Then it said, "The elders said, 'One that does good like a mother,' and I have done him good, and I have got this that the elders said. But go up again to the master, and tell him the gazelle is very ill, and it has not drunk the gruel of red millet."

So the old woman returned, and found the master and the mistress drinking coffee. And when he heard what the gazelle had said, he cried: "Hold your peace, old woman, and stay your feet and close your eyes, and stop your ears with wax; and if the gazelle bids you come to me, say your legs are bent, and you cannot walk; and if it begs you to listen, say your ears are stopped with wax; and if it wishes to talk, reply that your tongue has got a hook in it."

The heart of the old woman wept as she heard such words, because she saw that when the gazelle first came to that town it was ready to sell its life to buy wealth for its master. Then it happened to get both life and wealth, but now it had no honor with its master.

And tears sprung likewise to the eyes of the sultan's wife, and she said, "I am sorry for you, my husband, that you should deal so wickedly with that gazelle"; but he only answered, "Old woman, pay no heed to the talk of the mistress: tell it to perish out of the way. I cannot sleep, I cannot eat, I cannot drink, for the worry of that gazelle. Shall a creature that I bought for an eighth trouble me from morning till night? Not so, old woman!"

The old woman went downstairs, and there lay the gazelle, blood flowing from its nostrils. And she took it in her arms and said, "My son, the good you did is lost; there remains only patience."

And it said, "Mother, I shall die, for my soul is full of anger and bitterness. My face is ashamed, that I should have done good to my master, and that he should repay me with evil." It paused for a moment, and then went on, "Mother, of the goods that are in this house, what do I eat? I might have every day half a basinful, and would my master be any the poorer? But did not the elders say, 'He that does good like a mother!'"

And it said, "Go and tell my master that the gazelle is nearer death than life."

So she went, and spoke as the gazelle had bidden her; but he answered, "I have told you to trouble me no more."

But his wife's heart was sore, and she said to him: "Ah, master, what has the gazelle done to you? How has he failed you? The things you do to him are not good, and you will draw on yourself the hatred of the people. For this gazelle is loved by all, by small and great, by women and men. Ah, my husband! I thought you had great wisdom, and you have not even a little!"

But he answered, "You are mad, my wife."

The old woman stayed no longer, and went back to the gazelle, followed secretly by the mistress, who called a maidservant and bade her take some milk and rice and cook it for the gazelle.

"Take also this cloth," she said, "to cover it with, and this pillow for its head. And if the gazelle wants more, let it ask me, and not its master. And if it will, I will send it in a litter to my father, and he will nurse it till it is well."

And the maidservant did as her mistress bade her, and said what her mistress had told her to say, but the gazelle made no answer, but turned over on its side and died quietly.

When the news spread abroad, there was much weeping among the people, and Sultan Darai arose in wrath, and cried, "You weep for that gazelle as if you wept for me! And, after all, what is it but a gazelle, that I bought for an eighth?"

But his wife answered, "Master, we looked upon that gazelle as we looked upon you. It was the gazelle who came to ask me of my father, it was the gazelle who brought me from my father, and I was given in charge to the gazelle by my father."

And when the people heard her they lifted up their voices and spoke:

"We never saw you, we saw the gazelle. It was the gazelle who met with trouble here, it was the gazelle who met with rest here. So, then, when such an one departs from this world we weep for ourselves, we do not weep for the gazelle."

And they said furthermore:

"The gazelle did you much good, and if anyone says he could have done more for you he is a liar! Therefore, to us who have done you no good, what treatment will you give? The gazelle has died from bitterness of soul, and you ordered your slaves to throw it into the well. Ah! leave us alone that we may weep."

But Sultan Darai would not heed their words, and the dead gazelle was thrown into the well.

When the mistress heard of it, she sent three slaves, mounted on donkeys, with a letter to her father the sultan, and when the sultan had read the letter he bowed his head and wept, like a man who had lost his mother. And he commanded horses to be saddled, and called the governor and the judges and all the rich men, and said:

"Come now with me; let us go and bury it."

Night and day they traveled, till the sultan came to the well where the gazelle had been thrown. And it was a large well, built round a rock, with room for many people; and the sultan entered, and the judges and the rich men followed him. And when he saw the gazelle lying there he wept afresh, and took it in his arms and carried it away.

When the three slaves went and told their mistress what the sultan had done, and how all the people were weeping, she answered:

"I too have eaten no food, neither have I drunk water, since the day the gazelle died. I have not spoken, and I have not laughed."

The sultan took the gazelle and buried it, and ordered the people to wear mourning for it, so there was great mourning throughout the city.

Now after the days of mourning were at an end, the wife was sleeping at her husband's side, and in her sleep she dreamed that she was once more in her father's house, and when she woke up it was no dream.

And the man dreamed that he was on the dust-heap, scratching. And when he woke, behold! that also was no dream, but the truth.

The Brown Bear of Norway

(FROM *THE LILAC FAIRY BOOK*)

There was once a king in Ireland, and he had three daughters, and very nice princesses they were. And one day, when they and their father were walking on the lawn, the king began to joke with them, and to ask them whom they would like to be married to. "I'll have the king of Ulster for a husband," says one; "and I'll have the king of Munster," says another; "and," says the youngest, "I'll have no husband but the Brown Bear of Norway." For a nurse of hers used to be telling her of an enchanted prince that she called by that name, and she fell in love with him, and his name was the first name on her tongue, for the very night before she was dreaming of him. Well, one laughed, and another laughed, and they joked with the princess all the rest of the evening. But that very night she woke up out of her sleep in a great hall that was lighted up with a thousand lamps; the richest carpets were on the floor, and the walls were covered with cloth of gold and silver, and the place was full of grand company, and the very beautiful prince she saw in her dreams was there, and it wasn't a moment till he was on one knee before her, and telling her how much he loved her, and asking her wouldn't she be his queen. Well, she hadn't the heart to refuse him, and married they were the same evening.

"Now, my darling," says he, when they were left by themselves, "you must know that I am under enchantment. A sorceress that had a beautiful daughter wished me for her son-in-law; but the mother got power over me, and when I refused to wed her daughter she made me take the form of a bear by day, and I was to continue so till a lady would marry me of her own free will, and endure five years of great trials after."

Well, when the princess woke in the morning, she missed her husband from her side, and spent the day very sadly. But as soon as the lamps were lighted in the grand hall, where she was sitting on a sofa covered with silk, the folding doors flew open, and he was sitting by her side the next minute.

584

So they spent another happy evening, but he warned her that whenever she began to tire of him, or ceased to have faith in him, they would be parted for ever, and he'd be obliged to marry the witch's daughter.

She got used to find him absent by day, and they spent a happy twelvemonth together, and at last a beautiful little boy was born; and happy as she was before, she was twice as happy now, for she had her child to keep her company in the day when she couldn't see her husband.

At last, one evening, when herself, and himself, and her child were sitting with a window open because it was a sultry night, in flew an eagle, took the infant's sash in his beak, and flew up in the air with him. She screamed, and was going to throw herself out the window after him, but the prince caught her, and looked at her very seriously. She bethought of what he said soon after their marriage, and she stopped the cries and complaints that were on her tongue. She spent her days very lonely for another twelvemonth, when a beautiful little girl was sent to her. Then she thought to herself she'd have a sharp eye about her this time; so she never would allow a window to be more than a few inches open.

But all her care was in vain. Another evening, when they were all so happy, and the prince dandling the baby, a beautiful greyhound stood before them, took the child out of the father's hand, and was out of the door before you could wink. This time she shouted and ran out of the room, but there were some of the servants in the next room, and all declared that neither child nor dog passed out. She felt, somehow, as if it was her husband's fault, but still she kept command over herself, and didn't once reproach him.

When the third child was born she would hardly allow a window or a door to be left open for a moment; but she wasn't the nearer to keep the child to herself. They were sitting one evening by the fire, when a lady appeared standing by them. The princess opened her eyes in a great fright and stared at her, and while she was doing so, the lady wrapped a shawl round the baby that was sitting in its father's lap, and either sank through the ground with it or went up through the wide chimney. This time the mother kept her bed for a month.

"My dear," said she to her husband, when she was beginning to recover, "I think I'd feel better if I was to see my father and mother and sisters once more. If you give me leave to go home for a few days I'd be glad." "Very well," said he, "I will do that, and whenever you feel inclined to return, only mention your wish when you lie down at night." The next morning when she awoke she found herself in her own old chamber in her father's palace. She rang the bell, and in a short time she had her mother and father and married sisters about her, and they laughed till they cried for joy at finding her safe back again.

In time she told them all that had happened to her, and they didn't know what to advise her to do. She was as fond of her husband as ever, and said she was sure that he couldn't help letting the children go; but still she was afraid beyond the world to have another child torn from her. Well, the mother and sisters consulted a wise woman that used to bring eggs to the castle, for they had great faith in her wisdom. She said the only plan was to secure the bear's skin that the prince was obliged to put on every morning, and get it burned, and then he couldn't help being a man night and day, and the enchantment would be at an end.

So they all persuaded her to do that, and she promised she would; and after eight days she felt so great a longing to see her husband again that she made the wish the same night, and when she woke three hours after, she was in her husband's palace, and he himself was watching over her. There was great joy on both sides, and they were happy for many days.

Now she began to think how she never minded her husband leaving her in the morning, and how she never found him neglecting to give her a sweet drink out of a gold cup just as she was going to bed.

One night she contrived not to drink any of it, though she pretended to do so; and she was wakeful enough in the morning, and saw her husband passing out through a panel in the wainscot, though she kept her eyelids nearly closed. The next night she got a few drops of the sleepy posset that she saved the evening before put into her husband's night drink, and that made him sleep sound enough. She got up after midnight, passed through the panel, and found a beautiful brown bear's hide hanging in the corner. Then she stole back, and went down to the parlor fire, and put the hide into the middle of it till it was all fine ashes. She then lay down by her husband, gave him a kiss on the cheek, and fell asleep.

If she was to live a hundred years she'd never forget how she wakened next morning, and found her husband looking down on her with misery and anger in his face. "Unhappy woman," said he, "you have separated us for ever! Why hadn't you patience for five years? I am now obliged, whether I like or no, to go a three days' journey to the witch's castle, and marry her daughter. The skin that was my guard you have burned it, and the egg-wife that gave you the counsel was the witch herself. I won't reproach you: your punishment will be severe without it. Farewell for ever!"

He kissed her for the last time, and was off the next minute, walking as fast as he could. She shouted after him, and then seeing there was no use, she dressed herself and pursued him. He never stopped, nor stayed, nor looked back, and still she kept him in sight; and when he was on the hill she was in the hollow, and when he was in the hollow she was on the hill. Her life was almost leaving her, when, just as the sun was setting, he turned up a lane, and went into a little house. She crawled up after him, and when she got inside there was a beautiful little boy on his knees, and he kissing and hugging him. "Here, my poor darling," says he, "is your eldest child, and there," says he, pointing to a woman that was looking on with a smile on her face, "is the eagle that carried him away." She forgot all her sorrows in a moment, hugging her child, and laughing and crying over him. The woman washed their feet, and rubbed them with an ointment that took all the soreness out of their bones, and made them as fresh as a daisy. Next morning, just before sunrise, he was up, and prepared to be off, "Here," said he to her, "is a thing which may be of use to you. It's a scissors, and whatever stuff you cut with it will be turned into silk. The moment the sun rises, I'll lose all memory of yourself and the children, but I'll get it at sunset again. Farewell!" But he wasn't far gone till she was in sight of him again, leaving her boy behind. It was the same to-day as yesterday: their shadows went before them in the morning and followed them in the evening. He never stopped, and she never stopped, and as the sun was setting he turned up another lane, and there they found their little daughter. It was all joy and comfort again till morning, and then the third day's journey commenced.

But before he started he gave her a comb, and told her that whenever she used it, pearls and diamonds would fall from her hair. Still he had his memory from sunset to sunrise; but from sunrise to sunset he traveled on under the charm, and never threw his eye behind. This night they came to where the youngest baby was, and the next morning, just before sunrise, the prince spoke to her for the last time. "Here, my poor wife," said he, "is a little hand-reel, with gold thread that has no end, and the half of our marriage ring. If you ever get to my house, and put your half-ring to mine, I shall recollect you. There is a wood yonder, and the moment I enter it I shall forget everything that ever happened between us, just as if I was born yesterday. Farewell, dear wife and child, for ever!" Just then the sun rose, and away he walked towards the wood. She saw it open before him and close after him, and when she came up, she could no more get in than she could break through a stone wall. She wrung her hands and shed tears, but then she recollected herself, and cried out, "Wood, I charge you by my three magic gifts, the scissors, the comb, and the reel—to let me through"; and it opened, and she went along a walk till she came in sight of a palace, and a lawn, and a woodman's cottage on the edge of the wood where it came nearest the palace.

She went into the lodge, and asked the woodman and his wife to take her into their service. They were not willing at first; but she told them she would ask no wages, and would give them diamonds, and pearls, and silk stuffs, and gold thread whenever they wished for them, and then they agreed to let her stay.

It wasn't long till she heard how a young prince, that was just arrived, was living in the palace of the young mistress. He seldom stirred abroad, and every one that saw him remarked how silent and sorrowful he went about, like a person that was searching for some lost thing.

The servants and conceited folk at the big house began to take notice of the beautiful young woman at the lodge, and to annoy her with their impudence. The head footman was the most troublesome, and at last she invited him to come and take tea with her. Oh, how rejoiced he was, and how he bragged of it in the servants' hall! Well, the evening came, and the footman walked into the lodge, and was shown to her sitting-room; for the lodge-keeper and his wife stood in great awe of her, and gave her two nice rooms for herself. Well, he sat down as stiff as a ramrod, and was talking in a grand style about the great doings at the castle, while she was getting the tea and toast ready. "Oh," says she to him, "would you put your hand out at the window and cut me off a sprig or two of honeysuckle?" He got up in great glee, and put out his hand and head; and said she, "By the virtue of my magic gifts, let a pair of horns spring out of your head, and sing to the lodge." Just as she wished, so it was. They sprung from the front of each ear, and met at the back. Oh, the poor wretch! And how he bawled and roared! and the servants that he used to be boasting to were soon flocking from the castle, and grinning, and huzzaing, and beating tunes on tongs and shovels and pans; and he cursing and swearing, and the eyes ready to start out of his head, and he so black in the face, and kicking out his legs behind him like mad.

At last she pitied him, and removed the charm, and the horns dropped down on the ground, and he would have killed her on the spot, only he was as weak as water, and his fellow-servants came in and carried him up to the big house.

Well, some way or other the story came to the ears of the prince, and he strolled down that way. She had only the dress of a countrywoman on her as she sat sewing at the window, but that did not hide her beauty, and he was greatly puzzled after he had a good look, just as a body is puzzled to know whether something happened to him when he was young or if he only dreamed it. Well, the witch's daughter heard about it too, and she came to see the strange girl; and what did she find her doing but cutting out the pattern of a gown from brown paper; and as she cut away, the paper became the richest silk she ever saw. The witch's daughter looked on with greedy eyes, and, says she, "What would you be satisfied to take for that scissors?" "I'll take nothing," says she, "but leave to spend one night outside the prince's chamber." Well, the proud lady fired up, and was going to say something dreadful; but the scissors kept on cutting, and the silk growing richer and richer every inch. So she promised what the girl had asked her.

When night came on she was let into the palace and lay down till the prince was in such a dead sleep that all she did couldn't awake him. She sung this verse to him, sighing and sobbing, and kept singing it the night long, and it was all in vain:

> "Four long years I was married to thee;
> Three sweet babes I bore to thee;
> Brown Bear of Norway, turn to me."

At the first dawn the proud lady was in the chamber, and led her away, and the footman of the horns put out his tongue at her as she was quitting the palace.

So there was no luck so far; but the next day the prince passed by again and looked at her, and saluted her kindly, as a prince might a farmer's daughter, and passed one; and soon the witch's daughter passed by, and found her combing her hair, and pearls and diamonds dropping from it.

Well, another bargain was made, and the princess spent another night of sorrow, and she left the castle at daybreak, and the footman was at his post and enjoyed his revenge.

The third day the prince went by, and stopped to talk with the strange woman. He asked her could he do anything to serve her, and she said he might. She asked him did he ever wake at night. He said that he often did, but that during the last two nights he was listening to a sweet song in his dreams, and could not wake, and that the voice was one that he must have known and loved in some other world long ago. Says she, "Did you drink any sleepy posset either of these evenings before you went to bed?" "I did," said he. "The two evenings my wife gave me something to drink, but I don't know whether it was a sleepy posset or not." "Well, prince," said she, "as you say you would wish to oblige me, you can do it by not tasting any drink to-night." "I will not," says he, and then he went on his walk.

Well, the great lady came soon after the prince, and found the stranger using her hand-reel and winding threads of gold off it, and the third bargain was made.

That evening the prince was lying on his bed at twilight, and his mind much disturbed; and the door opened, and in his princess walked, and down she sat by his bedside and sung:

"Four long years I was married to thee;
Three sweet babes I bore to thee;
Brown Bear of Norway, turn to me."

"Brown Bear of Norway!" said he. "I don't understand you." "Don't you remember, prince, that I was your wedded wife for four years?" "I do not," said he, "but I'm sure I wish it was so." "Don't you remember our three babes that are still alive?" "Show me them. My mind is all a heap of confusion." "Look for the half of our marriage ring, that hangs at your neck, and fit it to this." He did so, and the same moment the charm was broken. His full memory came back on him, and he flung his arms round his wife's neck, and both burst into tears.

Well, there was a great cry outside, and the castle walls were heard splitting and cracking. Everyone in the castle was alarmed, and made their way out. The prince and princess went with the rest, and by the time all were safe on the lawn, down came the building, and made the ground tremble for miles round. No one ever saw the witch and her daughter afterwards. It was not long till the prince and princess had their children with them, and then they set out for their own palace. The kings of Ireland and of Munster and Ulster, and their wives, soon came to visit them, and may every one that deserves it be as happy as the Brown Bear of Norway and his family.

Janni and the Draken

(FROM *THE GRAY FAIRY BOOK*)

Once there was a man who shunned the world, and lived in the wilderness. He owned nothing but a flock of sheep, whose milk and wool he sold, and so procured himself bread to eat; he also carried wooden spoons, and sold them. He had a wife and one little girl, and after a long time his wife had another child. The evening it was born the man went to the nearest village to fetch a nurse, and on the way he met a monk who begged him for a night's lodging. This the man willingly granted, and took him home with him. There being no one far nor near to baptize the child, the man asked the monk to do him this service, and the child was given the name of Janni.

In the course of time Janni's parents died, and he and his sister were left alone in the world; soon affairs went badly with them, so they determined to wander away to seek their fortune. In packing up, the sister found a knife which the monk had left for his godson, and this she gave to her brother.

Then they went on their way, taking with them the three sheep which were all that remained of their flocks. After wandering for three days they met a man with three dogs who proposed that they should exchange animals, he taking the sheep, and they the dogs. The brother and sister were quite pleased at this arrangement, and after the exchange was made they separated, and went their different ways.

Janni and his sister in course of time came to a great castle, in which dwelt forty Draken, who, when they heard that Janni had come, fled forty fathoms underground.

So Janni found the castle deserted, and abode there with his sister, and every day went out to hunt with the weapons the Draken had left in the castle.

One day, when he was away hunting, one of the Draken came up to get provisions, not knowing that there was anyone in the castle. When he saw Janni's sister he was terrified, but she told him not to be afraid, and by-and-by they fell in love with each other, for every time that Janni went to hunt the sister called the Drakos up. Thus they went on making love to each other till at length, unknown to Janni, they got married. Then, when it was too late, the sister repented, and was afraid of Janni's wrath when he found it out.

One day the Drakos came to her, and said: "You must pretend to be ill, and when Janni asks what ails you, and what you want, you must answer: 'Cherries,' and when he inquires where these are to be found, you must say: 'There are some in a garden a day's journey from here.' Then your brother will go there, and will never come back, for there dwell three of my brothers who will look after him well."

Then the sister did as the Drakos advised, and next day Janni set out to fetch the cherries, taking his three dogs with him. When he came to the garden where the cherries grew he jumped off his horse, drank some water from the spring, which rose there, and fell directly into a deep sleep. The Draken came round about to eat him, but the dogs flung themselves on them and tore them in pieces, and scratched a grave in the ground with their paws, and buried the Draken so that Janni might not see their dead bodies. When Janni awoke, and saw his dogs all covered with blood, he believed that they had caught, somewhere, a wild beast, and was angry because they had left none of it for him. But he plucked the cherries, and took them back to his sister.

When the Drakos heard that Janni had come back, he fled for fear forty fathoms underground. And the sister ate the cherries and declared herself well again.

The next day, when Janni was gone to hunt, the Drakos came out, and advised the sister that she should pretend to be ill again, and when her brother asked her what she would like, she should answer "Quinces," and when he inquired where these were to be found, she should say: "In a garden distant about two days' journey." Then would Janni certainly be destroyed, for there dwelt six brothers of the Drakos, each of whom had two heads.

The sister did as she was advised, and next day Janni again set off, taking his three dogs with him. When he came to the garden he dismounted, sat down to rest a little, and fell fast asleep. First there came three Draken round about to eat him, and when these three had been worried by the dogs, there came three others who were worried in like manner. Then the dogs again dug a grave and buried the dead Draken, that their master might not see them. When Janni awoke and beheld the dogs all covered with blood, he thought, as before, that they had killed a wild beast, and was again angry with them for leaving him nothing. But he took the quinces and brought them back to his sister, who, when she had eaten them, declared herself better. The Drakos, when he heard that Janni had come back, fled for fear forty fathoms deeper underground.

Next day, when Janni was hunting, the Drakos went to the sister and advised that she should again pretend to be ill, and should beg for some pears, which grew in a garden three days' journey from the castle. From this quest Janni would certainly never return, for there dwelt nine brothers of the Drakos, each of whom had three heads.

The sister did as she was told, and next day Janni, taking his three dogs with him, went to get the pears. When he came to the garden he laid himself down to rest, and soon fell asleep.

Then first came three Draken to eat him, and when the dogs had worried these, six others came and fought the dogs a long time. The noise of this combat awoke Janni, and he slew the Draken, and knew at last why the dogs were covered with blood.

After that he freed all whom the Draken held prisoners, among others, a king's daughter. Out of gratitude she would have taken him for her husband; but he put her off, saying: "For the kindness that I have been able to do to you, you shall receive in this castle all the blind and lame who pass this way." The princess promised him to do so, and on his departure gave him a ring.

So Janni plucked the pears and took them to his sister, who, when she had eaten them, declared she felt better. When, however, the Drakos heard that Janni had come back yet a third time safe and sound, he fled for fright forty fathoms deeper underground; and, next day, when Janni was away hunting, he crept out and said to the sister: "Now are we indeed both lost, unless you find out from him wherein his strength lies, and then between us we will contrive to do away with him."

When, therefore, Janni had come back from hunting, and sat at evening with his sister by the fire, she begged him to tell her wherein lay his strength, and he answered: "It lies in my two fingers; if these are bound together then all my strength disappears."

"That I will not believe," said the sister, "unless I see it for myself."

Then he let her tie his fingers together with a thread, and immediately he became powerless. Then the sister called up the Drakos, who, when he had come forth, tore out Janni's eyes, gave them to his dogs to eat, and threw him into a dry well.

Now it happened that some travelers, going to draw water from this well, heard Janni groaning at the bottom. They came near, and asked him where he was, and he begged them to draw him up from the well, for he was a poor unfortunate man.

The travelers let a rope down and drew him up to daylight. It was not till then that he first became aware that he was blind, and he begged the travelers to lead him to the country of the king whose daughter he had freed, and they would be well repaid for their trouble.

When they had brought him there he sent to beg the princess to come to him; but she did not recognize him till he had shown her the ring she had given him.

Then she remembered him, and took him with her into the castle.

When she learnt what had befallen him she called together all the sorceresses in the country in order that they should tell her where the eyes were. At last she found one who declared that she knew where they were, and that she could restore them. This sorceress then went straight to the castle where dwelt the sister and the Drakos, and gave something to the dogs to eat which caused the eyes to reappear. She took them with her and put them back in Janni's head, so that he saw as well as before.

Then he returned to the castle of the Drakos, whom he slew as well as his sister; and, taking his dogs with him, went back to the princess and they were immediately married.

The Fox and the Lapp

(FROM *THE BROWN FAIRY BOOK*)

Once upon a time a fox lay peeping out of his hole, watching the road that ran by at a little distance, and hoping to see something that might amuse him, for he was feeling very dull and rather cross. For a long while he watched in vain; everything seemed asleep, and not even a bird stirred overhead. The fox grew crosser than ever, and he was just turning away in disgust from his place when he heard the sound of feet coming over the snow. He crouched eagerly down at the edge of the road and said to himself: "I wonder what would happen if I were to pretend to be dead! This is a man driving a reindeer sledge, I know the tinkling of the harness. And at any rate I shall have an adventure, and that is always something!"

So he stretched himself out by the side of the road, carefully choosing a spot where the driver could not help seeing him, yet where the reindeer would not tread on him; and all fell out just as he had expected. The sledge-driver pulled up sharply, as his eyes lighted on the beautiful animal lying stiffly beside him, and jumping out he threw the fox into the bottom of the sledge, where the goods he was carrying were bound tightly together by ropes. The fox did not move a muscle though his bones were sore from the fall, and the driver got back to his seat again and drove on merrily.

But before they had gone very far, the fox, who was near the edge, contrived to slip over, and when the Laplander saw him stretched out on the snow he pulled up his reindeer and put the fox into one of the other sledges that was fastened behind, for it was market-day at the nearest town, and the man had much to sell.

They drove on a little further, when some noise in the forest made the man turn his head, just in time to see the fox fall with a heavy thump on to the frozen snow. "That beast is bewitched!" he said to himself, and then he threw the fox into the last sledge of all, which had a cargo of fishes. This was exactly what the cunning creature wanted, and he wriggled gently to the front and bit the cord which tied the sledge to the one before it so that it remained standing in the middle of the road.

Now there were so many sledges that the Lapp did not notice for a long while that one was missing; indeed, he would have entered the town without knowing if snow had not suddenly begun to fall. Then he got down to secure more firmly the cloths that kept his goods dry, and going to the end of the long row, discovered that the sledge containing the fish and the fox was missing. He quickly unharnessed one of his reindeer and rode back along the way he had come, to find the sledge standing safe in the middle of the road; but as the fox had bitten off the cord close to the noose there was no means of moving it away.

The fox meanwhile was enjoying himself mightily. As soon as he had loosened the sledge, he had taken his favorite fish from among the piles neatly arranged for sale, and had trotted off to the forest with it in his mouth. By-and-by he met a bear, who stopped and said: "Where did you find that fish, Mr. Fox?"

"Oh, not far off," answered he; "I just stuck my tail in the stream close by the place where the elves dwell, and the fish hung on to it of itself."

"Dear me," snarled the bear, who was hungry and not in a good temper, "if the fish hung on to your tail, I suppose he will hang on to mine."

"Yes, certainly, grandfather," replied the fox, "if you have patience to suffer what I suffered."

"Of course I can," replied the bear, "what nonsense you talk! Show me the way."

So the fox led him to the bank of a stream, which, being in a warm place, had only lightly frozen in places, and was at this moment glittering in the spring sunshine.

"The elves bathe here," he said, "and if you put in your tail the fish will catch hold of it. But it is no use being in a hurry, or you will spoil everything."

Then he trotted off, but only went out of sight of the bear, who stood still on the bank with his tail deep in the water. Soon the sun set and it grew very cold and the ice formed rapidly, and the bear's tail was fixed as tight as if a vice had held it; and when the fox saw that everything had happened just as he had planned it, he called out loudly:

"Be quick, good people, and come with your bows and spears. A bear has been fishing in your brook!"

And in a moment the whole place was full of little creatures each one with a tiny bow and a spear hardly big enough for a baby; but both arrows and spears could sting, as the bear knew very well, and in his fright he gave such a tug to his tail that it broke short off, and he rolled away into the forest as fast as his legs could carry him. At this sight the fox held his sides for laughing, and then scampered away in another direction. By-and-by he came to a fir tree, and crept into a hole under the root. After that he did something very strange.

Taking one of his hind feet between his two front paws, he said softly:

"What would you do, my foot, if someone was to betray me?"

"I would run so quickly that he should not catch you."

"What would you do, mine ear, if someone was to betray me?"

"I would listen so hard that I should hear all his plans."

"What would you do, my nose, if someone was to betray me?"

"I would smell so sharply that I should know from afar that he was coming."

"What would you do, my tail, if someone was to betray me?"

"I would steer you so straight a course that you would soon be beyond his reach. Let us be off; I feel as if danger was near."

But the fox was comfortable where he was, and did not hurry himself to take his tail's advice. And before very long he found he was too late, for the bear had come round by another path, and guessing where his enemy was began to scratch at the roots of the tree. The fox made himself as small as he could, but a scrap of his tail peeped out, and the bear seized it and held it tight. Then the fox dug his claws into the ground, but he was not strong enough to pull against the bear, and slowly he was dragged forth and his body flung over the bear's neck. In this manner they set out down the road, the fox's tail being always in the bear's mouth.

After they had gone some way, they passed a tree-stump, on which a bright colored woodpecker was tapping.

"Ah! those were better times when I used to paint all the birds such gay colors," sighed the fox.

"What are you saying, old fellow?" asked the bear.

"I? Oh, I was saying nothing," answered the fox drearily. "Just carry me to your cave and eat me up as quick as you can."

The bear was silent, and thought of his supper; and the two continued their journey till they reached another tree with a woodpecker tapping on it.

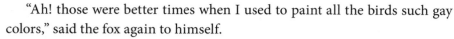

"Ah! those were better times when I used to paint all the birds such gay colors," said the fox again to himself.

"Couldn't you paint me too?" asked the bear suddenly.

But the fox shook his head; for he was always acting, even if no one was there to see him do it.

"You bear pain so badly," he replied, in a thoughtful voice, "and you are impatient besides, and could never put up with all that is necessary. Why, you would first have to dig a pit, and then twist ropes of willow, and drive in posts and fill the hole with pitch, and, last of all, set it on fire. Oh, no; you would never be able to do all that."

"It does not matter a straw how hard the work is," answered the bear eagerly, "I will do it every bit." And as he spoke he began tearing up the earth so fast that soon a deep pit was ready, deep enough to hold him.

"That is all right," said the fox at last, "I see I was mistaken in you. Now sit here, and I will bind you." So the bear sat down on the edge of the pit, and the fox sprang on his back, which he crossed with the willow ropes, and then set fire to the pitch. It burnt up in an instant, and caught the bands of willow and the bear's rough hair; but he did not stir, for he thought that the fox was rubbing the bright colors into his skin, and that he would soon be as beautiful as a whole meadow of flowers. But when the fire grew hotter still he moved uneasily from one foot to the other, saying, imploringly: "It is getting rather warm, old man." But all the answer he got was: "I thought you would never be able to suffer pain like those little birds."

The bear did not like being told that he was not as brave as a bird, so he set his teeth and resolved to endure anything sooner than speak again; but by this time the last willow band had burned through, and with a push the fox sent his victim tumbling into the grass, and ran off to hide himself in the forest. After a while he stole cautiously and found, as he expected, nothing left but a few charred bones. These he picked up and put in a bag, which he slung over his back.

By-and-by he met a Lapp driving his team of reindeer along the road, and as he drew near, the fox rattled the bones gaily.

"That sounds like silver or gold," thought the man to himself. And he said politely to the fox:

"Good-day, friend! What have you got in your bag that makes such a strange sound?"

"All the wealth my father left me," answered the fox. "Do you feel inclined to bargain?"

"Well, I don't mind," replied the Lapp, who was a prudent man, and did not wish the fox to think him too eager; "but show me first what money you have got."

"Ah, but I can't do that," answered the fox, "my bag is sealed up. But if you will give me those three reindeer, you shall take it as it is, with all its contents."

The Lapp did not quite like it, but the fox spoke with such an air that his doubts melted away. He nodded, and stretched out his hand; the fox put the bag into it, and unharnassed the reindeer he had chosen.

"Oh, I forgot!" he exclaimed, turning round, as he was about to drive them in the opposite direction, "you must be sure not to open the bag until you have gone at least five miles, right on the other side of those hills out there. If you do, you will find that all the gold and silver has changed into a parcel of charred bones." Then he whipped up his reindeer, and was soon out of sight.

For some time the Lapp was satisfied with hearing the bones rattle, and thinking to himself what a good bargain he had made, and of all the things he would buy with the money. But, after a bit, this amusement ceased to content him, and besides, what was the use of planning when you did not know for certain how rich you were? Perhaps there might be a great deal of silver and only a little gold in the bag; or a great deal of gold, and only a little silver. Who could tell? He would not, of course, take the money out to count it, for that might bring him bad luck. But there could be no harm in just one peep! So he slowly broke the seal, and untied the strings, and, behold, a heap of burnt bones lay before him! In a minute he knew he had been tricked, and flinging the bag to the ground in a rage, he ran after the fox as fast as his snow-shoes would carry him.

Now the fox had guessed exactly what would happen, and was on the look out. Directly he saw the little speck coming towards him, he wished that the man's snow-shoes might break, and that very instant the Lapp's shoes snapped in two. The Lapp did now know that this was the fox's work, but he had to stop and fetch one of his other reindeer, which he mounted, and set off again in pursuit of his enemy. The fox soon heard him coming, and this time he wished that the reindeer might fall and break its leg. And so it did; and the man felt it was a hopeless chase, and that he was no match for the fox.

So the fox drove on in peace till he reached the cave where all his stores were kept, and then he began to wonder whom he could get to help him kill his reindeer, for though he could steal reindeer he was too small to kill them. "After all, it will be quite easy," thought he, and he bade a squirrel, who was watching him on a tree close by, take a message to all the robber beasts of the forest, and in less than half an hour a great crashing of branches was heard, and bears, wolves, snakes, mice, frogs, and other creatures came pressing up to the cave.

When they heard why they had been summoned, they declared themselves ready each one to do his part. The bear took his crossbow from his neck and shot the reindeer in the chin; and, from that day to this, every reindeer has a mark in that same spot, which is always known as the bear's arrow. The wolf shot him in the thigh, and the sign of his arrow still remains; and so with the mouse and the viper and all the rest, even the frog; and at the last the reindeer all died. And the fox did nothing, but looked on.

"I really must go down to the brook and wash myself," said he (though he was perfectly clean), and he went under the bank and hid himself behind a stone. From there he set up the most frightful shrieks, so that the animals fled away in all directions. Only the mouse and the ermine remained where they were, for they thought that they were much too small to be noticed.

The fox continued his shrieks till he felt sure that the animals must have got to a safe distance; then he crawled out of his hiding-place and went to the bodies of the reindeer, which he now had all to himself. He gathered a bundle of sticks for a fire, and was just preparing to cook a steak, when his enemy, the Lapp, came up, panting with haste and excitement.

"What are you doing there?" cried he; "why did you palm off those bones on me? And why, when you had got the reindeer, did you kill them?"

"Dear brother," answered the fox with a sob, "do not blame me for this misfortune. It is my comrades who have slain them in spite of my prayers."

The man made no reply, for the white fur of the ermine, who was crouching with the mouse behind some stones, had just caught his eye. He hastily seized the iron hook which hung over the fire and flung it at the little creature; but the ermine was too quick for him, and the hook only touched the top of its tail, and that has remained black to this day. As for the mouse, the Lapp threw a half-burnt stick after him, and though it was not enough to hurt him, his beautiful white skin was smeared all over with it, and all the washing in the world would not make him clean again. And the man would have been wiser if he had let the ermine and the mouse alone, for when he turned round again he found he was alone.

Directly the fox noticed that his enemy's attention had wandered from himself he watched his chance, and stole softly away till he had reached a clump of thick bushes, when he ran as fast as he could, till he reached a river, where a man was mending his boat.

"Oh, I wish, I do wish, I had a boat to mend too!" he cried, sitting up on his hind-legs and looking into the man's face.

"Stop your silly chatter!" answered the man crossly, "or I will give you a bath in the river."

"Oh, I wish, I do wish, I had a boat to mend," cried the fox again, as if he had not heard. And the man grew angry and seized him by the tail, and threw him far out in the stream close to the edge of an island; which was just what the fox wanted. He easily scrambled up, and sitting on the top, he called: "Hasten, hasten, O fishes, and carry me to the other side!" And the fishes left the stones where they had been sleeping, and the pools where they had been feeding, and hurried to see who could get to the island first.

"I have won," shouted the pike. "Jump on my back, dear fox, and you will find yourself in a trice on the opposite shore."

"No, thank you," answered the fox, "your back is much too weak for me. I should break it."

"Try mine," said the eel, who had wriggled to the front.

"No, thank you," replied the fox again, "I should slip over your head and be drowned."

"You won't slip on *my* back," said the perch, coming forward.

"No; but you are really *too* rough," returned the fox.

"Well, you can have no fault to find with *me*," put in the trout.

"Good gracious! are *you* here?" exclaimed the fox. "But I'm afraid to trust myself to you either."

At this moment a fine salmon swam slowly up.

"Ah, yes, you are the person I want," said the fox; "but come near, so that I may get on your back, without wetting my feet."

So the salmon swam close under the island, and when he was touching it the fox seized him in his claws and drew him out of the water, and put him on a spit, while he kindled a fire to cook him by. When everything was ready, and the water in the pot was getting hot, he popped him in, and waited till he thought the salmon was nearly boiled. But as he stooped down the water gave a sudden fizzle, and splashed into the fox's eyes, blinding him. He started backwards with a cry of pain, and sat still for some minutes, rocking himself to and fro. When he was a little better he rose and walked down a road till he met a grouse, who stopped and asked what was the matter.

"Have you a pair of eyes anywhere about you?" asked the fox politely.

"No, I am afraid I haven't," answered the grouse, and passed on.

A little while after the fox heard the buzzing of an early bee, whom a gleam of sun had tempted out.

"Do you happen to have an extra pair of eyes anywhere?" asked the fox.

"I am sorry to say I have only those I am using," replied the bee. And the fox went on till he nearly fell over an asp who was gliding across the road.

"I should be *so* glad if you would tell me where I could get a pair of eyes," said the fox. "I suppose you don't happen to have any you could lend me?"

"Well, if you only want them for a short time, perhaps I could manage," answered the asp; "but I can't do without them for long."

"Oh, it is only for a very short time that I need them," said the fox; "I have a pair of my own just behind that hill, and when I find them I will bring yours back to you. Perhaps you will keep these till them." So he took the eyes out of his own head and popped them into the head of the asp, and put the asp's eyes in their place. As he was running off he cried over his shoulder: "As long as the world lasts the asps' eyes will go down in the heads of foxes from generation to generation."

And so it has been; and if you look at the eyes of an asp you will see that they are all burnt; and though thousands and thousands of years have gone by since the fox was going about playing tricks upon everybody he met, the asp still bears the traces of the day when the sly creature cooked the salmon.

Motikatika

(From *The Crimson Fairy Book*)

O nce upon a time, in a very hot country, a man lived with his wife in a little hut, which was surrounded by grass and flowers. They were perfectly happy together till, by-and-by, the woman fell ill and refused to take any food. The husband tried to persuade her to eat all sorts of delicious fruits that he had found in the forest, but she would have none of them, and grew so thin he feared she would die. "Is there nothing you would like?" he said at last in despair.

"Yes, I think I could eat some wild honey," answered she. The husband was overjoyed, for he thought this sounded easy enough to get, and he went off at once in search of it.

He came back with a wooden pan quite full, and gave it to his wife. "I can't eat *that*," she said, turning away in disgust. "Look! there are some dead bees in it! I want honey that is quite pure." And the man threw the rejected honey on the grass, and started off to get some fresh. When he got back he offered it to his wife, who treated it as she had done the first bowlful. "That honey has got ants in it: throw it away," she said, and when he brought her some more, she declared it was full of earth. In his fourth journey he managed to find some that she would eat, and then she begged him to get her some water. This took him some time, but at length he came to a lake whose waters were sweetened with sugar. He filled a pannikin quite full, and carried it home to his wife, who drank it eagerly, and said that she now felt quite well.

When she was up and had dressed herself, her husband lay down in her place, saying: "You have given me a great deal of trouble, and now it is my turn!"

"What is the matter with you?" asked the wife.

"I am thirsty and want some water," answered he; and she took a large pot and carried it to the nearest spring, which was a good way off.

"Here is the water," she said to her husband, lifting the heavy pot from her head; but he turned away in disgust.

"You have drawn it from the pool that is full of frogs and willows; you must get me some more." So the woman set out again and walked still further to another lake.

"This water tastes of rushes," he exclaimed, "go and get some fresh." But when she brought back a third supply he declared that it seemed made up of water-lilies, and that he must have water that was pure, and not spoilt by willows, or frogs, or rushes. So for the fourth time she put her jug on her head, and passing all the lakes she had hitherto tried, she came to another, where the water was golden like honey. She stooped down to drink, when a horrible head bobbed up on the surface.

"How dare you steal my water?" cried the head.

"It is my husband who has sent me," she replied, trembling all over. "But do not kill me! You shall have my baby, if you will only let me go."

"How am I to know which is your baby?" asked the ogre.

"Oh, that is easily managed. I will shave both sides of his head, and hang some white beads round his neck. And when you come to the hut you have only to call 'Motikatika!' and he will run to meet you, and you can eat him."

"Very well," said the ogre, "you can go home." And after filling the pot she returned, and told her husband of the dreadful danger she had been in.

Now, though his mother did not know it, the baby was a magician and he had heard all that his mother had promised the ogre; and he laughed to himself as he planned how to outwit her.

The next morning she shaved his head on both sides, and hung the white beads round his neck, and said to him: "I am going to the fields to work, but you must stay at home. Be sure you do not go outside, or some wild beast may eat you."

"Very well," answered he.

As soon as his mother was out of sight, the baby took out some magic bónes, and placed them in a row before him. "You are my father," he told one bone, "and you are my mother. You are the biggest," he said to the third, "so you shall be the ogre who wants to eat me; and you," to another, "are very little, therefore you shall be me. Now, then, tell me what I am to do."

"Collect all the babies in the village the same size as yourself," answered the bones; "shave the sides of their heads, and hang white beads round their necks, and tell them that when anybody calls 'Motikatika,' they are to answer to it. And be quick for you have no time to lose."

Motikatika went out directly, and brought back quite a crowd of babies, and shaved their heads and hung white beads round their little black necks, and just as he had finished, the ground began to shake, and the huge ogre came striding along, crying: "Motikatika! Motikatika!"

"Here we are! here we are!" answered the babies, all running to meet him.

"It is Motikatika I want," said the ogre.

"We are all Motikatika," they replied. And the ogre sat down in bewilderment, for he dared not eat the children of people who had done him no wrong, or a heavy punishment would befall him. The children waited for a little, wondering, and then they went away.

The ogre remained where he was, till the evening, when the woman returned from the fields.

"I have not seen Motikatika," said he.

"But why did you not call him by his name, as I told you?" she asked.

"I did, but all the babies in the village seemed to be named Motikatika," answered the ogre; "you cannot think the number who came running to me."

The woman did not know what to make of it, so, to keep him in a good temper, she entered the hut and prepared a bowl of maize, which she brought him.

"I do not want maize, I want the baby," grumbled he "and I will have him."

"Have patience," answered she; "I will call him, and you can eat him at once." And she went into the hut and cried, "Motikatika!"

"I am coming, mother," replied he; but first he took out his bones, and, crouching down on the ground behind the hut, asked them how he should escape the ogre.

"Change yourself into a mouse," said the bones; and so he did, and the ogre grew tired of waiting, and told the woman she must invent some other plan.

"To-morrow I will send him into the field to pick some beans for me, and you will find him there, and can eat him."

"Very well," replied the ogre, "and this time I will take care to have him," and he went back to his lake.

Next morning Motikatika was sent out with a basket, and told to pick some beans for dinner. On the way to the field he took out his bones and asked them what he was to do to escape from the ogre. "Change yourself into a bird and snap off the beans," said the bones. And the ogre chased away the bird, not knowing that it was Motikatika.

The ogre went back to the hut and told the woman that she had deceived him again, and that he would not be put off any longer.

"Return here this evening," answered she, "and you will find him in bed under this white coverlet. Then you can carry him away, and eat him at once."

But the boy heard, and consulted his bones, which said: "Take the red coverlet from your father's bed, and put yours on his," and so he did. And when the ogre came, he seized Motikatika's father and carried him outside the hut and ate him. When his wife found out the mistake, she cried bitterly; but Motikatika said: "It is only just that he should be eaten, and not I; for it was he, and not I, who sent you to fetch the water."

The Bear

(From *The Gray Fairy Book*)

Once on a time there was a king who had an only daughter. He was so proud and so fond of her, that he was in constant terror that something would happen to her if she went outside the palace, and thus, owing to his great love for her, he forced her to lead the life of a prisoner, shut up within her own rooms.

The princess did not like this at all, and one day she complained about it very bitterly to her nurse. Now, the nurse was a witch, though the king did not know it. For some time she listened and tried to soothe the princess; but when she saw that she would not be comforted, she said to her: "Your father loves you very dearly, as you know. Whatever you were to ask from him he would give you. The one thing he will not grant you is permission to leave the palace. Now, do as I tell you. Go to your father and ask him to give you a wooden wheel-barrow, and a bear's skin. When you have got them bring them to me, and I will touch them with my magic wand. The wheel-barrow will then move of itself, and will take you at full speed wherever you want to go, and the bear's skin will make such a covering for you, that no one will recognize you."

So the princess did as the witch advised her. The king, when he heard her strange request, was greatly astonished, and asked her what she meant to do with a wheel-barrow and a bear's skin. And the princess answered, "You never let me leave the house—at least you might grant me this request." So the king granted it, and the princess went back to her nurse, taking the barrow and the bear's skin with her.

As soon as the witch saw them, she touched them with her magic wand, and in a moment the barrow began to move about in all directions. The princess next put on the bear's skin, which so completely changed her appearance, that no one could have known that she was a girl and not a bear. In this strange attire she seated herself on the barrow, and in a few minutes she found herself far away from the palace, and moving rapidly through a great forest. Here she stopped the barrow with a sign that the witch had shown her, and hid herself and it in a thick grove of flowering shrubs.

Now it happened that the prince of that country was hunting with his dogs in the forest. Suddenly he caught sight of the bear hiding among the shrubs, and calling his dogs, hounded them on to attack it. But the girl, seeing what peril she was in, cried, "Call off your dogs, or they will kill me. What harm have I ever done to you?" At these words, coming from a bear, the prince was so startled that for a moment he stood stock-still, then he said quite gently, "Will you come with me? I will take you to my home."

"I will come gladly," replied the bear; and seating herself on the barrow it at once began to move in the direction of the prince's palace. You may imagine the surprise of the prince's mother when she saw her son return accompanied by a bear, who at once set about doing the house-work better than any servant that the queen had ever seen.

Now it happened that there were great festivities going on in the palace of a neighboring prince, and at dinner, one day, the prince said to his mother: "This evening there is to be a great ball, to which I must go."

And his mother answered, "Go and dance, and enjoy yourself."

Suddenly a voice came from under the table, where the bear had rolled itself, as was its wont: "Let me come to the ball; I, too, would like to dance."

But the only answer the prince made was to give the bear a kick, and to drive it out of the room.

In the evening the prince set off for the ball. As soon as he had started, the bear came to the queen and implored to be allowed to go to the ball, saying that she would hide herself so well that no one would know she was there. The kind-hearted queen could not refuse her.

Then the bear ran to her barrow, threw off her bear's skin, and touched it with the magic wand that the witch had given her. In a moment the skin was changed into an exquisite ball dress woven out of moon-beams, and the wheel-barrow was changed into a carriage drawn by two prancing steeds. Stepping into the carriage the princess drove to the grand entrance of the palace. When she entered the ball-room, in her wondrous dress of moon-beams, she looked so lovely, so different from all the other guests, that every-one wondered who she was, and no one could tell where she had come from.

From the moment he saw her, the prince fell desperately in love with her, and all the evening he would dance with no one else but the beautiful stranger.

When the ball was over, the princess drove away in her carriage at full speed, for she wished to get home in time to change her ball dress into the bear's skin, and the carriage into the wheel-barrow, before anyone discovered who she was.

The prince, putting spurs into his horse, rode after her, for he was determined not to let her out of his sight. But suddenly a thick mist arose and hid her from him. When he reached his home he could talk to his mother of nothing else but the beautiful stranger with whom he had danced so often, and with whom he was so much in love. And the bear beneath the table smiled to itself, and muttered: "I am the beautiful stranger; oh, how I have taken you in!"

The next evening there was a second ball, and, as you may believe, the prince was determined not to miss it, for he thought he would once more see the lovely girl, and dance with her and talk to her, and make her talk to him, for at the first ball she had never opened her lips.

And, sure enough, as the music struck up the first dance, the beautiful stranger entered the room, looking even more radiant than the night before, for this time her dress was woven out of the rays of the sun. All evening the prince danced with her, but she never spoke a word.

When the ball was over he tried once more to follow her carriage, that he might know whence she came, but suddenly a great waterspout fell from the sky, and the blinding sheets of rain hid her from his sight.

When he reached his home he told his mother that he had again seen the lovely girl, and that this time she had been even more beautiful than the night before. And again the bear smiled beneath the table, and muttered: "I have taken him in a second time, and he has no idea that I am the beautiful girl with whom he is so much in love."

On the next evening, the prince returned to the palace for the third ball. And the princess went too, and this time she had changed her bear's skin into a dress woven out of the starlight, studded all over with gems, and she looked so dazzling and so beautiful, that everyone wondered at her, and said that no one so beautiful had ever been seen before. And the prince danced with her, and, though he could not induce her to speak, he succeeded in slipping a ring on her finger.

When the ball was over, he followed her carriage, and rode at such a pace that for long he kept it in sight. Then suddenly a terrible wind arose between him and the carriage, and he could not overtake it.

When he reached his home he said to his mother, "I do not know what is to become of me; I think I shall go mad, I am so much in love with that girl, and I have no means of finding out who she is. I danced with her and I gave her a ring, and yet I do not know her name, nor where I am to find her."

Then the bear laughed beneath the table and muttered to itself.

And the prince continued: "I am tired to death. Order some soup to be made for me, but I don't want that bear to meddle with it. Every time I speak of my love the brute mutters and laughs, and seems to mock at me. I hate the sight of the creature!"

When the soup was ready, the bear brought it to the prince; but before handing it to him, she dropped into the plate the ring the prince had given her the night before at the ball. The prince began to eat his soup very slowly and languidly, for he was sad at heart, and all his thoughts were busy, wondering how and where he could see the lovely stranger again. Suddenly he noticed the ring at the bottom of the plate. In a moment he recognized it, and was dumb with surprise.

Then he saw the bear standing beside him, looking at him with gentle, beseeching eyes, and something in the eyes of the bear made him say: "Take off that skin, some mystery is hidden beneath it."

And the bear's skin dropped off, and the beautiful girl stood before him, in the dress woven out of the starlight, and he saw that she was the stranger with whom he had fallen so deeply in love. And now she appeared to him a thousand times more beautiful than ever, and he led her to his mother. And the princess told them her story, and how she had been kept shut up by her father in his palace, and how she had wearied of her imprisonment. And the prince's mother loved her, and rejoiced that her son should have so good and beautiful a wife.

So they were married, and lived happily for many years, and reigned wisely over their kingdom.

Jack My Hedgehog

(FROM *THE GREEN FAIRY BOOK*)

There was once a farmer who lived in great comfort. He had both lands and money, but, though he was so well off, one thing was wanting to complete his happiness: he had no children. Many and many a time, when he met other farmers at the nearest market town, they would tease him, asking how it came about that he was childless. At length he grew so angry that he exclaimed: "I must and will have a child of some sort or kind, even should it only be a hedgehog!"

Not long after this his wife gave birth to a child, but though the lower half of the little creature was a fine boy, from the waist upwards it was a hedgehog, so that when his mother first saw him she was quite frightened, and said to her husband, "There now, you have cursed the child yourself." The farmer said, "What's the use of making a fuss? I suppose the creature must be christened, but I don't see how we are to ask anyone to be sponsor to him, and what are we to call him?"

"There is nothing we can possibly call him but Jack my Hedgehog," replied the wife.

So they took him to be christened, and the parson said: "You'll never be able to put that child in a decent bed on account of his prickles." Which was true, but they shook down some straw for him behind the stove, and there he lay for eight years. His father grew very tired of him and often wished him dead, but he did not die, but lay on there year after year.

Now one day there was a big fair at the market town to which the farmer meant to go, so he asked his wife what he should bring her from it. "Some meat and a couple of big loaves for the house," said she. Then he asked the maid what she wanted, and she said a pair of slippers and some stockings. Lastly he said, "Well, Jack my Hedgehog, and what shall I bring you?"

"Daddy," said he, "do bring me a bagpipe." When the farmer came home he gave his wife and the maid the things they had asked for, and then he went behind the stove and gave Jack my Hedgehog the bagpipes.

When Jack had got his bagpipes he said, "Daddy, do go to the smithy and have the house cock shod for me; then I'll ride off and trouble you no more." His father, who was delighted at the prospect of getting rid of him, had the cock shod, and when it was ready Jack my Hedgehog mounted on its back and rode off to the forest, followed by all the pigs and asses which he had promised to look after.

Having reached the forest he made the cock fly up to the top of a very tall tree with him, and there he sat looking after his pigs and donkeys, and he sat on and on for several years till he had quite a big herd; but all this time his father knew nothing about him.

As he sat up in his tree he played away on his pipes and drew the loveliest music from them. As he was playing one day a King, who had lost his way, happened to pass close by, and hearing the music he was much surprised, and sent one of his servants to find out where it came from. The man peered about, but he could see nothing but a little creature which looked like a cock with a hedgehog sitting on it, perched up in a tree. The King desired the servant to ask the strange creature why it sat there, and if it knew the shortest way to his kingdom.

On this Jack my Hedgehog stepped down from his tree and said he would undertake to show the King his way home if the King on his part would give him his written promise to let him have whatever first met him on his return.

The King thought to himself, "That's easy enough to promise. The creature won't understand a word about it, so I can just write what I choose."

So he took pen and ink and wrote something, and when he had done Jack my Hedgehog pointed out the way and the King got safely home.

Now when the King's daughter saw her father returning in the distance she was so delighted that she ran to meet him and threw herself into his arms. Then the King remembered Jack my Hedgehog, and he told his daughter how he had been obliged to give a written promise to bestow whatever he first met when he got home on an extraordinary creature which had shown him the way. The creature, said he, rode on a cock as though it had been a horse, and it made lovely music, but as it certainly could not read he had just written that he would *not* give it anything at all. At this the Princess was quite pleased, and said how cleverly her father had managed, for that of course nothing would induce her to have gone off with Jack my Hedgehog.

Meantime Jack minded his asses and pigs, sat aloft in his tree, played his bagpipes, and was always merry and cheery. After a time it so happened that another King, having lost his way, passed by with his servants and escort, wondering how he could find his way home, for the forest was very vast. He too heard the music, and told one of his men to find out whence it came. The man came under the tree, and looking up to the top there he saw Jack my Hedgehog astride on the cock.

The servant asked Jack what he was doing up there. "I'm minding my pigs and donkeys; but what do you want?" was the reply. Then the servant told him they had lost their way, and wanted some one to show it them. Down came Jack my Hedgehog with his cock, and told the old King he would show him the right way if he would solemnly promise to give him the first thing he met in front of his royal castle.

The King said "Yes," and gave Jack a written promise to that effect.

Then Jack rode on in front pointing out the way, and the King reached his own country in safety.

Now he had an only daughter who was extremely beautiful, and who, delighted at her father's return, ran to meet him, threw her arms round his neck and kissed him heartily. Then she asked where he had been wandering so long, and he told her how he had lost his way and might never have reached home at all but for a strange creature, half-man, half-hedgehog, which rode a cock and sat up in a tree making lovely music, and which had shown him the right way. He also told her how he had been obliged to pledge his word to give the creature the first thing which met him outside his castle gate, and he felt very sad at the thought that she had been the first thing to meet him.

But the Princess comforted him, and said she should be quite willing to go with Jack my Hedgehog whenever he came to fetch her, because of the great love she bore to her dear old father.

Jack my Hedgehog continued to herd his pigs, and they increased in number till there were so many that the forest seemed full of them. So he made up his mind to live there no longer, and sent a message to his father telling him to have all the stables and outhouses in the village cleared, as he was going to bring such an enormous herd that all who would might kill what they chose. His father was much vexed at this news, for he thought Jack had died long ago. Jack my Hedgehog mounted his cock, and driving his pigs before him into the village, he let every one kill as many as they chose, and such a hacking and hewing of pork went on as you might have heard for miles off.

Then said Jack, "Daddy, let the blacksmith shoe my cock once more; then I'll ride off, and I promise you I'll never come back again as long as I live." So the father had the cock shod, and rejoiced at the idea of getting rid of his son.

Then Jack my Hedgehog set off for the first kingdom, and there the King had given strict orders that if anyone should be seen riding a cock and carrying a bagpipe he was to be chased away and shot at, and on no account to be allowed to enter the palace. So when Jack my Hedgehog rode up the guards charged him with their bayonets, but he put spurs to his cock, flew up over the gate right to the King's windows, let himself down on the sill, and called out that if he was not given what had been promised him, both the King and his daughter should pay for it with their lives. Then the King coaxed and entreated his daughter to go with Jack and so save both their lives.

The Princess dressed herself all in white, and her father gave her a coach with six horses and servants in gorgeous liveries and quantities of money. She stepped into the coach, and Jack my Hedgehog with his cock and pipes took his place beside her. They both took leave, and the King fully expected never to set eyes on them again. But matters turned out very differently from what he had expected, for when they had got a certain distance from the town Jack tore all the Princess's smart clothes off her, and pricked her all over with his bristles, saying: "That's what you get for treachery. Now go back, I'll have no more to say to you." And with that he hunted her home, and she felt she had been disgraced and put to shame till her life's end.

Then Jack my Hedgehog rode on with his cock and bagpipes to the country of the second King to whom he had shown the way. Now this King had given orders that, in the event of Jack's coming the guards were to present arms, the people to cheer, and he was to be conducted in triumph to the royal palace.

When the King's daughter saw Jack my Hedgehog, she was a good deal startled, for he certainly was very peculiar looking; but after all she considered that she had given her word and it couldn't be helped. So she made Jack welcome and they were betrothed to each other, and at dinner he sat next her at the royal table, and they ate and drank together.

When they retired to rest the Princess feared lest Jack should kiss her because of his prickles, but he told her not to be alarmed as no harm should befall her. Then he begged the old King to place a watch of four men just outside his bedroom door, and to desire them to make a big fire. When he was about to lie down in bed he would creep out of his hedgehog skin, and leave it lying at the bedside; then the men must rush in, throw the skin into the fire, and stand by till it was entirely burnt up.

And so it was, for when it struck eleven, Jack my Hedgehog went to his room, took off his skin and left it at the foot of the bed. The men rushed in, quickly seized the skin and threw it on the fire, and directly it was all burnt Jack was released from his enchantment and lay in his bed a man from head to foot, but quite black as though he had been severely scorched.

The King sent off for his physician in ordinary, who washed Jack all over with various essences and salves, so that he became white and was a remarkably handsome young man. When the King's daughter saw him she was greatly pleased, and next day the marriage ceremony was performed, and the old King bestowed his kingdom on Jack my Hedgehog.

After some years Jack and his wife went to visit his father, but the farmer did not recognize him, and declared he had no son; he had had one, but that one was born with bristles like a hedgehog, and had gone off into the wide world. Then Jack told his story, and his old father rejoiced and returned to live with him in his kingdom.

The Adventures of a Jackal

(FROM *THE ORANGE FAIRY BOOK*)

In a country which is full of wild beasts of all sorts there once lived a jackal and a hedgehog, and, unlike though they were, the two animals made great friends, and were often seen in each other's company.

One afternoon they were walking along a road together, when the jackal, who was the taller of the two, exclaimed:

"Oh! there is a barn full of corn; let us go and eat some."

"Yes, do let us!" answered the hedgehog. So they went to the barn, and ate till they could eat no more. Then the jackal put on his shoes, which he had taken off so as to make no noise, and they returned to the high road.

After they had gone some way they met a panther, who stopped, and bowing politely, said:

"Excuse my speaking to you, but I cannot help admiring those shoes of yours. Do you mind telling me who made them?"

"Yes, I think they *are* rather nice," answered the jackal; "I made them myself, though."

"Could you make me a pair like them?" asked the panther eagerly.

"I would do my best, of course," replied the jackal; "but you must kill me a cow, and when we have eaten the flesh I will take the skin and make your shoes out of it."

So the panther prowled about until he saw a fine cow grazing apart from the rest of the herd. He killed it instantly, and then gave a cry to the jackal and hedgehog to come to the place where he was. They soon skinned the dead beasts, and spread its skin out to dry, after which they had a grand feast before they curled themselves up for the night, and slept soundly.

Next morning the jackal got up early and set to work upon the shoes, while the panther sat by and looked on with delight. At last they were finished, and the jackal arose and stretched himself.

"Now go and lay them in the sun out there," said he; "in a couple of hours they will be ready to put on; but do not attempt to wear them before, or you will feel them most uncomfortable. But I see the sun is high in the heavens, and we must be continuing our journey."

The panther, who always believed what everybody told him, did exactly as he was bid, and in two hours' time began to fasten on the shoes. They certainly set off his paws wonderfully, and he stretched out his forepaws and looked at them with pride. But when he tried to *walk*—ah! that was another story! They were so stiff and hard that he nearly shrieked every step he took, and at last he sank down where he was, and actually began to cry.

After some time some little partridges who were hopping about heard the poor panther's groans, and went up to see what was the matter. He had never tried to make his dinner off *them*, and they had always been quite friendly.

"You seem in pain," said one of them, fluttering close to him, "can we help you?"

"Oh, it is the jackal! He made me these shoes; they are so hard and tight that they hurt my feet, and I cannot manage to kick them off."

"Lie still, and we will soften them," answered the kind little partridge. And calling to his brothers, they all flew to the nearest spring, and carried water in their beaks, which they poured over the shoes. This they did till the hard leather grew soft, and the panther was able to slip his feet out of them.

"Oh, thank you, thank you," he cried, skipping round with joy. "I feel a different creature. Now I will go after the jackal and pay him my debts." And he bounded away into the forest.

But the jackal had been very cunning, and had trotted backwards and forwards and in and out, so that it was very difficult to know which track he had really followed. At length, however, the panther caught sight of his enemy, at the same moment that the jackal had caught sight of him. The panther gave a loud roar, and sprang forward, but the jackal was too quick for him and plunged into a dense thicket, where the panther could not follow.

Disgusted with his failure, but more angry than ever, the panther lay down for a while to consider what he should do next, and as he was thinking, an old man came by.

"Oh! father, tell me how I can repay the jackal for the way he has served me!" And without more ado he told his story.

"If you take my advice," answered the old man, "you will kill a cow, and invite all the jackals in the forest to the feast. Watch them carefully while they are eating, and you will see that most of them keep their eyes on their food. But if one of them glances at *you*, you will know that is the traitor."

The panther, whose manners were always good, thanked the old man, and followed his counsel. The cow was killed, and the partridges flew about with invitations to the jackals, who gathered in large numbers to the feast. The wicked jackal came among them; but as the panther had only seen him once he could not distinguish him from the rest. However, they all took their places on wooden seats placed round the dead cow, which was laid across the boughs of a fallen tree, and began their dinner, each jackal fixing his eyes greedily on the piece of meat before him. Only one of them seemed uneasy, and every now and then glanced in the direction of his host. This the panther noticed, and suddenly made a bound at the culprit and seized his tail; but again the jackal was too quick for him, and catching up a knife he cut off his tail and darted into the forest, followed by all the rest of the party. And before the panther had recovered from his surprise he found himself alone.

"What am I to do *now*?" he asked the old man, who soon came back to see how things had turned out.

"It is very unfortunate, certainly," answered he; "but I think I know where you can find him. There is a melon garden about two miles from here, and as jackals are very fond of melons they are nearly sure to have gone there to feed. If you see a tailless jackal you will know that he is the one you want." So the panther thanked him and went his way.

Now the jackal had guessed what advice the old man would give his enemy, and so, while his friends were greedily eating the ripest melons in the sunniest corner of the garden, he stole behind them and tied their tails together. He had only just finished when his ears caught the sound of breaking branches; and he cried: "Quick! quick! here comes the master of the garden!" And the jackals sprang up and ran away in all directions, leaving their tails behind them. And how was the panther to know which was his enemy?

"They none of them had any tails," he said sadly to the old man, "and I am tired of hunting them. I shall leave them alone and go and catch something for supper."

Of course the hedgehog had not been able to take part in any of these adventures; but as soon as all danger was over, the jackal went to look for his friend, whom he was lucky enough to find at home.

"Ah, there you are," he said gaily. "I have lost my tail since I saw you last. And other people have lost theirs too; but that is no matter! I am hungry, so come with me to the shepherd who is sitting over there, and we will ask him to sell us one of his sheep."

"Yes, that is a good plan," answered the hedgehog. And he walked as fast as his little legs would go to keep up with the jackal. When they reached the shepherd the jackal pulled out his purse from under his foreleg, and made his bargain.

"Only wait till to-morrow," said the shepherd, "and I will give you the biggest sheep you ever saw. But he always feeds at some distance from the rest of the flock, and it would take me a long time to catch him."

"Well, it is very tiresome, but I suppose I must wait," replied the jackal. And he and the hedgehog looked about for a nice dry cave in which to make themselves comfortable for the night. But, after they had gone, the shepherd killed one of his sheep, and stripped off his skin, which he sewed tightly round a greyhound he had with him, and put a cord round its neck. Then he lay down and went to sleep.

Very, very early, before the sun was properly up, the jackal and the hedgehog were pulling at the shepherd's cloak.

"Wake up," they said, "and give us that sheep. We have had nothing to eat all night, and are very hungry."

The shepherd yawned and rubbed his eyes. "He is tied up to that tree; go and take him." So they went to the tree and unfastened the cord, and turned to go back to the cave where they had slept, dragging the greyhound after them. When they reached the cave the jackal said to the hedgehog:

"Before I kill him let me see whether he is fat or thin." And he stood a little way back, so that he might the better examine the animal. After looking at him, with his head on one side, for a minute or two, he nodded gravely.

"He is quite fat enough; he is a good sheep."

But the hedgehog, who sometimes showed more cunning than anyone would have guessed, answered:

"My friend, you are talking nonsense. The wool is indeed a sheep's wool, but the paws of my uncle the greyhound peep out from underneath."

"He is a *sheep*," repeated the jackal, who did not like to think anyone cleverer than himself.

"Hold the cord while *I* look at him," answered the hedgehog.

Very unwillingly the jackal held the rope, while the hedgehog walked slowly round the greyhound till he reached the jackal again. He knew quite well by the paws and tail that it was a greyhound and not a sheep that the shepherd had sold them; and as he could not tell what turn affairs might take, he resolved to get out of the way.

"Oh! yes, you are right," he said to the jackal; "but I never can eat till I have first drunk. I will just go and quench my thirst from that spring at the edge of the wood, and then I shall be ready for breakfast."

"Don't be long, then," called the jackal, as the hedgehog hurried off at his best pace. And he lay down under a rock to wait for him.

More than an hour passed by and the hedgehog had had plenty of time to go to the spring and back, and still there was no sign of him. And this was very natural, as he had hidden himself in some long grass under a tree!

At length the jackal guessed that for some reason his friend had run away, and determined to wait for his breakfast no longer. So he went up to the place where the greyhound had been tethered and untied the rope. But just as he was about to spring on his back and give him a deadly bite, the jackal heard a low growl, which never proceeded from the throat of any sheep. Like a flash of lightning the jackal threw down the cord and was flying across the plain; but though his legs were long, the greyhound's legs were longer still, and he soon came up with his prey. The jackal turned to fight, but he was no match for the greyhound, and in a few minutes he was lying dead on the ground, while the greyhound was trotting peacefully back to the shepherd.

The Adventures of the Jackal's Eldest Son

(FROM *THE ORANGE FAIRY BOOK*)

Now, though the jackal was dead, he had left two sons behind him, every whit as cunning and tricky as their father. The elder of the two was a fine handsome creature, who had a pleasant manner and made many friends. The animal he saw most of was a hyæna; and one day, when they were taking a walk together, they picked up a beautiful green cloak, which had evidently been dropped by some one riding across the plain on a camel. Of course each wanted to have it, and they almost quarreled over the matter; but at length it was settled that the hyæna should wear the cloak by day and the jackal by night. After a little while, however, the jackal became discontented with this arrangement, declaring that none of his friends, who were quite different from those of the hyæna, could see the splendor of the mantle, and that it was only fair that he should sometimes be allowed to wear it by day. To this the hyæna would by no means consent, and they were on the eve of a quarrel when the hyæna proposed that they should ask the lion to judge between them. The jackal agreed to this, and the hyæna wrapped the cloak about him, and they both trotted off to the lion's den.

The jackal, who was fond of talking, at once told the story; and when it was finished the lion turned to the hyæna and asked if it was true.

"Quite true, your majesty," answered the hyæna.

"Then lay the cloak on the ground at my feet," said the lion, "and I will give my judgment." So the mantle was spread upon the red earth, the hyæna and the jackal standing on each side of it.

There was silence for a few moments, and then the lion sat up, looking very great and wise.

"My judgment is that the garment shall belong wholly to whoever first rings the bell of the nearest mosque at dawn to-morrow. Now go; for much business awaits me!"

All that night the hyæna sat up, fearing lest the jackal should reach the bell before him, for the mosque was close at hand. With the first streak of dawn he bounded away to the bell, just as the jackal, who had slept soundly all night, was rising to his feet.

"Good luck to you," cried the jackal. And throwing the cloak over his back he darted away across the plain, and was seen no more by his friend the hyæna.

After running several miles the jackal thought he was safe from pursuit, and seeing a lion and another hyæna talking together, he strolled up to join them.

"Good morning," he said; "may I ask what is the matter? You seem very serious about something."

"Pray sit down," answered the lion. "We were wondering in which direction we should go to find the best dinner. The hyæna wishes to go to the forest, and I to the mountains. What do you say?"

"Well, as I was sauntering over the plain, just now, I noticed a flock of sheep grazing, and some of them had wandered into a little valley quite out of sight of the shepherd. If you keep among the rocks you will never be observed. But perhaps you will allow me to go with you and show you the way?"

"You are really very kind," answered the lion. And they crept steadily along till at length they reached the mouth of the valley where a ram, a sheep and a lamb were feeding on the rich grass, unconscious of their danger.

"How shall we divide them?" asked the lion in a whisper to the hyæna.

"Oh, it is easily done," replied the hyæna. "The lamb for me, the sheep for the jackal, and the ram for the lion."

"So I am to have that lean creature, which is nothing but horns, am I?" cried the lion in a rage. "I will teach you to divide things in that manner!" And he gave the hyæna two great blows, which stretched him dead in a moment. Then he turned to the jackal and said: "How would you divide them?"

"Quite differently from the hyæna," replied the jackal. "You will breakfast off the lamb, you will dine off the sheep, and you will sup off the ram."

"Dear me, how clever you are! Who taught you such wisdom?" exclaimed the lion, looking at him admiringly.

"The fate of the hyæna," answered the jackal, laughing, and running off at his best speed; for he saw two men armed with spears coming close behind the lion!

The jackal continued to run till at last he could run no longer. He flung himself under a tree panting for breath, when he heard a rustle among the grass, and his father's old friend the hedgehog appeared before him.

"Oh, is it you?" asked the little creature; "how strange that we should meet so far from home!"

"I have just had a narrow escape of my life," gasped the jackal, "and I need some sleep. After that we must think of something to do to amuse ourselves." And he lay down again and slept soundly for a couple of hours.

"Now I am ready," said he; "have you anything to propose?"

"In a valley beyond those trees," answered the hedgehog, "there is a small farmhouse where the best butter in the world is made. I know their ways, and in an hour's time the farmer's wife will be off to milk the cows, which she keeps at some distance. We could easily get in at the window of the shed where she keeps the butter, and I will watch, lest some one should come unexpectedly, while you have a good meal. Then you shall watch, and I will eat."

"That sounds a good plan," replied the jackal; and they set off together.

But when they reached the farmhouse the jackal said to the hedgehog: "Go in and fetch the pots of butter and I will hide them in a safe place."

"Oh no," cried the hedgehog, "I really couldn't. They would find out directly! And, besides, it is so different just eating a little now and then."

"Do as I bid you *at once*," said the jackal, looking at the hedgehog so sternly that the little fellow dared say no more, and soon rolled the jars to the window where the jackal lifted them out one by one.

When they were all in a row before him he gave a sudden start.

"Run for your life," he whispered to his companion; "I see the woman coming over the hill!" And the hedgehog, his heart beating, set off as fast as he could. The jackal remained where he was, shaking with laughter, for the woman was not in sight at all, and he had only sent the hedgehog away because he did not want him to know where the jars of butter were buried. But every day he stole out to their hiding-place and had a delicious feast.

At length, one morning, the hedgehog suddenly said:

"You never told me what you did with those jars?"

"Oh, I hid them safely till the farm people should have forgotten all about them," replied the jackal. "But as they are still searching for them we must wait a little longer, and then I'll bring them home, and we will share them between us."

So the hedgehog waited and waited; but every time he asked if there was no chance of getting jars of butter the jackal put him off with some excuse. After a while the hedgehog became suspicious, and said:

"I should like to know where you have hidden them. To-night, when it is quite dark, you shall show me the place."

"I really *can't* tell you," answered the jackal. "You talk so much that you would be sure to confide the secret to somebody, and then we should have had our trouble for nothing, besides running the risk of our necks being broken by the farmer. I can see that he is getting disheartened, and very soon he will give up the search. Have patience just a little longer."

The hedgehog said no more, and pretended to be satisfied; but when some days had gone by he woke the jackal, who was sleeping soundly after a hunt which had lasted several hours.

"I have just had notice," remarked the hedgehog, shaking him, "that my family wish to have a banquet to-morrow, and they have invited you to it. Will you come?"

"Certainly," answered the jackal, "with pleasure. But as I have to go out in the morning you can meet me on the road."

"That will do very well," replied the hedgehog. And the jackal went to sleep again, for he was obliged to be up early.

Punctual to the moment the hedgehog arrived at the place appointed for their meeting, and as the jackal was not there he sat down and waited for him.

"Ah, there you are!" he cried, when the dusky yellow form at last turned the corner. "I had nearly given you up! Indeed, I almost wish you had not come, for I hardly know where I shall hide you."

"Why should you hide me anywhere?" asked the jackal. "What is the matter with you?"

"Well, so many of the guests have brought their dogs and mules with them, that I fear it may hardly be safe for you to go among them. No; don't run off that way," he added quickly, "because there is another troop that are coming over the hill. Lie down here, and I will throw these sacks over you; and keep still for your life, whatever happens."

And what did happen was, that when the jackal was lying covered up, under a little hill, the hedgehog set a great stone rolling, which crushed him to death.

The Adventures of the Younger Son of the Jackal

(FROM *THE ORANGE FAIRY BOOK*)

Now that the father and elder brother were both dead, all that was left of the jackal family was one son, who was no less cunning than the others had been. He did not like staying in the same place any better than they, and nobody ever knew in what part of the country he might be found next.

One day, when we was wandering about he beheld a nice fat sheep, which was cropping the grass and seemed quite contented with her lot.

"Good morning," said the jackal, "I am so glad to see you. I have been looking for you everywhere."

"For *me*?" answered the sheep, in an astonished voice; "but we have never met before!"

"No; but I have *heard* of you. Oh! You don't know what fine things I have heard! Ah, well, some people have all the luck!"

"You are very kind, I am sure," answered the sheep, not knowing which way to look. "Is there any way in which I can help you?"

"There *is* something that I had set my heart on, though I hardly like to propose it on so short an acquaintance; but from what people have told me, I thought that you and I might keep house together comfortably, if you would only agree to try. I have several fields belonging to me, and if they are kept well watered they bear wonderful crops."

"Perhaps I might come for a short time," said the sheep, with a little hesitation; "and if we do not get on, we can part company."

"Oh, thank you, thank you," cried the jackal; "do not let us lose a moment." And he held out his paw in such an inviting manner that the sheep got up and trotted beside him till they reached home.

"Now," said the jackal, "you go to the well and fetch the water, and I will pour it into the trenches that run between the patches of corn." And as he did so he sang lustily. The work was very hard, but the sheep did not

624

grumble, and by-and-by was rewarded at seeing the little green heads poking themselves through earth. After that the hot sun ripened them quickly, and soon harvest time was come. Then the grain was cut and ground and ready for sale.

When everything was complete, the jackal said to the sheep:

"Now let us divide it, so that we can each do what we like with his share."

"You do it," answered the sheep; "here are the scales. You must weigh it carefully."

So the jackal began to weigh it, and when he had finished, he counted out loud:

"One, two, three, four, five, six, seven parts for the jackal, and one part for the sheep. If she likes it she can take it, if not, she can leave it."

The sheep looked at the two heaps in silence—one so large, the other so small; and then she answered:

"Wait for a minute, while I fetch some sacks to carry away my share."

But it was not sacks that the sheep wanted; for as soon as the jackal could no longer see her she set forth at her best pace to the home of the greyhound, where she arrived panting with the haste she had made.

"Oh, good uncle, help me, I pray you!" she cried, as soon as she could speak.

"Why, what is the matter?" asked the greyhound, looking up with astonishment.

"I beg you to return with me, and frighten the jackal into paying me what he owes me," answered the sheep. "For months we have lived together, and I have twice every day drawn the water, while he only poured it into the trenches. Together we have reaped our harvest; and now, when the moment to divide our crop has come, he has taken seven parts for himself, and only left one for me."

She finished, and giving herself a twist, passed her woolly tail across her eyes; while the greyhound watched her, but held his peace. Then he said:

"Bring me a sack." And the sheep hastened away to fetch one. Very soon she returned, and laid the sack down before him.

"Open it wide, that I may get in," cried he; and when he was comfortably rolled up inside he bade the sheep take him on her back, and hasten to the place where she had left the jackal.

She found him waiting for her, and pretending to be asleep, though she clearly saw him wink one of his eyes. However, she took no notice, but throwing the sack roughly on the ground, she exclaimed:

"Now measure!"

At this the jackal got up, and going to the heap of grain which lay close by, he divided it as before into eight portions—seven for himself and one for the sheep.

"What are you doing that for?" asked she indignantly. "You know quite well that it was I who drew the water, and you who only poured it into the trenches."

"You are mistaken," answered the jackal. "It was *I* who drew the water, and *you* who poured it into the trenches. Anybody will tell you that! If you like, I will ask those people who are digging there!"

"Very well," replied the sheep. And the jackal called out:

"Ho! You diggers, tell me: Who was it you heard singing over the work?"

"Why, it was you, of course, jackal! You sang so loud that the whole world might have heard you!"

"And who it is that sings—he who draws the water, or he who empties it?"

"Why, certainly he who draws the water!"

"You hear?" said the jackal, turning to the sheep. "Now come and carry away your own portion, or else I shall take it for myself."

"You have got the better of me," answered the sheep; "and I suppose I must confess myself beaten! But as I bear no malice, go and eat some of the dates that I have brought in that sack." And the jackal, who loved dates, ran instantly back, and tore open the mouth of the sack. But just as he was about to plunge his nose in he saw two brown eyes calmly looking at him. In an instant he had let fall the flap of the sack and bounded back to where the sheep was standing.

"I was only in fun; and you have brought my uncle the greyhound. Take away the sack, we will make the division over again." And he began rearranging the heaps.

"One, two, three, four, five, six, seven, for my mother the sheep, and one for the jackal," counted he; casting timid glances all the while at the sack.

"Now you can take your share and go," said the sheep. And the jackal did not need twice telling! Whenever the sheep looked up, she still saw him flying, flying across the plain; and, for all I know, he may be flying across it still.

Dapplegrim

(FROM THE RED FAIRY BOOK)

There was once upon a time a couple of rich folks who had twelve sons, and when the youngest was grown up he would not stay at home any longer, but would go out into the world and seek his fortune. His father and mother said that they thought he was very well off at home, and that he was welcome to stay with them; but he could not rest, and said that he must and would go, so at last they had to give him leave. When he had walked a long way, he came to a King's palace. There he asked for a place and got it.

Now the daughter of the King of that country had been carried off into the mountains by a Troll, and the King had no other children, and for this cause both he and all his people were full of sorrow and affliction, and the King had promised the Princess and half his kingdom to anyone who could set her free; but there was no one who could do it, though a great number had tried. So when the youth had been there for the space of a year or so, he wanted to go home again to pay his parents a visit; but when he got there his father and mother were dead, and his brothers had divided everything that their parents possessed between themselves, so that there was nothing at all left for him.

"Shall I, then, receive nothing at all of my inheritance?" asked the youth.

"Who could know that you were still alive—you who have been a wanderer so long?" answered the brothers. "However, there are twelve mares upon the hills which we have not yet divided among us, and if you would like to have them for your share, you may take them."

So the youth, well pleased with this, thanked them, and at once set off to the hill where the twelve mares were at pasture. When he got up there and found them, each mare had her foal, and by the side of one of them was a big dapple-gray foal as well, which was so sleek that it shone again.

"Well, my little foal, you are a fine fellow!" said the youth.

"Yes, but if you will kill all the other little foals so that I can suck all the mares for a year, you shall see how big and handsome I shall be then!" said the Foal.

So the youth did this—he killed all the twelve foals, and then went back again.

Next year, when he came home again to look after his mares and the foal, it was as fat as it could be, and its coat shone with brightness, and it was so big that the lad had the greatest difficulty in getting on its back, and each of the mares had another foal.

"Well, it's very evident that I have lost nothing by letting you suck all my mares," said the lad to the yearling; "but now you are quite big enough, and must come away with me."

"No," said the Colt, "I must stay here another year; kill the twelve little foals, and then I can suck all the mares this year also, and you shall see how big and handsome I shall be by summer."

So the youth did it again, and when he went up on the hill next year to look after his colt and the mares, each of the mares had her foal again; but the dappled colt was so big that when the lad wanted to feel its neck to see how fat it was, he could not reach up to it, it was so high? and it was so bright that the light glanced off its coat.

"Big and handsome you were last year, my colt, but this year you are ever so much handsomer," said the youth; "in all the King's court no such horse is to be found. But now you shall come away with me."

"No," said the dappled Colt once more; "here I must stay for another year. Just kill the twelve little foals again, so that I can suck the mares this year also, and then come and look at me in the summer."

So the youth did it—he killed all the little foals, and then went home again.

But next year, when he returned to look after the dappled colt and the mares, he was quite appalled. He had never imagined that any horse could become so big and overgrown, for the dappled horse had to lie down on all fours before the youth could get on his back, and it was very hard to do that even when it was lying down, and it was so plump that its coat shone and glistened just as if it had been a looking-glass. This time the dappled horse was not unwilling to go away with the youth, so he mounted it, and when he came riding home to his brothers they all smote their hands together and crossed themselves, for never in their lives had they either seen or heard tell of such a horse as that.

"If you will procure me the best shoes for my horse, and the most magnificent saddle and bridle that can be found," said the youth, "you may have all my twelve mares just as they are standing out on the hill, and their twelve foals into the bargain." For this year also each mare had her foal. The brothers were quite willing to do this; so the lad got such shoes for his horse that the sticks and stones flew high up into the air as he rode away over the hills, and such a gold saddle and such a gold bridle that they could be seen glittering and glancing from afar.

"And now we will go to the King's palace," said Dapplegrim—that was the horse's name, "but bear in mind that you must ask the King for a good stable and excellent fodder for me."

So the lad promised not to forget to do that. He rode to the palace, and it will be easily understood that with such a horse as he had he was not long on the way.

When he arrived there, the King was standing out on the steps, and how he did stare at the man who came riding up!

"Nay," said he, "never in my whole life have I seen such a man and such a horse."

And when the youth inquired if he could have a place in the King's palace, the King was so delighted that he could have danced on the steps where he was standing, and there and then the lad was told that he should have a place.

"Yes; but I must have a good stable and most excellent fodder for my horse," said he.

So they told him that he should have sweet hay and oats, and as much of them as the dappled horse chose to have, and all the other riders had to take their horses out of the stable that Dapplegrim might stand alone and really have plenty of room.

But this did not last long, for the other people in the King's Court became envious of the lad, and there was no bad thing that they would not have done to him if they had but dared. At last they bethought themselves of telling the King that the youth had said that, if he chose, he was quite able to rescue the Princess who had been carried off into the mountain a long time ago by the Troll.

The King immediately summoned the lad into his presence, and said that he had been informed that he had said that it was in his power to rescue the

Princess, so he was now to do it. If he succeeded in this, he no doubt knew that the King had promised his daughter and half the kingdom to anyone who set her free, which promise should be faithfully and honorably kept, but if he failed he should be put to death. The youth denied that he had said this, but all to no purpose, for the King was deaf to all his words; so there was nothing to be done but say that he would make the attempt.

He went down into the stable, and very sad and full of care he was. Then Dapplegrim inquired why he was so troubled, and the youth told him, and said that he did not know what to do, "for as to setting the Princess free, that was downright impossible."

"Oh, but it might be done," said Dapplegrim. "I will help you; but you must first have me well shod. You must ask for ten pounds of iron and twelve pounds of steel for the shoeing, and one smith to hammer and one to hold."

So the youth did this, and no one said him nay. He got both the iron and the steel, and the smiths, and thus was Dapplegrim shod strongly and well, and when the youth went out of the King's palace a cloud of dust rose up behind him. But when he came to the mountain into which the Princess had been carried, the difficulty was to ascend the precipitous wall of rock by which he was to get on to the mountain beyond, for the rock stood right up on end, as steep as a house side and as smooth as a sheet of glass. The first time the youth rode at it he got a little way up the precipice, but then both Dapplegrim's fore legs slipped, and down came horse and rider with a sound like thunder among the mountains. The next time that he rode at it he got a little farther up, but then one of Dapplegrim's fore legs slipped, and down they went with the sound of a landslip. But the third time Dapplegrim said: "Now we must show what we can do," and went at it once more till the stones sprang up sky high, and thus they got up. Then the lad rode into the mountain cleft at full gallop and caught up the Princess on his saddle-bow, and then out again before the Troll even had time to stand up, and thus the Princess was set free.

When the youth returned to the palace the King was both happy and delighted to get his daughter back again, as may easily be believed, but somehow or other the people about the Court had so worked on him that he was angry with the lad too. "Thou shalt have my thanks for setting my Princess free," he said, when the youth came into the palace with her, and was then about to go away.

"She ought to be just as much my Princess as she is yours now, for you are a man of your word," said the youth.

"Yes, yes," said the King. "Have her thou shalt, as I have said it; but first of all thou must make the sun shine into my palace here."

For there was a large and high hill outside the windows which over-shadowed the palace so much that the sun could not shine in.

"That was not part of our bargain," answered the youth. "But as nothing that I can say will move you, I suppose I shall have to try to do my best, for the Princess I will have."

So he went down to Dapplegrim again and told him what the King desired, and Dapplegrim thought that it might easily be done; but first of all he must have new shoes, and ten pounds of iron and twelve pounds of steel must go to the making of them, and two smiths were also necessary, one to hammer and one to hold, and then it would be very easy to make the sun shine into the King's palace.

The lad asked for these things and obtained them instantly, for the King thought that for very shame he could not refuse to give them, and so Dapplegrim got new shoes, and they were good ones. The youth seated himself on him, and once more they went their way, and for each hop that Dapplegrim made, down went the hill fifteen ells into the earth, and so they went on until there was no hill left for the King to see.

When the youth came down again to the King's palace he asked the King if the Princess should not at last be his, for now no one could say that the sun was not shining into the palace. But the other people in the palace had again stirred up the King, and he answered that the youth should have her, and that he had never intended that he should not; but first of all he must get her quite as good a horse to ride to the wedding on as that which he had himself. The youth said that the King had never told him he was to do that, and it seemed to him that he had now really earned the Princess; but the King stuck to what he had said, and if the youth were unable to do it he was to lose his life, the King said. The youth went down to the stable again, and very sad and sorrowful he was, as anyone may well imagine. Then he told Dapplegrim that the King had now required that he should get the Princess as good a bridal horse as that which the bridegroom had, or he should lose his life. "But that will be no easy thing to do," said he, "for your equal is not to be found in all the world."

"Oh yes, there is one to match me," said Dapplegrim. "But it will not be easy to get him, for he is underground. However, we will try. Now you must go up to the King and ask for new shoes for me, and for them we must again have ten pounds of iron, twelve pounds of steel, and two smiths, one to hammer and one to hold, but be very particular to see that the hooks are very sharp. And you must also ask for twelve barrels of rye, and twelve slaughtered oxen must we have with us, and all the twelve ox-hides with twelve hundred spikes set in each of them; all these things must we have, likewise a barrel of tar with twelve tons of tar in it." The youth went to the King and asked for all the things that Dapplegrim had named, and once more, as the King thought that it would be disgraceful to refuse them to him, he obtained them all.

So he mounted Dapplegrim and rode away from the Court, and when he had ridden for a long, long time over hills and moors, Dapplegrim asked: "Do you hear anything?"

"Yes; there is such a dreadful whistling up above in the air that I think I am growing alarmed," said the youth.

"That is all the wild birds in the forest flying about; they are sent to stop us," said Dapplegrim. "But just cut a hole in the corn sacks, and then they will be so busy with the corn that they will forget us."

The youth did it. He cut holes in the corn sacks so that barley and rye ran out on every side, and all the wild birds that were in the forest came in such numbers that they darkened the sun. But when they caught sight of the corn they could not refrain from it, but flew down and began to scratch and pick at the corn and rye, and at last they began to fight among themselves, and forgot all about the youth and Dapplegrim, and did them no harm.

And now the youth rode onwards for a long, long time, over hill and dale, over rocky places and morasses, and then Dapplegrim began to listen again, and asked the youth if he heard anything now.

"Yes; now I hear such a dreadful crackling and crashing in the forest on every side that I think I shall be really afraid," said the youth.

"That is all the wild beasts in the forest," said Dapplegrim; "they are sent out to stop us. But just throw out the twelve carcasses of the oxen, and they will be so much occupied with them that they will quite forget us." So the youth threw out the carcasses of the oxen, and then all the wild beasts in the forest, both bears and wolves, and lions, and grim beasts of all kinds, came. But when

632

they caught sight of the carcasses of the oxen they began to fight for them till the blood flowed, and they entirely forgot Dapplegrim and the youth.

So the youth rode onwards again, and many and many were the new scenes they saw, for traveling on Dapplegrim's back was not traveling slowly, as may be imagined, and then Dapplegrim neighed.

"Do you hear anything?" he said.

"Yes; I heard something like a foal neighing quite plainly a long, long way off," answered the youth.

"That's a full-grown colt," said Dapplegrim, "if you hear it so plainly when it is so far away from us."

So they traveled onwards a long time, and saw one new scene after another once more. Then Dapplegrim neighed again.

"Do you hear anything now?" said he.

"Yes; now I heard it quite distinctly, and it neighed like a full-grown horse," answered the youth.

"Yes, and you will hear it again very soon," said Dapplegrim; "and then you will hear what a voice it has." So they traveled on through many more different kinds of country, and then Dapplegrim neighed for the third time; but before he could ask the youth if he heard anything, there was such a neighing on the other side of the heath that the youth thought that hills and rocks would be rent in pieces.

"Now he is here!" said Dapplegrim. "Be quick, and fling over me the ox-hides that have the spikes in them, throw the twelve tons of tar over the field, and climb up into that great spruce fir tree. When he comes, fire will spurt out of both his nostrils, and then the tar will catch fire. Now mark what I say—if the flame ascends I conquer, and if it sinks I fail; but if you see that I am winning, fling the bridle, which you must take off me, over his head, and then he will become quite gentle."

Just as the youth had flung all the hides with the spikes over Dapplegrim, and the tar over the field, and had got safely up into the spruce fir, a horse came with flame spouting from his nostrils, and the tar caught fire in a moment; and Dapplegrim and the horse began to fight until the stones leapt up to the sky. They bit, and they fought with their fore legs and their hind legs, and sometimes the youth looked at them. And sometimes he looked at the tar, but at last the flames began to rise, for wheresoever the strange horse bit or wheresoever he kicked he hit upon the spikes in the hides, and at length he had to yield. When the youth saw that, he was not long in getting down from the tree and flinging the bridle over the horse's head, and then he became so tame that he might have been led by a thin string.

This horse was dappled too, and so like Dapplegrim that no one could distinguish the one from the other. The youth seated himself on the dappled horse which he had captured, and rode home again to the King's palace, and Dapplegrim ran loose by his side. When he got there, the King was standing outside in the courtyard.

"Can you tell me which is the horse I have caught, and which is the one I had before?" said the youth. "If you can't, I think your daughter is mine."

The King went and looked at both the dappled horses; he looked high and he looked low, he looked before and he looked behind, but there was not a hair's difference between the two.

"No," said the King; "that I cannot tell thee, and as thou hast procured such a splendid bridal horse for my daughter thou shalt have her; but first we must have one more trial, just to see if thou art fated to have her. She shall hide herself twice, and then thou shalt hide thyself twice. If thou canst find her each time that she hides herself, and if she cannot find thee in thy hiding-places, then it is fated, and thou shalt have the Princess."

"That, too, was not in our bargain," said the youth. "But we will make this trial since it must be so."

So the King's daughter was to hide herself first.

Then she changed herself into a duck, and lay swimming in a lake that was just outside the palace. But the youth went down into the stable and asked Dapplegrim what she had done with herself.

"Oh, all that you have to do is to take your gun, and go down to the water and aim at the duck which is swimming about there, and she will soon discover herself," said Dapplegrim.

The youth snatched up his gun and ran to the lake. "I will just have a shot at that duck," said he, and began to aim at it.

"Oh, no, dear friend, don't shoot! It is I," said the Princess. So he had found her once.

The second time the Princess changed herself into a loaf, and laid herself on the table among four other loaves; and she was so like the other loaves that no one could see any difference between them.

But the youth again went down to the stable to Dapplegrim, and told him that the Princess had hidden herself again, and that he had not the least idea what had become of her.

"Oh, just take a very large bread-knife, sharpen it, and pretend that you are going to cut straight through the third of the four loaves which are lying on the kitchen table in the King's palace—count them from right to left—and you will soon find her," said Dapplegrim.

So the youth went up to the kitchen, and began to sharpen the largest bread-knife that he could find; then he caught hold of the third loaf on the left-hand side, and put the knife to it as if he meant to cut it straight in two. "I will have a bit of this bread for myself," said he.

"No, dear friend, don't cut, it is I!" said the Princess again; so he had found her the second time.

And now it was his turn to go and hide himself; but Dapplegrim had given him such good instructions that it was not easy to find him. First he turned himself into a horse-fly, and hid himself in Dapplegrim's left nostril. The Princess went poking about and searching everywhere, high and low, and wanted to go into Dapplegrim's stall too, but he began to bite and kick about so that she was afraid to go there, and could not find the youth. "Well," said she, "as I am unable to find you, you must show yourself;" whereupon the youth immediately appeared standing there on the stable floor.

Dapplegrim told him what he was to do the second time, and he turned himself into a lump of earth, and stuck himself between the hoof and the shoe on Dapplegrim's left fore-foot. Once more the King's daughter went and sought everywhere, inside and outside, until at last she came into the stable, and wanted to go into the stall beside Dapplegrim. So this time he allowed her to go into it, and she peered about high and low, but she could not look under his hoofs, for he stood much too firmly on his legs for that, and she could not find the youth.

"Well, you will just have to show where you are yourself, for I can't find you," said the Princess, and in an instant the youth was standing by her side on the floor of the stable.

"Now you are mine!" said he to the Princess.

"Now you can see that it is fated that she should be mine," he said to the King.

"Yes, fated it is," said the King. "So what must be, must."

Then everything was made ready for the wedding with great splendor and promptitude, and the youth rode to church on Dapplegrim, and the King's daughter on the other horse. So everyone must see that they could not be long on their way thither.

The Nunda, Eater of People

(FROM *THE VIOLET FAIRY BOOK*)

Once upon a time there lived a sultan who loved his garden dearly, and planted it with trees and flowers and fruits from all parts of the world. He went to see them three times every day: first at seven o'clock, when he got up, then at three, and lastly at half-past five. There was no plant and no vegetable which escaped his eye, but he lingered longest of all before his one date tree.

Now the sultan had seven sons. Six of them he was proud of, for they were strong and manly, but the youngest he disliked, for he spent all his time among the women of the house. The sultan had talked to him, and he paid no heed; and he had beaten him, and he paid no heed; and he had tied him up, and he paid no heed, till at last his father grew tired of trying to make him change his ways, and let him alone.

Time passed, and one day the sultan, to his great joy, saw signs of fruit on his date tree. And he told his vizir, "My date tree is bearing"; and he told the officers, "My date tree is bearing"; and he told the judges, "My date tree is bearing"; and he told all the rich men of the town.

He waited patiently for some days till the dates were nearly ripe, and then he called his six sons, and said: "One of you must watch the date tree till the dates are ripe, for if it is not watched the slaves will steal them, and I shall not have any for another year."

And the eldest son answered, "I will go, father," and he went.

The first thing the youth did was to summon his slaves, and bid them beat drums all night under the date tree, for he feared to fall asleep. So the slaves beat the drums, and the young man danced till four o'clock, and then it grew so cold he could dance no longer, and one of the slaves said to him: "It is getting light; the tree is safe; lie down, master, and go to sleep."

So he lay down and slept, and his slaves slept likewise.

A few minutes went by, and a bird flew down from a neighboring thicket, and ate all the dates, without leaving a single one. And when the tree was stripped bare, the bird went as it had come. Soon after, one of the slaves woke up and looked for the dates, but there were no dates to see. Then he ran to the young man and shook him, saying:

"Your father set you to watch the tree, and you have not watched, and the dates have all been eaten by a bird."

The lad jumped up and ran to the tree to see for himself, but there was not a date anywhere. And he cried aloud, "What am I to say to my father? Shall I tell him that the dates have been stolen, or that a great rain fell and a great storm blew? But he will send me to gather them up and bring them to him, and there are none to bring! Shall I tell him that Bedouins drove me away, and when I returned there were no dates? And he will answer, 'You had slaves, did they not fight with the Bedouins?' It is the truth that will be best, and that will I tell him."

Then he went straight to his father, and found him sitting in his verandah with his five sons round him; and the lad bowed his head.

"Give me the news from the garden," said the sultan.

And the youth answered, "The dates have all been eaten by some bird: there is not one left."

The sultan was silent for a moment: then he asked, "Where were you when the bird came?"

The lad answered: "I watched the date tree till the cocks were crowing and it was getting light; then I lay down for a little, and I slept. When I woke a slave was standing over me, and he said, 'There is not one date left on the tree!' And I went to the date tree, and saw it was true; and that is what I have to tell you."

And the sultan replied, "A son like you is only good for eating and sleeping. I have no use for you. Go your way, and when my date tree bears again, I will send another son; perhaps he will watch better."

So he waited many months, till the tree was covered with more dates than any tree had ever borne before. When they were near ripening he sent one of his sons to the garden: saying, "My son, I am longing to taste those dates: go and watch over them, for to-day's sun will bring them to perfection."

And the lad answered: "My father, I am going now, and to-morrow, when the sun has passed the hour of seven, bid a slave come and gather the dates."

"Good," said the sultan.

The youth went to the tree, and lay down and slept. And about midnight he arose to look at the tree, and the dates were all there—beautiful dates, swinging in bunches.

"Ah, my father will have a feast, indeed," thought he. "What a fool my brother was not to take more heed! Now he is in disgrace, and we know him no more. Well, I will watch till the bird comes. I should like to see what manner of bird it is."

And he sat and read till the cocks crew and it grew light, and the dates were still on the tree.

"Oh my father will have his dates; they are all safe now," he thought to himself. "I will make myself comfortable against this tree," and he leaned against the trunk, and sleep came on him, and the bird flew down and ate all the dates.

When the sun rose, the head-man came and looked for the dates, and there were no dates. And he woke the young man, and said to him, "Look at the tree."

And the young man looked, and there were no dates. And his ears were stopped, and his legs trembled, and his tongue grew heavy at the thought of the sultan. His slave became frightened as he looked at him, and asked, "My master, what is it?"

He answered, "I have no pain anywhere, but I am ill everywhere. My whole body is well, and my whole body is sick I fear my father, for did I not say to him, 'To-morrow at seven you shall taste the dates'? And he will drive me away, as he drove away my brother! I will go away myself, before he sends me."

Then he got up and took a road that led straight past the palace, but he had not walked many steps before he met a man carrying a large silver dish, covered with a white cloth to cover the dates.

And the young man said, "The dates are not ripe yet; you must return to-morrow."

And the slave went with him to the palace, where the sultan was sitting with his four sons.

"Good greeting, master!" said the youth.

And the sultan answered, "Have you seen the man I sent?"

"I have, master; but the dates are not yet ripe."

But the sultan did not believe his words, and said; "This second year I have eaten no dates, because of my sons. Go your ways, you are my son no longer!"

And the sultan looked at the four sons that were left him, and promised rich gifts to whichever of them would bring him the dates from the tree. But year by year passed, and he never got them. One son tried to keep himself awake with playing cards; another mounted a horse and rode round and round the tree, while the two others, whom their father as a last hope sent together, lit bonfires. But whatever they did, the result was always the same. Towards dawn they fell asleep, and the bird ate the dates on the tree.

The sixth year had come, and the dates on the tree were thicker than ever. And the head-man went to the palace and told the sultan what he had seen. But the sultan only shook his head, and said sadly, "What is that to me? I have had seven sons, yet for five years a bird has devoured my dates; and this year it will be the same as ever."

Now the youngest son was sitting in the kitchen, as was his custom, when he heard his father say those words. And he rose up, and went to his father, and knelt before him. "Father, this year you shall eat dates," cried he. "And on the tree are five great bunches, and each bunch I will give to a separate nation, for the nations in the town are five. This time, I will watch the date tree myself." But his father and his mother laughed heartily, and thought his words idle talk.

One day, news was brought to the sultan that the dates were ripe, and he ordered one of his men to go and watch the tree. His son, who happened to be standing by, heard the order, and he said:

"How is it that you have bidden a man to watch the tree, when I, your son, am left?"

And his father answered, "Ah, six were of no use, and where they failed, will you succeed?"

But the boy replied: "Have patience to-day, and let me go, and to-morrow you shall see whether I bring you dates or not."

"Let the child go, Master," said his wife; "perhaps we shall eat the dates— or perhaps we shall not—but let him go."

And the sultan answered: "I do not refuse to let him go, but my heart distrusts him. His brothers all promised fair, and what did they do?"

But the boy entreated, saying, "Father, if you and I and mother be alive to-morrow, you shall eat the dates."

"Go then," said his father.

When the boy reached the garden, he told the slaves to leave him, and to return home themselves and sleep. When he was alone, he laid himself down and slept fast till one o'clock, when he arose, and sat opposite the date tree. Then he took some Indian corn out of one fold of his dress, and some sandy grit out of another. And he chewed the corn till he felt he was growing sleepy, and then he put some grit into his mouth, and that kept him awake till the bird came.

It looked about at first without seeing him, and whispering to itself, "There is no one here," fluttered lightly on to the tree and stretched out his beak for the dates. Then the boy stole softly up, and caught it by the wing.

The bird turned and flew quickly away, but the boy never let go, not even when they soared high into the air.

"Son of Adam," the bird said when the tops of the mountains looked small below them, "if you fall, you will be dead long before you reach the ground, so go your way, and let me go mine."

But the boy answered, "Wherever you go, I will go with you. You cannot get rid of me."

"I did not eat your dates," persisted the bird, "and the day is dawning. Leave me to go my way."

But again the boy answered him: "My six brothers are hateful to my father because you came and stole the dates, and to-day my father shall see you, and my brothers shall see you, and all the people of the town, great and small, shall see you. And my father's heart will rejoice."

"Well, if you will not leave me, I will throw you off," said the bird.

So it flew up higher still—so high that the earth shone like one of the other stars.

"How much of you will be left if you fall from here?" asked the bird.

"If I die, I die," said the boy, "but I will not leave you."

And the bird saw it was no use talking, and went down to the earth again.

"Here you are at home, so let me go my way," it begged once more; "or at least make a covenant with me."

"What covenant?" said the boy.

"Save me from the sun," replied the bird, "and I will save you from rain."

"How can you do that, and how can I tell if I can trust you?"

"Pull a feather from my tail, and put it in the fire, and if you want me I will come to you, wherever I am."

And the boy answered, "Well, I agree; go your way."

"Farewell, my friend. When you call me, if it is from the depths of the sea, I will come."

The lad watched the bird out of sight; then he went straight to the date tree. And when he saw the dates his heart was glad, and his body felt stronger and his eyes brighter than before. And he laughed out loud with joy, and said to himself, "This is *my* luck, mine, Sit-in-the-kitchen! Farewell, date tree, I am going to lie down. What ate you will eat you no more."

The sun was high in the sky before the head-man, whose business it was, came to look at the date tree, expecting to find it stripped of all its fruit, but when he saw the dates so thick that they almost hid the leaves he ran back to his house, and beat a big drum till everybody came running, and even the little children wanted to know what had happened.

"What is it? What is it, head-man?" cried they.

"Ah, it is not a son that the master has, but a lion! This day Sit-in-the-kitchen has uncovered his face before his father!"

"But how, head-man?"

"To-day the people may eat the dates."

"Is it true, head-man?"

"Oh yes, it is true, but let him sleep till each man has brought forth a present. He who has fowls, let him take fowls; he who has a goat, let him take a goat; he who has rice, let him take rice." And the people did as he had said.

Then they took the drum, and went to the tree where the boy lay sleeping.

And they picked him up, and carried him away, with horns and clarionets and drums, with clappings of hands and shrieks of joy, straight to his father's house.

When his father heard the noise and saw the baskets made of green leaves, brimming over with dates, and his son borne high on the necks of slaves, his heart leaped, and he said to himself "To-day at last I shall eat dates." And he called his wife to see what her son had done, and ordered his soldiers to take the boy and bring him to his father.

"What news, my son?" said he.

"News? I have no news, except that if you will open your mouth you shall see what dates taste like." And he plucked a date, and put it into his father's mouth.

"Ah! You are indeed my son," cried the sultan. "You do not take after those fools, those good-for-nothings. But, tell me, what did you do with the bird, for it was you, and you only who watched for it?"

"Yes, it was I who watched for it and who saw it. And it will not come again, neither for its life, nor for your life, nor for the lives of your children."

"Oh, once I had six sons, and now I have only one. It is you, whom I called a fool, who have given me the dates: as for the others, I want none of them."

But his wife rose up and went to him, and said, "Master, do not, I pray you, reject them," and she entreated long, till the sultan granted her prayer, for she loved the six elder ones more than her last one.

So they all lived quietly at home, till the sultan's cat went and caught a calf. And the owner of the calf went and told the sultan, but he answered, "The cat is mine, and the calf mine," and the man dared not complain further.

Two days after, the cat caught a cow, and the sultan was told, "Master, the cat has caught a cow," but he only said, "It was my cow and my cat."

And the cat waited a few days, and then it caught a donkey, and they told the sultan, "Master, the cat has caught a donkey," and he said, "My cat and my donkey." Next it was a horse, and after that a camel, and when the sultan was told he said, "You don't like this cat, and want me to kill it. And I shall not kill it. Let it eat the camel: let it even eat a man."

And it waited till the next day, and caught some one's child. And the sultan was told, "The cat has caught a child." And he said, "The cat is mine and the child mine." Then it caught a grown-up man.

After that the cat left the town and took up its abode in a thicket near the road. So if any one passed, going for water, it devoured him. If it saw a cow going to feed, it devoured him. If it saw a goat, it devoured him. Whatever went along that road the cat caught and ate.

Then the people went to the sultan in a body, and told him of all the misdeeds of that cat. But he answered as before, "The cat is mine and the people are mine." And no man dared kill the cat, which grew bolder and bolder, and at last came into the town to look for its prey.

One day, the sultan said to his six sons, "I am going into the country, to see how the wheat is growing, and you shall come with me." They went on merrily along the road, till they came to a thicket, when out sprang the cat, and killed three of the sons.

"The cat! The cat!" shrieked the soldiers who were with him. And this time the sultan said:

"Seek for it and kill it. It is no longer a cat, but a demon!"

And the soldiers answered him, "Did we not tell you, master, what the cat was doing, and did you not say, "'My cat and my people?'"

And he answered: "True, I said it."

Now the youngest son had not gone with the rest, but had stayed at home with his mother; and when he heard that his brothers had been killed by the cat he said, "Let me go, that it may slay me also." His mother entreated him not to leave her, but he would not listen, and he took his sword and a spear and some rice cakes, and went after the cat, which by this time had run of to a great distance.

The lad spent many days hunting the cat, which now bore the name of "the Nunda, eater of people," but though he killed many wild animals he saw no trace of the enemy he was hunting for. There was no beast, however fierce, that he was afraid of, till at last his father and mother begged him to give up the chase after the Nunda.

But he answered: "What I have said, I cannot take back. If I am to die, then I die, but every day I must go and seek for the Nunda."

And again his father offered him what he would, even the crown itself, but the boy would hear nothing, and went on his way.

Many times his slaves came and told him, "We have seen footprints, and to-day we shall behold the Nunda." But the footprints never turned out to be those of the Nunda. They wandered far through deserts and through forests, and at length came to the foot of a great hill. And something in the boy's soul whispered that here was the end of all their seeking, and to-day they would find the Nunda.

But before they began to climb the mountain the boy ordered his slaves to cook some rice, and they rubbed the stick to make a fire, and when the fire was kindled they cooked the rice and ate it. Then they began their climb.

Suddenly, when they had almost reached the top, a slave who was on in front cried:

"Master! Master!" And the boy pushed on to where the slave stood, and the slave said:

"Cast your eyes down to the foot of the mountain." And the boy looked, and his soul told him it was the Nunda.

And he crept down with his spear in his hand, and then he stopped and gazed below him.

"This *must* be the real Nunda," thought he. "My mother told me its ears were small, and this one's are small. She told me it was broad and not long, and this is broad and not long. She told me it had spots like a civet-cat, and this has spots like a civet-cat."

Then he left the Nunda lying asleep at the foot of the mountain, and went back to his slaves.

"We will feast to-day," he said; "make cakes of batter, and bring water," and they ate and drank. And when they had finished he bade them hide the rest of the food in the thicket, that if they slew the Nunda they might return and eat and sleep before going back to the town. And the slaves did as he bade them.

It was now afternoon, and the lad said: "It is time we went after the Nunda." And they went till they reached the bottom and came to a great forest which lay between them and the Nunda.

Here the lad stopped, and ordered every slave that wore two cloths to cast one away and tuck up the other between his legs. "For," said he, "the wood is not a little one. Perhaps we may be caught by the thorns, or perhaps we may have to run before the Nunda, and the cloth might bind our legs, and cause us to fall before it."

And they answered, "Good, master," and did as he bade them. Then they crawled on their hands and knees to where the Nunda lay asleep.

Noiselessly they crept along till they were quite close to it; then, at a sign from the boy, they threw their spears. The Nunda did not stir: the spears had done their work, but a great fear seized them all, and they ran away and climbed the mountain.

The sun was setting when they reached the top, and glad they were to take out the fruit and the cakes and the water which they had hidden away, and sit down and rest themselves. And after they had eaten and were filled, they lay down and slept till morning.

When the dawn broke they rose up and cooked more rice, and drank more water. After that they walked all round the back of the mountain to the place where they had left the Nunda, and they saw it stretched out where they had found it, stiff and dead. And they took it up and carried it back to the town, singing as they went, "He has killed the Nunda, the eater of people."

And when his father heard the news, and that his son was come, and was bringing the Nunda with him, he felt that the man did not dwell on the earth whose joy was greater than his. And the people bowed down to the boy and gave him presents, and loved him, because he had delivered them from the bondage of fear, and had slain the Nunda.

Herr Lazarus and the Draken

(FROM *THE GRAY FAIRY BOOK*)

Once upon a time there was a cobbler called Lazarus, who was very fond of honey. One day, as he ate some while he sat at work, the flies collected in such numbers that with one blow he killed forty. Then he went and ordered a sword to be made for him, on which he had written these words: "With one blow I have slain forty." When the sword was ready he took it and went out into the world, and when he was two days' journey from home he came to a spring, by which he laid himself down and slept.

Now in that country there dwelt Draken, one of whom came to the spring to draw water; there he found Lazarus sleeping, and read what was written on his sword. Then he went back to his people and told them what he had seen, and they all advised him to make fellowship with this powerful stranger. So the Draken returned to the spring, awoke Lazarus, and said that if it was agreeable to him they should make fellowship together.

Lazarus answered that he was willing, and after a priest had blessed the fellowship, they returned together to the other Draken, and Lazarus dwelt among them. After some days they told him that it was their custom to take it in turns to bring wood and water, and as he was now of their company, he must take his turn. They went first for water and wood, but at last it came to be Lazarus's turn to go for water. The Draken had a great leathern bag, holding two hundred measures of water. This Lazarus could only, with great difficulty, drag empty to the spring, and because he could not carry it back full, he did not fill it at all, but, instead, he dug up the ground all round the spring.

As Lazarus remained so long away, the Draken sent one of their number to see what had become of him, and when this one came to the spring, Lazarus said to him: "We will no more plague ourselves by carrying water every day. I will bring the entire spring home at once, and so we shall be freed from this burden."

But the Draken called out: "On no account, Herr Lazarus, else we shall all die of thirst; rather will we carry the water ourselves in turns, and you alone shall be exempt."

Next it comes to be Lazarus's turn to bring the wood. Now the Draken, when they fetched the wood, always took an entire tree on their shoulder, and so carried it home. Because Lazarus could not imitate them in this, he went to the forest, tied all the trees together with a thick rope, and remained in the forest till evening. Again the Draken sent one of them after him to see what had become of him, and when this one asked what he was about, Lazarus answered: "I will bring the entire forest home at once, so that after that we may have rest."

But the Draken called out: "By no means, Herr Lazarus, else we shall all die of cold; rather will we go ourselves to bring wood, and let you be free." And then the Draken tore up one tree, threw it over his shoulder, and so carried it home.

When they had lived together some time, the Draken became weary of Lazarus, and agreed among themselves to kill him; each Draken, in the night while Lazarus slept, should strike him a blow with a hatchet. But Lazarus heard of this scheme, and when the evening came, he took a log of wood, covered it with his cloak, laid it in the place where he usually slept, and then hid himself. In the night the Draken came, and each one hit the log a blow with his hatchet, till it flew in pieces.

Then they believed their object was gained, and they lay down again.

Thereupon Lazarus took the log, threw it away, and laid himself down in its stead. Towards dawn, he began to groan, and when the Draken heard that, they asked what ailed him, to which he made answer: "The gnats have stung me horribly."

This terrified the Draken, for they believed that Lazarus took their blows for gnat-stings, and they determined at any price to get rid of him. Next morning, therefore, they asked him if he had not wife or child, and said that if he would like to go and visit them they would give him a bag of gold to take away with him. He agreed willingly to this, but asked further that one of the Draken should go with him to carry the bag of gold. They consented, and one was sent with him.

When they had come to within a short distance of Lazarus's house, he said to the Draken: "Stop here, in the meantime, for I must go on in front and tie up my children, lest they eat you."

So he went and tied his children with strong ropes, and said to them: "As soon as the Draken comes in sight, call out as loud as you can, 'Drakenflesh! Drakenflesh!'"

So, when the Draken appeared, the children cried out; "Drakenflesh! Drakenflesh!" and this so terrified the Draken that he let the bag fall and fled.

On the road he met a fox, which asked him why he seemed so frightened. He answered that he was afraid of the children of Herr Lazarus, who had been within a hair-breadth of eating him up.

But the fox laughed, and said: "What! you were afraid of the children of Herr Lazarus? He had two fowls, one of which I ate yesterday, the other I will go and fetch now—If you do not believe me, come and see for yourself; but you must first tie yourself on to my tail."

The Draken then tied himself on to the fox's tail, and went back thus with it to Lazarus's house, in order to see what it would arrange. There stood Lazarus with his gun raised ready to fire, who, when he saw the fox coming along with the Draken, called out to the fox: "Did I not tell you to bring me all the Draken, and you bring me only one?"

When the Draken heard that he made off to the right-about at once, and ran so fast that the fox was dashed in pieces against the stones.

When Lazarus had got quit of the Draken he built himself, with their gold, a magnificent house, in which he spent the rest of his days in great enjoyment.

The Goblin Pony

(FROM *THE GRAY FAIRY BOOK*)

Don't stir from the fireplace to-night," said old Peggy, "for the wind is blowing so violently that the house shakes; besides, this is Hallow-e'en, when the witches are abroad, and the goblins, who are their servants, are wandering about in all sorts of disguises, doing harm to the children of men."

"Why should I stay here?" said the eldest of the young people. "No, I must go and see what the daughter of old Jacob, the rope-maker, is doing. She wouldn't close her blue eyes all night if I didn't visit her father before the moon had gone down."

"I must go and catch lobsters and crabs" said the second, "and not all the witches and goblins in the world shall hinder me."

So they all determined to go on their business or pleasure, and scorned the wise advice of old Peggy. Only the youngest child hesitated a minute, when she said to him, "You stay here, my little Richard, and I will tell you beautiful stories."

But he wanted to pick a bunch of wild thyme and some blackberries by moonlight, and ran out after the others. When they got outside the house they said: "The old woman talks of wind and storm, but never was the weather finer or the sky more clear; see how majestically the moon stalks through the transparent clouds!"

Then all of a sudden they noticed a little black pony close beside them.

"Oh, ho!" they said, "that is old Valentine's pony; it must have escaped from its stable, and is going down to drink at the horse-pond."

"My pretty little pony," said the eldest, patting the creature with his hand, "you mustn't run too far; I'll take you to the pond myself."

With these words he jumped on the pony's back and was quickly followed by his second brother, then by the third, and so on, till at last they were all astride the little beast, down to the small Richard, who didn't like to be left behind.

On the way to the pond they met several of their companions, and they invited them all to mount the pony, which they did, and the little creature did not seem to mind the extra weight, but trotted merrily along.

The quicker it trotted the more the young people enjoyed the fun; they dug their heels into the pony's sides and called out, "Gallop, little horse, you have never had such brave riders on your back before!"

In the meantime the wind had risen again, and the waves began to howl; but the pony did not seem to mind the noise, and instead of going to the pond, cantered gaily towards the sea-shore.

Richard began to regret his thyme and blackberries, and the eldest brother seized the pony by the mane and tried to make it turn round, for he remembered the blue eyes of Jacob the rope-maker's daughter. But he tugged and pulled in vain, for the pony galloped straight on into the sea, till the waves met its forefeet. As soon as it felt the water it neighed lustily and capered about with glee, advancing quickly into the foaming billows. When the waves had covered the children's legs they repented their careless behavior, and cried out: "The cursed little black pony is bewitched. If we had only listened to old Peggy's advice we shouldn't have been lost."

The further the pony advanced, the higher rose the sea; at last the waves covered the children's heads and they were all drowned.

Towards morning old Peggy went out, for she was anxious about the fate of her grandchildren. She sought them high and low, but could not find them anywhere. She asked all the neighbors if they had seen the children, but no one knew anything about them, except that the eldest had not been with the blue-eyed daughter of Jacob the rope-maker.

As she was going home, bowed with grief, she saw a little black pony coming towards her, springing and curveting in every direction. When it got quite near her it neighed loudly, and galloped past her so quickly that in a moment it was out of her sight.

How Some Wild Animals Became Tame Ones

(FROM *THE BROWN FAIRY BOOK*)

Once upon a time there lived a miller who was so rich that, when he was going to be married, he asked to the feast not only his own friends but also the wild animals who dwelt in the hills and woods round about. The chief of the bears, the wolves, the foxes, the horses, the cows, the goats, the sheep, and the reindeer, all received invitations; and as they were not accustomed to weddings they were greatly pleased and flattered, and sent back messages in the politest language that they would certainly be there.

The first to start on the morning of the wedding-day was the bear, who always liked to be punctual; and, besides, he had a long way to go, and his hair, being so thick and rough, needed a good brushing before it was fit to be seen at a party. However, he took care to awaken very early, and set off down the road with a light heart. Before he had walked very far he met a boy who came whistling along, hitting at the tops of the flowers with a stick.

"Where are you going?" said he, looking at the bear in surprise, for he was an old acquaintance, and not generally so smart.

"Oh, just to the miller's marriage," answered the bear carelessly. "Of course, I would much rather stay at home, but the miller was so anxious I should be there that I really could not refuse."

"Don't go, don't go!" cried the boy. "If you do you will never come back! You have got the most beautiful skin in the world—just the kind that everyone is wanting, and they will be sure to kill you and strip you of it."

"I had not thought of that," said the bear, whose face turned white, only nobody could see it. "If you are certain that they would be so wicked—but perhaps you are jealous because nobody has invited *you*?"

"Oh, nonsense!" replied the boy angrily, "do as you see. It is your skin, and not mine; I don't care what becomes of it!" And he walked quickly on with his head in the air.

The bear waited until he was out of sight, and then followed him slowly, for he felt in his heart that the boy's advice was good, though he was too proud to say so.

The boy soon grew tired of walking along the road, and turned off into the woods, where there were bushes he could jump and streams he could wade; but he had not gone far before he met the wolf.

"Where are you going?" asked he, for it was not the first time he had seen him.

"Oh, just to the miller's marriage," answered the wolf, as the bear had done before him. "It is rather tiresome, of course—weddings are always so stupid; but still one must be good-natured!"

"Don't go!" said the boy again. "Your skin is so thick and warm, and winter is not far off now. They will kill you, and strip it from you."

The wolf's jaw dropped in astonishment and terror. "Do you *really* think that would happen?" he gasped.

"Yes, to be sure, I do," answered the boy. "But it is your affair, not mine. So good-morning," and on he went. The wolf stood still for a few minutes, for he was trembling all over, and then crept quietly back to his cave.

Next the boy met the fox, whose lovely coat of silvery gray was shining in the sun.

"You look very fine!" said the boy, stopping to admire him, "are you going to the miller's wedding too?"

"Yes," answered the fox; "it is a long journey to take for such a thing as that, but you know what the miller's friends are like—so dull and heavy! It is only kind to go and amuse them a little."

"You poor fellow," said the boy pityingly. "Take my advice and stay at home. If you once enter the miller's gate his dogs will tear you in pieces."

"Ah, well, such things *have* occurred, I know," replied the fox gravely. And without saying any more he trotted off the way he had come.

His tail had scarcely disappeared, when a great noise of crashing branches was heard, and up bounded the horse, his black skin glistening like satin.

"Good-morning," he called to the boy as he galloped past, "I can't wait to talk to you now. I have promised the miller to be present at his wedding-feast, and they won't sit down till I come."

"Stop! stop!" cried the boy after him, and there was something in his voice that made the horse pull up. "What is the matter?" asked he.

"You don't know what you are doing," said the boy. "If once you go there you will never gallop through these woods any more. You are stronger than many men, but they will catch you and put ropes round you, and you will have to work and to serve them all the days of your life."

The horse threw back his head at these words, and laughed scornfully.

"Yes, I am stronger than many men," answered he, "and all the ropes in the world would not hold me. Let them bind me as fast as they will, I can always break loose, and return to the forest and freedom."

And with this proud speech he gave a whisk of his long tail, and galloped away faster than before.

But when he reached the miller's house everything happened as the boy had said. While he was looking at the guests and thinking how much handsomer and stronger he was than any of them, a rope was suddenly flung over his head, and he was thrown down and a bit thrust between his teeth. Then, in spite of his struggles, he was dragged to a stable, and shut up for several days without any food, till his spirit was broken and his coat had lost its gloss. After that he was harnessed to a plough, and had plenty of time to remember all he had lost through not listening to the counsel of the boy.

When the horse had turned a deaf ear to his words the boy wandered idly along, sometimes gathering wild strawberries from a bank, and sometimes plucking wild cherries from a tree, till he reached a clearing in the middle of the forest. Crossing this open space was a beautiful milk-white cow with a wreath of flowers round her neck.

"Good-morning," she said pleasantly, as she came up to the place where the boy was standing.

"Good-morning," he returned. "Where are you going in such a hurry?"

"To the miller's wedding; I am rather late already, for the wreath took such a long time to make, so I can't stop."

"Don't go," said the boy earnestly; "when once they have tasted your milk they will never let you leave them, and you will have to serve them all the days of your life."

"Oh, nonsense; what do *you* know about it?" answered the cow, who always thought she was wiser than other people. "Why, I can run twice as fast as any of them! I should like to see anybody try to keep me against my will."

And, without even a polite bow, she went on her way, feeling very much offended.

But everything turned out just as the boy had said. The company had all heard of the fame of the cow's milk, and persuaded her to give them some, and then her doom was sealed. A crowd gathered round her, and held her horns so that she could not use them, and, like the horse, she was shut in the stable, and only let out in the mornings, when a long rope was tied round her head, and she was fastened to a stake in a grassy meadow.

And so it happened to the goat and to the sheep.

Last of all came the reindeer, looking as he always did, as if some serious business was on hand.

"Where are you going?" asked the boy, who by this time was tired of wild cherries, and was thinking of his dinner.

"I am invited to the wedding," answered the reindeer, "and the miller has begged me on no account to fail him."

"O fool!" cried the boy, "have you no sense at all? Don't you know that when you get there they will hold you fast, for neither beast nor bird is as strong or as swift as you?"

"That is exactly why I am quite safe," replied the reindeer. "I am so strong that no one can bind me, and so swift that not even an arrow can catch me. So, good-bye for the present, you will soon see me back."

But none of the animals that went to the miller's wedding ever came back. And because they were self-willed and conceited, and would not listen to good advice, they and their children have been the servants of men to this very day.

The Cottager and His Cat

(FROM *THE CRIMSON FAIRY BOOK*)

Once upon a time there lived an old man and his wife in a dirty, tumble-down cottage, not very far from the splendid palace where the king and queen dwelt. In spite of the wretched state of the hut, which many people declared was too bad even for a pig to live in, the old man was very rich, for he was a great miser, and lucky besides, and would often go without food all day sooner than change one of his beloved gold pieces.

But after a while he found that he had starved himself once too often. He fell ill, and had no strength to get well again, and in a few days he died, leaving his wife and one son behind him.

The night following his death, the son dreamed that an unknown man appeared to him and said: "Listen to me; your father is dead and your mother will soon die, and all their riches will belong to you. Half of his wealth is ill-gotten, and this you must give back to the poor from whom he squeezed it. The other half you must throw into the sea. Watch, however, as the money sinks into the water, and if anything should swim, catch it and keep it, even if it is nothing more than a bit of paper."

Then the man vanished, and the youth awoke.

The remembrance of his dream troubled him greatly. He did not want to part with the riches that his father had left him, for he had known all his life what it was to be cold and hungry, and now he had hoped for a little comfort and pleasure. Still, he was honest and good-hearted, and if his father had come wrongfully by his wealth he felt he could never enjoy it, and at last he made up his mind to do as he had been bidden. He found out who were the people who were poorest in the village, and spent half of his money in helping them, and the other half he put in his pocket. From a rock that jutted right out into the sea he flung it in. In a moment it was out of sight, and no man could have told the spot where it had sunk, except for a tiny scrap of paper floating on the water. He stretched down carefully and managed to reach it, and on opening it found six shillings wrapped inside. This was now all the money he had in the world.

The young man stood and looked at it thoughtfully. "Well, I can't do much with this," he said to himself; but, after all, six shillings were better than nothing, and he wrapped them up again and slipped them into his coat.

He worked in his garden for the next few weeks, and he and his mother contrived to live on the fruit and vegetables he got out of it, and then she too died suddenly. The poor fellow felt very sad when he had laid her in her grave, and with a heavy heart he wandered into the forest, not knowing where he was going. By-and-by he began to get hungry, and seeing a small hut in front of him, he knocked at the door and asked if they could give him some milk. The old woman who opened it begged him to come in, adding kindly, that if he wanted a night's lodging he might have it without its costing him anything.

Two women and three men were at supper when he entered, and silently made room for him to sit down by them. When he had eaten he began to look about him, and was surprised to see an animal sitting by the fire different from anything he had ever noticed before. It was gray in color, and not very big; but its eyes were large and very bright, and it seemed to be singing in an odd way, quite unlike any animal in the forest. "What is the name of that strange little creature?" asked he. And they answered, "We call it a cat."

"I should like to buy it—if it is not too dear," said the young man; "it would be company for me." And they told him that he might have it for six shillings, if he cared to give so much. The young man took out his precious bit of paper, handed them the six shillings, and the next morning bade them farewell, with the cat lying snugly in his cloak.

For the whole day they wandered through meadows and forests, till in the evening they reached a house. The young fellow knocked at the door and asked the old man who opened it if he could rest there that night, adding that he had no money to pay for it. "Then I must give it to you," answered the man, and led him into a room where two women and two men were sitting at supper. One of the women was the old man's wife, the other his daughter. He placed the cat on the mantel shelf, and they all crowded round to examine this strange beast, and the cat rubbed itself against them, and held out its paw, and sang to them; and the women were delighted, and gave it everything that a cat could eat, and a great deal more besides.

After hearing the youth's story, and how he had nothing in the world left him except his cat, the old man advised him to go to the palace, which was only a few miles distant, and take counsel of the king, who was kind to everyone, and would certainly be his friend. The young man thanked him, and said he would gladly take his advice; and early next morning he set out for the royal palace.

He sent a message to the king to beg for an audience, and received a reply that he was to go into the great hall, where he would find his Majesty.

The king was at dinner with his court when the young man entered, and he signed to him to come near. The youth bowed low, and then gazed in surprise at the crowd of little black creatures who were running about the floor, and even on the table itself. Indeed, they were so bold that they snatched pieces of food from the King's own plate, and if he drove them away, tried to bite his hands, so that he could not eat his food, and his courtiers fared no better.

"What sort of animals are these?" asked the youth of one of the ladies sitting near him.

"They are called rats," answered the king, who had overheard the question, "and for years we have tried some way of putting an end to them, but it is impossible. They come into our very beds."

At this moment something was seen flying through the air. The cat was on the table, and with two or three shakes a number of rats were lying dead round him. Then a great scuffling of feet was heard, and in a few minutes the hall was clear.

For some minutes the King and his courtiers only looked at each other in astonishment. "What kind of animal is that which can work magic of this sort?" asked he. And the young man told him that it was called a cat, and that he had bought it for six shillings.

And the King answered: "Because of the luck you have brought me, in freeing my palace from the plague which has tormented me for many years, I will give you the choice of two things. Either you shall be my Prime Minister, or else you shall marry my daughter and reign after me. Say, which shall it be?"

"The princess and the kingdom," said the young man.

And so it was.

The Language of Beasts

(FROM *THE CRIMSON FAIRY BOOK*)

Once upon a time a man had a shepherd who served him many years faithfully and honestly. One day, whilst herding his flock, this shepherd heard a hissing sound, coming out of the forest near by, which he could not account for. So he went into the wood in the direction of the noise to try to discover the cause. When he approached the place he found that the dry grass and leaves were on fire, and on a tree, surrounded by flames, a snake was coiled, hissing with terror.

The shepherd stood wondering how the poor snake could escape, for the wind was blowing the flames that way, and soon that tree would be burning like the rest. Suddenly the snake cried: "O shepherd! for the love of heaven save me from this fire!"

Then the shepherd stretched his staff out over the flames and the snake wound itself round the staff and up to his hand, and from his hand it crept up his arm, and twined itself about his neck. The shepherd trembled with fright, expecting every instant to be stung to death, and said: "What an unlucky man I am! Did I rescue you only to be destroyed myself?" But the snake answered: "Have no fear; only carry me home to my father who is the King of the Snakes." The shepherd, however, was much too frightened to listen, and said that he could not go away and leave his flock alone; but the snake said: "You need not be afraid to leave your flock, no evil shall befall them; but make all the haste you can."

So he set off through the wood carrying the snake, and after a time he came to a great gateway, made entirely of snakes intertwined one with another. The shepherd stood still with surprise, but the snake round his neck whistled, and immediately all the arch unwound itself.

"When we are come to my father's house," said his own snake to him, "he will reward you with anything you like to ask—silver, gold, jewels, or whatever on this earth is most precious; but take none of all these things, ask rather to understand the language of beasts. He will refuse it to you a long time, but in the end he will grant it to you."

Soon after that they arrived at the house of the King of the Snakes, who burst into tears of joy at the sight of his daughter, as he had given her up for dead. "Where have you been all this time?" he asked, directly he could speak, and she told him that she had been caught in a forest fire, and had been rescued from the flames by the shepherd. The King of the Snakes, then turning to the shepherd, said to him: "What reward will you choose for saving my child?"

"Make me to know the language of beasts," answered the shepherd, "that is all I desire."

The king replied: "Such knowledge would be of no benefit to you, for if I granted it to you and you told any one of it, you would immediately die; ask me rather for whatever else you would most like to possess, and it shall be yours."

But the shepherd answered him: "Sir, if you wish to reward me for saving your daughter, grant me, I pray you, to know the language of beasts. I desire nothing else"; and he turned as if to depart.

Then the king called him back, saying: "If nothing else will satisfy you, open your mouth." The man obeyed, and the king spat into it, and said: "Now spit into my mouth." The shepherd did as he was told, then the King of the Snakes spat again into the shepherd's mouth. When they had spat into each other's mouths three times, the king said:

"Now you know the language of beasts, go in peace; but, if you value your life, beware lest you tell any one of it, else you will immediately die."

So the shepherd set out for home, and on his way through the wood he heard and understood all that was said by the birds, and by every living creature. When he got back to his sheep he found the flock grazing peacefully, and as he was very tired he laid himself down by them to rest a little. Hardly had he done so when two ravens flew down and perched on a tree near by, and began to talk to each other in their own language: "If that shepherd only knew that there is a vault full of gold and silver beneath where that lamb is lying, what would he not do?" When the shepherd heard these words he went straight to his master and told him, and the master at once took a wagon, and broke open the door of the vault, and they carried off the treasure. But instead of keeping it for himself, the master, who was an honorable man, gave it all up to the shepherd, saying: "Take it, it is yours. The gods have given it to you." So the shepherd took the treasure and built himself a house. He married a wife, and they lived in great peace and happiness, and he was acknowledged to be the richest man, not only of his native village, but of all the country-side. He had flocks of sheep, and cattle, and horses without end, as well as beautiful clothes and jewels.

One day, just before Christmas, he said to his wife: "Prepare everything for a great feast, to-morrow we will take things with us to the farm that the shepherds there may make merry." The wife obeyed, and all was prepared as he desired. Next day they both went to the farm, and in the evening the master said to the shepherds: "Now come, all of you, eat, drink, and make merry. I will watch the flocks myself to-night in your stead." Then he went out to spend the night with the flocks.

When midnight struck the wolves howled and the dogs barked, and the wolves spoke in their own tongue, saying:

"Shall we come in and work havoc, and you too shall eat flesh?" And the dogs answered in their tongue: "Come in, and for once we shall have enough to eat."

Now among the dogs there was one so old that he had only two teeth left in his head, and he spoke to the wolves, saying: "So long as I have my two teeth still in my head, I will let no harm be done to my master."

All this the master heard and understood, and as soon as morning dawned he ordered all the dogs to be killed excepting the old dog. The farm servants wondered at this order, and exclaimed: "But surely, sir, that would be a pity?"

The master answered: "Do as I bid you"; and made ready to return home with his wife, and they mounted their horses, her steed being a mare. As they went on their way, it happened that the husband rode on ahead, while the wife was a little way behind. The husband's horse, seeing this, neighed, and said to the mare: "Come along, make haste; why are you so slow?" And the mare answered: "It is very easy for you, you carry only your master, who is a thin man, but I carry my mistress, who is so fat that she weights as much as three." When the husband heard that he looked back and laughed, which the wife perceiving, she urged on the mare till she caught up with her husband, and asked him why he laughed. "For nothing at all," he answered; "just because it came into my head." She would not be satisfied with this answer, and urged him more and more to tell her why he had laughed. But he controlled himself and said: "Let me be, wife; what ails you? I do not know myself why I laughed." But the more he put her off, the more she tormented him to tell her the cause of his laughter. At length he said to her: "Know, then, that if I tell it you I shall immediately and surely die." But even this did not quiet her; she only besought him the more to tell her.

Meanwhile they had reached home, and before getting down from his horse the man called for a coffin to be brought; and when it was there he placed it in front of the house, and said to his wife:

"See, I will lay myself down in this coffin, and will then tell you why I laughed, for as soon as I have told you I shall surely die." So he lay down in the coffin, and while he took a last look around him, his old dog came out from the farm and sat down by him, and whined. When the master saw this, he called to his wife: "Bring a piece of bread to give to the dog." The wife brought some bread and threw it to the dog, but he would not look at it.

Then the farm cock came and pecked at the bread; but the dog said to it: "Wretched glutton, you can eat like that when you see that your master is dying?" The cock answered: "Let him die, if he is so stupid. I have a hundred wives, which I call together when I find a grain of corn, and as soon as they are there I swallow it myself; should one of them dare to be angry, I would give her a lesson with my beak. He has only one wife, and he cannot keep her in order."

As soon as the man understood this, he got up out of the coffin, seized a stick, and called his wife into the room, saying: "Come, and I will tell you what you so much want to know"; and then he began to beat her with the stick, saying with each blow: "It is that, wife, it is that!" And in this way he taught her never again to ask why he had laughed.

The Twelve Huntsmen

(FROM *THE GREEN FAIRY BOOK*)

Once upon a time there was a King's son who was engaged to a Princess whom he dearly loved. One day as he sat by her side feeling very happy, he received news that his father was lying at the point of death, and desired to see him before his end. So he said to his love: "Alas! I must go off and leave you, but take this ring and wear it as a remembrance of me, and when I am King I will return and fetch you home."

Then he rode off, and when he reached his father he found him mortally ill and very near death.

The King said: "Dearest son, I have desired to see you again before my end. Promise me, I beg of you, that you will marry according to my wishes"; and he then named the daughter of a neighboring King who he was anxious should be his son's wife. The Prince was so overwhelmed with grief that he could think of nothing but his father, and exclaimed: "Yes, yes, dear father, whatever you desire shall be done." Thereupon the King closed his eyes and died.

After the Prince had been proclaimed King, and the usual time of mourning had elapsed, he felt that he must keep the promise he had made to his father, so he sent to ask for the hand of the King's daughter, which was granted to him at once.

Now, his first love heard of this, and the thought of her lover's desertion grieved her so sadly that she pined away and nearly died. Her father said to her: "My dearest child, why are you so unhappy? If there is anything you wish for, say so, and you shall have it."

His daughter reflected for a moment, and then said: "Dear father, I wish for eleven girls as nearly as possible of the same height, age, and appearance as myself."

Said the King: "If the thing is possible your wish shall be fulfilled"; and he had his kingdom searched till he found eleven maidens of the same height, size, and appearance as his daughter.

Then the Princess desired twelve complete huntsmen's suits to be made, all exactly alike, and the eleven maidens had to dress themselves in eleven of the suits, while she herself put on the twelfth. After this she took leave of her father, and rode off with her girls to the court of her former lover.

Here she enquired whether the King did not want some huntsmen, and if he would not take them all into his service. The King saw her but did not recognize her, and as he thought them very good-looking young people, he said, "Yes, he would gladly engage them all." So they became the twelve royal huntsmen.

Now, the King had a most remarkable Lion, for it knew every hidden or secret thing.

One evening the Lion said to the King: "So you think you have got twelve huntsmen, do you?"

"Yes, certainly," said the King, "they *are* twelve huntsmen."

"There you are mistaken," said the Lion; "they are twelve maidens."

"That cannot possibly be," replied the King; "how do you mean to prove that?"

"Just have a number of peas strewed over the floor of your ante-chamber," said the Lion, "and you will soon see. Men have a strong, firm tread, so that if they happen to walk over peas not one will stir, but girls trip, and slip, and slide, so that the peas roll all about."

The King was pleased with the Lion's advice, and ordered the peas to be strewn in his ante-room.

Fortunately one of the King's servants had become very partial to the young huntsmen, and hearing of the trial they were to be put to, he went to them and said: "The Lion wants to persuade the King that you are only girls"; and then told them all the plot.

The King's daughter thanked him for the hint, and after he was gone she said to her maidens: "Now make every effort to tread firmly on the peas."

Next morning, when the King sent for his twelve huntsmen, and they passed through the ante-room which was plentifully strewn with peas, they trod so firmly and walked with such a steady, strong step that not a single pea rolled away or even so much as stirred. After they were gone the King said to the Lion: "There now—you have been telling lies—you see yourself they walk like men."

"Because they knew they were being put to the test," answered the Lion; "and so they made an effort; but just have a dozen spinning-wheels placed in the ante-room. When they pass through you'll see how pleased they will be, quite unlike any man."

The King was pleased with the advice, and desired twelve spinning-wheels to be placed in his ante-chamber.

But the good-natured servant went to the huntsmen and told them all about this fresh plot. Then, as soon as the King's daughter was alone with her maidens, she exclaimed: "Now, pray make a great effort and don't even *look* at those spinning-wheels."

When the King sent for his twelve huntsmen next morning they walked through the ante-room without even casting a glance at the spinning-wheels.

Then the King said once more to the Lion: "You have deceived me again; they *are* men, for they never once looked at the spinning-wheels."

The Lion replied: "They knew they were being tried, and they did violence to their feelings." But the King declined to believe in the Lion any longer.

So the twelve huntsmen continued to follow the King, and he grew daily fonder of them. One day whilst they were all out hunting it so happened that news was brought that the King's intended bride was on her way and might soon be expected. When the true bride heard of this she felt as though a knife had pierced her heart, and she fell fainting to the ground. The King, fearing something had happened to his dear huntsman, ran up to help, and began drawing off his gloves. Then he saw the ring which he had given to his first love, and as he gazed into her face he knew her again, and his heart was so touched that he kissed her, and as she opened her eyes, he cried: "I am thine and thou art mine, and no power on earth can alter that."

To the other Princess he dispatched a messenger to beg her to return to her own kingdom with all speed. "For," said he, "I have got a wife, and he who finds an old key again does not require a new one."

Thereupon the wedding was celebrated with great pomp, and the Lion was restored to the royal favor, for after all he had told the truth.

The Fox and the Wolf

(FROM *THE ORANGE FAIRY BOOK*)

At the foot of some high mountains there was, once upon a time, a small village, and a little way off two roads met, one of them going to the east and the other to the west. The villagers were quiet, hard-working folk, who toiled in the fields all day, and in the evening set out for home when the bell began to ring in the little church. In the summer mornings they led out their flocks to pasture, and were happy and contented from sunrise to sunset.

One summer night, when a round full moon shone down upon the white road, a great wolf came trotting round the corner.

"I positively *must* get a good meal before I go back to my den," he said to himself; "it is nearly a week since I have tasted anything but scraps, though perhaps no one would think it to look at my figure! Of course there are plenty of rabbits and hares in the mountains; but indeed one needs to be a greyhound to catch *them*, and I am not so young as I was! If I could only dine off that fox I saw a fortnight ago, curled up into a delicious hairy ball, I should ask nothing better; I would have eaten her then, but unluckily her husband was lying beside her, and one knows that foxes, great and small, run like the wind. Really it seems as if there was not a living creature left for me to prey upon but a wolf, and, as the proverb says: 'One wolf does not bite another.' However, let us see what this village can produce. I am as hungry as a schoolmaster."

Now, while these thoughts were running through the mind of the wolf, the very fox he had been thinking of was galloping along the other road.

"The whole of this day I have listened to those village hens clucking till I could bear it no longer," murmured she as she bounded along, hardly seeming to touch the ground. "When you are fond of fowls and eggs it is the sweetest of all music. As sure as there is a sun in heaven I will have some of them this night, for I have grown so thin that my very bones rattle, and my poor babies are crying for food." And as she spoke she reached a little plot of grass, where the two roads joined, and flung herself under a tree to take a little rest, and to settle her plans. At this moment the wolf came up.

At the sight of the fox lying within his grasp his mouth began to water, but his joy was somewhat checked when he noticed how thin she was. The fox's quick ears heard the sound of his paws, though they were soft as velvet, and turning her head she said politely:

"Is that you, neighbor? What a strange place to meet in! I hope you are quite well?"

"Quite well as regards my health," answered the wolf, whose eye glistened greedily, "at least, as well as one can be when one is very hungry. But what is the matter with you? A fortnight ago you were as plump as heart could wish!"

"I have been ill—very ill," replied the fox, "and what you say is quite true. A worm is fat in comparison with me."

"He is. Still, you are good enough for me; for 'to the hungry no bread is hard.'"

"Oh, you are always joking! I'm sure you are not half as hungry as I!"

"That we shall soon see," cried the wolf, opening his huge mouth and crouching for a spring.

"What are you doing?" exclaimed the fox, stepping backwards.

"What am I doing? What I am going to do is to make my supper off you, in less time than a cock takes to crow."

"Well, I suppose you must have your joke," answered the fox lightly, but never removing her eye from the wolf, who replied with a snarl which showed all his teeth:

"I don't want to joke, but to eat!"

"But surely a person of your talents must perceive that you might eat me to the very last morsel and never know that you had swallowed anything at all!"

"In this world the cleverest people are always the hungriest," replied the wolf.

"Ah! how true that is; but—"

"I can't stop to listen to your 'buts' and 'yets,'" broke in the wolf rudely; "let us get to the point, and the point is that I want to eat you and not talk to you."

"Have you no pity for a poor mother?" asked the fox, putting her tail to her eyes, but peeping slyly out of them all the same.

"I am dying of hunger," answered the wolf, doggedly; "and you know," he added with a grin, "that charity begins at home."

"Quite so," replied the fox; "it would be unreasonable of me to object to your satisfying your appetite at my expense. But if the fox resigns herself to the sacrifice, the mother offers you one last request."

"Then be quick and don't waste my time, for I can't wait much longer. What is it you want?"

"You must know," said the fox, "that in this village there is a rich man who makes in the summer enough cheeses to last him for the whole year, and keeps them in an old well, now dry, in his courtyard. By the well hang two buckets on a pole that were used, in former days, to draw up water. For many nights I have crept down to the palace, and have lowered myself in the bucket, bringing home with me enough cheese to feed the children. All I beg of you is to come with me, and, instead of hunting chickens and such things, I will make a good meal off cheese before I die."

"But the cheeses may be all finished by now?"

"If you were only to see the quantities of them!" laughed the fox. "And even if they *were* finished, there would always be *me* to eat."

"Well, I will come. Lead the way, but I warn you that if you try to escape or play any tricks you are reckoning without your host—that is to say, without my legs, which are as long as yours!"

All was silent in the village, and not a light was to be seen but that of the moon, which shone bright and clear in the sky. The wolf and the fox crept softly along, when suddenly they stopped and looked at each other; a savory smell of frying bacon reached their noses, and reached the noses of the sleeping dogs, who began to bark greedily.

"Is it safe to go on, think you?" asked the wolf in a whisper. And the fox shook her head.

"Not while the dogs are barking," said she; "someone might come out to see if anything was the matter." And she signed to the wolf to curl himself up in the shadow beside her.

In about half an hour the dogs grew tired of barking, or perhaps the bacon was eaten up and there was no smell to excite them. Then the wolf and the fox jumped up, and hastened to the foot of the wall.

"I am lighter than he is," thought the fox to herself, "and perhaps if I make haste I can get a start, and jump over the wall on the other side before he manages to spring over this one." And she quickened her pace. But if the wolf could not run he could jump, and with one bound he was beside his companion.

"What were you going to do, comrade?"

"Oh, nothing," replied the fox, much vexed at the failure of her plan.

"I think if I were to take a bit out of your haunch you would jump better," said the wolf, giving a snap at her as he spoke. The fox drew back uneasily.

"Be careful, or I shall scream," she snarled. And the wolf, understanding all that might happen if the fox carried out her threat, gave a signal to his companion to leap on the wall, where he immediately followed her.

Once on the top they crouched down and looked about them. Not a creature was to be seen in the courtyard, and in the furthest corner from the house stood the well, with its two buckets suspended from a pole, just as the fox had described it. The two thieves dragged themselves noiselessly along the wall till they were opposite the well, and by stretching out her neck as far as it would go the fox was able to make out that there was only very little water in the bottom, but just enough to reflect the moon, big, and round and yellow.

"How lucky!" cried she to the wolf. "There is a huge cheese about the size of a mill wheel. Look! look! did you ever see anything so beautiful!"

"Never!" answered the wolf, peering over in his turn, his eyes glistening greedily, for he imagined that the moon's reflection in the water was really a cheese.

"And now, unbeliever, what have you to say?" and the fox laughed gently.

"That you are a woman—I mean a fox—of your word," replied the wolf.

"Well, then, go down in that bucket and eat your fill," said the fox.

"Oh, is that your game?" asked the wolf, with a grin. "No! no! The person who goes down in the bucket will be *you*! And if *you* don't go down your head will go without you!"

"Of course I will go down, with the greatest pleasure," answered the fox, who had expected the wolf's reply.

"And be sure you don't eat all the cheese, or it will be the worse for you," continued the wolf. But the fox looked up at him with tears in her eyes.

"Farewell, suspicious one!" she said sadly, and climbed into the bucket.

In an instant she had reached the bottom of the well, and found that the water was not deep enough to cover her legs.

"Why, it is larger and richer than I thought," cried she, turning towards the wolf, who was leaning over the wall of the well.

"Then be quick and bring it up," commanded the wolf.

"How can I, when it weighs more than I do?" asked the fox.

"If it is so heavy bring it in two bits, of course," said he.

"But I have no knife," answered the fox. "You will have to come down yourself, and we will carry it up between us."

"And how am I to come down?" inquired the wolf.

"Oh, you are really very stupid! Get into the other bucket that is nearly over your head."

The wolf looked up, and saw the bucket hanging there, and with some difficulty he climbed into it. As he weighed at least four times as much as the fox the bucket went down with a jerk, and the other bucket, in which the fox was seated, came to the surface.

As soon as he understood what was happening, the wolf began to speak like an angry wolf, but was a little comforted when he remembered that the cheese still remained to him.

"But where *is* the cheese?" he asked of the fox, who in her turn was leaning over the parapet watching his proceedings with a smile.

"The cheese?" answered the fox; "why I am taking it home to my babies, who are too young to get food for themselves."

"Ah, traitor!" cried the wolf, howling with rage. But the fox was not there to hear this insult, for she had gone off to a neighboring fowl-house, where she had noticed some fat young chickens the day before.

"Perhaps I did treat him rather badly," she said to herself. "But it seems getting cloudy, and if there should be heavy rain the other bucket will fill and sink to the bottom, and his will go up—at least it may!"

The Norka

(From *The Red Fairy Book*)

Once upon a time there lived a King and Queen. They had three sons, two of them with their wits about them, but the third a simpleton. Now the King had a deer park in which were quantities of wild animals of different kinds. Into that park there used to come a huge beast—Norka was its name—and do fearful mischief, devouring some of the animals every night. The King did all he could, but he was unable to destroy it. So at last he called his sons together and said, "Whoever will destroy the Norka, to him will I give the half of my kingdom."

Well, the eldest son undertook the task. As soon as it was night, he took his weapons and set out. But before he reached the park, he went into a *traktir* (or tavern), and there he spent the whole night in revelry. When he came to his senses it was too late; the day had already dawned. He felt himself disgraced in the eyes of his father, but there was no help for it. The next day the second son went, and did just the same. Their father scolded them both soundly, and there was an end of it.

Well, on the third day the youngest son undertook the task. They all laughed him to scorn, because he was so stupid, feeling sure he wouldn't do anything. But he took his arms, and went straight into the park, and sat down on the grass in such a position that the moment he went asleep his weapons would prick him, and he would awake.

Presently the midnight hour sounded. The earth began to shake, and the Norka came rushing up, and burst right through the fence into the park, so huge was it. The Prince pulled himself together, leapt to his feet, crossed himself, and went straight at the beast. It fled back, and the Prince ran after it. But he soon saw that he couldn't catch it on foot, so he hastened to the stable, laid his hands on the best horse there, and set off in pursuit. Presently he came up with the beast, and they began a fight. They fought

668

and fought; the Prince gave the beast three wounds. At last they were both utterly exhausted, so they lay down to take a short rest. But the moment the Prince closed his eyes, up jumped the beast and took to flight. The Prince's horse awoke him; up he jumped in a moment, and set off again in pursuit, caught up the beast, and again began fighting with it. Again the Prince gave the beast three wounds, and then he and the beast lay down again to rest. Thereupon away fled the beast as before. The Prince caught it up, and again gave it three wounds. But all of a sudden, just as the Prince began chasing it for the fourth time, the beast fled to a great white stone, tilted it up, and escaped into the other world, crying out to the Prince: "Then only will you overcome me, when you enter here."

The Prince went home, told his father all that had happened, and asked him to have a leather rope plaited, long enough to reach to the other world. His father ordered this to be done. When the rope was made, the Prince called for his brothers, and he and they, having taken servants with them, and everything that was needed for a whole year, set out for the place where the beast had disappeared under the stone. When they got there, they built a palace on the spot, and lived in it for some time. But when everything was ready, the youngest brother said to the others: "Now, brothers, who is going to lift this stone?"

Neither of them could so much as stir it, but as soon as he touched it, away it flew to a distance, though it was ever so big—big as a hill. And when he had flung the stone aside, he spoke a second time to his brothers, saying:

"Who is going into the other world, to overcome the Norka?"

Neither of them offered to do so. Then he laughed at them for being such cowards, and said:

"Well, brothers, farewell! Lower me into the other world, and don't go away from here, but as soon as the cord is jerked, pull it up."

His brothers lowered him accordingly, and when he had reached the other world, underneath the earth, he went on his way. He walked and walked. Presently he espied a horse with rich trappings, and it said to him:

"Hail, Prince Ivan! Long have I awaited thee!"

He mounted the horse and rode on—rode and rode, until he saw standing before him a palace made of copper. He entered the courtyard, tied up his horse, and went indoors. In one of the rooms a dinner was laid out. He sat down and dined, and then went into a bedroom. There he found a bed, on which he lay down to rest. Presently there came in a lady, more beautiful than can be imagined anywhere but in a fairy tale, who said:

"Thou who art in my house, name thyself! If thou art an old man, thou shalt be my father; if a middle-aged man, my brother; but if a young man, thou shalt be my husband dear. And if thou art a woman, and an old one, thou shalt be my grandmother; if middle-aged, my mother; and if a girl, thou shalt be my own sister."

Thereupon he came forth. And when she saw him she was delighted with him, and said:

"Wherefore, O Prince Ivan—my husband dear shalt thou be!—wherefore hast thou come hither?"

Then he told her all that had happened, and she said:

"That beast which thou wishest to overcome is my brother. He is staying just now with my second sister, who lives not far from here in a silver palace. I bound up three of the wounds which thou didst give him."

Well, after this they drank, and enjoyed themselves, and held sweet converse together, and then the Prince took leave of her, and went on to the second sister, the one who lived in the silver palace, and with her also he stayed awhile. She told him that her brother Norka was then at her youngest sister's. So he went on to the youngest sister, who lived in a golden palace. She told him that her brother was at that time asleep on the blue sea, and she gave him a sword of steel and a draught of the Water of Strength, and she told him to cut off her brother's head at a single stroke. And when he had heard these things, he went his way.

And when the Prince came to the blue sea, he looked—there slept the Norka on a stone in the middle of the sea; and when it snored, the water was agitated for seven miles around. The Prince crossed himself, went up to it, and smote it on the head with his sword. The head jumped off, saying the while, "Well, I'm done for now!" and rolled far away into the sea.

After killing the beast, the Prince went back again, picking up all the three sisters by the way, with the intention of taking them out into the upper world: for they all loved him and would not be separated from him. Each of them turned her palace into an egg—for they were all enchantresses—and they taught him how to turn the eggs into palaces, and back again, and they handed over the eggs to him. And then they all went to the place from which they had to be hoisted into the upper world. And when they came to where the rope was, the Prince took hold of it and made the maidens fast to it. Then he jerked away at the rope and his brothers began to haul it up. And when they had hauled it up, and had set eyes on the wondrous maidens, they went aside and said: "Let's lower the rope, pull our brother part of the way up, and then cut the rope. Perhaps he'll be killed; but then if he isn't, he'll never give us these beauties as wives."

So when they had agreed on this, they lowered the rope. But their brother was no fool; he guessed what they were at, so he fastened the rope to a stone, and then gave it a pull. His brothers hoisted the stone to a great height, and then cut the rope. Down fell the stone and broke in pieces; the Prince poured forth tears and went away. Well, he walked and walked. Presently a storm arose; the lightning flashed, the thunder roared, the rain fell in torrents. He went up to a tree in order to take shelter under it, and on that tree he saw some young birds which were being thoroughly drenched. So he took off his coat and covered them over with it, and he himself sat down under the tree. Presently there came flying a bird—such a big one that the light was blotted out by it. It had been dark there before, but now it became darker still. Now this was the mother of those small birds which the Prince had covered up. And when the bird had come flying up, she perceived that her little ones were covered over, and she said, "Who has wrapped up my nestlings?" and presently, seeing the Prince, she added: "Didst thou do that? Thanks! In return, ask of me anything thou desirest. I will do anything for thee."

"Then carry me into the other world," he replied.

"Make me a large vessel with a partition in the middle," she said; "catch all sorts of game, and put them into one half of it, and into the other half pour water; so that there may be meat and drink for me."

All this the Prince did. Then the bird—having taken the vessel on her back, with the Prince sitting in the middle of it—began to fly. And after flying some distance she brought him to his journey's end, took leave of him, and flew away back. But he went to the house of a certain tailor, and engaged himself as his servant. So much the worse for wear was he, so thoroughly had he altered in appearance, that nobody would have suspected him of being a Prince.

Having entered into the service of this master, the Prince began to ask what was going on in that country. And his master replied: "Our two Princes—for the third one has disappeared—have brought away brides from the other world, and want to marry them, but those brides refuse. For they insist on having all their wedding-clothes made for them first, exactly like those which they used to have in the other world, and that without being measured for them. The King has called all the workmen together, but not one of them will undertake to do it."

The Prince, having heard all this, said, "Go to the King, master, and tell him that you will provide everything that's in your line."

"However can I undertake to make clothes of that sort? I work for quite common folks," says his master.

"Go along, master! I will answer for everything," says the Prince.

So the tailor went. The King was delighted that at least one good workman had been found, and gave him as much money as ever he wanted. When his tailor had settled everything, he went home. And the Prince said to him:

"Now then, pray to God, and lie down to sleep; to-morrow all will be ready." And the tailor followed his lad's advice, and went to bed.

Midnight sounded. The Prince arose, went out of the city into the fields, took out of his pocket the eggs which the maidens had given him, and, as they had taught him, turned them into three palaces. Into each of these he entered, took the maidens' robes, went out again, turned the palaces back into eggs, and went home. And when he got there he hung up the robes on the wall, and lay down to sleep.

Early in the morning his master awoke, and behold! there hung such robes as he had never seen before, all shining with gold and silver and precious stones. He was delighted, and he seized them and carried them off to the King. When the Princesses saw that the clothes were those which had been theirs in the other world, they guessed that Prince Ivan was in this world, so they exchanged glances with each other, but they held their peace. And the master, having handed over the clothes, went home, but he no longer found his dear journeyman there. For the Prince had gone to a shoemaker's, and him too he sent to work for the King; and in the same way he went the round of all the artificers, and they all proffered him thanks, inasmuch as through him they were enriched by the King.

By the time the princely workman had gone the round of all the artificers, the Princesses had received what they had asked for; all their clothes were just like what they had been in the other world. Then they wept bitterly because the Prince had not come, and it was impossible for them to hold out any longer; it was necessary that they should be married. But when they were ready for the wedding, the youngest bride said to the King:

"Allow me, my father, to go and give alms to the beggars."

He gave her leave, and she went and began bestowing alms upon them, and examining them closely. And when she had come to one of them, and was going to give him some money, she caught sight of the ring which she had given to the Prince in the other world, and her sisters' rings too—for it really was he. So she seized him by the hand, and brought him into the hall, and said to the King:

"Here is he who brought us out of the other world. His brothers forbade us to say that he was alive, threatening to slay us if we did."

Then the King was wroth with those sons, and punished them as he thought best. And afterwards three weddings were celebrated.

The Enchanted Deer

(FROM *THE LILAC FAIRY BOOK*)

A young man was out walking one day in Erin, leading a stout cart-horse by the bridle. He was thinking of his mother and how poor they were since his father, who was a fisherman, had been drowned at sea, and wondering what he should do to earn a living for both of them. Suddenly a hand was laid on his shoulder, and a voice said to him:

"Will you sell me your horse, son of the fisherman?" and looking up he beheld a man standing in the road with a gun in his hand, a falcon on his shoulder, and a dog by his side.

"What will you give me for my horse?" asked the youth. "Will you give me your gun, and your dog, and your falcon?"

"I will give them," answered the man, and he took the horse, and the youth took the gun and the dog and the falcon, and went home with them. But when his mother heard what he had done she was very angry, and beat him with a stick which she had in her hand.

"That will teach you to sell my property," said she, when her arm was quite tired, but Ian her son answered her nothing, and went off to his bed, for he was very sore.

That night he rose softly, and left the house carrying the gun with him. "I will not stay here to be beaten," thought he, and he walked and he walked and he walked, till it was day again, and he was hungry and looked about him to see if he could get anything to eat. Not very far off was a farm-house, so he went there, and knocked at the door, and the farmer and his wife begged him to come in, and share their breakfast.

"Ah, you have a gun," said the farmer as the young man placed it in a corner. "That is well, for a deer comes every evening to eat my corn, and I cannot catch it. It is fortune that has sent you to me."

"I will gladly remain and shoot the deer for you," replied the youth, and that night he hid himself and watched till the deer came to the cornfield; then he lifted his gun to his shoulder and was just going to pull the trigger, when, behold! instead of a deer, a woman with long black hair was standing there. At this sight his gun almost dropped from his hand in surprise, but as he looked, there was the deer eating the corn again. And thrice this happened, till the deer ran away over the moor, and the young man after her.

On they went, on and on and on, till they reached a cottage which was thatched with heather. With a bound the deer sprang on the roof, and lay down where none could see her, but as she did so she called out, "Go in, fisher's son, and eat and drink while you may." So he entered and found food and wine on the table, but no man, for the house belonged to some robbers, who were still away at their wicked business.

After Ian, the fisher's son, had eaten all he wanted, he hid himself behind a great cask, and very soon he heard a noise, as of men coming through the heather, and the small twigs snapping under their feet. From his dark corner he could see into the room, and he counted four and twenty of them, all big, cross-looking men.

"Some one has been eating our dinner," cried they, "and there was hardly enough for ourselves."

"It is the man who is lying under the cask," answered the leader. "Go and kill him, and then come and eat your food and sleep, for we must be off betimes in the morning."

So four of them killed the fisher's son and left him, and then went to bed.

By sunrise they were all out of the house, for they had far to go. And when they had disappeared the deer came off the roof, to where the dead man lay, and she shook her head over him, and wax fell from her ear, and he jumped up as well as ever.

"Trust me and eat as you did before, and no harm shall happen to you," said she. So Ian ate and drank, and fell sound asleep under the cask. In the evening the robbers arrived very tired, and crosser than they had been yesterday, for their luck had turned and they had brought back scarcely anything.

"Someone has eaten our dinner again," cried they.

"It is the man under the barrel," answered the captain. "Let four of you go and kill him, but first slay the other four who pretended to kill him last night and didn't because he is still alive."

Then Ian was killed a second time, and after the rest of the robbers had eaten, they lay down and slept till morning.

No sooner were their faces touched with the sun's rays than they were up and off. Then the deer entered and dropped the healing wax on the dead man, and he was as well as ever. By this time he did not mind what befell him, so sure was he that the deer would take care of him, and in the evening that which had happened before happened again—the four robbers were put to death and the fisher's son also, but because there was no food left for them to eat, they were nearly mad with rage, and began to quarrel. From quarrelling they went on to fighting, and fought so hard that by and bye they were all stretched dead on the floor.

Then the deer entered, and the fisher's son was restored to life, and bidding him follow her, she ran on to a little white cottage where dwelt an old woman and her son, who was thin and dark.

"Here I must leave you," said the deer, "but to-morrow meet me at midday in the church that is yonder." And jumping across the stream, she vanished into a wood.

Next day he set out for the church, but the old woman of the cottage had gone before him, and had stuck an enchanted stick called "the spike of hurt" in a crack of the door, so that he would brush against it as he stepped across the threshold. Suddenly he felt so sleepy that he could not stand up, and throwing himself on the ground he sank into a deep slumber, not knowing that the dark lad was watching him. Nothing could waken him, not even the sound of sweetest music, nor the touch of a lady who bent over him. A sad look came on her face, as she saw it was no use, and at last she gave it up, and lifting his arm, wrote her name across the side—"the daughter of the king of the town under the waves."

"I will come to-morrow," she whispered, though he could not hear her, and she went sorrowfully away.

Then he awoke, and the dark lad told him what had befallen him, and he was very grieved. But the dark lad did not tell him of the name that was written underneath his arm.

On the following morning the fisher's son again went to the church, determined that he would not go to sleep, whatever happened. But in his hurry to enter he touched with his hand the spike of hurt, and sank down where he stood, wrapped in slumber. A second time the air was filled with music, and the lady came in, stepping softly, but though she laid his head on her knee, and combed his hair with a golden comb, his eyes opened not. Then she burst into tears, and placing a beautifully wrought box in his pocket she went her way.

The next day the same thing befell the fisher's son, and this time the lady wept more bitterly than before, for she said it was the last chance, and she would never be allowed to come any more, for home she must go.

As soon as the lady had departed the fisher's son awoke, and the dark lad told him of her visit, and how he would never see her as long as he lived. At this the fisher's son felt the cold creeping up to his heart, yet he knew the fault had not been his that sleep had overtaken him.

"I will search the whole world through till I find her," cried he, and the dark lad laughed as he heard him. But the fisher's son took no heed, and off he went, following the sun day after day, till his shoes were in holes and his feet were sore from the journey. Nought did he see but the birds that made their nests in the trees, not so much as a goat or a rabbit. On and on and on he went, till suddenly he came upon a little house, with a woman standing outside it.

"All hail, fisher's son!" said she. "I know what you are seeking; enter in and rest and eat, and to-morrow I will give you what help I can, and send you on your way."

Gladly did Ian the fisher's son accept her offer, and all that day he rested, and the woman gave him ointment to put on his feet, which healed his sores.

At daybreak he got up, ready to be gone, and the woman bade him farewell, saying:

"I have a sister who dwells on the road which you must travel. It is a long road, and it would take you a year and a day to reach it, but put on these old brown shoes with holes all over them, and you will be there before you know it. Then shake them off, and turn their toes to the known, and their heels to the unknown, and they will come home of themselves."

The fisher's son did as the woman told him, and everything happened just as she had said. But at parting the second sister said to him, as she gave him another pair of shoes:

"Go to my third sister, for she has a son who is keeper of the birds of the air, and sends them to sleep when night comes. He is very wise, and perhaps he can help you."

Then the young man thanked her, and went to the third sister.

The third sister was very kind, but had no counsel to give him, so he ate and drank and waited till her son came home, after he had sent all the birds to sleep. He thought a long while after his mother had told him the young man's story, and at last he said that he was hungry, and the cow must be killed, as he wanted some supper. So the cow was killed and the meat cooked, and a bag made of its red skin.

"Now get into the bag," bade the son, and the young man got in and took his gun with him, but the dog and the falcon he left outside. The keeper of the birds drew the string at the top of the bag, and left it to finish his supper, when in flew an eagle through the open door, and picked the bag up in her claws and carried it through the air to an island. There was nothing to eat on the island, and the fisher's son thought he would die of food, when he remembered the box that the lady had put in his pocket. He opened the lid, and three tiny little birds flew out, and flapping their wings they asked,

"Good master, is there anything we can do for thee?"

"Bear me to the kingdom of the king under the waves," he answered, and one little bird flew on to his head, and the others perched on each of his shoulders, and he shut his eyes, and in a moment there he was in the country under the sea. Then the birds flew away, and the young man looked about him, his heart beating fast at the thought that here dwelt the lady whom he had sought all the world over.

He walked on through the streets, and presently he reached the house of a weaver who was standing at his door, resting from his work.

"You are a stranger here, that is plain," said the weaver, "but come in, and I will give you food and drink." And the young man was glad, for he knew not where to go, and they sat and talked till it grew late.

"Stay with me, I pray, for I love company and am lonely," observed the weaver at last, and he pointed to a bed in a corner, where the fisher's son threw himself, and slept till dawn.

"There is to be a horse-race in the town to-day," remarked the weaver, "and the winner is to have the king's daughter to wife." The young man trembled with excitement at the news, and his voice shook as he answered:

"That will be a prize indeed, I should like to see the race."

"Oh, that is quite easy—anyone can go," replied the weaver. "I would take you myself, but I have promised to weave this cloth for the king."

"That is a pity," returned the young man politely, but in his heart he rejoiced, for he wished to be alone.

Leaving the house, he entered a grove of trees which stood behind, and took the box from his pocket. He raised the lid, and out flew the three little birds.

"Good master, what shall we do for thee?" asked they, and he answered, "Bring me the finest horse that ever was seen, and the grandest dress, and glass shoes."

"They are here, master," said the birds, and so they were, and never had the young man seen anything so splendid.

Mounting the horse he rode into the ground where the horses were assembling for the great race, and took his place among them. Many good beasts were there which had won many races, but the horse of the fisher's son left them all behind, and he was first at the winning post. The king's daughter waited for him in vain to claim his prize, for he went back to the wood, and got off his horse, and put on his old clothes, and bade the box place some gold in his pockets. After that he went back to the weaver's house, and told him that the gold had been given him by the man who had won the race, and that the weaver might have it for his kindness to him.

Now as nobody had appeared to demand the hand of the princess, the king ordered another race to be run, and the fisher's son rode into the field still more splendidly dressed than he was before, and easily distanced everybody else. But again he left the prize unclaimed, and so it happened on the third day, when it seemed as if all the people in the kingdom were gathered to see the race, for they were filled with curiosity to know who the winner could be.

"If he will not come of his own free will, he must be brought," said the king, and the messengers who had seen the face of the victor were sent to seek him in every street of the town. This took many days, and when at last they found the young man in the weaver's cottage, he was so dirty and ugly and had such a strange appearance, that they declared he could not be the winner they had been searching for, but a wicked robber who had murdered ever so many people, but had always managed to escape.

"Yes, it must be the robber," said the king, when the fisher's son was led into his presence; "build a gallows at once and hang him in the sight of all my subjects, that they may behold him suffer the punishment of his crimes."

So the gallows was built upon a high platform, and the fisher's son mounted the steps up to it, and turned at the top to make the speech that was expected from every doomed man, innocent or guilt. As he spoke he happened to raise his arm, and the king's daughter, who was there at her father's side, saw the name which she had written under it. With a shriek she sprang from her seat, and the eyes of the spectators were turned towards her.

"Stop! stop!" she cried, hardly knowing what she said. "If that man is hanged there is not a soul in the kingdom but shall die also." And running up to where the fisher's son was standing, she took him by the hand, saying,

"Father, this is no robber or murderer, but the victor in the three races, and he loosed the spells that were laid upon me."

Then, without waiting for a reply, she conducted him into the palace, and he bathed in a marble bath, and all the dirt that the fairies had put upon him disappeared like magic, and when he had dressed himself in the fine garments the princess had sent to him, he looked a match for any king's daughter in Erin. He went down into the great hall where she was awaiting him, and they had much to tell each other but little time to tell it in, for the king her father, and the princes who were visiting him, and all the people of the kingdom were still in their places expecting her return.

"How did you find me out?" she whispered as they went down the passage.

"The birds in the box told me," answered he, but he could say no more, as they stepped out into the open space that was crowded with people. There the princes stopped.

"O kings!" she said, turning towards them, "if one of you were killed to-day, the rest would fly; but this man put his trust in me, and had his head cut off three times. Because he has done this, I will marry him rather than one of you, who have come hither to wed me, for many kings here sought to free me from the spells, but none could do it save Ian the fisher's son."

The White Wolf

(FROM *THE GRAY FAIRY BOOK*)

Once upon a time there was a king who had three daughters; they were all beautiful, but the youngest was the fairest of the three. Now it happened that one day their father had to set out for a tour in a distant part of his kingdom. Before he left, his youngest daughter made him promise to bring her back a wreath of wild flowers. When the king was ready to return to his palace, he bethought himself that he would like to take home presents to each of his three daughters; so he went into a jeweler's shop, and bought a beautiful necklace for the eldest princess; then he went to a rich merchant's and bought a dress embroidered in gold and silver thread for the second princess, but in none of the flower shops nor in the market could he find the wreath of wild flowers that his youngest daughter had set her heart on. So he had to set out on his homeward way without it. Now his journey led him through a thick forest. While he was still about four miles distant from his palace, he noticed a white wolf squatting on the roadside, and, behold! on the head of the wolf, there was a wreath of wild flowers.

Then the king called to the coachman, and ordered him to get down from his seat and fetch him the wreath from the wolf's head. But the wolf heard the order and said: "My lord and king, I will let you have the wreath, but I must have something in return."

"What do you want?" answered the king. "I will gladly give you rich treasure in exchange for it."

"I do not want rich treasure," replied the wolf. "Only promise to give me the first thing that meets you on your way to your castle. In three days I shall come and fetch it."

And the king thought to himself: "I am still a good long way from home, I am sure to meet a wild animal or a bird on the road, it will be quite safe to promise." So he consented, and carried the wreath away with him. But all along the road he met no living creature till he turned into the palace gates, where his youngest daughter was waiting to welcome him home.

That evening the king was very sad, remembering his promise; and when he told the queen what had happened, she too shed bitter tears. And the youngest princess asked them why they both looked so sad, and why they wept. Then her father told her what a price he would have to pay for the wreath of wild flowers he had brought home to her, for in three days a white wolf would come and claim her and carry her away, and they would never see her again. But the queen thought and thought, and at last she hit upon a plan.

There was in the palace a servant maid the same age and the same height as the princess, and the queen dressed her up in a beautiful dress belonging to her daughter, and determined to give her to the white wolf, who would never know the difference.

On the third day the wolf strode into the palace yard and up the great stairs, to the room where the king and queen were seated.

"I have come to claim your promise," he said. "Give me your youngest daughter."

Then they led the servant maid up to him, and he said to her: "You must mount on my back, and I will take you to my castle." And with these words he swung her on to his back and left the palace.

When they reached the place where he had met the king and given him the wreath of wild flowers, he stopped, and told her to dismount that they might rest a little.

So they sat down by the roadside.

"I wonder," said the wolf, "what your father would do if this forest belonged to him?"

And the girl answered: "My father is a poor man, so he would cut down the trees, and saw them into planks, and he would sell the planks, and we should never be poor again; but would always have enough to eat."

Then the wolf knew that he had not got the real princess, and he swung the servant-maid on to his back and carried her to the castle. And he strode angrily into the king's chamber, and spoke.

"Give me the real princess at once. If you deceive me again I will cause such a storm to burst over your palace that the walls will fall in, and you will all be buried in the ruins."

Then the king and the queen wept, but they saw there was no escape. So they sent for their youngest daughter, and the king said to her: "Dearest child, you must go with the white wolf, for I promised you to him, and I must keep my word."

So the princess got ready to leave her home; but first she went to her room to fetch her wreath of wild flowers, which she took with her. Then the white wolf swung her on his back and bore her away. But when they came to the place where he had rested with the servant-maid, he told her to dismount that they might rest for a little at the roadside. Then he turned to her and said: "I wonder what your father would do if this forest belonged to him?"

And the princess answered: "My father would cut down the trees and turn it into a beautiful park and gardens, and he and his courtiers would come and wander among the glades in the summer time."

"This is the real princess," said the wolf to himself. But aloud he said: "Mount once more on my back, and I will bear you to my castle."

And when she was seated on his back he set out through the woods, and he ran, and ran, and ran, till at last he stopped in front of a stately courtyard, with massive gates.

"This is a beautiful castle," said the princess, as the gates swung back and she stepped inside. "If only I were not so far away from my father and my mother!"

But the wolf answered: "At the end of a year we will pay a visit to your father and mother."

And at these words the white furry skin slipped from his back, and the princess saw that he was not a wolf at all, but a beautiful youth, tall and stately; and he gave her his hand, and led her up the castle stairs.

One day, at the end of half a year, he came into her room and said: "My dear one, you must get ready for a wedding. Your eldest sister is going to be married, and I will take you to your father's palace. When the wedding is over, I shall come and fetch you home. I will whistle outside the gate, and when you hear me, pay no heed to what your father or mother say, leave your dancing and feasting, and come to me at once; for if I have to leave without you, you will never find your way back alone through the forests."

When the princess was ready to start, she found that he had put on his white fur skin, and was changed back into the wolf; and he swung her on to his back, and set out with her to her father's palace, where he left her, while he himself returned home alone. But, in the evening, he went back to fetch her, and, standing outside the palace gate, he gave a long, loud whistle. In the midst of her dancing the princess heard the sound, and at once she went to him, and he swung her on his back and bore her away to his castle.

Again, at the end of half a year, the prince came into her room, as the white wolf, and said: "Dear heart, you must prepare for the wedding of your second sister. I will take you to your father's palace to-day, and we will remain there together till to-morrow morning."

So they went together to the wedding. In the evening, when the two were alone together, he dropped his fur skin, and, ceasing to be a wolf, became a prince again. Now they did not know that the princess's mother was hidden in the room. When she saw the white skin lying on the floor, she crept out of the room, and sent a servant to fetch the skin and to burn it in the kitchen fire. The moment the flames touched the skin there was a fearful clap of thunder heard, and the prince disappeared out of the palace gate in a whirlwind, and returned to his palace alone.

But the princess was heart-broken, and spent the night weeping bitterly. Next morning she set out to find her way back to the castle, but she wandered through the woods and forests, and she could find no path or track to guide her. For fourteen days she roamed in the forest, sleeping under the trees, and living upon wild berries and roots, and at last she reached a little house. She opened the door and went in, and found the wind seated in the room all by himself, and she spoke to the wind and said: "Wind, have you seen the white wolf?"

And the wind answered: "All day and all night I have been blowing round the world, and I have only just come home; but I have not seen him."

But he gave her a pair of shoes, in which, he told her, she would be able to walk a hundred miles with every step. Then she walked through the air till she reached a star, and she said: "Tell me, star, have you seen the white wolf?"

And the star answered: "I have been shining all night, and I have not seen him."

But the star gave her a pair of shoes, and told her that if she put them on she would be able to walk two hundred miles at a stride. So she drew them on, and she walked to the moon, and she said: "Dear moon, have you not seen the white wolf?"

But the moon answered, "All night long I have been sailing through the heavens, and I have only just come home; but I did not see him."

But he gave her a pair of shoes, in which she would be able to cover four hundred miles with every stride. So she went to the sun, and said: "Dear sun, have you seen the white wolf?"

And the sun answered, "Yes, I have seen him, and he has chosen another bride, for he thought you had left him, and would never return, and he is preparing for the wedding. But I will help you. Here are a pair of shoes. If you put these on you will be able to walk on glass or ice, and to climb the steepest places. And here is a spinning-wheel, with which you will be able to spin moss into silk. When you leave me you will reach a glass mountain. Put on the shoes that I have given you and with them you will be able to climb it quite easily. At the summit you will find the palace of the white wolf."

Then the princess set out, and before long she reached the glass mountain, and at the summit she found the white wolf's palace, as the sun had said.

But no one recognized her, as she had disguised herself as an old woman, and had wound a shawl round her head. Great preparations were going on in the palace for the wedding, which was to take place next day. Then the princess, still disguised as an old woman, took out her spinning-wheel, and began to spin moss into silk. And as she spun the new bride passed by, and seeing the moss turn into silk, she said to the old woman: "Little mother, I wish you would give me that spinning-wheel."

And the princess answered, "I will give it to you if you will allow me to sleep to-night on the mat outside the prince's door."

And the bride replied, "Yes, you may sleep on the mat outside the door."

So the princess gave her the spinning-wheel. And that night, winding the shawl all round her, so that no one could recognize her, she lay down on the mat outside the white wolf's door. And when everyone in the palace was asleep she began to tell the whole of her story. She told how she had been one of three sisters, and that she had been the youngest and the fairest of the three, and that her father had betrothed her to a white wolf. And she told how she had gone first to the wedding of one sister, and then with her husband to the wedding of the other sister, and how her mother had ordered the servant to throw the white fur skin into the kitchen fire. And then she told of her wanderings through the forest; and of how she had sought the white wolf weeping; and how the wind and star and moon and sun had befriended her, and had helped her to reach his palace. And when the white wolf heard all the story, he knew that it was his first wife, who had sought him, and had found him, after such great dangers and difficulties.

But he said nothing, for he waited till the next day, when many guests—kings and princes from far countries—were coming to his wedding. Then, when all the guests were assembled in the banqueting hall, he spoke to them and said: "Hearken to me, ye kings and princes, for I have something to tell you. I had lost the key of my treasure casket, so I ordered a new one to be made; but I have since found the old one. Now, which of these keys is the better?"

Then all the kings and royal guests answered: "Certainly the old key is better than the new one."

"Then," said the wolf, "if that is so, my former bride is better than my new one."

And he sent for the new bride, and he gave her in marriage to one of the princes who was present, and then he turned to his guests, and said: "And here is my former bride"—and the beautiful princess was led into the room and seated beside him on his throne. "I thought she had forgotten me, and that she would never return. But she has sought me everywhere, and now we are together once more we shall never part again."

The Dragon and His Grandmother

(FROM *THE YELLOW FAIRY BOOK*)

There was once a great war, and the King had a great many soldiers, but he gave them so little pay that they could not live upon it. Then three of them took counsel together and determined to desert.

One of them said to the others, "If we are caught, we shall be hanged on the gallows; how shall we set about it?" The other said, "Do you see that large cornfield there? If we were to hide ourselves in that, no one could find us. The army cannot come into it, and to-morrow it is to march on."

They crept into the corn, but the army did not march on, but remained encamped close around them. They sat for two days and two nights in the corn, and grew so hungry that they nearly died; but if they were to venture out, it was certain death.

They said at last, "What use was it our deserting? We must perish here miserably."

Whilst they were speaking a fiery dragon came flying through the air. It hovered near them, and asked why they were hidden there. They answered, "We are three soldiers, and have deserted because our pay was so small. Now if we remain here we shall die of hunger, and if we move out we shall be strung up on the gallows." "If you will serve me for seven years," said the dragon, I will lead you through the midst of the army so that no one shall catch you." "We have no choice, and must take your offer," said they. Then the dragon seized them in his claws, took them through the air over the army, and set them down on the earth a long way from it.

He gave them a little whip, saying, "Whip and slash with this, and as much money as you want will jump up before you. You can then live as great lords, keep horses, and drive about in carriages. But after seven years you are mine." Then he put a book before them, which he made all three of them sign.

"I will then give you a riddle," he said; "if you guess it, you shall be free and out of my power." The dragon then flew away, and they journeyed on with their little whip. They had as much money as they wanted, wore grand clothes, and made their way into the world. Wherever they went they lived in merrymaking and splendor, drove about with horses and carriages, ate and drank, but did nothing wrong.

The time passed quickly away, and when the seven years were nearly ended two of them grew terribly anxious and frightened, but the third made light of it, saying, "Don't be afraid, brothers, I wasn't born yesterday; I will guess the riddle."

They went into a field, sat down, and the two pulled long faces. An old woman passed by, and asked them why they were so sad. "Alas! what have you to do with it? You cannot help us." "Who knows?" she answered. "Only confide your trouble in me."

Then they told her that they had become the servants of the Dragon for seven long years, and how he had given them money as plentifully as blackberries; but as they had signed their names they were his, unless when the seven years had passed they could guess a riddle. The old woman said, "If you would help yourselves, one of you must go into the wood, and there he will come upon a tumble-down building of rocks which looks like a little house. He must go in, and there he will find help."

The two melancholy ones thought, "That won't save us!" and they remained where they were. But the third and merry one jumped up and went into the wood till he found the rock hut. In the hut sat a very old woman, who was the Dragon's grandmother. She asked him how he came, and what was his business there. He told her all that happened, and because she was pleased with him she took compassion on him, and said she would help him.

She lifted up a large stone which lay over the cellar, saying, "Hide yourself there; you can hear all that is spoken in this room. Only sit still and don't stir. When the Dragon comes, I will ask him what the riddle is, for he tells me everything; then listen carefully what he answers."

At midnight the Dragon flew in, and asked for his supper. His grandmother laid the table, and brought out food and drink till he was satisfied, and they ate and drank together. Then in the course of the conversation she asked him what he had done in the day, and how many souls he had conquered.

"I haven't had much luck to-day," he said, "but I have a tight hold on three soldiers."

"Indeed! three soldiers!" said she. "Who cannot escape you?"

"They are mine," answered the Dragon scornfully, "for I shall only give them one riddle which they will never be able to guess."

"What sort of a riddle is it?" she asked.

"I will tell you this. In the North Sea lies a dead sea-cat—that shall be their roast meat; and the rib of a whale—that shall be their silver spoon; and the hollow foot of a dead horse—that shall be their wineglass."

When the Dragon had gone to bed, his old grandmother pulled up the stone and let out the soldier.

"Did you pay attention to everything?"

"Yes," he replied, "I know enough, and can help myself splendidly."

Then he went by another way through the window secretly, and in all haste back to his comrades. He told them how the Dragon had been outwitted by his grandmother, and how he had heard from his own lips the answer to the riddle.

Then they were all delighted and in high spirits, took out their whip, and cracked so much money that it came jumping up from the ground. When the seven years had quite gone, the Fiend came with his book, and, pointing at the signatures, said, "I will take you underground with me; you shall have a meal there. If you can tell me what you will get for your roast meat, you shall be free, and shall also keep the whip."

Then said the first soldier, "In the North Sea lies a dead sea-cat; that shall be the roast meat."

The Dragon was much annoyed, and hummed and hawed a good deal, and asked the second, "But what shall be your spoon?"

"The rib of a whale shall be our silver spoon."

The Dragon-made a face, and growled again three times, "Hum, hum, hum," and said to the third, "Do you know what your wineglass shall be?"

"An old horse's hoof shall be our wineglass."

Then the Dragon flew away with a loud shriek, and had no more power over them. But the three soldiers took the little whip, whipped as much money as they wanted, and lived happily to their lives' end.

The Enchanted Pig

(FROM *THE RED FAIRY BOOK*)

Once upon a time there lived a King who had three daughters. Now it happened that he had to go out to battle, so he called his daughters and said to them:

"My dear children, I am obliged to go to the wars. The enemy is approaching us with a large army. It is a great grief to me to leave you all. During my absence take care of yourselves and be good girls; behave well and look after everything in the house. You may walk in the garden, and you may go into all the rooms in the palace, except the room at the back in the right-hand corner; into that you must not enter, for harm would befall you."

"You may keep your mind easy, father," they replied. "We have never been disobedient to you. Go in peace, and may heaven give you a glorious victory!"

When everything was ready for his departure, the King gave them the keys of all the rooms and reminded them once more of what he had said. His daughters kissed his hands with tears in their eyes, and wished him prosperity, and he gave the eldest the keys.

Now when the girls found themselves alone they felt so sad and dull that they did not know what to do. So, to pass the time, they decided to work for part of the day, to read for part of the day, and to enjoy themselves in the garden for part of the day. As long as they did this all went well with them. But this happy state of things did not last long. Every day they grew more and more curious, and you will see what the end of that was.

"Sisters," said the eldest Princess, "all day long we sew, spin, and read. We have been several days quite alone, and there is no corner of the garden that we have not explored. We have been in all the rooms of our father's palace, and have admired the rich and beautiful furniture: why should not we go into the room that our father forbad us to enter?"

"Sister," said the youngest, "I cannot think how you can tempt us to break our father's command. When he told us not to go into that room he must have known what he was saying, and have had a good reason for saying it."

"Surely the sky won't fall about our heads if we *do* go in," said the second Princess. "Dragons and such like monsters that would devour us will not be hidden in the room. And how will our father ever find out that we have gone in?"

While they were speaking thus, encouraging each other, they had reached the room; the eldest fitted the key into the lock, and snap! the door stood open.

The three girls entered, and what do you think they saw?

The room was quite empty, and without any ornament, but in the middle stood a large table, with a gorgeous cloth, and on it lay a big open book.

Now the Princesses were curious to know what was written in the book, especially the eldest, and this is what she read:

"The eldest daughter of this King will marry a prince from the East."

Then the second girl stepped forward, and turning over the page she read:

"The second daughter of this King will marry a prince from the West."

The girls were delighted, and laughed and teased each other.

But the youngest Princess did not want to go near the table or to open the book. Her elder sisters however left her no peace, and will she, nill she, they dragged her up to the table, and in fear and trembling she turned over the page and read:

"The youngest daughter of this King will be married to a pig from the North."

Now if a thunderbolt had fallen upon her from heaven it would not have frightened her more.

She almost died of misery, and if her sisters had not held her up, she would have sunk to the ground and cut her head open.

When she came out of the fainting fit into which she had fallen in her terror, her sisters tried to comfort her, saying:

"How can you believe such nonsense? When did it ever happen that a king's daughter married a pig?"

"What a baby you are!" said the other sister; "has not our father enough soldiers to protect you, even if the disgusting creature did come to woo you?"

The youngest Princess would fain have let herself be convinced by her sisters' words, and have believed what they said, but her heart was heavy.

Her thoughts kept turning to the book, in which stood written that great happiness waited her sisters, but that a fate was in store for her such as had never before been known in the world.

Besides, the thought weighed on her heart that she had been guilty of disobeying her father. She began to get quite ill, and in a few days she was so changed that it was difficult to recognize her; formerly she had been rosy and merry, now she was pale and nothing gave her any pleasure. She gave up playing with her sisters in the garden, ceased to gather flowers to put in her hair, and never sang when they sat together at their spinning and sewing.

In the meantime the King won a great victory, and having completely defeated and driven off the enemy, he hurried home to his daughters, to whom his thoughts had constantly turned. Everyone went out to meet him with cymbals and fifes and drums, and there was great rejoicing over his victorious return. The King's first act on reaching home was to thank Heaven for the victory he had gained over the enemies who had risen against him. He then entered his palace, and the three Princesses stepped forward to meet him. His joy was great when he saw that they were all well, for the youngest did her best not to appear sad.

In spite of this, however, it was not long before the King noticed that his third daughter was getting very thin and sad-looking. And all of a sudden he felt as if a hot iron were entering his soul, for it flashed through his mind that she had disobeyed his word. He felt sure he was right; but to be quite certain he called his daughters to him, questioned them, and ordered them to speak the truth. They confessed everything, but took good care not to say which had led the other two into temptation.

The King was so distressed when he heard it that he was almost overcome by grief. But he took heart and tried to comfort his daughters, who looked frightened to death. He saw that what had happened had happened, and that a thousand words would not alter matters by a hair's-breadth.

Well, these events had almost been forgotten when one fine day a prince from the East appeared at the Court and asked the King for the hand of his eldest daughter. The King gladly gave his consent. A great wedding banquet was prepared, and after three days of feasting the happy pair were accompanied to the frontier with much ceremony and rejoicing.

After some time the same thing befell the second daughter, who was wooed and won by a prince from the West.

Now when the young Princess saw that everything fell out exactly as had been written in the book, she grew very sad. She refused to eat, and would not put on her fine clothes nor go out walking, and declared that she would rather die than become a laughing-stock to the world. But the King would not allow her to do anything so wrong, and he comforted her in all possible ways.

So the time passed, till lo and behold! one fine day an enormous pig from the North walked into the palace, and going straight up to the King said, "Hail! oh King. May your life be as prosperous and bright as sunrise on a clear day!"

"I am glad to see you well, friend," answered the King, "but what wind has brought you hither?"

"I come a-wooing," replied the Pig.

Now the King was astonished to hear so fine a speech from a Pig, and at once it occurred to him that something strange was the matter. He would gladly have turned the Pig's thoughts in another direction, as he did not wish to give him the Princess for a wife; but when he heard that the Court and the whole street were full of all the pigs in the world he saw that there was no escape, and that he must give his consent. The Pig was not satisfied with mere promises, but insisted that the wedding should take place within a week, and would not go away till the King had sworn a royal oath upon it.

The King then sent for his daughter, and advised her to submit to fate, as there was nothing else to be done. And he added:

"My child, the words and whole behavior of this Pig are quite unlike those of other pigs. I do not myself believe that he always *was* a pig. Depend upon it some magic or witchcraft has been at work. Obey him, and do everything that he wishes, and I feel sure that Heaven will shortly send you release."

"If you wish me to do this, dear father, I will do it," replied the girl.

In the meantime the wedding-day drew near. After the marriage, the Pig and his bride set out for his home in one of the royal carriages. On the way they passed a great bog, and the Pig ordered the carriage to stop, and got out and rolled about in the mire till he was covered with mud from head to foot; then he got back into the carriage and told his wife to kiss him. What was the poor girl to do? She bethought herself of her father's words, and, pulling out her pocket handkerchief, she gently wiped the Pig's snout and kissed it.

By the time they reached the Pig's dwelling, which stood in a thick wood, it was quite dark. They sat down quietly for a little, as they were tired after their drive; then they had supper together, and lay down to rest. During the night the Princess noticed that the Pig had changed into a man. She was not a little surprised, but remembering her father's words, she took courage, determined to wait and see what would happen.

And now she noticed that every night the Pig became a man, and every morning he was changed into a Pig before she awoke. This happened several nights running, and the Princess could not understand it at all. Clearly her husband must be bewitched. In time she grew quite fond of him, he was so kind and gentle.

One fine day as she was sitting alone she saw an old witch go past. She felt quite excited, as it was so long since she had seen a human being, and she called out to the old woman to come and talk to her. Among other things the witch told her that she understood all magic arts, and that she could foretell the future, and knew the healing powers of herbs and plants.

"I shall be grateful to you all my life, old dame," said the Princess, "if you will tell me what is the matter with my husband. Why is he a Pig by day and a human being by night?"

"I was just going to tell you that one thing, my dear, to show you what a good fortune-teller I am. If you like, I will give you a herb to break the spell."

"If you will only give it to me," said the Princess, "I will give you anything you choose to ask for, for I cannot bear to see him in this state."

"Here, then, my dear child," said the witch, "take this thread, but do not let him know about it, for if he did it would lose its healing power. At night, when he is asleep, you must get up very quietly, and fasten the thread round his left foot as firmly as possible; and you will see in the morning he will not have changed back into a Pig, but will still be a man. I do not want any reward. I shall be sufficiently repaid by knowing that you are happy. It almost breaks my heart to think of all you have suffered, and I only wish I had known it sooner, as I should have come to your rescue at once."

When the old witch had gone away the Princess hid the thread very carefully, and at night she got up quietly, and with a beating heart she bound the thread round her husband's foot. Just as she was pulling the knot tight there was a crack, and the thread broke, for it was rotten.

Her husband awoke with a start, and said to her, "Unhappy woman, what have you done? Three days more and this unholy spell would have fallen from me, and now, who knows how long I may have to go about in this disgusting shape? I must leave you at once, and we shall not meet again until you have worn out three pairs of iron shoes and blunted a steel staff in your search for me." So saying he disappeared.

Now, when the Princess was left alone she began to weep and moan in a way that was pitiful to hear; but when she saw that her tears and groans did her no good, she got up, determined to go wherever fate should lead her.

On reaching a town, the first thing she did was to order three pairs of iron sandals and a steel staff, and having made these preparations for her journey, she set out in search of her husband. On and on she wandered over nine seas and across nine continents; through forests with trees whose stems were as thick as beer-barrels; stumbling and knocking herself against the fallen branches, then picking herself up and going on; the boughs of the trees hit her face, and the shrubs tore her hands, but on she went, and never looked back. At last, wearied with her long journey and worn out and overcome with sorrow, but still with hope at her heart, she reached a house.

Now who do you think lived there? The Moon.

The Princess knocked at the door, and begged to be let in that she might rest a little. The mother of the Moon, when she saw her sad plight, felt a great pity for her, and took her in and nursed and tended her. And while she was here the Princess had a little baby.

One day the mother of the Moon asked her:

"How was it possible for you, a mortal, to get hither to the house of the Moon?"

Then the poor Princess told her all that happened to her, and added "I shall always be thankful to Heaven for leading me hither, and grateful to you that you took pity on me and on my baby, and did not leave us to die. Now I beg one last favor of you; can your daughter, the Moon, tell me where my husband is?"

"She cannot tell you that, my child," replied the goddess, "but, if you will travel towards the East until you reach the dwelling of the Sun, he may be able to tell you something."

Then she gave the Princess a roast chicken to eat, and warned her to be very careful not to lose any of the bones, because they might be of great use to her.

When the Princess had thanked her once more for her hospitality and for her good advice, and had thrown away one pair of shoes that were worn out, and had put on a second pair, she tied up the chicken bones in a bundle, and taking her baby in her arms and her staff in her hand, she set out once more on her wanderings.

On and on and on she went across bare sandy deserts, where the roads were so heavy that for every two steps that she took forwards she fell back one; but she struggled on till she had passed these dreary plains; next she crossed high rocky mountains, jumping from crag to crag and from peak to peak. Sometimes she would rest for a little on a mountain, and then start afresh always farther and farther on. She had to cross swamps and to scale mountain peaks covered with flints, so that her feet and knees and elbows were all torn and bleeding, and sometimes she came to a precipice across which she could not jump, and she had to crawl round on hands and knees, helping herself along with her staff. At length, wearied to death, she reached the palace in which the Sun lived. She knocked and begged for admission. The mother of the Sun opened the door, and was astonished at beholding a mortal from the distant earthly shores, and wept with pity when she heard of all she had suffered. Then, having promised to ask her son about the Princess's husband, she hid her in the cellar, so that the Sun might notice nothing on his return home, for he was always in a bad temper when he came in at night. The next day the Princess feared that things would not go well with her, for the Sun had noticed that some one from the other world had been in the palace. But his mother had soothed him with soft words, assuring him that this was not so. So the Princess took heart when she saw how kindly she was treated, and asked:

"But how in the world is it possible for the Sun to be angry? He is so beautiful and so good to mortals."

"This is how it happens," replied the Sun's mother. "In the morning when he stands at the gates of paradise he is happy, and smiles on the whole world, but during the day he gets cross, because he sees all the evil deeds of men, and that is why his heat becomes so scorching; but in the evening he is both sad and angry, for he stands at the gates of death; that is his usual course. From there he comes back here."

She then told the Princess that she had asked about her husband, but that her son had replied that he knew nothing about him, and that her only hope was to go and inquire of the Wind.

Before the Princess left the mother of the Sun gave her a roast chicken to eat, and advised her to take great care of the bones, which she did, wrapping them up in a bundle. She then threw away her second pair of shoes, which were quite worn out, and with her child on her arm and her staff in her hand, she set forth on her way to the Wind.

In these wanderings she met with even greater difficulties than before, for she came upon one mountain of flints after another, out of which tongues of fire would flame up; she passed through woods which had never been trodden by human foot, and had to cross fields of ice and avalanches of snow. The poor woman nearly died of these hardships, but she kept a brave heart, and at length she reached an enormous cave in the side of a mountain. This was where the Wind lived. There was a little door in the railing in front of the cave, and here the Princess knocked and begged for admission. The mother of the Wind had pity on her and took her in, that she might rest a little. Here too she was hidden away, so that the Wind might not notice her.

The next morning the mother of the Wind told her that her husband was living in a thick wood, so thick that no axe had been able to cut a way through it; here he had built himself a sort of house by placing trunks of trees together and fastening them with withes and here he lived alone, shunning human kind.

After the mother of the Wind had given the Princess a chicken to eat, and had warned her to take care of the bones, she advised her to go by the Milky Way, which at night lies across the sky, and to wander on till she reached her goal.

Having thanked the old woman with tears in her eyes for her hospitality, and for the good news she had given her, the Princess set out on her journey and rested neither night nor day, so great was her longing to see her husband again. On and on she walked until her last pair of shoes fell in pieces. So she threw them away and went on with bare feet, not heeding the bogs nor the thorns that wounded her, nor the stones that bruised her. At last she reached a beautiful green meadow on the edge of a wood. Her heart was cheered by the sight of the flowers and the soft cool grass, and she sat down and rested for a little. But hearing the birds chirping to their mates among the trees made her think with longing of her husband, and she wept bitterly, and taking her child in her arms, and her bundle of chicken bones on her shoulder, she entered the wood.

696

For three days and three nights she struggled through it, but could find nothing. She was quite worn out with weariness and hunger, and even her staff was no further help to her, for in her many wanderings it had become quite blunted. She almost gave up in despair, but made one last great effort, and suddenly in a thicket she came upon the sort of house that the mother of the Wind had described. It had no windows, and the door was up in the roof. Round the house she went, in search of steps, but could find none. What was she to do? How was she to get in? She thought and thought, and tried in vain to climb up to the door. Then suddenly she be-thought her of the chicken bones that she had dragged all that weary way, and she said to herself: "They would not all have told me to take such good care of these bones if they had not had some good reason for doing so. Perhaps now, in my hour of need, they may be of use to me."

So she took the bones out of her bundle, and having thought for a moment, she placed the two ends together. To her surprise they stuck tight; then she added the other bones, till she had two long poles the height of the house; these she placed against the wall, at a distance of a yard from one another. Across them she placed the other bones, piece by piece, like the steps of a ladder. As soon as one step was finished she stood upon it and made the next one, and then the next, till she was close to the door. But just as she got near the top she noticed that there were no bones left for the last rung of the ladder. What was she to do? Without that last step the whole ladder was useless. She must have lost one of the bones. Then suddenly an idea came to her. Taking a knife she chopped off her little finger, and placing it on the last step, it stuck as the bones had done. The ladder was complete, and with her child on her arm she entered the door of the house. Here she found everything in perfect order. Having taken some food, she laid the child down to sleep in a trough that was on the floor, and sat down herself to rest.

When her husband, the Pig, came back to his house, he was startled by what he saw. At first he could not believe his eyes, and stared at the ladder of bones, and at the little finger on the top of it. He felt that some fresh magic must be at work, and in his terror he almost turned away from the house; but then a better idea came to him, and he changed himself into a dove, so that no witchcraft could have power over him, and flew into the room without touching the ladder. Here he found a woman rocking a child. At the sight of her, looking so changed by all that she had suffered for his sake, his heart was moved by such love and longing and by so great a pity that he suddenly became a man.

The Princess stood up when she saw him, and her heart beat with fear, for she did not know him. But when he had told her who he was, in her great joy she forgot all her sufferings, and they seemed as nothing to her. He was a very handsome man, as straight as a fir tree. They sat down together and she told him all her adventures, and he wept with pity at the tale. And then he told her his own history.

"I am a King's son. Once when my father was fighting against some drag-ons, who were the scourge of our country, I slew the youngest dragon. His mother, who was a witch, cast a spell over me and changed me into a Pig. It was she who in the disguise of an old woman gave you the thread to bind round my foot. So that instead of the three days that had to run before the spell was broken, I was forced to remain a Pig for three more years. Now that we have suffered for each other, and have found each other again, let us forget the past."

And in their joy they kissed one another.

Next morning they set out early to return to his father's kingdom. Great was the rejoicing of all the people when they saw him and his wife; his father and his mother embraced them both, and there was feasting in the palace for three days and three nights.

Then they set out to see her father. The old King nearly went out of his mind with joy at beholding his daughter again. When she had told him all her adventures, he said to her:

"Did not I tell you that I was quite sure that that creature who wooed and won you as his wife had not been born a Pig? You see, my child, how wise you were in doing what I told you."

And as the King was old and had no heirs, he put them on the throne in his place. And they ruled as only kings rule who have suffered many things. And if they are not dead they are still living and ruling happily.

The Clever Cat

(From *The Orange Fairy Book*)

Once upon a time there lived an old man who dwelt with his son in a small hut on the edge of the plain. He was very old, and had worked very hard, and when at last he was struck down by illness he felt that he should never rise from his bed again.

So, one day, he bade his wife summon their son, when he came back from his journey to the nearest town, where he had been to buy bread.

"Come hither, my son," said he; "I know myself well to be dying, and I have nothing to leave you but my falcon, my cat and my greyhound; but if you make good use of them you will never lack food. Be good to your mother, as you have been to me. And now farewell!"

Then he turned his face to the wall and died.

There was great mourning in the hut for many days, but at length the son rose up, and calling to his greyhound, his cat and his falcon, he left the house saying that he would bring back something for dinner. Wandering over the plain, he noticed a troop of gazelles, and pointed to his greyhound to give chase. The dog soon brought down a fine fat beast, and slinging it over his shoulders, the young man turned homewards. On the way, however, he passed a pond, and as he approached a cloud of birds flew into the air. Shaking his wrist, the falcon seated on it darted into the air, and swooped down upon the quarry he had marked, which fell dead to the ground. The young man picked it up, and put it in his pouch and then went towards home again.

Near the hut was a small barn in which he kept the produce of the little patch of corn, which grew close to the garden. Here a rat ran out almost under his feet, followed by another and another; but quick as thought the cat was upon them and not one escaped her.

When all the rats were killed, the young man left the barn. He took the path leading to the door of the hut, but stopped on feeling a hand laid on his shoulder.

"Young man," said the ogre (for such was the stranger), "you have been a good son, and you deserve the piece of luck which has befallen you this day. Come with me to that shining lake yonder, and fear nothing."

Wondering a little at what might be going to happen to him, the youth did as the ogre bade him, and when they reached the shore of the lake, the ogre turned and said to him:

"Step into the water and shut your eyes! You will find yourself sinking slowly to the bottom; but take courage, all will go well. Only bring up as much silver as you can carry, and we will divide it between us."

So the young man stepped bravely into the lake, and felt himself sinking, sinking, till he reached firm ground at last. In front of him lay four heaps of silver, and in the midst of them a curious white shining stone, marked over with strange characters, such as he had never seen before. He picked it up in order to examine it more closely, and as he held it the stone spoke.

"As long as you hold me, all your wishes will come true," it said. "But hide me in your turban, and then call to the ogre that you are ready to come up."

In a few minutes the young man stood again by the shores of the lake.

"Well, where is the silver?" asked the ogre, who was awaiting him.

"Ah, my father, how can I tell you! So bewildered was I, and so dazzled with the splendors of everything I saw, that I stood like a statue, unable to move. Then hearing steps approaching I got frightened, and called to you, as you know."

"You are no better than the rest," cried the ogre, and turned away in a rage.

When he was out of sight the young man took the stone from his turban and looked at it. "I want the finest camel that can be found, and the most splendid garments," said he.

"Shut your eyes then," replied the stone. And he shut them; and when he opened them again the camel that he had wished for was standing before him, while the festal robes of a desert prince hung from his shoulders. Mounting the camel, he whistled the falcon to his wrist, and, followed by his greyhound and his cat, he started homewards.

His mother was sewing at her door when this magnificent stranger rode up, and, filled with surprise, she bowed low before him.

"Don't you know me, mother?" he said with a laugh. And on hearing his voice the good woman nearly fell to the ground with astonishment.

"How have you got that camel and those clothes?" asked she. "Can a son of mine have committed murder in order to possess them?"

"Do not be afraid; they are quite honestly come by," answered the youth. "I will explain all by-and-by; but now you must go to the palace and tell the king I wish to marry his daughter."

At these words the mother thought her son had certainly gone mad, and stared blankly at him. The young man guessed what was in her heart, and replied with a smile:

"Fear nothing. Promise all that he asks; it will be fulfilled somehow."

So she went to the palace, where she found the king sitting in the Hall of Justice listening to the petitions of his people. The woman waited until all had been heard and the hall was empty, and then went up and knelt before the throne.

"My son has sent me to ask for the hand of the princess," said she.

The king looked at her and thought that she was mad; but, instead of ordering his guards to turn her out, he answered gravely:

"Before he can marry the princess he must build me a palace of ice, which can be warmed with fires, and wherein the rarest singing-birds can live!"

"It shall be done, your Majesty," said she, and got up and left the hall.

Her son was anxiously awaiting her outside the palace gates, dressed in the clothes that he wore every day.

"Well, what have I got to do?" he asked impatiently, drawing his mother aside so that no one could overhear them.

"Oh, something quite impossible; and I hope you will put the princess out of your head," she replied.

"Well, but what *is* it?" persisted he.

"Nothing but to build a palace of ice wherein fires can burn that shall keep it so warm that the most delicate singing-birds can live in it!"

"I thought it would be something much harder than that," exclaimed the young man. "I will see about it at once." And leaving his mother, he went into the country and took the stone from his turban.

"I want a palace of ice that can be warmed with fires and filled with the rarest singing-birds!"

"Shut your eyes, then," said the stone; and he shut them, and when he opened them again there was the palace, more beautiful than anything he could have imagined, the fires throwing a soft pink glow over the ice.

"It is fit even for the princess," thought he to himself.

As soon as the king awoke next morning he ran to the window, and there across the plain he beheld the palace.

"That young man must be a great wizard; he may be useful to me." And when the mother came again to tell him that his orders had been fulfilled he received her with great honor, and bade her tell her son that the wedding was fixed for the following day.

The princess was delighted with her new home, and with her husband also; and several days slipped happily by, spent in turning over all the beautiful things that the palace contained. But at length the young man grew tired of always staying inside walls, and he told his wife that the next day he must leave her for a few hours, and go out hunting. "You will not mind?" he asked. And she answered as became a good wife:

"Yes, of course I shall mind; but I will spend the day in planning out some new dresses; and then it will be so delightful when you come back, you know!"

So the husband went off to hunt, with the falcon on his wrist, and the greyhound and the cat behind him—for the palace was so warm that even the cat did not mind living in it.

No sooner had he gone, than the ogre who had been watching his chance for many days, knocked at the door of the palace.

"I have just returned from a far country," he said, "and I have some of the largest and most brilliant stones in the world with me. The princess is known to love beautiful things, perhaps she might like to buy some?"

Now the princess had been wondering for many days what trimming she should put on her dresses, so that they should outshine the dresses of the other ladies at the court balls. Nothing that she thought of seemed good enough, so, when the message was brought that the ogre and his wares were below, she at once ordered that he should be brought to her chamber.

Oh! what beautiful stones he laid before her; what lovely rubies, and what rare pearls! No other lady would have jewels like those—of that the princess was quite sure; but she cast down her eyes so that the ogre might not see how much she longed for them.

"I fear they are too costly for me," she said carelessly; "and besides, I have hardly need of any more jewels just now."

"I have no particular wish to sell them myself," answered the ogre, with equal indifference. "But I have a necklace of shining stones which was left me by father, and one, the largest engraven with weird characters, is missing. I have heard that it is in your husband's possession, and if you can get me that stone you shall have any of these jewels that you choose. But you will have to pretend that you want it for yourself; and, above all, do not mention me, for he sets great store by it, and would never part with it to a stranger! To-morrow I will return with some jewels yet finer than those I have with me to-day. So, madam, farewell!"

Left alone, the princess began to think of many things, but chiefly as to whether she would persuade her husband to give her the stone or not. At one moment she felt he had already bestowed so much upon her that it was a shame to ask for the only object he had kept back. No, it would be mean; she could not do it! But then, those diamonds, and those string of pearls! After all, they had only been married a week, and the pleasure of giving it to her ought to be far greater than the pleasure of keeping it for himself. And she was sure it *would* be!

Well, that evening, when the young man had supped off his favorite dishes which the princess took care to have specially prepared for him, she sat down close beside him, and began stroking his head. For some time she did not speak, but listened attentively to all the adventures that had befallen him that day.

"But I was thinking of you all the time," said he at the end, "and wishing that I could bring you back something you would like. But, alas! what is there that you do not possess already?"

"How good of you not to forget me when you are in the midst of such dangers and hardships," answered she. "Yes, it is true I have many beautiful things; but if you want to give me a present—and to-morrow is my birthday— there *is* one thing that I wish for very much."

"And what is that? Of course you shall have it directly!" he asked eagerly.

"It is that bright stone which fell out of the folds of your turban a few days ago," she answered, playing with his finger; "the little stone with all those funny marks upon it. I never saw any stone like it before."

The young man did not answer at first; then he said, slowly:

"I have promised, and therefore I must perform. But will you swear never to part from it, and to keep it safely about you always? More I cannot tell you, but I beg you earnestly to take heed to this."

The princess was a little startled by his manner, and began to be sorry that she had every listened to the ogre. But she did not like to draw back, and pretended to be immensely delighted at her new toy, and kissed and thanked her husband for it.

"After all I needn't give it to the ogre," thought she as she dropped off to sleep.

Unluckily the next morning the young man went hunting again, and the ogre, who was watching, knew this, and did not come till much later than before. At the moment that he knocked at the door of the palace the princess had tired of all her employments, and her attendants were at their wits' end how to amuse her, when a tall negro dressed in scarlet came to announce that the ogre was below, and desired to know if the princess would speak to him.

"Bring him hither at once!" cried she, springing up from her cushions, and forgetting all her resolves of the previous night. In another moment she was bending with rapture over the glittering gems.

"Have you got it?" asked the ogre in a whisper, for the princess's ladies were standing as near as they dared to catch a glimpse of the beautiful jewels.

"Yes, here," she answered, slipping the stone from her sash and placing it among the rest. Then she raised her voice, and began to talk quickly of the prices of the chains and necklaces, and after some bargaining, to deceive the attendants, she declared that she liked one string of pearls better than all the rest, and that the ogre might take away the other things, which were not half as valuable as he supposed.

"As you please, madam," said he, bowing himself out of the palace.

Soon after he had gone a curious thing happened. The princess carelessly touched the wall of her room, which was wont to reflect the warm red light of the fire on the hearth, and found her hand quite wet. She turned round, and— was it her fancy? or did the fire burn more dimly than before? Hurriedly she passed into the picture gallery, where pools of water showed here and there on the floor, and a cold chill ran through her whole body. At that instant her frightened ladies came running down the stairs, crying:

"Madam! madam! what has happened? The palace is disappearing under our eyes!"

"My husband will be home very soon," answered the princess—who, though nearly as much frightened as her ladies, felt that she must set them a good example. "Wait till then, and he will tell us what to do."

So they waited, seated on the highest chairs they could find, wrapped in their warmest garments, and with piles of cushions under their feet, while the poor birds flew with numbed wings hither and thither, till they were so lucky as to discover an open window in some forgotten corner. Through this they vanished, and were seen no more.

At last, when the princess and her ladies had been forced to leave the upper rooms, where the walls and floors had melted away, and to take refuge in the hall, the young man came home. He had ridden back along a winding road from which he did not see the palace till he was close upon it, and stood horrified at the spectacle before him. He knew in an instant that his wife must have betrayed his trust, but he would not reproach her, as she must be suffering enough already. Hurrying on he sprang over all that was left of the palace walls, and the princess gave a cry of relief at the sight of him.

"Come quickly," he said, "or you will be frozen to death!" And a dreary little procession set out for the king's palace, the greyhound and the cat bringing up the rear.

At the gates he left them, though his wife besought him to allow her to enter.

"You have betrayed me and ruined me," he said sternly; "I go to seek my fortune alone." And without another word he turned and left her.

With his falcon on his wrist, and his greyhound and cat behind him, the young man walked a long way, inquiring of everyone he met whether they had seen his enemy the ogre. But nobody had. Then he bade his falcon fly up into the sky—up, up, and up—and try if *his* sharp eyes could discover the old thief. The bird had to go so high that he did not return for some hours; but he told his master that the ogre was lying asleep in a splendid palace in a far country on the shores of the sea. This was delightful news to the young man, who instantly bought some meat for the falcon, bidding him make a good meal.

"To-morrow," said he, "you will fly to the palace where the ogre lies, and while he is asleep you will search all about him for a stone on which is engraved strange signs; this you will bring to me. In three days I shall expect you back here."

"Well, I must take the cat with me," answered the bird.

The sun had not yet risen before the falcon soared high into the air, the cat seated on his back, with his paws tightly clasping the bird's neck.

"You had better shut your eyes or you may get giddy," said the bird; and the cat, you had never before been off the ground except to climb a tree, did as she was bid.

All that day and all that night they flew, and in the morning they saw the ogre's palace lying beneath them.

"Dear me," said the cat, opening her eyes for the first time, "that looks to me very like a rat city down there, let us go down to it; they may be able to help us." So they alighted in some bushes in the heart of the rat city. The falcon remained where he was, but the cat lay down outside the principal gate, causing terrible excitement among the rats.

At length, seeing she did not move, one bolder than the rest put its head out of an upper window of the castle, and said, in a trembling voice:

"Why have you come here? What do you want? If it is anything in our power, tell us, and we will do it."

"If you would have let me speak to you before, I would have told you that I come as a friend," replied the cat; "and I shall be greatly obliged if you would send four of the strongest and cunningest among you, to do me a service."

"Oh, we shall be delighted," answered the rat, much relieved. "But if you will inform me what it is you wish them to do I shall be better able to judge who is most fitted for the post."

"I thank you," said the cat. "Well, what they have to do is this: To-night they must burrow under the walls of the castle and go up to the room were an ogre lies asleep. Somewhere about him he has hidden a stone, on which are engraved strange signs. When they have found it they must take it from him without his waking, and bring it to me."

"Your orders shall be obeyed," replied the rat. And he went out to give his instructions.

About midnight the cat, who was still sleeping before the gate, was awakened by some water flung at her by the head rat, who could not make up his mind to open the doors.

"Here is the stone you wanted," said he, when the cat started up with a loud mew; "if you will hold up your paws I will drop it down." And so he did. "And now farewell," continued the rat; "you have a long way to go, and will do well to start before daybreak."

"Your counsel is good," replied the cat, smiling to itself; and putting the stone in her mouth she went off to seek the falcon.

Now all this time neither the cat nor the falcon had had any food, and the falcon soon got tired carrying such a heavy burden. When night arrived he declared he could go no further, but would spend it on the banks of a river.

"And it is my turn to take care of the stone," said he, "or it will seem as if you had done everything and I nothing."

"No, I got it, and I will keep it," answered the cat, who was tired and cross; and they began a fine quarrel. But, unluckily, in the midst of it, the cat raised her voice, and the stone fell into the ear of a big fish which happened to be swimming by, and though both the cat and the falcon sprang into the water after it, they were too late.

Half drowned, and more than half choked, the two faithful servants scrambled back to land again. The falcon flew to a tree and spread his wings in the sun to dry, but the cat, after giving herself a good shake, began to scratch up the sandy banks and to throw the bits into the stream.

"What are you doing that for?" asked a little fish. "Do you know that you are making the water quite muddy?"

"That doesn't matter at all to me," answered the cat. "I am going to fill up all the river, so that the fishes may die."

"That is very unkind, as we have never done you any harm," replied the fish. "Why are you so angry with us?"

"Because one of you has got a stone of mine—a stone with strange signs upon it—which dropped into the water. If you will promise to get it back for me, why, perhaps I will leave your river alone."

"I will certainly try," answered the fish in a great hurry; "but you must have a little patience, as it may not be an easy task." And in an instant his scales might be seen flashing quickly along.

The fish swam as fast as he could to the sea, which was not far distant, and calling together all his relations who lived in the neighborhood, he told them of the terrible danger which threatened the dwellers in the river.

"None of us has got it," said the fishes, shaking their heads; "but in the bay yonder there is a tunny who, although he is so old, always goes everywhere. He will be able to tell you about it, if anyone can." So the little fish swam off to the tunny, and again related his story.

"Why *I* was up that river only a few hours ago!" cried the tunny; "and as I was coming back something fell into my ear, and there it is still, for I went to sleep, when I got home and forgot all about it. Perhaps it may be what you want." And stretching up his tail he whisked out the stone.

"Yes, I think that must be it," said the fish with joy. And taking the stone in his mouth he carried it to the place where the cat was waiting for him.

"I am much obliged to you," said the cat, as the fish laid the stone on the sand, "and to reward you, I will let your river alone." And she mounted the falcon's back, and they flew to their master.

Ah, how glad he was to see them again with the magic stone in their possession. In a moment he had wished for a palace, but this time it was of green marble; and then he wished for the princess and her ladies to occupy it. And there they lived for many years, and when the old king died the princess's husband reigned in his stead.

The Magician's Horse

(FROM *THE GRAY FAIRY BOOK*)

Once upon a time, there was a king who had three sons. Now it happened that one day the three princes went out hunting in a large forest at some distance from their father's palace, and the youngest prince lost his way, so his brothers had to return home without him.

For four days the prince wandered through the glades of the forest, sleeping on moss beneath the stars at night, and by day living on roots and wild berries. At last, on the morning of the fifth day, he came to a large open space in the middle of the forest, and here stood a stately palace; but neither within nor without was there a trace of human life. The prince entered the open door and wandered through the deserted rooms without seeing a living soul. At last he came on a great hall, and in the center of the hall was a table spread with dainty dishes and choice wines. The prince sat down, and satisfied his hunger and thirst, and immediately afterwards the table disappeared from his sight. This struck the prince as very strange; but though he continued his search through all the rooms, upstairs and down, he could find no one to speak to. At last, just as it was beginning to get dark, he heard steps in the distance and he saw an old man coming towards him up the stairs.

"What are you doing wandering about my castle?" asked the old man.

To whom the prince replied: "I lost my way hunting in the forest. If you will take me into your service, I should like to stay with you, and will serve you faithfully."

"Very well," said the old man. "You may enter my service. You will have to keep the stove always lit, you will have to fetch the wood for it from the forest, and you will have the charge of the black horse in the stables. I will pay you a florin a day, and at meal times you will always find the table in the hall spread with food and wine, and you can eat and drink as much as you require."

The prince was satisfied, and he entered the old man's service, and promised to see that there was always wood on the stove, so that the fire should never die out. Now, though he did not know it, his new master was a magician, and the flame of the stove was a magic fire, and if it had gone out the magician would have lost a great part of his power.

One day the prince forgot, and let the fire burn so low that it very nearly burnt out. Just as the flame was flickering the old man stormed into the room.

"What do you mean by letting the fire burn so low?" he growled. "I have only arrived in the nick of time." And while the prince hastily threw a log on the stove and blew on the ashes to kindle the glow, his master gave him a severe box on the ear, and warned him that if ever it happened again it would fare badly with him.

One day the prince was sitting disconsolate in the stables when, to his surprise, the black horse spoke to him.

"Come into my stall," it said, "I have something to say to you. Fetch my bridle and saddle from that cupboard and put them on me. Take the bottle that is beside them; it contains an ointment which will make your hair shine like pure gold; then put all the wood you can gather together on to the stove, till it is piled quite high up."

So the prince did what the horse told him; he saddled and bridled the horse, he put the ointment on his hair till it shone like gold, and he made such a big fire in the stove that the flames sprang up and set fire to the roof, and in a few minutes the palace was burning like a huge bonfire.

Then he hurried back to the stables, and the horse said to him: "There is one thing more you must do. In the cupboard you will find a looking-glass, a brush, and a riding-whip. Bring them with you, mount on my back, and ride as hard as you can, for now the house is burning merrily."

The prince did as the horse bade him. Scarcely had he got into the saddle than the horse was off and away, galloping at such a pace that, in a short time, the forest and all the country belonging to the magician lay far behind them.

In the meantime the magician returned to his palace, which he found in smoldering ruins. In vain he called for his servant. At last he went to look for him in the stables, and when he discovered that the black horse had disappeared too, he at once suspected that they had gone together; so he mounted a roan horse that was in the next stall, and set out in pursuit.

As the prince rode, the quick ears of his horse heard the sound of pursuing feet.

"Look behind you," he said, "and see if the old man is following." And the prince turned in his saddle and saw a cloud like smoke or dust in the distance.

"We must hurry," said the horse.

After they had galloped for some time, the horse said again: "Look behind, and see if he is still at some distance."

"He is quite close," answered the prince.

"Then throw the looking-glass on the ground," said the horse. So the prince threw it; and when the magician came up, the roan horse stepped on the mirror, and crash! his foot went through the glass, and he stumbled and fell, cutting his feet so badly that there was nothing for the old man to do but to go slowly back with him to the stables, and put new shoes on his feet. Then they started once more in pursuit of the prince, for the magician set great value on the horse, and was determined not to lose it.

In the meanwhile the prince had gone a great distance; but the quick ears of the black horse detected the sound of following feet from afar.

"Dismount," he said to the prince; "put your ear to the ground, and tell me if you do not hear a sound."

So the prince dismounted and listened. "I seem to hear the earth tremble," he said; "I think he cannot be very far off."

"Mount me at once," answered the horse, "and I will gallop as fast as I can." And he set off so fast that the earth seemed to fly from under his hoofs.

"Look back once more," he said, after a short time, "and see if he is in sight."

"I see a cloud and a flame," answered the prince; "but a long way off."

"We must make haste," said the horse. And shortly after he said: "Look back again; he can't be far off now."

The prince turned in his saddle, and exclaimed: "He is close behind us, in a minute the flame from his horse's nostrils will reach us."

"Then throw the brush on the ground," said the horse.

And the prince threw it, and in an instant the brush was changed into such a thick wood that even a bird could not have got through it, and when the old man got up to it the roan horse came suddenly to a stand-still, not able to advance a step into the thick tangle. So there was nothing for the magician to do but to retrace his steps, to fetch an axe, with which he cut himself a way through the wood. But it took him some time, during which the prince and the black horse got on well ahead.

But once more they heard the sound of pursuing feet. "Look back," said the black horse, "and see if he is following."

"Yes," answered the prince, "this time I hear him distinctly."

"Let us hurry on," said the horse. And a little later he said: "Look back now, and see if he is in sight."

"Yes," said the prince, turning round, "I see the flame; he is close behind us."

"Then you must throw down the whip," answered the horse. And in the twinkling of an eye the whip was changed into a broad river. When the old man got up to it he urged the roan horse into the water, but as the water mounted higher and higher, the magic flame which gave the magician all his power grew smaller and smaller, till, with a fizz, it went out, and the old man and the roan horse sank in the river and disappeared. When the prince looked round they were no longer to be seen.

"Now," said the horse, "you may dismount; there is nothing more to fear, for the magician is dead. Beside that brook you will find a willow wand. Gather it, and strike the earth with it, and it will open and you will see a door at your feet."

When the prince had struck the earth with the wand a door appeared, and opened into a large vaulted stone hall.

"Lead me into that hall," said the horse, "I will stay there; but you must go through the fields till you reach a garden, in the midst of which is a king's palace. When you get there you must ask to be taken into the king's service. Good-bye, and don't forget me."

711

So they parted; but first the horse made the prince promise not to let anyone in the palace see his golden hair. So he bound a scarf round it, like a turban, and the prince set out through the fields, till he reached a beautiful garden, and beyond the garden he saw the walls and towers of a stately palace. At the garden gate he met the gardener, who asked him what he wanted.

"I want to take service with the king," replied the prince.

"Well, you may stay and work under me in the garden," said the man; for as the prince was dressed like a poor man, he could not tell that he was a king's son. "I need someone to weed the ground and to sweep the dead leaves from the paths. You shall have a florin a day, a horse to help you to cart the leaves away, and food and drink."

So the prince consented, and set about his work. But when his food was given to him he only ate half of it; the rest he carried to the vaulted hall beside the brook, and gave to the black horse. And this he did every day, and the horse thanked him for his faithful friendship.

One evening, as they were together, after his work in the garden was over, the horse said to him: "To-morrow a large company of princes and great lords are coming to your king's palace. They are coming from far and near, as wooers for the three princesses. They will all stand in a row in the courtyard of the palace, and the three princesses will come out, and each will carry a diamond apple in her hand, which she will throw into the air. At whosesoever feet the apple falls he will be the bridegroom of that princess. You must be close by in the garden at your work. The apple of the youngest princess, who is much the most beautiful of the sisters, will roll past the wooers and stop in front of you. Pick it up at once and put it in your pocket."

The next day, when the wooers were all assembled in the courtyard of the castle, everything happened just as the horse had said. The princesses threw the apples into the air, and the diamond apple of the youngest princess rolled past all the wooers, out on to the garden, and stopped at the feet of the young gardener, who was busy sweeping the leaves away. In a moment he had stooped down, picked up the apple and put it in his pocket. As he stooped the scarf round his head slipped a little to one side, and the princess caught sight of his golden hair, and loved him from that moment.

But the king was very sad, for his youngest daughter was the one he loved best. But there was no help for it; and the next day a threefold wedding was celebrated at the palace, and after the wedding the youngest princess returned with her husband to the small hut in the garden where he lived.

Some time after this the people of a neighboring country went to war with the king, and he set out to battle, accompanied by the husbands of his two eldest daughters mounted on stately steeds. But the husband of the youngest daughter had nothing but the old broken-down horse which helped him in his garden work; and the king, who was ashamed of this son-in-law, refused to give him any other.

So as he was determined not to be left behind, he went into the garden, mounted the sorry nag, and set out. But scarcely had he ridden a few yards before the horse stumbled and fell. So he dismounted and went down to the brook, to where the black horse lived in the vaulted hall. And the horse said to him: "Saddle and bridle me, and then go into the next room and you will find a suit of armor and a sword. Put them on, and we will ride forth together to battle."

And the prince did as he was told; and when he had mounted the horse his armor glittered in the sun, and he looked so brave and handsome, that no one would have recognized him as the gardener who swept away the dead leaves from the paths. The horse bore him away at a great pace, and when they reached the battle-field they saw that the king was losing the day, so many of his warriors had been slain. But when the warrior on his black charger and in glittering armor appeared on the scene, hewing right and left with his sword, the enemy were dismayed and fled in all directions, leaving the king master of the field. Then the king and his two sons-in-law, when they saw their deliverer, shouted, and all that was left of the army joined in the cry: "A god has come to our rescue!" And they would have surrounded him, but his black horse rose in the air and bore him out of their sight.

Soon after this, part of the country rose in rebellion against the king, and once more he and his two sons-in-law had to fare forth to battle. And the son-in-law who was disguised as a gardener wanted to fight too. So he came to the king and said: "Dear father, let me ride with you to fight your enemies."

"I don't want a blockhead like you to fight for me," answered the king. "Besides, I haven't got a horse fit for you. But see, there is a carter on the road carting hay, you may take his horse."

So the prince took the carter's horse, but the poor beast was old and tired, and after it had gone a few yards it stumbled and fell. So the prince returned sadly to the garden and watched the king ride forth at the head of the army accompanied by his two sons-in-law. When they were out of sight the prince betook himself to the vaulted chamber by the brook-side, and having taken counsel of the faithful black horse, he put on the glittering suit of armor, and was borne on the back of the horse through the air, to where the battle was being fought. And once more he routed the king's enemies, hacking to right and left with his sword. And again they all cried: "A god has come to our rescue!" But when they tried to detain him the black horse rose in the air and bore him out of their sight.

When the king and his sons-in-law returned home they could talk of nothing but the hero who had fought for them, and all wondered who he could be.

Shortly afterwards the king of a neighboring country declared war, and once more the king and his sons-in-law and his subjects had to prepare themselves for battle, and once more the prince begged to ride with them, but the king said he had no horse to spare for him. "But," he added, "you may take the horse of the woodman who brings the wood from the forest, it is good enough for you."

So the prince took the woodman's horse, but it was so old and useless that it could not carry him beyond the castle gates. So he betook himself once more to the vaulted hall, where the black horse had prepared a still more magnificent suit of armor for him than the one he had worn on the previous occasions, and when he had put it on, and mounted on the back of the horse, he bore him straight to the battle-field, and once more he scattered the king's enemies, fighting single-handed in their ranks, and they fled in all directions. But it happened that one of the enemy struck with his sword and wounded the prince in the leg. And the king took his own pocket-handkerchief, with his name and crown embroidered on it, and bound it round the wounded leg. And the king would fain have compelled him to mount in a litter and be carried straight to the palace, and two of his knights were to lead the black charger to the royal stables. But the prince put his hand on the mane of his faithful horse, and managed to pull himself up into the saddle, and the horse mounted into the air with him. Then they all shouted and cried: "The warrior who has fought for us is a god! He must be a god."

And throughout all the kingdom nothing else was spoken about, and all the people said: "Who can the hero be who has fought for us in so many battles? He cannot be a man, he must be a god."

And the king said: "If only I could see him once more, and if it turned out that after all he was a man and not a god, I would reward him with half my kingdom."

Now when the prince reached his home—the gardener's hut where he lived with his wife—he was weary, and he lay down on his bed and slept. And his wife noticed the handkerchief bound round his wounded leg, and she wondered what it could be. Then she looked at it more closely and saw in the corner that it was embroidered with her father's name and the royal crown. So she ran straight to the palace and told her father. And he and his two sons-in-law followed her back to her house, and there the gardener lay asleep on his bed. And the scarf that he always wore bound round his head had slipped off, and his golden hair gleamed on the pillow. And they all recognized that this was the hero who had fought and won so many battles for them.

Then there was great rejoicing throughout the land, and the king rewarded his son-in-law with half of his kingdom, and he and his wife reigned happily over it.

The Grateful Beasts

(FROM *THE YELLOW FAIRY BOOK*)

There was once upon a time a man and woman who had three fine-looking sons, but they were so poor that they had hardly enough food for themselves, let alone their children. So the sons determined to set out into the world and to try their luck. Before starting their mother gave them each a loaf of bread and her blessing, and having taken a tender farewell of her and their father the three set forth on their travels.

The youngest of the three brothers, whose name was Ferko, was a beautiful youth, with a splendid figure, blue eyes, fair hair, and a complexion like milk and roses. His two brothers were as jealous of him as they could be, for they thought that with his good looks he would be sure to be more fortunate than they would ever be.

One day all the three were sitting resting under a tree, for the sun was hot and they were tired of walking. Ferko fell fast asleep, but the other two remained awake, and the eldest said to the second brother, "What do you say to doing our brother Ferko some harm? He is so beautiful that everyone takes a fancy to him, which is more than they do to us. If we could only get him out of the way we might succeed better."

"I quite agree with you," answered the second brother, "and my advice is to eat up his loaf of bread, and then to refuse to give him a bit of ours until he has promised to let us put out his eyes or break his legs."

His eldest brother was delighted with this proposal, and the two wicked wretches seized Ferko's loaf and ate it all up, while the poor boy was still asleep.

When he did awake he felt very hungry and turned to eat his bread, but his brothers cried out, "You ate your loaf in your sleep, you glutton, and you may starve as long as you like, but you won't get a scrap of ours."

Ferko was at a loss to understand how he could have eaten in his sleep, but he said nothing, and fasted all that day and the next night. But on the following morning he was so hungry that he burst into tears, and implored his brothers to give him a little bit of their bread. Then the cruel creatures laughed, and repeated what they had said the day before; but when Ferko continued to beg and beseech them, the eldest said at last, "If you will let us put out one of your eyes and break one of your legs, then we will give you a bit of our bread."

At these words poor Ferko wept more bitterly than before, and bore the torments of hunger till the sun was high in the heavens; then he could stand it no longer, and he consented to allow his left eye to be put out and his left leg to be broken. When this was done he stretched out his hand eagerly for the piece of bread, but his brothers gave him such a tiny scrap that the starving youth finished it in a moment and besought them for a second bit.

But the more Ferko wept and told his brothers that he was dying of hunger, the more they laughed and scolded him for his greed. So he endured the pangs of starvation all that day, but when night came his endurance gave way, and he let his right eye be put out and his right leg broken for a second piece of bread.

After his brothers had thus successfully maimed and disfigured him for life, they left him groaning on the ground and continued their journey without him.

Poor Ferko ate up the scrap of bread they had left him and wept bitterly, but no one heard him or came to his help. Night came on, and the poor blind youth had no eyes to close, and could only crawl along the ground, not knowing in the least where he was going. But when the sun was once more high in the heavens, Ferko felt the blazing heat scorch him, and sought for some cool shady place to rest his aching limbs. He climbed to the top of a hill and lay down in the grass, and as he thought under the shadow of a big tree. But it was no tree he leant against, but a gallows on which two ravens were seated. The one was saying to the other as the weary youth lay down, "Is there anything the least wonderful or remarkable about this neighborhood?"

"I should just think there was," replied the other; "many things that don't exist anywhere else in the world. There is a lake down there below us, and anyone who bathes in it, though he were at death's door, becomes sound and well on the spot, and those who wash their eyes with the dew on this hill become as sharp-sighted as the eagle, even if they have been blind from their youth."

"Well," answered the first raven, "my eyes are in no want of this healing bath, for, Heaven be praised, they are as good as ever they were; but my wing has been very feeble and weak ever since it was shot by an arrow many years ago, so let us fly at once to the lake that I may be restored to health and strength again." And so they flew away.

Their words rejoiced Ferko's heart, and he waited impatiently till evening should come and he could rub the precious dew on his sightless eyes.

At last it began to grow dusk, and the sun sank behind the mountains; gradually it became cooler on the hill, and the grass grew wet with dew. Then Ferko buried his face in the ground till his eyes were damp with dewdrops, and in a moment he saw clearer than he had ever done in his life before. The moon was shining brightly, and lighted him to the lake where he could bathe his poor broken legs.

Then Ferko crawled to the edge of the lake and dipped his limbs in the water. No sooner had he done so than his legs felt as sound and strong as they had been before, and Ferko thanked the kind fate that had led him to the hill where he had overheard the ravens' conversation. He filled a bottle with the healing water, and then continued his journey in the best of spirits.

He had not gone far before he met a wolf, who was limping disconsolately along on three legs, and who on perceiving Ferko began to howl dismally.

"My good friend," said the youth, "be of good cheer, for I can soon heal your leg," and with these words he poured some of the precious water over the wolf's paw, and in a minute the animal was springing about sound and well on all fours. The grateful creature thanked his benefactor warmly, and promised Ferko to do him a good turn if he should ever need it.

Ferko continued his way till he came to a ploughed field. Here he noticed a little mouse creeping wearily along on its hind paws, for its front paws had both been broken in a trap.

Ferko felt so sorry for the little beast that he spoke to it in the most friendly manner, and washed its small paws with the healing water. In a moment the mouse was sound and whole, and after thanking the kind physician it scampered away over the ploughed furrows.

Ferko again proceeded on his journey, but he hadn't gone far before a queen bee flew against him, trailing one wing behind her, which had been cruelly torn in two by a big bird. Ferko was no less willing to help her than he had been to help the wolf and the mouse, so he poured some healing drops over the wounded wing. On the spot the queen bee was cured, and turning to Ferko she said, "I am most grateful for your kindness, and shall reward you some day." And with these words she flew away humming, gaily.

Then Ferko wandered on for many a long day, and at length reached a strange kingdom. Here, he thought to himself, he might as well go straight to the palace and offer his services to the King of the country, for he had heard that the King's daughter was as beautiful as the day.

So he went to the royal palace, and as he entered the door the first people he saw were his two brothers who had so shamefully ill-treated him. They had managed to obtain places in the King's service, and when they recognized Ferko with his eyes and legs sound and well they were frightened to death, for they feared he would tell the King of their conduct, and that they would be hung.

No sooner had Ferko entered the palace than all eyes were turned on the handsome youth, and the King's daughter herself was lost in admiration, for she had never seen anyone so handsome in her life before. His brothers noticed this, and envy and jealousy were added to their fear, so much so that they determined once more to destroy him. They went to the King and told him that Ferko was a wicked magician, who had come to the palace with the intention of carrying off the Princess.

Then the King had Ferko brought before him, and said, "You are accused of being a magician who wishes to rob me of my daughter, and I condemn you to death; but if you can fulfill three tasks which I shall set you to do your life shall be spared, on condition you leave the country; but if you cannot perform what I demand you shall be hung on the nearest tree."

And turning to the two wicked brothers he said, "Suggest something for him to do; no matter how difficult, he must succeed in it or die."

They did not think long, but replied, "Let him build your Majesty in one day a more beautiful palace than this, and if he fails in the attempt let him be hung."

The King was pleased with this proposal, and commanded Ferko to set to work on the following day. The two brothers were delighted, for they thought they had now got rid of Ferko for ever. The poor youth himself was heart-broken, and cursed the hour he had crossed the boundary of the King's domain. As he was wandering disconsolately about the meadows round the palace, wondering how he could escape being put to death, a little bee flew past, and settling on his shoulder whispered in his ear, "What is troubling you, my kind benefactor? Can I be of any help to you? I am the bee whose wing you healed, and would like to show my gratitude in some way."

Ferko recognized the queen bee, and said, "Alas! how could you help me? for I have been set to do a task which no one in the whole world could do, let him be ever such a genius! To-morrow I must build a palace more beautiful than the King's, and it must be finished before evening."

"Is that all?" answered the bee, "then you may comfort yourself; for before the sun goes down to-morrow night a palace shall be built unlike any that King has dwelt in before. Just stay here till I come again and tell you that it is finished." Having said this she flew merrily away, and Ferko, reassured by her words, lay down on the grass and slept peacefully till the next morning.

Early on the following day the whole town was on its feet, and everyone wondered how and where the stranger would build the wonderful palace. The Princess alone was silent and sorrowful, and had cried all night till her pillow was wet, so much did she take the fate of the beautiful youth to heart.

Ferko spent the whole day in the meadows waiting the return of the bee. And when evening was come the queen bee flew by, and perching on his shoulder she said, "The wonderful palace is ready. Be of good cheer, and lead the King to the hill just outside the city walls." And humming gaily she flew away again.

Ferko went at once to the King and told him the palace was finished. The whole court went out to see the wonder, and their astonishment was great at the sight which met their eyes. A splendid palace reared itself on the hill just outside the walls of the city, made of the most exquisite flowers that ever grew in mortal garden. The roof was all of crimson roses, the windows of lilies, the walls of white carnations, the floors of glowing auriculas and violets, the doors of gorgeous tulips and narcissi with sunflowers for knockers, and all round hyacinths and other sweet-smelling flowers bloomed in masses, so that the air was perfumed far and near and enchanted all who were present.

This splendid palace had been built by the grateful queen bee, who had summoned all the other bees in the kingdom to help her.

The King's amazement knew no bounds, and the Princess's eyes beamed with delight as she turned them from the wonderful building on the delighted Ferko. But the two brothers had grown quite green with envy, and only declared the more that Ferko was nothing but a wicked magician.

The King, although he had been surprised and astonished at the way his commands had been carried out, was very vexed that the stranger should escape with his life, and turning to the two brothers he said, "He has certainly accomplished the first task, with the aid no doubt of his diabolical magic; but what shall we give him to do now? Let us make it as difficult as possible, and if he fails he shall die."

Then the eldest brother replied, "The corn has all been cut, but it has not yet been put into barns; let the knave collect all the grain in the kingdom into one big heap before to-morrow night, and if as much as a stalk of corn is left let him be put to death."

The Princess grew white with terror when she heard these words; but Ferko felt much more cheerful than he had done the first time, and wandered out into the meadows again, wondering how he was to get out of the difficulty. But he could think of no way of escape. The sun sank to rest and night came on, when a little mouse started out of the grass at Ferko's feet, and said to him, "I'm delighted to see you, my kind benefactor; but why are you looking so sad? Can I be of any help to you, and thus repay your great kindness to me?"

Then Ferko recognized the mouse whose front paws he had healed, and replied, "Alas I how can you help me in a matter that is beyond any human power! Before to-morrow night all the grain in the kingdom has to

720

be gathered into one big heap, and if as much as a stalk of corn is wanting I must pay for it with my life."

"Is that all?" answered the mouse; "that needn't distress you much. Just trust in me, and before the sun sets again you shall hear that your task is done." And with these words the little creature scampered away into the fields.

Ferko, who never doubted that the mouse would be as good as its word, lay down comforted on the soft grass and slept soundly till next morning. The day passed slowly, and with the evening came the little mouse and said, "Now there is not a single stalk of corn left in any field; they are all collected in one big heap on the hill out there."

Then Ferko went joyfully to the King and told him that all he demanded had been done. And the whole Court went out to see the wonder, and were no less astonished than they had been the first time. For in a heap higher than the King's palace lay all the grain of the country, and not a single stalk of corn had been left behind in any of the fields. And how had all this been done? The little mouse had summoned every other mouse in the land to its help, and together they had collected all the grain in the kingdom.

The King could not hide his amazement, but at the same time his wrath increased, and he was more ready than ever to believe the two brothers, who kept on repeating that Ferko was nothing more nor less than a wicked magician. Only the beautiful Princess rejoiced over Ferko's success, and looked on him with friendly glances, which the youth returned.

The more the cruel King gazed on the wonder before him, the more angry he became, for he could not, in the face of his promise, put the stranger to death. He turned once more to the two brothers and said, "His diabolical magic has helped him again, but now what third task shall we set him to do? No matter how impossible it is, he must do it or die."

The eldest answered quickly, "Let him drive all the wolves of the kingdom on to this hill before to-morrow night. If he does this he may go free; if not he shall be hung as you have said."

At these words the Princess burst into tears, and when the King saw this he ordered her to be shut up in a high tower and carefully guarded till the dangerous magician should either have left the kingdom or been hung on the nearest tree.

Ferko wandered out into the fields again, and sat down on the stump of a tree wondering what he should do next. Suddenly a big wolf ran up to him, and standing still said, "I'm very glad to see you again, my kind benefactor. What are you thinking about all alone by yourself? If I can help you in any way only say the word, for I would like to give you a proof of my gratitude."

Ferko at once recognized the wolf whose broken leg he had healed, and told him what he had to do the following day if he wished to escape with his life. "But how in the world," he added, "am I to collect all the wolves of the kingdom on to that hill over there?"

"If that's all you want done," answered the wolf, "you needn't worry yourself. I'll undertake the task, and you'll hear from me again before sunset to-morrow. Keep your spirits up." And with these words he trotted quickly away.

Then the youth rejoiced greatly, for now he felt that his life was safe; but he grew very sad when he thought of the beautiful Princess, and that he would never see her again if he left the country. He lay down once more on the grass and soon fell fast asleep.

All the next day he spent wandering about the fields, and toward evening the wolf came running to him in a great hurry and said, "I have collected together all the wolves in the kingdom, and they are waiting for you in the wood. Go quickly to the King, and tell him to go to the hill that he may see the wonder you have done with his own eyes. Then return at once to me and get on my back, and I will help you to drive all the wolves together."

Then Ferko went straight to the palace and told the King that he was ready to perform the third task if he would come to the hill and see it done. Ferko himself returned to the fields, and mounting on the wolf's back he rode to the wood close by.

Quick as lightning the wolf flew round the wood, and in a minute many hundred wolves rose up before him, increasing in number every moment, till they could be counted by thousands. He drove them all before him on to the hill, where the King and his whole Court and Ferko's two brothers were standing. Only the lovely Princess was not present, for she was shut up in her tower weeping bitterly.

The wicked brothers stamped and foamed with rage when they saw the failure of their wicked designs. But the King was overcome by a sudden terror when he saw the enormous pack of wolves approaching nearer and nearer, and calling out to Ferko he said, "Enough, enough, we don't want any more."

But the wolf on whose back Ferko sat, said to its rider, "Go on! go on!" and at the same moment many more wolves ran up the hill, howling horribly and showing their white teeth.

The King in his terror called out, "Stop a moment; I will give you half my kingdom if you will drive all the wolves away." But Ferko pretended not to hear, and drove some more thousands before him, so that everyone quaked with horror and fear.

Then the King raised his voice again and called out, "Stop! you shall have my whole kingdom, if you will only drive these wolves back to the places they came from."

But the wolf kept on encouraging Ferko, and said, "Go on! go on!" So he led the wolves on, till at last they fell on the King and on the wicked brothers, and ate them and the whole Court up in a moment.

Then Ferko went straight to the palace and set the Princess free, and on the same day he married her and was crowned King of the country. And the wolves all went peacefully back to their own homes, and Ferko and his bride lived for many years in peace and happiness together, and were much beloved by great and small in the land.

The Jackal and the Spring

(FROM *THE GRAY FAIRY BOOK*)

Once upon a time all the streams and rivers ran so dry that the animals did not know how to get water. After a very long search, which had been quite in vain, they found a tiny spring, which only wanted to be dug deeper so as to yield plenty of water. So the beasts said to each other, "Let us dig a well, and then we shall not fear to die of thirst"; and they all consented except the jackal, who hated work of any kind, and generally got somebody to do it for him.

When they had finished their well, they held a council as to who should be made the guardian of the well, so that the jackal might not come near it, for, they said, "he would not work, therefore he shall not drink."

After some talk it was decided that the rabbit should be left in charge; then all the other beasts went back to their homes.

When they were out of sight the jackal arrived. "Good morning! Good morning, rabbit!" and the rabbit politely said, "Good morning!" Then the jackal unfastened the little bag that hung at his side, and pulled out of it a piece of honeycomb which he began to eat, and turning to the rabbit he remarked:

"As you see, rabbit, I am not thirsty in the least, and this is nicer than any water."

"Give me a bit," asked the rabbit. So the jackal handed him a very little morsel.

"Oh, how good it is!" cried the rabbit; "give me a little more, dear friend!"

But the jackal answered, "If you really want me to give you some more, you must have your paws tied behind you, and lie on your back, so that I can pour it into your mouth."

The rabbit did as he was bid, and when he was tied tight and popped on his back, the jackal ran to the spring and drank as much as he wanted. When he had quite finished he returned to his den.

In the evening the animals all came back, and when they saw the rabbit lying with his paws tied, they said to him: "Rabbit, how did you let yourself be taken in like this?"

"It was all the fault of the jackal," replied the rabbit; "he tied me up like this, and told me he would give me something nice to eat. It was all a trick just to get at our water."

"Rabbit, you are no better than an idiot to have let the jackal drink our water when he would not help to find it. Who shall be our next watchman? We must have somebody a little sharper than you!" and the little hare called out, "I will be the watchman."

The following morning the animals all went their various ways, leaving the little hare to guard the spring. When they were out of sight the jackal came back. "Good morning! good morning, little hare," and the little hare politely said, "Good morning."

"Can you give me a pinch of snuff?" said the jackal.

"I am so sorry, but I have none," answered the little hare.

The jackal then came and sat down by the little hare, and unfastened his little bag, pulling out of it a piece of honeycomb. He licked his lips and exclaimed, "Oh, little hare, if you only knew how good it is!"

"What is it?" asked the little hare.

"It is something that moistens my throat so deliciously," answered the jackal, "that after I have eaten it I don't feel thirsty any more, while I am sure that all you other beasts are for ever wanting water."

"Give me a bit, dear friend," asked the little hare.

"Not so fast," replied the jackal. "If you really wish to enjoy what you are eating, you must have your paws tied behind you, and lie on your back, so that I can pour it into your mouth."

"You can tie them, only be quick," said the little hare, and when he was tied tight and popped on his back, the jackal went quietly down to the well, and drank as much as he wanted. When he had quite finished he returned to his den.

In the evening the animals all came back; and when they saw the little hare with his paws tied, they said to him: "Little hare, how did you let your-self be taken in like this? Didn't you boast you were very sharp? You under-took to guard our water; now show us how much is left for us to drink!"

"It is all the fault of the jackal," replied the little hare, "He told me he would give me something nice to eat if I would just let him tie my hands behind my back."

Then the animals said, "Who can we trust to mount guard now?" And the panther answered, "Let it be the tortoise."

The following morning the animals all went their various ways, leaving the tortoise to guard the spring. When they were out of sight the jackal came back. "Good morning, tortoise; good morning."

But the tortoise took no notice.

"Good morning, tortoise; good morning." But still the tortoise pretended not to hear.

Then the jackal said to himself, "Well, to-day I have only got to manage a bigger idiot than before. I shall just kick him on one side, and then go and have a drink." So he went up to the tortoise and said to him in a soft voice, "Tortoise! tortoise!" but the tortoise took no notice. Then the jackal kicked him out of the way, and went to the well and began to drink, but scarcely had he touched the water, than the tortoise seized him by the leg. The jackal shrieked out: "Oh, you will break my leg!" but the tortoise only held on the tighter. The jackal then took his bag and tried to make the tortoise smell the honeycomb he had inside; but the tortoise turned away his head and smelt nothing. At last the jackal said to the tortoise, "I should like to give you my bag and everything in it," but the only answer the tortoise made was to grasp the jackal's leg tighter still.

So matters stood when the other animals came back. The moment he saw them, the jackal gave a violent tug, and managed to free his leg, and then took to his heels as fast as he could. And the animals all said to the tortoise:

"Well done, tortoise, you have proved your courage; now we can drink from our well in peace, as you have got the better of that thieving jackal!"